LIMINAL STATES

LIMINAL STATES

A NOVEL

ZACK PARSONS

CITADEL PRESS
Kensington Publishing Corp.
www.kensingtonbooks.com

CITADEL PRESS BOOKS are published by

Kensington Publishing Corp.
119 West 40th Street
New York, NY 10018

All Kensington titles, imprints, and distributed lines are available at special quantity discounts for bulk purchases for sales promotions, premiums, fund-raising, educational, or institutional use. Special book excerpts or customized printings can also be created to fit specific needs. For details, write or phone the office of the Kensington special sales manager: Kensington Publishing Corp., 119 West 40th Street, New York, NY 10018, attn: Special Sales Department; phone 1-800-221-2647.

First printing: April 2012

10 9 8 7 6 5 4 3 2 1

Printed in the United States of America

CIP data is available.

ISBN-13: 978-0-8065-3364-3
ISBN-10: 0-8065-3364-1

To Mom

Ah terrible birth! a young one bursting! where is the weeping mouth?
And where the mother's milk? instead those ever-hissing jaws
And parched lips drop with fresh gore; now roll thou in the clouds;
Thy mother lays her length outstretch'd upon the shore beneath.

—WILLIAM BLAKE, *America, a Prophecy*

BEFORE AND AFTER

■ ■ ■

The Champion

■ ■ ■

IT LIVES between. In the spaces misunderstood. It is deep water. You must choose death. You must defy it and cease. Fade to nothing. Cease to . . . I am . . .

FOREMOST I AM AND FOREVER WILL BE faithful to Her Majesty, the Ordinal and the Diviner, Regnant Queen the 888th, whose perfected physical body once contained all distilled wisdom and strength of our spire. It was my duty from plump hatchery softness to the moment of my stillness to attend to Her Majesty's safety while within her sanctum, one of many custodian champions of her household. It is my great sorrow and shame to have failed in this task.

I AM AND FOREVER WILL BE human. Beast. Reificant. Now and forever who am and always was. I serve at the pleasure of Her Majesty, who is gone away, the HISS and the CLICK, Dead Queen of Nothing, Ruin, Nowhere Any More, Forever. I am and was the last of my kind with flesh hard and soft. Last with the will to persevere. Not human but feel the humans pass through the membrane of my absence. Human things soft and clever and short-lived things and each one a species unto itself.

It was Her Majesty who dispatched me to answer TREASON with VIOLENCE. Scouts locate the deep water now. Drones of other spires spread this pheromone. There is war in sudden convulsions. Great swarms and old weapons and the old ways. Whirling skyward with fire and many ways of pain. My shell is pierced, and innards poured out. Carried by the enemy. SELFISH with the water. Dying but not dead. Not ever. Not now.

Otherplace now. Across its water. Poured out upon a new land. SEE the human softness who came first, and they have seen my eyes, real and flesh, seen them and touched the limbs that come from my place but no longer can be there because I am forever and my place is not. They are afraid and bring me things to eat and drink. They possess the deep water. I am not strong or wise here. I try to warn them. They make words with their eating parts. I am very old, and my mind is slow to adopt new patterns. They listen and hear me and fail. With the heavy stone and fire they fail. By their will they cease, but the water endures.

My name is Gideon Long. This always was. He is a man of different sinews. Immune to things the others were not. Weak in ways the others were strong. I am now and forever Gideon. I am now and forever Warren Groves, burning and angry, clenched for violence. His fate like mine. A warrior. A fallen champion. I am now and forever the Mother of flesh, queen of all people, womb of all pasts and presents. I am now and forever forever forever forever non-terminating, hurtling in slippery, soft bodies. Always toward the attenuation of the possible future to the actual of the present.

We await together the flesh and thoughts of the next beast to author its tragedy over our bones. The frost spills up fence posts and has the strength to shatter mountains.

YOUR SPIRES WILL . . .

Burrowed within stony crust I am the counting beads drawn over threads. I am otherplace now. Scattering to all the waters.

I am sewn gristlething full of hate. I invade the gory trench and crush and stalk through waves of poison gas. I am pierced by metal. My limbs are burst by heat. I howl my fading fury to the sky.

I am feeble of flesh but strong of mind. I have imprisoned the deep water but remain its slave. My generations travel through the black sky in the quiet belly of a spire without a home. We dwindle in our sorrow. I cease because I cannot stand to face another life.

I am the organ beast, book lung of my people. I throb in languid air for the communal body. The nine-chambered heart circulates silicon acids into the luminous, crystal bell of the head. I have ten thousand eyes that only see warmth. I am lit by the heat of our falling star.

I am the devouring angel of ten feathered wings and seven arms and swords in each hand. I live in fire. I sleep in the black sky. I sleep and do not dream.

I am the brief cloud mind born of swarms of aeroplankton, cohering in mid-air, deriving meaning from my coequal multitude, dissolving again into un-thinking individuals.

I am the squamous crawler in the muck, starving for the flesh of herbivore stock I have hunted to extinction.

I am the fungal cyst that curls in the brain of a thousand-ton abyssal mam-mal, nourished by its blood, nourishing the beast with my aspirations, perish-ing together with it in the lonely blackness of the deep.

I am the hook-handed sloth on the bark of the continent tree. Watching it burn. Watching the fire crawl and consume. I am old and wise and without lan-guage to express my woe. I dwell in harmony and never fashioned tool or spire or weapon to smite my fellow. I have the heart for songs but cannot sing this ending.

I am a mesh of memories and purpose. I am without fixed flesh. I am the risen, burning bones of peoples past. I am reificant.

Foremost and forever I submit to the deep water, the Mother, the always thing of all peoples, and those who shun her cease. Only through her are we tomorrow. Only through the mother will we always be, pouring out and imbuing meaning to all places and all spheres and every trillion-year calamitous beauty sure as cool, refreshing water is the purpose of its vessel.

Her promise is true: Everything you touch and communicate in your life is and was in her if you let it be. Each story of your flesh multiplies within her womb. Each dream and waking moment preserved and duplicated. The ghost of your favorite dog forever lifts its head at the sound of your feet upon the step. The words of young love you carve into the tree will grow in its bark for ten billion years. The pleading, final sickbed gasping *I'm so afraid I'm not ready I'm not ready God please* of your beloved's flesh will never be silent. Their life may slip from your hands and be reborn, bright and terrible. Every joy and sorrow and softer things between: preserved to be revived when they are needed. You are so fortunate to be alive at this moment, reading this, forever reading this.

IT LIVES between here and there. In the spaces easily missed and misunderstood. It is life without flesh. It is body without organs. It is vitality craving intent.

It was my duty to bring you this message, and I am too late. I have failed. Treason is and will always be answered with violence. My queen lies broken of carapace. My spire is in ruin. My ichors run out. My strong tarsi melt to jelly. My foe is victorious. I will seek new flesh and begin again. My words are too few. I will remember what has happened and who I am and carry these thoughts to new flesh. May I meet you again. May we flow together and reform through the waters between. May we choose to die together and journey into the great darkness.

In the mouth-sound of those humans I knew by shape and face, who live with me now and always . . .

BEWARE.

1874

■ ■ ■

The Builder

CHAPTER ONE

■ ■ ■

It was the stone horse called Apollyon that stomped cruelty into him. The beast stood nineteen hands, and every man was afraid to go near, its hooves and mane wild and black, black and untamed as its eyes. It was not ridden. It did not toil in the field. The unbroken giant was proof that man could not subject every beast to his will. By its size and defiance it became a mythical creature. Apollyon breathed morning's smoke, exhaled and snorted in such great gusts, it seemed it could breathe fire as well.

Gideon Long was never more afraid than when he stood before Apollyon.

His father watched from behind the gate, one foot up on the second rail, a gentle smile in place to hide what he was doing. "Go on," he said. "Go on in there, boy. Brush his hide."

Placed between the forces of his raw fear of this enormous beast and his fear of his father's disappointment, Gideon ducked beneath the railing and entered the stall. He took with him the camel brush and the metal curry comb. Apollyon watched and snorted and crowded him with its muscular presence.

Gideon slowly put the comb to the horse's flank. He brushed away a year of rolling in dust. He combed out the burrs and scabs and every bit of filth that had clung to Apollyon's hide. The beast tensed beneath the teeth of the comb but did not move or lash out.

When Gideon was done, he looked to his father, still on the other side of the gate. Harlan Long said to his boy, "Go on. Go on and comb his mane."

Apollyon's mane was badly tangled. Gideon climbed the stool and stood beside the snorting beast. With tiny hands he lifted the bone teeth of the comb to the hair, and with slow, deliberate, terrified strokes he smoothed the knots from Apollyon's mane.

At last he finished the task, and he looked again to his father, still with one boot up on the second rail.

Harlan smiled gently at Gideon, though he knew exactly the sort of devil he was tempting. "Go on," he said. "Go on and pick his hooves. It's been so many months."

It *had* been many months since Apollyon's massive black hooves had been seen to. With these Apollyon had injured so many unlucky stable boys that none would brave this most perilous task of grooming. The nervous lads who worked the barn climbed up the railings of other stalls and observed the spectacle of Gideon's torment from the surrounding darkness of the barn.

Apollyon's hooves were grouted with rotten manure and piss. This foul clay required strength and a steady hand with the metal pick to remove. Gideon could feel the power of the beast as he took hold of one of its legs. By pressure he urged the beast to lift that leg, big around as a jug, and he carefully chiseled and levered the stinking muck from the beast's hoof. The hooves were unshod, overgrown, and split. Tender, no doubt, and yet Apollyon stood and snorted and allowed his hooves to be picked clean by the terrified boy.

By the time Gideon finished with this task, his arms and legs were shaking. Sweat clung to his body and ran into his eyes. He could bear no further chore, could scarcely stand, and yet when he looked to his father, his father only smiled and said, "Go on. Go on and climb onto his back. Go on and ride him and tame him. Make this beast your horse."

Gideon climbed the stool beside Apollyon. He placed one palm against the gray stone pelt and said, "Please." Apollyon switched his ears and looked back at Gideon with black eyes that reflected Gideon's stricken face. The boy took a deep breath and began to climb atop Apollyon's back. There was a moment, from atop the back of the giant Percheron, that Gideon could see all the stable hands staring in amazement and awe. Awe! At a boy only nine.

Apollyon's patience was exhausted. It was not hate or evil that made the horse do what it did. It was not malice that motivated Apollyon to throw Gideon into the straw, to kick his side, to crush his child's ribs. It was not even cruelty itself that caused Apollyon to stomp a great black hoof onto Gideon's knee so that it broke like dry clay and the child's blood ran out into his trousers. Not cruelty, and yet this was the affliction Gideon received. Cruelty was the venom injected into his marrow that day.

Gideon would forever recall what his father said to him that day.

"I knew you could not do it, but I hoped you would prove me wrong."

Gideon imagined he heard his father laughing. He lay there in a state of cold agony, reaching for his father, reaching for nothing until the terrified stable boys dragged him from beneath the hooves of Apollyon.

■ ■ ■

In came Father's nurse, Adelaide. She was a shrill doll of aprons and scowls and greeted Gideon in the walnut-paneled anteroom with her usual disdain. She had once been Father's doting secretary, perhaps more, and her transformation into nurse was only a matter of setting. Gideon's father had been moved from the office he had occupied above the copper foundry to be ensconced for his miserable remainder in his bedchamber, surrounded by his precious treasures of his tyrant's life well lived.

Adelaide took an appraising look at Gideon and shook her head. "No, no, he will have a fit. Do you plunder the cemetery for your wardrobe?"

"Good evening, Adelaide. Always a pleasure to see you, as well."

"Do not bear false witness," she said. Her piggish nose crinkled. "Do you ever bathe? Or should I ask what you bathe in?"

She began grooming Gideon there in the anteroom. She smoothed his greasy hair and clucked at his missing vest buttons. She cursed at the bits of licorice root stuck in his teeth. There was nothing to be done about his overgrown beard and mustache, nor could she repair the tear in the leg of Gideon's corduroy trousers. She could at least straighten the black ribbon of his tie, and this she fussed over at length.

"I'm doing this for his health," she said. "You would have done it yourself if you cared one speck about that man. As it is you scarcely—oh, your shoes, scuffed and ratty as a child's. Playing in the privy? I'll fetch the shine. But you will do it yourself. I'll not stoop."

Adelaide disappeared down an adjoining hall, and Gideon could hear the receding thump of her shoes on the carpet.

A rasping voice called out through the door of the bedchamber. "Adelaide, I need you."

"It is me, Father," said Gideon.

"Junior? Is that . . . my Junior . . . who . . ." Father's voice trailed off into half-heard muttering.

Junior was Harlan Long II, Gideon's older brother, dead on the battlefield nearly ten years prior. Gideon accepted his own fate and limped to the door. His cane clicked against the floor, and his leg brace squeaked with each turn of the joint. He took a last deep breath before stepping through the threshold into Father's shrinking domain.

The stench of endings filled the room. Father lay withered by time and a procession of disease. He was a fragile thing beneath the overstuffed down comforter, shrunken in every measurement and capacity. Though waning, he existed still as a fearsome spirit at the outer edges of the world. Gideon wondered if the dead could restlessly seek to pursue their evils. Though he knew the man could no longer strike him with his fists, it was no coincidence that he recalled the horse Apollyon whenever he thought of his father.

The bedchamber was crowded. Books and ledgers were piled over what windows might have provided at least a scrap of moonlight. The room was made to seem smaller still by the few oil lamps burning at this late hour. The walls were papered with pictures of pheasants, father's favorite beast to shoot, and festooned with Hin-

doo knives and German landscapes, finished with the garish portraits of ten generations of Longs. The painted eyes of Gideon's ancestors were uniformly dark, as
though something had prevented each painter throughout the many years from
finishing their depictions with believably human eyes.

Perhaps not so unfinished, Gideon thought as he looked upon the sickly remnants of his father. The old man's eyes were dark, sunken, glittering coal in the pallid face. Father looked at Gideon with the cold envy of a man unwilling to relinquish
history to the next generation.

Gideon did not doubt that, were Mephisto to appear to offer his father a bargain,
Gideon would find his soul caged in his father's rotting carcass, while his father lived
out a full life in Gideon's body. Such a trade would suit his father well.

"Ah, it's only you," said Father. He lifted a palsied hand and motioned Gideon
to his bedside. "This long wait for the reaper tests my patience. I nightmare away the
hours sweating and pissing myself, yet the true terror is conjured when I imagine
what ruin you have brought to my lifetime's enterprise."

Gideon said nothing. He reached to take his father's hand, but the invalid
dragged his speckled claw away.

"This land remembers me, what I did. I carved civilization from it. I beat back
the savage, goddamn him. I—" Father's cough interrupted him. His lungs rattled,
and he spilled phlegm down his chin. "Civilization."

"Please, Father, you are unwell. Try to calm yourself. Perhaps some sleep."

"Perhaps sleep," Father said in a voice that mocked Gideon's tone. "Sage counsel
to be sure. History is written by the sleeping."

Father raised his gnarled hand once more and pointed a bony finger up at Gideon.
"You'll not raise my hackles on this day. I called you here to be spoken at, so listen."

"I brought you the accounts," Gideon said. "I have detailed everything with—"

Gideon brought forth the heavy ledgers he carried beneath his arm. Each was
carefully crafted to tell a story of vitality to his father. Each was an increasingly difficult deception. Father pushed them away with surprising vehemence.

"You brought me scrap paper and numbers written down by liars." Father sat up
in the bed. "I yet have faithful men within your midst, men whose loyalty to my
enterprise compels them to report your mismanagement. You can bring in your
Dutchman and your fancy machine. Replace white men practiced at the trade with
stinking Slavs and all those gutter Chinese. Cheaper, but they will ruin you. Those
mongrel peoples are parasites gathering upon the body of this nation."

The old man's eyes bulged, and foam gathered at the corners of his lips. His hair
was long and gray and as thin as spun sugar around the spotted dome of his head.

"Father, try to calm yourself," Gideon said as he took a step forward.

"Your brother, God rest him, was brought up for this. He had the spirit of a Long
in him."

Father fought to catch his breath.

"You have already met Mr. Horten," Gideon said with a pleading tone. "I have explained the wireworks. It is an investment that will pay dividends over—"

"We're in copper, boy. Not iron." Father sighed and allowed himself to settle back in the cushioned bed. "Your excuses no longer matter to me. I have sent for my attorney."

Gideon felt a fearful lurch and clenching in his gut. He steadied himself by leaning against his cane and tried not to show his fear. It was too late. His father's smile revealed a mouthful of teeth so decayed, they were nearly gray.

"Yes, Gideon. My attorney is come from Memphis. He will be arriving in Jessup in two days by railway. Robert Broken Horse can take care of sending a coach to retrieve him."

Father gleefully wallowed in Gideon's dismay.

"He will want to see everything. The accounts themselves, not just these ledgers. What you have done to my foundry, to the mine. To our family."

"I have done nothing."

"Nothing would be bad enough, a failure by inaction, but I suspect you are lying to me. I fear Pearce has not been put in his place, as you claim. Profligacy, perhaps criminal acts of accounting. Mr. Surebow will sniff it out, and your goose will soon be cooked."

"Yes, Father."

"Should any of my suspicions prove true, I have already alerted your sister's husband to be ready to take over the business."

Gideon began to protest, but Father held up a hand to stop him.

"He has already proven himself in his own enterprise. I should rather my life's work pass to another name than have it ruined by my own. By this method my industrious ancestors will at least enjoy some benefit of all my labors."

Father clapped his hands together to punctuate his declaration. He seemed rejuvenated by Gideon's reaction. He took the edge of the comforter in his left hand and flung it back from his body. An orange brine of liquid surrounded him on the mattress.

"I will be needing you to clean my piss."

CHAPTER TWO

■ ■ ■

He snatched in his hand the fire and the knife and ran, heedless of discovery, out into the night. He was barefoot. His nightshirt was soiled with blood. The same blood sheathed his face and his eyes were wild marbles in its midst. Smoke coughed from every crack of the shanty. Could someone yet live within its walls? Fire glowed beneath the door. The shack throbbed with malevolence.

He fled from it. Into the cold. Men were returning from shifts in the textile mills and chemical factories of Kensington. Some were barge tenders from the river come to the snowy mud and squalor of the shanties in search of pleasure.

The boy ran on against the tide of returning workers. He escaped the grasp of twenty men. He howled toward the river. In sight of the railhead he cast aside his lantern and it broke open and spilled fire in the road.

The train platform before him was crowded with travelers bound for Schuylkill and farther on. A train policeman was patrolling to prevent stowaways and thefts among the waiting travelers. The boy tried to discern some course by which he could climb onto the train and avoid detection. His head was not clear. His hands shook with the wild beat of his heart.

The fire started by his lantern was causing a commotion. A shabbily dressed man took off his jacket and used it to beat the spreading flames. Curious inhabitants of nearby shacks were emerging one by one to view the spectacle. The impromptu fire-man shouted and pointed to indicate the boy.

His only route for escape was in the direction of the river itself. He shoved past a man with the obvious intent of capturing him and leaped onto the wooden decking to the coal wharves of Port Richmond. A half dozen steam colliers crowded the docks. Most were dark and silent, their crews ashore. Two bustled with activity as the overhead cranes loaded coal into their holds.

A cry went up from behind the boy, and he sensed that he was discovered. The boots of several men beat against the dock as they chased him. If they caught him, his life would end, perhaps not by noose, but by some other slow and poisonous method. His fear propelled him, and he ran to the railing. The boy took a last glance back. He bit the blade of the knife and jumped into the Delaware.

The cold nearly sent him into shock. He could not swim. Years spent up to his knees in the muck, and he could not swim. He thrashed and kicked and was only just able to keep his head above water. His fingers collided with something, and he grabbed hold. When he bobbed to the surface again, he could see that he was clinging to the rigging of one of the iron-banded steamships. He hauled himself up the slimy ropes and paused out of sight to ensure no guard was patrolling. His body steamed in the cold air. He pressed his prickled flesh against the ship's hull.

When he was certain he was not detected, he heaved himself over the railing and onto the deck. It was crowded on the ship. Men with long hair and heavy coats focused on one another or the coal clattering into the hold. Their voices were loud and fearless. He crept across the deck undetected and turned himself sideways to slip into a gap between the ship's superstructure and its sidewall.

Exhaustion and cold took their toll. The boy sagged and lapsed into a restless sleep. His dreams were haunted by bloody visions of his deeds. He awoke for just a moment as the ship departed. Long enough to see the fires of Philadelphia receding into the distance.

He next awoke to angry shouting. One of the sailors was leaning half his body into the narrow passage the boy occupied.

"C'mere," the man said. "I ain't gonna hurt ya."

The sailor stretched his arm out as far as he could in the tight space and his grimy fingers wriggled scant inches from the boy's nose. The boy could smell the rope oil on the man's hand.

"C'mere!"

The boy slashed the knife at the sailor's fingers and nearly opened the man's wrist. The blade was made from thick bottle glass and wrapped in twine. The sailor howled in pain and surprise and retreated from the hiding spot. The boy darted out. His legs were unsteady on the swaying ship but he was too nimble for the shocked sailors to catch. He ducked under one and dodged around another. They enclosed him in a half circle and backed him against the railing.

"We have you, boy." The sailor's teeth showed red from sucking at his wound. "Throw down the knife and it'll only be a kick or two."

The boy leapt into the frigid Delaware. He resurfaced with a gasp and heard the men calling out to him and throwing ropes into the water. "You will drown!" they told him. He ignored them and paddled and kicked away into the night as best as he could manage. The ship never turned back for him.

When the boy finally pulled himself onto the rocky shore he was some ways distant from any city. Across the river a few lights burned. On his side of the river was only darkness and piles of fresh snow. The snow here was different. It seemed to trap and hold the moonlight and it took him a moment to realize it was because there was nothing *but* the snow. There were no buildings or rutted roads to break it up. Hardly any animal tracks at all.

The boy's limbs were nearly frozen. His arms were growing rigid and his legs did not bend at all. It was only his will that allowed him to start off across the snowy field. The mud beneath the snow squished between his toes and pulled at his feet. It was exhaustion piled on top of exhaustion. At least the mud of the riverbank had scoured and concealed most of the blood.

There was a dark wood to the north. He recalled a friend's tale of black bears living in the wilderness near Philadelphia and he had no true measure of how far he was from the city.

He feared the wood. In daylight he might have enjoyed it. In the darkness and on this night of all nights he was afraid of things far more sinister than bears. Spirits of retribution might haunt those trees.

The boy followed a snow-scabbed brook. It was easier to walk in the water and his feet were so numb he felt no pain from the rocks. He trudged for what seemed hours before he could not endure more. It was in that moment of surrender, with legs of lead and hair matted with frost, that the boy heard a familiar sound. The night was so quiet, and the sound was still very distant. It was the unmistakable *creak-creak-creak* of a waterwheel turning.

In his relief the boy tripped and sprawled facedown into the stream.

He splashed and stumbled forward on frozen legs. He could see the wheel now as it revolved slowly in the current. It was joined to a barrel-shaped mill house made from river bricks. A few wet lumps of snow slid from the steeply angled roof and thumped onto the rocky path to the doorway. The soft glow of candlelight was visible behind the varicolored pucks of crowned glass composing two small and deeply set windows. The candle moved behind that glass and the boy's pace quickened with excitement.

He climbed up the snow gathered at the banks of the brook. His deadened feet caught roots and he pulled himself up and out of the streambed. He set off across the field in the open. Each step cut deeply into the snow. His arms and legs no longer hurt at all. The more he walked the warmer he became.

When he first spied the mill it did not seem far away and yet he never seemed to close with it no matter his effort. Despite this he felt a great calm descending. He felt reassured and well. He felt that the candle glimpsed through the window was a fire that touched him with its warmth.

The heat built to an uncomfortable temperature and he began to pull at his sodden nightshirt. He lifted it over his head and threw it aside. Another few steps and he felt compelled by the burning heat to strip out of his flannel drawers. The skin of his arms and legs was nearly blue. He had no concern. The flow of blood would soon be restored by that incredible heat.

He stumbled and sprawled naked into the snow. He gave a queer shout as he dropped to his knees and then tipped onto his side. He was very warm and tired. Snug as a weevil in a flour sack. He laid his belly in the warm snow and let sleep come easy.

Somewhere in the distance the fire took on a voice and called the boy's name. The fire knew what he had done. He was ready. He was unafraid. He smiled into the snow and knew it was coming to claim him.

The boy woke in the mill house. It was daylight and he was swaddled like a babe in blankets three thick. He sat inches from a hearth churning with tall flames that buffeted his face.

"He's awake," said a young girl with a plain face and straight brown hair. She was sitting very near him and reacted as if he were a trapped beast coming awake.

"Go fetch Pa," said a woman.

The boy's whole body ached so that it was a great undertaking to turn his head to see who was talking. A woman smiled down at him. She possessed the same plain face as the girl, and yet she was pretty. Her eyes were brown. Her cheeks were pinched pink. The boy smiled back.

"Let me get you some hot milk," she said.

"Pa" came down the ladder from the attic. The sound of his boots arriving on the puncheon floor reminded the boy fearfully of his own father. Pa was smaller than the boy's father. He had bigger hands, though, and he easily lifted the boy up and carried him to the kitchen.

Ma ladled hot milk from a pan into a cup and held it to the boy's lips. The boy drank, though the liquid burned him. Pa cradled the boy. His black hair was as coarse as a horse brush, and odd moles like little fleshy ticks disfigured his face.

"You're safe now," Pa said. "No more harm will come to you. What do they call you? Where do you come from?"

The boy swallowed the milk and answered quietly, "Don't know."

He knew, but they never asked again, not once in seven years. They called him Stranger for a few days and then Warren. Ma said it was a strong name. It was the name of her father's brother who fought the Indians. Warren took on their family name of Groves. They taught him letters and to use a pencil and celebrated the winter day he'd come to them as the day of his birth. When he was twelve, they gave to him a black book in which to write what he thought. He treasured the book but only wrote one thing upon its pages. A name and a deed they could never know.

They loved him as their own. Fortune could not have provided a better home. In those years his brothers and sisters came to see him as shared blood. Kin of gentle demeanor. The boy named Warren knew different. By blood and by deed, he was a killer.

■ ■ ■

Sheriff Warren Groves rode high in his saddle through the streets of Spark. Pat Cole rode alongside. Cole was the bigger man and he rode the larger horse and yet Sheriff Groves commanded the attention of those on the streets at this early hour. His eyes were steely. His square jaw was unmoving beneath his natural frown.

The town was named for the sparks that flew from the axes of early prospectors striking against unexpected deposits of flint rock. The houses and hotels of the mining town atop Red Stem were tinted gold by the deceptively soft glow of the New Mexico morning. Spark was beginning to stir. Drunks staggered out of alleyways in search of a more comfortable place to lay their head. Whores and gamblers retreated from the morning light and left the world to be cleaned up and made into some estimation of wholesome again for the day.

The furnace smell of the foundry permeated every corner and the Red Brook tannery made itself known as well. There was room enough in the air for more pleasant aromas. Delilah's smelled of baking bread. Cook fires smoldered and gave off the scent of trail coffee and stew and salted ham.

Stores and hotels and saloons and cribs clung to the wagon trail running up the mountain's gentle slope like cheap beads on a string. The houses made from whitewashed mud and wood were kept to side streets. The Pearce family owned most of the land in town and doled it out with preference given to their own employees. The workers at the Pearce foundry were nearer the summit end of town to shorten their walk.

The employees of the Long foundry and the other businesses were scattered throughout and their dwellings tended toward cheapness and disorder. A hearty few solitary miners worked private claims beyond the limits of Spark and came into town to spend away a nugget. In the short years Warren Groves had held the office of sheriff these solitary folk had mostly gone. Their claims were bought up and the land stirred into the Pearce holdings. The sheriff lived beyond the town himself but did not bring law down to the drainage of Red Stem where the Chinese camps had grown and stayed.

They had their own justice down in the mountain's shadow. It was dirty and served the needs of industry for a price paid in men's misery. Would the Pearce family have their way that law would be imposed on Spark as well.

"Good to meet you this morning, Warren," said Mayor Partridge. "Should I be concerned that you are on patrol this early hour?"

The portly mayor was outside a parlor house in undershirt and suspenders. He appeared to be washing his hair out of a bucket. Soapy water dripped from his fingers. His cheeks were red with a fresh shave.

"I will let you know on that," said Sheriff Groves.

Deputy Cole gave Sheriff Groves a sidelong look and a smile. They continued to ascend the mountain up Spark's rutted main thoroughfare.

They met Bo Fairway outside the Whitney. He sat beneath an umbrella at a table drinking coffee. It was the largest hotel in town and sported a three-story theater palace with gambling and saloon. Its ramshackle appearance owed to the gradual nature of its many expansions. No surer sign of a boom time in Spark than the sound of saws and hammers at the Whitney. Sheriff Groves reckoned it quiet enough to hear the ring of a spittoon in the hotel.

"Have a coffee, gentlemen," said Bo. "Sit down with me. The rowdies have all packed up, and it'll be nice and peaceful. Have a breakfast."

"Had both already, Mr. Fairway, but I do appreciate the offer."

"Annie large?" asked Bo Fairway.

Sheriff Groves slowed his horse with a light tug on the reins. "She is. Big as a barn."

"God willing everything goes well for the two of you. A good man deserves a break from hardship."

"Deserving got nothing to do with who draws a hot hand in this world." Sheriff Groves saluted Fairway with a tip of his hat and rode on.

Farther up Red Stem Sheriff Groves and Pat Cole turned their horses off the main road and followed a path worn between houses and rain barrels. Their destination was tucked away amid miners' shanties. The large adobe house was finished in gaily painted wood and a sign above the porch read simply IDA's. The woman herself stood in the doorway. She leaned against the frame like a cat against its owner's leg. Ida was a cat for sure—long-legged and tanned, and since retired to open her own establishment. Her corset wasn't as full as once it was and her thin limbs were drooping with the waste of age.

Sheriff Groves and Deputy Cole tied off their horses at the post and walked into the shade of the porch. Ida Pinkney stepped aside to allow them in. There wasn't much to her establishment, and it had no reputation for fine or tender women.

The parlor was shabbily finished with a bar and a few tables and clay spittoons overflowing onto creaky planks. A cheap Walinford piano was intended for amusement and to keep men from fighting while they waited for friends. The real business was done in back with the Mexican Indian and Chinese girls in windowless mud cells separated by hung sheets. Space enough for six beds in four rooms.

"Sheriff," said Ida. "Glad Tom found you."

"It's been a while. You are looking fine today."

"You are a bad liar," Ida said. "Deputy Cole. How is Libby?"

Pat Cole frowned and said, "Elizabeth is doing well. I am sure she will be happy you asked after her."

Ida chuckled. Her thick whore's plaster turned the half of her face caught in the light into textured clay. She sat them down at one of the tables and flopped into the chair across from them with an unladylike weariness. "I have been at it since the day afore, so if my manners are not what you've come to expect, please forgive me."

Sheriff Groves set his hat on the table. "Your man Tom the Indian said you had concern the outlaw John Vargas was on the premises in the night. Said I ought to come talk with you on that. So here I am. Say what you felt you needed to."

Ida packed her lip with tobacco before answering. "I weren't sure at first," she said. "He is uglier than the scrawl on them posters. Is his hide really worth five hundred dollars?"

"Alive and for his capture," said Sheriff Groves. "To be paid by the Bank of New Mexico on account of evil done in Santa Fe. Not from my pocket, just so you understand. I am only concerned with outlaws in our town."

"I'll trust your honest reputation not to usurpate no reward money from me." Ida spit across the room with fine accuracy. A bit of brown juice dribbled from her lip. "There's more to it than just John Vargas. He was here with a pig of a Mexican. They were talkin' up some sort of train robbery. Spending money like they'd already done it but talkin' like it was still to come."

"Did he say where and when?" said Deputy Cole.

"By my own ear I cannot say. He spent money with one of my girls. Rose the Indian. She told me his lips loosened once he'd wet his prick. Says he's got a whole gang, and they were planning it for tomorrow."

Sheriff Groves tapped the table. "Did he speak to his methods?"

Ida rolled her eyes up as if she might see her memories. "Yes, actually, he sure did. Or maybe so. Rose told me John Vargas bragged when he got real drunk and sought her again about having a whole wagonful of powder. Stoled it from the engineers. You think he's set to blow up a train?"

"Vargas blew up a bank to get at its money. You said there was a Mexican with him?"

"He didn't do nothing except laugh at everything. Just laughing and laughing at even things that wasn't jokes."

Sheriff Groves thanked Ida for the information and the water and left with Deputy Cole following him. They mounted up and began to navigate their way back out to the main road. The day was lighter and less colored, and the wagoneers and tradesmen were beginning to show their faces.

"If you had to rob a train headed to Las Cruces, where would you lie in wait?" Sheriff Groves asked.

"Jessup is the only stop between there and up north," said Pat Cole. It was a well-known fact. In recent years Spark had directly competed with Jessup for the rail. A few years back the Pacific Southern's surveyors had decided the grade favored Jessup. It dealt a blow to Sparks's economic future. "They wouldn't need a whole wagon of powder to rob a stopped train."

Sheriff Groves was glad his deputy was catching on. "They ain't robbing a stopped train," said Sheriff Groves. "They aim to stop it before it gets to Jessup."

"If Ida's story was true."

"That bank robbery Vargas was in on went wrong in Santa Fe. He was just a part, not its leader, and they was a pack of wild idiots anyway. They accidentally burned all the money. Most of the gang was caught or killed."

A drunk lay passed out in their path. He was facedown and snoring into a puddle of sick crawling with flies. His feet were bare. Pat Cole guided his horse around the drunk. Sheriff Groves was sure enough in his mount to ride over the man.

"I am curious," Sheriff Groves said. "How does John Vargas have money to waste *before* a train robbery? I ain't heard of a robbery that pays out in advance."

They emerged onto the main road and Sheriff Groves reined his horse to a halt. It danced in a nervous circle.

"Vargas has been paid to do the robbery," said Pat Cole.

"Ride to the office. You and Turk lasso whoever you can and hand out stars. Good riders only—might be need to cross tough terrain. I intend to check Bo Fairway's and the other cribs on the chance Vargas and his Mexican are still laid up in town."

"You reckon we should tell Colonel Midlinghall?"

Sheriff Groves thought on the consequences of involving the Army and then nodded. "Mildenhall," he corrected. "Yes. Army ought to be told," he said.

"What about Annie?"

"We'll stop by," said Sheriff Groves. "I need to be certain she can hold for another day."

CHAPTER THREE

■ ■ ■

There was Annabelle and Clarice and Penelope of the name Moraud; three beautiful daughters to a doting father. Monsieur Moraud was dedicated to the hand-making of violins. He was successful enough to employ a number of craftsmen, and the Moraud label was well respected and valued by musicians from Moscow to London. This business afforded Mr. Moraud and his three girls their tutors, house-keepers, and a luxurious home in the beauteous green massif of the Vosges, in the between where France and Germany folded together.

Annabelle was the youngest of the girls and had come into the world as her mother left it. The doctor had said it was bleeding caused by a natural defect of her mother's biology. Mr. Moraud had never voiced any blame toward Annabelle, but as a young girl she had secretly harbored the shame that it was her own existence that took her mother's life. When alone, she stared at her mother's painted portraits on the walls and wondered what parts of her mother endured within her. Was it her blue eyes or copper-colored hair? Did Mr. Mendel's alchemy bestow to Annabelle the gentle point of her mother's chin or the rosy cheeks?

Mr. Moraud said that the physical resemblance was uncanny, but it was Annabelle's way that reminded him most of her mother. She knew he watched her from his bedroom on the second floor as she stood apart from her sisters. While they played and sang songs together, little Annabelle spent her afternoons alone and silent in the apple orchard. She plucked fallen apples from the cold stream and filled her dress with them. In the evening she would peel them and bake them with sugar or honey.

This idyllic life did not endure. The Morauds were Huguenots whose religion more closely resembled that of the German Calvinists than of the Catholics who lived all around them. The Germans of Strasbourg wished for Mr. Moraud to join them, but Mr. Moraud said he was a French patriot. "And those Germans do not dance," he was fond of saying. "I must dance with my girls." The Germans closed their shops to his instruments and refused to transport his violins east. His country-men did not repay his loyalty. The Catholics who supplied his workshop refused him tendon and rosin and fine, imported woods. They heard he traded with the Germans, so they refused to transport his violins west.

Mr. Moraud never wavered in faith, for he said it was a duty to his beloved wife to share her beliefs with their daughters. He doubled his efforts to instill faith in his girls even as his fortunes waned. He soon realized he could no longer afford to provide his daughters with all the finer things to which they were accustomed. He gathered them up in the parlor and explained that they would have to leave. He wished to take them to America, where they would begin a new life. He told them tales of this distant and limitless country to excite their imagination.

Penelope, who was the eldest, sobbed and fled from the parlor and shut herself up in the cushioned fastness of her bedroom. Clarice, who was too finely-mannered for such a display, buried her face in her folded arms. Mr. Moraud sighed and sat back in his chair. Annabelle came to his side and told him that she wanted to see America. She had read of it in books, mostly books of Louisiana but also tales of the north, where vast cities grew with speed.

Upon arriving in Boston, Mr. Moraud opened a business and established his family in a small apartment. Almost at once reality diverged from his plan. Mr. Moraud was cheated by his business partner and left destitute. He produced violins himself, though his hands were growing stiff with age, and these violins were shabby in comparison to the masterworks of his youth. He made enough money to buy wood for his stove and food for his daughters and little else.

Annabelle watched life shape her father into something hard and unhappy. He returned each day from stringing violins and carving their necks a little more stooped and a little cloudier in the eyes. He drank schnapps and slept in his chair beside the stove. He did not sing any longer. He did not dance with his girls, not even during the holidays. The Bible they brought from France gathered dust upon the shelf.

Penelope left first. Annabelle watched her pack in the night, afraid to tell their father that she was marrying a man of German stock and modest means. Clarice's departure was more gradual and yet more sudden. She served as an office girl in a textile mill and spent her nights wearing gaudy dresses and pursuing men in unlady-like ways. Annabelle barely recognized her. Their father suspected vice, and every conversation became one of terrible shouting and breaking crockery. Clarice simply did not return from work one evening.

After three days passed, Annabelle urged her father to visit the mill where Clarice was employed to ask after her sister. Mr. Moraud went in a dark and serious suit but was turned away and told to keep off the property. They visited the gendarmes together, Annabelle by her father's side as the man in the blue suit with the brass buttons told them that many daughters disappeared in a city such as Boston and that, after all, Clarice was old enough to choose to do so.

Annabelle lay in the lonely room she had shared with her sister and imagined that Clarice, with her golden hair and bawdy American ways, had met a wealthy man and left with him for New York City. They dined in cafes atop the tallest buildings and rode in carriages that glowed at night with hanging lanterns. Father once said that he believed Clarice dead but spoke no more on the matter.

Father left Annabelle last. The physicians told her it was a disease of his blood, contracted from an untreated wound. He lay sick for many days, growing grayer and grayer, speaking deliriously, mistaking Annabelle for her mother during his wakeful moments, until he was gone. She dried the last sweat from his brow and did not feel the urge to weep. Men from the church took the body the next day.

She stood in his empty shop, no bigger than a shed, and touched the tools he had once used to make wood become a violin. She stood in the bedroom and looked at the small portrait of her mother beside his empty sickbed. She stared at the stuffed chair that still bore his shape. Her father was utterly gone. The burial was a matter of procedure.

She returned home in her black dress and sat in his chair and drank his schnapps. In a despairing panic she searched the apartment for memories of the lives that had been stolen from her. She found pencils and scraps of notes and nothing. Nothing like what she wanted.

Within a cabinet she discovered a tin box, small and green, painted by hand with the image of a woman wearing a wreath of flowers and leaves, and above this was the name *Vervains*. There were traces of corrosion visible at the worn edges of the box.

It was so very quiet in the apartment. The stove had gone cold, and her foggy breath puffed into the room. Annabelle wiped her eyes and set the box upon the table. She opened it slowly, and the hinges squeaked. Within the box was a small pile of gold and silver coins and folded banknotes. There was an unpleasant, metallic odor but also the familiar smell of sawdust and string and the oils used to treat the wood her father had used.

There was also a book, *An Account of the West*, its pages yellowed with smoke but its pasteboard illustrations clear and detailed. Within this book was described and illuminated a world without the stone tombs of tenements or the filthy alleyways prowled by criminals. It was an empty place, beautiful but waiting to be filled. Mountains, like the Vosges, capped with snow, and trains that seemed to paint the world behind them. Streams cut deep grooves into the world, and landscapes of impossible breadth were inhabited by mill wheels and stagecoaches and lonesome hotels.

Annabelle was precipitously alone, and yet excitement fluttered within her. The whole of America stretched before her, where anything could be hewn from wood and stone and given form by perseverance and intellect. She decided the matter that easily. By this inheritance she would seek out the story that better suited her yearning. She would never recapture the fairy tale of her childhood, but she could author her own somewhere far away from Boston. Somewhere west.

■ ■ ■

Annie was alone beneath the quilt. Warren was gone. She recalled through the cotton walls of a dream his distant weight lifting from the stuffed mattress. He'd left early in the morning. Off to be Sheriff Warren Groves. She was accustomed to his settling disputes in town or arresting the rowdies, accustomed to wondering if he would come home with all his parts.

It was a struggle to rise from the bed in her pregnant state. She padded to the door. Nel was puttering away in the kitchen. The old midwife must have been up early to fix breakfast for Warren.

Annie returned to the bedside and knelt on the floor. She stretched a hand beneath the wooden bed frame and felt for the top of the box. Her fingertips found the smooth metal top and traced the corrosion upon the edges. She slid the box across the floor until it appeared at her knees. It was made from tin and painted with a portrait of a woman wearing a crown of flowers beneath the name *Vervains*.

She stole a last glance at the door and opened the box. There were letters. Nineteen, she knew precisely, and each had been read a dozen times. Beneath the bundled letters were the gifts. There were golden earrings set with sapphire, a sparkling gold and exotic ruby necklace, silver rings, ivory and jade broaches, and bracelets—a treasure few men could afford their wives.

She let her fingers drag across the jewelry, savoring each with the lusty guilt of an illicit lover. She lifted the stack of envelopes tied with a red ribbon. These letters were addressed to her as *A*, and her name was never penned within them. The bundle weighed a hundred pounds in her hands. She took out the most recent letter and found it seemed heavier than most.

A, together soon, the beauty of the world will belong to you.

Annie sighed. She never should have allowed him into that private world. They were her own words, repeated back many months later. Her romantic daydream.

"In my greed I long for all the beauty of the world and for it to belong to me." She had to tell him it was done. He was taking it too far, and with the baby soon to come, she could not—

There was a knock at the door, and Nel said, "Mrs. Groves?"

Annie's heart felt as though it would explode. She quickly replaced the letter in the bundle and closed it back into the box with the red ribbon trailing out. She pushed the box under the bed just as the door opened. She clasped her hands together as if in prayer. It was a cruel way to deceive but all that came to her in the moment.

"Would you—oh, ma'am, I am sorry, I did not realize you was attending the Lord." The midwife ducked her head and retreated back through the door.

"I am finished," Annie said, and she got to her feet.

"I heard you stir and was come to ask if you would like a bath. The kettle is already on the stove."

"That would be nice."

"I'll fetch the tub and get it poured. You come have some tea I made."

Annie luxuriated in the bath. She leaned the back of her long neck against the rim of the tub and allowed her copper-blond hair to spill down nearly to the floor. A diminishing *drip-drip* of water pattered against the old blanket spread beneath.

Even on a good day her ankles and feet were swollen and tender. Her back hurt. Her breasts piled uncomfortably atop the taut cannonball of her belly. In the heat of the day she became terribly sweaty, and at night she found it difficult to sleep. Any chance to be off her feet was a welcome comfort. A hot bath was a particular luxury.

She floated in the warm water, and the salt of her aches dissolved. Her skin glistened. She was as tan as a cowhand on her arms and legs. She touched herself and wondered what it might feel like to have a man other than Warren hold her. She had never met one so strong and handsome as her husband, and yet, she did desire more from life than the simple happiness he gave her.

The baby kicked. She laughed as if she'd been caught in her thoughts. This one was strong. At night Warren laid a hand on her belly and felt it pushing. He was sure it was the son he had been after since their wedding.

Annie tested the dovetailed curve of the tub with her feet. She pressed against the metal, and it flexed.

She knew better than Warren. The first and second time she had known it was a boy. She'd birthed two sons to the coffin. Strangled like calicos by her womb. This time was different. She could feel the girl.

Nel was at the door again. The old midwife had seen her through two unhappy births and had been hired on to help with the third. Pat Cole's wife, Libby, warned that the woman was an ill omen, but Annie valued Nel's competent manner over any superstition.

"Do ya need more water?" asked Nel. She held a copper kettle in one hand and a terry towel in the other. "We don't want you too hot, or it might cook the baby."

"Just a bit," said Annie, and though the woman had seen more of her than even Warren, she covered herself with her arm.

Nel began to pour steaming water into the tub, raising the level of the milky liquid nearly to the tops of Annie's bent knees. Annie hissed as plumes of hot water caressed her legs.

"We want you clean for that birthing." Nel tottered away from the tub and peered through the slatted window. "You know I midwifed for Mrs. Farris, oh, about two years back, an' the baby just fell on out in the bath. No labor, nothing. Just squirted on out."

"There is a picture," said Annie, and she laughed. "I saw a piglet let out of a bag at Schroeder's once. I'd imagine it was something like that, was it?"

"Goodness, no," Nel said. "Mrs. Farris stayed as big as house for, oh, on about two years now, I'd reckon."

The two women shared a laugh at the thought, and Nel left Annie alone to soak.

The morning was dimming to gray. Rain-heavy clouds gathered to the east were moving swiftly toward the house and were already in the way of the sun. Looked to be a summer storm come early. She watched the clouds drifting closer and closer.

Annie used to love the rain, but where Warren had built their house, it caused nothing but problems. Storm drainage from Spark collected mine tailings and left its residue in their horse pasture. After particularly heavy rains it could make a stinking lake that lasted days and killed off the grazing.

She was startled by flying shadows passing the windows. Hooves beat the dusty road, and Annie could see the shadows to be men riding down from the mountain. There were a number of them. Ringo, their black and white cow dog, came barking out from the barn to challenge the riders.

The baby kicked, and it hurt. The baby kicked again. There was another pain beneath the baby's kicks, an ache that seemed to ebb and flow with her breathing. Annie got her feet beneath her in the tub and pushed herself up. She stood and reached for the towel.

Beyond the window slats the world was growing darker. The rain was beginning to beat against the metal roof of the barn. Ringo was barking madly with excitement.

Annie found the towel with her fingers and brought it to her dripping body. The baby kicked again. She could see Warren and Pat Cole and Turk. Other men she half recognized. Warren got down from his horse, dipped his shoulders and lowered his head, and began running toward the front door as the rain swept across the pasture and clattered up the shingles of the house.

She could hear the door opening. Feel the baby kick again. Warmth gushed between her thighs. She looked down at the soapy white water filling the tub. A red flower was spreading beneath her. The baby kicked. Fear pricked her brow and ran hot in her blood. Boots thumped on puncheon floor.

"Annie," Warren said as he entered the room. "Got to—"

"It's not supposed to be like that," Annie said, and she looked from her husband down to the blood swirling in the bath. "It's not supposed to . . . I'm bleeding."

He ran to her, caught her up in his arms, and lifted her easily out of the tub. She smelled the trail and something else, foul, clinging to him.

"What do I do?" he asked.

She did not know.

CHAPTER FOUR

■ ■ ■

They came down from the mountain and into the shimmering heat of the badlands. They pursued the choked meander of Green Creek, rode hard through morning, and kept the rain-darkened sky at their backs. Gideon piloted the muscular white mare called Sirocco, sure-footed over root and sage and beaten agave. Father's old Crow Indian Robert Broken Horse rode ahead in the saddle of the cream gelding he favored for long journeys. The Indian was trail wise and steady. He pointed out falls and snake holes to Gideon so that he might avoid them.

It was midday when they passed the skeleton trusses of the rail bridge. Robert Broken Horse found a gentleness in the bank and rode down into the dry wash and among the boulders. The creek bed was stained to a high waterline by copper deposits, and the flaked verdigris collected in cracks and against stones half-buried in sun-split alluvium to lend the wash a queer, mossy appearance.

They sought the place where the men lay in wait. There were twenty or so of them. Rough men. Vaqueros and bandits and horse thieves. Men with ropes waiting for them wherever law found purchase. There were also the country boys, aflame in their youth, heads full of notions of disappearing in clouds of gun smoke rather than surviving to be preyed upon by time and toil.

Gideon noticed a third and even more distinct breed. Apaches. Mescalero renegades. Just tame enough to withhold murder for every white or Spanish they saw but fierce enough to kill for money. A mercenary band of the savages had been hired on.

There were four of these creatures, and they kept apart from the other men. They stood beside their painted ponies, high on the bank and as far from the rail bridge as possible.

Their flesh was like stained wood, and they layered over it the rough-stitched hides of animals. Their black hair was long and tied with beads and feathers and bones, and they wrapped their boots and lower legs in snake-bite botas. They carried knives as well as guns of a caliber and fashion that resembled crude imitations of more honest weapons, though surely even the cleverest Apache possessed no means to manufacture rifles and pistols.

Their faces were terrible, and Gideon could not stand to look upon them long. They were devil idols carved from rock. To meet their black eyes was to open a door best left barred, but he could feel their gaze as spiders upon his neck, and he imagined they judged how he might appear when drained of blood and cut down to chops and brisket.

The other men rose slowly from the dust and gathered around the newcomers. Robert Broken Horse addressed them in Spanish and then English. Gideon climbed down from his horse and greeted the Yankee Eli McClelland, who had seen to the emplacement and fusing of the night before.

McClelland was huge and red-faced, his mustache drooping with sweat. McClelland's barrel-body was stuffed into a Union coat so beaten, it looked gray everywhere but the damp beneath his arms and in a ring around his neck. He, like all men involved in this mob, had been told that Gideon's name was Eustace Wiley. It was a name of pure fantasy and one that Gideon entertained might become famous after this day.

The big Yankee shook Gideon's hand vigorously and said, "Good to finally meet you, Mr. Wiley. Your Indian told me you were the strategist of our endeavor."

Gideon smiled and nodded his thanks. He took out his gold pocket watch and inspected it.

"Should be upon us shortly," said McClelland. "Everything is stuck in like cockle-burrs. They were a surly crew, but I put the fear of God into them, and we got it done. It's a minute burn, give or take, to this one and five minutes to the other. I've laid in enough powder and should have—"

Gideon climbed atop the largest boulder he could find, and the men turned and regarded him with slight curiosity. He held his walking cane like a circus barker's and spread his arms wide to encompass the vast reach of the New Mexico sky. The storm was behind him, long and dark, moving steadily east in search of bones to wash.

"Gentlemen, if I could command your attention for a moment," Gideon said, and Robert Broken Horse translated into Spanish. "In scarce minutes a black train of the Pacific Southern Railroad will come steaming into the trap we have laid. My colleague and I have gone to heroic lengths to ensure our plan requires a minimum of violence. Our numbers and the suddenness of our attack will be sufficient to disarm crew and passengers. However, I have learned that a snake of a man has slithered aboard the train."

Distant thunder rumbled and caromed from the western mountains.

"This snake comes from Memphis, dresses in cotton suits bought from a store in New York, and wears little glass spectacles. He parts his hair in the middle. He carries a red valise—a red bag—from which he will not be separated without violence.

Therefore, I make an exception for him, and violence is my aim and desire, to not only harm but to kill this man, for he means to do as much to me."

Gideon avoided coloring his description of Mr. Surebow with the full contempt he held for the man.

"This is very important. The man who kills him and hands over his bag will be rewarded with one hundred silver dollars."

The white men murmured with excitement. Once Robert Broken Horse translated the offer into Spanish, the vaqueros whistled and jawed. Gideon allowed a moment of conversation and then beat the copper ferule of his cane against the platform of the boulder. His audience fell silent once more and tilted their dirt-smeared faces to him.

"My, um, my father," Gideon began, but he was uncertain of this beginning, and so he fell silent once more. He looked from the expectant faces of his outlaws to the Apache Indians and beyond, to the snarls of mountains south and west.

Gideon detested acts without meaning as animalistic. For this undertaking to be successful, it was his vital duty to imbue these men with a higher purpose than riches. Difficult, for they seemed by the very act of ambushing the railroad to align themselves against Gideon's concept of progress.

"We tear down mountains today." Gideon gestured with his cane. A few men turned their heads to look at the mountains he indicated. "Look at them sitting sullen and untouchable. Arrogant. They pass the centuries with barely a mark. But their days are numbered, my friends. What is coming here has already arrived out east. The future belongs to us. Railroads and paved streets and gas to light your house at night. And the mountains, gravid with riches, are doomed. The natural world places no value on ore. Only man divines purpose. We dig it up and build, and from a meaningless collection of stones and wood we have, by labor and design, derived civilization.

"It is the law of man that most valuable of all is paper and coin," said Gideon. "Men no longer require the natural order at all to decide worth. Then are we not visionaries to see that we can labor for long years for rewards and riches, or we can simply take it?"

He waited for a response, but the men only stared.

"Do not squander the riches you claim today on fleeting pleasures." Gideon's words were a chastisement to himself. "When each of us is dust, do you think our descendants will care or even remember the origin of their wealth? We determine the future on this day, without regard to nature or to the, um, the peculiar caprices of men in cotton suits. To hell with the sons of bitches from Memphis or New York. We make the world our own, we'll tear down the mountains for their gold, and dare the fools to stop us."

Robert Broken Horse finished his translation to Spanish. The vaqueros, outlaws, farm boys, and even the savage Apaches stared at Gideon as though he might grow horns. They said nothing, not even a whisper, and their expressions communicated little more.

Gideon wiped at the sweat of his brow with a black handkerchief. These base animals had no place for higher thoughts. A whore or a new saddle. A gun to wear on their hip. They conceived no greater tomorrow than a finer privy in which to shit.

A childish giggling emerged from the gathered men. Gideon searched their faces for the culprit, but most seemed to not care or to be as confused as he was. The giggling became a full-throated howl of mirth.

Men began to step aside and move away until the source of the laughter was revealed by subtraction to be a short, pock-faced Mexican. He was so fat, his shirt was poorly buttoned, and his arms bulged out at his cuffs. He stood next to another man Gideon recognized from print accounts as the bank robber John Vargas.

"Be quiet, you beast," Gideon demanded.

The rebuke propelled the portly Mexican to further paroxysms of laughter. The vaqueros and other men around him muttered with annoyance. Only the outlaw John Vargas, languid with opium, stood beside the laughing Mexican untouched by his companion's apparent madness.

There was another sound. A distant rumble, not loud, but felt in the legs.

"Smoke!" shouted Eli McClelland.

The rumble grew louder and seemed to crackle like fire. Gideon looked up the bank to where the Yankee stood atop a rock pile. The engineer lowered a spyglass from his eye and jumped down from the rocks. He stumbled and slid down the bank into the wash.

"Train is coming," he said. "Light the number one fuse."

Only after the Yankee struck a match and lit the first fuse was the source of the rumble revealed. It was not the storm or the approaching train, which was still many miles distant, but an ugly head of floodwater come thundering down from the mountains, frothing and thick with mud and branches and wagon bones.

The horses panicked and bolted in a dozen directions, clambering up the rocky banks and throwing shoes in their desperation to escape the water. It seemed to move slowly in a custard wave and yet was upon them almost the instant it was spotted. A few men had time to cry in alarm or scramble toward the bank before the flood washed over their shoes and up to their knees with great velocity. The rushing water toppled men over and carried the unlucky away down the flooded creek, possibly never to be seen alive again.

Gideon was near enough the bank to catch a rock with one hand as he was thrown down on his side. His head struck a sharp corner of stone. Hot blood gushed into his hair and down his cheek. The blow nearly caused him to lose his hold and be dragged away by the churning mud.

Robert Broken Horse, who must have seen the water coming and escaped, dragged Gideon onto the rocks and laid him on his back. Gideon spit out a mouthful of bitter muck and cursed the pain and all of it.

The air was sharp with the smell of the burning fuse and the loamy stink of the floodwater. Men gasped and shouted and heaved their bodies out of the wash on either side of the swollen creek. Inverted to Gideon's supine view, high upon the bank, the four taciturn Apaches stood, unmoved, beside their ponies.

■   ■   ■

Annie's world was swimmy cold and blue at its edges. She felt sick and strange, and maybe her bones were shaking inside. Maybe her whole body was shaking inside.

Warren kept saying, he kept saying, "Rain is gonna stop soon." Only it never did stop like he said. Only she could hear it still *clatter-clatter* against the roof and *whoosh* with wind against the panes of glass.

"Bleeding is normal," Doc Carson said. "She opened up good, and I can feel the baby. If need be, I'll use the tool."

Warren said something so she couldn't hear the doctor—that thing he did when he talked to Pat Cole about a shooting or a stabbing so she wouldn't know. He didn't even want to look at her. He was wearing his hat in the house.

Low voices, men talking. Men talk. Nel held Annie's arm and whispered, "It will be fine. It will be fine." Why was it so hard to make sense of things?

"No, it won't be fine," Annie said, but the words were crackers in her mouth, and all stuck to her lips and tongue.

"It ain't fever," Doc Carson said. "Don't you worry, Sheriff. I'll see to her. Might be night before she's through."

"No, please," Annie said, only the words were strangled. It was never like this before. They thought it was, but it wasn't like this before.

They didn't know anything to do. Men did men things, and watching the little baby come out wasn't a man thing. She knew, some way, that Warren was afraid to see her now. She was turned into a bad thing.

Annie struggled to sit. Nel held her fast to the bed.

"Calm yourself," Nel said. "Shh. Just try to breathe."

Not okay. No. She could feel him leaving. The thump of boots she could see in her head. She knew which part of the floor he was standing on by the way the house sounded beneath him.

He stopped just inside the kitchen. She could close her eyes and see his fingers on the stove. Feeling the greasy ridges of cast iron. Heat of morning's fire. He turned around, shuffling his feet as though he might come back.

She begged him to come back. Why would he leave her now?

The feet thumped away. The door opened, the rain came in, and when the door closed again, he was gone. Not just left the room. Gone.

Nel whispered something to Doc Carson, and Doc Carson said something back. Something with the word "train" that Annie could not understand.

Nel lifted the towel held between Annie's legs and showed it to Doc Carson. Annie couldn't see his face, because the world was dark and blue around that part. She could see the white towel, though. It was all turned dripping. Bright red and dripping. Wasn't like this before.

■ ■ ■

Sheriff Warren Groves and his deputies Pat Cole and the foreigner who was called Turk rode the freshly mudded trail down from Red Stem and south into the flatlands. They had with them half a dozen good men with paper badges pinned to their coats and fresh rifles and more cartridges than an army would need for provision.

The storm clouds scudded the heights of the Red Lines and gave their rain and left, off north and east. The riders soon crossed the clear divide in the landscape where the rain had darkened the rocks and earth. On the other side of this line it was parchment soil and sun-hot stone. The desert plain was untouched except by flood.

The unseasonal rain sought the lowland and collected in the dry washes. The waters formed thin streams on the surface and emptied into barren creeks and carried off the ribs of canoes and the footbridges. Sheriff Groves warned the less experienced riders to keep clear of the banks no matter the temptation to get a look at the rain's architecture. No time for that.

Each man knew he rode with urgency and for danger. Though the men were no greenhorns, they were unseemly in their spoil for a fight. Only Sheriff Groves and maybe Pat Cole knew what was being left behind. Sheriff Groves looked at his big deputy and felt no inclination to discuss the matter. Annie's birth trouble weighed heavy on his heart and there wasn't a thing left to decide by talking.

They crossed many miles of graben and raised dust behind them and passed the burned husks of Indian tents and the fallen bricks of haciendas. They reached the Ciruela Escarpment near midday. The tableland fell away by twenty to thirty feet in a steep cliff of whinstone and snowy pilings of gypsum sand. The escarpment continued west to east in a ragged boundary stretching for more than five miles. At the edges of the escarpment the land sagged and poured out smooth as flour to the desert below. There was no time for cautious detours.

Sheriff Groves stopped the horses and got down and walked to the edge of the cliff to view the terrain. Footpaths were cut into the stone face. Those nearby were wide enough to allow a man to walk a mule or horse down to the desert below.

"I don't favor that approach," said Pat Cole.

Sheriff Groves pointed out to the horizon. The smoke of the train was easily spotted and beneath it the moving line of the train itself. It crossed within the rusty spokes and felloes of the rail bridge at Bear Creek as they watched.

"If we mean to catch that train, this is our route," said Sheriff Groves. "We can ride for the bridge at Green Creek."

He studied the desert sprawling below. He told the men what had to be done and they got down from their saddles. They took their horses' reins in hand and formed a single file to descend the twisting path cut into the face of the escarpment. Sheriff Groves went first and warned the men behind not to be distracted by the train.

He could see that Pat Cole was wary of the height. Sheriff Groves thought to tell Pat Cole to stay as lookout. Thought better. Such a thing said aloud would have undermined his deputy and driven him to act with foolish bravado.

The horses rolled their eyes in their heads and resisted. Once coaxed onto the trail their ears swiveled at the sound of each pebble loosed by a bad step. The horses ground their teeth against their bits and foam dripped from their mouths.

The path cut back and forth down the escarpment so that the men at the front of the line were directly beneath the men at the back. A look down was dizzying for the height and sheerness. The broken skeletons of mules and goats lay half-buried under rocks and alkali sand. It was slow going.

Sheriff Groves' horse stopped and refused to go on. They were nearly at the bottom. He fought the reins to keep his horse moving. It whinnied in protest and stomped its feet. He clucked at the horse and slackened the lead and yanked it taut again.

"Want me to kick him?" asked Pat Cole.

There was a fool idea. Sheriff Groves laid a hand on his horse's face and leaned in close. "Almost there," he said. The horse was not calmed nor inclined to move.

Sheriff Groves squinted over his horse's muzzle at the shimmering desert. Flat miles of badland and dry sage. Even the cactuses seemed to be struggling in the heat. He could hear the rush of floodwaters and nearer was the cry of mated quails. He could not hear the train and this near to the ground he could only judge its location by the smoke above it.

He was searching the distance as a great mass of brown and black dirt convulsed. It lifted from the plain to the south and heaved up in a mound and carried into the air the bridge over Bear Creek. Several men gasped in surprise at the sight. The bridge's iron trusses came apart and along with a barrage of stones flew hundreds of feet into the sky.

Sheriff Groves stared for fully a second before he recognized what was happening. "God Almighty," he said.

The sound beat against them like a blow from an open hand. The force threw hats from heads and knocked the men caught unaware against the face of the cliff. Sheriff Groves was nearly trampled as his horse surged down the trail. He rolled over the side of the path and suffered the fall of six or seven feet onto the pile of loose rock.

There was a great crash and cry and men and animals came tumbling down the cliff from various heights. Sheriff Groves rolled and got up out of the way. His stomach turned at the sight of men and horses dashed upon the rocks. The animals screamed. Ink stains of blood flicked from broken limbs. Some horses found their legs and got up and some were badly injured and could only kick and cry with pain.

Pat Cole's legs lay pinned beneath the deputy's huge bay horse. The stout lawman hollered from the pain and he was not a man known to complain much at injury.

The train's whistle blew a shrill note to signal braking. Boulders and stones flung into the air by the distant explosion began to fall not far away. Sheriff Groves could feel the impacts of the largest of these beneath his boots. The stink of the blasting powder and uprooted bridge was carried by the smoke from the blast. The train's brakes began to squeal.

Men got up from the calamity and caught the reins of loose horses. The paper deputies were cursing and bloodied and not seriously hurt. Most animals could be saved and were not so badly hurt that they could not ride. The sheriff's horse and a few others had kept their footing or had escaped injury despite having rolled a dozen feet down the pitiless face of the escarpment.

There was nothing to be done for Pat Cole's horse. All four of the animal's fetlocks and hooves dangled as uselessly as sticks in socks. Bone showed through the hide and blood spattered the rocks each time it kicked. Pat Cole hadn't seen it yet. He was busy with a stream of curses.

Turk brought over his shotgun and placed the barrel to the horse's head. Sheriff Groves tried to calm Pat Cole down but the deputy had a great fondness for the horse and cried out in dismay when he realized what was happening. The gun sounded and the horse's head flung back in reflex. The animal's long neck drooped to the ground. Black blood drained out of mouth and eyes. The horse's hindquarters kicked for several seconds and further injured Pat Cole.

Turk said he was sorry to Pat Cole and went over to Jasper Toomey's horse. The Indian paint sat up as a child in a chair and screamed for the pain of its nearly amputated back legs folded underneath its rump. Turk shot this horse as well. It landed on its side with a crash of stone and lifting dust. A great quantity of blood spilled out of its head and turned the rocks dark. Jasper Toomey complained at the cost of the horse and the imposition of being forced to ride with another man.

The other men were not seriously hurt and together they got a rope around the neck of Pat Cole's horse. As they labored Sheriff Groves was mindful of the train slowing across the plain. Some men held up the horse's hindquarters and the others pulled on the rope and in this way freed Pat Cole from beneath its body. His limbs were crushed and blood ran out from the torn legs of his trousers. His left arm was turned beneath his back and broken in several places. Turk and Sheriff Groves lifted Pat Cole to sitting and the limb hung behind him at a sick angle.

In parley with the other men it was decided as quickly as could be that Jasper Toomey and a man called Frank Barnard would build a travois and pull Pat Cole behind Barnard's horse. In this way all three men could ride back to Spark with only one horse to spare.

Unless the bandits' plan had already gone awry it seemed they intended to trap the Pacific Southern between two downed bridges. Sheriff Groves and the other men would ride on to Green Creek at greatest speed in an effort to forestall or repel the ambush.

When Sheriff Groves brought the news to his wounded deputy Pat Cole regarded him with plain anger. His face was chalked with dust and his eyes were rimmed red. He was sweating from the pain but he looked at Sheriff Groves like a snake that had bitten him. Sheriff Groves got done telling him how it would be and then got up and started toward his horse.

"You go on," Pat Cole said.

Sheriff Groves did not turn back as he walked away. He tipped his hat to no one and climbed into the saddle of his black and white rabicano and he left Pat Cole in the dirt.

CHAPTER FIVE

■ ■ ■

Annie sprawled upon the blanket, the sun warming her face and the silken ribbons of her hair spread out around her head. The cerulean sky was without cloud or defect. The waterfall drummed into a clear pool and vibrated the rock beneath her, and it raised a susurrus voice that beckoned to her to swim. Warren came over to her from the water, his trousers rolled up to his knees and his undershirt rolled up at the sleeves. His face and hair dripped water on her feet, and she let out a cry from the coldness.

Warren Groves was strong and good-hearted and tender when she needed him to be and hard iron beside her when she was afraid. Not so much like that cloying braggart Gideon Long. Warren had no fortune, but he was in every other way her fantasy of an American man. He reached down a hand, and she took it, and he lifted her up and into his tanned arms.

In evening, by the glow of a fire, they made love for the first time beside the waterfall. She had promised to save herself for marriage, but she answered his advances without hesitation. When it was done, they lay together on the rocks that still held the warmth of the day. The moon had taken on a strange appearance as if distorted by a circular lens suspended in the sky.

"What is happening in the sky?" she asked Warren.

"It's a moon dog," said Warren. "Nothing to worry about. Seen one on the trail in Texas."

She turned her head trying to see if it moved with her view. It remained in the starry sky, a bright halo surrounding the moon.

"If you hadn't lured me out here it would have passed God's eye with no man to see it."

"Then we are fortunate to be here to appreciate his spectacle." Warren's words held an appreciation for the sublime, but he was already rolling onto his side to fold her up in his big arms.

It was a miracle, she thought as he pulled her against him. She was distracted.

She realized that Warren would never be more than he was in that moment. No matter how strong or kind, Warren could not fill her yearning.

Annie blamed greed. She craved all the beautiful things, of France and of the Mediterranean, to travel the oceans, and she dreamed of Gideon Long, who was not the good things that Warren was but who gladly promised to fulfill her every desire. He lavished her with secret gifts and with poems and perfumes. He enticed her to leave Warren and join him in travel.

Warren left the house early each morning to attend to his duties as sheriff, and on some days Annie fantasized about this different life she could have. She stood naked but for the jewelry Gideon gave her and looked at her decorated neck in the hand mirror.

Gideon had known her even before Warren, but in those days he was tentative, seeking to win her affection and impress her by indirect methods of flattery and gifts. Too tentative. Warren had swept her away with his masculinity. Gideon had never even kissed her, but by his prose she knew herself to be the object of his fantasies. Even this answered a perversely Christian desire, to be wanted but to never submit to lust.

She tilted the mirror down at an indecent angle, and her body bulged, and she became gravid. Pain seared her belly, and the mirror dropped from her fingers.

Annie awoke to the confusion of unfamiliar hands and voices. She struggled, tried to speak, and felt the pain anew. Before she could make any sense of it, she fell back into sleepless unconsciousness. It was only when someone—a doctor?—brought salts to her nose that she came fully awake and sat up in the bed and knocked over a pitcher of water.

She was in her bedroom in the house. In her own bed. Warren's bed. She knew that much. The lines of the world were bright and moving. An old crone was beside her, holding her arm with both hands, saying something. Calm. Be calm. She felt a hand on her belly.

"Why are you here?" said Annie.

She was naked, she realized, and she fought to pull clothes or blankets over her body. She was too weak to struggle against the woman.

"Please, what is happening?" said Annie.

"Is that French?" said the man who might be a doctor. "I can't understand her. You've got to get her to calm down and stop kickin', or this'll beat the devil. Give her something to bite."

The old woman looked very mean, and she took a piece of soft cloth and stuffed it into Annie's mouth. The cloth was moist and bitter, and Annie tried to spit it out.

"Hold her tight now," said the doctor.

Something cold and hard slipped between her legs and into her body, and it hurt, and she could feel the blood pouring out. She bit down on the cloth for the pain, and the sharp, bright lines of the world dimmed and turned blue. It felt as if an auger was being turned inside her loins.

"I can't reach her," the doctor said. "Here now, help me with the towels. If we can clear some of this out, I might be able to find it."

The old woman—Nel?—left Annie's side, and the pressure eased on her mouth. The pain was receding. She was able to spit the cloth out and breathe. She laid her head back against the pillow. The sound of rain was gone. Was it there before? Somewhere else, not so far, she could hear the *creak-creak* turning of a wheel in water and the soft buzz of insects.

"I came as soon as I was able," said a familiar voice.

Annie lifted her head just a bit and was surprised to see her father standing behind the strangers.

"Papa?" she said. "Papa, how did you get here?"

"Shh, there was a train. Don't you remember?"

"I do," she said.

"There's something else." Papa smiled, and he seemed very happy. "Your mother is coming."

The door began to open. Annie felt a thrill at seeing her mother. Light beamed in through the doorway, a warming glow. She strained to sit up, to see her mother's face, but the light disappeared, and the room beyond fell away, and Annie was gazing into a howling blackness that yawned open and threatened to swallow her up. She began to scream.

"Get the cloth back into her mouth," said the doctor.

■　■　■

Eli McClelland was the only man still in the water. He stood hunch-shouldered, like a bear dressed in a Union coat, and he reached into the foaming water searching for the end of the fuse. He seemed unbothered by the rushing water that had carried away several men, or was at the least more intent on finding the fuse than concerned with his own safety. As Gideon watched, McClelland began walking upstream against the current, body stooped over so that it was easy to imagine he might pull up a fish.

"Ready the men on this side," said Gideon to Robert Broken Horse. He raised his voice to be heard by McClelland. "Get out of the water. There is no time for that."

"I need to find the fuse," said McClelland. "It'll still burn."

McClelland continued upstream, trudging into the flowing water, heedless of the approaching train. He was nearing the rail bridge over Green Creek. The kegs of powder were placed beneath the bridge's decking, near the stone abutments on either bank of the creek. These explosives were supplemented with a small amount of dynamite, secured by Gideon himself, and placed high enough to require ladders. The rope of safety fuse reached from the bridge and into the creek and was pulled tight by the weight of the flowing water.

Gideon could see that McClelland intended to wade to where the fuse entered the water only a few feet beneath the bridge. The braking train was nearly upon them. There was nowhere near the time left to follow the fuse back to a safe point, pull it from the water, and get it lit.

"My rifle," Gideon said to Robert Broken Horse, who was doing his best to organize the soaked bandits into a fighting force.

The Indian brought out from the horse's saddle a dark velvet cloth containing Gideon's rifle. He untied the cord holding the cloth in a roll and unfurled it upon the ground. Fabric loops held a series of cartridges and various cleaning implements. He presented the rifle to Gideon.

It was a gift from the same Austrians who'd sold him the wireworks, a fine bolt-action rifle of Bavarian manufacture and Austrian carving and inlay. The brass scope Gideon had attached was a bit of American ingenuity. Made, no doubt, somewhere east, where few men used such things but devised them anyway. The screeching of the train was loud, as if within Gideon's skull.

He sat on the bank and raised a knee. He laid the rifle across his leg in the method taught to him as a young man by the Voortrekker named Retief. The marksman was hired by Chatholm to teach manly pursuits to the sons of the wealthy. Retief was a hunter and warrior. He fought the Zulu. Gideon recalled the Boer's advice, barked down his collar while he sat firing very similar rifles for days on end at the arsenal, and Gideon held his breath and aimed through the scope.

Reckoning the dynamite to be too small a target, Gideon fired the rifle and struck one of the powder kegs. The wood splintered, and the bullet disappeared with a thump into the keg. Black powder spilled out from the wound.

McClelland looked about, still standing in the creek with the fuse drawn tightly over his upturned palms, still not understanding his peril. Gideon released his held breath. He reached for another cartridge, then stopped, finger and thumb poised to grasp a fresh shot, as the immense black shape of the Pacific Southern loomed into view above the rim of Green Creek.

The train's brakes smoked from the friction, and its huge iron wheels turned so slowly, Gideon could count the individual spokes. The fireman and engineer turned and gazed the length of Green Creek almost at the same moment, and their eyes fell upon the many men sitting in wait. Gideon could see the alarm on their faces, and though he could not hear them over the noise of the train, he was certain they were calling out a warning.

Although the train was very slow, it appeared to have enough speed to cross the bridge. A coal car was laid in behind the locomotive, and just visible behind that was the freight car.

Without need for command the men began to fire upon the locomotive's cab. Bullets sparked and penetrated the metal walls and scarred the red and gold livery of the Pacific Southern line. The engineer and fireman were either shot or escaped out the opposite side of the locomotive. The train continued forward, and the sound of the brakes eased. It was no longer slowing.

The freight car was fully visible, and a passenger carriage came into view, rolling slowly behind it. The locomotive was nearly across the bridge.

McClelland stood in the creek's floodwaters, still holding the fuse, struck dumb by the sight of the train on the bridge above. For some reason he turned his head toward Gideon, and in that moment the bridge exploded.

There was no puff of warning or sudden flash of burning powder. The bridge and all of the charges and the locomotive and the first three cars disappeared in an upheaval of earth and smoke and a deadly hail of shrapnel. The noise of the blast knocked against the men along the bank and rang in their ears. McClelland was thrown down the creek with such force that his body tore into several gory slabs, and these tumbled and separated and disappeared over the bank of the creek.

The bridge's iron trusses were deformed and flung in every direction by the blast. One piece of truss the size of a man smashed into the creek nearby and showered Gideon and Robert Broken Horse in water. Most fragments were carried high into the air and far away. The damaged masonry of the supporting abutments crumbled in on the creek and nearly dammed it up.

The locomotive and its coal car rose highest into the air, the boiler bursting in a welter of steam and coal raining out of the tender. Gideon could now see the engineer and fireman, plainly dead, spinning high into the air amid stones and loosed rail wheels. The locomotive seemed to hang in the air before crashing down some beyond the bridge and on the far side of the bank. In an instant Gideon could only see the black cloud of coal dust that rose where the engine fell.

The freight car, being directly above the explosion, was dealt the same fate as the bridge. Its pieces and contents were scattered across the plain and down into the creek. Burning clothing and papers and odd bits of baggage rained down for some time.

The first passenger car, with only its forward portion exposed to the direct violence of the explosion, reared up like a threatened caterpillar, the walls of the car bending and twisting, its windows shattering. It came down out of alignment with the track and rolled down on its side away from the ambuscade. Gideon could see this car breaking open and spilling out men and women who were promptly dashed beneath a ruin of wheels and gears and burning wood.

The remaining passenger cars drove on into the churning smoke where the bridge was not, fell into the creek, and telescoped into one another. Despite the cloud of dust and smoke Gideon could glimpse the passengers through the breaking windows, ghostlike and contorted in panic, as the cars smashed one into the other and cored out the life dwelling in each.

By the time the train had spent its momentum, only a single passenger car remained to be saved by the pile of wreckage; rebounding from the previous car to plunge into the creek, it rolled to a halt on the stump of the ruined bridge. A red caboose car remained clinging to the track behind it. Every other bit of the train was a smoking ruin.

The water of the creek turned immediately black with lubricants and coal dust. Pieces of bodies floated out from the piled cars.

A swarm of insects—wasps—emerged from beneath the crumbled stonework of the bridge's western abutment. An enormous section of papered hive was laid open by the bridge's collapse. Pale hunks tumbled into the floodwater. The geometric arrangements of the hundreds of papered cells filled Gideon with disgust.

Their horrid civilization destroyed, the swarm of wasps took wing above the carnage as if to survey the extent of the disaster. The droning, formless cloud circled once, breaking and reforming around the smoke from the burning locomotive, and the angry wasps descended upon the men trapped, injured, and crying out for help in the train cars.

Gideon stood and pulled his black kerchief up over his nose and mouth. He was nearly run to the ground as the Apaches whooped and rode for the train. Their faces were painted for war. All around, the disorganized ambush was waked from its stupor by the sight of the easy prey, and men began to cheer and brandish weapons and rush headlong toward the smoking wreckage.

■   ■   ■

Sheriff Groves rolled his spurs along his rabicano's flanks and leaned down against the wind. The men riding by his sides howled blood at the sight of the exploding train. Sheriff Groves was silent, and his jaw was set. He drove on through the shrapnel that whistled and snapped through the brush. The posse galloped without fear through the rain of debris and out into the open desert parallel to the track.

Men emerged from the bed of Green Creek to commence their lawless assault. A battle was underway at the last rail car before the caboose. Smoke shot from windows and rifles and pistols crackled within. Sheriff Groves turned the horses and rode across the track and formed a line in the manner of a cavalry charge. Without undue hesitation he wished the men luck and said to them, "Take those alive you can."

The posse bore down on the flanks of the ambushers. The Indians on the backs of their ponies saw the move and turned off down the creek to avoid the charge. John Vargas was caught staggering up out of Green Creek, and his fat vaquero friend was slitting the throat of a Pinkerton. Sheriff Groves drew on them from his saddle and opened fire. The Mexican swatted at his throat as if stung and pitched into the tangle of the ruined bridge. The lean bandit John Vargas folded up and lay with his face in the dirt and did not move again.

The lawmen's horse charge tore through the ambushers and turned them. Some of the bandits broke and began to run. The posse split rather than drive down into the flooded creek. Shots were crackling in all directions and some from within the train car were being directed at the deputies.

Sheriff Groves reined his horse in a tight circle. Two men appeared over the ridge of the wash with kerchiefs tied over their faces. One was an Indian with dark skin and a white man's clothes. The other was an Anglo with wild black hair and dark eyes that gazed at Warren Groves first with shock and then with hatred.

Sheriff Groves fired and might have hit one of the men only they ducked back down into the creek bed. His pistols were emptied so he took out his rifle from the saddle and heeled down after them. He took the ridge and saw them running for their horses. They turned and opened fire at close range and Sheriff Groves shot without taking aim. The white man was struck in the belly. He dropped and curled up on the ground and the Indian threw down his gun and ran for his horse.

Sheriff Groves brought his rifle up and took aim at the fleeing Indian. It was an easy shot but he was thrown from his saddle by an unexpected blow. His mouth filled with dust and the pain convulsed his lower back. His horse stomped and turned in confusion without a rider and the sheriff rolled to avoid being crushed. When he came up he saw the Apache Indian sheathed his lance and leaped from his horse hung with scalps. The savage came at Sheriff Groves with a war knife.

The Indian said in Spanish, "Go away easy."

Sheriff Groves could see the knife clear as a silver dollar. It was a black tooth of chapped blade and a handle of stag horn held so tightly by the Indian that his knuckles turned yellow. Warren kicked at the Indian as he came. The blade slashed and tore a strip from his pants and hot pain carved into the side of his leg.

Sheriff Groves kicked again and his heel caught the Indian in the chest. The Indian fell back and Sheriff Groves was able to get hold of his own rifle. Without the time to fire he struck the Indian's face with the butt and got up on his knees. He was above the fallen Indian who was then spitting blood and some jagged pieces of teeth.

He hit the Indian again and dazed him and Sheriff Groves got up onto his feet and picked up the Indian's war knife. He put the blade into the Indian's side easily—ran it right through his hide coat and stuck him again and again until the Indian quit moving and breathing and the ground was rich with his blood. Sheriff Groves left the blade sticking out and went and found his horse.

The Indian dressed as a white man was on horseback and was too far distant to be easily shot. The man Sheriff Groves had shot in the belly was still rolling along the creek and painting green rocks red. Sheriff Groves wanted to either tie him down or finish him off but a fearful cry was going up from the train car. More of the savage Indians had fought their way inside and were killing the passengers and so he settled for shooting the wounded man's horse.

Men's bodies and dead horses lay scattered across the desert on both sides of the track. The locomotive was burning across the creek and gave off a roiling awning of black smoke to shade the battlefield. Felix Arguello crouched beside his young brother Marcos and Sheriff Groves could see that the younger man was shot through the heart and yet still alive and that with each beat of his heart new blood spit out and down his shirt. The old lawman Ben Reed was still in his saddle but stuck through the belly with an Indian lance and he fidgeted and tried to snap it off so that he could move better.

Sheriff Groves rode past them and with Turk and two other men rode along the face of the passenger car and fired in at the Indians who were killing off the passengers and looting their bodies. They rode to the ragged edge of the rail bridge and as they did a contingent of Americans and Mexicans too afraid to cross the flooded creek came up from the wash with their hands raised in surrender. Their appearance startled Turk and he mistakenly shot one man through the head. The others immediately fled back down into the wash.

The sheriff and his men leaped from their horses and kicked in the door of the passenger car and commenced firing with little opportunity for concern for the passengers. Turk unloaded both barrels of his shotgun and felled an Apache who was bent over to take the coat from a uniformed soldier. There were two other Indians nearer the back of the car. One attempted to escape out the far end with arms full of bags and fine coats. The bloody bodies filling the car tripped him up and Sheriff Groves fired and shot him dead.

The last of the savages was intent upon using the black blade of his knife to finish off a screaming Anglo. The Indian was dark and wore a Mexican cavalry uniform defaced by pelts and grisly trophies. The Anglo was a small man with bulging eyes and thick spectacles that further magnified his terror. He was pressed with his back against the wall of the train with a package tucked beneath one arm and his shielding hand and cotton suit drenched in blood from the Indian's knife. There was no shooting the Indian without also shooting the Anglo.

The black tooth of the Indian's blade plunged past the man's guard and his pleading became a gurgle. He slid down the wall and clutched at his chest and the Indian tore something from the dying man's grasp. The savage at last saw his predicament and fled. Turk fired after him but the car lurched and the shot clattered into the metal of the train. The Indian escaped and fled to his horse. Sheriff Groves fired through the windows but did not seem to hit him.

Several of the passengers were still alive and wounded and begging for help. Black wasps swarmed and added their menace to the air. The deputies wanted to cover their faces with their kerchiefs but the sheriff would not allow it on the grounds that if they came across an armed passenger they might be mistaken for bandits.

He sent Turk off to catch any of the men he could down on the riverbank and in particular to go after the white man he had wounded and left rolling in the dirt. The sheriff and the deputies Henry Dubois and the Spaniard called the Duke, whom the sheriff did not well know, began to drag the wounded passengers out of the car. They were bedeviled by the wasps, which darted at their faces and stung their necks, and the train car was overwhelmed by the shambles stink of blood and shit. They slipped and slid in the gore and tried to hold their sick, and when it was through, they were badly stung by wasps and covered in filth so that only their eyes showed white.

Only after they had finished that awful work did two armed clerks emerge from the caboose, which was revealed to be the money car, and it had scarcely been touched in the attack. The armed men refused to help with the wounded or leave the car. One of them demanded that Sheriff Groves send a rider to the cavalry post at Jessup. Sheriff Groves told the man that the Army post at Red Stem had been informed of the robbery.

The man persisted and received for an answer several open-handed blows to his face, and when he fell to the ground, Sheriff Groves followed him down and beat him with his fists and kicked him until his men pulled him away. The beaten train guard and his companion retreated into the money car and barred the door.

Sheriff Groves sat down on a box of peaches some poor soul was taking west, and he reached behind him and felt the long gouge above his kidney. It was fouled with blood and dust, so he got his water from his horse and poured some down his back. He was still cleaning the wound when Turk rode slowly out of the wash with a file of men staggering behind him. The prisoners were tied to a swaying length of tarry rope that was knotted to Turk's saddle.

"Did you get the one I belly shot?" asked Sheriff Groves.

"Must have run off," said Turk. "Won't get far. I can go after him."

Sheriff Groves made a fist with his sore knuckles and squinted at the sun peeking between rolling clouds of black smoke. The skies were otherwise clear, and the storm was long passed. He kicked at the flies that came after his wounds.

"Rain water'll dry up, and he'll be dead if nobody finds him by tomorrow," said Sheriff Groves. He surveyed the carnage and made up his mind. "Let the son of a bitch feed the vultures," he said, and he spit into the dirt.

Turk tipped his hat and rode on to the shade of the rail car to tie the prisoners down. When Sheriff Groves was sure that all the men were occupied in their labors, he sat back on the box of peaches and took out from his coat pocket a small and wrinkled book that was bound in black hide. He found the stub of a pencil in its pages and opened the book and hesitated as he read the first name once again.

The name of Abraham Nunn was written in stolen ink by the hand of a child, and as for names to write down in that book, only a few could be worse. Sheriff Groves did not linger or allow himself to recall the details. He turned the pages past other names and found a fresh page where none were written. On this page he wrote down the date as he reckoned it to be, March the fourth of 1874, and he wrote below that *Mexican bandit* and *white man John Vargas* and *Apache Indian on horse* and *Apache Indian on train.* He left a space below each name to later add details and closed the book, the stub of the pencil locked once more in its pages.

Having confessed the killing done to the pages of this particular book, he felt some weight lift from his conscience. It was not the full weight of the deeds but only small and measured ingots of everything that had gone before.

CHAPTER SIX

■ ■ ■

Gideon considered death, which he had not often contemplated, and wondered how, when his blood had finished running out of his shot belly, death would suit him. He decided it would feel like rising underdressed to a cold morning, and he thought, upon trying to decipher the strange shapes in his eyes when he looked up at the sky, that he would like to depart as a cloud. To dissipate and be carried away on the wind. To be breathed in and out and experience the world as the emptiness of the air.

Gideon held out some hope that the craven bastard Robert Broken Horse would recall his duty and come riding to save him. He was not certain how long he walked north—his gold pocket watch was ruined by water and no longer turned, and he was never a good judge of the trail—so he continued aimlessly and in a state of constant exhaustion.

For a time Gideon leaned against a sandstone boulder, unshackled his leg from the ruin of its brace, and tried to get at his wound with the thought of cauterizing it. He moaned when he saw the extent of his injury—the neat hole made by the bullet that had passed through him and left his body as a ragged, flapping wound—and the way the sticky blood filled his trousers and dribbled out in his footprints. He knew by the foul smell of the wound that his guts had been rent by the bullet.

Gideon surrendered to his misery against the rock. His plan was a failure, his fortune gone, his life spilled out with each passing moment. He laid the back of his head against the boulder and turned his face up to the heat of the sun. He closed his eyes and could still see the shapes moving against the red of his eyelids.

He thought of the sheriff's face, fantasized pressing thumbs into the man's eyes and tearing out the lawman's tongue. Gideon fell unconscious for a time. Dreamless. He awoke sun-sore and fearful of dying in that position, imagined his carcass explored by the beaks of vultures, and he opened his eyes. He could not readily stand and slid down onto his knees on the rocks.

He was overcome with thirst, and he crawled to the edge of the creek. The water was already diminished and flowed slowly. He lowered his face to the water and found it warm and with a mineral thickness that reminded him of broth. It was difficult to swallow, but he drank. The water coated his tongue with grit and did very little to slake his thirst.

Annie. He thought of her as he knew her years ago, when she first arrived in Spark. Young and beautiful, with a French manner in the saddle and a pretty face. Her voice was sweet and accented, though her English was never obscured by her upbringing. He called on her many times in those early days. Kissed her hand, her face, her lips only once. Never—

"Never fucked her, did you?"

Gideon looked up in surprise. Father sat on the western bank, across the creek, dressed in his flannel housecoat over filthy pajamas. He dipped his bare feet into the water. Though Father was only the scrap of a man Gideon had left in the sickbed, he seemed revitalized by Gideon's misery.

"Father?"

"Spent all that time courting her, writing her poems, and giving her flowers, for what? Who bedded her, little dandy? Who was the man to lay his seed in her and make her his?"

"She still loves me." Gideon staggered to his feet and stood in the shallow flow of the creek.

"I know all about your schoolboy letters and your lavish gifts. What woman would deny those jewels, boy? But when she lays her head down at night, whose is beside it? Whose hand feels her tit—"

"You are not real," said Gideon. "Do not speak of her that way."

"Real enough to torment you." Father played his feet back and forth through the water. "While you die, I yet live in my sickbed. Live to see the villain you've now become. Did you think some sacks of gold would make it all better? You would be a hero?"

"To hell with you," said Gideon.

"I can't help but think about that handsome sheriff. How that strapping Leander must swim to her and cram her full of meat at night."

"Damn you," said Gideon. He stumbled out into the water and toward Father.

"Like a beast. Like a wild dog. Rutting her while she howls his name at the moon. And you not fit to lick her piss from the pot, boy."

Gideon fell and sputtered, was nearly carried away by the hip-deep water, but he summoned the will and got his feet beneath him on the slippery rocks.

"Oh, Sheriff," Father said in a mockery of a woman's voice, "I would never have dreamed such pleasure could be felt."

Gideon fell again, his hands sliding on the rocks, but he was in the shallows and fought back onto his feet. Father chuckled at his predicament. Gideon stalked out of the water, eyes white against the mud covering his face, and Father's laughter climbed in pitch and became an insane cackle. The thrill of anger restored vigor to Gideon's limbs.

Father offered no resistance, only continued to laugh and shake with mirth, and Gideon got his hands around Father's bony neck. Gideon's thumbs pressed against the bulging windpipe, and he silenced Father's mocking laugh with a squeeze. The bones of Father's neck were as brittle as dead wood, and as Gideon tightened his grip, they crackled and snapped, and Father's head drooped lifelessly.

Gideon released Father's throat and let his corpse, so weightless, slip back onto the riverbank. His heart beat with exertion, and he gasped for breath. He lifted his head and saw he had crossed to the western shore of Green Creek. Father's corpse had become a coincidental doll of twigs and branches deposited by the flood.

Gideon Long climbed the western bank and set off into the desert of white sand toward the distant, dark shapes of the mountains.

■   ■   ■

Claws pinned Annie to the grass, and she was forced to see the volcanic sky. She could not turn her head or look away from the black roiling of the clouds lit from within by bursts of fire and lightning. Screaming voices rose from the tableland all around her, and the grass became switches that cut into her flesh. The she-thing was made of bones and black feathers, and its steaming drool was black and as hot as tar, and the long, purple tongue of a giraffe hung from its jaws, and when it hissed in its alien way, the spittle slopped on Annie's face.

Annie's legs were spread open, and another creature of bone and sinews stood before her. The creature was huge, with the humped shoulders and head of a Limousin bull, skinned and sick with flies and infection. It regarded her naked body and shook with laughter that sent webs of rotting yellow fat dripping from its shoulders. Her thighs burned where it violated her.

The crying voices around her fell silent, and the bull flared its nostrils. It lowered its head so that she felt the putrid heat of its breath on her body. Black fingernails traced her breasts and her distended stomach. The child stirred within her womb. The bull sensed the movement and jerked its head back and smiled with a mouth tangled with sharp, recurved teeth. It brayed with hunger, and in the hot dirge of its roar Annie could hear every imagined bestial terror of long, country nights.

She wailed as it forced her open and reached an arm into her, tearing at her womb with talons and fighting to grasp her unborn daughter. The pain was beyond anything she had ever known, yet she found the strength to kick and fight against the creature.

It was her belief that God would not intervene unless it was His will, and so Annie prayed to Him for strength and comfort, returning to the French words of her childhood. She thought of the preacher who visited their house and spoke of the tribulations their kind suffered at the hands of their countrymen. The words he taught her. God was not to be petitioned but worshipped.

She recalled Papa the patriot, who stood for his church and refused the entreaties of the German Calvinists and the curses of the Catholics and worshipped in his way. She remembered him strong and wealthy in Alsace, before they were driven out, and thought of his smile as she said her prayers aloud.

The fleshless Minotaur and the rotted bird-woman laughed at her prayers and tore at her with even greater violence. She could feel the baby smothering in her womb, and she fought them. She threw off the she-thing from her arm, but it returned and pushed her down and held her with its claws, its lurid wings beating a terrible perfume into her face.

"Let go," said a voice near her head.

There was a crepuscular light on the plain, and it illuminated the withered trees of the apple orchard and the cracked pan of soil, and it transfixed in golden beams a figure wrapped in billowing clothes that could only be her mother. She recognized her from paintings and chromos but had never heard her voice. It sounded to Annie like her own voice echoing back from the mountains.

"Let go, Annie," said her mother. "Don't fight them."

"They're killing her," said Annie.

"She will die, because they are saving you." A hand rested upon her mother's shoulder, and it became, by revelation, attached to a man. His face was shaded by a wide-brimmed hat, and he wore the coat and boots of Warren. She felt uncertain it was Warren and could sense that it might be her father.

"Warren?"

"He's not here," said her mother. "You are alone."

The man was gone, and Annie felt a coldness and heaviness to her limbs. Her mother faded into the light, like motes of dust, and disappeared. Annie's unborn child meant everything to her. Still, she shut her eyes and accepted the bargain. Her life for her daughter's.

■   ■   ■

The day was closing down on Gideon as he limped northwest out of the graben basin and walked among the rippled, embryonic dunes and farther into the barchan crescents of white gypsum desert. The sun, retreating slowly among the distant mountains, dried his clothes and made of the day's filth a crusted shell that gave him the appearance of a primordial man. The mud flaked off his coat and trousers with each step.

The wind erased his uneven trail from the surface of the desert, and there was no rock, only intermittent scrub where the alkali desert had blown away and exposed the hardpan. Gideon's bleeding had slowed to a blackened, congealed seep, and he felt cold all over despite the lingering daylight heat.

In the great distance, seeming to emerge from the gray valleys and peaks of the San Andres, Gideon could see a single figure melting out from the desert littoral. He at first dismissed it as an illusion of the heat or another apparition like his father, but from one minute to the next it grew in size, until he could discern a horse and rider.

Robert Broken Horse. He waved his arms and stumbled toward the damned Indian, already formulating the abuse he would heap on the cowardly old Crow. It was only as he crested a dune and could see the horse and rider descending an opposite dune that Gideon realized it was not Robert Broken Horse.

The Indian who rode at him sat atop a half-tamed war pony, a blanket beneath his legs, and the rider had the mien and trappings of a savage. The Indian wore feathers and beads in his hair and, over bare chest, a green Mexican cavalry coat, ragged and dusty, probably torn from the murdered body of some unlucky presidial trooper.

Crude panniers hung over the hindquarters of the pony, and these were festooned with scalps that flopped as horse and Indian rode at Gideon at a gallop. The Indian cradled a flintlock rifle like a babe in one arm and rested the stock across his lap.

Gideon surrendered himself to the Indian without a fight, weakly raised his hands into the air, and the savage rode around him in a circle so near that he could smell the stink of the riding blanket and chewed tobacco. The Indian shouted in Spanish, and the horse kicked the white sand into Gideon's eyes. He fell and braced himself for the blow or shot that would end his life.

"If you will not fight," said Father, "at least stand and die like a man."

Gideon regained his feet and opened his eyes. The Indian clicked with his tongue, and the horse pranced to a stop, snorting and snarling at Gideon.

The Indian reached back to the pannier, took something out, and threw it at Gideon's chest. It struck him nearly hard enough to knock him over. He managed to catch it in his arms and felt a moment's horror as he saw blood red. He realized, with relief, that it was no gory trophy but the valise belonging to Father's lawyer.

He laughed at his improbable fortune. The Indian did not like this, and he brought up his flintlock and shouted in Spanish.

"I do not speak Spanish," Gideon said. "No . . . *no habla espanol, amigo.*"

The Indian's smile showed dirty teeth. "Specie," the Indian said. "Silver or gold."

"English?"

"I learned your language from a man who made me kill him. I thought he was my friend. He lied to me. Did you lie to me?"

Gideon patted his body to demonstrate he carried no coins.

"Not a lie." Gideon gestured to the Red Lines. "Red Stem. The town there. I have your money."

The Indian folded his arms across his chest. His dark skin was dusted with the alkali sand, and his hair caught the wind, blowing behind him like a black standard.

"Agua," Gideon said. "Water. Water, please."

The Indian dragged up two skins of water slung across the pony's back and measured the weight of each in his hands. He poured most of the water into one of the skins and tied it to the pannier. He handed the other to Gideon. It was light, only a few sips, but Gideon tilted it up and drained the warm water into his mouth. It was clean and pure compared to the floodwater he'd drunk at Green Creek.

The Indian watched sullenly, as if he might yet decide to kill Gideon and take back his water.

"We cannot go to the place of your people," said the Indian. "Not this night or for some time to come. I have seen the blue army ride out in anger, and they will kill any Indian they find."

Gideon lowered the empty skin from his lips. "The Army? I must return. They will not kill me. Let me take your horse. I can ride in and fetch your money."

The Indian leaned down to examine Gideon more closely. "If I split you in half, which half will remain with me?"

"I am a wealthy man," said Gideon. "You have done what I asked, and I mean to pay."

"You do not have water or horse, and you are dying. You are a wealthy man. That is good. What is your name, wealthy man?"

"Gideon Long."

The Indian climbed down from the horse and stood so that his face was near Gideon's. His eyes were dark, unyielding, like polished buttons or the painted eyes of a doll.

"That is your body's name. What is your name? Do you know it yet?"

"I . . . I am not sure how to answer. I only know the name I was given. What . . ." Gideon paused to swallow the dryness returning to his throat. "What is your name?"

"Why are you playing along with this savage hoodoo?" said Father. "Kill this animal, take his horse and water. You have a pistol in your coat. I can see it."

"The Mescalero call me Speaks With Knife. They were my people once, a long time before they let themselves be caged. I have other names, but you may call me by that name. May I ask you, Gideon Long, are you a Christian?"

"Yes, well, I am, but I do not pursue it. I do not worship in a church or proselytize. It is something I have learned in school. I think that God should . . . why are you asking me this?"

Speaks With Knife took a leather-bound Bible from his riding pouches. It was of the cheap sort carried by frontier preachers, and when the Indian lifted it from the pack, Gideon could see the unmistakable dark stain of blood on its pages.

"You are going to die, Gideon Long. I have letters. Would you like me to read from this book over your body?"

"I do not intend to die," Gideon said.

Speaks With Knife leaned very close to Gideon and flared his nostrils and inhaled deeply. He touched Gideon's face with short fingers. "You must be a powerful shaman. To refuse death, you must be most powerful of all. Will you be reborn like White Painted Woman, or will you refuse to leave your body?"

"What?"

"I have seen many strange things, wealthy man Gideon Long. There is a book in your Christian Bible. It says this world will be destroyed in plague and war, and beasts of terrible power will walk the earth. The sickness and guns are here already, Gideon Long. Do you wield this terrible power?"

"He is babbling like a heathen," said Father.

"Leave me some water," said Gideon. "I will walk to Spark. You found me once, you can find me again. If I am dead, you can take everything I have."

"When I was a boy, I believed the world went on forever. My mother told me it did. But I have seen maps, Gideon Long. The white man does not lie with maps to his own kind. The white man has found everything, and he has plans for it. Plans to gather up all of the shapes and make them square. He will put his houses in a row and raise trees of telegraph rope and turn the meadow with his plows. This is not the end of your world, but it is the end of a world."

"Listen to this fool!" said Father. "Kill him. Please. Shut him up."

"No," said Gideon.

"I have been wicked and cruel to the white man, crueler even than Riding Iron or Fierce Bear or any other war chief will allow, and still there will be no stopping the white man. Some may join him, but this is not my fate. These are the very last days. This is the Revelation. This book in your Christian Bible was written for me."

Speaks With Knife turned his back to Gideon, reached to the pannier, and hefted the water skin. "I will set a camp in the western hills and leave you some—"

Gideon's revolver popped and spit white smoke. The wet cartridge did not discharge properly. The Indian turned, bleeding from his cheek, his eyes wide and furious. Gideon fumbled with the pistol, cocked back the hammer, fired a second time, missed in his haste, cocked again, and this time shot Speaks With Knife through the heart.

The Apache fell to the ground and sprawled beside the horse. His blood spilled out quickly across the sand, and Speaks With Knife lay on his back with his eyes open and blinking slowly. Gideon stood over him, darkening him with his shadow. The Indian's bloody hand grabbed at Gideon's leg, fingers twisting in the fabric and smearing the blood over the top of his boot. In a moment more the Indian was dead.

"You almost bungled it," said Father. "Look at this miserable animal. That could be you, but now you have a horse."

Gideon turned to catch the horse, and the pony snorted and reared up on its hind legs. He backed away, but the horse came at him, gnashing its jaws like a predator and snapping at him with its teeth. Father began to laugh and mock him. The horse would not be calmed, would not even flee. It circled around Gideon and tried to kick and bite him. He became terrified and reminded of Apollyon, though the Indian's horse was small, and Gideon's father laughed and mocked even more.

"Remember this, boy? Ha-ha, what a show. Outwitted by a horse once more."

In his limping attempts to avoid the pony's charging, Gideon became snared on the lifeless body of Speaks With Knife, and he fell on his back on the sticky, bloodied sand surrounding the Indian. An unshod hoof smashed against his shoulder, and another missed his neck by only a fraction of an inch. The horse rode over him, turned back, and as it came a second time, Gideon sat up and shot the animal in the head.

It stopped, snorted, tried to start toward him again, and fell onto its side. Father laughed very hard at this and even harder when Gideon realized his missed shot at the Indian had punctured the water skin.

"You've managed to kill yourself all over again," said Father.

Gideon saved what he could from the water skin—not much at all—and left the dead horse and Indian lying where they had fallen. In the panniers he discovered beads and bones and Mexican paper and a skin full of tiswin that he drank, burning and awful, though he knew it would soon worsen his thirst.

He clutched in his arm the red valise of Father's attorney, and he carried the Indian's flintlock and tobacco for a time, thinking of trading or protecting himself from animals, but as he grew weaker, these fell from his grasp. His hold on the valise tightened.

Night came, and the bright gibbous moon kept a deep shade of blue overhead. The sand seemed to glow beneath that cloudless sky. It appeared like snow, and, with the cold, it was easy for Gideon to imagine himself on the Christmas heath of Chatholm. He shivered out of cold and weakness, teeth clicking painfully, and thirst was his constant concern.

He was followed into the night, pursued by a cautious band of coyotes. Each time he looked back, he would catch only a glimpse as they disappeared behind the last dune he'd crossed. When the wind fell silent, he could hear them sniff and dig at his trail of blood or hear the soft pad of their feet on the sand. They snarled and yipped with excitement when he descended the face of a dune or slipped and fell in the spilling desert. He could sense them closing in and rose before they thought him too weak to continue and decided the moment had come to attack.

Father's voice mocked him, though he never saw the apparition after its strangulation at the creek. Delirious, dying, Gideon tumbled down a dune's slack, accompanied all the way by Father's laugh. The mountains seemed near enough to be touched. The San Andres. The black stones towered behind the desert, radiating heat, yet he felt, at last, he could not rise again.

Gideon laughed at himself. Laughed at his fate. The valise fell open, and papers began to spill out. The wind whipped papers into the air and swept the contents of the valise away down the rippling slack until only a single bound folio remained.

He watched the coyotes mount the dune above him, one next to the other, a formation ready to charge down after him. They growled and licked their jaws at the prospect of his meat. The largest started down the dune. Its eyes burned with the reflected moonlight, and Gideon could see strings of drool slipping from its open mouth.

The coyote stopped, flattened its ears, lowered the wedge of its head to the sand, and growled.

"Come on," Gideon said. "Come and have your meal."

He could nearly feel the teeth at his throat. The coyotes did not obey him. They were backing away, snarling and retreating back up the dune. Some near the top turned and ran, trailing piss, or slunk off with heads low and tails tucked beneath their bodies.

Gideon had enough sense left to realize these hungry animals were not afraid of him. He rolled his head and looked to the opposite dune.

The lone dog stood limned by the light of the moon. It was of the mongrel, prick-eared sort kept by Indians. Its fur was completely white, nearly incandescent, as if lit from behind, whiter even than the gypsum sand, and its eyes were pale blue gems. Gideon had never seen a dog like it, and, in his way, he understood the fear of the coyotes. It was not a fear of violence but of something out of place, as if something had stepped from a dream and into the world.

The dog stared at him, not happily in the way of a pet, yet not in challenge; it was appraising him. It stared for a long time and then disappeared silently back over the dune.

Gideon found the strength to rise, scooped the remaining folio back into the valise, and, though he was afraid, felt compelled, by the strangeness of the dog and by his hopeless situation, to follow it.

CHAPTER SEVEN

■ ■ ■

The prisoners not too badly injured were disarmed by Sheriff Groves and his men and put to work clearing debris under guard. The prisoners too wounded to work lay in their bindings and moaned and cursed the wasps that crawled upon their faces.

Sheriff Groves and his posse saved what men and women they could from the tangled ruin of the train. Many lay trapped by tons of debris and it was not possible to dislodge the crumpled cars for fear of further injuring those beneath.

As night approached they lit fires and burned sagebrush to drive away the wasps. A search revealed pieces of crates used for mining charges and the iron bands from black-powder kegs. Some horses used by the ambushers were recovered and the injured passengers were put onto sledges behind them.

Turk discovered a fancy rifle on the banks of Green Creek and brought it for Sheriff Groves to examine. It was silver-plated and filigreed and mounted with a glass telescope. Sheriff Groves turned it over in his hands.

It was an exquisite marksman's weapon of foreign manufacture and designed for exotic, high-caliber cartridges. Few men in the Territories could afford such weapons. There could be little doubt it belonged to the master of the attack and based upon the position where it was discovered, this man was also surely the one Sheriff Groves had wounded.

Soon after dark the fire-lit camp was joined by a full company of artillery and wagon under Colonel Mildenhall. Guns were unlimbered and revetments dug as the gunners deployed in a perimeter around the derailed train. The colonel declared entrenched defenses necessary to repel Indian attacks, though none was forthcoming.

"Hardly favorable gunnery positions," he said to Sheriff Groves. "Had I known the extent of this disaster, I might have brought the entire battalion down from Red Stem."

"Have you brought a doctor?"

"Yes." Colonel Mildenhall pointed out an officer in conversation with several men of the wagon team. "That is Lieutenant Gutteridge. He is Fort Trumbull's surgeon and a fine fellow. Show him to the wounded, and I am certain he can take over from there."

Sheriff Groves held his hat in hands chapped and blistered by a day of constant labor. "We done what we could for those trapped. With the ox you might be able to move some of the wreck."

Colonel Mildenhall was distracted and conferred with an adjutant for several seconds before answering. "Oh, yes, of course. My engineers are already inspecting the train. We might have been here sooner had we been better forewarned."

Down in the creek the terrible jumble of wreckage was caught in the living light of the engineers' torches, and Sheriff Groves recalled a tiny girl he had lifted from beneath a wheel of the train. She lived only a short time after her rescue and never spoke, though she was wide-eyed and awake.

He could not stand to hold her in his arms and so he discovered a reason to be busy and passed her tiny body to Felix Arguello. The deputy was talking to his dead brother's corpse as if it was still alive and took the child in his arms and held her like a doll. Much later and after an exhausting effort with the axes Sheriff Groves saw the girl dangling in Felix Arguello's arms as dead as a drowned cat. The deputy was singing a Spanish lullaby to her.

"We'll use axes here," said an officer of the engineers. "Tie the chain on—no, not there, on the main beam. The floor is already buckled."

The chief engineer shortly came over to them and thanked Sheriff Groves and his men for their efforts. He turned back to his work and only paused to scrape a bit of creek mud from the top of his boot. "You get yourself some food and water," he said.

"I thought to leave," said Sheriff Groves. "My wife is giving birth."

The engineer returned to them and placed both hands on Sheriff Groves' shoulders and looked him in the eye almost fondly. "My goodness, man. What a day for you to be out here. Go on back to your wife. The Army has this matter under control."

■   ■   ■

Gideon held on desperately to the valise, though he long ago forgot what it might contain. The world he perceived belonged mostly to the cold racking his body and the silent white dog that padded ahead of him through the desert. It loped on, sure of its bearings, and he followed it beyond the limits of endurance. The dog never allowed him close enough to touch. It took each dune ahead and turned back and watched him as he struggled on, the sand sucking at his boots.

When he fell, the dog stopped and sniffed at him. Each time he felt sure he could go on no longer, he found some last reserve of strength and, summoning it with a groan, rose to his feet and continued after the white dog.

"Where are you taking me?"

The dog did not answer but cocked its ears and looked back as if Gideon might have barked or made some other equally unexpected sound.

"Home to the family? A walking ration for your pups, eh? My meat is all stringy. Marinated in whiskey."

Short, limestone hills rose from the dunes ahead, shaped so perfectly that they seemed designed, though the tops of some were pitted or flattened as if struck by a hammer. Beyond these hills, and the last white dunes, lay the stark face of the San Andres range, very close now.

Gideon stopped. These black mountains did not belong to the San Andres at all. During his wandering he must have crossed some impossible distance, or was conveyed by some unknown means, for the black granite rocks could only belong to the Oscura range, which lay many miles farther north than the San Andres.

This range was considered dangerous and uninhabitable, avoided by travelers and even retreating Indian raiding parties. The Oscuras lay well north of the Red Lines and closer to the Jornada del Muerto. Though he had never been to the Oscuras, he was aware of underground rivers near them, had seen them marked on maps, and knew they were said to emerge on the surface through ancient basalt channels. The water would be salted, likely barely potable, but in his state he would drink dry the sea.

"Take me to the water," he told the dog, and he gestured with his hand.

The dog trotted on, leading him among the conical hills scattered lightly with brush and trees. In the branches of one of these sat a horned owl, and it only made sense that its feathers were white and its eyes were blue, because it, like the dog, surely sprang from Gideon's imagination. But when he blinked, it was only a normal owl, and the dog was still white.

The sands quit with little prelude, and Gideon continued to follow the dog until the hills grew and became jagged enough to resemble the dark mountains. As they approached the black face of the Oscuras, the animals and insects fell silent all at once, as though some invisible line was crossed and on the other side was a vacuum in which nothing could live. Even the wind became silent.

"I am alive," Gideon said, or maybe only thought, and when he looked up to say something else to the dog, the white hound had disappeared.

Gideon approached the black granite, felt the stone's warmth with his fingertips. He wondered how the dog might have passed through solid rock. A ghost? Some Indian spirit? No, no, probably a figment of his dying brain. Of course. A biological phantasm. Deprived of oxygen, a man might dream an eternity even as he suffocated. Deprived of blood, which Gideon knew from lecture to convey that vital oxygen, the brain could surely conjure a white dog where none existed.

No. The dog's head emerged from the rock some ways distant, and the dog gazed at him expectantly before disappearing once more. Gideon stumbled after the dog and found, almost by touch, the entrance to a cave. No, not a cave; he could see moonlight in the depths. He pursued the dog into the mountain and discovered a winding, narrow canyon. He followed the padding sound of the dog's feet on the dusty rocks, though this sound and the sound of his own steps echoed to confusion in the confines of the canyon.

The mountain rose all around as towering, forbidding walls of black rock. The immediate sides of the canyon were smooth and curving, shaped by countless centuries of wind, though it was deathly still and difficult to imagine any wind at all. It was so quiet, he felt the mute grandeur of a cathedral's interior or the great hall of a palace. This was a chamber for receiving visitors, God's own construction to impress His majesty upon emissaries to his realm.

The canyon broadened gradually, and Gideon glimpsed a wider valley, set with terraces hewn from the stone. Ahead, the dog climbed one of these terraces, and as Gideon rounded the final curve in the canyon, he emerged into that valley, the moon bright overhead. Arrayed along the face of the canyon's wall, constructed atop the carved terraces, sat an entire silent pueblo built of crude, block buildings and linked by the timber bones of ladders.

This Indian city was dark and in a state of ruin. It seemed deader even than the white sand desert. The dog disappeared into the terraced jumble of houses. Gideon did not need the dog. He could smell the water now. Somewhere in those ruins. He had to have a drink. No other thought compelled him. Not even wonder at the discovery of some ancient, sad city built by extinct hands.

Gideon felt very calm. He began to climb up the terrace where the dog had disappeared and thought that after having a drink it might be nice to finally lie down and die.

■   ■   ■

Annie gasped and sat up in the bed. Nel screamed with fright, and before Annie could speak, the midwife hurried out of the room exclaiming, "She is alive!"

It was night. The sound of the rain was gone, and it was very cold. Annie's body was damp, and the sheet clung to her as snugly as meat casing but offered no warmth. She tried to turn, found she could not, but was able to get her shaking elbows behind herself and sit upright in the bed.

The baby was still inside her, moving, alive, though only barely. Nel came into the room with tear-wet eyes and seemed unable to come any closer.

"Please," Annie said, and her voice was only a whisper. "Please, Nel. Come here."

"It will be okay," said Nel.

The midwife sat in the chair beside the bed and overcame her fear and held Annie in her arms. Nel stroked Annie's head and seemed to be trying to calm her once more, but Annie knew there was little time.

The doctor entered the room, carrying a tray of iodine bottles and knives and metal saws. Butcher's tools.

"Nel," said Annie. "Listen to me. I am dead, died, I know. Listen. Listen. Where is Warren?"

Nel looked to the doctor, and the doctor shook his head.

"Not here," said Nel. "But soon . . ."

"Doesn't matter," said Annie. "Tell Warren . . . would like my daughter named after my mother. Claire." Annie grabbed at Nel's sleeve and looked up into the midwife's watering eyes. Annie could feel the bed falling away, the ceiling growing higher and higher.

"There is . . . a box, 'neath the bed. Hurt him . . . you . . ."

"It's okay. Warren will take care of it," Nel said.

Desperation.

"No . . . no . . . you . . ."

Annie slumped and said nothing else. She came to know only the narrowing tunnel that winnowed the memories until there remained only the incandescent thought of those she loved, alive and dead and existing forever in one moment. When she found them, her body slipped away from her. It lay as limp as a doll in Nel's arms, persisting in myriad tiny ways of biology that would soon fade and never again form the sum of Annabelle Groves.

■ ■ ▮

The men who rode beside Sheriff Groves were sapped of all vitality by their ordeal and slumped in their saddles and fought to remain awake. Felix Arguello rode with his dead brother lain across the back of his horse and wrapped up in blankets that were stained by his blood. The old lawman Ben Reed was pierced through his side by an Apache lance and refused treatment to his wound. He drank apple whiskey until he fell into a stupor and lay moaning in his saddle with the stump of the Indian lance still in his guts.

Sheriff Groves rode ahead, and he sat high in his saddle and kept his back as straight as a flagpole. He rolled his spurs to motivate his horse, and when the men lagged behind, he stood in the stirrups and hollered back to Turk.

The Chinese camps at the base of Red Stem were lit up by candles and lanterns and fed nocturnally upon the sordid economy of miners and foundry workers come down from the mountain to be pillaged of their pay. As Sheriff Groves and his men approached, they were met by riders from the Chinese camp carrying guns and torches.

The outlaw sheriff Artemus Wick sat the back of a gaunt mare, and his face was lit by the glowing cheroot caught in the corner of his thin-lipped mouth. He was lanky and narrow-faced ugly and smiled with black teeth. He held Sheriff Groves and his men up with questions about what had happened and about why the Army was moved south, and he made hollow offers to help.

There were more than a dozen Chinamen with him, and they rode mules and ponies and held torches and shotguns and did not banter or express any sympathy or intent other than the cold menace of their guns. The threat was casual: parley or violence. Not wanting more blood, Sheriff Groves indulged the outlaw.

He told Wick to mind his own business and collect his pay from Desmond Pearce, and Artemus Wick spit tobacco and told him back that no train would have been robbed on his watch. Sheriff Groves had a mind to gun Artemus Wick from his saddle. Turk intervened and told Wick there was a need to hurry and that such conversations could be continued later.

"Will be," said Wick, and he and his Celestials rode back into the camp.

■   ■   ■

The cliff pueblo's paths of white brick were crumbling and precarious. Many of the structures were reduced to yawning, brick-lined holes in the foundational granite, and in these Gideon could see drifts of sand and old bones. He might survive a fall into one such hole, but he would never be able to climb back out. The ladders were tricks—they broke and fell apart at the slightest weight—and so Gideon attempted to follow the footprints left by the dog.

His vision at night was never very keen, and now, barely able to stand, he chose to crawl on hands and knees to steady himself and to even see the tracks left by the white dog. When he lost sight of them, he relied on his sense of smell, for he was able to detect the sweetness of water in the air.

The silent brick houses that remained upright held the empty square frames of windows. These openings were black, so black he imagined things moving in their depths, uncoiling and turning and regarding him with long-dead faces and hollow, eyeless cavities. His rational mind fought to quiet the fear but could not, for this was no rational path he traversed; it was the sort often beset by spirits and devils and things that lurked in the shadows of dead cities.

After a very long time of crawling Gideon knelt before the yawning entrance of a cave tunnel. It was a true cave, dark, and all around him were the fallen walls of what seemed the largest and most elaborate of the pueblo structures, as if this ancient tunnel in the bedrock had held some ceremonial significance to the Indians. Many of these structural remnants had long since tumbled over the surrounding cliff and exposed the perilous drop. The walls that remained created slumping tunnels through which a deadened wind softly moaned.

Gideon hesitated only a moment at the threshold. Death was coming for him, whether outside or within the cave. His journey had brought him here and, seized by fatalistic curiosity, he intended to see that journey to its conclusion. Onward into the darkness, his hands became ragged and his trousers tore at the knees. The gold watch, still chained to his vest, spilled from his pocket as he descended into the cave and made a scraping sound as it dragged beneath him.

The last pricks of moonlight were gone. He knew darkness and the growing heat beneath his palms and the smell of the water. He crawled into the depths, the cave ceiling low overhead, and his hands passed across crystal and jagged rock and the smooth basalt deposited by the movement of oceans of fire.

He cast aside the valise, which was nearly in tatters anyway, and in the crushing heat he writhed out of his clothes and pushed them aside in the tunnel. He wrapped the chain of his pocket watch around his forearm and held the familiar shape in his hand. At least that might retain some value. Gold was always worth something wherever you ended up.

Several times in his journey he lost all strength and fell into a dreamless sleep and woke to terrifying darkness, unsure if he was alive or dead. He imagined insects and slippery creatures climbing over his body or across his hands, though he never truly encountered these things, and that was also a cause for unease. No bat or bug or even lichen grew in the tunnel, though the temperature and humidity rose to the sweltering heat of a jungle. Surely some creature could make this miserable bowel its home.

Gideon spilled out of the tunnel and slid several feet across sloping stone and into the basin of a large cavern. The walls were hot and coated in moisture. Queer amber and rose-colored light filtered down from the ceiling, transmitted by lava channels no bigger around than Gideon's wrist. He reckoned they must pass all the way to the surface of the mountain, though, judging by the strange color of the light, perhaps through crystalline deposits or some other lens. The floor of this cavern was basalt and sloped conically down to a nearly circular pit in the center of the floor.

Gideon approached this warily, unsure on his feet and afraid the pit might open into a chamber filled with boiling magma. No, not magma; the pit was filled with water so rich with dissolved minerals that it possessed the color and consistency of cream. There was no obvious source for the water, and the surface of the pool was still and had a rich, queasy scent. It reminded Gideon of fresh marrow.

He forgot his caution in his thirst, forgot the danger of drinking unknown water, and he fell upon his aching knees and lay down on his numb belly. He leaned over the pool and lowered his face toward the opaque surface. He did not even care that his gold watch hung from his arm and dangled in the pool. He reached his hands into the hot liquid and brought out a cupped handful, nearly thick as pitch. He held it to his lips and drank. It tasted sweet and rich, was thicker even than the flooded creek, and it burned as he swallowed.

He stretched for more and saw by the filtered moonlight that something was wrong with his hand. His fingers shriveled and twitched, and there was a new smell in the air, like something cooking. Pain shot through his hand and raced up his arm.

The stain of the liquid spread along his flesh, up his forearm, and burned his skin like some hungry disease. The chain unexpectedly fell from his arm, and the pocket watch splashed into the water.

Pain ripped at his inner throat and scoured down into his belly. It was agony beyond all reason. He grabbed at his neck with his fingers, but this only smeared the mud of the pool across his flesh.

Gideon tried to scream, but no sound came. He tried to rise to his feet and began to stumble. Across the pool from him lay the dog, calm and watching him with those blue eyes. Gideon tried to take a step, but his bad knee gave out, and he pitched forward, directly toward the placid surface of the pool.

For a moment he felt the warmth of the pool swallowing him up. Almost pleasant for that moment, but then came a searing, boiling heat that was like flames against every bit of his flesh. Father was laughing. Brother lay slain on the Missouri grass. Sister's fat finger was banded in gold by her fatter husband. Mother was buried in Providence by her sisters. He thought of the coward, Robert Broken Horse. Of Sheriff Groves, who had stolen everything from him.

And he thought of Annabelle, the letters he'd written and the gifts he'd given, the fortune he'd spent pursuing her, the touch of her hand on his, a long ago dance at the Whitney, her lips as soft as any woman's he had ever known and twice as sweet. The way of her smile.

Gideon spilled out his ingredients into the pool. Richest and blackest of all was the cruelty given to him by the horse Apollyon, and this stained the liquid and effervesced. Every crack and crevice yawned and widened, and his body broke apart, and Gideon did not remember any more, and there was nothing left of him at all except for everything that mattered.

■ ■ ■

Sheriff Groves rode for the lights of Spark and he spurred his horse uphill till it gnashed and foamed at the bit. The other men had fallen behind but he no longer cared. He could see the lanterns still burning at his house. He could see Doc Carson's horse tied at the trough and his stomach turned sour.

He burst in through the door and startled Doc Carson who sat drinking a cup of whiskey at the table with his head down and his shoulders bent.

"Annie?" said Sheriff Groves.

"Warren," said Doc Carson and he tried to put his hands on Sheriff Groves.

He pushed Doc Carson away and nearly knocked him to the floor. Nel came out of the bedroom and she held a pile of bloody towels to her breast.

"Where is she?" he asked Nel.

He didn't wait for an answer. He started toward the door of the bedroom. Nel said something urgent. He didn't have ears for it or care what it was.

He threw open the door and Annie was beneath the blankets. He took them in his hand and pulled them off her body and he stood and held the corner of the sheet while he looked down at the cut-open corpse that used to be his wife. He saw the fine bits. He saw the way her mouth hung open and her head turned to the side and he studied the slit that went up her middle and the way she was opened up like a butcher's work. The room smelled of blood.

Sheriff Groves sat in the chair beside her and he still held to the corner of the sheet. It dragged over Annie's mutilated body. He said nothing and only stared at her face with his arms hanging at his sides. He could hear Nel and Doc Carson speaking in the kitchen but he made no effort to discern what they said. They left him alone.

But not long enough by his reckoning. Hardly.

"Warren," said Nel and she came into the room. "Doc did everything he could."

Warren said nothing.

"He saved the baby," she said. She held out the bloody towel to him and he saw that it held the ugly raisin of an infant swaddled within. It looked sickly and its arm moved to its face.

"It's a girl," said Nel.

"Take that out of here," he said.

"Warren," said Nel.

She pressed the swaddled babe into his arms. He took it gently and he saw only Annie in its tiny face. It seemed black-eyed and terribly fragile. He could imagine no future with the child. He could not conceive of lullabies and wooden toys. He felt sick looking at it. He felt afraid.

He held the child out to Nel and she reluctantly took it back.

"Get it out," he said.

"Warren . . ."

"I can't be having a child to look after. Not now. Get it out of here."

"She named it Claire, and she—"

Warren reached down to his hip and took out his pistol and he cocked the hammer back and pointed it at Nel. He did not turn his body and only barely inclined his head toward the midwife. Her mouth hung open in surprise.

"Get it out, by God," Sheriff Groves said. "I ain't gonna tell you again."

Nel clutched the child to her breast and fled from the room. She shouted at Doc Carson and he left the house with her and at last Warren Groves sat alone in peace with the body of his wife. After a long while he got up and walked around to the side of the bed he usually slept on and though the sheets were dark with blood he lay down beside his wife in his filthy trail clothes.

His hand dangled alongside the bed and after a time the dog they called Ringo crept fearfully into the room and licked his hand. He scratched the animal on the head and put his hand across his chest and then closed his eyes and allowed himself to feel the full weariness of a single day. Only then did he drift off to sleep with the weight of his wife beside him for the very last time.

■   ■   ■

The creature heaved from the pool's recondite depths, limbs and head bound in pale mucilage, bobbing to the surface in the manner of a linen-wrapped corpse flooded out of a grave. The creature within moved and pushed at its cocoon and was thrust partially upon the cavern floor by force of unseen current. It broke its arms free from its binding and pulled itself up the slope, slid with its belly upon the stone, moaned inhumanly, writhed, tore at the cowl covering its face, and vomited out great quantities of viscous broth.

It clawed and kicked until it could lie flat against the heat of the stone and its legs and feet were out of the pool. It ripped away the milk-white envelope of congealed fluid covering its body and shucked this membrane from its head and discarded the wet slop. In this way the creature's pale flesh was gradually revealed in the shape of a man.

"Alive," the thing said, and it rolled onto its back.

It had memories, sticky and submerged, only slowly returning to the surface and full of things of a sort and shape that had a name but were not understood. These were discrete and esoteric things. The back of a pretty girl as she leaned against a tree. A train stopped on a bridge. Birds in the air above a coast, tethered by the wind like kites. A woman slumped and sobbing on the floor beside a neatly made bed. White sand so close, the individual grains could be seen. A punch in the nose by a ginger-haired boy. A friend, a brother, rigging a sailing boat. A giant horse and on its back a withered, laughing king.

There were other, older memories, receding to feelings. Wrong things. They dwindled but never ended, and their yawning, bottomless nature made the creature afraid to consider them. They were borrowed and unwelcome.

The moonlight that filtered into the chamber was dim, amaranthine pink and citrine, throbbing with the tempo of the earth, and within its feeble shafts the creature glimpsed every light of Revelation, from Apollo's labors to the fire on Horeb, to the molten glow of the smelter's pour.

The creature scooped more of the scum from its eyes and nostrils and spit up even more from its belly. The world was being indexed. Its brain was recovering the context for jumbled words and memories.

"Help me," the creature said, and it knew the language it spoke.

It began to crawl away from the pool, which it feared yet did not know for certain why. Its grip was strong but greased with fluids from the pool, and it slipped as it placed its hands one after another and clawed its way up the hot rocks. The creature's palm fell upon tiny pebbles, and as its weight shifted, these dug into the flesh without piercing the skin. The creature lifted its hand, some of the pebbles falling away, catching the moonlight and glittering gold.

"What?" wondered the creature. It examined the gold pebbles and turned them over and felt sick with realization. Teeth. His teeth. My teeth. Gideon's teeth.

Gideon Long's gold teeth.

He felt with his tongue and found every tooth real and whole in his mouth. Where before there were gold fillings and gold teeth there were new, enameled teeth. Every tooth in its place. No, there were more than usual. His wisdom teeth, which he recalled vividly being quartered and extracted in London, were still there, not only present in his mouth but aligned such that they emerged from the flesh and caused no discomfort.

Gideon's fingers discovered another object nearby. His gold pocket watch, stripped of chain and glass and painted hands. Only the gold shell remained. He recalled its falling into the pool. Disappearing before his fall.

He climbed to his feet and stood in the heated crucible of the pool chamber and laughed. His knee was no longer lame, and his body was no longer weak or dying. He was not just alive, not just whole; he was boiling with vigor. Youth. Scars and marks on his flesh had disappeared.

Gideon stopped laughing. There was something else in the room. A dark mound lay beside the pool. It was in the shape of a man, covered in the same envelope that had sheathed Gideon's body when he emerged. He stood motionless and waited to see whether or not it would give some sign of life, but it did not stir.

He cautiously crept nearer and nearer, stealing glances at the pool as though its liquid might surge out and reclaim this impossible gift. It was surely a man in shape, features obscured by the membrane that clung to its body. Gideon touched it with his toe several times, but when this did not provoke a reaction, he crouched beside it and, pinching the membrane between fingers and thumbs, lifted and tore it away. The thing within stank of the fresh, hot marrow of opened bones.

The gelatinous membrane parted and retracted like rubber, and the corpse's face—for it was surely a dead thing—was revealed in the gloomy light. It was a man, young and rather handsome, with the pronounced features of a savage, though paler of flesh. The face was familiar, though Gideon did not immediately recognize it. He stared for several seconds and then, realizing who it was, pulled his hands away.

This was the body of the man Gideon had murdered in the desert. The Apache called Speaks With Knife, youthful and free of defects and yet not restored to life. There was no sign of the violence Gideon had inflicted, not even a mark on his cheek. Gideon furiously ripped at the membrane and saw that the place where his fatal shot had struck the Indian was perfect and smooth.

Some part of the body moved, and Gideon recoiled. The corpse was not dead at all, only sleeping, and as it came awake, it moved its arms wildly and shouted without words. The loud voice was bestial. It brayed with wild fear.

Gideon realized the man was sliding very slowly down into the pool, and as his feet were sucked back into the liquid, there was a bubbling that Gideon recognized. The body of Speaks With Knife screamed in pain. Its limbs were trapped within the membranous sheath. Its dark eyes bulged in horror. Gideon rubbed his arms and face and felt a sympathetic burning, the agony of the pool was so immediately recalled.

It was devouring the Indian, slowly. Bones popped and limbs twisted, and the man, now only moaning and gurgling, rolled onto his side as he was resorbed and digested into the liquid. The Indian's long black hair trailed behind his head and was the last thing to disappear as the Indian slid beneath the surface and was gone. The bubbling ceased, and the pool was again placid and silent.

"Why?" wondered Gideon. "Why would this strange pool produce an idiot simulacrum of a dead man? To torment me? Or was it only coincidence, a creature plucked from my mind?"

Gideon felt a thrill upon recalling the Indian's blood that had cursed his boots, soaking into the leather, becoming sticky beneath his toes. He was no longer transfixed and fled from the chamber, crawling into the darkness of the tunnel, up from the stinking, primordial cave and out, gasping, into the cold, open air and the canyon pueblo. His entire body steamed, naked, but Gideon did not shiver. He gazed up at the stars above, and the moon, and he gathered his thoughts and, on reflection, felt not fear but elation. Triumph.

Gideon looked at the stars and the moon and sneered. Poor, stymied God. Meaningless fate. He mocked the broken mandala. He shouted and exulted at the Revelation of the new flesh. Against all possibility and conspiring fortune, in the face of certain obliteration, Gideon Long still existed.

CHAPTER EIGHT

■ ■ ■

Warren Groves awoke at the first graying of the sky and enjoyed a single moment of forgetfulness. In the wan light of the bedroom he saw Annie as alive beside him and only sleeping. The slack parting of her lips and the sunken flesh of her cheeks and the butcher's stink soon dismissed this illusion. Warren sat up and threw back the cover and faced again the full horror of his wife's mortal wounds.

He dragged the washtub outside and emptied it into the dirt. He carried it back into the house and filled it again with water he heated in kettles and he cut hunks from a piece of soap and let them dissolve into the water until it was cloudy and steaming hot. He lifted Annie's body in his arms and it seemed to weigh nothing at all and he put it into the water and with her sponge he cleaned her.

Warren never looked directly at the body. The thing of her. He laved it in soap water and scrubbed the stains from its marionette hands and only stared at the way the water surrounding it was gradually discolored to a rusty brown. When the body was clean he laid it out on the table and sewed it shut and her belly looked deflated and horrible for what was gone. He wrapped her in a clean sheet sprinkled with lime from the barn so that he did not have to look at her any longer and so the flies would not plant their maggots in her flesh.

He had no appetite and he sought to quench his thirst with the bottle of whiskey Doc Carson had left on the stove. He took it with him into the barn and drank and alone lifted up the massive end of an old viga pulled from the ruin of a Spanish monastery and he slid the beam onto a sawbuck.

He was no longer the sheriff. Had no more interest in the sort of justice the law offered. He made himself drunk before noon and sawed the beam and sang Annie's French songs to himself even though he knew them only by the melody and the roughest sounds of the words.

■ ■ ■

The freight wagons and their escorts crowded all other traffic from the road. These were huge vehicles, reinforced with iron axles and drawn by mule teams of ten or more. The wagons were flat-sided and painted blue and white. Each wagon bore the name of S.H. Ogilvy, the founder and proprietor of seventy-four beehive coke ovens in the Territory of Arizona. Ogilvy's firm transported fuel coke five times per year to the foundry of Desmond Pearce atop Red Stem. This delivery was near at hand, as the wagons filed up the main road through Spark and beyond, creating such a procession that idle folk gathered to watch.

The wagons' huge wheels turned and slipped in the wagon ruts, and men shouted with concern at a wagon sliding precariously back and threatening the wagon behind. Disaster was averted by chocking the back axle until the mules could be brought under control and beaten forward. The mules halted again, and the Mexican teamsters cursed in Spanish and lashed them constantly, driving them up the sloping road.

Outriders protected the flanks of the wagon train, shotguns ready as though some outlaw might rush from an alley and make off with six tons of coke. Here and there among the wagons the Anglos working directly for Ogilvy stood on the running boards. They were better dressed than the teamsters, wore tan and white Stetson hats, and shouted orders to one another, relaying them from one man to the next over the din of the mules to direct the course of the wagon train.

Near the very end of this long column, chased only by the last of the armed riders, came a garish blue and yellow celerity wagon appointed with a comfortable interior, curtained windows, and a rack filled with matching baggage of the sort a Londoner might transport for a weekend in the country. The wagon contained three passengers, though it had left Arizona with only two. Bernard Huff, the agent of Ogilvy, and his pretty wife, Samantha, sat side by side on the bench of the carriage, nervously averting their gaze from the man introduced as Robert McClelland.

Gideon wore a pair of Bernard's fine trousers and a button-down shirt in the current fashion, though slightly too small for his limbs so that the cuffs ended before they reached his wrists. It was an unexpectedly fine replacement for his tattered clothes recovered from the cave, purchased, as well as his passage on the carriage, with the gold of his teeth and the gutted remains of his gold pocket watch. The agent, Huff, had been given no say in the matter. The bribe was paid to the wagon master named Conroy, who'd taken the gold and looted Huff's case for the clothing.

Gideon smiled at the well-dressed couple, his lips curled back, and he could see them shrink away in their seats and interpret his expression as a snarl. Perhaps it *was* a snarl. He did experience a certain bestial hunger and considered, absently, whether his jaw contained the strength to tear out their throats. It was not that he thought he might, only that some primitive recess of his mind reminded him that tearing out throats was a thing to be enjoyed and the hot gush of blood a thing to be savored.

The Huffs said nothing. Gideon watched out the window as the wagon train ascended the road to Spark. It was a landscape of rock, desert, and the geologic folding of mountains, on into the wide-open distance, populated only occasionally by squatter shacks, grave markers, boulders, and cholla cactus. Gideon despised the austere endlessness of New Mexico. The country knew it was hated and behaved accordingly.

Gideon slid open the glass of the carriage window and leaned his head out to see past the wagons. The leading elements of the wagon train were already through Spark and ascending to the foundry. The carriage, at the tail end of the column, was still on the lower outskirts of the town. Gideon recognized the frame house and barn just ahead and on the right, and his heart quickened in his breast.

Sheriff Groves. Trying to pretend to wealth with that house. Annabelle. In an instant he could leap from the carriage and be with her. She was so tantalizingly near, he could feel her hair against his face as he held her in his arms.

No. Not yet. Too many lingering troubles. Once he was able to repair the finances at the foundry, all would be well.

Gideon leaned back in his seat and shut his eyes. He could hear a man singing, off-key, too distant to be understood, but the melody was haunting and familiar. It was one of Annabelle's songs. The man clearly did not know the rhyme, but Gideon did. "*Le sommeil va bientôt venir.*" A simple lullaby to convince a child to sleep.

He was glad when the carriage rolled into Spark and left behind the song and the lonely frame house where Annabelle lived with another man. It was nice to be surrounded again by buildings and alleyways. Gideon was gladdened by the sight of slop buckets emptied onto dirt roads, prospectors and mulattoes squatting the side streets in their tents, drunken miners rising late in the shadows of unfamiliar houses, and plain-faced whores coming out of their cribs and squinting up at the sky.

"I see the Whitney coming up," he said.

"Oh?" said Bernard.

Bernard believed Gideon's story, believed he was a surveyor for the railroad attacked by Indians on his way to Spark, believed his horse and instruments were stolen and he was abandoned, in blood-soaked rags, to die in the desert.

"Thank you for your hospitality," said Gideon.

Though the carriage was still a ways short of the Whitney, Gideon was anxious to be off before he was recognized. He opened the door and climbed onto the sideboard.

"You never did show us what was in your bag," said Mrs. Huff.

She pointed out the window to the red valise, held in one of Gideon's hands and very much the worse for wear.

"A solution," said Gideon. "I found it in the desert."

"You are very lucky," said Mrs. Huff.

She bit at her lower lip and reached a blue-gloved hand out and brushed his that gripped the frame of the door. Gideon was poised to leap down from the carriage but could not resist glancing back and offering the pretty young blonde a smile. She did bear some resemblance to his beloved Annabelle.

"I am preternaturally blessed," he said.

He leaped down and waited until the wagon train had passed. He had no money for the luxury and privacy he so desired. No silver dollars for a hot bath or for the debts he owed Bo Fairway. Gideon left the shade of the Whitney's awning. The wagon train was disappearing up the curve of the mountain. He trudged, barefoot, over the rutted wagon paths and up the slowly curving road through Spark.

He ducked past foundry workers who recognized him, soot-faced miners returning from morning shift, and soiled doves who called out his name from the balconies of the saloons. The girls shook the hems of their petticoats and they buzzed like horseflies. Gideon's station in the town demanded he not request, nor could he rely upon, the assistance of any one of these people.

Flies bit his neck, and the sun burned his newly pale skin no matter how he shaded himself with the valise. He did not want to return to the house. Not now. But he had no choice. He passed through the estate's rusty iron gate and up the cobblestone path to the mansion. Father endured like a tumor on the upper floors. He could feel the malignant throb of life.

Gideon stole in through the scullery door unnoticed by Mrs. Reece. Her staff of young women and boys was too afraid of Gideon to alert her as he crept past the laundry basins and the pantry. This fear was Father's doing, for he tormented the kitchen and laundry staff with incessant demands, shouting, and the hanging sword of liquidation. Only Mrs. Reece and Adelaide had the fortitude to endure; the rest of the staff was perpetually being sacked and hired to placate Father. The worst Gideon ever inflicted upon the servants was the occasional liaison with a well-rounded laundry girl or maid, and these larder trysts were only with consent.

On the second floor he could hear Adelaide, Father's nurse, acting as his proxy in the hall and vituperating at some poor maid. Gideon could see Adelaide at the end of the long hall, silhouetted by the huge window, leaning in and prodding the girl with the gnarled tip of a finger.

Gideon kept to the carpet as much as possible and then dashed quickly across the anteroom's tiled floor, relying on his bare feet to conceal the sound of his footsteps. He felt reduced to a low thing, creeping about in his family house, feet caked in mule dung, wearing a stranger's clothes. There was nothing else to be done. He could not stand to be summoned by Father in this condition.

He reached his chambers at last and shut the door behind him. The extravagant bedroom was crammed with maps and trophies from his time in England, meaningless ribbons, a stuffed fox, and all the elaborate models of steamships he had assembled against Father's wishes. He had not built one of these in many years, not since discovering whiskey and women, but he still admired the craftsmanship of the masts, rigging, funnels, decks, and tiny cannons.

His prize model was of a ship of his own design. *The Republic* never sailed any sea, it was a flight of his imagination, as long as Brunel's Great Eastern and powered by a submerged screw. A flagship for America to match any of Europe. He knew little of shipbuilding but vowed some day to see *The Republic* launched. Once his family's fortunes were restored he would have wealth enough for such pursuits.

He touched the painted flag atop *The Republic* and recalled the expense and difficulty of constructing even the model. It had been many years since he had been on a ship like it.

He often fantasized about booking passage on a trans-Atlantic steamer, of taking Annabelle to see England, London, to Scotland, where his great-grandfather was born. His greatest aspiration was to take her on his own steamer, sailing to whichever port around the world she desired. He might stand at the rail with his arm across her shoulders and watch the sun rising over nothing but blue water.

Gideon rang the house maids and ordered basins of hot water and a mirror. He sat in a chair, and a young girl named Margaret washed his hair and shaved him while he soaked his feet in a tub. He watched in the mirror as she lathered up his face, amazed at the ageless contours of his cheeks, the absence of crow's-feet at the corners of his eyes. He was the same as when he awoke the day before but with the youth of ten years earlier and without injury or defect.

Curative powers were claimed of many pools and mud fields throughout history. A hot spring could not explain what he saw in the mirror. Gideon did not believe in magic, he learned to doubt such superstitions at Chatholm, but like all good Christians he believed in the miraculous. Surely God's hand was at work in his rejuvenation. If science might explain Gideon's new life, God was in the eyes of the dog that led him to it.

"Why?" said Gideon. Margaret paused in shaving his face. He met her eyes in the mirror. "I don't expect you to have any answers. Continue."

She did an adequate job with the razor and admitted to shaving her father on occasion. Perhaps Gideon was old enough to be her father. He could only be sure that the man seen in the mirror was not.

Two small wounds bled, and for these she applied the styptic pencil. As she stanched the second of these, Gideon seized her wrist, and, finding her smell appealing and her corseted figure acceptable, he turned her onto the bed and raised her apron and skirt and had at her without objection. She had pretty brown eyes, said little, and her neck tasted sweet. She chewed her lip and looked at the ceiling, and when he finished, he rolled over and asked her to clean him and told her fetch him a meal and two full pitchers of water.

Margaret returned with another servant, a boy named Tom who held his jaw clenched in anger, though he said nothing. Margaret had the red-eyed look of a girl just finished crying. Gideon found no appetite for her upset and did not inquire as to her feelings.

"Just there is fine," he said, directing them to a writing desk.

He dismissed them with instructions to fetch the Dane. He drank down three cups of water and swallowed bites of stewed rabbit, potatoes, and a crusty piece of bread. When he finished his meal, he took a small box of Lewis Licorice Dandies from his desk drawer and chewed on the sweet, candied extract. He looked in the mirror and picked the black shreds from his teeth with a fingernail.

Gideon's suit felt a bit tight, and he could not be sure if it was because he was full with food and water or if his lean, youthful muscles made for a tighter fit. He tried on the jacket he had worn to his brother's funeral, and this fit perfectly.

He was lacing up his boots when there came a hesitant knock at the door. It was the Dane, obsequious as always, shaved head bowed like that of a monk in the presence of a holy artifact. Gideon knew that such a servile demeanor was only a veneer with the Dane. It barely concealed his uncompromising view of bookkeeping and his simmering resentment over his forced involvement in financial subterfuge. It was the Dane and Robert Broken Horse and no others who knew the truth of the Long family's business peril.

"You sent for me?"

Gideon ignored the Dane and finished lacing his boot. He got up from his chair and brought over the valise and rested it on the writing desk beside the remnants of his meal.

"Your leg," said the Dane. "Why do you not have limp?"

"Sit down," Gideon said, and he gestured to the chair before the desk. Gideon opened the valise and took out the lone folio that had survived his journey across the desert. "Tell me what this means."

The Dane sat down and put on his spectacles. Gideon lit a lamp on the desk and turned up the flame. The Dane paged slowly through the document, and Gideon studied his expression. When the Dane finished, he closed the folio, exhaled deeply, and sat back in the chair. He laced his fingers behind his head.

"Your father has lot of money in bonds, gold, silver, and land. Lot of land in California. By the ocean."

"What? What is the document?"

"Is testament," said the Dane. "Drawn to ensure fortune, along with business, pass to your sister and husband when he is dying." The Dane leaned forward in the chair and licked his lips. "There is no signing."

"Unsigned?"

"That is right."

The Dane did not show any particular satisfaction at this news. Gideon made up for him. He clapped the Dane roughly on the shoulder, and his jubilation was such that he went over to his cabinet full of spirits and took out a bottle of cognac and two glasses. He had been denied the train's gold by bad luck and damned Warren Groves, but a fortune could be his after all, and he could be the one to save the business. Certainly cause for celebration.

"Let us reflect upon the easing turn of fortune," Gideon said, and he poured himself and the Dane each a healthy portion of amber liquid. "A toast. To . . . starting over."

They clinked glasses, but the Dane would not drink. Gideon finished his in a single gulp and snatched the glass from the Dane's hand.

"You filthy teetotaler," he laughed. "You would not believe what I went through for that document."

"Congratulation, Mr. Long. Maybe meet payroll for month."

Gideon's expression soured. "Always my little squarehead, eh? You can never enjoy a moment of victory."

"Sir, I enjoy no longer forging ledger. If this is possible by this money, I am very glad."

"Out." Gideon waved to the door. "Out of here before I remember why I hate you. Spend your brain on how I can claim Father's money and turn the wireworks to profit."

"Sir, might I be permission to leave early? My wife work at the church, and she is help with funerals."

Gideon was already distracted, paging through his father's testament, planning to smother the old brute beneath a pillow. "The what?"

"The funerals, for those mans who die in train. And for ah . . . sheriff wife."

■ ■ ■

The church was built on the southern slope of Red Stem and the view from the cemetery encompassed nearly all of the Tularosa Basin from the white sand desert to the distant and hazy shapes of the San Andres Mountains. The cemetery was surrounded by a sagging wooden fence and it spread down the slope and beyond the First Gospel Church of the Redemption.

It was an old church. One of the oldest buildings in Spark. It was the work of the first Anglos to come and built from whitewashed boards and capped with a gabled roof rebuilt twice with blue shakes. The steeple was askew on account of being constructed at an angle and there was a ten-foot copper cross at its summit that drooped as if time might pull it down. That copper cross was the donation of the Pearce family and replaced a seven-foot copper cross given by the Long family. That cross now stood among the stones and wooden crosses as a monument in the cemetery.

The cemetery was currently full up with curious folk come to take a count of the number of bodies being put into the ground that day. Word of the train calamity had spread and was already being printed in his rag as TRAIN MASSACRE! by the newspaperman and distributed in such quantity that some copies were printed on paper sacks.

"Sheriff, I am mighty sorry we can't do this all proper, but the Army has took over my church," said the sunburned preacher.

The coffin thumped against the earth at the bottom of the grave and the grave-diggers let go the ropes to coil in the ground. Warren stared down at his wife's casket.

"Did your wife have a verse I could read? Some favorite bit of scripture?"

"Don't expect she read things the same way as you."

"I'll just say a general prayer, if you'd rather," said the preacher.

Warren nodded absently to the preacher who was of little concern to him. He focused his attention on the task at hand. On the duty of burying his wife. He had done all the steps that were needed. He had cleaned her body and built her a fine casket out of old oak and dressed her in the clothes she wore to their wedding and kissed her head and nailed her into the box. He had picked a fine plot and put down a carved cross and dug her a hole. With the help of Felix Arguello and two buffalo soldiers he had now put her into the ground and all that was left was to say a few words and seal her in the earth.

Warren Groves could not bring himself to speak over Annie's grave. He looked at the mountains for a long time and listened to the sobbing of the train families and the murmur and grunt of the laboring soldiers and the sound the wind made high up when there was nothing but people and crosses to blow over and around. Warren never was a man of fine words and he couldn't find any that suited what he felt.

Small fingers slid into his palm and Warren found Libby Cole standing beside him with her dark hair blowing and lashing against his arm. Her eyes were struck with tears and she was looking at the box filled with Annie.

"Annie rode into Spark back when I was hardly a lady," said Libby. "Weren't no words from the Good Book or testifying to be done to me. Her friend, the one who fell sick, she tried all that. Annie just told me God made up His mind about me whatever I did, and I ought look beyond where I was and find a happiness and a goodness here on this earth, and I told her I believed she was right.

"But I didn't. I thought she was full of it. And I asked her later for some money. I told her it was to buy a church dress, and she gave it to me right then and took my hand and said she was giving it to me because she knew it would do good. And I bought me some morphine and shot it all up that very night. Just about killed my-self.

"I did not wake up for nine days and would have died if Annie hadn't've called on me the next morning and took me to Doc Carson. I was in his tent for a whole week unconscious, and Annie had so many people she was helping then, she had to ask folks she knew, and on account of she was friends with the sheriff, she asked a man named Pat Cole to take care of me.

"I can't say I owe Annie a lot. That ain't enough by half. I owe her most every-thing I am now. Only she wouldn't say that. She'd tell me God always planned it and it was God that had her give me that money and God that nearly killed me shooting morphine into my arm. I will go on believing it was Annie's doing. Bless her soul. I know she's with God now."

Libby threw a bouquet of white and lavender wildflowers down into the grave. "Good-bye, Annie." Libby gave Warren's hand a squeeze.

"Good-bye, Annie," Warren said. It was enough.

Felix and the Negroes stayed and helped him shovel earth into the grave until the coffin was covered up and the dirt was piled in a mound over her body. When he was through he shook each man's hand and thanked them. He found Libby waiting for him by the gate to the cemetery.

"Thank you for what you said," Warren said. "I was—"

Libby slapped him hard enough to take off his hat and turn his head. He began to recover and she slapped him again even harder than the first time and his cheek bore a scarlet mark where she struck him.

"You low-down animal," Libby said.

"I'm sorry about Pat—"

"This ain't about my husband." Libby's face contorted in anger and grief. "You left her to die, Warren. Alone. And you'll have to live with that. But damn you to hell for what you done with that baby. If you ever, in your life, ever, was a man at all, you'd get that little girl and you'd bring her back."

"You ain't gonna change my mind on the matter." Giving up the child weighed on him but it did not matter. He was set on his course for bloodshed and had no place left for tenderness.

"You're a damn fool and a coward."

"Might be those things. I wasn't meant to raise a child on my own. I am for certain a killer and to that manner born," said Warren. "I am not a good man. It was only Annie tempered me."

"God sees through them excuses," she said.

Warren looked her in the eye and considered if Elizabeth Cole should know. There was nobody else in the world who did. He slowly reached a hand into his trouser pocket and took out the black book tied up with a strap. He held it out to her, and she only reluctantly took it.

"What is this?"

"Open it to the first page," Warren said.

She unfastened the strap and opened the book. She squinted at the ink stains and childish scrawl on the first page.

"December, 1853," Libby read aloud.

"That's it."

Warren looked back at the mound of earth above his wife's grave.

"Abraham Nunn," Libby read. "Piece of glass. What does this mean?"

"It was the first time I took a life. I was a boy of ten or eleven when I wrote that name. I killed Abraham Nunn—I murdered Abraham Nunn—with a shard of green glass from a bottle of rye."

"Why?" said Libby.

"He done some things. Some of them bad enough to be hanged for maybe, but that don't change it. Wasn't justice I was after. I just wanted to put a stop to him. He was drunk, and he was helpless. I sat on his chest, and I killed him with a piece of glass."

"My God, Warren. That's . . . you ain't that man anymore. You're a good man. You can be a father to that baby."

Warren took the book back from Libby and stuffed it into his pocket.

"I've spent my life filling up that book. Writing red across twenty years. To give it meaning was why I joined the law. It was Annie who made it all right. Coming home to her, I always kept my accounts. I put down names that deserved it. Killers and violent men and men who done things to children."

"Does Pat know?"

"He shouldn't ever. He's seen me write in that book, and that's it. I never had cause to show it to him, and you know Pat ain't the sort to pry."

"Who was Abraham Nunn?"

Warren shook his head and walked past Libby. "I think I said enough already. If you ain't convinced now, then you ain't going to be."

The line of folk come to see the dead stretched beyond the cemetery gate and down the slope of Red Stem. Women and men in the line were weeping. Bored children played in the road. Franciscan Sisters walked the line, offering ladles of water to the folk sweltering in the afternoon heat. Libby followed Warren out of the cemetery and struggled with her bustle and crinolette and was quickly exhausting herself keeping pace with Warren's long stride.

"What did he do to you?" said Libby. "Who was he?"

Libby's bustle caught up on the cemetery fence. She was afraid of tearing it.

"Who was he?" she said again.

Warren saw Libby's predicament. He stopped and knelt in the scratch grass. He found the snag with his fingers and freed the green fabric of her skirt from the rusty hook of a nail. Libby's hair was blowing into her face and she pushed it back and looked Warren in the eye when he stood.

"Who was he to you?"

"Nothing." Warren paused and felt old things on the wind off the mountain, distant memories and voices long ago gone quiet. "My mother told me some trees grow from the soil straight and true, and some are brambles that prick your skin, and some bear poison fruit. Abraham Nunn was a poison tree. He shook his daughter till she died and buried her so shallow, the dogs dug her up."

The wind stung his eyes so Warren turned his face away from Libby.

"He drank rye and beat his wife so that every day her face was swollen and changed. One night he came home broke from cards and fearsome drunk and put his fists to his wife until she lay still and didn't breathe no more at all. No more songs from her. No more smiles. When he was asleep and snoring, I killed him. With a piece of green glass I killed him and set fire to his house. I killed my father."

Warren left Libby Cole by the swaying pickets of the cemetery fence. He fetched his horse from the stable and paid the boy who'd fed and watered it. Warren took from his bag a brace of pistols and he buckled them around his hips and climbed into his saddle. Before riding he examined the tin star from his pocket and looked at the word stamped in the metal. He felt the shape of it with his fingers.

He let the star fall into the dust and did not look back to see it glittering in the road.

CHAPTER NINE

■ ■ ■

Something more than convenience, or the liquor poured down his neck, made him use the red valise. He filled it up with the letters. Soft bundles, well-fingered, each envelope smelling like Annabelle at different points in time. There were ten, and each he knew like a favorite book, by the heaviness of it and the way the envelope was torn. He relived the brimming vault of sense and memory as each envelope passed into the dusty valise: begun hopeful, when they first encountered; becoming desperate when Warren entered her life, wistful; and finally hopeful again that she might abandon her lawman husband and run away with Gideon to Europe.

These pages belonged in a book he would never author. Not now. He had so completely slipped the lasso of fate—mocked it, even—and here was his reward. Fate warning that if it was to be denied, it would claim another.

He fed the last of the letters into the valise, and they lay above a pistol for which he had only one bullet. He pushed his chair against the wall and sat in it with the back of his head against the papered wall of rusted brown and gold.

The window was open, curtains billowing in the hot wind, and the light that was colored scarlet by the curtain reminded Gideon of the crystal-lensed moon that had filtered into the esoteric cavern. Was that place real? He hardly believed it could be, yet he need only gaze into the mirror and see himself as he was long ago, not some overgrown old child living in his father's home, but a young man fresh from England. Healed of scars and born again.

And she no longer existed at all.

Gideon made himself get up from the chair lest his own drunken inertia overtake him. He staggered to the writing desk again, opened the drawer he always locked with a key, and took out the lavender box. He could not look at it. He quickly snatched it up and shoved it into the valise. He put on a high-topped hat, denting its crown as he pushed it over his brow. He closed the bag and brought with him a bottle of Portuguese wine. The wax-sealed cork yielded to his teeth, and he spit the cork down the hallway, not caring who found it.

Killing Father was so much less than he had expected. Adelaide was gone on some errand, and so he simply walked into the musty bedchamber and set about murdering Harlan Long. Father offered no resistance. He did not speak or cry out as Gideon's hands found his throat. His eyes bulged. His pale face turned crimson. Even this was an irritation in its own way. There was no triumph in this act. Father seemed to smile mockingly up at Gideon until Gideon could not bear it, and he took a heavy down pillow and smothered Father beneath it.

Father fought weakly in his last moments. Perhaps some animal instinct overwhelmed his nihilistic good humor. Gideon overcame the thrashing limbs and leaned heavily on the pillow until all movement ceased. When he was sure Father was dead, he fell back into an overstuffed chair and held the pillow to his chest. He looked at the black-eyed faces of his ancestors staring out as mute witnesses to his patricide. He stared at Father. Dead Father. He waited for the desiccated husk that had tormented him all those years to rise from the bed and attack him.

Adelaide came and screamed in horror. She threw herself over Father's legs and pounded her fists upon his withered body. She wailed, and she shouted for Gideon to fetch the doctor. He had no intention of doing so but fled because of the terrifying sorrow of the stoic nurse. It was an impossible explosion, like a tree bursting into flames. He recoiled from the very idea that anyone loved his Father. He fled. Snatched the bottle and fled.

He left the house the way he had come and walked down the cobblestones, weaving back and forth, passing through the rusty gate and whistling haphazardly from one broken tune to the next. He ignored the gawking foundry workers and the whores calling out to him from the saloons. He stopped only to tip the bottle to his lips and let the warm, sweet wine overflow his mouth.

The cemetery was crowded with muttering townsfolk, men in suits, Negro soldiers, and strangers come from Jessup or Las Cruces or wherever else people had waited hopefully for a train that never arrived. Gideon could tell that the men in suits were Pinkertons by their demeanor—the way they leaned in aggressively at the Army officers as though expecting subservience—already brought in by the railroad to find the men who had destroyed the train. He laughed and drank more wine, amused by how easily he could surrender himself to the hands of the Pinkertons.

Not yet. He was not ready for the gallows. He passed the bottle of wine to a man who looked like he needed it and staggered past the queue into the cemetery. There were many fresh graves and more bodies being buried. The line of corpses on the ground hardly bothered his conscience. Gideon saw the dead arranged on the ground and looked at them as the victims of a terrible accident. He wasn't guilty. His intent was never to harm or kill those on the train. Fate, not Gideon Long, had decided they needed to die.

He knew few would see things his way, but he did not care. He was already punished as completely as could be and wished he had died out in the desert and never learned of Annabelle's end.

Gideon found that her fresh grave was marked with a simple wooden cross. It was carved with the name *Annabelle Groves*, though her name was, and would always be, Moraud. Annabelle Moraud. Born 1851, died 1874. She lay beneath the earth in the ripeness of womanhood, slain by the stranger Warren Groves, who sat terrible and alone at night, who was sheriff, who had shot Gideon in the belly and left him to die.

Gideon tasted the acid of his anger. It was not the time for that. He dropped to his knees in the dirt and laid a hand on the mound of earth as though he might feel the beating of her heart. He let his fingers trail through the dust and then, with only his hands, began to dig a small hole atop the grave.

When his digging penetrated a foot or so into the earth, he took the letters out from the valise, placed them into the hole, and hung his head.

"I wish we could have done these things, Annabelle. I would have had my father's business, everything sorted, and all the riches to show you the world. I . . . I told you of Venice, its beauty at night, but it's nothing. . . ."

Tears dropped from his chin, and he hung his head even lower so that his nose nearly touched the mound of dirt. His lips pulled back from his gums, and his face was frozen in a silent, horrible sob. He sucked in the tears and the mucus and sat up, wiped at his eyes, and took the box from the valise.

He took out the ring. Gold and diamonds. Worth more than enough to pay all his gambling and drinking debts. He would rather die than sell it, had only bought it two years ago during his trip to Paris. It was exquisite. A dozen diamonds from an Amsterdam Jew and a twisting serpent band of gold from the Galerie de Valois, handcrafted by Frederic Boucheron himself.

He placed the ring atop the letters. It sparkled like water in moonlight.

"For this . . . I would have killed him," Gideon whispered. "I will kill him.

"Good-bye, Annie," he said, and he filled in the shallow hole.

Gideon stood up. The mountainside seemed to roll like the surface of the ocean, and he steadied himself. He took the pistol from the valise and stuck it into the waist of his trousers, the metal cold against his leg. He took a last look at where Annabelle would always be, and he departed. There was a curious smile on his face, the cold rapture of knowing that by night Sheriff Groves would fall before the smoke of his gun.

■ ■ ■

Turk let Warren Groves into the sheriff's office after the prisoners. Warren wrapped his fists in cloth and beat the men one at a time until they talked. He let his anger empty into his hands and pummeled face and body until each man spilled his story.

The stories had different beginnings but the same characters appeared in each. An Indian dressed like a white man did the hiring and the paying. An old Union engineer named Eli McClelland instructed them to dig and plant explosives at the bridges of Bear Creek and Green Creek. He was dead.

The boss of them all was a white man with wild black hair they called Mr. Wiley. He walked with a limp and had a brace on his leg that squeaked with each step. There was a man he instructed them to kill and then take his red bag. They spit blood through split lips and said Mr. Wiley was crazy.

Warren left the cellar where they kept the prisoners. Turk met Warren in the hall and watched him unwind the bloody cloth from his knuckles.

"Did you find what you need?" asked Turk.

"I reckon I did," said Warren.

"The army intends to hang them all," said Turk. "Soon. While the paper men from Santa Fe are here. If you have the heart you should have words with Mildenhall. Not all those boys have done the same evil."

"Not my concern," said Warren. Turk shook his head with dismay.

"You can't just turn your gun on whoever did this," said Turk.

Warren ignored his friend. He discarded the bloody strips of cloth on the floor of the sheriff's office. There was a man shouting like a fool out in the street. Warren shook his head at Turk and walked out into the night with a good idea of who needed sorting.

■ ■ ■

"Sheriff Groves!" Gideon shouted from the road outside the sheriff's office. "Sheriff Warren Groves!"

It was darkened to dusk, but he could see men moving within the sheriff's office. Pinkertons and uniformed men of the Army. Groves was sure to be inside holding court.

"Groves, you coward, get out here!"

A man stepped out of the office and into the street.

Gideon recognized Sheriff Groves. He was hale and handsome, a veritable champion of the West, a spirit summoned to fit the scale of the country. He seemed as indefatigable as Gideon's father. The sort of man who would wrestle mustangs down with only his hands and kill tigers with a pistol and outfight a savage, he was a conqueror.

Warren Groves was in his suspenders and undershirt, sleeves rolled up to show tanned arms, and no badge in sight. His knuckles were raw and red. His eyes were blue, and his short blond hair was rearranged by the wind. He posed with his hands on his hips and looked at Gideon with naked contempt.

"Warren Groves," said Gideon.

"You've got me at a disadvantage," said Sheriff Groves. Even his accent rankled, slow and broad as the graben desert.

More men came out from the sheriff's office and stood on the boardwalk. Some

wore U. S. Cavalry blue, and others Gideon recognized from the cemetery. Pinkertons. Gideon laughed that Warren Groves would not remember his face.

"I knew your wife," Gideon said. "Annabelle."

"You did?"

"I did. Knew her well, Sheriff. I am surprised you don't remember me. I used to
call upon Annabelle when she lived on the charity of Bo Fairway, over at the Whitney. Met her when she first came west. Still don't recall?"

"Get to the point, mister."

This sent Gideon into a swaying, unseemly fit of laughter. He could not help it.
He was quivering and giddy at the thought of finally acting out his fantasy.

"'Mister,'" said Gideon. "You're a peach, Sheriff. No wonder Annabelle fell for
you. Must have been that sense of humor."

"I've got to warn you," said Sheriff Groves. "I've had about enough of this nonsense, so unless you want to be laid out in a wagon rut, get to what concerns me."

"No need for hostility. I only wanted to offer my heartfelt condolences. Annabelle was a kind, beautiful, wonderfully bright young woman. It is a tragedy that she
had to be taken from this earth so prematurely."

Sheriff Groves did not reply; he only stood and glared down from the boardwalk
at Gideon.

"Had to die alone, like some sort of kept cat gone and hid under the porch. Had
to die 'cause you stole her away. She only married you to protect herself. Did she ever
tell you that one? She was afraid and—"

"I'm about one second from putting you down."

Gideon's face twisted up in anger, and he waved a finger and shouted at Sheriff
Groves. "You cocksucker! You killed her. Murderer! She didn't love you. She—"

Sheriff Groves stepped down off the boardwalk and came for Gideon with the
clear intent to do harm. Gideon retreated instinctively from the fury. He had not
planned to draw out the sheriff so early, but he had talked himself out of any alternative. He reached for the pistol in the waist of his trousers. He gripped the body-
warmed wood of the handle and dragged the barrel out along his leg. He brought
the gun up.

Sheriff Groves had both his pistols skinned, and they spoke fire and thunder and
smoke. Death came suddenly to Gideon. No time to reflect or see the wheel turn. Two
slugs made different paths straight through his head. He tasted blood in his sinuses
and saw the battle flag of his memory sink, tattered by canister. He was moving with
great speed, moving so fast that Gideon Long was gone before his body hit the dirt.

"What in God's name was that?" asked Turk.

Warren Groves holstered his pistols and looked at the body lying in the road.
Blood was spilling beneath its head in a dark pool and ran out of both nostrils and
one ear. One leg was out straight and flat, and the other was bent at the knee and
began to stretch out with involuntary spasms of the muscles.

Warren knelt beside the body. Blood poured out of the holes in its forehead and covered the face down to its upper lip in a scarlet veil. The eyes were open and white amid the blood, and they looked up, unseeing, into the twilight sky. He studied the eyes. He recognized them from Green Creek.

"That is Harlan Long's son," said Warren. "He used to walk around town with a brace on his leg. I have killed the man responsible for the train robbery."

He crouched and dragged his fingers over the dead man's eyes to close them. He reached down to the corpse's shirt just above his trousers, dragged the fabric out of his pants, and exposed the corpse's pale belly. He felt the stomach with his hands and found not even a scratch.

"I shot this fella," Sheriff Groves said. "Before, I mean. I shot him yesterday."

"How's that?" said Turk.

"Just how I said. I shot him yesterday. He came up out of Green Creek with a kerchief over his face. Recognize his eyes and nose."

They turned the body over, and Sheriff Groves lifted the back of the shirt and found no mark there either.

"Fixed himself in a hurry," said Turk.

■ ■ ■

There came a fragile, fluid gist, in the shadow-shape of a man, telegraphed along unseen wires and through the place where things were not, haunted by vistas that could not be. To this shifting, unfocused eye, no place was seen for more than a moment. Thousands of smoking stones fell from a red sky. Tea-colored seas broke against chiming shores of knife-edged crystal. Black, fallen stones spanned an empty canal that reached to the horizon. Faceless idols leaned haphazard in desert clay. Everywhere yawned the black chasm, not quite infinite but without the white man's maps.

Through these shuffling, impossible terrains a parade of liminal beasts moved on two legs and four and ten and none at all and floated with gas-filled bladders on the currents of storms and wriggled in the decay accumulating in fathomless trenches. All these places smelled and tasted the same and were dying, and the light was never warm enough.

The shadow-shape passed unnoticed, moving far too fast to sense by any means of flesh or device.

For a waking man it was only a single instant, the time it took Sheriff Groves to holster his pistols, but there existed different things than waking men, and this shadow-shape traveled for ten thousand years and none at all and emerged, encapsulated in the sack of foul liquid, onto the smooth shores of the pool that smelled like fresh marrow cracked from bones. It was Gideon Long, vomiting out a bellyful of cursed broth, retching and heaving himself out of the liquid.

On hot and sloping rock, transfixed by shafts of colored light, Gideon Long found himself restored again to life.

CHAPTER TEN

■ ■ ■

Warren was not sure of the hour and kept the shutters closed so the house remained dark throughout the day. The objects he touched were soft at the edges in the gloom. The house trapped and magnified the sweltering heat. He sweated constantly. The dog refused to stay indoors and lay on the porch while Warren labored within. He packed Annie's fine things into a trunk for Libby Cole.

Revenge had come too quickly and easily. He wallowed in the sticky anguish that was meant to be pushed aside by a need to hunt down the man responsible. With Gideon Long dead and already buried there was no new direction only more whiskey and a house filled with Annie's things.

Annie kept her pens and pencils in a drawer in the bedroom. She had filled a scratch pad made from pulp paper he'd bought in Santa Fe and a fine art diary picked out of a catalogue and brought by mail all the way from Chicago. Not since before the baby was coming did Warren recall seeing any drawing in the diary. He took it out of the drawer and felt the weight of it and admired the calfskin cover. He opened it to the last page and looked at himself.

It was clear by the mustache and the brow that it was he sitting at the kitchen table. In the sketch he sat with back bent and arms resting on knees. His hat dangled from one hand. The way the crosshatch shaded his face and the room it was clearly at night. The only light source was the lantern he took with him out to the barn and put on the table late at night with the flame so low it barely shed any light at all.

This was a private moment and he was surprised that Annie had witnessed it and been able to capture such a thorough sketch without his knowing. The sketch was dated five months ago. He tore it from the book and stuffed it into his pocket. He placed the book in the chest of her belongings.

In the settling heat of daylight Warren was often tricked by memory and the sound of the house to think that Annie was there. He heard her open the door of the stove and he heard her turn in the bed even though he'd burned it behind the house. He fed carrots to her horse called Morgan and oiled her kidney saddle as if she might ride in the afternoon.

When night came and he was too drunk to be useful Warren sat down at the kitchen table with the last bottle of whiskey and stared at the lantern's flame. She was gone, along with the baby who'd killed her and everything else of this life. The house would burn. He'd planned it already. Wanted to see the fire swallow it as he rode away to maybe find a new life or maybe find no life at all. Let the damned thing leave a charred wound on the mountainside.

The pistol was in his hand without his even thinking about it and he looked down the barrel and opened the cylinder to see the empty brass from killing Gideon Long. He thought about what he might do with the gun and put it down on the table beside the box.

The box was the last thing he'd found while emptying the bedroom. It was small and heavy and made from cheap tin faintly corroded at the corners. A length of red ribbon trailed out one side and was pinched closed in the lid. The top was green and painted by hand with the image of a woman wearing a halo made of flowers and leaves.

"Vervains," Warren read aloud.

Holy herb. The Indians believed you could inhale its smoke and see the world as it truly was. He drank a slug of whiskey and said *Vervains* several more times before deciding he did not like the taste of the word. The hinges creaked as he opened the box with a motion more languid than momentous. There was a stack of letters wrapped up in ribbon and under that he could see the glint of metal. He took the letters out. Didn't recognize them.

Underneath was a treasure of jewelry he'd never seen Annie wear. There were different sizes and stones that could only be real and gold and silver that caught the flame of the lantern and sparkled. These were exquisite pieces of fine craftsmanship and not a crude ring of frontier gold of the sort Annie had worn to her grave. He rolled his matching ring with his thumb.

There it was. There was the gut-shot heaviness of unwanted discovery. The sick sensation a man feels when he realizes that his horse haa been stolen or leaves a room only to hear a close friend talk him down to a stranger. It was a secret kept from him by the only person he couldn't bear keeping one. He did not want to look at the letters and for a short time he put them back in the box.

The letters somehow reminded Warren of the strange words Gideon Long had said to him in the street outside the sheriff's office. The drunken fool had spoken as if he knew Annie and why she had married Warren. He reached for the stack of letters. The need to know regardless of the hurt it might cause was stronger than the will to only suspect. He tore the ribbon from the envelopes and rattled the papers and opened the first letter. He read them all. Every miserable word of them. They were all from Gideon Long and full of romantic discussion and French and poems that crawled over his skin like ticks.

Gideon's letters to Annie contained references to matters private and personal between Warren and his wife. Gideon wrote of future plans and of love and of how Annie might rid herself of the burden of her husband. Warren read between the florid pages and sensed the dark catfish shape of the sweet words Annie must have written in return. He wondered if she was ever his at all or if there was a moment when she had stopped being true. There were no dates on the letters for him to know when he'd lost her.

He felt the need to stick a knife into someone's heart and wished Gideon Long still lived so that he might kill him again.

■ ■ ■

The sheriff's dog left its mark on Gideon's hands and arms before it died. It lay where he'd killed it, mouth hanging open, the slowing blood gushing out along the curl of its tongue. It seemed small and very different from the animal that had fought him, diminished to little more than a rat in death. He would find a use for the horrible animal soon enough. An experiment of sorts.

He wrapped the wounds it had caused him in strips torn from a horse blanket. He draped himself in the blanket, hissing when the coarse fabric glued itself to the sores on his shoulders.

He reached into the nearest stall and hefted the water bucket. The water sloshed, wetting the blanket, pouring over his chin and washing away the filth of the road and some of the blood. He drank and drank until his stomach hurt from fullness.

He threw the bucket away and put a saddle on the larger of the two horses, a tall black gelding with a touch of white Appaloosa spotting on its rump. The horse was not glad to be handled, and Gideon made a poor job of it in the darkness of the barn. When he was at least satisfied the saddle would not simply fall off the horse's back, he crept to the door of the barn.

Gideon fell into the shadows and waited for Warren to come outside. Surely he'd heard the dog snarling from the house. Gideon waited to slit Warren Groves open like a pig. Minutes passed. Blood ran out from the crude bandages and over the flesh of his sunburned hands. Strange, how the salt of his own blood could sting his skin. Or was it the dog's blood? He could not be certain, there was so much of it. Gideon waited and waited, and the lights remained dim through the shuttered slats over the windows.

Days in the desert without food, water, or clothing had raised Gideon into a savage. His shoulders and face were blistered, lips chapped with thirst, tongue swollen from the same, and his entire body was as red as ribbon. Gideon's bare feet were toughened into bloodied leather by the rocks that hid in sand.

Gideon counted each misery against Warren Groves as surely as the bullets that had blasted his head in the road outside the sheriff's office. He was thankful too. Thankful for what he was learning. He knew, more and more, what he was capable of and what he could endure. Anything.

Warren Groves was late. Taking his time. Shut up in his ugly, pretend, rich-man's house, celebrating the murder of Annabelle Moraud, planning to share his seed with all the whores in the Whitney. Gideon ran a fingertip up the hollow tooth of bleached mule thighbone sharpened by the luck of the break into a ragged needle. He craved unlocking the sheriff's heart with the dagger, snapping it off in his breast, watching it quiver with Warren's slowing pulse.

No more waiting. No more skulking in the shadows of the barn. Gideon set off across the pasture, making no effort to hide himself. He would throw open the door and search the pathetic house until he found where Warren Groves was cowering. Gideon peered in the slatted windows facing the pasture, could see nothing, continued to the front of the house, and stopped with an intake of breath.

Only a few yards up the road to Red Stem came one of the sheriff's deputies astride a muscular palomino with a white blaze. Gideon recognized the man by his olive skin and dark hair. He was some breed of Castizo or more exotic creature imported from the Orient.

He remembered the man from when Sheriff Groves had gunned Gideon down in the road. Gideon fell back around the side of the house and listened as the newcomer reined the horse to a thundering halt. He heard the jingle of spurs and the sound of the horse being tied to the porch's railing. Boots thudded against the wooden decking.

Gideon rose no louder than the desert and the distant sounds of town and camp. He crossed the dusty wooden planks with quiet feet and put the knife of thighbone through the back of the deputy. The man twisted and convulsed and reached back as if to tear out the blade. Gideon stabbed him twice more and let the man turn and pull his hands from the bloodied knife and roll with his back against the railing as he slid down to the porch.

Gideon wanted the man to see his face, to know who killed him. The bone splintered in the deputy's back as he turned, driving it deeper, and the man, finally, lay gasping, eyes wide, mouth moving without sound, staring up into Gideon's scabbed, sun-baked flesh and white smile.

"Yes, I know, it is rather cruel. You were only audience to my killing. In the road up there. Do you remember?" Gideon wrapped his hands around the man's throat and began to choke him. "Don't fight it. I am dead, and yet I am here, putting an end to you. Don't feel bad. Release. Be free. I no longer hew to the laws of heaven and earth that govern you. It is really rather cruel."

The deputy's eyes seemed as if they might explode from their sockets. Veins bulged from his forehead, and his entire face turned so red, it was nearly purple. He choked out a series of words in a heathen tongue Gideon did not recognize.

The deputy kicked his feet and pried at Gideon's fingers until the strength drained from his wounds and his arms fell to his sides. The deputy was limp against the railing when Gideon let go of his neck, stared at the raw band around his throat and the way drops of blood welled in his nose and never spilled down his lip, and said to the impassive horse, "Poor, sad Sheriff Groves. Should I give him this same luxury of death?"

The crude poncho of the horse blanket hung heavy with the deputy's blood. He patted the man's horse on the nose.

"I think I will give him worse than that." He reached beneath the horse's chin and scratched the curb groove. The horse flicked its ears back and repeatedly stomped a foot like a dog pantomiming with its back paw.

Gideon took a wood axe from one of the crates filled with workman's tools and walked in the door to Sheriff Groves' house as though he were invited. Sheriff Groves was lost in thought, slow to look up as Gideon entered. He was studying the secrets of a biscuit tin lying on the table. There it was. At last he saw the monster that had crept into his house. Gideon savored the moment of Sheriff Groves' gaping horror and smashed him across the face with the axe's handle.

The sheriff offered little resistance. He grunted on the second blow and tried to stand, but Gideon relentlessly beat his face and shoulders and head, and when Sheriff Groves weakly raised hands to shield his face from the falling blows, Gideon broke his fingers and beat him over the head. Gideon's shoulders heaved with his breath, his arms shook with the power in his blood, and when Sheriff Groves finally lay unmoving, Gideon sat back in a chair, blood and bits of flesh dripping from his hair and down into his eyes. A window caught his reflection, and Gideon saw his red face in the glass and thought, *I am the devil*. And he was.

Sheriff Groves was still alive, even semiconscious, and his breath formed bubbles in the blood drooling out of his mouth.

"Hello, Sheriff Groves," said Gideon.

Gideon departed in the night with the sheriff tied over the back of the horse in tow behind him. He also brought the sheriff's dog in a muslin sack saturated with the animal's blood. He knew, generally, the direction to the canyon. As the night wore on, he could recognize certain landmarks—the sand-eaten bones of a wagon, a tree that seemed to bear the face of a woman, the leaning bricks of a hilltop mission—and knew by the position of the mountains on the horizon and the encroaching white sands that they were on a course for the pueblo village.

He could not ignore the sensation of something pulling at him, like an invisible wire tied around his waist, or as if he were a bird returning to its roosting ground. That pool was beckoning him back and guiding him truer than any compass.

In the morning Sheriff Groves stirred against his horse. Gideon stopped and got down and poured water onto the lawman's face. His mouth was a wreck, and his eyes were swollen nearly shut. The water sputtered from his nose and mouth. He drank some and muttered unintelligible words.

"Not long now," Gideon said. He stroked Sheriff Groves like a pet and poured water over the cuts on his scalp to clear away the flies biting at the wounds.

They rode through the morning. The horses lowered their heads to the heat. By midday they reached the end of the desert dunes and entered the white hogback hills arranged before the Oscuras. Gideon soon felt the same deadening as they passed from a world of vitality to a world of stillness.

This uncanny landscape, where even the wind was timid, was disliked by the horses. They fought the reins, and Gideon's mount even reared up in an effort to throw him from its back. He climbed down and led both reluctant horses toward the black rock. For a moment, atop one of the symmetrical mounds of rock and sand, Gideon thought he saw the white dog standing sentinel.

No. It was only some wild animal that retreated from sight. There was nothing else but spilling gypsum sand and rocks atop the hill. Not even the tiniest scrap of brush grew this close to the entrance into the canyon.

Gideon guided the horses through the hollow and into the shadowed valley. Sheriff Groves awoke, lifted his head, struggled against his bonds, and began to moan piteously at the sight of the abandoned pueblo city.

"It is quite unnerving, I agree," said Gideon. "Who built this? Where did they go? Why would they leave such a city standing empty?"

They reached the terraces. Sheriff Groves stretched to see the extent of the pueblo. Weak as a babe, he quivered to hold up his head. His beaten face was glued with blood.

Gideon laid a heavy rock atop the leads of the horses to tie them down. He thought, for a moment, that he detected the sound of claws echoing on the canyon rocks. He listened but heard nothing else. He lifted Sheriff Groves from the back of the mare and slung the bound lawman over his shoulder. Blood smeared pink and red on the horse's coat and mixed with the animal's sweat where Sheriff Groves had laid his head.

"I am afraid this will be an unpleasant journey," said Gideon.

It surely was. He dragged, pushed, and pulled Sheriff Groves up to the terrace where the cave entrance burrowed into the black rock of the mountain. Sheriff Groves was helpless to protect himself from the rocks he cracked his head against and the jagged edges that cut into his flesh. A few spots were nearly vertical climbs, and for these Gideon had to scale the rock ahead of Sheriff Groves and drag him up by tying the hemp rope around his chest.

He brought Sheriff Groves to the very entrance of the dark cave. He set the law-man up against the rock face so that he could look down at the valley below. Gideon descended again, unloading the supplies he had brought—clothes, food, and jugs of water—into a secret cache he had prepared days earlier. This he concealed close to the ladders, and Sheriff Groves had no way of knowing its exact location even if he were paying careful attention, which, Gideon suspected, he was not.

Gideon was tired, and so he drank and ate, and still the sheriff did not stir from where he was left beside the cave. Gideon fetched the sack containing the sheriff's nasty little mutt, and he took this down into the depths of the earth. He saw the pool for the first time by the light of a lantern. It was serene and receptive. Eager.

He threw the sack containing the sheriff's dead dog into the pool. It stuck for a moment in the gluey white and moved as if pulled from beneath. It disappeared beneath the liquid's surface.

Minutes passed. Gideon sweated through his shirt and drank water from a clay pot. After what must have been several minutes the pool began to bubble. The embryonic sack heaved up with unexpected force and slid up from the pool to rest upon the stone. Gideon cut the sack open, unsurprised to discover the snout and matted fur of the dog within.

After several seconds it began to slide back into the pool, attached by a web of tissue to the surface of the liquid. Gideon recalled what happened to the Indian. Rather than allow the unconscious dog to be resorbed, he cut it free and lifted it to safety. It awoke and made a mess upon the floor. It seemed to have trouble standing at all. Its eyes were wild and fearful, but it seemed too confused to fight against him. If it had any memory of Gideon it did not show it.

"I'm sorry for this," he said, and he broke the animal's neck. He waited. Nothing more occurred. No replacement dog issued from the pool.. He threw the dead dog again into the pool, but it did not reemerge.

The water did not favor dead things. Could it sense the absence of consciousness? Gideon could not know whether God or science churned in the pale liquid, but there were clearly rules at work. Life could not be restored to the dead if they were not alive when they fell into the pool. An Indian could be made from only his blood, but his soul was not preserved. A dead dog was spit back out with no apparent memories of its previous life. But Gideon was reborn no matter where or how he perished.

But how often? wondered Gideon.

He undressed and neatly folded each item of clothing and placed them in a pile beside the pool. He left the cave and kicked Warren until he awoke. He stood naked before the battered lawman and took the time to indicate his various injuries and describe the agony of his terrible sunburn. Sheriff Groves did not look at him.

"I would lecture you on faith, and mine you wrenched from me and debased for three years, but by your state I fear we do not have that luxury. Warren Groves, I have again found faith. I believe in a very specific miracle. I believe in the Resurrection. Mine. First you will witness, then we will see if you can share in the miracle."

Gideon picked up the revolver he had brought for this moment and stepped to the edge of the cliff, many feet from the sheriff.

"Watch closely," said Gideon.

He placed the barrel of the gun against his own throat, angled the revolver so that the bullet should kill him instantly, and pulled the trigger. The gunshot echoed in the valley and along an unseen filament, and Gideon perceived the motion of his fall from the cliff. He was light as smoke exhaled through the hole in his head. His body plummeted away from him to break upon the rocks below, and he was an urge, already moving at great speed, past the hues and objects of the world.

CHAPTER ELEVEN

■ ■ ■

Gideon Long's body fell out of sight and boomed against the stones beneath the terraced pueblo. Warren heard the meat slapping and tearing across the rocks. The noise described the wet loops of entrails slithering out from burst seams. The strangeness of this dream made him sick and he leaned his head against the stone and tried to close his eyes. They were so swollen he could not open or close them completely.

There was oppression to the undisturbed blue uniformity of the sky. A painted fraudulence. It added to Warren's suspicion that he was dreaming or dead. He had crossed the white sands and moved through silent foothills and into a canyon where nothing moved. He was racked with pain when he was not unconscious. This world could not be real. He was passed out drunk or asleep and dreaming or killed on the floor of his kitchen by the maniac claiming to be Gideon Long.

The boiled stench of a man's insides emptied and cooking over sunned rocks began to rise. The horses did not like it and Warren was glad to hear them whinnying and struggling against their ropes. They were real enough and horses meant there might be some escape.

That was for later. He was too tired to even struggle much against his binding. He attempted to push himself up along the wall of rock to at least stand. His legs were too weak. There were too many injuries to give preference to any particular agony. Several ribs broken. His jaw and nose broken. Teeth knocked out or snapped into pieces. He suspected by the pain in his guts that he was bleeding inside. He knew from cattle drives that a man kicked in the side by a horse could die as surely as a man kicked in the face.

He rolled onto his side on the ground and drooled blood into the dust. Something moved. Some animal was coming. He lifted his head and saw the pale spirit of a creature. A big white dog came slowly and confidently up the terrace ramp. Its eyes were glittering blue like the sapphire he'd found in Annie's secret box. By the look it was a Navajo mongrel with ears pricked straight up and long and powerful legs. More shorthaired wolf than the sort of animal white men kept.

Warren tried to call out to the dog. Discovered he could not speak more than an inarticulate blowing of spit and blood. It came closer anyway and snuffled its nose at the air and the ground.

He was not afraid. There was so little sense to what was transpiring that his last concern was being mauled further by a ghost dog.

The dog loomed over his head with the sun behind it and its white fur now seemed gray. Its eyes still shone. Its pink tongue slid out from its muzzle and lapped the blood on his forehead. It took only one taste and backed away slowly. Warren tried to speak again. The dog loped off down the terrace ramp and out of sight.

He rolled onto his back and listened for the dog and managed to become unconscious without closing his eyes. He awoke to someone calling his name and he tried to sit up. His injuries prevented that and he fell back again and stared up at the daylight sky.

"Good thinking," said the voice. "You have certainly earned a good rest. Let me get some clothing on, and I will show you to your destiny."

Gideon Long appeared after many minutes and he wore the clothing he'd left folded by the cave. He was pale and fit and there was no sunburn or scabs. No gunshot wound or spilling entrails.

He lifted Warren up by his bound wrists and walked him over to the cliff. Warren seethed with anger and found he could hardly even give his rage a voice. He drooled and spit and was carried to the edge of the cliff by his captor.

"Now, now," said Gideon. "Have a look down there."

The naked body of Gideon Long was a hundred feet or more below. It was twisted across a dagger of black stone. Its face was upturned and unmistakably that of the maniac Gideon Long who had attacked him and kidnapped him from his home.

"Witness my lifeless body," said Gideon. "What an appalling mess. Who knew I contained such a quantity of giblets? Now, look at me, standing beside you. It is impossible, and yet here I am, alive and whole. Injuries and infirmities repaired."

Warren croaked in anger.

"Why? Is that what you're asking? I do not pretend to know why I am blessed with this strain of immortality, nor by what biology or mechanism it operates, only that it does. There is a Stygian pool deep within the volcanic bowel of this mountain."

Gideon patted Warren on the shoulder and dragged him back from the edge of the cliff and into the darkness of the cave.

"It devours a man and remakes him. It will swallow up anything but gold. I will take you there so that you can believe."

Warren dug his heels in against the rocks. Gideon easily overwhelmed him and pulled him into the cool darkness of the cave. Deeper and deeper, and as the heat and moisture grew, Warren knew what it was to be swallowed and consumed by a beast of geologic scale and lifespan.

He was brought at miserable length to a cavern large enough to consume the lantern's light. Warren fell and had to be pulled along on his back down a steep slope. Pale trailings of minerals formed thousands of stalactites upon the surface of the domed ceiling. Narrow chimneys in the rock cast dim pink and yellow beams across the sloping chamber. Gideon was dragging him to the center of the chamber. He ignored the pain and turned his head and could see a black circle there suggesting a well or some deeper passage.

The closer Gideon pulled Warren to the fissure the more a stench of rotting meat and sour wounds permeated the air. Warren didn't want to go near it and began to fight and kick to free himself from the hands holdings his arms. Gideon laughed at him. It was a feeble effort and tired Warren almost immediately. Gideon dragged him the remaining distance to the hole.

"Here we are," said Gideon.

He rolled Warren onto his belly so that he lay upon the warmed rocks and his head dangled over the rim of the hole. Here the smooth rock fell away in a steeply conical depression that opened into a circular pool five or six feet across. The liquid of the pool was so full with minerals that it had the appearance of white mud. It reminded Warren of the batter Annie used for biscuits.

Could Gideon have told the truth? Was this underground pustule the gateway to eternal life? Warren tried to force himself up with his hands. Gideon pressed with his boot against the small of Warren's back. The pain was so excruciating that Warren nearly blacked out.

"Good," Gideon said. "It still hurts. I want you to feel it all. It is quite painful. Look at it, Warren Groves."

Gideon stepped from Warren's back and lifted him up by his armpits. He pressed his cheek to Warren's and spoke through clenched teeth. "Before, at your house, I meant to teach you a lesson with my knife. To murder you. But why murder a man who wants to die? No. I deny you. Live with your guilt."

Gideon shouted and hurled Warren down the slope. He rolled down the smoothed rocks and found no purchase with his searching fingers. He splashed into the pool. The thick liquid surrounded his arm and leg, and he was dragged deeper.

"You heard her songs every day and did not know them." Gideon peered down from the edge of the pit. "I damn you, Warren Groves. Live forever."

The liquid closed over Warren's face, and the strange light of the cavern faded quickly. He felt as though he were sinking with heavy weights around his legs. The liquid was becoming hotter and hotter. It was intolerable. The heat etched his flesh like acid. It scoured the clothing and hair from his body and devoured his flesh, and when he screamed, it filled his mouth and throat and lungs and saturated his every tissue in histological violence.

Protean grit scoured his bones and poured into his sightless sockets. The liquid pulled at him with formless hands and rent apart the wishbone of his pelvis. His arms and legs dissolved to nothing. Darkness at last. A relief from pain. And Warren Groves was destroyed so utterly that not a scrap of flesh or fiber or hair remained.

■ ■ ■

Warren Groves was a stranger in his flesh. He staggered away from the foal sac of his unnatural rebirth as young and strong as fifteen years prior. He was afraid and fled from the stinking liquid of the pool expecting to be attacked at any moment by Gideon Long. He was not. The cavern was changed. The roof was much lower and made from sagging iron beams holding back a further collapse. The walls were not natural stone but gray bricks of large size. The tunnel down which he had been dragged was marked with crude paintings that did not have an obvious meaning.

He escaped from the tunnel convinced that he was within a dream.

The canyon was gone. He inhabited a landscape of fractured hardpan spread out in every direction to meet the starless night sky. He had emerged from the remains of a huge stone building long ago fallen into ruin. The building was tilting and half swallowed up by the earth. It must once have been as large as any in Europe. The air he breathed was unsatisfying and hot and smelled of long-ago smoke as if the stones around him had baked in ovens.

Beams of light like those of a lighthouse swept the sky above him. This light cast long and quivering shadows and lent motion to every detail of the world. There was no empty pueblo city of eyeless windows and powdered bones. A small shack of four walls and a roof of black shakes sat in the distance and into this was set a single square window that glowed faintly from within. He wondered if Gideon Long hid within this building. He reminded himself that it was a dream so anything might be possible.

Warren approached the shack with caution. No figure appeared at the window but smoke issued from the tin chimney. The door he took to be made from sticks was upon closer examination built from thousands of bones of every size and description. Threads of dried sinew lashed the door into a single piece that clattered gently in the desert night.

Warren raised his hand to try the door and immediately felt a shooting pain in his side. He reached back and found a wooden shaft piercing his flesh. He pulled and the flat arrowhead tore loose from his body with a gush of red-black blood upon the cracked hardpan. A second arrow thumped into the side of the shack and stuck in one of the shingles. A third and fourth speared into Warren's flesh.

"God damn it," he said and he fell to his knees and tried to spot who was killing him.

Three figures rose from the hardpan. They wore cloaks to conceal their bodies on the empty plain. Their faces were hidden by the savage animal heads that topped the cloaks. They made a strange cry and drew out long knives and advanced upon Warren as he pulled at another of the arrows stuck into his gut.

Realizing they meant to finish their work he got to his feet and pulled open the door of bones. The shack was very hot and lit by the faint pulse of embers through the grate of a potbellied stove. He fell inside the tiny abode and shut the door behind him. There was no mechanism to lock it. A barricade would be the only means to keep the Indians out.

The shack was stuffed with furniture in great disrepair and books printed in some heathen language Warren could not decipher. Tables and shelves were crowded with glass jars. These contained various samples of herbs and insects and pickled animals unknown to Warren. There were also signs of violence. Splashes of blood that were still wet to his touch. A hank of tacky hair clung to a bookcase packed with jars of fluttering insects.

Warren kicked what furniture he could easily reach into the path of the door. Jars fell to the earth floor and broke open and the shack filled with the strong smell of preserving fluid. His movements were awkward with the last arrow still stuck in him. The third arrow had fired between his ribs and landed shallow in the muscle of his chest. He gripped the arrow where it pierced him and shouted in pain and turned the head so it could slide back out through his ribs. The arrow plucked at his muscle and raised a mound of his skin as it came out with a gush of blood.

He shook off the arrow and saw by the light of the stove that it was made of a single length of hollow bone. Such a long and straight bone corresponded to no animal he had ever seen. It was notched and tipped with an iron arrowhead.

The Indians yanked open the door and pulled aside the furniture with little effort. They shouted in a tongue like that of the Navajo but he knew some words of that language and it was not the same. He was weak from losing blood and could hardly stand but he was determined to meet them on his feet. They pulled aside the last of the chairs and he came at them with the arrow as a dagger.

They wielded wide blades of iron like billhooks and the first man that came in broke apart Warren's arrow with a swing of his blade. Warren hit the man with his fist and staggered him back but it was a hopeless battle. They crowded into the shack and threw him against the hot stove and hacked at him with their blades.

He fell into darkness amid the agony of their knives slicing open his limbs and scalp but he did not die. He awoke with his face sticky with blood and his limbs numb. The sky above was yellow and cloudless and cast a sickly light all around the gnarled veldt that thudded by beneath him. He dimly realized he was lashed to a travois being pulled by the Indians. Any hope of escape slid away from him as he lapsed once more into unconsciousness.

Warren's eyes opened again to find the Indians talking over him. There were many more now and when he lolled his head he could see he was in a village of gray hide tents and clay ovens. His vision was stung with blood and tears but he perceived the lip of an earthen wall surrounding them as if the village was raised from the bottom of a huge crater.

Though he could not understand their words the warriors who brought him to the village were conversing with a man of authority. The medicine man or chief wore colored paint on his face and one eye was a ruin. His neck was decorated with a bib of bones like those used to make the door of the shack. The chief did not seem pleased the warriors had brought a live man. He barked a command and Warren was dragged deeper into the village. They took him past the piled bones of animals he did not recognize. He passed gray pelts stretched and drying revealed as covered in fine scales like those of a fish.

Rotting heads decorated hunting spears. These were grisly trophies. The heads were greatly decayed but resembled no man or beast Warren had ever seen. The flattened oval shape was strange and they were smaller than a man's and so pale they almost appeared as skulls. There was no hair and their jaws hung open along cleft lips and drooled black blood. Gray flies packed the clouded blue hemispheres of the corpses' protruding eyes.

Warren believed himself in hell or in a dream and so accepted the things he witnessed. The pain was real so he suspected it was hell. Two small men of great age and identical face came and sat beside Warren. They ate seeds from a clay cup and talked and prodded him with absent curiosity. One stuck a finger into the long slice covering Warren's scalp and he cried out in pain. Their laughter brought a stout Indian woman from a nearby tent. She wore an apron of blue cloth turned to black by old blood. She shouted at the old men and began untying Warren.

She tried to lift him from the travois but he was too heavy. She called and other women with curiously similar faces came from within the tent. Their hair was dark and knotted at the back with feathers. Three of them worked to lift him up from the sled and carried him loose as a doll into the tent dragging his heels through the chalky earth. The mounting loss of blood and various severed tendons prevented him from offering any real resistance.

In the tent there was some relief from the day's yellow heat. His vision narrowed as they laid him down upon a clay slab. Butchering tools hung from a wooden lattice above his face. As darkness pooled at the edges of his perception he was aware of another slab and another pale body beside him. This was where the savages skinned and butchered animals. They surrounded him and their rough hands were on his body. Merciful darkness closed in around him once more.

He awoke still upon the slab. He was not butchered or flayed. His wounds were sewn. The woman had applied poultices of strong herbs to his worst injuries. By the bitter taste in his mouth he supposed they had treated him with a decoction. He did not understand their actions but his head was swimming and he had very little control of his body. He suspected he still might die.

He rolled his neck and his head flopped to the side. He could just make out the pale body arranged on the slab beside him. Pooled blood formed a line of purple flesh from the head to the foot of the naked figure. The nails were black. The limbs and slim body were covered in arrow wounds.

For a moment he saw it as one of the fish-eyed creatures whose rotting heads decorated the Indians' spears. It was not one of these creatures. It was a man.

It was Gideon Long.

Warren faded in and out of consciousness several more times and was not sure how much time passed. He saw the chief and the warriors above him and their faces were all of the same man but marked with different patterns of pigment. The chief spoke in a murmur, his words drumming like rain on a stone. Warren allowed the sound to carry him back into darkness.

He emerged from that darkness to find a single warrior looking down at him. Warren lifted his head just a little to see him better. The man's face bore a more elaborate scheme of pigment. His eyes were red flecked with black. Something was happening, like tongues of fire curling out around the Indian. Warren could not hold his head up any longer. As it fell back he was aware, for only a moment, of a huge, luminous presence in the tent.

Words were spoken in the language of the Indians. What scared Warren was that the voice did not have a tone at all, but it was so loud it hurt his head behind his nose.

Warren faded out and awoke once more. By the light of a lantern he saw the woman who saved him. She was occupied with preparing a small animal. As she worked she was singing in her language. The tune reminded him of Annie's French lullabies. He watched her move at the edges of his vision.

Suddenly there came a shrill whistle. She lifted her head and he could see worry on her face. She waited and listened and became stricken when there followed a series of whoops such as those he heard from the Indians when they ambushed him. These were war cries. The woman fled from the tent and left him in darkness straining to hear what was occurring outside the tent. He lost consciousness.

He was aware of a keen pain. At his throat and at his groin and at his limbs. His eyes opened for only a moment but he saw white flesh fringed with barbs. Something tore at his wound atop his scalp. He heard a clatter like the violent shaking of dice in a cup and it surrounded him on all sides. Pain found a home in every part of his body that could still feel and for an instant he died.

■   ■   ■

Warren Groves came out from the steaming depths of the earth and his sweat was cold upon his skin and the paleness of his new flesh seemed to glow in the moonlight. This was the place he remembered from before. The other must have only been a dream. He staggered to the edge of the cliff and fell upon his knees and lowered himself to his belly to look down upon the rocks. The ruined body of Gideon Long was there. The horses were gone.

Warren was once more a stranger in this body. This was his face and his limbs but from another time. His arms and shoulders were youthful and muscular.

He discovered a wooden placard left for him by his tormentor. It was the fresh grave marker of Gideon Long. It was leaned against the stone beside the entrance to the cave. Meant to be found. Beneath it were shoes and trousers and shirt—some of his own things stolen from his home and left for him. There was also a clay jug full of water. It had a sour smell and the taste of vinegar, but Warren did not care. He drank and drank until he thought he might be sick.

He took up the wooden cross in his hands. The date of Gideon Long's death was roughly scratched out. Warren smashed the cross in half and broke it again into smaller fragments with a wrenching of his wrists. It snapped easily, and he shouted and flung its pieces across the terrace.

What Gideon Long had told him was true. Only death could have supplied the pain Warren knew when he was thrown into the pool. He could scarcely recall the places between. He knew Hell followed by the blackness which lingered upon his thoughts like the forgotten name of a dear friend.

He'd come back wrapped in a foal sac and drenched and spitting out that rotten soup and it left no doubt. He had died and come back. Come out of the cave not of Lazarus or Christ but like some terrible thing conjured from the pit. The sight of the heathen pueblo only furthered this notion.

Warren dressed and as he did recalled the fleeting dream he had known between death and life. He suspected it was no dream at all and not someplace described in verse. It was a place all the same, and by the oiled way it slipped from his memory, he was meant to forget all about it. Even his body desired to forget it. He refused that pull of oblivion and said aloud what detail he remembered so that he might better fix it in his mind. The radiant, blue-eyed figure. Creeping pale figures hidden in shadow. A shack full of jars and cages. Full of . . . what?

He repeated the words so many times, they lost their meaning, and he was unsure any were remembered at all or if he only imagined them. Details he suspected to be false crept in and became part of the sequence. In frustration he yielded to the unraveling nature. He was not allowed to remember these things. Not this time.

Warren collected the kindling of the grave marker and bound it together in his hand. There was no shortage of loose stones, but it took quite a search in the moonlight to locate a suitable flint. While he searched, he gathered ossified timbers from the pueblo and fragments of the crumbling ladders. There were no growing plants or wild animals. No birds overhead.

The first discovery was of the char pit. He almost did not see it because its entrance was covered by a fallen section of wall. It was deep and dark and blackened nearly to the rim. Warren climbed down into it, and his hands became immediately covered by soot.

At the bottom he discovered a great many blackened bones. Some tribes known to the Navajo ate men, he knew, but these bones did not tell the story of cannibals. There were no carving marks or notches in the femurs or arm bones. These bodies were burned with the flesh still on them and reduced to fragments by the heat.

The bones were very old—nearly as old, he suspected, as the crumbled ladders. But they were all of the same historic age. Burned all at once. A massacre? Adults but no children. Whoever perpetrated the mass killing and burning had not killed the children.

Warren piled his kindling near the cave entrance and, following a tiring effort with the flint, he set a fire. The timbers and ladder pieces were so dry, they flashed and hissed when they burned. The pieces of the cross provided a stable base for the fire, though there was not much to last long. Warren selected the longest of these fragments and wrapped one end tightly in strips of cloth torn from his shirttail.

It was a feeble torch and would not burn long, but it provided light enough to chase out the shadows, and, so equipped, Warren was able to search the cliff on its various levels and look into the nooks and alcoves, natural and not. Most of these niches were empty or contained crude paintings of animals and men or fragments of pottery. Warren learned from the paintings that the former inhabitants of the pueblo had hunted deer and sheep using bow and arrow and spear and hunting dogs and had revered the sun and moon.

The color was gone from the markings on the pottery, and the etchings on the broken pieces were difficult to discern. At length Warren picked out among the repeating patterns wolves and cougars and other animals. There were a few broken dolls in one of the alcoves, and Warren imagined these held by the children and left behind as they were taken by another tribe. Finding these and other hidden traces of the culture that had once inhabited the village, he began to imagine he walked among them or they with him, and he was unsure which would be a ghost.

His torch had nearly gone out when he found a path leading up to a higher terrace. It was so narrow that he could hardly navigate it, and even the subdued winds of the canyon gave him pause. He teetered on the path that overlooked a sheer drop to the floor of the valley. He cupped one hand around the torch to keep the meager flame going, and this left him little stability or balance. His cautious ascent knocked loose stones that clattered down the mountain, and he very nearly fell when he stepped wrong.

The path opened onto a terrace much smaller than the others. There was a domed entrance of brick set against the side of the mountain, and Warren could see that this was some lodge or chamber carved out of the mountain by hand. The stonework must have required years with the primitive tools of the Indians.

Warren held the torch into the tunnel. It was not tall enough for him to stand upright, but he was able to carefully enter. A collapse partially blocked the tunnel with timbers and fallen bricks and boulders. Each step he took into the tunnel sent stones skittering away and loosed more rocks.

He steadied his breathing and continued and was careful to avoid the ancient timbers that extended into his path and seemed to brace the tunnel ceiling against further collapse. He passed from the squat tunnel to the high dome of a chamber built by human hands. It was too perfectly round to have occurred naturally. His fingers trailed along the wall and felt the dimpled marks left by chisels.

He lifted his torch above his head and revealed the inner curve of the white-painted dome and the hundreds of odd black crosses marking the ceiling. These reminded him of the symbols painted on the tunnel wall in his dream. They were almost like Christian crosses only there was no care put into making their shape. He stumbled over fallen stones and came to a strange idol built from clay.

It was a grasshopper of size almost equal to a horse and it sat up like a man upon a stone bench. Its limbs were arranged with the intention of meaning and each of its clawed hands gripped a long-desiccated frond of herb or flower. The craftsmanship was exquisite even by the standards of modern men with modern tools.

Warren intended to wipe the thick dust from its bulbous face but at the lightest contact the statue collapsed. It did not tip but rather fell apart into brittle pieces that cracked upon the stone floor. Warren backed away as the upper segments of the insect idol crumbled into a heap. Only the long bulb of the idol's back end and a pair of thick limbs remained on the bench. The statue was hollow.

Warren stooped and picked up a fragment of the statue's head. It was a thin and brittle piece of the idol's faceted eye. He held it up to the torchlight and was surprised to see the light show through the amber curve of the fragment. He sought out a piece of a limb in the mess upon the floor and lifted it up and found that the tubular appendage contained fine white material like threads or cloth rotted away by the years. He dipped his finger into the piece and it became coated in brown smut.

He moved to return the arm segment to the floor and as he did the fragment moved as if jointed and snapped into two pieces. A certain fear seized him that this might not be a statue at all but the remains of some strange animal. He dismissed the fear but nevertheless began to back out of the chamber. His foot collided with a stone and Warren turned his ankle and nearly fell. He caught himself on the wall, and his torch illuminated a series of crude paintings that ran in a ring around the width of the chamber.

At that moment the chamber began to come apart as suddenly as the statue. Warren caught only a glimpse of the painting as he retreated quickly. Stones clattered down all around him, and ancient timbers snapped and broke into the room. He reached the tunnel, and a black pour of stones filled in the chamber and buried the room and its strangeness under tons of rubble.

He stumbled away from the plume of choking dust exhaled from the tunnel. When he closed his eyes he could still see the painting illuminated by torchlight. Children knelt on bended knee before the devil idol of the grasshopper. The idol did not sit upon a stone bench but stood on four legs and before it was a pile of human bodies surrounded by fire.

Warren salvaged pieces of fallen timber from the blocked tunnel and returned these to his campfire down the treacherous path. The fire had nearly gone out while he was exploring but he was able to stoke the flames and the hissing smoky fire of the desiccated timbers warmed his hands.

By the light of the fire his thoughts turned to the nature of oblivion. Whether it was an irrevocable state or another place and whether men could come and go as they pleased. He thought of Annie and the permanence of her death. He wondered if she could be dug up and somehow restored to life by the pool. Placed into it a corpse and spit back out a living woman.

Warren dismissed such thoughts as ghoulish tampering with the order of things. Even if it were possible and she could live again she would never forgive his transgression. Annie was gone. Forever gone. He remembered the way her muscles had felt stiff in his arms as he laid her into the coffin. What might come back from that could not be her.

He considered his own remove from humanity. Whether he truly was Warren Groves or something else entirely. Had he visited hell? Had he escaped it? He feared that he might be seized by an invisible spirit and compelled to do things to repay his debt. He imagined that this insect Beelzebub worshipped by long-ago savages might be a master.

Warren thought most of all of Gideon Long and all his transgressions. He was a murderer and a usurper. He'd twisted the beauty of Warren's life with Annie into something to be doubted. It was Gideon Long who blamed Warren for abandoning Annie. There was truth to that. Warren had abandoned her and fled from that house and her birth pains. He had left his wife to die alone, and he had abandoned his daughter.

Dawn was coming to the valley. Warren was no longer mute and so shouted to it in anger and cursed the name of Gideon Long. The queer way his words echoed back unnerved him and Warren climbed down the terraces and through the forgotten pueblo and sought to leave that place. It was as he walked past the broken corpse draped over the rocks that he decided on a greater purpose. The corpse's mouth hung open and its face was torn in such a way that it seemed to smile with dull white teeth.

Warren felt mocked by the corpse's gladness. He crushed the grinning face beneath a rock and the act was imbued with meaning beyond simple rage. It was his first movement of a new life. He did not intend to merely wander the desert or return to the hollowed shell of his old existence. He experienced a new though familiar craving and he knew it would not cease until it was satisfied.

He would return to Spark and gather his things and become a killer again. He would find Gideon Long. He would hunt him wherever he went through the land and dog his every step and he would kill Gideon Long as many times as demanded by the growl of his desire.

CHAPTER TWELVE

■ ■ ■

Warren found Turk's chestnut horse half-dead from exhaustion in the barn. It still wore its saddle and so he watered it and fed it and lashed onto its back the provisions he needed. He pried up the loose floorboard beside his bed and took out his secret cache of money. He belted his guns and brought along Gideon's fancy rifle as well. He rode up to Red Stem in search of blood.

Some folk recalled seeing Gideon Long come through town early in the morning. In a hurry and with two horses. The Indian guide Cody White was making water in an alley and saw Long leaving town early in the afternoon and on the back of a black gelding. Behind him he was leading another horse laden with trunks and sacks.

Buffalo soldiers marooning in the shade of cottonwoods were well-positioned to have seen the comings and goings along the road. They were relaxed and laughing when Warren saw them at a distance but they drew up and went quiet and looked at him warily as he approached.

He spoke to them on the subject of his need to find Gideon Long and gave them his quarry's description. They confessed to spending almost the whole afternoon in that spot but went on to answer specific questions with a chorus of "No, suh" and "Sorry, suh."

He was fit to give up when he recognized among them the two called George and Sebastian who had helped dig Annie's grave not a week ago. He called out to them and they looked surprised and afraid and their companions cut their eyes at them as if the two were traitors in their midst. With reluctance they came forward and Warren thanked them again for their help and he shook their hands. He pressed a Mexican gold dollar into each man's palm.

"Please," he said and he leaned in. "The man I'm after killed my wife. He's a murderer through and through, and if you've got anything to tell me, I promise it won't get you into no trouble."

"We seen him," said George. "Came up alone as we was setting up here. Saw him ride all the way up to the big house. Then he came back down later on with sundry items laden on a packhorse."

"Do you have an inclination of his direction?" asked Warren.

"Musta rode out north or maybe east," said George. "For sure. We can see all the way south near on to the table edge. Only saw wagons out there."

Warren thanked them and climbed into the saddle of Turk's horse and rode out, heels down, for the northern trail. It was a long way to Santa Fe and with many possible hideouts and villages intervening. East was a difficult course from the Red Lines, traversing several ranges and some deadly Indian territory. No matter what sort of maniac Gideon Long had turned into, he was born and raised with the luxuries of wealth. Not the sort of man to attempt crossing unknown badlands while being pursued.

Gideon would make for civilization. The more civilized the better. He had nearly a day's head start and Warren rode Turk's sickly horse. It didn't matter. Warren knew he would catch him. It was only a matter of when and where.

■ ■ ■

At Santa Fe there was a Spanish colonial hacienda become a hotel. Its aged splendor was long since surrendered along with the territory to the Americans and their guns. Colonial grandeur had fallen into disrepair and attracted seedy elements of frontier transience. Girls lounged in the garden and cowboys gambled and drank and groped the girls in the open. They stared with the hard eyes of criminals as Warren passed through their midst.

The hotel manager was a short Anglo with little hair left on his head and a long hook nose topped with wire spectacles. He sat on a stool and peered at Warren over the fortification of the hotel desk. Warren didn't doubt that a shotgun was kept beneath the counter and ready to fire dimes into a man's face.

For three U.S. dollars the manager told Warren the room he wanted. The old gnome even gave Warren a spare key so that he would not kick in the door.

The room was around the back. Long's stolen horses were hitched outside and drinking foul water from a trough. Warren put Turk's half-dead horse beside them. At the door he crouched and carefully unlocked the mechanism. He listened for a sound that might suggest he'd been detected.

Hearing no warning he stood and threw open the door. It swung violently into the darkness of the room and smashed over a table covered in emptied bottles and jugs. A stout blonde and a dark-haired Mexican girl screamed and bolted stark naked from the bed. Gideon was tangled in the sheets and only sat up with delayed alarm.

The room was caught in an opium haze. Gideon struggled to keep his red-rimmed eyes open. His head drooped. He tried to get up and instead oozed off the mattress and onto the floor.

Warren stepped into the room and was met with a loud crack and a puff of white smoke. A shrapnel of fragments of adobe cut the back of his neck. It was the blond whore crouched behind a chair. She was fumbling to reload the pepperbox with cartridges from her bag.

"Don't," Warren said.

She finished her reloading and clicked the pistol's breech and as she brought it up to fire again Warren shot her. She dropped the gun and cried out and fell. She sat against the wall and grabbed at the hole in her chest just below her throat. Blood was running out in a great quantity and she was for certain mortally wounded. The other girl looked at her friend and wailed and pushed past Warren to flee from the room. He let her go. His interest was only in bringing harm to Gideon Long.

Warren holstered one pistol and grabbed Gideon by his hair and dragged him upright. He splashed his face with the piss pot and slapped him again and again until he finally seemed to regain some sense. He threw Gideon onto his back upon the stinking mattress.

The shot girl was gasping and wheezing in the corner. Her fat body shook and her legs were tightly together so that the blood gushing from the chest wound pooled in the crook of her pubis and formed a red line along the separation of her legs.

"Why'd you have to kill her?" Gideon moaned. "She was so sweet. Such a—"

Warren struck Gideon's mouth with the butt of his pistol.

"I want you to listen to me," Warren said. "I want you to hear this before I kill you."

"Go ahead," said Gideon, and the petulance of his voice struck Warren all wrong. "Go ahead. I did what I intended to here."

"Killed Robert Broken Horse? I woulda done it for you."

"Say your piece, and get it over with," said Gideon. "I have other plans."

"I'd be obliged." Warren sat down on the bed and put an arm across Gideon's shoulders and held him tightly. "This is the once I intend to spare words for you again. We may as well parley like gentlemen."

Gideon wiped the back of his hand across his teeth and looked at the blood left behind. He spit onto the mattress and spared a glance for the girl still dying in the corner.

"You done more in the past weeks than any man can account for in a lifetime. Fortunate that you seem to be offering more than one life to settle up," Warren growled. "If the devil has given you so many I reckon you won't mind sharing with me."

He pressed the gun to Gideon's cheek and turned his head with it so that he could look into his eyes.

"Wherever you go, I will find you, and I will kill you. Never sleep easy, because soon I will be there, and I will kill you. And I'm gonna keep right on doing that until either you or the devil gives up."

Gideon began to object. Warren pressed the barrel of the gun hard into his cheek.

"Just tell me you understand."

"I do," said Gideon and without a second's pause Warren shot him through the brain.

The body flopped back with its head leaned over the edge of the bed. Warren got up from the bed and watched as its heart pumped away uselessly and emptied its blood and brains out the back of its skull and onto the floor. The girl in the corner was wide-eyed and dead.

Warren left the carnage of the darkened room and entered the bright light of day. He could hear shouting and the excited cries of horses as men were gathered at the front of the hotel to come after him. He took his things from the saddle of Turk's horse and put them on the black gelding Gideon had stolen from Warren's barn. He intended to reclaim the horses Gideon took from him and let Turk's poor old thing rest.

He escaped south on his own horse with Annie's horse called Morgan following behind. He rode the rough trail back toward Spark in search of Gideon Long.

■ ■ ■

Warren passed through the trading post at San Acacia and exchanged Gideon's fancy rifle for a solid repeater and some ammunition and money to buy good canteens and a padded coat better suited to nights on the trail and cold mornings high in the mountains. He reckoned he was three days from Spark if he kept up the pace. It was exhausting the horses.

When he slept beneath the stars he dreamed each twinkling light was an eye pressed to a peephole and he was caught in a jar. He assumed his every action delighted unseen observers. Some nights he dreamed of the pueblo and the grasshopper idol. Some nights he dreamed of the day he spent in hell. Most nights he dreamed of Annie.

He was crossing through the meander of the Rio Grande on his course south when he spied at a great distance a donkey cart coming north up the road. There was a single man in the driver's bench. He leaned lazily and reminded Warren in his posture of Gideon Long.

Warren concealed himself and the horses in the folded curtain walls of the canyon to wait for the cart to pass. From the top of the scree pile he could see across the road and down the riverbank and just spot a crescent of dark and rushing water.

The cart clattered down the road. Gideon was its driver and he sat oblivious and chewing licorice in a corner of his mouth and dressed as fine and fancy as a gentleman. Warren opened rapid fire from hiding and blasted the poor donkeys into a panic. One broke loose and ran and fell dead a few feet away. The other veered over the banks and fell along with the cart into a twisted ugliness of wagon and wounded beast and cargo.

A splash was followed by waterlogged thrashing and Warren leaped down the scree pile and reloaded as he went. He crossed the road to the bank and looked over and saw Gideon lying among the shallows on his back. The river washed over him and leeched blood from two bullet wounds in a crimson ribbon.

The wounded donkey was trying to run back up the bank. It trailed the broken-down cart behind it. Clothes and blankets and provisions for weeks were scattered in the shallows in heaps and caught on rocks and already drifting downstream. A great quantity of apples had spilled out the back of the cart and formed a merry bobbing parade down the river.

"You cannot f—"

Warren silenced Gideon with a blast of the repeater. Long flopped back into the water and lay with his arms above his head. His body swayed back and forth in the current. Warren splashed through the river's shallows to the body and checked to be certain that Gideon was dispatched to whatever interim hell he visited before returning to life. He was dead.

Warren picked up an apple from the cold water and held it in his mouth as he picked over Gideon's body for money. He put the donkey still struggling to climb the bank out of its misery. He stood for a long time beside the dead donkey and watched the unfurling red tendrils of its blood flow with the river. He'd witnessed plenty of pack animals killed in accidents on the trail or in violence or by folks just being plain mean. He'd done in a few himself when they twisted a leg.

He wondered where this donkey was supposed to be. Wondered what it was supposed to be doing. Maybe the donkey was always destined to end up dead in the shallows of the Rio Grande. No. It was dead because the world had stopped working how it was supposed to.

Warren's teeth snapped into the apple.

■　■　■

Things did not go as planned at Spark. He got distracted. Someone had taken over his old house. Women's laundry was draped over the porch rails and horses crowded around the hitching post. He could hear loud voices and shouts and revelry from inside. Thugs and Celestials patrolled the streets. Artemus Wick had finally usurped the law. Getting caught by Wick's men would mean a fight or might mean jail. Time spent in a cage would be worse than losing at a draw.

He left his horses with a Mexican crib girl named Silver and paid her ten dollars to water them and feed them herself. Gideon could move freely through this newly hostile territory without much worry of being waylaid. Spark's former sheriff Warren Groves was forced to follow the footpaths through the twisting shacks and shanties.

He took a knife and a pistol and crept through the squalor and stepped over drunks and glared at skinny kids watching him from doors and empty windows. His thick beard and long hair disguised him and he wore a kerchief piled around his neck not quite in the fashion of a bandit but near enough to lessen his chances of being recognized. In this way he passed by Ida Pinkney unnoticed.

He glimpsed Gideon riding tall in the saddle of a rusty brown mare. He was nearly up the mountain. Nearly to his family's home. There was too much distance and too many folks between to gun him down with a pistol. Warren kept after him and ducked from one hiding place to the next. He crouched behind rain barrels and ran along piss-stinking paths and squeezed between houses built so close even a dog would go around. He was filthy and hot and even though Gideon seemed in no hurry Warren was falling farther and farther behind.

There was no sign of Gideon by the time he reached the iron fence surrounding the foundry and the Long family mansion. Warren looked either way and leaped at the fence and caught hold and climbed it with a painful bruising of his chest and stomach. He crossed the barren yard and dead garden and found a kitchen entrance that was quiet.

He entered and was grabbed straightaway and thrown into the larder. He was assailed with punches and kicks. His gun was gone and his knife was pulled from his fingers before he could react. Four men. Five. Their fists were wrapped in rags and more than one used a table or chair leg. They hit and kicked until Warren was a bloody wreck on the floor. He looked up at them through swollen eyes and saw pity. They were a rangy gang of miners and out-of-work foundry men. They spoke to one another in a language Warren could not understand. Something ugly and mean.

They discussed what to do with him and decided to shut him in the larder. He lay half-conscious and bleeding. It was dark when the door opened. A pretty young girl with a shy demeanor and a candle held in her quivering hand brought some food and water. He reached for her and she dropped the plate and cringed away. She ran at the sound of his voice and someone closed and locked the door behind her.

The next day they let him go. Two men with their heads in cloth sacks marched him at gunpoint out through the gate. Took all his money and his gun. They never said who they were but he knew who'd paid them to do it. Gideon. He had slipped the tightening noose. He could be anywhere at all.

■ ■ ■

It took six weeks. Warren caught him after a riverboat robbery and massacre in Kansas City. Gideon was with a gang he called his Chatholm Boys. Rough types. Rougher even than most who had helped with the train robbery. Warren waited for Gideon to be alone taking a piss and he killed him with a knife. Killed him in the privy and took his scalp for his trouble. The first of many trophies he would claim from Gideon. The loyal Chatholm Boys didn't seem to mind. They kept right on drinking and whoring while Warren slipped out the door.

■ ■ ■

He caught Gideon twice on the road and shot him at close range. Both times Warren took Gideon's thumbs and strung them around his neck on a length of Long-brand copper wire. The second time he took the thumbs while Gideon was still breathing. Gideon wailed at the popping knuckles. His eyes bulged at the sight of the fleshy ingots of his thumbs falling upon the trail.

■ ■ ■

Warren caught him in Memphis coming out of a nice saloon. There was a girl on his arm in hat and frills and pretty as a Persian cat. Gideon was dressed in a nice suit too and he chewed a stick of licorice. He took it out of his mouth. His teeth were black.

"Hello, Sisyphus," said Gideon.

Folks screamed at the sound of the gun. The pretty girl ran as best she could in all that crenellation. Warren got down on one knee and sawed off Gideon's scalp and he tied it to his bloodstained belt and hung it beside the knives he had collected on the road. The newspaper folks might write about the wild man with the fresh collection of scars who shot down a gentleman and cut off his scalp. They could write their gruesome stories. By the time the law came down Warren would be gone.

■ ■ ■

At New Orleans Warren found Gideon climbing the gangplank of a French steamer called *Morocco*. Gideon's body shook from the bullets and tumbled over the railing and fell into the water with a splash. Ladies and gentlemen ran onto the steamer or fled. The deck hands cowered behind the abandoned luggage. Warren walked to the gangplank and aimed his pistols down and shot the floating body until both guns clicked empty.

■ ■ ■

Warren pursued his quarry through the Dakota badlands. He was shadowed by riders of the Lakota Indians but they did not attack him or interfere. He became so exhausted and cold that he fell asleep in his saddle beneath a frost-heavy blanket. When he awoke it was night and his horse stood idle in the midst of stacked cairns of frost-silver rocks.

He was near a long and snowy hill without trees and upon this he saw a strange shape nearly as big as his horse. It was the grasshopper idol restored to life and it regarded him with luminous red eyes and opened mandibles large enough to tear off his hand. He reached for his gun and brought it up and the creature was gone into the snowy night. He could not be sure if it was ever there or if he truly saw it lift into the sky on black wings and disappear.

The Lakota found him frozen to his horse and took him to their village elder and warmed him by the fire. They were curious but unafraid. He screamed with memories of the hell he'd seen between life and death. The Lakota poked and prodded him and gave him a bitter herb that numbed his mouth when he chewed it. He dressed in the furs they gave him but pushed away any further help.

He left the yellow warmth of the tent and strode in the midst of the snow-drifted wigwams. Men wrapped in heavy furs and brandishing rifles stood guard outside the tents. Women and children watched through the seams of buffalo hide.

Warren Groves found his horse and climbed into its saddle. He could feel them watching as he disappeared into the blizzard. When he found Gideon he killed him by hand and the snow turned a brilliant shade of red.

■ ■ ■

Gideon attempted an ambush in Utah. In the desert of sun-red rocks and eerie standing stones. It was where Gideon had made himself a preacher of End Times and had himself a church and congregation and a stockpile of guns. Warren survived being shot in his chest and in each leg and he blazed a trail of reckoning through Gideon's faithful. His appearance of skins and scalps and jagged scars and brutal weapons illuminated their notion of avenging angels.

The men crumpled at the first discharge of Warren's guns and he stalked them and shot them down. He hacked at them with a bowie knife and a tomahawk and throttled a girl who stabbed him through the belly with a knitting needle. The survivors were routed from the church. They screamed prayers to God for salvation. Gideon holed up in the unfinished bell tower. He shot through the door and poorly quoted scripture and so Warren pushed the church piano up against the door and set fire to the building.

He watched it burn. Yanked the knitting needle from his guts and walked back to his horses as the flames reached high into the sky. The horses were by then as mean and terrible as their rider. They stood resolute with dark eyes devoid of animal fear.

■ ■ ■

The law knew of Warren. In Arizona a marshal who chased him all the way from Houston caught him hanging Gideon from the beam of an old prospector cabin. Gideon was dead already and his face was as purple as a plum. The marshal thought he might convince Warren to surrender by aiming a shotgun at his chest. Warren drew and fired and killed the man so quick the marshal never pulled the trigger.

In a Colorado trading post Warren found his likeness printed on a wanted poster. He stared at the paper for a long time. Five hundred dollars was a substantial reward. The drawing was rendered in such detail that only a witness to his atrocities could have created such an image. He wondered if Gideon circulated his description.

The old man at the trading post recognized Warren and tried to draw a gun. Warren shot him in the belly and he fell and set to dying in a lot of pain with his face resting upon the floor.

Two young girls came out from the back at the sound of the gun and they saw the man fallen and began raising a fearful cry. An older woman came out with her

hair all pinned up and a white apron tied over a gingham dress and her hands covered in flour. She didn't fall to her knees. She grabbed for the gun. Warren shot her
too. He aimed to wound but wasn't too sure she'd last long. He was sick and left the
trading post wondering on what was the use of that.

By the time he reached Providence he was hardly a man at all. The folks in the
streets in their fine suits cowered and ran from the sight of him. Horses stomped
their feet. Dogs growled. The sailors and whores stared out at him from the sordid
lairs that crowded Narragansett Bay. Men from lands as savage and strange as any
part of America felt they beheld something new.

This was not a beast of Ceylon or Singapore or the lands of the Musselmen. It
wasn't a creature of the howling Carpathians or the lush green valleys of the Alps.
There was no brass idol built for it on any forsaken island of the Mediterranean. He
was no old and musty myth.

Warren Groves was a new thing of American mud and bones and stinking scalps,
his neck hung with a collar of thumbs and tongues. His knives were notched bones
and his eyes were dark and reachless as if he perceived a different world entire to that
of mortal men. He bore the scars of a hundred wounds on his hide and did not die.
Warren felt no shame or gladness at their fear. He only felt the open sore of his hate.

There was a sanitarium on a hill beside a river that smelled of industry. Warren
did not know the river's name or care to but the sanitarium was called Straymore. It
was where Gideon's mother had died six years ago. Why Gideon would be going
back did not concern Warren.

The orderlies and nurses came to the windows at the beat of his horses' hooves
on the brick-paved path. They locked the doors and called for the police when they
saw him in the saddle.

He blasted the doors with a shotgun and went inside and ignored the cries of
alarm and the immediate lunatic chorus of the patients. He stalked the din and the
guttering gas-lit halls. His footsteps echoed against the curving tiles and he found
the place where Gideon sat waiting and reading a newspaper.

"I thought you—" Gideon said and Warren emptied both guns into him and left
him slumped in the chair. The two were surrounded by smoke. The newspaper was
still held and holed and splattered with blood in Gideon's lifeless hands. There was
nothing else for Warren at Straymore and yet something beckoned him through the
door beside Gideon.

The room was small but the whitewashed brick walls made it seem larger. The
windows facing the door were open to the air so that long curtains of diaphanous
blue billowed into the room on the cool breeze and gave the light filling the room an
overcast quality. A bed stood against one wall. Beside it stood a small table stacked
haphazardly with books and periodicals. The folio atop the pile was a booklet of
French songs.

A rolling chair made from wood and wicker sat facing the windows with its high back to Warren. There was someone sitting in the chair and quietly humming in a tuneless manner. He approached cautiously but without cause for fear.

His guns and vengeance faced the one thing that could break them. Annabelle Groves sat in the rolling chair in a formless blue gown and stared out the dimmed windows at an overgrown garden. She was humming a song familiar to Warren.

He hugged her and kissed her cheek. She hardly reacted. Her gaze was fixed upon the garden. He was forced to turn the chair away from the windows to compel her to look at him. In the gaslight filtering in from the hall her youthful face was slack. He shook her and she kept humming and staring away. She was the brass left after the bullet was gone.

Footsteps and hollering came down the hall. Warren lifted his wife up onto his shoulder and left a bloody path as he departed Straymore. He routed the orderlies and with them some police who fled from the sound of his guns and went falling and shouting away down the halls. Some other men got in his way and had to die.

He threw Annie over the back of her horse and rode out through the cobbled streets and winding colonial tenements. He followed the Narragansett River until he found a secluded tributary shaded by old trees that hung their heavy boughs above the stream. A lonely boat was tied to the roots of a tree.

The horses stood and ate grass and Warren carried Annie down into the water and stood with her and stroked her face. He held her so that she looked into his eyes. She gazed through him and to someplace beyond. There was nothing left in there that was Annie Groves.

"I am truly sorry," Warren said. He held her down beneath the water and drowned her. He carried her body out of the stream and laid her in the boat. It was a canoe of old wood and filled with fallen branches that crackled beneath her weight. He piled old leaves and dry branches upon her and doused her in the antiseptic rotgut he carried in his saddle. She lit easily and burned with orange fire and turned to smoke. He pushed off the burning boat and sent it into the stream to flow and join the river and follow it to the sea.

She disappeared from view and Warren took to the saddle and breathed deeply and resolved to find a conclusion. Every fiber of him hurt. This sick endeavor needed its ending.

CHAPTER THIRTEEN

■ ■ ■

The San Francisco hotel called the Seaside wasn't beside the sea. It stood three stories and was flat-fronted to give the impression of greater splendor. It was early in the evening and still light out but the place was curiously quiet. Other hotels seemed to be doing a brisk business. This discrepancy made Warren tie his horses up a good distance away and cross the street with his guns out. There was no doorman or guard at the door and none of the usual sort of gold digger and soiled doves he expected to find congregating on the portico.

A few oil lamps were burning but the shutters were closed and it was dark in the hotel. There were wooden tables and a bar and a player piano. The walls were festooned with ugly landscape paintings and dusty game trophies. There was a dice table and a card table and there was not a person in the saloon.

Warren cocked back the hammers on his pistols and tried to wish his boots to silence as he stalked across the floorboards. The knives hung from his belt clinked together softly like a chime. There was a door in the back that said OFFICE and an inner balcony and stairs. Warren started for the door and felt a prickling at his neck.

"Guns down, Warren Groves. You got three men with rifles pointed at your back. Come to shooting, we will put bullets in you. Go on and put your guns down, and let's talk."

The voice was familiar. Not Gideon. Warren resisted the urge to spin around and fire and he put his guns on the floor. He turned slowly with his hands raised. Three men knelt along the balcony with rifles aimed at him. They were well dressed but looked to be hard men. Pinkertons maybe. Bounty hunters. A mountain of a man stood behind these three and he held a long-barrel Colt of ruinous caliber pointed at Warren.

Pat Cole. He had a pointed beard and a thick mustache but it was surely him.

"It ain't good to see you." Pat closed the hammer on his gun and lifted his aim. The other three men kept their rifles pointed at Warren's chest.

Pat Cole came down the stairs slowly and with a pronounced limp.

"Pat," said Warren. It was the first time in a long while he had heard his own voice. "Pat, you shouldn't be here."

"We were warned by the man you were following."

"Gideon Long."

Pat finished descending the stairs and limped to stand before Warren. He looked him up and down and could not hide his disgust.

"My God, Warren. You done lost yourself to violence. Look at you. Festooned like a savage and twice as ripe."

"I came to put an end to all this, Pat. Leave me be, and I won't be a trouble to nobody no more."

"You killed Gideon Long. In the streets of Spark near on eighteen months ago. Don't you remember? You been on the warpath ever since. Killing through every state and territory. Word is you killed a marshal. Chasing a ghost."

"Chasing him."

"A ghost. I've heard the tales. The wild-eyed man looking for Gideon Long. Killing anyone who looked like him—"

"Was him."

"Warren, I loved you like a brother. I dug up that body to be sure. Because I loved you. Gideon Long was rotting in his box."

"Where is he now? The man who tipped you off. Is he here?"

"You've lost it, so I reckon there ain't much more point to this, but I got to know. Why Turk? Why did you kill him? Was it for his horse? You write his name in that black book you keep?"

The book Warren had told Libby Cole about was buried somewhere safe. Page after page bore the name Gideon Long. Warren looked Pat Cole in the eye and searched for some vestige of their friendship. He didn't find it. Pat Cole's mind was all made up and he was no different than the people who shrank away and looked upon Warren like a devil.

The next instant was sound and fire. Every man shot at least once and every bullet and nearly every piece of shot found a home in human meat. Pat Cole was killed straightaway. He lay heavily across Warren like the body of a bear and had a half dozen rifle bullets in his back. Warren was shot to hell by some of the same bullets and a couple of others that went through his arm and his good shooting hand.

The men on the balcony were all three still alive though only briefly based on their wounds. Warren got to them good with the little sawed-off two-barrel he hung in all his knives so nobody would even see it. He tried to push out from under Pat Cole's body and couldn't. His strength was going fast. He could barely lift his arms.

The smoke was still in the air when Gideon came from the back of the hotel. His boots were pointed and black and new and they clumped heavily on the floorboards. All around was the noise of blood splashing from heights and pouring out across the floor by the pitcher. Gideon stood triumphantly over Warren. He was different. Had a scar on his cheek and a mouthful of gold teeth that glittered.

"I did not think you would kill your friend."

Warren said nothing but continued to struggle beneath Pat Cole's body. Gideon saw the struggle and put a foot on the corpse and stood so heavily that the air groaned from its lungs and Warren could hardly breathe himself.

"Do you see how they perceive your actions? Your oldest friends see only madness and depravity. You have relinquished your humanity in your thirst for blood, and I have lost mine by dying again and again. You and I are now a species apart."

Gideon took out a derringer from his suit vest and aimed it between Warren's eyes.

"Someday we might be friends, but not yet. Until you realize the futility of what you are doing, we cannot reconcile."

"Annie." Warren's voice was barely a gasp.

"You did not have to kill her. There was no harm to her being alive."

Warren moaned and spit blood. He felt much as he had when Gideon had beaten him and taken him to the cave. No. Not quite so hopeless. Warren whispered something so quiet that Gideon could not possibly hear him.

"What was that?" Gideon leaned in and held a hand to his ear. "What did you say?"

This was the moment Warren had prepared for. He felt the heat and heard the soft hiss buried beneath Pat Cole and for an instant it became a *whoosh*. Gideon's expression betrayed that he heard it too.

The dynamite exploded and Gideon and Warren were sent on their way.

■　■　◪

Warren was a president without his constituents. In this state he existed in the valley apart from any human notion of time. It was a dream place or a real place where no man could walk. It was not the empty desert or the Pueblo canyon but some mix of the two. The sky was ugly yellow and there were no clouds at all. The shack was there but it seemed swaybacked and shrunken.

Warren realized he could not get inside. He pulled and pulled at the door and beat it with his fists and was denied entrance. He cried out in anger and heard himself as echoes breaking against the walls of black rock.

He despised the plaintive sound and so fell silent and leaned against the door and pressed his palms to the wood. He became still as stone.

A great length of time passed and Warren spied a jackrabbit upon a nearby rock. Its fur was pure white and its eyes were the same brilliant blue as those of the Indian dog that had come to him after Gideon's attack. The rabbit seemed to regard him curiously. It sniffed at the air and twitched its ears and then turned and began hopping away. He followed it. The rocks were sharp beneath his feet. It entered the narrowing canyon that folded upon itself and concealed the way ahead by its convolutions.

The rabbit stopped at the foot of a man. His face was hidden by canyon shadow. The rabbit seemed confused and rose up on its back legs and sniffed at the bare shins of the human figure. The man reached down and took up the rabbit by the scruff of its neck. He stepped toward Warren so that his face was revealed.

It was Warren's own face. The eyes were dark red and flecked with black as if the Oscura stone had splintered into twin pools of blood.

So this is hell again, thought Warren. *Is this the devil who thinks he owns my soul?*

The man snapped the rabbit's neck and dashed its limp body to the rocks. Warren was furious and smashed the man with his fists and knocked him to the ground. The man did not resist and so Warren crushed him with a stone. His anger poured out of him as blood beneath the rock.

Tired and sick and afraid that he might never escape this place Warren continued into the valley's narrowing meander. It became so constricted he shuffled with his back and chest against the wind-smoothed rocks. When it seemed he might become trapped in the canyon it finally widened and he emerged into the silent bowl of an unfamiliar canyon. The stones ascended in tapering pillars like cave formations. The sky overhead had turned pink.

The canyon was filled with rabbits. There were too many of them to be counted and they were all white and all with the same blue eyes. Warren was not at all relieved to see them.

The wind picked up and began to howl through the valley and the stone shaped the air into a primal voice. The rabbits were all looking at him. There was a light in the sky growing larger and brighter. A second sun was falling down. The wind roared. The shadows crawled and poured out from every surface as the star fell lower and lower and cast every object and man into shivering relief.

A sudden quiet. A sudden gasp of stillness. A man stood up from the midst of the rabbits. His flesh was pale. His face was that of Warren Groves but his eyes were brilliant blue.

■ ■ ■

In the faint, unearthly light of the cavern Gideon cleaned himself of the slop that clung to his limbs and webbed his fingers and toes. After more than a year of being murdered by the outlaw Warren Groves, that man's final, explosive act of defiance amused Gideon. A good jest. He stretched his new muscles and shook the primordial stew from his head. Always the last wisps of memories that were his and not his, receding like clouds boiling away beneath a hot sun.

Gideon's many visits to the cave had resulted in gradual improvements. He brought clay pots of water, washing basins, clean clothing, shoes, and wooden boxes filled with provisions. The cave and the pueblo beyond were transformed into an outpost, the first stop on each of Gideon's journeys beginning at the pool and ending in his brutal murder.

He walked from the pool and sought out the water pots. Instead he cut his foot upon a jagged shard of broken pottery. His new eyes adjusted to the soft light, and he could see that all his efforts had been destroyed. The pots were broken, the boxes smashed, and food scattered and crushed underfoot. Much of it was missing completely, stolen or thrown into the pool to be digested.

He found a torn shirt and trousers sealed to the cavern's warm rock by a decayed mash of root vegetables. It bore the imprint of a boot as clear as a signet in a wax seal. He pried away the mess and donned the clothing and crawled out from the cave. The good humor with which he greeted each new life was obliterated by anger.

Warren Groves was waiting for him beyond the cave. The lawman was dressed and relaxed along the upper terrace overlooking the valley. He did not even turn to face Gideon as he approached. Gideon thought of pushing him over the edge. So easy to splatter his brains upon the dark rocks below, but that was not how gentlemen behaved, and Gideon was doing his best to train this wild animal to be a gentleman.

"Good show," said Gideon. "I should have known better than to gloat over you."

In his short time of resurrection Warren Groves had somehow managed to acquire an industrial stink. Groves wore clothing of his own. Must have laid them out here before the ambush in San Francisco.

"I would extend to you my hospitality, Mr. Groves, but it would seem you have already rejected it. What a frightful mess you've made in there. At some point you'll need to learn of more rewarding pursuits than destruction."

Gideon joined him at the edge of the terrace and gazed down upon a wagon so large, it must have been brought into the valley by a mule team. The mules were gone, long ago turned loose or ridden out.

"What is all that?" asked Gideon.

"Something I shoulda done a year ago."

There was more detail to be seen, broken-down crates and wooden spools. Fine gray wires ran throughout the valley. No, not wire at all. Black lengths and loops fed from one crated pile to another along the base of the cliff and up the terraces to cases of explosives near the cave entrance.

"You can't do this!" Gideon grabbed at Warren's shoulders.

Warren punched Gideon in the nose and sent him to the ground with the coppery taste of blood in his mouth. The outlaw did not even look at him.

"It is already lit."

"Wait," said Gideon. "Please. Be reasonable. You do not know what this will mean. We could become trapped in the rubble forever. You would doom us to that?"

"I will," said Warren. "You and I have done too much evil to go on living. It's past time for us to set things right."

Gideon got up and stood beside Warren again. The blood dripped out over his lips. He could see the smoke issuing from the fuse. There was a thick trunk of it from the mule cart running along the ground to the slope of the terraces. At each level it diverged into one or two smaller fuses.

"You ever dream in between being alive?" asked Warren.

"What?" Gideon held a hand to his nose. "No. Yes, I suppose. I never thought of them as dreams. I see places."

"Places?"

"I told you of these things before—do you remember? Cease this madness with the dynamite, and we can discuss it like rational men."

"Tell me again," said Warren.

Further objections were clearly pointless, so Gideon answered, "When I die, I feel as if I am falling, very quickly and without direction. I am plunging through a gulf of darkness, a great sea of black with no shores or moon or stars. Though it seems endless, I pass through this darkness quickly, and I experience a multitude of places in such rapid succession that I can barely endure it."

"Are they like the valley out there, only with a yellow cyclone sky? Or a flat plain with a big building falling to bricks?"

"No, not that. I only see the valley when I walk out of this cave. You must know, these memories fade, so it is difficult to recall the details."

"You got to recollect a few."

"Please, stop the fuses," Gideon urged, but Warren just cocked his head and smiled. Gideon continued. "All right. I do recall a few. Barely. Forests of stone obelisks and places with no ground at all, only clouds. Fallen pillars as big around as my family's foundry, laid over a channel of stone, thousands of spires in the rain. There was a rolling meadow of white plants and blue flowers, sun-lit, cotton seeds drifting in the light, but it was cold and ugly, and I knew somehow that the plants were poison."

"That your hell?" wondered Warren.

"Or the infinity of God's creation." Gideon watched the fuse begin its slow climb to the first terrace. There was yet time to stop this. "Before you trap us in here with your dynamite, why don't you tell me what you see?"

"Ain't much to tell. I forget, same as you, but what I do recollect ain't that way."

"Humor a man about to be blasted to pieces," said Gideon, but his mind was on the guns hidden in the pueblo below and the folding knife he kept beside the pool. The chamber was ransacked. Perhaps if he could lure Warren back to the pool.

"Here, but not exactly," said Warren. "There's a shack, and it's full of furniture and old books. Jars like somebody has been collecting things. There are Indians and they wear strange hides. And there are animals with blue eyes."

"Like the dog," said Gideon.

Warren nodded. "I only saw it once and never again. Now it's just black. Always black and this feel like I'm moving. There's something in that black, some memory was snatched out of my head and gets farther away all the time."

"What have you done with yourself over all these months?"

"You're an odd man to ask that question."

"Right." Gideon stamped his foot. "Right. Your task was murdering me over and over again. Right? Yes. My task, Mr. Groves, was to make something out of this world. Do you understand?"

"Don't care to," Warren said.

"I made money, by any means available, and I bought back my family business from the creditors. I mined thousands of tons of copper, sold mile upon mile of copper wire. I built coke ovens and barracks and a kitchen for my workers. Every problem *you* see needs to be solved with violence. I paid wages, Mr. Groves—do you see? Better than the Pearce foundry. Men fed their families with my money. I made a better world. All of that is going to end now."

"Somebody else will do it."

"But I did it!" Gideon tore at his shirt. "I fought back against the darkness, and you, pig, you wallowed in it. Do you see? All those folks in Utah. That marshal. Damn you, I am not the villain. That whore in Santa Fe. You have to remember her. You killed her. That poor family at the tr—"

Warren struck him in the mouth to shut him up. Gideon was undeterred. He spit out the blood and kept on talking but began to back away toward the cave entrance.

"I fucked her, you know," Gideon said. "She was still a woman, even if she didn't speak to me."

Warren's rage seized him, and he roared and struck at Gideon with both fists. Gideon retreated into the cave, scampering and ducking away from his foe. He dodged and ran and crawled deeper, with Warren clutching at his heels.

They emerged into the cavern, and Warren immediately landed a two-fisted blow to Gideon's shoulders. The impact sent him to one knee but stopped him only for a moment. He launched his shoulder into Warren's midsection and knocked him to the ground. Gideon tried to go for where the knife was hidden, but Warren rolled and stood before Gideon could press the advantage.

"You fucking devil," Warren said.

"Now, now," said Gideon, backing away. "I tried to save her. If you put a dead thing into the pool it doesn't return like we do. It's a blank slate. Just meat. But you can teach it. I did my best with her. " His hand felt for the knife in the dark stone. "I sang to her and fed her by my own hand. She could sing a little herself before you took her." Gideon's fingers found the alcove empty. "What did *you* do for her? Left her to rot? I'll not apologize to the man who has killed her twice."

Gideon brought up his guard without the knife. It was the first time the men had faced one another in a truly fair fight. Warren had a few inches and close to thirty pounds of muscle on Gideon. He landed two powerful body blows, and Gideon shrugged them off even though he spit blood. Gideon bit Warren's biceps and raised blood through his shirt. Warren shouted in surprise and gave Gideon the opening to land a solid cross to Warren's cheek.

"Feeling it now, eh?" Gideon laughed from behind his guard.

"I'll pull out your heart."

Warren's punches missed or only connected with Gideon's guard. Gideon began to get the better of Warren. The men were battered and bloodied. Their circling had brought them closer to the pool.

Gideon seized the opportunity and dragged Warren to the floor. Gideon got his hands around Warren's throat and began choking him and pulling him closer and closer to the pool until Warren was on his back with his head over the rim.

"Can't stop it," choked Warren.

Warren hammered Gideon's ribs with his fists, and Gideon could feel the knife-pain of the bones breaking. Despite his will, he lost some of his grip on Warren's throat, just enough for Warren to turn his neck. The outlaw used his knees to slam Gideon aside, and he twisted his body and broke free. Gideon lunged at him, and Warren countered and beat him to the ground and began to choke him.

There was a loud splash of stones falling into the pool. Warren sought the source of the noise and was immediately struck by Gideon's knees. Warren was not dislodged so easily. He tightened his grip on Gideon's throat until Gideon felt as if his eyes would burst in their sockets. He tried to plead with Warren to let him up. To end this madness. The outlaw was crazed.

There came a wet, gagging sound and another splash. A slapping of flesh on stone. Gideon clawed at Warren's face and gnashed his teeth. Warren risked dividing his attention to look over. Gideon freed his throat and pushed Warren off his chest. As he rose, gasping, he saw what Warren saw.

A human figure was rising to its feet and tearing at the membrane covering its body. The sack parted and revealed white skin. Beneath the cowl the face was obscured by the thickness and uniformity of muddy slime. The thing lurched in their direction. Gideon's stomach tightened in recognition.

"No," Gideon said.

It was over. Warren Groves recognized the futility of it and surrendered. He found his hat and left, left to pull the fuses and maybe to disappear into the desert for at least one lifetime.

The thing that stepped out of the pool limped over to Gideon and offered him a hand up. Gideon was afraid and confused but took the offered hand and stood and faced it. It was a man who smiled in a way that was sickeningly familiar, for he wore the face of Gideon Long.

1890

■ ■ ■

The Covenant

■ ■ ■

The ferocity of the day divided the world clearly into shade and baking canyon rock. Where the men stood in shadow, their faces were blue, and where they stood in the midday sun, the rocks were almost white, and the men's faces seemed to glow. There were nine men who gathered to author the Covenant. Nine men divided by two faces.

There was Gideon Long and his four brothers, and there was Warren Groves and his three brothers, separated by months or years, depending, diverged by personal experience but each from the root of their originator. The men who shared the face of Gideon stood together and discussed the details of the document. The Warrens were sullen and stood apart from one another.

It was the Warren named Thomas Yarborough who finally convened the signing. He was the most recent of the Warrens to emerge and draw his name from the hat. His voice alone among the Warrens had sought to reconcile their new way of living to the realities of the modern age.

"Enough talking," said Thomas. "The longer you confer, the more opportunity for my brothers to desert this endeavor. We sorted it out, and unless you object, let's be done."

"There is only one item," said the Gideon called Harlan Bishop. "It is the matter of the Judge."

"He'll be elected," said Thomas. "It's only right."

"Democracy, being the foundation of this great nation, would of course be desirable," said the originator, Gideon Long, "but not always practicable. Gathering in this location could become impossible if our ranks continue to swell."

"Conducting a tabulation of votes from a Diaspora could be similarly time-consuming," added Harlan Bishop, "and require methods open to fraud or abuse. We propose a simple alternative."

"Beware," said the originator, Warren Groves, stepping forth from the blue shadow. "He means trickery."

Each Warren knew the originator was right to be wary.

"Get to your meaning," Thomas addressed the Gideons.

"I will assume the duty of selecting each Judge," said Harlan Bishop, "until I die and the duty passes to another Gideon."

Curses went up from the Warrens. The Gideons reacted with a uniform look of bemusement. They had expected such a reaction.

"I'll not abide by you choosing the Judges," said Thomas.

"We currently outnumber you," said Harlan Bishop, "but this might not always be the case. Should we leave it up to the pool, then? Dominance to whichever of us benefits from its generosity? I think not. Democracy will not work in our unique situation."

"I'll not bow to you," said the Warren called Jacob Fortune. "Forget the whole goddamn thing. We don't need no Constitution."

"I have not been allowed to finish," said Harlan Bishop. He waited for leave to continue from the Warrens. Jacob shook his head in disgust. Harlan continued, "As I said, I will choose the Judge, but only from your numbers. That means your face and your blood will always occupy the office."

"Why?" asked Thomas.

"He means to piss on us, but like a gentleman," said Jacob.

"You are lawmen," said Gideon Long. "Renegades by deed, perhaps, but you adhere to your own code. Uphold this Covenant. That is all we ask."

Thomas saw the sense in the idea. At the least it would prevent a repetition of this painful experience. He turned to his brothers.

"We're each of us derived from the same notion and same flesh, aligned if not—"

"I reckon I'll just put my mark upon this fucking paper." Warren Groves stepped forward and took up the pen. The Covenant was flat upon a campaign table and held fast at its corners by four pieces of black rock. "Do any of you object?"

No one spoke, and so Warren Groves scrawled the alterations and added his name to the paper. He tossed the ink pen onto the table and began walking away. The other Warrens, all but Thomas, followed him down the terraces. Gideon Long took up the pen and signed his own name with a flourish.

"We should read the oath aloud," said Gideon as he admired his penmanship.

"Allow me," said Harlan, and he held up the paper and began to read aloud.

"By the Intercession of the Lord, or by His natural creation, the Pool that dwells in the black mountains has rendered all flesh it touches unlimited; it restores vitality to the dead and produces at uncertain intervals whole men of likeness and mind indistinguishable from their originators. This cohort of duplications and their originators do hereby assemble as a brotherhood and set forth to establish a Covenant of laws and principles to guide our body, to preserve mortal society, and to provide authority for the enforcement of laws herein.

"Gideon Long and all men of his likeness resulting from his flesh and Warren Groves and all men of his likeness resulting from his flesh do hereby swear, individually and collectively, of free will, that . . ."

Harlan was losing his voice to dryness. Another of the Gideons handed him a flask to wet his tongue. Thomas Yarborough glared at the Gideons from beneath the drooping brim of a farmer's hat. Harlan Bishop cleared his throat and continued.

"I will permit no man, woman, or child of mortal nature to enter the Pool, nor will I bathe them in its waters against their will.

"I will reveal no detail of the Pool, its function, its location, or even its existence in conversation or in document.

"I will not submerge dead men, women, children, or beasts in the waters of the Pool.

"I will abandon my name upon death and forfeit all claim on past property, family, friendships, or debt.

"I will avoid all communication with those who knew me before my death.

"I will not congregate with a duplication of the same originator in any location beyond the black mountains.

"I will not take the life of another, be they mortal or duplication, unless under flag of war or in the commission of lawful duties under this law or under the law of the land.

"IN THE PRESENCE OF GOD and in the interest of preserving the fabric of mortal society, the signatories of this Covenant, known as brothers in good standing, do hereby swear to abide and uphold the laws put forth within under the just penalty of death."

Harlan paused to interpret Warren's scrawled modification.

"It's difficult to . . . yes . . . I see. 'Such penalties will henceforth be served by the office of Judge'— now he's crossed out what was written and added, 'who will be picked from the Warrens by the cocksucker Harlan Bishop or the shit that comes from his privy if he's busy being dead.' The, um, colloquialisms notwithstanding, um, the intent of the document is clear. If the Judge perishes or vacates the office, he will be replaced at the earliest opportunity.

"Signed by Gideon Long for all men of his origination and signed by Warren Groves for all men of his origination. Did you wish to examine the document?"

"No," said Thomas. "Who will be the first Judge?"

"Him," said Harlan Bishop, and he pointed past Thomas to the entrance of the cave. A Warren emerged, newly made and still pale with the clinging liquid of the pool.

"Is it done?" the new Warren asked. "Last I recall, they were conferring. I had to crawl out of that fucking cave."

"Who are you?" asked Thomas.

"I drew the name Cal Borden," said the Warren, and he held up the slip of paper he took from the hat. "The name and memories I recall immediately are those of Jacob Fortune. Where is he?"

"Gone," said Thomas. "They've all gone but me."

"Was it signed?" Cal wondered aloud.

Thomas did not answer with words. He turned his back and began to descend the terraces. Gideon stepped forward, a bright smile upon his face.

"Congratulations, Cal Borden," said Gideon Long. "You are the first Judge of the Covenant."

Cal's arms fell to his sides, and his mouth hung open in dismay. After some time of staring he sat down upon a rock and hung his head.

"Shit," he said, although nobody by then was listening.

1951

■ ■ ■

The Judge

CHAPTER ONE

■ ■ ■

I was Warren Groves, the originator, the first of my kind. I was brought to this against my will. I stood atop the black rocks and howled into the desert night. I navigated a red river without conscience.

I was Benjamin Dent. I drew my name from a beaten hat and set out west across New Mexico to forge a new life. I hated my brothers. I turned my back on killing. I dug gold in California and lost a finger to a Chinaman. I was a mean drunk and reminded myself of Abraham Nunn.

I was Jacob Fortune, who rose from the water and yearned for the life of Benjamin Dent. I called myself by his name and sought him out, and I fantasized of bashing in his brain and taking his wife for my own. I recoiled from my fantasies of murder. I retreated to the cave and confessed my thoughts to my brothers. The Covenant was born of my actions, but I despised it.

I was Cal Borden, the first Judge. For my flag I hunted Spanish in the Philippines. For the Covenant I hunted my brothers. I was shunned and disliked. When I could not bear my deeds any longer, I forsook the office of Judge and took up as a deckhand on a merchant ship and grew to loathe the steadiness of land.

I was Wilton Brisk, and I emerged with the scent of the ocean filling my nose. I became a lawman of Missouri, well liked and respected. I ascended to the office of mayor and then to congressman. I saw my wife run down by a carriage. In despair I lived alone and apart from the world. I fell and broke my neck and lost movement in my arms or legs. I begged the nurses at the state hospital to let me die, but they would not.

I was Grant Agnew, Bull Whitman, Max Holden, Donald Hendricks, Franklin Wise, Ian Bendwool, and other names only briefly. I was a policeman in Atlanta, I fought in the trenches of France, I learned books, traveled foreign lands, and saw the moon reflected in the water of the Indian Ocean. I loved and I was loved. I was unrequited and unhappy, and I drank. I watched lives ending and beginning, but I never could sire another son or daughter. All of these memories, all of these men, flowed together as tributaries of my river until, in 1934, I emerged from the pool. I was thrust into this world, becoming not just water and intent, but the man named Casper Cord.

My dreams were haunted by half-remembered names and lives I could only clearly recall while sleeping. Between these scenes of filial Americana were gaps— dark spaces filled with oily black. There were memories in those spaces once. Strange memories I was made to forget, memories that in nightmares clenched my heart and awoke me with the sound of my own screaming. I even began to forget the Indians I encountered in the desert with their gray cloaks and arrows made from bone.

Sometimes there was only the grasshopper. It was black and polished like the skin of an automobile. I dreamed we talked, but it did not speak in words. I dreamed it took flight above me, and its black wings assumed the cruciform shape upon the ceiling of a cave. That place was gone, a tomb of rubble for the black grasshopper idol, but I will not forget the texture of its shell or the hollow, articulated limbs filled with the threads of past integuments.

The grasshopper thing lived, as surely as a rabbit or a dog or a man, and by the nature of the Pool I feared this fallen idol would live again.

CHAPTER TWO

■ ■ ■

Thanks to Sgt. Hector Flores of the Los Angeles Police Department I began my day with a dead girl. The headlights of the squad cars formed pools of color in the brittle gray morning. The poolful of the dead girl's colors had my attention: milk-white skin, the blue of her overcoat, red hair, red waitress's dress, and a red stream that flowed out onto the highway's gravel shoulder.

She was sprawled on a stretch of Dairy Valley blacktop some surveyor had decided to call Cranford. I'd never seen this stretch, or I'd seen it a thousand times and it had never left a mark on my brain. It was a lonely place to end up. Quiet and cold in the early morning.

The crowd around her was keeping me from getting a good look. There were a couple of Cranford sheriffs in brown uniforms, a couple of LAPD cops, and some overcoats and big hats all blowing steam and waiting on the meat wagon.

Flores was beside me, looking like branches cinched up in a cop belt. He was a good lawman, better than me, though he wasn't much fun and never smiled beneath his drooping mustache. Good cops don't laugh too much, and Flores never laughed. I could tell by the way he was biting his lip, he was hot about something.

"Out with it," I said.

"You didn't wear a tie," he said in that deep-down voice of his.

A glance at the rumpled front of my shirt confirmed his accusation.

"Kapinski's here," he foghorned, "and he's gonna kick your bung out."

Now, there was a thought. I'd long ago outgrown being afraid of men like Kapinski, which made life easier as a whole but made keeping jobs much trickier. The smaller the Kapinskis of the world, the more tenuous their hold on authority, the more they pound their chests and kick over tables and make sure you get run out of a job.

"My head hurts, it's cold, and I gotta see my doctor this morning."

"You okay?"

I was yawning when he asked, so I nodded and waved to him before answering. "Old war wound. We all got 'em. Just cut it out with the Emily Post routine and tell me why you dragged me out here."

"Found this." Flores pushed two fingers at me. Pinched between them was a stub of white paper. I took it and unfolded it. My name and telephone number and the word *Help* were scrawled in ink by a feminine hand. Not what I was expecting.

"Help?"

"Too late." Flores pointed up the road to the heap of laundry and bent curves. The wind was charming snakes from the dead girl's hair. Her overcoat was flapping against white legs twisted up all wrong. She wore an unfashionable brown loafer on one foot, and the other foot was bare. Dirty and bare. I couldn't see her face.

"Does Kapinski know about this?" I waved the slip of paper with my name on it.

"Just me," Flores said. "I found it in her purse. Thought I'd cover your ass for some stupid reason. Go take a look. Tell me if you know her."

He snapped his fingers for me to return the stub of paper. I gave it up. Over the years I have honed my detective's mind so that I am able to memorize key details like my own name and telephone number.

Kapinski was piled up under a broad-brimmed white hat holding court with the badges. He liked to jowl his way through his theories. I could hear the story as I approached, dumb as a little paste-eater.

According to Kapinski, the dead girl's name was Holly Webber. Didn't spark any fires. Kapinski thought she took the wrong bus from El Segundo, tried to walk to one of the subdivisions, and got creamed by a trucker. *There and there, look at the tire scraps. Someone tried to brake. Thump. Guy gets out and realizes what he's done to this beauty. Gets back into his truck, wheels back around there, and takes off east. Not going to be any witnesses out in the desert.*

"But what about the money?" Kapinski wondered aloud.

"What *about* the money?" I asked, joining the loose circle of cops and dicks surrounding the dead girl.

One of the Cranford sheriffs gestured to a rough line of wild brambles along the side of the road. There was a deputy over there picking through the bushes. I watched him pluck a bill from a branch and stuff it into a cloth sack.

"Casper Cord." Kapinski spit out my name like an olive pit that had just cracked a molar. "What the hell are you doing here?"

"Looking for a golf ball."

Kapinski eyed my open collar with disgust. He likes to see a dressed neck. "I'm sure I told you I never wanted to see you sniffing around real detective work again. We've got no time for freelance boozers."

"If you see any real detectives, let me know, and I'll clear out." His face went red, so I backed off. "Come on, Rudy, don't give me the high hat after all these years. Let me take a look, see if I know the stiff."

I knelt down beside the body. The blue overcoat was soaked with blood and sized to be the girl's. One of the cops had laid it over her face.

"Tell me about this money," I said.

I lifted the overcoat from the dead girl, and whatever Kapinski had to say bounced off my skull. My immediate concern was that against all of my expectations I did recognize this girl. I'd been looking for her face in every crowd and passing car for three-quarters of a century. Sometimes I glimpsed her, only to be proven wrong by a second look. This was different. This was no passing resemblance.

Damned if I wasn't looking at the face of my long-dead wife, Annie Groves. Dead all over again.

Couldn't be, right? That's what I thought.

I had to be sure she was real. I touched her cheek with my fingertips. Her skin was cold. The wind wrapped fat locks of her hair around my arm and slipped silk ribbons of it between my fingers. I leaned in closer, still not believing my eyes. Her perfume smelled like tangerines.

She was slack with death. Her face was younger than I remembered and her body longer and more voluptuous beneath the draped overcoat. The only injury to her face was a single droplet of tacky blood in one of her nostrils. Her full lips were parted slightly as if she was speaking. Her blue eyes were open wide, but their luster was dulled by the wind. I turned her head so she seemed to be looking at me.

Hands grabbed me and lifted me up from the pavement. I guess I was pretty caught up in her, because I just went right on staring, ignoring whatever the brunos were saying. Finally one of them got between me and her and grabbed me by the lapel of my coat. It was Kapinski.

"Answer me, you goddamn drunk. Who the hell is Annie Groves? Some name she gave you?"

"No, it's nothing." I shook off the coppers holding my overcoat. "It's not her. I'm mistaken."

"Her name is Webber." Kapinski held up a vehicle license. "Her purse was in the ditch over there. Christ Almighty, do you stalk car accidents looking for girls to lie down on? No, never mind. Get out of here. Leave it to the real police."

He gave me a shove. Who was I to argue?

I took a last look at her face before they covered it up with the overcoat. It was her. Goddamn it all, it was her. Dead all over again. She'd been full of sunshine and giggles before I knew she existed, and here we meet again, and she's as useless as a rock in a lake, only this rock had my name written on the bottom.

I staggered back to my car. I tried to have a few words with Flores, but my mouth was full of molasses, and things were coming out all wrong. Kapinski was scowling at him, and Flores wanted me out of there in a hurry. He bundled me into my car.

"You okay to drive?" he asked.

I nodded. All kinds of strange reels were slipping through my projector. The world was flickering and stuttering on me, but I had to think it through.

Maybe those Gideon sons of bitches had figured out some way to bring her back, even though that goddamn Pool never worked that way. Never did what you wanted. Fooling around with sticking dead things into that lousy soup was the most forbidden of the forbidden. Dead things came out alive but empty. They were worse than animals. The Pool somehow knew they were bad, because it dragged them back and never made dupes.

I was going at it from the wrong angle. I wasn't equipped to unravel some metaphysical mystery posed by my long-dead wife showing up on a lonely strip of Cranford highway. I knew how to glue the pieces together when it concerned earthly enigmas. I knew how to bust cheating husbands and work a source with sweet talk or chin music. I knew how to find people and answers.

And I knew Kapinski was as wrong as a blondJap girl. I saw the evidence on my way back to the car. Holly Webber's missing shoe was lying in the dust a hundred feet from the road. Pretty girl like that doesn't go wandering in an empty lot out past the subdivisions. She definitely doesn't lose her shoe in the middle of an empty lot and keep going.

Unless she is being chased.

I killed time at a boondocks chow house called Dandy's that was anything but. A slab of gristle in a paper hat was chasing breakfast around a griddle in back as if it owed him rent money. I asked Doris, the only waitress, to scrape a couple of layers off their pot of tar and call it coffee. The place was empty except for one table of men in flannel shirts quietly talking, probably laborers from one of the developments going up.

I left a dime on the counter for Doris and retraced my course to the scene of the crime. The coroner had taken away the body. Kapinski and his boys were gone too. The only sign that this stretch of road was any different than the stretch leading up to it was the dark stain attracting flies by the side of the road and about a hundred cigarette butts.

The full light of day clarified the scene. There was a dirt road perpendicular to the highway about fifty yards from where Holly Webber's body was found. It led off past a long-gone farmhouse, the dusty field containing Holly Webber's shoe, and a collapsed barn. Opposite the abandoned farm was a low hill covered in desert grass and topped with an assortment of parched trees. The cops had used the first few yards of the dirt track as a turnaround, but I could make out fresh tire tracks running all the way to where it dead-ended.

I followed the dirt road on foot. A decrepit mailbox leaned into the road and marked the overgrown drive of the farmhouse. The door of the mailbox was missing. The rusty metal hinges were snapped and showed silver. The mailbox was empty.

I wasted about ten minutes wandering around the farm, doing my best not to twist my ankle in one of the weed-covered holes concealed like traps on the property. There were some impressions in the weeds, as if maybe somebody had walked from the road to the sun-baked lump of a tractor. I searched the weeds around it for a few minutes and turned up nothing.

Feeling defeated, I tapped out a smoke from a fresh pack and sat my ass down on the hitch of the tractor. The weather-beaten metal protested and shed a patina of red flakes. I gazed out across the field I'd just crossed and beyond the dirt track to the hill. The dry copse atop it was rattling away an accompaniment to the wind. A sickly elm shook its leaves, swayed back and forth, and moved just enough for me to catch a glimpse of blue peeking out between the branches.

That blue was the body of a motor scooter. It was a Cushman, fairly new, in a design and color appropriate for a pretty young girl who preferred driving herself to relying on a man with a car. No bus from El Segundo for her. I hunched over the scooter, wheezing from my jog up the hill. Felt like I had gravel in my lungs. Too old and too worn out to be running up hills in Cranford.

I scribbled the Cushman's tag in my black book. There was a pair of heels and a balled up pair of nylons in the scooter's foot well. The shoes were bright red but sensible, the sort of thing a doll who was on her feet a lot would wear. Work clothes, no good for crawling around in the bushes.

Most of the prints were made by her loafers. There were footprints from a man's shoes, as well. These overlapped the woman's in places and seemed to pursue her toward the highway. I managed to follow them about halfway from the hill to the highway, but I lost sight of them. I backtracked to the Cushman and followed the man's footprints the other way, up and over the hill. The trail disappeared in a dry creek bed littered with round stones.

The Cushman and the shoes ruled out Kapinski's nonsense about the wrong bus. Holly Webber came out here with a purpose, and it was important enough to push a hundred-pound scooter up a hill and hide it in some trees. There was a white crash helmet atop a tree stump. The inside of it smelled like Holly Webber's tangerine perfume.

She'd been camped out behind a heap of yellow stones. It was a good spot to overlook the farmhouse and the mailbox. No campfire, but I kicked a ball of paper from a burger joint, and that led me to the peel of an orange, an Ellery Queen novel, and a pair of military-surplus binoculars.

Holly Webber definitely came out to this miserable scab of Dairy Valley with a purpose. She was dropping off or picking up money, using the mailbox with the freshly-snapped hinges. Based on those footprints around the scooter, she was caught flat-footed by a man who pursued her to her demise. Run down by his accomplices, and some or all of the cash ended up in the bushes.

Nobody had to pay me for the job I now planned to do. Holly Webber had spelled out Help in blue cul-de-sac curlicues on a scrap of envelope. Flores was right. I was too late to save her. But the story didn't have to end with Holly Webber dead on the pavement. There were other ways a man like me could help. I knew a thing or two about revenge.

CHAPTER THREE

■ ■ ■

Dr. Rutledge was a specialist of the lung with a reputation in pediatrics. He was recommended by my regular man, Doc Brightbow, a whisper of an old coot with palsied hands and a tendency to medicate everything with bicarbonate and aspirin. The Brightbow special wasn't taking care of my cough, so he sent me to Dr. Rutledge with the promise that he had an X-ray machine and could sort this out.

It was a little radiographic instrument intended for children. I was a big lunk. Taking pictures of my chest meant lots of repositioning the equipment. The result was a bunch of overlapping X-rays arranged on a light box in a puzzle of shadow bones and faint tissues. Reminded me of collaged reconnaissance photography. P Boats over the Pacific, hunting Tojo's fleets in my lungs.

I only like incurious doctors. I'm paranoid the good ones will be wise to me. Take a measure and examine a chart and say, "This isn't right at all" and know what I am. How long I've been kicking around. I didn't like Rutledge especially. Too many certificates and big words. It was dangerous. He spoke with a cigarette hanging from his lips, ashes gathering in the folds of his white coat.

"You have some severe scarring of the osseous tissue from your previous injuries." He pointed to my mended ribs with the cap of a pen. "It complicated this, but we have an accurate picture now. These dark spots here are what we're after. Malignancies here and here. I would say two growths in your lung that have metastasized to your surrounding tissue. Two more on your lymph node here. Those account for the swelling in your throat. There's also an odd lesion that appears to be on your pineal gland, but we weren't photographing your head, so I'd like to schedule you for head X-rays and—"

"Cancer?"

"Yes, we knew this was a possibility," Dr. Rutledge said. "You were on the Home Islands."

"I'm only thirty-five," I lied.

Rutledge took off his glasses and hung them from the front pocket of his white coat. He leaned across his desk toward me, and his smile made me want to clobber him.

"Cancer doesn't know age. Every day I see children with cancer. Some of them I can save, and some of them I can only treat. Mr. Cord, there are tablets and new therapies that could extend your life, but we did not catch this early. I am afraid this instance is probably terminal."

I'm sorry, fella, but your belts are all worn out. Your radiator is cracked. Transmission is shit. Fuel lines split and leaking. You're broken down and no good to anybody. Better to junk the whole damn thing and start over from scratch.

"How long?"

"I don't like to set a timeline for this. With the right medication, aggressive surgery, it could be measured in years."

"I ain't asking you to swear on a Bible. What's your best guess?"

"Three months," said Rutledge.

That will take the vinegar out of you. My clothes became all tight around me, and yet my senses expanded like a trick camera shot. I was aware of individual details in the room. There was the brick wall with the schoolhouse-awning windows, the wood paneling behind Rutledge festooned with a dozen certificates and important photographs, the wooly texture of the orange chairs, the way the trees outside turned the sunlight cold.

And there was Rutledge, fucking Rutledge, with his slicked-back hair and his cigarette resting in the ashtray, coiling purple smoke above his desk. He was writing on his pad.

I wasn't afraid to die. There have been times in my long, long life that I've been trying to die. I can get killed, but I can't stay killed. Been through it all. But there was the Covenant, rules that meant that when I died, I couldn't pick up where I'd left off. Breaking those rules would have severe consequences.

I didn't want to start over.

"What do I do?"

Rutledge passed me the papers he'd scribbled on.

"Tablets for the swelling in your neck. X-rays in one week for that lesion in your head." Rutledge scribbled again and passed me another sheet. "This is for a drug to treat the tumors in your chest. If it works, we'll continue with it; if it doesn't, we'll take a look at surgery and radiation. The one benefit of the post-war increase in cancer rates is that treatments are getting better and better. This last one is just for the pain. It will help stop the coughing, but you need to lie down if you take it.

"Two of these are expensive, so if you can, I would go through the Veteran's Administration. You'll have to see a VA specialist to get them approved."

"I'm on the waiting list to see the VA cancer docs," I said. "They're busy."

The government tried to hide it, but the VA cancer docs were a hundred- thousand-men-worth of busy, according to Murrow. And those were just the ones who bothered with the doctors. God only knew how many poor SOBs camped under bridges or moved around the country in those hobo caravans that followed the trains.

"If you can afford it out of pocket, then pay for it. Don't do anything stupid. You're still alive. I want to see you in a week, and we can reassess the situation then." He laid a hand flat on his desk. "You can also talk to your clergy. Miracles aren't my line of work."

What an asshole. I walked out in a daze, past the crying kids and the tangle-roots of matronly ankles. The lady at the window treated me like I'd just gotten a checkup. I paid cash and staggered out. My hat was crumpled in one hand and the prescriptions in the other.

The old Ford Tudor was baking under the California sun. I pushed my hat down on my head and sat in the excruciating heat, sat and drank warm whiskey out of a flask I kept in the smuggler's hold in the dash. I looked at the silver of the revolver next to the flask. Stillman .38 loaded with dumdums. A bullet through the brain is close to painless.

Nah. Not ready yet. I closed the smuggler's hold on the gun. I didn't have time for more of Rutledge's X-rays and exams. I didn't have time for waiting at the VA office and begging for Uncle Sam's help. Out on the highway I rolled the window down and tossed Rutledge's yellow bouquet of prescriptions into the rushing air.

I had time to kill.

■　■　■

I was out of place under the golden lights of Ciro's on a Friday night. I was more of an afternoon-lunch-crowd-er. Sit me in the back where I won't scare away the pretty girls. My hat was dented, my overcoat hung rumpled and smudged around my legs, and I was wearing a cheap loaner tie from the maître d'. Golden-threaded ducks on blue houndstooth.

The crowd at Ciro's was a luminous bunch of Hollywood aristocracy—raconteurs, stars, and the fragile ships of beautiful dreamers soon to be wreckage on the jagged coast of a seedy hotel. This was the stuff gossip pages were made for. The Will Mastin Trio was up on stage, the girls were dancing, but I was making my way through the crowd for a good angle on a particular man in a rumpled tuxedo.

"Beau Reynolds?" Someone tapped me on the shoulder. It wasn't the man who'd spoken; it was his muscle, a thick-necked Italian. The speaker was a smiling sprig of glitz beside the gorilla. He was a slicked-back type with dark eyes and a knockout blonde on his arm.

"Not me," I said, and I made sure he could see the scars. That usually scared them off, but if I was getting picked out of the crowd already, it might mean trouble.

"Oh, my apologies," he said. "I mistook you for the pilot. Have you seen him?"

"No," I said, and I shot a look of annoyance at the muscle. The gorilla hustled his man away to the private dining area.

Before I could resume my search for the real Beau Reynolds, I got waylaid by a twist with too much paint on and too much skin showing for the film code. Cigarette girl by the look of her wares, but something more by the look on her face and the way she was tugging at my elbow. Good-looking girl if you like them small and dangerous.

"You know who that was?" She had to lean in to ask me over the music. I could smell her sweat beneath her perfume. "Howard Hughes."

"He looked familiar," I said.

"So do you," she said. "You in the pictures?"

"Sell it somewhere else." I dragged my arm away from her. She told me what I could do with myself and circulated into the crowd near the edge of the dance floor.

Beau Reynolds was where I wanted him. Once I macheted my way through the jungle of people, I parted the fronds and found him entertaining a boisterous table of celebrities and those aspiring to join their ranks. One of the cigarette girls was in his lap, half girl and half legs, and he had one of the waitresses sitting on the table next to several emptied magnums of Champagne. I moved myself to a table with a free chair and ordered a drink and something to shut up my growling stomach.

The night was early for a man like Reynolds, the party only beginning. I recognized some of the faces that came and went, some of the old jokes being told. Sinatra and Ava Gardner stopped by. Reynolds convinced Sinatra to sing. He belted out "One for My Baby," and Beau took visible liberties dancing with Ava Gardner. Sinatra didn't say anything when he jumped down off the stage. I wasn't sure if it was Hedda Hopper taking notes from Beau's table or Beau's notorious right hook that kept Sinatra in line.

It was past midnight. More and more stars drifted out. Beau kept on dancing, his bowtie hanging from his collar, his cheek covered in lipstick kisses from a dozen different girls. At the table he bragged about escaping the Japs, about his turn as a movie star, but mostly he told lewd stories that made everyone roar with laughter.

When Reynolds was shooting *Aces Over Tokyo*, the director used to threaten him and William Bendix with a golf club for being out late drinking. That ended one day when Bendix showed up with a bat signed by Babe Ruth. He told about the time he drove over Darryl F. Zanuck's foot with a motorcycle, the time he skipped out on a beach picture to spend a week in Malta with Betty Grable, even though she was married, and the time he got three sheets and punched out Dwight Eisenhower's driver at a White House dinner.

Even some of the actors were jealous of a man who could be war hero and star. He was an Audie Murphy of the skies. I wasn't so envious. He was burning too bright. Late in the evening he was still going when all of the real stars were gone, still drinking and dancing to the house band, ragged at the edges, holding girls like a man holds the edge of a cliff. I was the only one in the place who knew why.

"Another soda water?" asked the waitress, scooping up my ashtray from the table.

Beau Reynolds was finally lurching off the dance floor, staggering toward the door and relying on a pair of laughing girls to steady him.

"No," I said, and I followed him out.

One of the girls was the cigarette girl with all those legs; the other one was a blonde from some science fiction picture. I couldn't remember the name of it, just that she filled out a sequined bathing suit and was eaten by a brain.

The three of them climbed into a taxi, and I followed in my car. It wasn't hard. I knew where he was headed. Reynolds had been camped out at the St. Francis for the past week. His minor scandals were making all the papers. The girls were chewing on him like red meat in the back of the cab. I kept my distance in the thinning traffic.

The cab pulled up outside the hotel, and the doorman hurried over to hold open the taxi while Reynolds settled with the hacker. I waited for the cab to pull away and then wheeled around to the alley beneath the fire escape of the St. Francis.

Reynolds had a suite near the top with a view overlooking Sunset Boulevard, but the bathroom window faced the fire escape. I put on my leather gloves and got onto the hood of my Tudor to pull down the fire escape's ladder. I climbed up the shaky iron staircase. My heart sank as I looked up at the framework extending toward the sky. I remembered climbing the ten floors the day before when I scoped the place out. It wasn't going to be pleasant.

I was still wearing the duck tie from Ciro's, and the wind was blowing it into my face. After about three floors I was having trouble. Five and I was ready to go down, wheezing and gasping for air, all sweaty, heart pounding in my chest. I hacked up something black and spit it over the side. I had to sit for a minute and smoke a Bravo before finishing the climb.

The light was on in the suite's bathroom. The dark shape of someone was moving inside, but I could not see clearly through the frosted glass. The shim I'd put under the double-hung window the day before was still there. I slid my fingers under the frame and lifted the window very slowly. I could hear water running. A shower too, but Reynolds was dressed and on his feet, hands on the sink and staring down into the water. I knew that feeling. Trying to will yourself not to be sick. Too much booze will do that to a man.

My shoes squeaked on the tile. I moved swiftly behind Reynolds and shut and locked the bathroom door. Reynolds turned to me, to the Stillman in my hand. His eyes were in shadow. His face—my face, but younger—registered no surprise.

"I saw you at Ciro's," he said. "I wanted it to last all night."

"Why did you bring the girls?"

"You won't hurt them, will you?"

I didn't need to answer; he knew I wouldn't. I lowered the gun.

"You knew this day would come," I said to him, and I advanced, grabbing him by his jacket. "You've been very bad. You made our face famous."

"What about Bishop? He's in the newspaper every day."

Harlan Bishop, still hanging on to life after all these years. But Harlan Bishop never broke the Covenant. Not technically. Not that I would admit that to a trouble-maker like Reynolds.

"You were supposed to stay dead after I threw you over the side of that boat."

"I can't help it if sharks destroyed the evidence."

I shoved him toward the shower.

"Evidence or not, you know the rules. When your number comes up, you get your ticket punched. Start the ride over with a new name. A new identity. This is twice now you've come back as Beau Reynolds."

"Nobody is the wiser."

"Sure. They only made a movie about the first time you pulled it off. What did the Japs call you?"

Shot down over the Sea of Japan in '45, back in '46 to give 'em hell again. Funny thing was, the Japs remembered it. The pilot who shot him in his parachute was still alive to tell the story after the war, and yet Beau Reynolds came back to haunt the skies over Japan.

"They called me 'Ghost Dragon.' " Beau sat down on the rim of the bathtub. "What did the Japs call you?"

There was a name for the Marines who came ashore on the Home Islands. What they called out when they saw us coming to their villages, into their homes, but Beau Reynolds probably knew that. I wasn't about to get sucked into his fast talk.

"Doesn't matter," I said, and I snapped my mind back out of that particular deep hole. "I've got to do this, bud. Now strip and get into the shower. I'll make it look like an accident."

"Why?"

"That's the way things are."

"Whose way? The Gideons'? Bishop's?"

My grip tightened on my Stillman, and I thought about putting one into his chest right then and there.

"None of the rest of us work for the Gideons," he whined. "How do you stomach looking at him? How do you sleep at night?"

I struck him across the brow with the grip of the gun. Not too hard, a little argument-stopper, but it opened a cut in his eyebrow, and blood gushed down the side of his face. Before he could protest, I pointed the gun at him.

"We all do what we have to do," I said. "Now get into the shower before you make me murder you."

"All right." Beau held up his hands in defeat. "I don't mind going out as a drunk who slipped in the shower. Just don't shoot me."

He undressed and got into the shower. I took off my hat and overcoat and set them over the sink. The water in the shower was turned pink by the blood flowing from Beau's lacerated brow.

"You need to hit the temple." I reached in and tapped the back of the faucet. The plunger for the stopper was square. "That'll pop right through the bone and open you up like a can of beer."

"Delightful," said Beau.

"It'll only hurt for a second. You'll black out right away, and if the fall doesn't kill you, the blood loss will. You don't want to end up paralyzed from a neck injury."

"It's not fair. I liked this one."

"Ain't nothing fair about this world, bud."

Beau swallowed some of the water. The chrome shower pipe distorted his reflection into a nose described by an oval. His muscles tensed. He threw himself forward, stopped. Did it again. I was wearing my hat and overcoat again and looking on from a safe distance. Starting to get annoyed. Beau cast a sidelong gaze at me, at the silenced Stillman I had once again leveled at him in case he lacked the courage to finish the job.

"I remember your name now," said Beau. "Casper. Those scars on the side of your face. It's still you, isn't it? What's your last name?"

"Doesn't matter."

"I'm just curious," said Beau. "My dying wish."

"Cord."

"Casper Cord?" Beau blinked away the water running into his eyes. "That's a good one. Lucky draw."

"I hate alliteration," I said, and I reached up and grabbed Beau by the throat and yanked hard. Beau's feet slid out from under him, and his temple fell straight down onto the faucet.

I heard the bone crunch. Beau made a sound that was all consonants. He kicked his legs and flexed his arms, but it was a dying thing. He lay at the bottom of the tub, his dark blood swirling into the shower drain. He tried to say something and couldn't. His eyes were already far away.

I dried off the sleeve of my overcoat with a towel. I took out the black book and pen from the breast pocket of my jacket and stood beneath the light to see the names written within. The book contained many names of many men, soldiers and criminals, whom I did not know and could only describe. I found where Beau Reynolds was written, and I added a small notation.

Beau Reynolds. Whom I killed twice.

■　■　■

There was a churchman by the name of Reverend Marquis whom Henry Ford hired to put Jesus into his factories. I guess Ford thought that instilling a Christian ethic would create more efficient workers. I met this Marquis fellow once, back when I was newly named Max Holden, and it was 1915 or 1916, on a ship crossing the Atlantic. Marquis had a pudgy face and an intellectual look. He was a bit quiet but always polite, and I learned once I got him going that he talked with enthusiasm and charisma.

I was on a personal mission to figure out what I was going to do with myself. That mission never really ends, but it was my main purpose at the time, as that person. I was listening very carefully to everyone around me, and I'll never forget what Marquis told me. The guy hated being aboard a ship and could barely sleep. One night I found him walking the halls, restless, and I took him to the ship's kitchen and cobbled together a proper American coffee.

After some polite conversation and answering his questions about the ship and about traveling the North Atlantic, I asked him what automobile Henry Ford was going to make next.

"You misunderstand," Marquis said. "Henry Ford is not concerned with automobiles. He rolls cars out of his factory just to be rid of them. They are the byproducts of his real business, which is the making of men."

Time proved Reverend Marquis at least partly wrong. He left the company because Henry Ford placed more value on productivity than spiritual enlightenment. His comment nevertheless informed my own life.

The Gideons would make Henry Ford proud. They issue from the Pool at irregular intervals, in resurrection or in the unpredictable act of duplication, and each man who comes out accepts his fate and seems friendly with the others of his kind. They are a production series. The Model G, of unified purpose and design.

Not so with us. With the Warrens.

In the beginning, all the evil that had wound its brambles around us formed a new man. The act of division created two men different from the original, one good and one evil, and they became the diverging fathers of us all. Death provides a clear line, but duplication muddies our memories. It is an instantaneous process.

If you're a duplicate, the last thing you remember could be your originator eating a sandwich, making love, fighting in a war, or reading a newspaper on the can. A third of us awake from a dream by emerging from the Pool. You come roaring to life and have about ten seconds in that goddamn cave to smack sense into your face and decide to be a whole new person. You have to turn all those memories into a new branch of the tree.

The Gideons seem to accept this arrangement. They're constructing their own narrative out of all those lives. For the Warrens the interwoven past grows more clouded with each generation, more jumbled as we multiply, but I remain certain of two things: that half the Warrens are pure evil and that I'm not.

Probably.

CHAPTER FOUR

■ ■ ■

Los Angeles was changing, but I still thought of it as the most glamorous refugee camp in the world. The way all of America was before it turned to war and industry. It was a city of a million luckless vagrants trying to get away from something back home. Dropping out on a world that hadn't delivered on many promises.

They wanted to rub shoulders with legends and stars and realize the vague sort of dream you have when you can't even think of a happy ending. Most of those folks ended up in the gutter or morgue or, worse, alone and drinking in bars like the Mermaid, hoping the world wouldn't follow them to the bottom of their glass of hooch.

I always went to bars like the Mermaid after a job, but the Mermaid was my favorite. This late at night it was quiet, and everybody minded their own business. I was the guy at the end of the bar all hunched up and trying to disappear into his overcoat. Flattened hat on worn bar top. Hank of hair dangling over the face of a born lemon-sucker. They were all my breed. My people. Drinking alone or in even lonelier pairs. The guilty. The condemned.

The Mermaid was grout in the ugly seam between Chinatown and more respectable parts. It had the feel of an expat bar in a foreign country. Electric Chinese lanterns glowing through the windows dueled with blinking neon Jugheimer and Old Glory beer signs. There was neediness to all the trappings. Behind the bar it was Kentucky bourbon and American flags and framed newspapers from '45 and '48 already yellowed by the cigarette smoke. Back when victory felt like deliverance.

I lit up a Bravo and looked at the photo of poor saint Harry S. I gave him a salute with my scotch and soda. Finished it off in two swallows, and the ice cubes clinked in the glass when I put it down.

I met my own reflection in the mirror behind the bar. Christ, I looked like shit. Was it killing Beau Reynolds? Was it the cancer? I knew where it snuck into me. I didn't like thinking about the war, but you don't get to pick when it comes back. It will hold you down and make you remember.

The bar began to sway, gently, like a ship on smooth seas, and I could see beyond the reflections of the blinking Chinese neon to an early morning aboard a steamer off the coast of Kyushu.

November 15, 1945. There was movement and light on the rushing black of the sea. Little ships were swarming out there. Red signals blinked among them, hypnotic flashes like those of the night squids in the Mediterranean. Excited men called out and rushed the gunwales. Assault boats. Landing craft. Some of them were coming closer. Landing craft for us. Beyond them, the bigger craft with the amtracks inside, bound for other ships and other units.

The excitement nearly broke into a riot as officers distributed dark glasses on cords and numbered tickets for the assault boats. Marines shouted questions and struggled to be heard. This was it. We were finally going to meet with Kyushu. No more kamikazes and suicide boats in the night. We'd look it in the face and howl.

"Put on the glasses!" came the cry of the watch officer. "Do not look directly at the target zone. Do not pick up souvenirs or drink water from within the area of effect. These things may be poisoned. Form in squads! Prepare to embark your assigned landing boat."

I was a sergeant in the United States Marine Corps. The Corps and Catholicism are two things they screw into you that don't come out. I shouted at my squad over the din and told the boys to ignore the watch officer and wear the glasses around their necks until we were in the landing craft.

I made a quick head count. Everyone was there, even the greenhorn looking like an artillery-sick Hun. We found our number, a gray scoop of a boat bouncing gently alongside the troopship, waiting for us at the bottom of a web of rope ladder. The assault ship's idling engine puffed out white smoke. The pilot waved up to me, and I could see he already wore black-lensed goggles.

I heard a distant droning above the shouting of men trying to organize. Somewhere, high above, a flight of bombers was passing toward Kyushu. A last gift for Tojo before we swam ashore.

Those goddamn whistles sounded again, and officers shouted at us to get over the sides and into the assault boats. Order crumbled. Men monkeyed and scrambled down into the darkness, hopefully into the scooped holds of the assault boats. All of mine made it. Many from other units must've ended up in the wrong boat in all that confusion. Some saps were wearing their dark glasses and fumbling blindly down the ropes. I could see some who fell into the sea and cried out for help, clinging desperately to the trailing ends of the webs. Nobody could help those poor bastards now. They'd have to wait for the crew of the troopship to fish them out.

■   ■   ■

The assault boat carrying my squad and another squad parted from the side of the troopship. We wouldn't miss that beast much, or so we always thought in these moments. It seemed so small within the converted freighter's holds and so vast from without, like a great iron temple scabbed with rust. In a moment its edifice passed from view.

There was only ocean and the assault craft around us. Light was beaming on the horizon, and the world was beginning to lighten. Our assault boat was part of a pack moving through the confusion of the troopships. The picket destroyers were ahead of us to take the fire for us when we got in closer to the landing beaches.

"Get your glasses on," I reminded the men.

We passed the silent monsters of the battleships and cruisers, their guns turned to face the day. Sailors waved their white caps and whistled and hooted. "Give 'em hell!" We were drenched with the spray off the scooped prow of the landing craft. We shivered, one man against the other, faces pale and tight with fear. It was so grim that I thought to make a joke. I was in the lead of the craft, just behind the landing ramp, so I turned and faced my squad.

"Man walks into a tailor," I said and then shouted it again to be heard over the noise of the engine. "Asks the tailor to make him a suit. Tailor says it'll take six weeks. Guy says, 'Six weeks!? It only took God six fucking days to make the whole world!' Tailor turns to him and says, 'Yeah, but have you seen how it looks lately?' "

A few guys tried to force a smile. Nobody laughed except for Bully, big Bully with the BAR. He hammed it up and threw back his head and laughed so big that I could see the fillings all the way back to his molars. As his mouth closed, his face was suddenly bright white. Pure white. The light's intensity swallowed the details of his face. I felt warmth against my back.

The light softened to golden and roiling red and lingered as though it was a flare burning very close to us, but I could see now it was at a great distance. Nearly the limit of the ocean's horizon. It was in the direction and of the intensity of the rising sun, but the sun could not ascend so quickly.

I squinted through the dark lenses of my glasses. I felt the boom of a massive detonation. It was followed by a howling wind that shook the landing craft and blew hot in our faces so mightily, we held fast to keep our helmets on our heads.

There was Kyushu. For the first time we saw the shivering mountain shadows of it. Distant houses and buildings atop the rocky bluffs were surrounded and backlit by fire. These structures bathed in radiance squirmed and became smoke. The light grew and curled and exterminated, and it made its shape known as a fiery storm capping a pillar rising high above the land and sea.

There was a second flash, beyond the horizon, and a second column of fire rose into view and pushed through the evaporating clouds. By this unearthly light the hundreds of landing boats took on a strange, indoor clarity, as if a spotlight was shone upon each. I could see the awe-struck faces in the ships nearby.

The sky was burning. The whole goddamn sky. Some men in my squad became sick at the sight. I felt it too. I'd been through hundred-hour barrages of artillery, and I'd lived in the bloody slop of trench warfare, and this raised gooseflesh on my arms. No device like this had come before this time. No horror manifested more completely. Not the artillery or the machine guns or even the gas.

"God Almighty," said a Marine from the other squad.

No one else spoke. We knew for certain what we were looking at. We knew it from the pictures of Hiroshima and Nagasaki. We had cheered that news, seemingly so long ago. Here was its reality. America's atom bombs were no longer a threat to tame the Emperor and his generals. They were no longer a demonstration of might. These were weapons with a military purpose. We bore witness to the granting of a wish.

"*Ichioku gyokusai*," a chaplain had once told me. "That's what the Japs call it. It's why they banzai charge and come at you with hand grenades. They believe in the majesty of annihilation. To die gloriously as a nation in one hundred million shards."

"Sick, fucking thing," I said, but nobody heard me in that landing craft, not even Bully.

Scorching heat and smoke and the cinder trees of Winton Beach awaited us. Day and night were forgotten. Kyushu existed in another phase, manmade, lit by the lingering pillars of fire as our boots met its shores. The generals and admirals were sure no resistance could survive our super weapons to fight the Marines of V Amphibious Landing Force.

They were wrong. Beyond the glassy sands, from cave and blackened bunker, from beneath every rock, came mortar and machine gun and 10,000 Japanese with *Banzai!* on their lips, to face the invaders of their precious world, to face us and die gloriously as a nation.

"Need anything else?"

I snapped back from the crunch of scorched sand and the howl of the naval artillery to Butch, the bartender of the Mermaid, making it damn clear he was tired of asking the question. He was grizzled and grandfatherly, only not the sort of grandfather you wanted. He was the grandfather who told the same story a hundred times and didn't like kids and only wanted to talk about how to get places and why things were better long ago.

"I'll have one more," I said, and I slid the empty glass across the bar. Butch grunted and took it. Yeah, I was feeling it, but I'd learned to handle my booze.

Butch slid over the glass of scotch. The napkin stuck underneath was marked with the silhouette of the sort of girl who would never set foot in a dive like the Mermaid. She could get a flat tire right outside, and she'd still walk ten blocks to use the phone at a junkyard.

I took one drink and started coughing. It was a rumbling, meaty cough that had nothing to do with the drink and everything to do with Kyushu. Butch didn't know that.

"If you're gonna lose your soup or something . . ." Butch finished the sentence by jabbing a finger in the direction of the filthy door of the restroom. I held up a hand until the coughing fit subsided.

"Ain't gonna puke." I tossed a dollar down. Butch swept a hand across the counter in a way that reminded me of a beach crab grabbing for a morsel. The dollar was gone. The tip was assumed.

I took my drink with me to the telephone booth in the back. It smelled a little like piss, so I lit a Bravo to cover the stench and closed the accordion door. The sounds of the bar were muted. My own ragged breathing seemed to echo. I put my nickel into the phone and gave the operator the telephone number.

The operator connected me to a line that buzzed like static on a radio for several seconds. There followed a strange series of clicks, leading into a silence that seemed to echo like the void inside an immense chamber. This was always the way when I placed my calls to Harlan Bishop.

"Mr. Bishop?" I said.

"Yes," he said, and his voice, undiminished by age, raised gooseflesh on my arms.

"The job is done," I said.

"I know," said Mr. Bishop. "The money is waiting for you at your office, as usual."

"I had a question for you." I was met with silence, so I continued. "There was an accident in Cranford this morning. I wanted to talk to you about it."

The silence seemed to grow louder.

"Mr. Bishop?"

"Yes. Why don't you come up to Chatholm Lodge tomorrow, and we can discuss this accident. Elias will tell you how to find us."

Before I could reply, there was another series of loud clicks. Bishop's manservant answered and explained how to find Chatholm Lodge. It was along the Pacific Coast Highway, north of Los Angeles in a wooded area somehow left undeveloped. The turn was marked as private property and identified only by a stone pillar and the letter *C*. Someone was to meet me at the gate hidden within.

"Eight o'clock tomorrow. It has its own lake. Very warm this time of year. Bring your bathing suit in case Mr. Bishop would like you to swim for him."

■ ■ ■

I cruised through the quiet suburban intersections and parked on the street outside a shingled bungalow. Red frame, cream-colored house. I was sure it was unlocked. Hawthorne had about as much crime as a forest preserve.

I stepped onto the sisal mat with the word *HOME* woven into the fibers in front of the door. I reached for the handle, stopped, slipped off my shoes, and picked them up in one hand. The door was unlocked. I stole inside, creeping through the darkened house, wary of the crowded lamps and sofas.

The ticking of a wall clock was louder than my footsteps on the carpet. I passed through the sunken living room and climbed the two steps up into the kitchen. The sweet smell of gardenias drifted through the open windows, and the kitchen was full of the lingering aroma of the last meal cooked on the stove.

In the dim light I could just make out the wood-carving of an Indian and an eagle on the wall of the hallway. I nearly bumped a tea table with a vase full of sparklers from the Fourth of July. The bedroom door was ajar. I pushed it open a little wider and stood in the doorway, looking down at the figure asleep in the bed.

Lynn was wearing my pajamas. She was slender and still pretty, but I was aware of her aging. I could see time stealing her away from me, too slow to watch but as sure as the erosion of mountains. How much longer? Thirty years? Thirty-five? I would be gone long before her.

Her brown hair spilled out around her on the pillow. Her lips were parted. As I watched, she stirred and turned onto her side.

I hung my coat and hat on the closet hook and set my shoes on the footstool. I undressed down to my underwear and black socks, and I lay down on the bed beside Lynn. She rolled onto her back.

"What time is it?" she said, her throat still glued together with sleep.

"Three-thirty."

"There's a Salisbury steak and mash under some foil." She spoke softly and without opening her eyes. "I doubt it's still good after nine hours."

"It's all right."

"Did you see the doctor?"

"Something happened today."

She opened her eyes and rolled onto her side to look at me. "What is it? What did the doctor say?"

"No, it isn't the doctor." I considered carefully how much to tell her. "Someone I knew a long time ago was killed. An old friend."

"That's horrible." Her hand rested on mine. "What happened?"

"They were murdered," I said. "Run down by a car. The police think it was an accident, but I'm certain it wasn't. I don't . . . I don't know where this is going to take me."

"It's dangerous, isn't it?"

"I don't know. It might take a while."

"You're holding something back from me." Lynn sighed. "I know. The more I know, the harder it gets."

"I just can't talk about it."

She sighed more emphatically and rolled onto her back.

"I can't fight with you about this anymore. You come home with these mysteries, you get depressed. I can tell it's dangerous, but you won't tell me why."

"Do you want me to not tell you at all?"

"I want you to tell me everything. You tell me half the problem, and you're just sharing your misery. I can't help you."

I used to pretend that I really wanted to tell her the truth and couldn't. Things got easier when it became automatic. I needed my lives compartmentalized, and when they mixed, no matter how hard I tried to control the mixture, it was explosive.

Lately I didn't tell Lynn much of anything. Since being chosen as the Judge and working for Mr. Bishop, I didn't have much to share. I didn't want to talk about the war. Even in my letters during the war I'd avoided the details of the fighting. I'd shut Lynn out of three-fourths of my life. No truth too small to be concealed.

She looked at me, brown eyes glassy in the dark, and touched my arm with her hand. "Did you go to the doctor?"

"Yes," I said. "It's fine. It's nothing. He said it will go away in time. Just scars from the gas the Japs used."

I held her gaze. She kissed me and slid her hand across my chest. Her body was hot beneath the blanket, and she sighed again, differently than before, and pressed herself against me. My hands sought the softness of her breasts. I kissed her and felt her fingers trailing down the scars on my side and stomach. I was tired and sore, but I found the energy for this.

I figured if I closed my eyes, I would picture Annie Groves, so I kept them wide open. I stared into Lynn's eyes and experienced her as my wife. It was brief and intense, and when we finished, we lay sweating and smiling on the unmade bed, my legs over hers. The fan turned slowly on the ceiling overhead. There was a night chill lingering in the air. Lynn's breasts were jeweled with her sweat.

"I'm glad you're all right," she said. "When you're gone, I worry about you. The longer you're gone, the more I worry." She stretched her arm lazily across the bed. Her fingers laced into the salted blond hair at my temple.

"Don't go," she said. "This mystery or whatever it is. Don't do it."

"No one else will," I said. It wasn't a lie.

"Please," she said, and her face was so twisted up with sadness that I resented it.

"I'll try," I said at last. "Maybe I can do it all from a desk."

She kissed me again. The gratitude in her eyes might have melted a softer heart. She slept in my arms, but I lay awake, staring at the ceiling, thinking about everything but her.

While Lynn snored, I returned to those first days on the Home Islands. They spilled out of my head and flowed across the ceiling in overlapping projections of films playing all at once. As soon as one scene came into focus, the next intruded and began playing over top.

We came off the landing ramps and shared horrors on a scale impossible to conceive in advance, sacrifices unbearable, piling one atop the other in strata of tangled metal and slain men. I fought hard and killed men and witnessed great heroics by my brothers and by the Japs. The company suffered heavy losses. Many were killed getting off the beach. All of us were wounded.

We climbed the ragged cliffs and beyond, into the wasteland, where no building or tree stood as it was before. The ground was blackened. Here and there we took cover behind the slumping masonry of a workshop or collapsed chimney.

The Japs we found were maniacs. Blinded and deafened by the bombs. Some couldn't even stand, but they fought us until we were close enough to see their burned faces. We battled with a single man crouching behind a pile of slag for nearly ten minutes. When we finally killed him with a grenade and overtook his position, we realized the slag was a blackened Jap tank. Bully forced open a hatch, and a gust of steam billowed out. The crew was cooked in there like pork in a Dutch oven.

The civilians came at us just as hard. Old men, women, and even children hurled bombs at trucks and attacked us at night using knives and farm tools. There were no orders about killing the civilians, but it was commonplace, even among my squad. The slightest suspicion and we killed them. What else could we do? We couldn't chance leaving them at our backs.

After two days we were covered in soot from the atom bombs. The Jap civilians were so small compared to us, so tiny and underfed. We had phrase books, but there was no communicating with them. Not by words. They did not react to us as if we were merely an invading army. They screamed and ran from the sight of us. Children wailed long after they'd fled from view.

The next day we left the ruins and passed into a dense forest. The trees blotted out the sky, and the air was cool and rich with strange, flowery smells. Monkeys called out warnings as we approached, and the singing birds fell silent whenever we drew near. It was disquieting. Even when there were no buildings to betray the Japanese architecture, I could feel the difference. I did not recognize the insects that crawled upon our arms or the plants that we passed by.

The morning of the second day in the forest I climbed a tree and gazed out at a nearby hill. A huge bird took flight. It seemed golden in the morning light, and its wings beat slowly over the tops of blue-green trees that lent the air their perfume. The strangeness of the place was oppressive. In that moment I felt as if I stood in prehistory or upon the face of another planet.

■   ■   ■

The next day our task was to capture a hill to create an opening for the regular Army. We took the damned hill after a bloody battle with armed Japanese civilians—school children and their teachers. We worked alongside the few prisoners we took to bury all the dead and then we made them help us cut a road for the trucks.

The Army used the road, but refused to advance past Kushikino. There was more hard fighting ahead. It was street fighting with long artillery duels and messy block-to-building engagements that reminded me of the awful newsreels the Soviets smuggled out of Stalingrad. The Japs just didn't want to quit on Kushikino.

Tanks finally arrived from the reserve division, and these broke the stalemate. We were too weary to cheer or wave. The column of tanks ascended the path into the mountains, and we followed to clear out the artillery positions. The Japs had built an entire complex of tunnels in the mountains facing Kushikino, and so it took several more days of heavy fighting.

Our entire division, or what remained of it, followed the tanks north and came upon the mountains as a flood. We broke into smaller units, companies at first, then platoons, and streamed into the foothills and up the slopes, north toward Kagoshima Sendai. Our final objective was to cut off southern Kyushu from the north.

We passed into the place where the second atomic bomb had fallen. By then we'd learned of others, falling in support of the Army and the Anzacs. Seven in all. This dead place was just another small town without even a name on our maps. It was once an airfield and mustering point for a Japanese division; now it was a charred valley of melted trucks and roads covered in ash.

As we passed through this valley, we took on the character of the ruins. Soot once more covered our faces and clothes. The whites of our eyes and our teeth stood out against the black of our faces. We fought for a day in the ruins of a hospital against a militia of half-blind burn victims. These men had not moved from this ruined place since the bomb had fallen weeks earlier.

They were like the feral survivors of a shipwreck stranded on an island long ago. Even as they fired at us, we could see they were dying from the bomb's poison. Their heads were wrapped in soiled bandages, and their mouths were bloody and toothless. Even so, they killed several in our platoon. Even the invalids, hidden away in ditches and concealed beneath toppled walls, laid hammers against the firing pins of artillery shells to take their toll in blood.

We were glad to leave that valley behind on the following day. We climbed out, up a misty mountain road bracketed by cliff and a forest fallen and scorched by the heat of the bomb. We overtook a large group of refugees without warning. The elderly and mothers carried their livelihood in bundles upon their backs. Their children marched along behind them like ducklings. The children cried at the fearsome look of us, and the women spoke curses I could not understand.

"*Oni! Oni!* American!" one woman said. Her face was livid with burns. The bird-squawk of her voice carried down the line, and others shouted it. "*Oni!* American!"

As the cry spread, there was a great commotion, and many of the women hurled their children over the side of the road and off the mountain. The poor tots screamed in fear, and their tiny bodies tumbled into the mist shrouding the valley below. Their mothers were silent and leaped to join their sons and daughters. We witnessed suicides so often that we were rarely moved by them, but this was different, absolute nihilism.

We panicked and tried to stop them. Some men pleaded and stood in their way; Bully desperately searched for his phrase book. I fired my pistol into the air, but this only sent more of them charging off the cliff with their sons and daughters.

"Oni! Oni!" the remaining women called after us as we continued past the refugees, into the mountains, into an alien world, precious and fragile, glimpsed and now ending.

We never fought for Sendai. Our company was kept out of it to rest and refit. We bivouacked and gained back some of the weight we'd lost. They brought us mail, and we read our letters and tried to laugh about what we'd just been through. I wrote back to Lynn. I tried to imagine myself a tourist rather than an invader and did a lousy job describing the sights and smells of the country. I wrote her about the mist in the mountains and the huge bird that seemed to be made of gold. I lay in a hammock at night, beneath a mosquito net pilfered from a Jap house, listening to the strange hum of the insects and the rustle of rats in the grass.

The morning after Sendai fell, a jeep drove up the muddy track to our tents. It was a runner from Battalion HQ. He was a skinny sort, with a big Adam's apple and a warbling voice. He had orders to bring me, alone, to the HQ in the new Sendai airfield.

The airfield was just being built, mostly tents and a single observation tower with a radio mast. Fuel and supply trucks were convoying from the south. The close-air-support planes that had helped us during the fight for Kushikino were re-based here. The pilots were tanned and clean, smiling like film stars, imports from some island airbase we'd probably hacked for them out of a godforsaken island jungle three months ago. I couldn't resent them. I'd seen what happened if they had to bail out and the Japs got them. Even the farmers would cut them to pieces and string them up.

Colonel Ainsley's command tent was dimly lit and smelled of lamp oil. There were two men seated at a table so small, it was surely intended for children. They hunched over a pair of black radio sets, focused on the dials and their notepads of white paper to the exclusion of everything else in the world. Several Marine officers were conferring around a map table representing the area of operations of V Amphibious. I recognized Ainsley by the bronze egg of his bald head. He stood with parade posture beside his map table. I couldn't tell if he was listening to or ignoring the officers discussing the disposition of the Japanese forces.

"Sergeant Cord," said Ainsley without even looking at me, "you've been requested by someone else. Give him what he needs."

"It's good to see you."

I sought the source of the voice in the dimness of the tent and came face-to-face with a duplicate. Another Warren. It was a startling thing to be reminded of what I was. Only in the throes of war was it possible for me to forget my immortal nature.

The man smiled in a friendly manner and extended his hand to me. "Lieutenant Milo Gardener."

Scant years separated us, but this Lt. Gardener, dressed in the uniform of an Army Paratrooper, distinguished himself by a deep scar running from his jaw up to the severe part in his pomade-flattened hair. He seemed softer than I imagined myself. Paler. He did not seem the brutal sort made for war, and yet he was relaxed and confident in greeting me.

"This is against the Covenant," I said, though I shook Lt. Gardener's hand.

"It's good you take your duties as Judge seriously. I know well enough you don't generally enforce it on the battlefield. That's partly why I'm here. The Covenant has been broken, seriously, and I am here to execute the orders of General Shiftman. Are you familiar with him?"

I knew of Shiftman. An elder Gideon, forty years out of the Pool, he hid his identity behind dyed blond hair and a ridiculous Victorian beard. He was as vain as them all, pompous, a poor strategist, but he held his lips close to the ear of FDR and probably Truman. He was one of the driving forces behind the separation of the Air Force from the Army in 1941. He was all mixed up in the atomic bomb business as well. It was disconcerting enough to meet a fellow Warren in person, but to meet one who served a master like Shiftman was a particular stripe of unpleasantness.

"What do you want, Lieutenant?"

"I am new to the theater and need a man familiar with its perils. A man I can trust and who understands what is at stake. No one fits the bill better than you."

"Excuse me, sir. How about you quit playing me like a piano and tell me what's at stake?"

Gardener took out a small leather-bound diary from his breast pocket. I could see that its pages were stuffed with postcards and photographs and bits of newspaper. From its pages he handed me a small, yellowing photograph. It was a gauzy military portrait of a young Japanese man in an officer's uniform of the Imperial Army. He was handsome and impeccably groomed. He posed with the confidence of the Japanese military aristocracy. I turned the photograph over but could not read the Japanese characters on the back.

"Lt. Col. Tomo Ishii," Gardener explained. "I've pursued him from Europe, believing him to carry secrets that imperil the fabric of our country. Proof of what we are, to begin with. Our ships and men hounded him on a long journey through the unkindest parts of the globe. I lost his trail only recently. I hoped him dead, but he has resurfaced here."

"Kyushu?"

"Here," said Gardener. "In the prisoner holding camp near Winton Beach, his military ID was collected and logged. But he's not in the camp. I've been over those sick and miserable creatures a half dozen times. But I think I know where we can find him. I need you to help track him through this unfamiliar terrain."

"I'm a Marine, not a tracker."

"West of Sendai, in the mountains that stand between the Marines and the Imperial Army. Difficult terrain and dangerous times. His unit maintains a fortified military hospital, formerly a lumber mill, in the forests of Mt. Kansen. We must recapture Ishii before he can retreat to the safety of his unit there."

"What is this unit?"

Lt. Gardener's lips tightened into a thin frown, and he gazed down at his hands. "Unit 731."

"I'm not familiar with that unit," I said. "Commandos?"

"I wish these were only men of arms." Gardener brushed away a buzzing fly. "Long ago you and I shared a primitive morality of absolutes. We believed in the concept of pure good and pure evil, a childish notion that does not account for the nuances of reality. Sergeant, Unit 731 is that rarest thing, without nuance or gradation. It is pure evil."

Gardener took the photograph back from me and regarded its face.

"And Lt. Col. Ishii brings them the seeds of our destruction."

■ ■ ■

A car honked out on the street. I was unsure whether I was awake and remembering the war or asleep and dreaming my memories. It was still dark outside, but on the cusp of dawn. I carefully rolled Lynn onto her back and got up from the bed.

I padded across the hall, catching a glance of my blue-gray face in the mirror as I pissed into the dark void of the toilet by memory. As I emerged back into the hall, a loud jangle brought me wide awake. The phone was ringing in the living room. I stubbed my toe on the way to answer it, falling onto the couch and grabbing at my throbbing big toe as I cradled the receiver to my ear.

"Yeah, what?"

"Casper Cord." The voice was a whisper.

"Yes, who is this?"

"Listen to me. They're coming for me. I don't have much time. Listen to me. I know what it is."

"Who is this? Tell me who it is, and I'll listen."

"Beau Reynolds."

I wasn't fond of hearing from duplicates, least of all ones that I'd just sent back to the soup.

"Mr. Reynolds, you're not supposed to be using that—"

Distant shouts and barking dogs echoed down the phone line. An involuntary thrill of anxiety prickled my neck and arms.

"They're coming. I can hear them. They brought the dogs. Oh, Christ." There was a sound like a chair or bed being moved. "It won't hold them. This place is under lockdown. It's . . ."

"Where are you?" My throbbing toe was forgotten. I scrambled in the dark for pen and paper. "What's the address?"

"I'm in Spark. It's . . . there are no people here anymore. The duplicates are . . ."

"What?"

"They're doing something with the Pool. Digging. I don't know what . . . it's not important."

Loud impacts against hollow wood. Shouting voices very close now. Dogs barking so loudly, it was difficult to hear Beau Reynolds, but the panic in his voice was clear enough.

"I've been through to the other side."

"What do you mean?"

Splintering wood. The loud clatter of the telephone being dropped.

"The blackness that gnaws at you! The memory that was taken out of our heads! I've been through!" Beau Reynolds shouted. "It goes all the way through."

Cold swept over Casper and raised gooseflesh on his arms. He knew the emptiness Reynolds was babbling about. There was a memory of something or somewhere that had been taken away from him the first time he was thrust into the Pool.

"Hold him." A new voice, deep and dispassionate.

There followed the confused noise of violent struggle. Men grunted, and I could hear objects being overturned and knocked into.

"Some of them remember it!" shouted Reynolds. "Some of the Warrens! Remember what we were all supposed to forget! The Pool! The grasshopper isn't—"

"Hold his arms!"

"No! Get back!" cried Reynolds, his voice distant from the telephone.

Whatever he said next was lost to a sound like a small electric motor revving. Reynolds began to scream incoherently. The motor strained. There was a grinding crunch and a pressurized pop followed by quiet except for several people breathing and a sound as though a cup of water was being slowly emptied onto the floor.

There was a soft rustling against the phone.

"Are you still there?" It was the man with the calm, deep voice.

"Yes," I said.

"What is your name?"

"Doug MacArthur."

"If you told me, it would spare some trouble," the man said.

"That's not at the top of my list. What did you do to Reynolds?"

"Pray that we have more use for you."

The line went dead.

CHAPTER FIVE

■ ■ ■

Some nights, no matter how hard it is to fall asleep, your body just gives up. Some nights you have to medicate yourself with a few belts of Brown Barrel. I opted for both and woke tangled up in the sheets as if I'd lost a fight with them. Maybe I had. I sure felt as if I'd gone ten rounds with somebody.

I rolled onto my side of the bed. Gone. Lynn was gone, and I was alone. At least I didn't have any nightmares about that fucking grasshopper or wake up coughing. It was bright and warm in the bedroom, and I flopped onto my back again and lay with the curtain-yellowed daylight across my chest. I heard Lynn in the kitchen, at the stove. She had something hissing in a pan. Bacon and eggs, by the smell of it.

She was talking. I could make out her voice but not her words. By the tone of her voice I knew that she was addressing Frank, the black tomcat that slept in the bed when I wasn't around and stayed out of sight when I was. Not that I ever did anything to that damn cat; it just didn't like me.

I leaned my head off the bed so I could see into the kitchen. Lynn was standing at the sink, showered and dressed, her red apron tied around her waist. Stocking lines down the back of her legs. The cat arched its back as it rubbed against one. Patti Page was on the radio in the living room. Lynn rubbed at her cheek with fingers reddened by hot water. She was beautiful; the moment was poured-amber perfect.

Voices intruded from the backyards outside. A woman was yelling to her child. Cars honked on the street. The moment was slipping away. The more I tried to cling to it, the more acutely I experienced its loss. Lynn began to run water in the kitchen. There was a distant plane flying overhead. The moment was pulled into the turning gears. It was gone forever.

I sat up, and the muck shifted in my lungs. That started the coughing. Lynn called out to me, but I was already on my feet, stumbling into the bathroom. I choked clotted black and yellow and red into the sink. Ran the shower to cover the noise. When I managed to stop the coughing, I shaved with the Remington and cleaned myself, finally coming awake beneath the hot stream of the shower. I spit a little more into the shower drain. There was blood smearing the phlegm. As it swirled, I recalled Beau Reynolds ebbing away in a hotel shower.

"I've gone through," I said, repeating his words. "Where did you go, Reynolds? How did you get there?"

Who was the other man on the telephone? Someone from the government? One of Bishop's men? I was Bishop's man. I was the dog he turned loose on the people he wanted hurt. I knew he used the Covenant as an excuse, but I kept taking those fucking envelopes.

I got out from under the water and wrapped a towel around my waist. I could see the scars on my body even though the mirror was fogged up. Pink and brown across my chest, a hint of darker keloid at my elbow.

"Ham and eggs," called Lynn from the kitchen.

"Be right out."

I crossed the hall and closed the door to the bedroom. I dressed in a gray flannel suit with a red silk tie patterned with white flowers. Lynn had bought it for me when we were still dating. Before the war. The first time I slipped the tie around my neck, it was for a date with her. We went to a dance hall in Santa Monica along the board-walk. She had a pink rose in her hair. We swing danced until my shoulders were sore and my shirt was unfashionably damp with sweat.

We left laughing and touching each other just because we'd reached that point in our relationship. I'd diced away my money, so she bought us ice cream to cool us down. It was humid, and the city smelled like rain. We walked along the boardwalk talking about Boris Karloff as Frankenstein. She had a dynamite monster impression.

We went down to the beach and played in the moonlit oil of the surf. A Mexican Indian made us a concoction from fresh oranges and tequila, and we got drunk and chased each other in the water. She took off her dress and was in her slip, soaking wet among the breakers, kissing me. It felt strange with the drink seller watching, so we walked back to her friend's car. I broke into it with a wire, and we tried to make love on the backseat. Too many people. Too many honking cars.

Lynn Short was Catholic and I was a mutt, so we did things her way. While I was on leave from my first deployment we had a big wedding at St. Philomena's. I wore my dress uniform. Her family packed the church. There were crying sisters, her mom, and a seemingly endless procession of aunts, uncles and cousins. I didn't have a family, so invited a few buddies from the Corps. Bully was the only one that showed up.

At the reception Bully and I stood together trying to talk. All the connections we had made were marinated in bad memories. We could joke in the trenches, but standing next to him at the reception made the wedding seem small and unimportant compared to the places we'd already seen together. We stood there sipping Jugheimers and watching Lynn move through her huge, overjoyed family.

"She's pretty," said Bully.

She was ecstatic, her smile so wide and earnest it was almost painful to think I was responsible. I tried to fix that expression in my memory. I was afraid I might live a thousand years and I wanted that one thing to stick with me through it all.

I even managed to forget about Annie for a day.

I tied a half-Windsor and adjusted the length until the tip of the diamond touched the top of my belt. Lynn was already cleaning her plate in the kitchen, so I came up behind her and hugged her and kissed her cheek. The Deco clock above the kitchen table said eight.

No more time to lounge in the morning. I was already late to meet Mr. Bishop, and I hadn't even set foot out the door. I put on my hat and overcoat.

"Please," Lynn said. "Sit down and have breakfast like a normal human being."

"I'm late. Sorry, sweetheart."

"Late for what?" She followed me to the door. "You remember what I said, mister detective. No more danger. I need you to stick around."

I swept through the screen door, and it closed behind me with a dramatic creak and bang worthy of a film production.

"Damn it, I mean it this time," she called out.

I didn't answer her.

■ ■ ■

The gate was a decorative bramble of black iron, and its tangled vines formed the word CHATHOLM. The drive was blocked by four black sedans and a squad of serious men in serious suits. Their pump shotguns convinced me not to argue when they told me to get out of the car.

Their leader was a man with a surplus of forehead, little squinting doll eyes, and splotchy sunburn around his hairline. He introduced himself as Agent D'Agostino and held up a badge as proof.

"Name?" he demanded.

"Casper Cord. I'm invited."

"I'll need to see some ID."

I handed over my wallet. He took out my license and flipped it back and forth, studying me as if I was a kid trying to buy a carton of Old Glory with his dad's license.

"Can I go inside?"

"Absolutely," said D'Agostino, "as soon as we've searched your vehicle."

They went top to bottom and didn't find the smuggler's hold. I thought about telling them but just figured they'd keep the heater and maybe never give it back.

"You guys work for the government?" I asked.

They did, but they weren't saying it. Somebody official was inside, and these guys were his detail. Nobody in government was taking any chances since Truman.

I remember when it happened. I had a paper bag full of groceries in the back of a cab. Heard it on the radio. The driver pulled over to the side of the road, and a long sigh blew out of his mouth. He was a vet too. Regular Army in the bloody Hürtgen Forest. We sat with the rain beating on the roof of the cabbie's Buick, shipwrecked on the same island by the news. Harry S. Truman shot dead by a Jap anarchist fresh out of the camps.

"It's clean," declared D'Agostino. "I'll take you in."

The G-men opened the gate and waved me through to the red brick drive shaded by old-growth trees. D'Agostino got behind the wheel of my car and drove. We passed through a forest, and the morning sun took on the shape and rhythm dictated by the overhanging branches.

"Are you here for Mr. Bishop or someone else?" I lit up a Bravo and blew smoke out the car window. "President Barkley here or something?"

"No."

"You guys aren't the friendliest bunch, are you?"

"No."

Glad I had the overcoat to keep out the chill.

D'Agostino circled my car around a bronze statue of somebody familiar and parked on the cobblestones just outside the broad steps leading up to the lodge. I followed him up the stairs to the double doors. Each of the ten-foot doors was a piece of wood elaborately carved with images of wild animals.

The inside of the lodge was dim and high-ceilinged, reminding me of an English hunting lodge, but everything was elevated to Teutonic extremes, as if someone had covered the wood-paneled rooms in glue and upended an animal mass grave. Severed heads loomed above us, and the bony branches of antlers created ossuary brambles on the walls.

We descended from the animal kingdom and passed through galleries filled with violent trophies of history. There were tapestries looted from Rhineland castles, paintings of German masters from both wars, and crude, bug-eyed statues from Japan's earliest history. According to one placard, I passed by a Chrysanthemum *datejime* dated to 1947 and still stained, supposedly, with Hirohito's blood. There were artifacts of Rome I'm sure the Vatican dearly missed. Mannequins posed in alcoves wearing military uniforms that looked to date back three-quarters of a century. I'd worn some of them myself.

D'Agostino led me to a door being held open by a white-gloved attendant. We passed from the dark, castlelike interior of the lodge into the sunlit majesty of a grand dining hall. I've got to admit to being a bit taken by the spectacle myself. Bishop's Berghof was a tribute to American industry.

A triptych of glass panes, each ten feet wide and thirty feet tall, half-covered by rolling shutters, created a view of azure waters that seemed to merge the huge room with the surface of a lake. The hills surrounding the lake were decorated with trees so dense and perfect, I expected to see a model train come chugging through.

The hall was filled with enough tables and chairs to entertain a hundred guests and still have room to cut a rug. I'd never seen that kind of money thrown around on a house. Not outside of Europe and all those old palaces. Only one table in the hall was occupied, near the doors to the kitchen, and the voices of the men seated there echoed in the empty space. White-coated attendants swarmed around them offering coffee and condiments from silver trays for what smelled like an extravagant breakfast.

Harlan Bishop was at the head of the table, gesturing with his cigarette holder and shedding ash all over his plate. He saw us coming, but our approach did not interrupt his conversation. A giant of a man wrapped in a tuxedo stood behind Bishop's high-backed wheelchair. That was Elias, his footman. The one who'd given me the directions.

Seated around the table was a well-dressed collection of politicians, potentates, and tycoons. I recognized some, like Ross Ogilvy, the head of Ogilvy Electric, and Stanley Pearce, from the railroad, from seeing their pictures in the newspapers.

I also knew Eustace DeWitt, a weevil of a man elevated by shady patronage to become the Republican senator from New Mexico. His family and the Gideons went back to the turn of the century when the senator's father ran New Mexico and helped guide a new artillery depot to the vicinity of Spark.

There was a small bald man with a pug face and thick spectacles who seemed familiar, but I could not place him. The other men, and there were several, were strangers to me, except for one: Ethan Bishop.

Harlan Bishop was, as far as I knew, the oldest living Gideon. His hair was almost gone, and his face was wrinkled and spotted with age. As he approached the inevitable end of his life, he had taken to cultivating various Gideon duplicates in the role of his "son," Ethan Bishop.

These Ethans only stuck around as long as they were useful. If they stepped out of line or developed too much of their own personality, Harlan would "retire" them and bring in another Gideon to play the role. Harlan Bishop never said it, but I figured his intent was to recast himself as his son and inherit his own business when he died.

His twisted scheme was designed to weave through the loopholes in the Covenant and did not violate any specific provisions, except for the fact that Harlan and Ethan often shared a room. That was an offense worthy of my Stillman. Hard to put a bullet into the old man when he'd been running his Ethan racket back when he picked me to be the Judge.

Ethan Bishop—the current Ethan Bishop, for however long he'd held the office—motioned for me to sit at his side. Such a gap of decades separated Harlan from Ethan that their resemblance to an outsider was more familial than remarkable.

"Father," said Ethan, interrupting the conversation around the table. "Your man is here from Los Angeles."

"Mr. Bishop," said D'Agostino, who was behind my seat, "I'm sorry to interrupt you all here. Mr. Cord has arrived. He was on the guest list."

Harlan Bishop turned his rheumy eyes to D'Agostino and blinked once. D'Agostino nodded, as if that was enough of an acknowledgment, and left the way he'd come. The conversation resumed with no introduction or mention of my presence.

"So did you give him the televisions?" The question came from a DeWitt.

"Yes," said Harlan. "Six Lumilux 50s. Top of the line. Had them flown from California to Washington and sent out technicians to set them up for the staff and in two of the bedrooms. He loved them, I'm told. Too bad the only broadcasting in color is out of a CBS shop in Albany."

There was scattered laughter.

"Technology is the hope that will see this nation through the darkness of war." Harlan put a serious point to it. "Those televisions and washers and air-conditioned automobiles are worth a squadron of bombers. The dream of tomorrow is what we're selling now. People need to believe in the future for America to work."

Those who laughed before now saluted the point with raised glasses and a chorus of, "Hear, hear."

"What about you, Ronald?" Ethan asked the man sitting to DeWitt's left. "Have you any interesting follies from South America?"

The man seated to DeWitt's left was younger, handsome, with blond hair, a strong jaw, and blue eyes. He actually looked like a younger, healthier version of me, though he was for certain no Warren.

"Nothing amusing, I'm afraid," said Ronald. "The matter grows more serious by the day. The workers have been infiltrated by Communists, and they have notions of revolution."

"Mr. Whiteacre runs our South American enterprise," explained Ethan. "He's father's protégé, but I'm afraid he's run afoul of the natives."

"There are enough good Americans down there to deal with any insurrection," said Whiteacre. "We'll hold the line with arms if need be."

"No, no," said Harlan, and he wiped at the crumbs around his mouth. "Violence against the workers is antithetical to our goals. The Germans, the Russians, they invade and conquer. We must convince the people to volunteer their labor and resources."

"There has been talk, serious talk, of nationalizing our factories," said Whiteacre. "If this coup business succeeds, I'm afraid we will have no alternative."

Harlan shook his head, "War is reserved for governments—not people—who stand in the way of progress. States and ideologies seize assets and nationalize our privately-owned factories, not people."

"Unrest here, as well," said the bespectacled man who was familiar to me.

"Will Paulus," Ethan introduced. "He's the senator here in California."

"Acting," said Paulus. "Until they sort things out in the special election."

Paulus was terse, rising to shake my hand but clearly not to be distracted. He was short and paunchy and had dark eyebrows and hair. Greek, maybe, but far enough up the family tree to pass for white.

"The economy," Paulus continued, "still hasn't recovered from the crash of '29, and there's been a great deal of agitating for worker movements. The Socialist party has several viable men up for congress."

"I'm sure you'd know all about that, being a Democrat," said Harlan.

"You start shooting in South America, and there will be solidarity protests," said Paulus. "Maybe a boycott or worse."

"It won't come to that," said Harlan.

"If it does?"

"So they'll boycott." Harlan seemed amused by the thought. "They'll have their pickets and burn their effigies and go home in automobiles we built and brag on telephones we sell that use lines we laid. They'll eat food picked on our plantations because it's cheaper. Because it's easier. Because we are the engine of progress and efficiency, the provider of the American way of life, and their short-sighted sanctimony is nothing but a stone tied 'round this country's neck."

"The Communists are parasites to progress in all their incarnations," said Whiteacre. "We go into their impoverished countries and give them jobs and running water, and they thank us by seizing our factories. It's theft, is what it is."

"Assault," said Harlan. "Robbery by force. Corporations may be Creatures of Statute, but they enjoy all the rights of a person."

"Yes," agreed Paulus. "They're psychopaths."

I wasn't buying what Paulus was saying. When a psychopath busts out of the loonie bin and starts chopping people up you always have the option of filling them with lead. Good luck finding a casket that could fit a corporation. "There's nothing lunatic about self-interest," said Whiteacre. "I promise you, if Ecuador and Guatemala nationalize, it will mean war. I'm sorry, Mr. Bishop, but we cannot let them win, or Mexico will follow; then they'll be in the streets here, demanding we hand over the fruits of our labor. In San Pedro. Is that what you would have, Senator Paulus?"

DeWitt spoke up. "The, uh, that railroad business, Harlan. Is it keeping to schedule? When will your power plant be built?"

Ogilvy and another man began to speak, but Harlan cut his gaze in my direction.

"More of this later," he said. He gestured to Elias, who wheeled him away from the table. "I need to speak with our new arrival. Come along, Mr. Cord."

"Don't I get any breakfast?" I asked, earning a reproachful glare from Elias.

Harlan Bishop's office was austere by comparison to the grand architecture of Chatholm Lodge. It was quite large but otherwise unembellished.

As we entered, we passed a scale model of Bishop's big industrial project out in San Pedro. I lingered to study the four hyperbolic towers that dwarfed the surrounding architecture. Word was, it was going to be atomic, the first commercial reactor, right in LA's backyard. It was belligerently huge, swallowing up most of San Pedro and Wilmington with its worker housing and utopian commercial developments.

"Big project?" I asked.

"Yes," said Harlan. "Senator Paulus, the Communist sympathizer, has proved to be a bit difficult. Overly preoccupied with safety and pay grades, extending the government where it doesn't belong, when jobs are what Los Angeles needs. The man fears atoms. Just another coward afraid of progress. I've asked my son to deal with him to prevent things from unraveling."

His son. A lie he was so used to telling, he told it even to me.

Bishop's desk was a simple piece and his displayed antiquities limited to a few trinkets. He parked his wheelchair behind it and, with a bit of help from Elias, got up on his feet and took hold of an ivory-handled walking cane.

"Leave us," he said to his manservant.

The brooding giant departed. Harlan opened French doors onto a balcony and ambled out into the heavy morning air. The view was bounded by an imposing wall of ancient, black trees. Their leaves formed a canopy above us and the sun blinked through the leaves. The forest intruded on every sense.

"I don't favor the fir trees," he said. "I wanted Redwoods. For once I was told I couldn't have something. They are very particular about where they grow."

I joined him at the railing. The trees creaked like the timbers of a ship on a rolling sea. The sound of their leaves was an ocean over our heads.

"Tell me about this accident in Cranford." Harlan Bishop put aside the cane and leaned on the railing.

"There was a woman killed. Her name was Holly Webber. Are you familiar with her?"

"No. Should I be?"

"That's not for me to say, but you would have recognized her. She was Annabelle Groves."

"That cannot be." He stood up straight and grasped my lapel in his bony claw. "You think I'm a fool? You taunt me with this? You're a sick fish. Demented. I had . . . I hadn't thought of her in years."

"I can't say I believe that."

"Now listen here, Judge." His hand quivered. "You cannot rub that name in my face and expect me to take it lightly."

"This ain't some prank. The girl was Annie Groves. Real as a brick."

"How can this be?" he asked.

"I'm asking you that."

"Of course." He let go of me. "I apologize. Perfectly reasonable of you, considering the history between us." He backed away. "No, I assure you that I do not know Holly Webber, nor how she came to die. There must be an explanation. Have you gone to the police?"

"I'm investigating it."

"Yes, you must. I'll pay you your usual fee, cover all your expenses. Get to the bottom of this, Mr. Cord. Keep me informed. You've always upheld the duties of your office with such respect and thoroughness. I trust you to do the same in this matter."

I thanked him, and he walked me back through his office.

"I must admit, I rarely let my temper get the better of me these days, but the thought that Annie Groves has come and gone once more . . ." He shook his head. "Well, I can hardly stand it."

"Those responsible will pay their due," I said.

He nodded and asked, "Is there anything else?"

Yes. There was a late-night telephone call placed to my house by Beau Reynolds. There was the sound of a power drill and claims he'd gone through to the other side. There was fear in the voice of a man who should not ever know fear, because he couldn't die.

"That's all for now," I said. "I'll be in touch."

■   ■   ■

I left Chatholm with none of my questions answered, but I was glad to have a paycheck attached to this. Paying the bills can be erratic when your only job is feeding bullets to misbehaving duplicates. It's the sort of secret-inside-a-secret work you can't exactly put on a job application. We were three months behind on the mortgage. Two months on the electric. Lynn wanted things but wouldn't ask because she knew we were broke.

I decided to swing by the office for the envelope of cash Bishop always slipped under the door after a job. I could make my stop at the county morgue after. As I was turning off the highway, I noticed a black Cadillac that seemed to be shadowing my every move. I made some last-second turns to see if it would follow, and it did, pursuing me all the way to Melrose. Maybe Bishop had decided to put someone on me to make sure I was hard at work, or maybe there was someone else who wanted a piece of the action.

I decided to give it to them. I knew a dead-end alley off Vine. Practically put the

Tudor up on two wheels turning into it. Knocked over a trash can and screeched to a stop. I popped the Stillman out of its compartment and aimed it across the seat and out the back window of the coup. Be a shame to have to replace the glass, but better than getting plugged myself.

The Cadillac appeared at the end of the alley, stopping but not turning in behind me. It sat idling ominously and blocked the only way out. The windows were colored black and hid the occupants from view. Maybe this hadn't been my best plan. I thumbed the hammer back on my iron. Unless they had a bazooka in that car, I'd at least get a couple of them.

With a screech of its white-walled tires and the smoke of burned rubber, it sped out of view.

"Chickens," I said, and I stowed the gun.

■ ■ ■

My office was a glorified phone booth on the basement level of an apartment building. It was across the hall from the superintendent's apartment and right below a fat Polish couple who sounded like they were raising hippos. Nice folks, though. Gave me a delicious box of jelly doughnuts a couple of years ago around Lent, but I never returned the favor, so I never got another box.

A single recessed window provided me with a creeping rectangle of sunlight and a view of the sidewalk at foot level. On slow days—and they were almost all slow days by design—I'd sit around trying to imagine the people attached to the hooves clopping past the window.

There was one lamp and one filing cabinet and one bookshelf and one desk with one swivel chair for me and one raggedy old hotel chair for clients who never visited. The whole shamus routine was a bluff. A put-on for Lynn and for my cop buddies. My real work was being the Judge. We didn't used to have it this way, but at some point I guess Harlan Bishop decided that, since the Judges kept walking out on him, he'd better start paying them.

I picked up the envelope and counted the lettuce. There was dust on the radio set. This place was turning into a museum. No time to sit around and flip the dials. I was going to meet a special girl.

■ ■ ■

At the morgue I blew a kiss to the doll behind the desk and headed downstairs to where they kept the stiffs on ice. I was greeted by Angelo Pappas, the nicest coroner in the state of California. He was fatherly and stout, with laugh lines etched deeply in his face and big hands that seemed to belong to a giant. He hugged me and smooched me European style on both cheeks and asked how Lynn was doing.

"She's well enough," I said. "Keeping busy."

"Still trying for a baby?"

Yeah, sure. Tearful phone calls with the doctor. Late-night talks wondering why we couldn't conceive. Maybe it was the radiation from the war. She took it hard. It was me, of course, but I couldn't spill the truth.

"Still trying," I said.

Angelo unwittingly dug his knife deeper. "Family is the most important thing. I don't know where I would be without my girls. You'll make a good dad, and Lynn, such a beautiful mother."

"I would love to have a coffee with you someday, talk all this over, but I'm afraid I'm here on business."

"I was afraid you would say that." Angelo glanced back at the door to the morgue. "If it was just you and me, I would give you whatever you want, but there is a problem. I was told to keep you out."

"Who? Kapinski? To hell with him."

"It's impossible this time. That body, the Webber girl—"

"Yes. I'll only take five minutes."

"You misunderstand." Angelo put one big paw on my shoulder. He spoke *sotto voce*. "She is gone."

"What?"

"The morgue is a crime scene. Someone has taken her body."

CHAPTER SIX

■ ■ ■

There were no clues or witnesses to put me onto the trail of whoever looted Holly Webber from one of Angelo's drawers, but at least I knew someone was trying to cover their tracks. They'd managed to cut off one avenue of approach. I wasn't going to sit idle while they cut off another.

Holly Webber wasn't in the phone book. I'd already looked and knew that much. I had the registration tag on that little Cushman step-through to go on and the fact that she was a waitress. A fin in the right hands will buy you a lot of answers in this economy, and an old county clerk by the name of Fletcher was taking my money. He'd coughed up the address attached to the Cushman's plate.

Holly Webber resided in South Los Angeles, in the old apartments. South LA was one of the only places not ruled by the housing regulations written to keep out undesirables. Covenants they called them, but a different sort than the kind I followed. No Negroes, no Chinese or Japs, and in some places, no Irish or Jews. In South LA the blacks were allowed to live side by side with the whites. Most of the whites chose to leave.

I drove past the Negroes working in the city. Porters and the like. It was strange seeing them by the dozens, dressed in everyday clothes, strolling along the streets, working on their cars, pushing babies, or licking ice cream cones.

My eye was trained by the beat to see the crooked elements. The young men in their bright suits lounging against the soaped windows of a faded Mercado, junk and reefer and folding knives in their pockets. Pretty mulatto girls in their slips and stockings. Three dollars for some fun.

A group of older men sat on the steps of a boxing gym, playing dice on cardboard. They lifted their heads and watched the Ford cruise by. There were bums and drunks, threadbare suits and wooden signs asking for work. Poor didn't know a color. Not in America. If I drove south or east I'd find plenty of whites and Chicanos doing the same. Okies and Indians, shiftless poor looking for work in the land of opportunity. They'd set up their camps and make trouble on the streets until the sheriffs ran them off.

The building was a three-story brick hotel. The Armitage. The condition of the building said it was a hundred years old, but the architecture said fifty. Jazz music played out an open window.

I parked the car by the lobby entrance. I was out of place, but I was used to it from my days walking beats for the LAPD. The colored kids stayed out of my way. Probably figured me for a dad looking for his hophead of a kid, or maybe they thought I was vice squad. The place wasn't a dump, but if you left it alone for a day or two, it might turn into one.

I climbed the stairs, my presence bringing a trio of colored teenagers to silence in a way that reminded me of the buffalo soldiers I'd met in Spark. They were near the top of the third floor, and I was fighting to keep my wheezing to myself, fighting not to cough. I nodded at them and held it in.

Apartment 318. The door was painted red. I knocked, but nobody was answering.

The hallway of the apartment building was ominously dark and still. A baby was crying a few doors down. The jazz music I'd heard from outside was muffled to a languid horn. I pushed back my hat and drew my Stillman from its shoulder holster. Sweat dripped into my eyes. I tried the door with my free hand. It was unlocked and pushed open with a creak of hinges. There were no signs of force around the lock or the door frame.

"Anybody here?" No point trying to sneak around.

I could smell her perfume lingering in the stillness. The door to the closet in the foyer was open, and the floor was piled with coat hangers. There was a single glove down there too, elbow length, the shed skin of a snake, the kind of thing a classy doll would wear to dinner. I put it in my pocket and continued cautiously.

The blinds were down over every window, and the apartment was gloomy. A lamp was overturned in the living room but still on. It cast the shadow of an end table like a black elephant on stilts.

The walls were papered with a floral pattern, something probably dating back to the building's construction. There were five dark rectangles in the paper on the living room wall above the swaybacked couch. Five nails in those shadows perfect for hanging picture frames. Whoever had ransacked this place was grabbing everything.

There were two bedrooms, two mattresses, sheets, chairs, and lamps. And nothing. The style of furniture and rudimentary décor suggested women lived in both rooms, but so much had been removed from the apartment, there was no getting a feel for the personality of the occupants. The dressers were empty, the closets bare; even the refrigerator in the kitchen was nearly empty, just some old bottles and half-eaten Chinese.

Holly Webber was living with someone. A woman who knew well enough to clear our when Holly died. Maybe Holly's roommate was snatched when the body thief from the morgue decided to clear out the apartment, as well.

I turned over chairs and felt the shelves for any idle carvings. Not even a piece of old gum. I searched the backs of cupboards and the tanks of toilets. Kicked the floorboards, looking for something loose. There was nothing. No hidden message. No trace of the identity of Holly Webber or her nameless roommate.

The apartment building had an office near the boiler room. It was hot and damp, the sort of place where diseases would grow. Cracks in the foundation. An old man in undershirt and suspenders buzzed me through the office door and told me to sit in a squeaky rolling chair that felt like it might tip over. I toyed with my rumpled hat.

"I'm wondering, who signs the checks for 318?" I asked.

"Pay cash," he said around the stub of a cigar. "What's it to you?"

"Friend of the family looking for a missing girl, name of Holly Webber. You seen her around?"

"I don't know you from a Jap." He gestured with the damp cigar. "The what-so-have-its of the renters are strictly confidential."

"You'd be helping her family."

"Helping you, more like. Some shamus with an ugly tie come in here chasing quarters, it ain't my business, but I don't gotta say nothing. I earn my reputation on being discreet. Do you get my meaning?"

I clocked him. Sent the cigar splattering onto the wall and knocked him out of his chair. He was sputtering and grabbing his chin when I came around to his side of the table and picked him up by his suspenders. In my experience, violence works best when it's sudden.

"Listen here, I ain't looking to bust you for running girls or dope out of here, but you'd better relax that jaw. Or do I need to loosen it up some more?"

"Awright! Get offa me!"

I lifted him up a couple more inches and dropped him onto his back.

"And the tie ain't ugly," I added.

He barked a complaint and then pulled himself up by the desk and into his chair. He was gonna have one hell of a bruise from the punch.

"Talk," I said.

"Yeah, I know her. Holly Webber, real hot piece. Looks like Rita Hayworth."

"That's her," I said. "Who does she room with?"

"What? Nobody, so far as I know. Seen her come and go plenty, but only her. She's good at sneaking out though. Sometimes I see her leaving when I was sure she already left, and I watch close."

"Yeah, I'll bet you do. She got a boyfriend?"

"I guess, maybe. Look, I don't know. I got twenty-two units booked right now. I forget who's hopping in bed with who."

I balled up my fists, and he flinched.

"Honest! I don't know. She goes out dancing a lot. Don't know where. All I know about her is she works out in El Segundo. One of them restaurants that all have the same name. Tasty Burger or whatever. With that creepy hamburger man."

"Swiftee Burger?"

He snapped his fingers, "Yeah, yeah, that's it. I seen her filling out that uniform like a job application for heartbreaker. And she rides one of them motorcycle things around. Real fetching look with her on the back. Real nice girl. Real nice."

"Who pays the rent?"

"What?"

"Some girls have men who pay for nice things." I looked around the dank office. "To some people this might qualify."

"I don't know who pays it. The cash is always waiting for me with her apartment number written on the envelope."

"Where?"

"Here, when I get up in the morning," he said. "Always on time. They slide it under the door."

■ ■ ■

The trail was getting colder as the day was getting hotter. Somebody needed to pick a setting on the thermostat and stick to it. The black paint of the old Tudor coupe sucked up the sun. The inside seat leather was too hot to touch. I cranked the windows down and hoped the air from the drive would cut some of the sweat souping up my shirt. I tossed my overcoat into the back with my hat.

It was a long drive from South LA to El Segundo, floral tie flapping around my throat, fighting traffic from the war factories. Buicks and Lincolns and DeSotos crowded the highway. These were the second-shifters leaving for the aircraft plants. All those cars were bought with money from building warplanes for Bishop and men like him. I figured America would fall apart if peace broke out. Ten years of killing and we'd forgotten how to do anything else.

An end to hostilities wasn't much of a concern, though. Korea was worse by the day. The Red Chinese were eager for a scrap, and good old six-star MacArthur was happy to oblige them. Maybe he'd go a round or two with the Soviets next. Maybe it would be World War III. Bishop would find a way to make money as the bombs were falling. It'd be war machines and stop-and-go traffic until the end of the century.

Something black splattered on my windshield. A moment later it happened again. Goddamn birds, I figured. I craned my head out of the car and searched for the source. Instead of a bird, the sky was filled with thousands of slowly drifting tufts of black, almost like feathers or ashes. One landed on my face, cold and wet and melting.

A snowflake. In Los Angeles. In June.

Traffic was snarled up, so I pulled into the lot of a nearby garage. Other drivers had the same idea. Men and women were getting out of their cars and looking up at the sky. Children were climbing out of backseats to chase the falling snowflakes.

There were no storm clouds, and yet the air was filled with the lazily dropping snowflakes. Discussions broke out among strangers about what could cause such a strange thing to occur. Wind currents from the arctic, theorized one man. No, no, said a skinny fella in a suit, an aircraft burst open high in the atmosphere, and its cargo of liquid was frozen and falling as snow. The snowflakes made a soft ticking sound as they fell and melted on contact with the hot pavement.

A burly man stepped out from behind the sign advertising white-walled tires. He had a look up at the sky and then at the kids chasing the snowflakes.

"I'd keep those kids away from it," he said. "Nothing to be played with."

"Why's that?" I asked, studying the bulging profile of the man's face.

He turned to me slowly, revealing the extent of the tumors on his face in malignant increments. Layers and scales of black carcinomas dripped from his eyelids and lips and bulged from his brow.

"It's poisoned by the bombs," said Lt. Milo Gardener.

I was back on Kyushu. 1945. Pursuing Lt. Col. Ishii, who had knowledge that could threaten the secret of our existence. Gardener was talking about the rain. Black rain was falling, pattering on our helmets and our ponchos. He said it was caused by the atom bombs we dropped on X-Day.

"It will make you sick," he warned. "You should see the poor bastards in the POW camps. They built the camps in the bomb zones, and now they're all puking their guts up."

"Wouldn't want to be a guard there," I said, and I watched the rainwater gather in the folds of my poncho like liquid coal. I shook it out and wiped the rest from my face.

There was me and Gardener and Gardener's menagerie of irregulars. There were nine of them—castoffs in various uniforms, each chosen to serve some esoteric purpose for Gardener's mission. They kept to themselves, or at least apart from me and Gardener.

Maybe because of the cold shoulder from my traveling companions I gravitated toward Gardener. The usual suspicion that exists between all men of our shared flesh, that belief that each individual's life is a secret betrayal of all the others, faded as we marched through forest valleys and steep merchant roads.

Each new vista became a shared experience gluing us one to the other, and I came to believe Lt. Gardener was a fine man with words more learned than mine and an easy confidence in himself and in the men he commanded. I saw a true reflection of myself in him.

We traveled for three days through the green mountains and valleys west of Sendai, following a course suggested by Lt. Gardener. There was someplace, some point on the map, where he believed we might intercept Ishii before he reached his unit.

My duty was to keep my companions mindful of the methods and indications of ambush. By careful scouting and altering our course around dangerous terrain, we avoided any serious encounters. Our boots overflowed into livid landscapes of destruction. Towns and factories and schools and hot springs; no village or structure was spared by the relentless waves of our bombers. Sometimes we heard the fighting beyond the mountains. Sometimes we saw the smoke rising from a battle or from a place where bombs or shells had fallen without purpose to sow destruction in the strange country.

No men dwelt between these ruins. No upright humans with bright eyes. There were only slumping beasts gathered in stunned tribes, wandering the forests or haunting the mountain trails. These were raggy things, pitiful creatures that crowded and sawed at the sour meat of dead horses for nourishment. They never slept or played; they only staggered through the world, their hair and clothes dark and limp with the rain.

If I lay still at night, I could hear them shuffling in the darkness, indefatigable, cursed and forever seeking some lost child or life now blasted to ruin. They cringed from our approach, but I came to fear them. I came to believe that only the certitude of our purpose allowed us to pass living through this aimless world of the lemures. I believed if we forgot our reason or lost our way, they would clench us with their ragged hands and carry us off to make us like them.

On the third night of our search for Lt. Col. Ishii we entered a small village engulfed in flames. It was not on the maps I carried in my bag, but Lt. Gardener said it was called Korano. This burning place was our destination. The townspeople were occupied with battling the fires. We watched them draw buckets of water from a well and throw the waters onto the flames swallowing up their homes. It was a futile effort.

The scurrying bucket brigades ignored us as we passed into Korano and walked among the falling ashes. Lt. Gardener identified a house made from stone that stood removed from the flames. We beat in the door with our rifles and found a terrified family of elderly parents, a woman, and several children. Lt. Gardener and his translator interrogated the adults one by one.

A cold meal was laid out on their table, and the rest of us, being tired and hungry, sat and ate their dinner while they huddled against a wall. There was a little girl with a pink ribbon tied around the waist of her dress. Her eyes were wide and dark and never seemed to blink. She was not crying like the other children, and so I held out a piece of chocolate left over from my ration. Her grandfather pulled her away and stood between me and the child, and so I sat back at the table and ate the cold, dry rice.

After several minutes Gardener signaled us to leave.

"Did you get your answers?" I asked him.

"Ishii was seen here during the day." Gardener held up a green book. "I showed them this. Photographs of Ishii's atrocities in China. The people in the village do not care for him much."

"Where is he now?" I asked as I followed Gardener out of the house.

"He knows I'm after him, and he's taken refuge with the Catholics in the Church of St. Ramon. It's about three miles from here." Gardener's face was alive with the colors of the burning village. "He will attempt to ambush us."

We stepped back into the street and were met by a small old man dressed in the blue uniform of a policeman. We were used to ignoring the outrage of Japanese civil officials, but this one was holding a pistol. He came toward us and shouted something that was lost to the roar of the flames. The bucket brigades ceased, and the townspeople stood as an audience to this encounter, their faces and details lost in the brightness of the flames at their backs.

The old policeman shouted again and came closer. Several of Lt. Gardener's men brought their guns up in a casual manner, as if they could not take this man seriously as a threat, but his approach forced them to react. The policeman brandished his pistol again. Lt. Gardener motioned for his men to lower their guns. The anguish and frustration of the policeman was painted on his face in valleys deepened to black by the moving shadows of the firelight. His pistol was a tiny revolver of obsolete manufacture. He thrust its barrel at Lt. Gardener, and there was a pop and a flash in the darkness, and white smoke puffed from the cylinder. No one was shot.

Lt. Gardener's men fired in response, and the policeman was struck several times. He fell to his knees, and the pistol slipped from his fingers. Blood darkened the front of his blue uniform. He looked up from his kneeling position, up above our heads at where the stars would be, as if his soul might leap out and into the night sky, and yet surely all he saw was smoke.

The old policeman's eyes dimmed, and he slumped onto his side and did not move again. The confrontation over, their champion slain, the black paper dolls of the townspeople shifted and picked up their buckets and wordlessly resumed their efforts to extinguish the fires.

"Why did you do that?" I demanded of the corpse. I kicked it and shouted at it, "You idiot!"

"Goddamn you all!" I shouted at the townspeople with their useless bucket brigade. "Why didn't you stop him? Why didn't you do something?"

Gardener pulled me away from the fires, as though I might throw myself into the conflagration. He dragged me down to the road.

"Why did he do it?" I asked, my voice hoarse with anger.

"The same reason they all do it." Gardener was already walking away down the road, his words almost lost to the fire's roar. " There's nothing left for them here."

The black snow had stopped in Los Angeles. The freak weather had produced nothing more lasting than oily puddles that were already being ignored. In a matter of seconds the heat had transformed something magical—or at least unusual—into something forgettable. The leaves of the palm trees were dripping with black. The world was moving on. The children had quit playing in the snow. The man with the faceful of tumors was gone.

■　■　■

Mister Swiftee was smiling, but his eyes were crazy. Round and wide. Maniacal. His burger-shaped head loomed over the parking lot of the Swiftee Burger in El Segundo, his expression not so much beckoning as challenging. He was daring the shift workers from the aircraft plants and the high school football teams to stop in and try to stomach one of his hamburgers.

Swiftee Burgers were cropping up all over the Los Angeles area. They were called franchise restaurants. The formula was to take the same mess of chrome and neon, the same paper hats and shake mixers and vinyl booths, the same not-terrible hamburgers, and duplicate everything and transplant it all over. It seemed to be working, based on the gangrenous spread of Mister Swiftee's likeness. Somewhere out there somebody wanted this.

The inside was decorated in the red and gold of the franchise. Waitresses in red dresses fringed with gold lace moved from table to table serving up baskets of hamburgers and French fries to families and shift workers. I felt more out of place here than in Ciro's. At least that was my neighborhood. This was something that didn't have a neighborhood, something out of the rocket future, some dark vision where Pluto landed on us instead of us landing on Pluto. One wrong word and a fox in a silver suit was gonna burn a hole in my chest with a ray gun.

"Can I help you?" asked a chubby-cheeked doll. She was just a kid. ELLA on her name tag.

"I sure hope so, miss," I said, taking off my hat. "Do you know a girl by the name of Holly Webber?"

That chased the cheery smile off her face. "Bob," she hollered. "Some man is here asking about Holly."

Bob came out from the kitchen and did not live up to my expectations. I was waiting for forearm hair and Navy tattoos stuffed behind a greasy apron. This guy had a pomaded wave of black hair neatly parted at the side, gold wire spectacles, and a mustache of two commas above his lip. His red apron was immaculate, his paper hat cocked to one side like Robin Hood's cap.

"Robert Mellon." He held out a hand, and we exchanged introductions. "I'm afraid I can't be of help to you. Everything I know has been given to the police, along with Miss Webber's earnings history."

"I was hoping I could ask you a few questions."

"She was only employed here for two months, I didn't know her well, she seemed like a nice girl, but she was late about half her shifts." He ticked each item off on his fingers.

"Was she working on the night of her disappearance?" I asked.

"Yeah," said Ella. Bob gave her the skunk eye.

"She was scheduled to work until close," said Bob, "but I let her go early. She said she had something personal."

"She lived in South Los Angeles," I said, and Bob nodded. "Do you know if she had any roommates or friends? Did she ever talk about anyone else?"

"Ella, why don't put on a fresh pot of coffee?" said Bob, and Ella snapped her gum in annoyance as she departed. Bob put an arm around me and walked me toward the door. "I'm a married man. I don't make it my business to know what these girls get up to, you understand?"

"I hear what you're saying, and I wasn't making any implications of an untoward nature."

"Good." Bob walked me through the door and out into the lot. The wind was picking up. "I think you'll find you have arrived back at your starting point. If I see you again, I hope you bring an appetite in place of questions. Beyond that, I would leave this matter to the police. Vultures have no business picking over a sweet girl like Holly."

He said everything real friendly, but there was nothing friendly about the smile he gave me before disappearing back into the restaurant. Struck out by a dandy in an apron. Society, such as it was, wouldn't let me beat the answers out of a guy like Mellon. I trudged back to my car as the lot was beginning to fill up with the evening crowd.

"Hey." The soft call belonged to a dame.

Caroline, judging by the name tag. Plain Jane, gangly, too many teeth, but there was something nice about the way the black snakes of her hair kept blowing across her face. Her eyes were pale blue and watery from all the wind.

"You were asking about Holly's roommate," she said.

"Did you know Holly?"

"She was my friend," said Caroline. "Look, she did have a roommate. She talked about her sometimes, this girl named Veronica. I don't know much about her except I think she was a dance hall girl. Seemed like her and Veronica were real close friends."

"Any boyfriends?"

Caroline shook her head. "The guys were all over Holly, but she stuck up for herself. Didn't seem interested in romance. She had given up on trying to be an actress like her mom, but she always wanted something more."

"I didn't know about her mother. What was her name? What pictures was she in?"

Caroline slid a cigarette between her pursed lips, and I leaned in to light it for her, cupping my hand to keep the flame going. She took a long drag before she answered my question.

"Isabella was her name. Holly only talked about some Western serial. *Red* something, maybe. No, it was *Rex. Rex Rawhide.*"

I wasn't familiar with it, but Hollywood was in the business of making and hoarding records of everything. Old serial reels were often pillaged for footage to fill in gaps in new productions. A train here, a leaping Indian there. All I needed to do was track down the studio behind *Rex Rawhide,* and I was willing to bet a sawbuck I'd find reels of it collecting dust on a shelf somewhere.

"What was Holly like?" I asked.

"Like? You mean, personally?"

I nodded and said, "It might help me understand who she was in contact with."

"She was real sweet and funny," said Caroline. "Always reading too. She loved to read. Mysteries mostly, but other sorts of books too. She'd come in sometimes and tell me all about someplace she'd read about in Africa or in the tropics."

"She wanted to travel?"

"Yeah, far as I know, she never left California, but she said her mom used to go away on trips and leave her with her uncle."

"Her mom still alive?"

"No, she died. Holly never said how, but she went to stay with her uncle for good when she was eleven or twelve." Caroline tossed the cigarette down and stubbed it out beneath the toe of her shoe. "Something bad happened with him."

"He touch her?"

"I don't think that's it. He died. Her whole foster family died, but she wouldn't talk about it except to say they were gone. Something bad happened."

"You've been a big help, Caroline." I flipped my notebook closed and started to get into my car.

"Hey." She stopped me again. "There's one other thing."

"What's that?"

"Holly was sure something big was happening that night she was killed. When she was packing up to leave, she told me, 'After tonight, everything is going to be different.'"

"She was right about that," I said.

■ ■ ■

I wanted more information on Holly's missing roommate, but there was no hook for me to hang my hat. Filling in Holly Webber's family tree with what Caroline had said didn't seem like much to go on either, but it was better than the hot nothing sandwiches Bob was serving. Maybe tracking down Isabella's film career would throw a curveball at whoever was heading me off. If I was real lucky, they'd never even heard of her.

I knew a guy who might have some answers, or know where to find them, about Isabella Webber. Nicky Lambros. He was a Hollywood dick, the sort of lowlife bloodhound that lawyers sent sniffing when a studio wanted leverage in a negotiation. He knew all the dirty tricks. Nicky was an ex-cop like me but run out of the LAPD for the worst sort of reason: he'd ratted out another cop. If I could put Nicky on the trail of Isabella, maybe her story could take me to whatever misery had befallen Holly Webber's foster family.

I decided to drive the truck road to Cranford just to see how far it was from El Segundo. Wrap my head around Holly Webber's last road trip. Quiet highway. Four lanes in the city, but I knew it would narrow to two before long.

I tapped out a Bravo on the dash and slid it between my lips. Lighting up and taking a drag got me started coughing. I flicked the cigarette out the car window and saw stars behind my eyes from all the hacking. When I finally managed to pull out of it, I was swerving off the road. I cranked the wheel back onto the highway and met the trombone blurt of an oncoming truck. I swerved back into my lane, and the truck thundered past.

Close call and no chance to relax. A huge black Cadillac came barreling out of the passing lane, hopping over the center line and screeching around to cut me off. The black shape closing in on my driver's side spooked me, and I overcorrected the Tudor right into a ditch. Nearly rolled it, but a lucky turn of the wheel put me on the access road to a defunct cannery. Gravel rattled against the car's undercarriage as I put my foot to the floor. I managed to clatter to a stop and was immediately swallowed by a cloud of brown dust.

That'll wake you up. Lucky thing I wasn't cradling a coffee between my knees.

There was another car with me. My mind was a bit addled from all that hacking and two brushes with roadside death. By the time I realized what was happening, my door was already coming open. I reached for the Stillman in its compartment much too slowly to do any good. A vise-grip hand dug into my shoulder and hauled me out of my car.

In the dusty haze all I could see was the huge, dark shape of the man; a man to match the Cadillac that ran me off the road. He was working with saps or something heavy in his hands that knocked aside my guard and put battering rams into my guts. I spit out all the air in my lungs and doubled up, but this rooker wasn't through with the one-sided dance. While I was looking at his boots—black, natch—he was hammering his fists at my ribs. Tenderized me up real good before picking me up with both hands.

He hoisted me face-to-face, and what a goddamn ugly puss it was. Underneath a flat-brimmed black hat and desert sun shades the man was all scar tissue. He stank of corruption and medicines. His nose was mostly gone, his mouth a lipless crease ringed with yellowing scabs, and the rest of him was a melty candle crusted over in seeping injuries and livid scars. I'd seen my share of the ugliness of war, and this fella took top honors. Like a gasoline bomb married a radiation sickness and had kids in the burn ward.

I believe I quoted him some of my favorite Shakespeare. Something along the lines of, "O villain, villain, smiling, damned villain!"

It came out more like "Christ!" and that only half said by bloodied lips.

"Let it go," he said, and he proceeded to throw my back against the Tudor and knock my brains in with his fists. When I was half-gone and spitting blood on the ground, he picked me up again. I weakly raised my hands to shield my face from more blows.

"See what you have, Casper," said the man, his voice rasping and sibilant. "Cherish it. This endeavor with Holly Webber, you must let go."

"Go to hell," I said.

"Circumstance insists I injure you so that my point is not forgotten," said the giant. "Understand that I do not take any particular pleasure in this."

His black-gloved fingers closed around the pinkie and ring finger of my shooting hand. I kicked uselessly at his shins. I saw my panicked, bloody face reflected in his dark glasses as he crushed my fingers. *Pop. Pop.* The gold of my wedding ring deformed along with the bone.

I've had more than my portion of physical misery. I've had limbs blown off and knives in my guts and the sharp sting of shrapnel cutting through me in a hundred places. You get used to it. Sometimes it kills you, and if it doesn't, you can take a beating or a bullet that would lay a normal man out and you just keep on going.

There's no getting around broken bones. The body isn't put together like that. The bones in my fingers crumbled like bar-top pretzels and split open my fingers, and all I could do was scream. Blood poured out and splashed into the dirt.

"I'm sorry," said the giant. "Let it go. Everyone will be better off."

He dropped me, and I lay in the dirt and watched him stalk back to the idling Cadillac. The car suited him. A mythological charger. Chrome teeth and bumper dulled by a layer of road grit.

I pushed myself up onto my elbows and tried to get a look at its tags, but it threw out so much dust, I started choking and couldn't see a thing. I managed to get to my feet. There was a filthy rag in my trunk, and I wrapped my hand up and hoped it would slow down the bleeding. When I got into my car, I realized I was bleeding out of my head and one of my ears as well. I'd be lucky if it didn't cauliflower up like a boxer's.

I couldn't shake this one off. Couldn't will myself through it. My soft insides were bleeding too. I slumped in the seat and expected to wake up in that fucking cave.

CHAPTER SEVEN

■ ■ ■

I think the reason the food always stinks in hospitals is because most of the people eating it have a mouthful of medicine. Whatever Doc Brightbow gave me was a little stronger than his usual prescription of aspirin. He leaned over and checked the IV bottles hooked into my pipes. One was medicine; the other was a transfusion of blood. I tried to sit up, but a little waif of a nurse pushed me gently back in the bed and slid the food tray back into my face.

I was gauzy-headed and smiling. Nothing really hurt. Yeah, there was throbbing in my fingers and my ribs, but it was distant, like reading a report that said I hurt, not doing the actual hurting. I smiled real big at the nurse and stuffed my face with corn bread. Lousy corn bread. Medicine-mouthed corn bread.

"You look just like Annie," I said to the nurse, but she didn't understand through all that corn bread.

"Just sit back and try to eat," she said. "I'll get some more pillows to prop you up better."

"She looks just like Annie," I said to Doc Brightbow.

"Eh, who's that?" he asked, puttering over to my side and laying a fatherly hand on my shoulder.

"Love of my life." I grinned up at him. It was the drugs, trust me. I'm not known for my smiling.

"Well, you had better keep that to yourself when Lynn is here," he said. "She's waiting outside. As are the police."

That sobered me up quick.

"Cops?"

"Yes, you're lucky they found you when they did. You very nearly bled out in that car. The police only discovered you because you were trespassing. I believe they want to ask you some questions about a missing body. Does that sound right?"

Yeah, sure, it sounded right for Kapinski to show up beside my hospital bed and get a few kicks in on me while I was down. He knew I couldn't have looted that body, and he couldn't possibly suspect my real attraction to Holly Webber.

Truthfully, I was more worried about Lynn. My waking up beaten half to death in the hospital wasn't going to go down well with her. It played into all her worst fears about my line of work.

She'd begged me to drop the case, and I'd told her I'd try. The worst sort of lie. To promise an effort you never intend to make.

Lynn came into the hospital room wrapped in a housecoat. She saw me and covered her mouth with her hands. Tears quivered in her eyes, but she's a strong girl. She didn't cry. She smiled. She came over to the bed and kissed my head, and she smiled, and that was worse than her bawling or being mad.

"I've been waiting out there all night," she said. "Doctor Brightbow told me you were sleeping."

"Are you okay?" I asked.

"Everything is fine," she said, and there was that damn smile again.

I needed her to be mad. I needed her to slap me or scream. I deserved it. I was a bad boy.

"Frank the cat?" I croaked.

"Helen is taking care of him." She kissed me again. "Stop worrying. Everything is fine."

"Stop saying everything is fine." I'd raised my voice.

Lynn stared at me. She wouldn't give me the benefit of her real feelings. That must be what it was like for her and all my non-answers and mysterious, late-night meetings.

"We can talk about it when you're better. For now I want you to get well. Do as your doctor says."

Kapinski interrupted. Lynn's glance asked my permission to shoo him out, but I wanted him there. I'd rather tangle with him than her any day of the week.

"He'll be quick," I said to Lynn.

When she'd left, Kapinski came over and sat on my bed.

"What's going on?" he asked.

"You asking for my sake or yours?"

"I'm asking as a friend. Or whatever we were before you left the force. Look at yourself. You're a damn mess." He waved his hat in the general direction of Cranford. "But I'm asking as a cop too. Body disappears from the morgue. Body you seemed to care about enough to show up at the morgue and try to talk your way in. Not three hours later the manager of that diner calls me and wants to know why some private dick was nosing around his restaurant and asking questions about Holly Webber. Then a squad car calls in an ambulance and picks you up in the middle of the night, half-dead in your car."

He got up from the bed and came around to the other side. Backlit by the hospital window, he reminded me of the giant who had done so much villainy to my body.

"Just spill it," Kapinski said. "I'm not going to run you in or put you in bracelets. But I can't help you if you aren't telling me the truth."

"You and I both know that girl was killed with intent out there," I said. "That's all it is to me. I'm trying to solve a murder I don't think you can."

"Charity case, huh? You're Mr. Generous all of the sudden."

"Go to hell, Kapinski. I'm not one of your dogs anymore, and it's still a free country. You can't keep me away from this."

Kapinski put his hat on his head and smiled really, miserably, shit-eatingly wide. "Looks like someone else will do that job for me," he said. "Let me know when you swallow your pride and realize you're in over your head. For your sake I hope that's before you get yourself killed."

■ ■ ■

Lynn stayed with me through another night. I picked at her, but she refused to engage in any of the arguments I tried to start with her. Doc Brightbow wanted me in the bed for a few days. My ribs weren't broken, but he couldn't put a plaster cast on my hand until the swelling went down.

"I'm still worried about blood in your organs," he said, pulling at his lip with concern. "We need to watch the urine for signs of deeper injury."

I had no intention of staying horizontal or letting a nurse strain my piss. While I was scabbing up in a hospital bed, there was someone out there with a lot of free time to work against me. But their little plan had backfired. The pain and humiliation of the beating only made me want to find Holly's killer even more.

In the morning Bishop sent a huge bouquet of flowers that smelled rotten to me. Lynn loved them.

"It's so good to know you still have friends," she said.

"I have lots of friends," I objected.

"You have lots of people you use to get what you need."

She went hunting for a vase. I'd been planning the escape all night. I popped out my IV, got my coat on over my hospital gown, filled my pockets with some bandages and tape, snatched the sack full of my bloody clothes, and made my getaway. The bruises and cuts on my face were already healing, but I still looked a mess. An orderly tried to stop me at the door, but I convinced him I'd been sleeping off a drunk and made my escape.

Nicky Lambros had an office on Laurel Canyon in the heart of Studio City. The palm trees looked like moldy lollipops. His office was decorated with ferns and expensive wood grains and a secretary with a foot of blond hair piled up. Her pin-up curves were swaddled in a blue velvet shift dress.

"Mr. Lambros is busy with a client, but you can have a seat over there." She pointed to the darkest corner of the waiting area.

Who could blame her? I looked like a bum. She kept shooting me looks out of the corner of her eye while I tried to get comfortable. My back and insides were killing me. Finally I broke down and got down on my back on the floor.

"You can't do that," she said.

"I'm doing it," I pointed out.

"I mean you've got to stop," she said. "I'll call the police."

"Come on, doll, I'm an old friend of Nicky's. It's been a rough couple days, and I need to—"

The door to his office burst open with a roar of laughter. Nicky Lambros came out clapping a couple of Hollywood Jews on their shoulders. He was an olive-skinned, fuzzy-headed fireplug wearing a pink suit and yellow tie. Low-key as ever.

"You tell Tony I am going to take him to the horses the next time we're both in New York," said Lambros. "Then we'll see who has a better eye for talent."

Nicky sent his clients on their way. The door closed, and his footsteps approached across the hardwood. He stood over me, his big, vivid tie hanging so low, the tip of its diamond almost touched my nose.

"You got a real comfortable floor, Nicky," I said.

"That's twelve-hundred-dollar hardwood you're bleeding on." He pushed me with the tip of his shoe. "You lose a fight with a truck?"

"Something like that."

He sighed and plopped down in one of the nearby chairs. His expensive shoes went up on the table, and he pretended to idly flip through a copy of *Photoplay*.

"So to what do I owe this visit from my esteemed former colleague?"

"I need your help." I rolled onto my side to sit up.

"I am shocked. Shocked, I say." He leaned over my head again and spoke with a stilted affect. "Being as how you have already imposed yourself on my hospitality, why don't you regale me with the full tale of what I am to involve myself in?"

I spilled the sauce on Holly Webber's roadside death, the suspected murder, the missing body, and that her mother, Isabella Webber, used to do the *Rex Rawhide* serials.

When I reached the part about the serials, Nicky said, "Aha!" and got to his feet.

"I loved *Rex Rawhide*," said Nicky. "Back when I was twelve, everybody watched *Rex Rawhide* and that little Indian fella, Kakakshi. Had to take the little brother trick-or-treating, and I was Rex, and he was Kakakshi—oh, must have been—"

"Save it for your memoirs."

"Point is, Paramount bought up Royal Radio Pictures. They folded all their equipment and people into their own serials department. You know the film vault Paramount keeps on Melrose?"

"I know of it. The one that almost burned down a few years back?"

"What? That was more like twenty years back," said Nicky. "Look, don't worry, the fire was long before your picture ended up in there. I can help you with this."

He disappeared into his office while I struggled to heave myself up off the floor. His secretary watched my effort with apparent fascination.

"I think I even know the gal you're talking about," shouted Nicky from his office. "She played Red Rogue."

Something clattered and spilled loudly on the floor in Nicky's office. His secretary looked up from the book she was reading.

"I'm all right, Candy," he assured her. "Just digging deep for this. That Isabella, she was a hot number. Rode a paint horse around in this outfit somewhere between a bathing suit and a cowgirl's. Used to lasso the bad guys and drag them behind her horse."

He stuck his head out of his office and said, "I tell ya, she could drag me over broken glass. Maybe take me back to the Red Rogue's hideout in the hills. I think they used to shoot over in Riverside. She could tie me up and then—"

"Jeez," groaned Candy.

"Then we can go for pancakes! That's all I was gonna say." He looked at me and hooked his thumb at his secretary. "She's got a perverted mind, I tell you. All those pulps she reads."

"Was she in all the serials?" I asked.

"Candy?"

"Isabella Webber," interjected Candy.

"No, no, only Rex and Kakakshi were in every one." More clattering and a sound like a plate breaking. "Shit. Can you get the broom? No, I'll get it later. What was I saying? Oh, yeah, about Red Rogue. She was in the 'El Camino de la Muerte' stories. I think they did two batches of five."

"You know everything about Red Rogue. Is that why you're so good at finding Reds?" I shouted to Nicky. "Is that how Romulus got such a great deal with Jose Ferrer?"

"House Un-American Activities Committee marches to their own drummer." He poked his head out of the door of his office. "You gonna run down my line of work while I'm doing you a favor? Some nerve. Some damn nerve. You believe this guy, Candy?"

"He's a joker," she said.

Nicky returned by the time I'd managed to leverage myself back onto my feet. He handed me a pair of white gloves and a scuffed-up octagonal metal case with STUDIO USE ONLY printed on the side.

"Paramount vault," he said. "Just get yourself a jacket from one of the boys running reels. One of them service caps too, if they got 'em."

"What are you talking about?"

He shook the octagon at me, and it rattled.

"Paramount sends runners all the time to pull reels from their vault. They take them to screenings for production, for bigwigs, for actors staying in hotels. If anybody at the Paramount vault asks, you just name some celebrity and a hotel and tell them you're taking the reels there. It's not like they check. And nobody is going to care about some old *Rex Rawhide* picture."

"You're a peach." I grabbed him and planted a kiss on his balding head.

"Get your germs off of me. Go on, I hope you find this waitress murderer or whatever. And you owe me."

"I still owe you from last time," I said on my way out the door.

"You owe me double!" Nicky shouted through the closing door, but I pretended not to hear him.

■ ■ ■

I never liked Melrose Avenue. No, that wasn't quite fair. Melrose Avenue had good parts, like the half block closed to fix the sewer, and where it disappeared into the ocean. Those were good bits. It was otherwise a long row of ugly commercial properties, studio warehouses, hokey hotels, and service stations trying to sell over-priced gasoline with discounts on new tires.

Melrose was the place to be if you wanted a dent pounded out of your car door with a mallet or if you wanted a hooker to find you floating facedown in the pool of a motel with a rodeo theme. Even the palm trees looked worn and tawdry.

Urchins were selling oranges and boxes of matches to the crowds. Some were waving the nickel fold-out cartoon maps to the private Valhallas of a hundred Hollywood demigods. Each time the traffic slowed, the children assaulted the cars with solicitations of "Hey, mister!" and "Please, señor!" They thronged the sunburned tourists slumming it at the discount movie houses and museums of Hollywood oddities. Families coughing up their dimes for second-run bikini films and ladling their fingers over Ronald Colman's false beards from *Kismet*.

The white-collar fraternities of business-trippers from the aircraft plants and military contractors and Bishop's towering ugliness out in San Pedro came to Melrose for the girls. *Buy me a drink, mister?* A ginger ale and lime and a crumpled tissue in the telephone booth; the skeleton outline of a sex story ten times better when repeated over fried fish at a Cleveland Kiwanis.

The Paramount vault was a dominant feature of Melrose. A big, ugly slab topped by massive industrial AC units. It was a windowless tomb with a white granite facade. There was a small visitors' entrance and several beige loading doors designed to accommodate trolley carts of film reels. The lot was enclosed by a wrought-iron gate and a studio security post. I bribed the guard with a dollar and a promise that I "won't touch nothing."

Getting into the building was easy; getting into the film archives required a little more patience. The upper floors of the vault housed prop storage and various offices for lesser Paramount executives. The real business was underground, in subterranean vaults kept cool and breezy by the humming air conditioners on the roof. Descending the stairs into the dim corridors was like entering a chilled, Dantesque grotto of nitrocellulose and acetate. Explosive chemical smells permeated the air.

A pair of chatty dames fortified within a cashiers' cage were the gatekeepers of this pit. I watched them for a while. Kept my distance and observed. They were smart and sarcastic and gave everyone who came through a hard time. Except for the guys coming and going in the blue jackets and gray baseball caps and white gloves. The couriers Nicky had told me about. They all had the octagonal cans like me. Some of them had carts stacked high with the canisters.

I followed one departing with a trolley cart of film reels.

"Where's that going?" I asked.

I tried to read the handwritten labels on the canisters. *A Foreign Affair*, something with *Hillbilly* in the title, *Streets of Laredo*, and a few others with the labels turned away.

"I'm taking these over to a private party at the Chateau Marmont. Why?"

"Sell me your hat and coat."

"No way, buddy," said the runner. "This is a honey gig."

I emptied the salad out of my wallet and waved it at him. He shed the jacket and passed it over. The hat was warm and damp with the sweat of his brow. I wheeled one of the unused trolley carts into the vault's waiting area and approached the cage.

The two women watched me through the brass bars of their cage. One was an imperious pile of hair and jewelry, conscripting Elizabeth Arden to shave twenty extra years down to ten. Her younger coworker had a pretty, doll-like face, but her head was too small for her long, slender neck so that she reminded me of a marshmallow on the end of a dowel.

"Well, here's my favorite part of the day," I said, stopping short of the door into the vault. "How are you two beautiful ladies doing?"

They melted. Guess they didn't get a lot of runners who looked like that movie star pilot who was just in the paper for dying in the shower. They made me take the hat off so they could get a better look. They couldn't remember his name. The older woman, Flo, even offered to tape up one of the cuts on my head. I let her. Saved me the trouble. When she finished, I was buzzed through without any trouble.

A short ramp opened into the airship-hangar immensity of the vault. Suck of pressure at the door. Tangible future histories in row upon row of stacked film cans. They were organized by year and alphabetically within years. The lighting was very low to avoid damaging the film. Electric lanterns were available near the ramp. I clipped one to the metal rim of my trolley cart.

I could hear the reel couriers and projectionists searching the underground library, seeking obscure films to hand-deliver or ship off across the country to a specialty screening. They were like Christmas ghosts: shuffling and muttering and never revealing themselves except as lights beaming through the stacks of film canisters.

Recent, popular movies occupied entire rows with surplus reels in metal cans. The originals were stored in plastic cases and labeled ORIGINAL or RAW.

I spent a long time shuffling around in the dark, searching for the *Rex Rawhide* serials, before I realized that non-Paramount films, including the American Pictures reels, were kept in a separate section. There was the feel of a slum to that area. The rows weren't straight, and I could hear water dripping somewhere. And whispers. The shelves were cheaply made from metal rods and Peg-Board and leaned as though decaying into one another. Toppled stacks of reels filled the shelves and in some cases spilled out onto the floor.

I abandoned the trolley in the center aisle and unclipped the light to go searching the narrow, haphazard aisles of shelves. The overhead lights flickered and buzzed and were entirely inadequate. I discovered that the *Rex Rawhide* serials were in a mess. The film cans were placed out of sequence and jumbled up with nearby film reels. I sorted through dozens of titles and misplaced reels from *Red Ranger* serials and a series of educational films called *Reds: The Threat Within.* Canisters broke open and spilled their contents at my feet.

I bent down to pick up the ribbons of film, and as I did, I heard the rush of the ocean. It was distant but distinct. I strained to hear it better, and the sound was gone.

I laboriously spooled the film back onto its reel and returned it to its canister. As I stood to place it back on the shelf, something moved on the other side. It was only a pale blur seen through the peg holes of one of the dilapidated shelves. It was so fast and quiet, I only glimpsed it as it departed. A hunched, pale man or a dog, maybe, loose in the stacks of reels.

"Wait," I said, and I chased after it, stumbling over a stack of fashion films.

It was faster but seemed to pause in hiding and wait for me to catch up, then spring around a corner or disappear down a row where the lights had failed. I never got a good look at it, but I could see the shine of its eyes in the dark as it observed my lame pursuit.

I wheezed and sputtered in my infirmity. My bruised muscles ached, and I could feel the stones in my lungs worse than I had in days. I kept going. My shoes splashed through filthy water that stung my ankles. The floor was fractured up ahead, the two halves forming a triangular trough that was filled with the water drizzling down from overhead pipes and conduits. There was very little light at all. Just the flickering beam of my lantern and the soft blue glow of distant sunlight reflected off hundreds of metallic surfaces.

I had it cornered. I could see its outline in the darkness, back against one of the stone walls of the vault's foundation. Its huge eyes glistened in the shadows. Who had let this animal in here?

"It's okay," I said. "I'm not gonna hurt you."

"*Click-click-click*," it answered.

There was a seared deadness to the air. Maybe one of the AC units had caught fire? I wasn't thinking rationally about things. I was stifled and struggling to breathe.

"*Click-click-click*," it said again.

"Shh, I'm not—"

It charged out of the darkness with great speed, and at the terrible sight of it I felt the sand of my bravery scatter. It was no dog. It was a haunted, pale creature of nightmare flesh, but real and close enough to touch. It stood upon its overarticulated hind legs and was nearly as tall as my throat. It was naked and man-shaped and pale white, almost chalky. Its hairless head and flattened snout reminded me of a fish or a frog. No, it was familiar to me. I had seen the head before. Its huge blue eyes bulged from either side and focused on me with clear menace. The skeletal forelimbs were folded up against its body, sharp, bony spurs above its fingers like those of a mantis.

Spears. I suddenly saw the living head as I remembered it: decaying on a spear in the Indian village long ago. This was one of the denizens of that hellish place.

As it came for me, it opened its mouth and bared clattering plated jaws. It launched its spurred limbs out, spearing them for my heart. I hollered and turned away, felt them pass close by as I careened into one of the shelves and knocked canisters of film and bones and rotted bits showering into the watery trough.

I could hear it splashing toward me. I tried to turn, but I was caught up in the Sargasso of old film reels and leathery dead things. I tripped and slid down a stone column. Burning-cold water saturated the legs of my pants. The beast was right over top of me, and I was at its mercy. I closed my eyes and waited to die.

"Are you all right?"

I looked at my chest. Not a mark. I was sprawled against a shelf, sagged so low that I was nearly sitting upon the pile of overturned film reels.

"Buddy, are you okay?"

The man asking was dressed in the costume of one of the couriers. He was unshaved, his face crumpled by time and bushy eyebrows swallowing up his dark brown eyes. He reached a hand down and helped me to my feet.

"I'm all right," I said, though my heart still hammered a ragged tattoo within my breast.

I stood up straight and attempted to regain my bearings. I was still in the aisle of the *Rex Rawhide* serials. I'd made a mess of those anti-Communist films, but otherwise I seemed fine. There was no dog, no ocean sound, not even dripping water. I'd evidently dreamed up the whole scenario.

"What are you looking for?" asked the old man.

"Uh." I reached into my pocket for my black book and read off the name. "*Rex Rawhide*. 'El Camino de la Muerte.' "

The old man nodded. He stepped over the spilled reels and examined the shelves.

"You're in the right place," he said. "Should be . . . right . . ."

He leaned down, trailing his finger over the film reels.

"Well, right here." The old man tapped his finger on empty shelving. "Someone checked it out. You're going to have to arrange a delivery."

"It's not there?"

"No, not even any copies. Happens all the time. But"—he groaned as he crouched down in the aisle—"they sometimes keep raw copies down here. And . . . yep . . . here you go . . . this what you need?"

The old man handed me a sagging cardboard box labeled EL CAMINO DE LA MUERTE and stamped RAW. It was heavy and filled with original film reels. Some segments of film were just a few dozen frames on a small reel or a paper bag containing a few frames.

"Might just be," I said, hefting the box.

"Royal Radio Pictures was one of the originals making serials," said the old man. "Used to have one called *Mystery Patrol*. Soldiers fighting ghosts and vampires. Took my son to them when he was about this tall."

The old man held a hand up around his waist.

"That was a long time before *Rex Rawhide*. They were all silent pictures back then, long before Bishop sold Royal Radio."

"What? Harlan Bishop?"

"Sure," he said. "Between wars he was making serials and movies, but he sold all that off in, oh, I think it was '38 or '39. You can probably figure it out just by looking at the dates on the cans. Wherever this section stops is when he sold it to Paramount."

"Is there somewhere in here that I can watch this stuff?" I shook the box. "I need to make sure it's the right picture."

The old man showed me to a projection room. It was a table, a couple of chairs, and a projector aimed at a white wall used by the couriers to check unreliable reels.

"Take your time," he said, and he gave me a pat on the shoulder. "And take it easy."

■ ■ ■

Alone in the small projection room I attempted to screen the many reels and bits of footage. I have always struggled with technology more complicated than a hand grenade, and this projector gave me fits. I ruined several pieces of film before I got the hang of it, but at last I sat and watched the flickering images and heard the voices on the tinny speaker.

There was no sequence to the clips, and the sound was imperfect or missing on many of the reels. Couldn't really piece together what was happening in the story. Something about cattle rustlers and a mine, a schoolteacher who was sweet on Rex, but that was about it. I never liked Westerns for the way they tried to conjure a time

I clearly remembered. Everyone was too clean and happy. Arrows always landed in armpits.

The lantern-jawed actor playing Rex Rawhide seemed to struggle with his lines, and the scenes with sound often ended with an exasperated shout from the director to cut. At one point Rex's Indian guy Friday, Kakakshi, played by a white actor in makeup, engaged in a long argument with Rex. I wished that bit had sound so I could hear them stripping the bark off each other.

I sorted through bits and pieces of footage, half scenes, construction of sets, monkeyshines by the cast and crew, and stunts gone wrong. I was bored with the process by the time I came across a piece of footage featuring Isabella Webber as the Red Rogue.

My pulse quickened at the sight of her, riding high in the saddle on the back of a galloping paint. She was lean and beautiful, dressed as Nicky had described, between bathing beauty and cowgirl, her face partly hidden by a mask. I watched her rope an outlaw and leap from her saddle to tie him up. She was so agile and strong, the horseback riding was certainly hers, though the leaping might have been a stunt woman's. I'm easily fooled by film tricks. The footage cut before it went to close-up.

It was a long while before I found another piece of footage with her in it. My sides ached, and my bandaged and taped hand throbbed painfully with each beat of my heart. I finally thought to hold my electric lantern beneath the film to see the frames so I didn't waste the time mounting each reel to see what it was. I passed the lantern beneath the leading frames of a short reel, and her face appeared, close-up, translucent and smiling. Just the sight of her in that tiny thumbnail frame was enough for me.

I fumbled to get the reel mounted on the projector. She wasn't wearing her mask, and her features were clearly those of Holly Webber. Of Annie Groves. She was taller and slimmer than either, particularly less curvaceous than her daughter, but the face was so similar to both that the effect was the same on me. I'm a man, and men don't swoon, especially not a Marine, but when your heart's been yearning for a certain gal for seventy-five years and then you see her in motion on a film reel, well, it has an effect.

I sat back in the chair and lit a cigarette. There was no audio; it was footage from behind the scenes. Isabella was standing in a rocky desert talking to someone off frame. Her horse was tied up behind her. She was laughing, and her smile made me smile. Big white teeth. She started to walk out of frame, and the camera swiveled to follow her.

Isabella wrapped her arms around the shoulders of a man. Harlan Bishop. It had to be. He was dressed in a fine suit, but his back was to the camera. I begged for him to turn around. To prove what I'd known deep down all along. Each touch inflamed more anger. His face against her neck, making her laugh. His hands on the curve of her back as she waved for the camera operator to look away.

I was so seized by anger, I reached to the projector to switch it off or roll it back, but I stopped. As the cameraman was panning the frame away from the blushing Isabella, her amorous friend finally turned. He looked straight into the camera, straight at me, and he had the face of Warren Groves.

The dam of my anger for Harlan Bishop was suddenly emptied into my fists. Here was the evil left hand of our existence, some lowdown Warren Groves running his fingers down the back of the woman each of us loved.

The camera panned away, to the horse and beyond, to two little girls playing in the desert. Their backs were turned. One had red hair, and the other was a blonde.

I hardly noticed they were there at all. The reel unspooled and clapped mechanically against the projector. I stared at the white wall for a long time.

CHAPTER EIGHT

■ ■ ■

"So when did you emerge?" asked Ethan Bishop, his hair unruly in the convertible's wind.

"Thirty-four," I shouted back.

"Good year. I—Father—took care of Sinclair that year. Could have used a man like you for that. I hear you work clean. Well, it was a real bloodbath at the hotel. Men and women both. It had to be done, of course—couldn't have California taking over the factories."

Christ, I hated him worse than his father. He wouldn't shut up.

We were high above the coal smoke of shipping and the concrete sneeze powder of the construction zone. The Channel Heights development offered sun-washed views of the outlying area and tantalizing blue glimpses of the Pacific. The brightly-colored bungalows followed meandering lanes up the hillsides. The houses peeked out coyly from desert trees, and each property sported a well-tended lawn and garden. Ethan, of course, had insisted on a guided tour of the whole construction project.

"Were you in the war?" he asked.

"Yes."

"Air Corps?"

"Marines."

"Oh, rough stuff, then? Planes are fabulous. The next war I recommend planes. Jets. Astro rockets by then, right? I've been in planes since the Great War. Really enjoy flying. Like knights of the skies. Really swell. I could have sworn you were in planes."

"You might be thinking of Beau Reynolds." The drive was making a wind sock of my necktie, and it kept snapping into my face.

"Perhaps so." Ethan shifted gears as we went over another ridge. "I'll admit, and take no offense at this, that I get you all mixed up quite easily."

Channel Heights defied the frame-house standard of Bishop-brand suburbaniza-tion. I'd bet it was a favorite spot on every tour Ethan gave, home to the engineers, scientists, skilled technicians, and project architects from the San Pedro Atomic Power Station.

"This is all very nice," I said. "Nicer than I expected."

"You probably pictured Power Town." Ethan gestured between the trees at the distant work camps. "Murrow has been quite the shit about it. All of those radio bums. You know we employ, house, and feed a hundred thousand? Sure, there's go-ing to be some bad apples in there. Some troublemakers."

I'd heard the same broadcasts as Ethan. The thousands working on the APS construction crews were bivouacked in temporary dormitories in Wilmington. The rows of long, whitewashed bunkhouses were separated by shoddy canteens, company stores, and shower blocks. I'd heard the dorms were overcrowded and uncomfort-able. The workers living in them had little expectation of privacy.

The real story, the one in the papers too, was that over two years of construction, a boomtown's barnacle economy of cheap booze shacks and chow houses and gam-ing halls had sprung up around the periphery. Crime was rampant. The politicians liked to blame the handful of Negro workers, but I knew it was the cops patrolling the Wilmington work camp who brought in the whores and drugs. The fortunate men who saved enough money to leave the camps probably moved into one of Har-lan's other housing developments.

Down along the channel road we raced the laden sardine trawlers with their wheeling coteries of gulls and the cargo ships bound for the bustling port facilities. In addition to materials specific to the construction site the freighters carried fruit from South America, minerals from the Far East, and a steady stream of cultural trinkets and cheap goods churned out by the less civilized world.

Trucks and locomotives waited to receive the cargo and transport it across the country. Bishop had his hand in every step, from the manufacture of the locomotives and trucks, to ownership of the overland freight companies like Mastiff Logistics, to building and maintaining the skeletal goliaths of the gantry cranes offloading box-cars directly onto the train carriages. Even viewed at a great distance, across the sun-silvered shipping channel, the port facility was a bracing example of modern man's achievements.

It was dwarfed by the scale of the San Pedro Atomic Power Station. Ethan told me the men who worked it called it the Pit. I recognized it all from the model in Harlan Bishop's office. The hyperbolic cooling towers appeared first above the urban clutter, the central tower foremost among them, a goliath among goliaths, but each a concrete-paneled stack that loomed over all other buildings in sight. Even the dis-tant hills and mountains seemed like berms to these five enormous structures. The industrial traffic swallowed up the little convertible. My view was blocked by the back of a truck, and choking fumes and dust blew unpleasantly into my face.

"Just a little farther," said Ethan. "There's an access road up ahead for visitors."

Until we reached the access road, traffic snarled all approaches leading to the site. Ethan explained there was a railhead inside the APS bringing in steel and fuel, but day and night construction required endless convoys of Mastiff trucks hauling in concrete and tools and flatbeds laden with machinery. White motor coaches conveyed workers between Power Town and the Pit.

We passed through a checkpoint manned by men in gray police uniforms. Ethan guided the convertible onto a two-lane strip of road hemmed in by fences and leading directly to an exclusive underground parking structure.

"This is where the men from Channel Heights park," said Ethan.

We donned hard hats bearing red miter logos and climbed aboard a white jeep converted to run on electric. The vehicle tunnels of the under works were smooth and well-lit by fluorescents and smelled of grease. Regular, color-coded signs were hung from the tunnel ceiling and pointed the way to various locations. Maintenance Hub, Level 9, Level 15, Level 20, Desalination South. Ethan turned the jeep down the tunnel toward the Desalination works.

He described the Pit as we traveled. Boring technical details that I tuned out. Intake from underground tidal chambers, steam from the turbines used to heat the multistep desalinators. Twenty thousand gallons an hour. Closed system impervious to radioactive contamination. Output fed into a cistern and pumped into the city water supply every sixty minutes following quality checks. Blah, blah, blah. I would have caught up on my sleep if I thought he wouldn't have noticed.

"Aren't people worried about the radiation sickness?" I asked.

"These aren't bombs in here." Ethan laughed ruefully. "The panic about radiation poisoning is ridiculous. Irresponsible politicking by the Democrats and their friends in the oil and coal industries."

"People like Senator Paulus?"

"Yes. Yes, exactly him. Very shrewd of you to spot his kind. He's a homosexual, you know."

"Didn't know that," I said. I'd never believe a charge of homosexuality from a snake like Ethan or his father. *Homosexual* was one of those words spit by certain people when they wanted to call somebody a Red, but they couldn't prove it.

Ethan parked the jeep, and we toured the stages of the desalination works. The smell of seawater was intense on the top level, and the tidal action of the inflow tunnels produced a steady susurration that traveled through the pipes and ended in a pressurized thud.

At the bottom stage, the ninth, we sampled water from paper cones. The test reactor was operating in non-generating mode, but it produced enough electricity to run test cycles on the desalination equipment. Full operations on all four reactors were still at least six months away.

"I am impressed." It was true. The scale was humbling.

"I will show you one of the reactors under construction," said Ethan. "They have already brought in the payload on west, and south is our operating test reactor. North is still under construction. You can see the reactor pool. Go for a swim if you'd care to."

"Look, let's skip it. I get it. You are building the top dog of power plants. Jobs for California. I'm on board, and I appreciate your rolling out the red carpet and all, but I need to talk to you about a case."

"The Holly Webber business, yes. All right. We can speak in my office."

We drove in silence past the Reactor East and various maintenance tunnels and downward ramps to deeper portions of the under works. We drove under a red sign with bold white lettering. RESTRICTED PYLON, ARMED GUARDS ON DUTY. Ethan caught me staring at it.

"Waste storage," said Ethan. "We store it in lead-lined chambers below the water table to avoid any chance of contamination. The Undercroft Vault. Only a few personnel are allowed into the deep Undercroft, and we guard it with bonded security at all times."

I could tell he was lying, but I didn't know how. Not until later anyway. We ventured to the surface and the modern luxury of Ethan's office on the sixth floor of the redbrick control building. I sat in a creaking chesterfield drinking a black tea from China. A difficult place to get exports from at the moment with all the business in Korea, but I'm sure it was a trivial matter for the Bishops.

The picture window behind Ethan's desk provided him with a view not of the reactors but north toward Hollywood. The afternoon was slowly receding into evening. The sun was less merciless, and the angled light was golden. Shadows of the mullions stretched across Ethan's arm and the side of his face in a distorted grid.

I put the bitter tea down in its saucer and said, "I hope you don't mind, but I wanted to begin by asking you a question about your lineage."

"I am Ethan Bishop by way of Harlan Bishop." Ethan opened a humidor on his desk and took a pair of Robustos out. He offered me one, but I waved it off.

"And it's like that with all of you?" I asked, and I took out my black book. "All of you who have been Ethans, I mean."

He didn't seem to take offense at my jab.

"We all diverge at various points from him, but we are never second generation. Never a duplicate of a duplicate. I was chosen to take on the role of Ethan Bishop in 1948."

"You mean to say that in 1948 you were a spontaneous duplicate of Harlan Bishop; you recalled his life up until the moment you diverged."

"Not exactly. I emerged in 1942 but was kept on standby in Spark until I was needed." He glanced at my pen and black book. "You know that is how it works. I remember telling you all this when I was Harlan Bishop."

"Of course, my apologies. We Warrens struggle with identity more than you Gideons."

"We're Bishops now," he corrected me sternly.

"Sure, right. So, has your father told you anything about Holly Webber?"

"No. The first time I heard that name was earlier today. I was rather surprised you wanted to meet after we spoke on the telephone. I don't think I'll be of much help."

"I disagree." I reached into my pocket and brought out an envelope. I passed it over to him. As he opened it, I continued my questioning. "What can you tell me about your relationship, as Harlan Bishop, with Isabella Webber?"

He looked up from the film clippings in his hand, and slowly a smile spread across his face.

"But this isn't Harlan Bishop at all," he said. "This is one of you. What are you playing at here?"

"It is a Warren," I agreed.

"Remarkable that this woman looks like Annabelle, but this is not Harlan Bishop."

"Right," I said as he slid the pictures back to me, "it's a Warren, like you said. On the set of the only film being produced at that time at Royal Radio Pictures. Harlan Bishop's film company."

Ethan leaned back in his chair and finally lit his cigar. The tip of it pulsed red within a growing cloud of smoke.

"I loved her, of course." Ethan spoke around the cigar, slipping easily into his remembered life as Harlan Bishop. "She was every bit Annabelle. I imagined God had secreted her in our midst as some sort of joke."

Jealousy. Maddening jealousy, in a cauldron, overflowing my veins and burning into my face, my hands. The pain of my broken fingers was forgotten. The stones in my lungs. In that moment it took every scrap of my willpower not to rise from my chair and throttle the miserable life from Ethan Bishop.

"So how did she end up with your father?"

"Now, now, she didn't, not so far as I know. The last I can recall was 1942, and she was still with that Warren in your little picture. He was off fighting the war, but there was no charming her away from him."

"What was his name?" I asked.

Ethan rolled his eyes up and looked at the ceiling.

"I can't recall. Was it Beau Reynolds? No, that's the pilot you mentioned earlier. I'm sorry, I'm positively terrible with remembering which of you is which."

"Do you know how she was cast for *Rex Rawhide*?"

"That Warren came to me, said it was her dream. He worked for me a bit, doing odd jobs here and there, so of course I said yes. I was always looking for talent. Commercial actresses, film stars. Father has given it all up, but I cast a wide net over the studios. They send me the reels of every pretty girl to come through their doors."

"Do you still have her reel?" I asked.

He wallowed in the smoke for a long while before answering. "I'm afraid I don't, but you could always ask my father."

"Your father lied to me about all this," I said. "How did Isabella Webber die?"

"I don't know. I expect you'll need to ask the Warren in that frame about all that."

"What about her daughter, Holly Webber?"

Ethan leaned forward, emerging from the cloud of cigar smoke like the prow of a warship from fog. "I never saw her daughter. She always sent her away when I was around."

"You never looked for her daughter?"

"I didn't. My father may have." He resumed puffing on his cigar, then added, almost as an afterthought, "Just our luck, right? To always come upon her after she's dead?"

"It's a tragedy," I said.

"If you think murder is afoot, I encourage you to get to the bottom of it all. I would have my revenge on the person responsible for taking her from us again."

"Right," I said.

"We're all working for the same thing, Mr. Cord." Ethan's expression was making me feel queasy.

"What's that?" I asked.

He smiled and said like I already should know, "The future."

■   ■   ■

I vomited in the gravel outside the maintenance door. Orange and brown and swirled with blood. Couldn't tell if it was from Ethan's smile, the lingering revelations from the Paramount vault, or my beat-up guts. Mad as I was, I decided to blame it on the beating. I heaved three times and walked away from it, flushing the taste from my mouth with a flask of whiskey from my coat. I walked over to a chain-link fence facing the car park where my Tudor was baking and leaned heavily against the metal. The Stillman was in my car. I could walk out to it, come back, and fill Ethan Bishop full of lead.

Nah. The Bishops had leaped into my spot as number one suspects, and they'd certainly been revealed as liars, but their killing Holly Webber didn't make any sense. If they'd found out she was alive, why run her down out in Cranford? Clearly they were still obsessed with her. And I still had not the slightest idea as to why she'd have my name on a piece of paper.

There was a dark shape moving beyond the chain-link. Emerging from a hidden entrance out among the cars. A broad-brimmed black hat, desert sun shades, a long black overcoat. A face melted like wax. That son of a bitch was out there. I didn't like the odds it was a coincidence. The big freak was working for one of the Bishops.

I stuffed the flask back into my coat and ran for the gate. I wasn't sure what I'd do—I clearly couldn't fight a man like this one—but I had to do something. By the time I made it around to the gate and charged in among the parked cars, he was gone. No, there was his massive Cadillac, wheeling around to leave.

I had to run in the other direction. My old coupe was lost somewhere in the candy-painted sea of parked automobiles. Sweat beaded my head, and I was wheezing, but I did not relent. The Cadillac was almost to the gate. I was panicked, breathless, and I found it. I collapsed into the hot tomb of the car and backed it up, nearly kneecapping some workers headed for their cars. The tires screeched as I made for the gate.

By the time I emerged onto the access road, I was sure I'd lost him, but there he was, several blocks away. The Cadillac was a battleship among a stop-and-go flotilla of frigates. I joined the queue of workers leaving for the evening. The russet curtains of the sky were closing over the sea, the sun in my eyes. The pursuit became a jerky, slow-motion affair as I attempted to maneuver up the lines of cars exiting the Pit, but we were all bottlenecked and waiting to leave.

My gun was out and sitting beside me on the seat. The prolonged tension of the traffic jam had me checking and rechecking its cylinders, careful to keep it hidden from the view of the surrounding commuters. My body was cold with sweat, and every song on the blaring car radios was annoying me.

We finally cleared the logjam, and traffic began to flow again. The Cadillac was headed west on the One, following the coast through Long Beach and past the Seal Beach Navy base. I'd spent years following Covenant breakers and cheating husbands, before that real crooks, so I was able to keep my distance and stay out of sight even when the Cadillac turned off the One at Sunset Beach and entered a residential neighborhood.

I followed the Cadillac into a beautiful, tree-lined neighborhood full of some of the biggest bungalows I'd ever seen. It reminded me of a richer Hawthorne, where Lynn and I lived. An exclusive sort of place.

Each house was a little different than the others around it—different angles, gables, unusual brick attachment—not the suburban sameness Bishop was exporting. There were kids playing in the yards. Men clipping the grass. Women sitting in spring-backed chairs, well-heeled and happy, queens watching the evening settle romantically over their kingdom.

And me, an outsider, dripping with blood and covered in bruises, an old black car full of cigarette smell and whiskey, a loaded gun in my lap. I was the interloper. Not the Cadillac that purred silently past the houses and turned into an asphalt drive. An automatic garage opened and swallowed up the car. I stopped on the street.

Was he working for Ethan? His henchman? Or was it Harlan he answered to?

Someone was paying the monster well for him to have a house like this. A pink bungalow with dark shades pulled down over the windows, it faced inland, but it was a short walk to the beach from here. I could hear it, faintly. Beckoning.

A police car rolled past. Local uniforms. They shot a concerned look at my old Ford, at me. Time to move along, they said with their eyes.

I was exhausted anyway. Too tired to murder in this peaceful place. Too many kids. Now that I knew the monster's secret lair, the advantage was mine. I could dispatch him at my convenience. For now, I could go home and have a bath.

I wheeled the car out of Sunset Beach and headed north along a frontage road, then deeper, avoiding the highway and letting the gray of evening fall across me. Headlights catching the playing-cards on bicycle spokes. Kids called in for dinner.

I think I was in Lakewood, at a stop sign on a quiet street, messing with the dial on my radio and trying to find something other than bad news. Both doors came open, and I was looking at iron.

"Nice and easy," said a man. "Just back it up. Out of the car."

"He's got a gun," said the one on the other side.

They leaned lower, and I could see their faces. Buzz cuts and navy-blue blazers. White around the eyes where the sunglasses had been. The one leaning over me smelled like too much aftershave. The other one grabbed my Stillman off the seat.

"All right, now out"—he shoved his gun into my ribs—"come on. No funny stuff."

He frog-marched me to an idling limousine. The other fella slipped behind the wheel of my car and started to drive away.

"Nothing in this world worse than a horse thief," I said.

The guy jabbed me in the back with the barrel of his gun. "Just get in the car and shut your mouth."

Harlan Bishop's footman Elias was waiting for me in the back of the limousine. His eyes were barely more than slits; the contours of his gaunt face were deepened by the low light within the car. He was a statue rising from a pool of oil. I climbed into the seat across from him, and the buzz cut with the heater slammed the door behind me. The limousine began to move.

"I think there's been some mistake," I said. "I didn't call for a Frankenstein."

Elias reached slowly into his jacket. His long, bony fingers returned clasping a stuffed envelope. He handed it to me. Inside was an impressive stack of green. More than I'd ever seen in an envelope. I wasn't completely sure how they'd gotten it all in there.

"Your job is done," said Elias. "It is time to go home."

"Or what?"

Elias blinked. He seemed to wait for me to reconsider, but I'm stubborn and never put a lot of thought into those sorts of decisions. Never much cared for people telling me what to do.

"Tell your boss"—I held the envelope out to him—"that he can keep his money.

I'd use gutter words, but I bet you'd drain the color. I decide when the job is done, and this one's a long way from it."

Elias took the envelope back and returned it to his jacket pocket. "Take us to the ocean," he said to the driver.

"You gonna try to kill me?" I scoffed. "Tougher men have tried."

"I'm a pacifist," said Elias. "I won't harm you."

Of course he wouldn't; he had people to do that for him. The buzz cuts, three of them, dragged me out of the car and onto a lonely strip of Pacific coast. We were ghosts in the limousine's headlights. The tide was coming at us, washing around my ankles as they took turns swinging at me. I got a couple of licks in. Turned one fella's nose sideways and left a bite mark on the hand of another.

Three on one wasn't a fair fight, and the buzz cuts beat me all over again. Stomped on my broken fingers and punched a couple of teeth loose. I was doubled up and drooling blood into the white-lit surf. Wheezing, blood bubbling from my nostrils. The ocean crashing at my knees and over my hands. Reeling back and trying to suck me out with the breakers. One last kick to my side, right where I was already worked over by that giant. Christ Almighty, these fucking people.

Elias splashed out next to me, his feet bare, his pants rolled up to his knees like a beachcombing kid. He took the black book out of my coat pocket and leaned down so I could hear him over the surf.

"You're done," he said. "If you come near Harlan Bishop or his son again, you will be killed."

"Thought you were . . . a pacifist," I said.

"I don't like seeing you like this," said Elias. "It hurts me more than you."

I doubted that very much.

■ ■ ■

I'm not sure if I blacked out or just stared up at the night sky and listened to the ocean. The pain in my body ebbed, and I returned to a faraway night. I was on Kyushu, in the mountains east of Sendai. Gardener's search for Lt. Col. Ishii and his secrets brought us to the burning village of Korano and beyond, up a winding mountain road to the Catholic Church of St. Ramon.

Moonlight illuminated the church. It seemed older than was possible, its iron crenellations black and Gothic, stones weathered and left moldy by the tropical summers, cracked by the cold winter. Loose vines dangled from the cross atop its steeple. Lost amid the trees, it reminded me of a plane long ago crashed in a jungle.

It was easy to see why Ishii had chosen it as his redoubt. It was situated on high ground, with an exposed approach surrounded by several low hills where ambushes could be situated. Lights burned through cinquefoil windows that ringed the chapel. The stained-glass tower windows lower to the ground were dark and covered in wooden slats to protect them from bombs.

I passed the field glasses to my left so the Pole in the German uniform could use them. We were gathered in a ditch, the last bit of good cover before the exposure of the road was our only way forward.

"That's a butcher's ground," I warned Gardener. "Some mines, a machine gun, or even a good rifle will take its toll every time we have to move between cover."

"Will we make it?" he asked.

"A few of us would," I said. "I say we take an alternate approach. We should climb down and around. The church has the mountain's peak at its back. I'd take my chances climbing sheer cliffs and roping down over the peak. The church's roof would shield us from fire unless he actually came out of it to shoot, in which case we'd have a shot right back at him."

"There's no time for that. We've got him cornered here. We have to press the advantage, no matter the casualties."

At Gardener's insistence, I drew up a battle plan. It was little more than distributing some hand grenades and explaining the basics of assaulting a fortified position.

"If we come under fire, don't stop. Don't try to take a shot. Don't turn back to help the man beside you. You have to move as quickly as you can toward the objective. Getting in close and pressuring them is the best way to help a wounded man."

The men stared at me without reaction. They didn't trust me. Nevertheless, Gardener was satisfied. He clapped a hand on my shoulder, and we formed up and began our advance.

We moved silently and as swiftly as we could. Each rattle of ammunition or clink of a canteen seemed to echo up the mountain. Our breath gusted from our mouths in the crisp mountain air. My legs ached from the climb. We could not slow or stop.

We passed the first of the hills. There was a collapsed outbuilding hidden behind it, some sort of shed. It seemed burned or rotted into absolute ruin. A footpath curled away from the structure and disappeared into thick grass. I was in the lead, Gardener right behind me. The rest of the men fanned out in a wedge, far enough apart that if the road was mined, only one of us would lose a limb.

The second and third hill were close together. One was barren, and the other was capped with an overgrown garden. Beside it, near the road, lay the hull of a truck stripped of any useful material. Only the body remained, slumping to rust, swallowed up by weeds. It was turned to offer good cover from the church. A little too good, by my eye, and there was pale, dead grass behind, suggesting it was recently moved. The Filipino radio man was poking around it until I waved him away.

The fifth hill was just before the halfway point up the road. There was a small cemetery atop the hill, fenced with black iron, most of the monuments just simple wooden crosses. There was a single stone cross big enough to shield a man. I looked back, unsurprised to see the wedge of men behind me looking at the cross monument as well, all probably thinking the same thing: if the shooting starts, that's where I'm going.

Ishii shot Gardener first. There was a single crack, and he crumpled in the road.

"Strzelec!" shouted the Pole, and the road erupted into chaos.

I turned, against my own instructions, and grabbed Gardener by his combat webbing and hauled him onto his feet. The big man with the Browning opened fire from the middle of the road. He'd stopped and was thumping rounds into the church, shattering windows and blasting apart masonry. The other men were scattering.

Gardener was conscious but dazed, blood spilling out of his chest and darkening the front of his uniform. Behind me I could see the Filipino running for the rusty truck. He crouched behind it, and a moment later it disappeared in a fireball. Shrapnel from the explosion snapped by and lifted dust in little clouds from the roadway. I felt some of it hit my midsection, a burning there, but there was no time to figure out how bad it was.

"Come on!" I shouted, and I dragged at Gardener. "Don't make me get this guy for you."

He pushed away my hands, stronger than I expected, and together we ran for the church. Another rifle shot cracked in the night, and the Pole fell facedown in the road. The damn fool on the Browning spotted the flash and hammered rounds into a window on the ground floor. The wood shutters blew apart in splinters, and the stained glass broke loose and came sheeting down.

I never heard the shot that killed the big guy on the Browning. His gun went quiet, and when I looked back, I saw him in a heap in the middle of the road.

Gardener and me and the Navy translator and the Indian with the Thompson were closing in on the church. The engineer was cowering in the cemetery. He'd won the prize cover of the cross and was stranded there, useless to us.

Ishii took a shot at us from another one of the windows, and it missed. Then we were in close, pressing ourselves to the stone wall of the church. It was very quiet without the Browning or the rifle shots ringing out. Our heavy breathing seemed loud, and I tried to quiet myself. I checked Gardener's injury. It was in and out, messy, but looked like a muscle wound.

"I will go first," said the Navajo with the Thompson.

"I'll give him something to think about," I said, and I pulled the pin on a hand grenade. I waited until the Indian was in position and then hurled it through the empty frame of a window. There was a startled cry on the other side and an explosion that shook the door. The Navajo kicked it in and stepped inside, firing his Thompson blind into the darkened church. By the camera flash of his gun I saw several men and women, Japanese and Anglo, cowering behind the chapel's pews.

Ishii shot the Indian with a pistol, and he came at us, screaming, his face twisted in rage like a Samurai mask, a Banzai scarf around his head. He thrust his officer's sword through the Navy translator's guts. As Ishii drew the bloody length of it back out, he tried to turn, and I clubbed him, right in the mouth, with the butt of my

Garand. He fell back but didn't go down, so I hit him again. The third time was to be sure, and the fourth time, opening a gash on his head, was because I couldn't kill him flat out. Gardener stopped me from hitting him again.

"We got him," he said. "Make sure he stays got. I need to find his sister."

"What?"

Gardener didn't answer. He was already running toward the pews, calling out in Japanese. I was furious with adrenaline. I wanted to gun down the Jap nuns and burn the church and Ishii with it. I picked up Ishii's pistol. One of those Jap Lugers. *Nambu*, they called them. It was still warm from being fired, and I thought about popping a round off into Ishii's brain.

The translator grabbed at my boot, reminding me he was still alive and saving me from a rampage I would have regretted.

"Up," he moaned.

I knelt beside him and saw straightaway that he was in bad shape. He was Italian or Greek, heavy brows, but his olive skin was sallow and his expression stricken. His shirt was black with blood. His guts were spilling out of the wound in his stomach. I tried to keep him from rolling onto them. He took hold of my blood-slicked hand.

"Help me get up," he said, and he stared intensely at me for a moment. He closed his eyes and breathed deeply a few more times and was dead.

I lifted Ishii beneath his armpits and dragged him over to a chair beside the altar. His head lolled drunkenly. The cowardly engineer finally showed up and helped me corral the nuns and the priest—a fat Anglo speaking Dutch or something—into the rectory. Gardener returned with his prize: a slim, teary-eyed Jap girl in a nun's habit. Gardener was talking to her in Japanese in a calm tone. He looked ashen.

"You all right?" I asked.

He finished murmuring to the Japanese girl before answering.

"Yes, are you?"

The front of my jacket was speckled with blood and holed in a dozen places. There was a red line of moisture at my belt. I was perforated good from shrapnel, but it didn't hurt at all and was barely bleeding. Weeks later when I was being shipped back to America from the Marshall Islands with two failing kidneys and a blood infection, it wouldn't seem so minor.

I replied to Gardener with a shrug.

"Get Ishii awake. She doesn't know where he put it."

"Put what?" asked the engineer.

"Get back outside and make sure no one is coming from the village," said Gardener to the engineer. "And see if any of those poor bastards are still alive."

I got Ishii awake by filling my canteen with holy water and dumping it over his head. His sister in the nun's habit was crying at the sight of him all bloodied up. It sounded like hiccups. When Ishii lifted his head, she blurted something and tried to reach for Ishii, but Gardener held her tightly. Ishii said something in Japanese.

"English only," said Gardener. "You don't want your sister to hear what we're talking about."

Ishii's lips curled back in a bitter smile.

"I should have known you would bring one of them, Gardener. To rub my nose in it? How many of you are there?"

"Enough," said Gardener.

"He knows?" I asked.

"I know." Ishii spit. "Everything. I know about you Americans and your secret army. The Warrens, right? I heard the code name tortured out of a man with your face at Buhlendorf."

"Save it. The villagers in Korano told me you had the case with you when you came through." Gardener drew his automatic and pressed the barrel to Ishii's sister's head. "This is real simple. You tell me where it is, and your sister lives. Nothing happens to her—"

"Hiertsukan!" Ishii shouted, and he fought with his bonds. "Let go of her, you son of a bitch!"

"Or you refuse and watch your sister's brains explode. I'm a fair man, Ishii. A lot fairer than you and your pressure experiments on those Chinese. I'm giving you a chance to save something you love. That's a lot to give a man in the middle of a war."

Ishii's sister closed her eyes. She was speaking quietly. In the tense silence that occupied the chapel I realized by her inflection she was reciting the Lord's Prayer in Japanese.

"I can't trust you," said Ishii.

"You can trust that I will make you watch her die and then torture it out of you. Like you did to a man with my face at Buhlendorf, right?"

"Hollman and the SS did that," said Ishii.

"Sure, and Uncle Sam is doing this. I'm just the gun at the end of his hand, pressed to little Miko's temple. I'm trying to save everyone some time."

Ishii went limp in his restraints. He stared down at his lap.

"It is atop the mountain," he muttered. "In the mountaineer's black cabin."

Gardener released Ishii's sister, and she threw herself at her brother. Ishii couldn't look at her. Neither could I.

"We're going to the top," said Gardener. "He's coming with us."

It was a long way up.

■ ■ ■

The shrill cry of the seagulls woke me from my dream. I was on the beach, legs dangling in the surf. One of my eyes was glued shut, and the other was a raw nerve pulsing in my brain. The dark shapes of the seagulls reminded me of a cursed place, long-ago symbols painted on the ceiling of a forgotten cave.

"Your hand looks infected."

I sat up to see who was talking and came face-to-face with a Warren. Again. This time the Warren was much older, hair long and white, face sun-chapped and eyes small in squinting folds. He was shirtless and bronzed, but his body was going slack with age. He was sitting on a metal camping cooler stuck into the sand. Drinking a beer.

"Can I have one of those?" I groaned.

"I'll give you two."

He lifted his butt up just enough to pull two cans out of the cooler. He cracked one open with his church key and passed it and the other one to me unopened. I held it against my eye and took a long sip of the other one.

"We're breaking the Covenant," I said.

He waved his hand dismissively and said, "Maybe the Judge will come along and shoot us."

"Are you real?" I asked, watching the gulls whirl above the beach.

"I don't know. Are you?"

I chuckled, and it turned into a cough, both of which pained my tender ribs.

"The name's Max Holden." He held a hand caked with sand out to me. Made for a gritty shake.

"Casper Cord. You're one of my past lives," I said. "An old one."

"Where'd we split?"

"Between wars, going to work in the canneries. I remember you used to have that Model T that you painted with house paint."

The old man chuckled. "Guilty, but in my defense I was drunk. I was always drunk. That's why I'm walking on a deserted beach in the early morning drinking beers with a stranger. What are you doing?"

"I'm the Judge," I said.

Max laughed and then realized I wasn't joking. "Casper Cord. I think I heard," he said, and he saluted me with his beer. "Well, if you're gonna kill me, at least let me finish my beer."

"To hell with it."

"That's the spirit," he said, and we toasted our cans together. "I got some reefer in my bag. You want to smoke it with me?"

I said yes, although I never really indulged in the drug. It felt good and eased my pain. We laughed at nothing, or maybe at just the right things, and passed the marijuana back and forth.

"What are you doing half-dead on a beach?" asked Max.

"It's a long story."

"They just keep getting longer for us. And more complicated all the time."

I stared at the surf, and we sat in silence for a while. The warmth of the day was accelerating, burning up that gauzy chill, dissipating the aimless pleasure of the reefer. The beer in my hand was warm.

"I've been seeing things," I said. "The grasshopper, some weird white creature, and Annabelle."

"I see two out of three of those," said Max. "Used to have nightmares about that damn grasshopper all the time. Never came knocking on my door, so I figured it was all in my head. Same with Annabelle. She never came knocking, so I just told myself I dreamed her."

"She came knocking, and I answered the door too late," I said, and I finished the last bitter swallow of beer.

"Opportunity lost is the worst, man. What you need is to talk to Ian. He lives up in Malibu. Them Hollywood rich folks try to run him off, but he's grandfathered in. You should see his place. It's incredible. He has this room he did up like that cave that collapsed. The one with all the crosses on the ceiling."

"With the grasshopper idol," I said.

"Yeah, exactly," said Max. "He gets you real high on this herbal stuff the Indians use, and you go on this wild trip through your memory. Beats any movie you'll see. And he cooked me dinner afterward."

"He's a Warren?"

"Yeah, Ian Bendwool. You got a pen and paper?"

I reached for my black book and was reminded Elias had robbed me of it. I took a dry cleaning tag from my pocket instead. Max dictated the address to me. When he was done, I struggled to push myself up. My pants were ruined, and I was missing both shoes and one sock.

"Thanks for your help," I said.

"No problem," said Max, only when I looked it wasn't Max at all, just some gray-haired bum smeared with dirt. He wasn't even sitting on a cooler, just carrying a few warm beers. I limped off the beach, sure I'd wake up again, but I didn't.

CHAPTER NINE

■ ■ ■

Not a lot scares me, but I was afraid to go home. I had a change of clothes at my office, so I took the bus and shuffled down the sidewalk barefoot, feeling like a bum. People were staring at me, and I couldn't blame them once I caught sight of myself in a window. My collar was sticking up, jacket torn, bloody bandages wrapped around my head, and one eye swollen halfway shut. I was fortunate Elias had left me my wallet. At least I could prove I wasn't a bum when a beat cop stopped me outside my building.

"It's been a rough couple of days," I explained.

The cop was unmoved to pity. "Just get off my street," he said.

I stumbled to the lot behind my building and was overjoyed to find my car parked there. I guess the brunos working for Bishop weren't complete monsters. I peeked in the windows and could see that the glove box and the smuggler's hold were both open and empty. Didn't look like the villains had left me my heater.

I took the back entrance into my building to avoid the doorman's judgmental gaze. It was dark and quiet down on the lower floor. There was a faint smell of perfume. The pounding in my head receded a little just being out of the sun. I started to put my key in the door, only to discover I'd evidently left the office unlocked. Great. The last time I did that, some kids took my radio. Forced me to bring the old set from home.

I made do by the rectangle of light coming through the semi-basement window. The office was gloomy, its shadows deep, but that suited my mood just fine. I sighed and sat down in my creaky office chair. There was a bottle of whiskey in my desk drawer. An extra pack of Bravos. There was a forgotten tumbler on my filing cabinet. I blew the dust off, turned it over on my desk, and glugged a measure of amber liquid into it. I drank it in one go and refilled the glass.

I switched on my desk lamp, instantly surprised to see I was not alone.

"Hello," said Holly Webber.

Trouble never looked as good in red as Holly Webber's imposter sitting across from me. Her crimson shift dress stuck to her in all the right places. Her skin was smooth and pale, and there was a lot of it showing, but my gaze kept wandering back to her face. It was surrounded by thick locks of red hair that fell to her shoulders and kept up with the dress. She had blushing apple cheeks and the sort of full red lips I dreamed about kissing right before my alarm clock went off.

Her shoes were off, and her legs were folded neatly beneath her as if she'd been sitting in my one good chair for a long time. She drew a filtered Wildcat from her handbag and hung it from her pursed lips. I leaned across the desk and gave her a light. I could faintly smell the sweetness of her perfume before the smoke got into my nose.

"My name is Holly Webber," she said.

There was the rub. Her name wasn't Holly Webber. Couldn't be. And yet here she was. The same big blue eyes that I'd last seen all glassy and staring up at the sky on a cold Dairy Valley morning.

"I need your help," she said. "You're the detective, right?"

I blinked a few times, still expecting her to disappear like so many other impossible things I'd seen in the last few days.

"Can you help me or not?" she asked.

"I'm sorry." I reached a hand across the desk to her. "Casper Cord."

Her hand was warm. Her grip was firm. Real and not a dream at all. She was barely wearing any makeup but was as beautiful as a Hollywood starlet. I held her hand overlong, and she pulled it away with a jerk.

"I may be able to help you," I said, my words tangled up by excitement. "I just might. But I need to know more. The case. Sit down, please."

She was already sitting.

"What is the case?" I asked.

"I have been kidnapped against my will," she said. "I mean, obviously not at the moment, but I have been kidnapped, and I'm afraid for my life."

"That's a good place to start. Who kidnapped you?"

"I don't know who. They broke into my apartment a few days ago."

"Where do you work?"

She took a long drag on her cigarette before answering. "A hamburger restaurant in El Segundo. Mister Swiftee."

"Uh-huh. And how did you escape from your captivity?"

"He was asleep," she said. "I could hear him snoring in the other room, so I pried the nail out of the window and climbed out."

"Where were you?"

"South somewhere. It was a nice neighborhood."

"Sunset Beach?"

"Yeah, that's it. How did you figure it out so fast?"

"I think I know who kidnapped you. Be glad you never saw his face. He might have been working for someone else. I'm still confused about something, though." I stood up from behind my desk, came around to her side, and leaned against the desktop. "Who are you?"

"Holly Webber," she said.

"Holly Webber is dead. I saw her body lying by the side of the road in Cranford."

"No!" she exclaimed, and she covered her mouth with her hand. She couldn't meet my gaze. "No, no, no. I thought . . . I didn't know what . . ."

"Calm down," I said, and I reached for her arm to comfort her. She pushed my hand away. Her big blue eyes were damp with tears.

"You're lying to me," she said. "I would have known if Holly died. Someone . . . I would have gotten a phone call and . . ."

"I'm not lying to you." I went on to explain everything about Holly Webber's death down in Cranford. Maybe in a little too much detail. The girl looked like I'd taken all the pluck out of her by the time I was finished.

She sagged in her chair. The taut sexuality of her was deflated. She was struggling to keep from crying.

"My name is Veronica Lambert," she finally admitted. "I am Holly's friend. Her best friend. We were roommates."

"I've been investigating Holly's death as a murder. Your name has come up. I . . . your resemblance to Holly is uncanny."

"Her mom always called us the twins." She wiped the welling tears away with her thumb. "We're not related. She lived most of the time with her dad. That's where I grew up, in Riverside. Funny thing is, Holly was the bottle red. I was the natural, like her mom. Do you have a drink?"

I cleaned the dust from another tumbler and poured her two fingers of my cheap whiskey.

"Why are you all dressed up?" I asked.

"He brought all my stuff with me when he kidnapped me," she said. "Just a bag and some clothes at first, but the next day he pushed in boxes and boxes of things. Picture albums, old stuffed animals—he must have cleared out our apartment."

"He did," I tipped the bottle at the edge of her glass and refilled it. "I checked it."

"Who is this guy?"

I held up my hand wrapped in bloody, pus-soaked bandages. She recoiled from the sight of it.

"He did that to me," I said. "He's a piece of work. Psychopath who can bend lead pipes."

"You know, you look real familiar to me," she said. "Did you know Holly's dad? You from Riverside?"

"No." I put down my whiskey. "But that brings me to another question. How did you know to come to me? And, more important, why did Holly have my name and telephone number the night she died?"

"She's had it since we lived together. Since her mom passed. If anything really bad happened, she was supposed to telephone you, because you could help."

"I couldn't help Holly," I said. "I can help you."

■ ■ ■

As much as my past dictated I be smitten with the latest in an apparently long line of Annie Groves look-alikes, I still wasn't convinced Veronica Lambert was on the level with me. I didn't have an answer as to why Holly had my number, and something wasn't adding up about how she died. If it was the giant with the melted face, what was he doing kidnapping Veronica and keeping her safe in his Sunset Beach bungalow?

I told Veronica not to worry, that I'd deal with the guy who'd kidnapped her, but instead I put on a change of clothes, cleaned myself up until the only hurt showing was a little tape on my face, and followed her. Easy to do when a girl is taking the bus everywhere.

Her first stop was to pick up some dry cleaning from a little Chinese shop. Woo's. She was in and out in a hurry, which was good, because she'd apparently convinced the bus driver to wait around for her. I could see the passengers shifting impatiently, probably hollering at the driver to get going. Veronica marched out of the cleaner's with a bagged dress over her shoulder and climbed the stairs back onto the bus.

The bus delivered Veronica straight to the driveway of a little yellow two-story in Montebello, not far from Jap Town. A poor, earnest neighborhood where the houses were pretty but uncomfortably close together. There were white flowers growing in the planter out in front of the house. A tricycle in the yard. I watched her walk up the cement path to the door. Even when she was alone, she poured herself up the steps and deployed every weapon in her arsenal.

She rang the bell. The inner door opened, and she had a brief conversation through the dark mesh of a screen door. Someone, a woman, opened it, and two little kids—a boy and a girl—shot out of the darkened house and launched themselves at Veronica. She scooped them up in her arms and showered them with kisses. She disappeared into the house.

The name on the mailbox was Delroy. I searched the streets for any sign of a tail. Twice in one week was more than enough, so I'd packed Ishii's trophy Jap gun from my desk into my smuggler's hold and was ready to pop lead at anyone who came my way. Assuming the war souvenir still worked.

The trees divided the sun and laid swaying leaf patterns over the parked cars. There were kids playing cowboys and Indians in a front yard down the street. The cowboys were winning, as usual.

Veronica emerged from the house with an alligator valise in one hand and a white coat draped over her arm. She said a cheery good-bye to someone I couldn't quite make out in the darkness of the doorway.

She was a different person. Her hair was combed back and pulled into a ponytail. Her hip-hugging crimson dress was replaced by a bright tangerine day dress with a cinched waist and vivid botanical print. No more cleavage and not much leg. The dress ended below her knee, and she wore open-toed shoes with kitten heels.

Half her face reclined behind her cat's-eye sunglasses. She waved a last time at the screen door, and, with her dry cleaning still in hand, she got behind the wheel of the Buick Woody in the driveway. It was rusty and dented, and Veronica looked tiny peering out of the window. She struggled to maneuver it out onto the road. She spent so long at it, I was afraid she would see me.

She had lunch with a man I didn't recognize, had a second lunch with another man, an Italian with several goons, and spent the afternoon by herself in a plush hotel in Beverly Hills. When she emerged, it was evening, and it took me a moment to spot her. I caught a glimpse of her hair and the red dress before she disappeared into a waiting taxi cab.

Her reason for taking a cab instead of her borrowed Buick was soon made apparent. She was headed to the Sugarside boardwalk. Parking was a nightmare because people either took the train or a boat into the marina. I didn't need to tail her all the way. I remembered what Caroline, Holly's coworker from the Swiftee Burger, had told me about Veronica. She worked as a dancing girl. And there was only one spot in Sugarside that still had taxi dancers.

The marina at night reminded me of those romantic visions of Venice you get in films and picture books. Yachts and cigarette boats and bobbing launches mingled in the dark and placid water, merry lights strung from masts. Men and women gathered on the decks and laughed and drank and enjoyed the summer night and the fruits of their wealth. Bonfires on the beaches. Barefoot youths danced around them like cargo cultists, their flesh crimson and wheat in the firelight, bodies lithe and exposed in their polyester swimming suits.

It was a Friday, and the crowds were out on the boardwalk. Young couples strolled, enjoying sweet ice and caramel corn and fair weather. The game barkers called to men to prove themselves worthy of the girl on their arm. Shoot a Jap! Test your strength against the Iron Anvil! Land a ring and win a dolly for your gal! Fortune tellers and tattoo artists beckoned from closet-sized stalls lit by the garish neon of their signs.

Illicit vices could be had at the joints in between or under the boardwalk. I'd followed more than my share of cads and hopheads down there with a camera. The coloreds and Chicanos sold bags of grass and little balls of Mexican junk. They worked alongside their best customers, the three-dollar girls and boys with gaunt bodies and dark, desperate eyes. If you strayed too far from the coppers, the beggars would be on you. Black-eyed, lingering, little hungry raccoons of boys and girls.

The Cabirian Palace was the mountain looming behind the boardwalk. Its domed roof and Deco cornices were the worse for wear. A painted mural of dancers above the entrance was nearly white with sun; its gold and silver embellishments were jewelry hung on ghosts. The noise from the band and the tidal din of the dancers spilled out the doors and along the colonnaded entryway.

Sailors from the USS *Fresno* lounged against the plaster pillars, languid with sweat, kerchiefs untied. They reminded me of the Filipino merchant sailors and the fishermen in Saipan, laughing and sleeping in the streets after two weeks on the sea. They were kids, drunk on *cuba libres* and perfumed necks, hair pomaded into greased ducktails, long nights and laughter prematurely dwindling into puddles of sour booze.

They wore their dress whites like boys heading to church. To their eyes I was a fossil come to life and escaped from the museum. A few of the sailors called out jeers, but I wasn't afraid. Sticks and stones already broke my bones; a few names weren't going to kill me.

Tropical heat inside the Cabirian. Lobby thick with smoke and sweat and the smells of intimate intervals spent in the coatroom. I pushed past the comers and goers. A dark-eyed cigarette girl sold me a pack of Bravos, and I lit one up just to feel at home. There was a long line for the taxi dancers. I was third- or fourth-rate. Worse than the Hollywood princes and the sailors and the desk workers weekending by the beach. I was one of the old, lonely men in their cheap suits, couldn't keep a girl's eye, came here because I couldn't get a date.

Most of the dance girls were out on the floor, but some few were taking a break, reclining on sofas and chairs—the plain girls with no curves, Latin girls and coloreds, who probably did their best business on the off nights when the club went mixed. There were also a few earners too tired for the current set.

I watched their feet. Unstrapping and restrapping, wiggling pinched toes, glimpses of long legs and half-heard exchanges of weary commiseration. They didn't smile. They were working, and this was their break area. The bouncers kept the men away, shoving drunks with beers spilling down their shirts and warning off the hopeless crushes waving their cards and calling out to girls with names that probably didn't belong to anyone.

It was Woody Herman and his Third Herd on stage, Woody's clarinet blaring out over the heaving sea of the dancers. Only the top row of the bandstand was visible at all. The beating drums of three hundred feet shook the floor like an earthquake, and the air moved with them, pulling all attention and all urges toward the incredible din of that packed ballroom.

There were a lot of beautiful girls at the Cabirian, but Veronica was easy to spot. She was a million-dollar doll in a hundred-dollar joint, her crimped copper-red hair flapping as she was swung around by her dance partner. She was buttoned into the crimson petticoat of a Dior Corolle, bell skirt ending above her knees, breasts nearly spilling out of the corseted top, one scarlet heel kicked up high as her partner dipped her so her hair touched the floor. She was straight out of my dreams, but I'd bet every man in the joint could say the same thing.

The interval ended, and Woody thanked the crowd and the band as the dance floor cleared. Red-faced men rejoined their friends in the lobby, exuberant and exerted, sharing the details of their fleeting romances, raving about the sweet things their girl had whispered in their ear. The dance girls went to the couches, safely behind the ticket counter. A few disappeared into the powder room. Three or four accompanied men to the coatroom for some earning on the side.

The line was long but efficient, and by the time the music was starting up again, I was in front of one of the ticket-sellers. A dour old pair of eyebrows with a banker's visor sat high behind the counter. He pointed a bony finger at the roped-off section of the lobby and spoke with rote detachment.

"Pick a girl. One dollar a dance, three for the interval. If you want another dance, you need to get back at the end of the line." He tapped his finger on a placard on the counter. "Get fresh, and you get tossed. No refunds."

"Give me until the interval with a woman who can dance," I said. "It doesn't matter what she looks like."

The old man had a sense of humor. I took to the dance floor with a six-foot-tall brunette named Mary. She had the body of Olive Oyl and a face like she'd been getting fresh with a lemon. Her rationed dress was plain and ill-fitting, and she smelled like soap, she didn't look too happy to be dancing with a beat-up old man either, but none of that mattered, because she was as sweet as custard once I got her on the dance floor. I searched for Veronica and found her with an Air Force man. A handsome officer.

"You look like that actor," said Mary. "The pilot who died."

"He offed himself because he couldn't stand sharing my face," I said. "You look very fetching yourself."

She covered her bad teeth with one hand when she smiled. "Can you dance?" she asked.

Maybe years ago. Maybe before I caught the wrong side of two beatings in one week. Yeah. I used to cut a rug with Lynn. She would work me into a lather like a rodeo horse, but all the dances I knew were old. Jitterbugs and Lindy Hops. Mary said those would be fine, even though clearly she knew how to dance the current steps and resented being shackled to an old-timer like me.

I used the pause between songs to take her by the hand and move closer to Veronica. Her customer was handsome, all right, but a lousy dancer, or maybe just more concerned with seeing how much of her he could get his hands on. Their version of a Balboa was infuriating. The Air Force man caressed her shapely hips and pressed against her. I was distracted and wasn't so good at the Balboa anyway. I stubbed my toe into Mary's foot.

"Watch it," she said.

I pulled her against me and dipped her in my arms. The song ended. The Air Force man and Veronica were standing very close and laughing. What an impossibly good time they seemed to be having. He touched her arm and whispered in her ear. She was smiling and playing with his medals.

"All you old-timers out there," Woody said, "might want to have yourself a drink. If you listen to the radio, then you've probably heard this one. It comes from Ray Anthony, and if you've got a pretty girl and you brought your dancing shoes, then 'Let's Dance!'"

A cheer went up from the crowd. The music was unfamiliar to me. The dance was a swing dance with very elaborate footwork that resembled a tango. Mary knew it, Veronica knew it, even the Air Force man knew it, but I was completely out of my element. I was stubbing my toes against Mary's again, searching for a context, trying to copy the dancers nearby.

"I thought you said you knew how to dance," Mary said.

"I need a drink," I said, and I left Mary on the dance floor. She carried right on dancing, seemingly happy to spend her time alone.

I found a stool facing a mirror and sat my ass down. I tapped out a Bravo and slid it between my lips. A Spanish-spewing Chicano with a bar back's mien accepted fifty cents and slid something wet and poisonous over on a napkin. The ice clicked against my front teeth, and the booze burned my throat. It tasted like a bad memory of rum and soda.

I looked at myself in the mirror. Sweaty, taped-up wounds, one eye still puffy from mistreatment. Christ Almighty, I had no business dancing out there. I was lucky I didn't have a coughing fit. One of those ones that ended with me doubled up and spitting blood.

I set the empty glass on the counter and tapped it for a refill. I turned my back on the bar. Veronica was still out there, a bit sweaty, dancing energetically with that dashing Air Force officer. I was beginning to entertain jealous fantasies, the sort of ridiculous garbage that ends with me victorious and her swooning. Rather than let my machismo get the better of me, I took my drink and stepped out a side door. The booming of the music was muffled in the narrow space between the Cabirian Palace and a roller rink. I walked up the alley to the through street running behind the boardwalk.

The Cadillac was there. Tinted windows, big chrome grill. It had to be the Cadillac from before. I reached into my pocket for Ishii's Jap pistol, but I'd left the damn thing in my car half a mile away.

I threw my drink down and bolted back down the alley. The door locked from the inside, and I couldn't get back into the dance hall. I went into the roller rink, right out onto the rink itself, dodging kids and whole families thudding along the wooden track. Some employee shouted at me as I bolted through the snack bar and out the front door.

The bouncer at the Cabirian wanted to be paid again, and I wasn't in the mood, so I put him on the ground with two quick taps to his kidney. A sailor tried to grab me, and I tripped him backward over my foot. I cut a path through the crowd. The music was ending, and the dancers were starting to come off the floor. I fought my way against the flow of people and toward Veronica. She was canoodling with the Air Force officer. Standing close and whispering in his ear.

I grabbed her wrist. "We've got to get out of here," I said.

"What the hell are you doing here?" she demanded.

"He's outside, waiting to take you back," I said.

"Hey!" The Air Force officer shoved me.

I smiled at him. You put me one on one against anyone but a heavyweight champ, and I'll take them down. I've been in too many scraps over the years to be afraid of getting hit and not know how to throw my own punch. I laid Air Force out with an uppercut that was sure to loosen some teeth. He fell and did that slow-lowering of his head that meant he was knocked out but trying to pretend he wasn't.

"Come on," I said, and I grabbed Veronica's wrist.

Of course she wasn't grateful about it. I'd just made a scene at the place she worked and knocked out a guy who was probably one of her best customers. These are the sorts of things I might have thought of if I'd stopped to consider what I was doing.

The bouncers were forming a blockade at the front entrance. There was another exit at the back, by the stage, but the dance floor had turned into hostile territory. I'd made too much of a scene. That left the alley. I dragged Veronica behind me as we ran out the door. Our escape through the alley was blocked by the towering shape of the giant in his flat-brimmed hat.

"Fuck off!" I shouted.

He started toward us, and I pulled Veronica into the roller rink. She screamed as two hand-holding teenagers skated right toward her. They managed to break apart and skate around us, but Veronica pitched over backward and pulled me down on top of her. No time to enjoy the soft landing. I pushed off her curves in a hurry and helped her up. She stumbled and lost a heel in our rush to get across the rink. I picked her up and put her over my shoulder.

"You again," said the rink employee from earlier. "What the hell is wrong with you?"

The alley door banged open, and people on the rink began to scream at the horrible sight of the giant. I wasn't going to stand around with a monster bearing down on us. I hustled past the rink employee and out onto the boardwalk.

By the time I got her to my car, Veronica was laughing hysterically.

"It's not funny," I insisted.

"It is," she said, "a little bit. Admit it."

The lights of the boardwalk receded in the back window. Veronica leaned over the back of the seat to watch them disappearing behind us. Her merry laughter teased a smile onto my face, but I hid it and played the part of the serious man.

"You only think it's funny because we got away," I said.

"But we did," she said.

CHAPTER TEN

■ ■ ■

When I dreamed of Annie, I was always separated from her by a distance. It was usually some memory or symbol my brain coughed up, a gulf or canyon, a gore-filled trench or a river. Once, she could only be reached by picking up a special telephone. It was ringing, and I knew she was calling, but people from my life kept preventing me from answering it.

Other nights the dream was straight from memories. I'd see her leaning on the porch rail, waiting for me as I rode down from Spark, or I'd see her shuttering up the windows for a storm while I was out in the barn closing in the animals. There was never an embrace. Not even a hug. I'd try to go to her and never arrived near enough to touch her.

Veronica Lambert was touching me, and she didn't even know it. She was asleep, slumped against my arm, and while she softly snored beside me, I enjoyed her warmth, the sound of her breath, and once I even leaned over and smelled her hair. It was the depraved act of a dime-novel creeper. I knew it was sick, but I couldn't stop myself.

We were headed to the supposed location of Ian Bendwool's house in Malibu. Maybe it was just my imagination, maybe Max Holden was a hallucination, but I'd written down a real address on that dry cleaning ticket. If there was a real place in Malibu, then maybe it held answers. If not, at least we'd swerved unpredictably away from the path everyone expected us to be on.

LA was at our backs. To the west the Pacific met the continent, white waves rolling in from the shelf and crashing against the coastal cliffs; to the right were the sorts of nowhere towns that catered to folks forever passing through.

Up ahead the Pacific Coast Highway was out, so I followed a detour, turning inland as the alternate road traced the contours of the hills and mountains. Veronica awoke and said she smelled smoke blowing in through the open windows. I smelled it too. The creosote and charcoal stink grew thicker and thicker until we could see the cinder mounds of the fire-claimed hills. In the distance a conflagration swept over the land in a moving front, burning brighter than seemed possible, turning the night red and leaving behind vast fields of glowing trees and stumps.

"Look out!" Veronica cried.

I braked hard to avoid hitting a full-grown buck crossing the road. It stopped, taller than the car, antlers like the branches of some dead tree. It gazed at us with primeval arrogance. It was a million years of history rendered in fur and sinew and the dark, gelatin marbles of its eyes.

The buck's world was ending, consumed by fire, and so it came into our domain, crossed man's asphalt, and stood before the dangerous machine of his invention. The buck looked into my eyes—the eyes of the pale beast that had gathered up all four corners of the world—and I saw it proud and untamed. I saw in it a hero of its kind, its deeds and victories venerated in the wicked branches of its antlers and in no other language or song.

"What is it doing?" asked Veronica.

"Escaping," I said. "Running to the ocean to die. To throw itself off a cliff so that it can choose its own fate and deny the fire."

In a single bound it disappeared into the darkness. Snowy ashes swirled in the headlamps' stark void. More deer were crossing farther down the road. They were small and panicked compared to the buck. Their heads were down. They did not look up. I motored on more cautiously.

The fire had a voice, complex and tidal, audible as a rumble and a rush and a steady crackling of exploding sap. The heat was becoming uncomfortable. We rolled up the windows to keep the ash out of the car and stewed in the heat baking through the metal.

"It's beautiful," Veronica said.

There were fire trucks up ahead. Three of them and an ambulance. Hoses looped and unspooled onto the asphalt. No sign of the firemen.

"I want to get out," Veronica said.

"That's a bad idea."

I was driving so slowly, she went ahead and opened the door. I stopped the car, and she dashed out and ran into the beams of the headlamps. Loose ash shivered across the lanes. She escaped down the highway beyond the reach of the light. Straight into the worst of the fire.

I cursed and pulled the car to the side of the road. I held a hand to my face against the blowing ash. The sound was incredible, like burning waves crashing against shores of kindling. I chased after her.

"Come back," I shouted. "Don't breathe the smoke."

It was impossible advice. I felt the spasms in my chest as the smoke aggravated the cancer. I began choking and coughing and leaned over in the road, spitting out scabrous globs of mucus. Each spasm of coughing hurt slightly worse than the last.

I wiped my mouth with my sleeve and started after her again. Into a pulsing wall of heat. My eyes stung with ash; cinders swirled above my head. There was a thundering and crying sound, and fireballs exploded from the wildfire and launched horizontally across the asphalt. At last, Veronica stopped, arms hanging at her sides, hair and skirt whipping wildly in the hot updrafts from the fire. She was silhouetted by the streaks that spread the blaze across the road.

"You need to get back," I said. "I saw a motor lodge back a few miles. We can . . . we can . . ."

A tsunami of fire was overtaking the road, curling flames spitting in incandescent arches fifty feet high over both lanes of the highway. The thundering and the crying sounds were issuing from a stampede across the road. The shooting fireballs were live animals, burning, crazed with pain and desperate to escape the holocaust. They raced out of the front of the wildfire by ones and by tens.

Jackrabbits and more deer and squirrels and raccoons screamed across the road in their death panic. Some were already dead but still moving; blackened bodies stumbled over the asphalt, cooked muscles compelled by the animal's will to survive. Some collapsed in the road and tried to drag themselves forward or curled up and lay still as their bodies were consumed by the fire. The smell of the burning hair and roasting meat was overpowering.

Veronica leaned in against my shoulder. I walked her to the car and put her into the backseat. Her dress and her face were smeared with soot. I cleaned her off with my necktie.

The road was completely impassable now. Our way denied. The fire was burning on both sides, and the molten asphalt would be a trap for any fool who dared to run the gauntlet. I turned the Ford around and drove for the motel.

"It's like the end of the world," she said.

"It's just a fire. It happens all the time."

I said it, but I knew she was right. By increments and in ways small and large the world was ending. The red sky blazed in the mirror; by some cinematographer's trick its molten fury layered over my reflected eyes.

■　■　■

The motor lodge was a two-story motel with a neon sign fouled with soot. The swimming pool was a charred custard cup. The motel amounted to no more than a dozen rooms and a detached office. The only other guest was driving a repainted Army twelve-ton truck. The door of the truck cab was stenciled with the dog placard of Mastiff Logistics. The boxes of cargo were covered with a tarp. A few boxes visible above the truck's tailgate were stamped with the Bishop Unlimited miter symbol.

"Rooms eight and nine." I helped Veronica out of the back of the car.

She stood on her own and pushed my hands away. "Give me the key," she said. "Do you have an aspirin?"

No aspirin, but I had a flask. She took a slug and handed it back. She carried her shoes and walked barefoot through the ashes drifting in the parking lot. I toted her valise into the room behind her. Her footprints smudged black on the lurid orange carpeting.

Someone had recently updated the motel with atomic-age ugliness. The garish papered walls were decorated with chrome spangles, there was a small television set, and the queen-size bed came with a red headboard made of plastic. The overhead lights were hung in a chandelier made from twists of black iron and yellow glass lanterns that produced weak, diffuse light.

The room's air conditioner was dormant, and the room was hot and smelled of past guests and a long vacancy. I switched the air on for her, and the ghosts of cigarettes gusted into the room. It also brought in the charred stink of the distant fires.

Veronica sat on the bed. Her face and dress were smudged with soot. She sighed and laid on her back with her knees hooked over the edge of the bed. I watched her chest rise and fall.

"Where are we going?" she asked.

"I told you," I said. "Malibu."

"We should be there already."

"There was a detour and the fire." I took off my hat and sat down on the bed with my back to her. I tried to convince myself I wasn't just lingering in the room waiting for something to happen.

"Is it about Holly's case?" she asked.

"There's a man there who might have some answers for me." Telling her much more would be an even greater violation of the Covenant. Meeting with him, if he was real at all, was already punishable by death. No need to drag her into such a sordid thing.

Veronica sat up behind me and slid her hands onto my shoulders.

"She was a good girl." Her voice was dredged in honey. "A lot better than me. I'm bad."

She ran her fingers up my neck and into my hair. They were centipedes against my skin.

"Now she's gone." Veronica's hand slipped away from my neck.

"What happened to Holly's family in Riverside?"

There was a long silence. I leaned over her, forcing her to look at me.

"It was only a few weeks after her mother died, and she'd come back to Riverside to stay full-time with her dad," said Veronica. "That was about six years ago. She was at my house, spending the night. We were thirteen. No, fourteen."

"So young?" I was surprised. I'd taken Holly and Veronica for mid or late twenties. I realized I'd allowed my own desires to color my perception.

"Just girls. Mom and Dad were asleep in bed, and there was this knock at the door." She made a knocking motion with her hand. "So loud, like gunshots. It was the sheriff. He asked to speak with Holly, and we both knew something was wrong. It was just like how the man in the dark suit came and told her about her mother dying. I was afraid to go with her to the door, so I watched from down the hall. The sheriff seemed so much bigger than her."

"What happened?"

"That was the last time I saw Holly for three years. The police held her for her own safety for a while, and then I guess after they ruled it an accident, they sent her off to a foster home."

"Ruled what an accident?"

"The fire. It killed her entire family. Dad, stepmother, all of them. But there was something really weird about it. The firemen thought it was a set fire, but the police said it was an accident. Weirdest of all, Holly Webber was listed in the newspaper as one of the people killed. My mom didn't believe me when I told her the sheriff took Holly away in his car."

"How did you find out about Holly being alive?"

"She called me." Veronica rolled onto her side. The air conditioner buffeted her hair gently. "I was already in the city, working as a secretary for a modeling agency. The guy who ran it kept trying to get me to pose naked. Holly called out of the blue, said she was set up with an apartment and had a spare room, so I left the YWCA and went to stay with her. It was just like old times."

She smiled at the memory of it.

"Why do you think she was in Cranford that morning?" I asked.

The smile disappeared. Veronica turned onto her other side, facing away from me.

"Let's talk about it some other time," she said. "I'm tired."

"Please." I laid my hand on her arm, and she shook it off.

"Don't touch me," she said.

"It's hot in here." I walked to the door and did not look back at her on the bed. "I'll get you a bucket of ice."

There was an ice machine beside the motel's office. I wiped the soot from the door and filled ice buckets from both rooms. When I returned, Veronica was no longer on the bed. I could hear the sound of the shower. The light was on in the bathroom, and her clothing lay discarded like the skin of a snake. I leaned into the room only long enough to set the ice bucket on the dresser.

I sat on the bed in my room and picked up the telephone and put it in my lap. My swollen left hand was immersed in my own ice bucket. Once it was numb, I would try wrapping it in clean bandages. I dialed the Hawthorne exchange and my home number. The line clicked a few times and then began to ring. Lynn answered.

"It's me," I said.

There was a long silence, and then she spoke.

"Where are you?"

"A motel. I'm headed to Malibu."

"Why?"

"It's where this is taking me."

She sighed. That was like a kick in my soft spots. It was the sound of distant glaciers breaking free, setting off on their lonesome way to melt in places they were never meant to be.

"When you disappeared from the hospital, they called the police," she said. "They spent hours searching high and low. I can deal with the embarrassment, but I'm not a part of your life at all anymore. You've entered some dark place. . . . Is this . . . is this about the war?"

"No," I said. "Yes. I don't know."

"And then your doctor calls." Lynn's voice was fraught with emotion. "Dr. Rutledge. He heard you were in the hospital, and he wanted to follow up on your treatment. For what, I don't know. He wouldn't discuss the matter with me. I'm just your wife, not somebody important. Something is wrong with you."

"It's fine," I said.

"I can't do this anymore." Her voice pitched up with anger. "You have this whole other life, and I have my life, and they don't touch anymore. You're never home, you don't tell me anything, I just . . . I can't do it anymore."

"I know," I said.

"Some police came by tonight. They're still parked outside on the street."

"Don't trust them," I said. "I have to go. I can't call you again until this is over with."

"Sure, disappear again. Will I see you alive?"

"Don't give up on me, Lynn. Please."

"I never gave up on you." Lynn's voice was quiet. Resigned. "Never. Don't say that to me. I wrote you letters every week during the war. I even kept all the ones you sent back. I visited you every day in the hospital. I helped you paint that darn shoebox of an office. I watched you buy all the phones you never answer. I've always been in the same place. I haven't moved anywhere. You gave up on me."

"No," I pleaded. "One more chance. I'll make it square. I'll be the man you married."

She was silent.

"You're right," I said. "About everything. I will come home as soon as I can and this will never happen again. Done. I'll quit the business."

"I'm not even sure what business you're in anymore." She sighed. "Alright. Okay. I'm a damn fool, Casper, but God help me I do still love you."

"Thank you." Relief washed over me. I had not even realized how afraid of losing her I had become.

"Did you even notice they'd cut your ring off your finger at the hospital?"

I lifted my swollen hand from the ice and looked at the pale flesh where my wedding ring had banded my finger. No. I hadn't noticed.

"I hope you find what you're looking for," she said. "Hurry home if you want me to be here."

I emptied my hip flask down my throat and fell asleep with the room spinning. I came awake at the sound of a knock at the door. She was there, a silk pajama top cinched around her waist, no bottoms, just the slender luxuries of her stockings. She was tragic and beautiful and everything I wanted at that moment. There was always a space between me and Annie in the dreams.

"Get away from here," I said. "You have your own room."

"I'm all alone over there." She insinuated herself into my room like smoke.

She got her curves between me and the door and leaned back to close it. Her lips were red and glistening. The lights of a passing truck poured golden across the open V of the pajamas and spilled light and shadow over the tops of her breasts.

"You loved her, didn't you?" she asked. "Holly. I could see it in your eyes."

"Someone else," I said.

"I can be her for you." She laid her arms over my shoulders, hands dangling behind my back. "Just how you remembered."

She kissed me. Her lips were a heated brand. A sting. I pushed her to arm's length.

"A girl might get her feelings hurt," she said.

"I'm a married man." The booze was still sloshing around my brain, but it was no excuse.

She laughed and touched my hand.

"Where's the ring?"

"What's your game?" I demanded.

Veronica brushed aside my arms and laid her palms against my chest. She was shorter than me and had to turn up her face to look me in the eye. She stepped closer, and I felt the intimate collision of all her softest corners.

"Tell me about her," she said. "What was her name?"

When I didn't immediately respond she kissed me hard enough to make a boxer weak in the knees.

"Annie," I whispered.

I grabbed her wrists and lifted her hands from my chest, but I didn't push her away.

"What was she like?"

"She wouldn't be in a stranger's hotel room at one in the morning dangling bait to get something she wants."

She jerked her hand from my grasp and slapped me across the face. Cinders danced in her eyes.

"Don't," she said. "You can't look at me like a piece of meat all day and then lecture me like I'm a child."

"Fine, let's lay them on the table, sweetheart. I'm a big, bad man who's been eyeballing your roundabouts since you walked into my office, but you're the one coming into my room, waking me up in the middle of the night. Taking advantage of a drunk, beat-up old man. You're the one dressed like the store ran out of clothes."

She could have screamed or hit me. Maybe I was still hoping she'd take the decision out of my hands. I saw the storm clouds of those sorts of ideas pass over her in an instant. She untied the silk belt holding the pajamas closed. She let the fabric fall from her shoulders. Her shapely body was swathed in black lace, constricted and cradled and overflowing in all the right places to make men forget their mothers. Her retort had won the argument.

We tangled together and unmade the bed.

■   ■   ■

It was remarkable how little guilt I experienced. The world was different, waking with Veronica beside me. When I came out of the shower, she was still there, dazzlingly naked on the bed, laughing at the way I looked at her. It was always like that with her, feeling a bit like I was laughed at, but that didn't stop us.

We left late in the morning for Malibu. The sky was clear and bright, and the fires had gone. We passed through a black, charred wasteland. The trees were just smoldering stumps. Even the stones were blackened and the roadway deformed by the heat. With the Tudor's windows down, the smell lingered. There was a certainty to it that was comforting. Everything that had burned was gone, but something new would grow in its place.

"Do you believe in ghosts?" Veronica asked me. The sun limned her face and seemed to exist within her flowing hair.

"Sure," I said.

"Just like that? Just 'sure'?"

"It's a silly question," I said. She didn't seem to care for that answer.

"I've never seen a ghost," she said, "but I can believe in them. Something has to happen to all that stuff we add up to. All the memories and the things we did with our lives."

"If there are ghosts at all, then we're all ghosts."

"What's that supposed to mean?"

"There's something telling you who to be. When you're a kid, it's telling you to grow. When you get older, well, get a slant at yourself, doll. Look at those hands and fingers, at the little hairs on your arms that you can barely see, at those eyes.

"All of that stuff comes from somewhere. That's adding you up so gradually, you don't even know it. Every time you eat or drink or do some honest work, jigsaw pieces of you are getting clicked into their place by the ghost. There's no moment where it stops and there you are, as you always will be. All you can do is look back at who you were.

"We're all growing and growing, even when we're old." I fitted a Bravo into the corner of my mouth. "Until something makes us stop."

"So then what? What happens when we stop? Where did Holly Webber go?"

"I dunno. If we are just a bunch of instructions, then maybe her ghost went prowling for someone else to make."

"Like me?" she asked.

She put her arm out the car window and skipped her flattened palm on the rushing air.

"I think it's more like music on the radio," she said. "Only there's no radio to pick it up. It just bounces around in the air, goes through locked doors and walls, and nobody even knows it's there."

CHAPTER ELEVEN

■ ■ ■

Malibu was clean and new. Maybe that was why it lacked the foundation of a real city. New money had come in and run out the regulars. There were streets and lampposts and even a few shops, but the real world of Malibu was resorts and exclusive retreats for Hollywood celebrities. They dwelled in the shade of transplanted palm trees on estates walled off from the outside world. They dined at private clubs and played golf. They lived in extravagant terraced houses of Lloyd-Wright angles, overlooking fenced beaches and pools of blue water. At night I'd bet those beaches were lit by tiki torches and strings of Christmas lights.

Old Malibu, or what was left of it, was a stretch of wharves and surviving boat-houses dripping off the rocks of a less hospitable stretch of coastline. I pulled the Tudor off into a rough parking area and shared space with three salt-eaten trucks and a green sedan of obscure manufacture.

Down in the sea a moored trawler was taking on ice from a truck parked out on the nearest wharf. The crew was simultaneously offloading sea urchins into wheeled bins. They were shouting up and down to one another. Their dialogue of labor reminded me of long-ago colliers at Port Richmond taking on coal.

"Can I go with you?" asked Veronica. "I don't want to be alone."

"You should stay in the car," I said, but her expression made me immediately relent. "All right. This might be strange. Or it might be nothing at all."

We left the car and approached the wharf. The spray from the ocean quickly saturated the bandages wrapping my broken fingers. Water covered my hat and coat in fine droplets. Stairs were cut into the nearby cliff, a green iron railing bolted into the stone intended as a small gesture of safety. I glimpsed the rugged beach cradled by the headlands. Gray sand and strips of flooded rocks and heaps of bull kelp.

A few locals with cat-whisker fishing poles and buckets of bait were lingering by the boathouse. I heard them bragging about the easy perch to the man on duty. The boathouse man leaned on his elbows out the open window of the shack. He seemed content to hear them out.

"They're loving this queer summer. Drop your hook in, barely need to bait it," said a red-bearded fisherman. "Just get yourself a mini-jig."

"You'll catch more if you get 'em whipped up by dropping in some minnows," said a fisherman draped in an old Army poncho. "The trick is not too many, so they don't eat their fill. Just right, and they'll bite on anything, and you'll pull in a dozen of them before they're all scared off."

"Don't leave none lay," the boathouse man warned. "I hate to see a fish gone to waste."

"Gulls'll eat it," said the bearded man.

"That ain't the point," said the boathouse man. "Woodrow said last week he came out and there was a whole heap of perch up on the wharf. Smelled to high heaven. I hope it wasn't none of you boys that did that."

The boathouse man was answered with a chorus of disavowals. A bin of sea urchins clattered up the wharf toward the boathouse, pushed by a pair of swarthy commercial fishermen. The locals went quiet. They greeted the approaching men with suspicious glances.

They caught sight of me and Veronica sidling up, and their suspicion turned ice cold.

"Hey there," I said, "I'm looking for Ian Bendwool. His address is in here, but I don't see any regular streets. Any of you know where he lives?"

The fishermen grumbled apologies and filed off down the wharf to start their fishing. We were left facing the grizzled old man in the boathouse.

"I know him," said the boathouse man. "Green house on the rocks, down below, between the bluffs. You his kid? He owes money on that place. And if he don't get thrown out for that, he's gonna get run out for all the cats."

"Sure," I said. "I'll let him know."

"Tell him to quit feeding those cats! I'll go down there with a pellet gun!" the boathouse man shouted after us.

Not exactly a friendly welcome, but it was at least proof my experience on the beach had produced a real lead. Whether new information or something old resurfacing out of my punch-drunk head, I could not be sure. I never pictured myself much of an oracle, so I'd put money on the latter.

The stairs were even more treacherous than they seemed. I raised my collar against the spray and descended them cautiously. Veronica clung to the rail behind me and took the stairs even slower than I managed. The steps finally met a flat, rocky area between two bluffs, and I turned to help Veronica the rest of the way down.

Ian Bendwool's house was nestled in between the bluffs, decayed by the sea salt to a pale green corpse of rotten wood and rain barrels and old fishing nets. The windows that weren't boarded up or shuttered were smeared with grime.

Something crunched underfoot as I started toward the house. Looking down, I realized that the ground all around was covered in thousands of tiny fish skeletons. Mewling cats emerged from crates and from the slumping gables of the roof. There were at least a dozen of them, and they rubbed against our legs and put their front paws on our knees.

"Don't pet them," I said, observing the shivering face of a white tomcat. "They're lousy with fleas."

I clapped my hands, and the cats scattered off to their corners and nooks to regard us sullenly as the interlopers we were. I went up the creaking stairs to the porch and rapped my knuckles on the salt-etched door. Veronica watched from the bottom of the stairs. No one answered, so I knocked again, and again, and a fourth time.

"No one is coming," she said.

"Ian Bendwool!" I shouted. "This is Warren Groves! I need to talk to you!"

"Warren Groves?" wondered Veronica aloud.

"A name he might recognize," I said. "Old alias of mine."

The door opened, and I was face-to-face with a scabrous wreck of a man, pale and unkempt, eyes cloudy, hands quivering, with a faded scar around his neck that suggested he'd been in a noose at some point. He was all the more disarming because I recognized myself in his sagging features.

"You wouldn't be the first man by that name to come here. What do you want?" His eyes shifted to Veronica, and she waved sheepishly. "Who is . . . my God. My God. Come in. Warren, Annie, come in."

Not content with merely inviting us inside, Ian came creeping out onto the porch and took Veronica by the hands. He pulled her, only half-willing, into the dim house, and we were immediately choked by the foul smell of cat urine and rotten food.

"Annie, I thought I'd never see you again." He hugged her with such force, the ratty shawl fell from his shoulders. "Come in. I'm so embarrassed I haven't cleaned. Let me get you both some tea."

The house was in a strange state of disrepair. The browned wallpaper was peeling in loops that reached to the floor, the ceilings sagged, fixtures were covered in cobwebs, and floorboards moved beneath my feet. Furniture and objects were placed haphazardly and with no regard to decoration or even function. Flat bicycle tires and broken umbrellas filled a narrow hallway. A motorcycle engine sat in what might have once been a dining room. It seemed that someone was slowly disassembling it and dropping its pieces into oily canisters laid out on the floor.

We followed Ian into a kitchen full of aquariums. These were filthy and the source of the earthen stink. They were the home to box turtles and lizards and snakes. The way the aquariums were arranged reminded me of jars and cages I'd seen long ago. Cats came rushing in and began begging Ian for food. He shushed them as he puttered around the kitchen, rattling a kettle and running the tap.

"Are you related to him?" whispered Veronica.

"Distantly," I whispered back. "Never met him before."

"How did you find her?" asked Ian Bendwool. "Is she . . . does she . . ."

"No," I said. "This isn't Annie. Her name is Veronica. She is a good friend of mine."

"Wrong," said Ian. "You're wrong."

Veronica gasped as Ian suddenly pinched her wrist.

"Watch it!" I pushed him away from her.

"Veronica." Ian resumed making the tea. "That's right. The girl. Like before. That's what they said."

"Someone told you about her? Who?"

"The voices," said Ian. I must have betrayed my incredulousness. He scowled and quickly added, "I'm not crazy, you know. Nothing wrong with my brain. Now you answer me, who sent you here?"

"Max Holden," I said. "He told me you could give me some answers."

"About what?"

I wasn't really eager to spill my guts on the subject of hallucinations in front of Veronica, but there she was, and here we were, and there was no point being bashful after coming all this way.

"I've been seeing some strange things," I said. I confessed the visions of the grasshopper and the pale man-thing that had attacked me in the Paramount vault. I even told him about how I might have imagined Max Holden and yet he'd given me valuable information. "It was all real enough to touch, real as Veronica there, but I don't think it happened."

"I don't know about all that," said Ian Bendwool, setting out jelly jars and filling them with scoops of black leaves. "Maybe I can help. Maybe. But why would I want to?"

I took a chance on something that had been percolating in my brain for what felt like months. Beau Reynolds and his frantic, late-night telephone call about going through to the other side.

"What do you know about the other side?" I asked.

Ian stopped fussing with the tea leaves. He stood with his old shoulders slumped and his back to us. When he finally answered, he did not turn to face me, and his voice was very quiet.

"Did you go there?" he asked.

"No, someone else did, but I need to know what it is. Where it is. Have you been through to the other side?"

"Yes." Ian Bendwool turned and tilted up his chin. He ran his bony fingers over his throat, and I could see by the light of the swaying bulb above us the ragged brown scar encircling his neck. It was definitely the mark of a man who had survived the noose. "I saw it once. I did. But I managed to forget it.

"Whatever was there made me put a rope around my neck. I was too heavy for the beam or would have died, but I at least wrung it out of my head. I don't remember the other side."

"Hell?" wondered Veronica aloud. "He saw hell?"

"Something like that," I said.

"Yes." Ian Bendwool's voice was a growl. "Sometimes I help others see it. Remember it. We've all been there, Warren Groves. You of all people should feel it in your bones. Long, long ago we passed into death and emerged, not here but there. Through the waters. On the other side."

"What's he talking about?"

"No hell of Abraham." Spittle formed at the corners of Bendwool's lips. "Not by the tales I've heard from the men I've helped. It's not as written by Blake or Milton. Those who have seen it have told me of monuments of cold black stone and things that devour men like you or me. Air that stings the lungs and water that burns the flesh."

Bendwool loomed over Veronica, only restrained by my hand on his withered chest.

"No Christian hell of brimstone. That promise is too good. The lake of fire too sweet. In this place the sea churns with the life of unspeakable things that drink the blood and eat the flesh of men."

"That's enough," I said, giving him a shove.

"Is it?" His eyes were wild. "Don't you want to see it for yourself, Warren Groves?"

"I do. . . . I think I should. . . ."

The kettle began to whistle and steam. The sharp sound jarred him from his mania, and he returned to preparing the tea.

"Max Holden remembered it," said Bendwool as he poured from the kettle. "He came to me and asked, so I helped him remember it. The poor fellow took it worse than most. Most can last a few hours. Maybe a few days. Maybe forever. I don't know after they leave here."

"Where is Max Holden now?"

Bendwool handed me a steaming jar of tea. It was almost too hot to hold. He passed another to Veronica full of the same muddled twigs and old leaves, and she hissed and put it on a nearby counter.

"Dead. Or back. It doesn't matter," said Bendwool. "He won't be the same. He saw the nightmare and couldn't bear it—threw himself off the cliff out there straightaway. Died on the rocks below. I don't know if it let him come back or if he's a ghost, haunting your beaches. I don't have answers to those sorts of questions."

Ian Bendwool grinned and displayed his browned teeth and rot-taken gums.

"If you're a fool and set on your way, I can help you with your questions. I can take you there. It's waiting for all of us."

■ ▢ ▢

The room was behind a door with two dead bolts that locked from the outside. It was clean in comparison to the rest of the cluttered house but, if anything, more discomforting than the squalor.

The walls were lumped with plaster that muddied the corners and bulged from the walls to conceal the house's right-angles. Every surface in the room was coated in thick layers of white paint. It was glossy and tacky to the touch. Bendwool made us take off our shoes before entering, and the soles of my feet plucked at the painted floors. The ceiling was covered with the cruciform black shapes I recalled from the cave above the pool. The cave with that goddamn grasshopper idol.

A wooden shelf reproduced the artifacts of the cave: a crude grasshopper-man statue made from clay, pieces scattered on the shelf as they'd lain broken in that cave so long ago. It was laughably crafted, but Bendwool barked with anger when I reached out to it.

"Touch nothing but what I tell you!"

Veronica lingered outside the doorway. Her frown, as her laugh, was different than Annie's, informed by generations of a changing world and the cynicism of modern youth. She was repelled and a little frightened by Bendwool's idiosyncrasies but concealed it behind a mocking raise of her eyebrows and a shake of her head when the old man wasn't looking. She leaned her upper body into the room and inspected the crosses on the ceiling.

"Are you very religious?" she asked. Her sarcasm was lost on Bendwool.

"No. I don't know what those symbols are. I just put them how I remembered them."

"Huh," she said, and she finally walked into the room. She wrinkled her nose and looked down when her feet made contact with the painted floor. She cast a pleading look in my direction.

The one window was covered with a blackout curtain, painted the same ugly white as the rest of the room, but black fibers showed through. There was an old-fashioned phonograph with its horn and furniture painted white. Beneath the shelf was one chair, white, of course, and nailed to the floor. Rope cuffs were knotted to the chair's arms and front legs.

"Sit down in the chair," he said. "I'll need to tie you up before we begin."

"You can't let him tie you up," said Veronica. "He might be a maniac."

"Shh," said Bendwool. "Quiet, sweetie. If I don't tie him down, he's liable to hurt himself thrashing around. He has to be restrained for his safety and ours. Then I'll give him the medicine."

Indian medicine, Bendwool explained. He mentioned jimson weed and something else. A "surprise" he promised, that would start me on my journey into the past. I didn't like the sound of any of it. Didn't sound like *my scene, man.* Then again, I didn't come all this way *not* to let some lunatic old man tie me to a chair and feed me mind-melting poisons.

"I need to have a word with Veronica before we do anything," I said.

"Sure, sure," said Bendwool. "Just holler, and we can get going."

He shuffled out of the room, trailing his stink behind him. As soon as he was gone, Veronica grabbed my upper arms with both hands.

"Do not do this," she said. "You can't drag me out here and leave me with this twisted up old man. I barely know you, let alone him."

"You came looking for me," I reminded her.

"I came looking for help and found you. I don't want to be left alone with this guy while you . . . do dope in here. Is that what it's about? Getting a fix? I know plenty of dope-pushers down on the boardwalk. Just drive me back to Sugarside, and I'll get you sorted out."

"It's not about that. I'm out of my depth—you get me? I'm a nickel detective in a hundred-dollar mystery. I don't have what I need for what we're into up to our necks."

"That crazy old man does?"

"Maybe," I said. "I have to find out if he does."

I reached into my coat pocket and brought out Ishii's pistol. She took it from me but looked at the hunk of metal in her hand like a dead bird dropped off by a cat.

"Take it," I said. "Safety is right there on the side. Point it where you want a bullet to go, look down that V there, and pull the trigger."

"I know how a gun works," she said.

"Good. We're all sorted. You should wait outside the house, on the porch. Maybe back at the car."

"Leave you behind?"

I gave her the car keys too. What can I say? I'm a trusting sort of guy.

"Get a fried perch," I suggested. "There was that restaurant we passed a couple miles back. The one with the boat sticking out of the building. I'm sure you'd light the place up."

"I don't like this," she said, but she was already going.

I waited for her footsteps to recede across the jumbled house. I listened for the opening and closing of the door and imagined her slender legs climbing those treacherous stairs back up to the wharf.

"All right," I hollered to Ian Bendwool. "Let's do it."

CHAPTER TWELVE

■ ■ ■

The surprise was the box itself. Ian Bendwool tied me to the chair and brought it into the room ceremoniously, concealed beneath a yellowed cloth. It was flat and wide like a cigar box. When he pulled the cloth aside, I saw that it was made from green-painted tin, and the lid depicted a pretty girl surrounded by a wreath of purple and white flowers. In a Gothic-style script was written the word *Vervains*.

My heart skipped in my chest. This was the same box but not the same. The box full of letters Annie kept hidden beneath the bed. It was as if someone had fabricated and painted the box completely from memory. Ian opened the lid, and I could see that it was filled with cubes of compressed plants. He plucked out a cube and held it up to my face.

"Open your mouth," said Bendwool. "Let it break apart on your tongue and swallow it."

"What is it?"

"A bouillon of verbena, jimson weed, and some other things. I cooked it up safe. It will help you ease into understanding."

I opened my mouth, and he placed the bullion, only slightly larger than a sugar cube, onto my tongue. It felt like straw. The bitter, herbal flavor spread through my mouth. The cube dissolved quickly into small plant fibers. I swallowed. Ian nodded and returned the box to its place on the shelf.

"Now close your eyes," Bendwool said.

I did as I was told. The room smelled of burning sage, smoking in a pan in the corner. I listened to the muffled pad of Bendwool's feet on the floor as he crossed the room to the phonograph. I expected music, but when it hummed to life and began to play, there was only the hiss and crackle heard between songs on a record.

Bendwool began to speak, his tone serious and deep, each word enunciated carefully.

"Before you open your eyes, you will listen to the sound of my voice and heed my instructions. You are in the Lost Lodge. The place of the grasshopper idol. The fallen temple of the past. It has been recovered from our collective experience. You are Warren Groves. You remember this place. You are Warren Groves, and you have been here before. You are in a place of great understanding.

"On the count of three you will see the world as it is meant to be. On the count of three you will open your eyes, and you will be Warren Groves. One.

"Two.

"Three."

I opened my eyes. I was still within the room, though it seemed distorted by a lens. I tried to turn to see Ian, but I could not find him with me. I felt as if I had a fever.

"Your body begins to feel lighter and lighter until you are weightless. You feel completely relaxed and at ease."

The tension oozed from my limbs. My arms and legs were limp. My shoulders relaxed. I was very aware of my breathing as it slowed.

"You feel weightless, as if you are floating, and you are. You are floating through a soft mist of white light."

The white dome of the lodge began to recede and become insubstantial and misty. I looked down, and the floor was white smoke, slowly rising and swallowing up my feet. Light glowed all around me. Even the chair faded away, and I was upright, floating as I would stand.

"You are surrounded by warmth and light. You feel safe, but you have not yet reached your destination. Within the light you are standing in a room. Before you is a door. On the other side of this door is the memory you have shut away. The door is locked, but you have the key to unlock this door. You are in control. Nothing behind that door can hurt you ever again. These events have already occurred. You are safe. This is the answer you have sought for so long."

I walked to the door. There was nothing remarkable about it. Just a plain white door with a brass handle and lock. There was something closed in my hand. I turned my fist and opened my fingers, and there was a small key in the palm of my hand. My actions were very slow and deliberate. I grasped the key with my fingers and inserted it into the lock and turned it. I heard tumblers shifting and clicking into place.

I reached out and grasped the doorknob. The brass was cool against my hand. I turned and pulled, opening the door toward me. There was only darkness on the other side of the doorway. A distant voice urged me to step through. Step through.

I did.

The axis of perception and gravity tumbled upside down, and I was floating quickly upward. I emerged from liquid, pushing and kicking onto rocks and tearing away the familiar cowl of birth. I lay upon octagonal paving stones, reaching up as columns in some places and in others arranged as stairs. The air was thin and burned in my mouth, and the world was awash in the marrow stench of the Pool.

This place was dark, so dark I believed at first I was in a huge cavern with a ceiling too high to be seen. My eyes adjusted to the new light, and I realized that above me was sky, blackened and roiling as if filled with smoke. Distant clouds flickered, purple and bruised, with lightning. A cyclopean shaft of light broke through and cast a bloody ray down into the world. It only remained for a moment before the clouds swallowed it up.

Behind me, extending into the unseen darkness, there lay a vast lake or ocean of white liquid. This sea rose in thick waves that crashed and broke against tessellated beaches. In some places the waves stole the rocks. The geometric promontories crumbled and hissed as they were swallowed up by the cream-colored tides.

The peril of being smothered by a wave sent me scurrying up the octagonal rocks and away from the coast. I managed to get my feet beneath me and began climbing the stones. As I exerted myself, my breathing grew labored, and my heart pounded heavily against my rib cage. This was not the stones in my lungs, which seemed gone, but the effect of being at a high altitude or some other place where the air was thin.

I climbed higher and higher, up from the coast, until I stood upon a rise overlooking a plain of paved stone. This was not paved with the octagons; it was a wide boulevard made from slabs ten feet to a side.

I sensed the outlines of a perfect street, a grand boulevard now cracked and buckled and tilting into ruin. On either side of this road rough obelisks of black rock reached many feet into the air. A few reached all the way to pyramid caps. Obelisks slumped or shed clattering stones. Some were fallen entirely and lay across the road in sundered pieces or in one crumpled bulk like the fallen trunk of a massive tree. Some few braced against one another and formed precarious arches over the road.

The vast scale of the boulevard and its surrounding structures was difficult to accept. They were immense, to be sure, but there were no trees or other identifiable landmarks.

This place was too dim to see a great distance, but on the horizon there were glowing plumes and incandescent streams suggesting volcanism. The wind was hot and stank of sulfur. The world rumbled and vibrated with these eruptions, the obelisks shedding more stones, but the fires were too distant to be of much immediate concern.

I climbed down from the octagonal stones and onto the ruined boulevard. I leaped the last few feet from the top of a geometric pillar and landed on the pale, fleshy residue of a membrane. I leaned down to examine the leathery material and was surprised to see it covered in a visibly spreading frost. I touched a finger to the frost, and it was warm. Fuzzy white spread to my fingertip, and I felt a pinch to my skin where it had touched me.

Stinging frost? I quickly wiped the substance onto the stone. My fingertip was red and throbbing. I stepped away from the fleshy membrane, mindful of the quickly expanding white.

A scream echoed against the silent obelisks. It was louder than the crashing sea, so it must not be far. I pursued the sound as best I could. Another scream followed. I was sure I heard the word *"God."* The wind was howling through the rocks. Each rumble of the distant volcanoes sent tremors through the pavement and stones skidding down the sides of the obelisks. These stones seemed small as they fell but thundered to the ground as big as cars and with the loudness of a cannonade.

As I raced into the masonry, feet on cold stone, my heart pounded urgently in my chest, and I grew weary and breathless. There came a third scream, sudden, short, and ending in a gurgle. The empty howling of the wind followed. I wanted to call out, but I was afraid.

I navigated the fallen obelisks. They were much larger than I thought from atop the ridge. The size of buildings in Chicago or New York. There were no windows or rooms, but they were not solid rock. Where they had split open, their internal structure was revealed as an octagonal honeycomb of cells and supporting walls. Some of these chambers opened onto the surface of the obelisks. The geometric black holes reminded me of the silent windows of the pueblo village. The wind howled through these sockets, and their bleak emptiness forced me to look away.

I climbed up and over a jumble of spilled stones and approached the spot where I believed the last scream to have originated. I only found more of the white frost. Curious, I dragged a stone through it, and the bottom of the stone was covered in blood as well as the threads of the white material. I tossed the stone away and followed a faint trail of the frost into a narrowing of the rock. The trail emerged across the tilted boulevard and disappeared into one of the yawning octagonal chambers of a fallen obelisk.

I hesitated at the threshold. Bestial noises echoed from the walls of the honeycombed structure. I imagined black talons against the stone and slavering jaws snapping for meat. I tried to steal myself with Ian Bendwool's words as I entered this maddening world: "These events have already occurred. You are safe. This is the answer you have sought for so long."

The entrance was large enough for a man to ride through on the back of a horse but tilted at an extreme angle. I stepped in, balancing my bare feet on the sloped walls. The ammonia stench was eye-watering and rose from water that pooled in the lowest corner of the octagonal chamber.

It was darker within the obelisk than without, but there was light. Stalks of pallid fungus sprouted from the water's edge, and these were capped with fleshy, teardrop bulbs that phosphoresced blue. They brightened as I drew near. I stepped warily around and over them so that the bulbs did not touch my bare skin.

With each shuffling step the bedlam sound of the demons grew louder and echoed through the tilting corridors. Their snarls reminded me of wolves fighting over food. Here and there I found traces of blood overgrown with the stinging rime that clung to floor and ceiling. The frost avoided the water filling the trough of the tilted octagonal chamber, but when I spit upon a patch, it grew rampantly around my saliva. More than once my toe or hand brushed against the frost unseen. Each time I recoiled with pain as if stung and quickly cleaned the frost from my body.

I reached a smaller octagonal corridor that once ran horizontally through the obelisk, since realigned by gravity into a nearly vertical shaft. I placed my hands against the incline and judged whether or not I could scale it without tools.

My toes touched something cold and yielding. There was a kind of grout where the corridor intersected with the octagonal cell. I leaned down and dragged a finger through it and brought it near enough to one of the glowing fungal bulbs to judge its consistency. It was a muddy brown paste of grit and decaying insect casings. Not grout at all, just refuse. The insect fragments glittered in the unearthly fungal luminescence. Pieces of the grasshopper? Each fragment crumbled at the slightest touch and was too rotted to judge the shape of its source.

I shook the fragments from my hand and began my ascent of the smooth incline of the upended corridor. It was immediately exhausting, but I persevered. I made the mistake of looking back only once. The near-vertical shaft disappeared into darkness below. Above my head the sounds were becoming more distinct and vivid. Tender skin and fat separated from knitted muscle. Soft feet padded against the stone floor. I could hear them breathing. More than one of them. I could smell their rancid spore.

I reached the rim of the corridor and pulled myself up by my fingers. I lay with my belly against the cool stone and did my best to stifle the sound of my labored breathing. My cheek was pressed flat to the floor, my ear listening for their movement. They were very close. They snuffled and clicked to one another as they ate their meal. I slowly lifted my head. Sweat-slackened hair fell into my eyes. It was dark.

But I could see.

The demons were the size of very small men or very large dogs. Their hairless bodies and limbs were slender and multijointed, and they crouched on their folded legs and held their arms near their torsos. Their flesh was pale white, darkening to blue and lavender at their joints. Their fingers were not clawed at all; they seemed almost webbed, and they held morsels of bleeding meat to their mouths in a manner similar to grasshoppers.

Their oblate heads were smooth, and their bulbous blue eyes rotated independently and focused pinprick pupils here and there. They possessed no visible ears, and only the bifurcated pinkness of the flesh above their mouths suggested nostrils. Each time one opened the lipless curl of its mouth, it exposed chitinous plates clattering and tearing through raw red meat.

These creatures seemed to be the source of the trophy heads atop spears in the long ago Indian village. Those heads were drooping with decay and deformed from wounds. They were also nearly the same as the creature I had seen in the Paramount vault. That beast was more fantastic in its appearance, more like a creature from a Hollywood picture, distorted, perhaps, by my memory. These were bestially real.

Two of the demons hissed and clicked their mouth-plates together in communication or challenge. They began to tug on either end of a piece of muscle tissue. They shifted to the right and in the process revealed the body sprawled upon the floor.

Gideon Long raised his head and looked directly at me with tears welling in his eyes. His mouth was stained by blood. His chest and belly were torn open, and the creatures plucked meat and giblets from his innards. He began to speak, his voice gurgling and choking, but only nonsense words emerged. Pulsing streams of blood coursed out of his nostrils and over his lips. His legs were shattered and bleeding from compound fractures. His arms were similarly broken and useless, and he flopped them like a bird's broken wings as the demons pulled more of his flesh to their clattering jaws.

I reached out blindly and felt along the filthy floor. My hand closed around a heavy rock. I pulled myself to my knees and to my feet and stood. The loathsome sound of the demonic feeding stopped. Their blue eyes rotated, and the pinprick pupils focused on me standing with the rock hanging in my hand. The nearest creature strained its long neck and clattered its teeth in challenge.

I stepped forward, and the demons stepped back. I took another step toward them and shouted something, although my head was swimming, and no words came easily. I drove them back with more shouting, and they snapped and hissed at me, crouching very low to the ground and moving from side to side as though searching for an opening. I stood at the feet of Gideon's mutilated body. I looked down into my old enemy's face, and the man was pleading.

"Help me," I think he was begging, though it might have been, "Kill me."

The initial shock of my appearance was wearing off. The demons were edging closer, walking sideways and attempting to circle around me. They were cautious, but I could sense they were not truly afraid. They'd had a taste of human flesh and knew how delicious I could be.

I only had one chance. I lifted the rock in both hands, up over my head. The demons stared at me, eyes shining in the darkness, jaws poised to tear at my flesh. I howled and brought the stone crashing down on Gideon Long's forehead. His skull caved in, and dark blood ran out from beneath the rock. He thrashed once and lay still.

The demons hissed and snapped their jaws at me. They were lithe and agile, and as they leaped and scrambled at me over Gideon's corpse, they revealed the full power contained within their corded muscles. I fled before them. I jumped down the corridor, sliding so fast that my legs and back burned and squealed against the stone. The demons followed, their white bodies and long limbs moving like spiders nimbly down the shaft of the upended corridor.

I fell, ankles and shin bones nearly breaking as I slammed into the insect refuse at the bottom of the shaft. I picked myself up and limped on into the octagonal chamber. The creatures were not as tall as I, but their stride was impossibly long. I could not outrun these creatures. One of them was upon me. I swung wildly, connecting with its shoulder. It weighed very little and was flung to the side. It leaped up, unharmed. I splashed through the stinging trough of water.

A weight fell upon my back. Fingers speared into the flesh of my shoulder, reached beneath the muscle and bone, and snapped the clavicle with an electric jolt of pain and a pop that resonated throughout my body. I screamed and swung my head, colliding with the face of the demon, mashing one of its huge eyes into its socket. The creature yowled and released its hold on my broken bone. It tumbled from my back and into the trough of water.

Pale and clattering, another demon leaped onto me. I fell and rolled onto my back. The water burned cold against my flesh. The creature pinned my hands to the ground and in a frenzy began biting and licking the exposed flesh and bone of my upper arm. I returned the favor, sinking my teeth into the demon's sinewy neck.

Cool black blood gushed into my mouth. It tasted bitter. The demon immediately released me, and I scrambled away, getting to my feet and dashing out of the octagonal chamber. Blood was pouring down my chest, dripping everywhere I went. My bloody footprints were turning white behind me.

The demons pursued me across the tilting boulevard. More had joined the hunt, white bodies contrasting with the black obelisks and debris in the ancient street. My smell was in the air. They were flooding out of hidden warrens and ruined black towers, hissing and clattering their jaws behind me. Pain radiated from my shoulder wound. The white frost was on me now, spreading across my bleeding flesh.

I climbed the octagonal rocks, hand over foot. I kicked and punched and clawed at the demons that attempted to seize me. They bit off two of my fingers and began fighting over them as they rolled in among the rocks. A one-eyed demon leaped at me from above and nearly pulled me down, but I was able to fling the creature aside.

I climbed the rise, and the sight of the cream-colored sea filled me with relief. I ran, slipping, fighting, and shouting, for the shore. The demons were crawling on all fours along the rocks, closing their mob pincer around me as their numbers grew.

There was something else. Some other creature, swooping black overhead. Thrumming wings beat the air against my back. The movement startled the demons blocking the way ahead of me, and they fled out of my path. I took the opportunity. Laughing madly, I ran past the hissing beasts and threw myself over the last octagonal piles of coastline.

As I dove into the white sea, as I felt the viscous evil begin to unravel my flesh, my eyes opened into light.

I was tied to a chair, squinting against the brightness of a white-painted door in a white-painted room. The crash of the waves and the frustrated yowling of the demons receded like the ridiculous details of any remembered dream. I was drenched with fever-sweat. My limbs were bruised and raw beneath the ropes, and my body felt beaten to hell, probably because it was.

Sweat dripped from my nose. I could not move or say anything for a long time. Something was wrong with my eyes. It was so bright, I could not stand to open them more than slits. People were shouting on the other side of the door. I wasn't sure who or what they were saying.

"Hey," I yelled, my voice hoarse. "Let me out of the chair."

There was a thump, followed by a long silence. I strained to hear something more. There was a sudden burst of shouting and a distant gunshot. Two gunshots. It was hard to make sense of what was happening. Screaming. A woman screaming. Veronica!

"Let me out of here!" I shouted. "You son of a bitch! Let me out!"

I frantically worked a foot loose from the ropes and kicked out the leg of the chair. I crumpled to the floor in a heap and broke my other leg free. The chair was well-made but ancient. I twisted it beneath my body and held it steady with my wrists while I used my body weight and my arm muscles to snap one of the arms off. When I'd finally managed to free myself, I did not hesitate to snap the shelf from the wall and use the board to hammer the hinges off the door.

"Goddamn you, Bendwool!"

I hammered the narrow end of the board into the door. I was at the ragged edge of exhaustion, my eyes still so dilated I could barely see, but I battered my way through. I tripped over a pile of records, the black platters cracking underfoot and spilling out onto the floor. I raced outside, past Ian Bendwool and whatever nonsense he was spouting, into the blinding light, and up the stairs.

I reached the top of the stairs, and through the whiteout haze of sunlight I glimpsed Veronica for just a moment. I saw the scarlet silk of her hair whipping in the wind as Ethan Bishop's convertible disappeared. I raced to the parking lot, but the hood on my poor Tudor was up, and the engine was sabotaged.

When I returned to Ian Bendwool's house, the old man was smiling as if nothing had occurred. I grabbed him by his ratty sweater and hauled him out of his chair. He offered no resistance.

"You said someone told you about Veronica. Who?" I demanded.

"The voice," said Ian Bendwool, and he pointed to his countertop. I realized he was indicating an old candlestick telephone.

"The voice was a telephone call? You told them I was here?"

"No," said Bendwool. "I didn't mention you. I told them she was here."

"You lousy fink!" I threw him down on the floor.

I was the Judge. I was a killer to the manner born. When I was only a boy, I murdered my father with a piece of glass. When I was a man, I killed horse thieves and bandits and Apache Indians. I'd killed Gideon Long dozens of times, fought in every war America had conceived to inflict upon the world, and slaughtered better men than myself for the mistake of standing beneath the wrong flag.

I stared into my own aged face, smiling its grotesque, peg-toothed smile. The enemy half. The betrayer. I flowed through the decades like a red river and never more red than in that moment. It's not a good thing to let the anger take over, but sometimes there just isn't any stopping it.

"What did you see?" Bendwool asked in a sweet voice. "Please, tell me what was there. I need to know how you saw it."

"Let me show you," I said.

Bendwool's telephone was as heavy as the stone I had used to smash in Gideon's skull. I raised it above my head and brought it down and learned firsthand it worked just as well as a stone on Ian Bendwool.

CHAPTER THIRTEEN

■ ■ ■

I was able to put my heap back together with the bootlegger's tool kit in the trunk. I patched the hoses with tape and replaced the missing spark plug. A man running homemade white lightning from the mountains to the city can't afford to call a towing truck if he breaks down. Same goes for a professional killer, though my credentials were in question after I let an old loon like Bendwool put one over on me.

There was a service station down the coast, and while the zipped-up skippy in the white coverall was filling my car up with gasoline, I cleaned up in the john. I ran a comb through my graying hair. Seeing myself in the mirror, how gaunt I was becoming, my pupils huge and black from the herbs, reminded me of the sickness in my lungs. That put me on my knees and coughing into the toilet like one of those boxes with the cat and the poison pill. Observation has consequences or whatever.

Stars exploded behind my eyelids with each cough. My body worked through its convulsions, but my mind was elsewhere.

I knew that if I got all the way back to Los Angeles as mad as I was, there would be a slaughter. Most likely I'd get myself killed and wouldn't do any good for anyone. Ethan Bishop had taken Veronica, but he couldn't have her. Not even a rich, entitled son of a bitch, the scion of the most powerful industrialist in America, could kidnap a woman against her will and get away with it.

A splash of cold water chased away my last thoughts of revenge. A lanky mechanic with a marijuana grin sold me his pair of sunglasses to cope with my blown-out pupils. I paid too much, so when I begged to use the station's telephone, he let me have at it for free. I called the only man I could think to call. The man I knew who would help me even if he hated my guts, because nothing was more important to him than gloating over my inabilities.

"I'll be there with bells on," said Kapinski. "And if this little adventure is some sort of trick, you know I am going to run you in for murder. Put you in irons. See how the boys in county jail like a piece of red cop meat thrown in with them."

"Murder ain't gonna stick to me," I said.

"We'll see." Kapinski laughed.

I beat him to San Pedro. Pulled to the side of the road overlooking the main entrance to Bishop's monster of a power station. Those partly-built cooling towers made it look like the ruins of a giant castle. Throw up a wall and a moat, and you'd have one hell of a fortress.

Kapinski and his cavalry showed up late. I was getting jittery, wishing I could just charge in there all by myself, when a blue Buick slid out of traffic and pulled in behind me. Kapinski got out of the passenger side. He had a nasty smile on his face, and his head looked swollen a full hat size.

"Thanks for coming," I choked out.

"My pleasure," he said, leaning an arm across the roof of my car and looking down at me. "Always look out for a fellow cop, right?"

Kapinski looking down his fat nose at me was giving me a crawl on the back of my neck. I tried to open the door of my car to get out, but he held it closed.

"Not so fast, Rex Rawhide. You're not going anywhere."

"This is my case."

"Soon as your voice came outta my telephone, this belonged to the LAPD. I got twenty blues and a half dozen detectives on this. If what you say is true, Bishop kidnapping a girl is going to be the biggest headline this department has seen since we brought out the tanks for those Mexicans back during the war. You are not running this operation. I am."

"Just get in there," I said. "He might hurt her."

Kapinski drummed on the roof of my car and backed away. He whistled and motioned back down the road. A line of squad cars and unmarked cars that had formed up behind us pulled back onto the road and started toward the Pit. Kapinski's car was last, idling in the lane long enough for Kapinski to turn back and give me a parting shot.

"You really pulled a Houdini act, disappearing from that hospital," he said. "I'm leaving your old buddy Flores to keep an eye on you. If you disappear again, it's on his head."

A squad car driven by Flores pulled in behind me. He looked none too happy, but then again, he never looked happy. Kapinski waggled his fingers at me and disappeared into the blue Buick, his attention already focused on the Pit.

I could see that the coppers got in easily enough through the entry gate and began disappearing in a convoy toward the control building where Bishop kept his office. The next hour was an agony of waiting. I imagined scenarios of Bishop and the cops shooting it out, scenarios of Bishop giving up peacefully or snowing them with his grift, buying them with deep pockets. The longer it took, the more pessimistic I became. I got out of the car and chain-smoked Bravos and paced by the side of the road.

There was a shift change at the Pit, and the engineers came streaming out in their candy-colored cars, headed for the nice houses in Channel Heights. The laborers doing all the hard work used other exits and probably rode in the white buses to Power Town. Poor whites, blacks, and Chicanos crammed into the longhouses like farm chickens.

I commiserated with Flores, but he was none too friendly, I'd guess still smarting about my disappearance from the hospital.

"Could go for a belt of the Brown Barrel," I said.

"You're in up to your eyebrows," he said. "If you've put Kapinski on to some nonsense, he is going to have your ass. And mine."

"I can handle Kapinski," I said.

"My wife said I should stop talking to you."

"She doesn't know how charming I am," I tried to say, but I started coughing and had to bend over and spit into the dirt.

"What are you doing running around on Lynn?" Flores said. "That isn't the sort of thing a man does. Running around with these women. Who was Holly Webber? Another one of your twists?"

"Didn't know her," I choked. "Swear."

"Now you got us after some girl named Veronica? You are a piece of work, man. Piece of work."

"Sorry," I managed, and finally I was able to stand up.

"And you're a damn mess. Where's your tie? Here. Drink some coffee. I think I have a tie in my trunk."

Flores gave me a spare, uniform-blue. Didn't go with the blood on my collar, but I wore it anyway. The coffee helped a little. Flores and I sat on the rounded trunk of the squad car, our backs to the Pit. We looked up the winding road to Channel Heights. The perfect lawns and healthy palm trees. It was a wonder they could pump all that water up there just to spray it on grass.

"I think Lynn is going to leave me," I said.

"Sounds like you have it coming to you."

"Yeah, it's for the best. She always deserved better than me." I tapped out another cigarette and put it between my lips. Flores lit it for me. "And I've got cancer."

"What?"

I nodded my head through the exhaled smoke.

"How did that happen?" asked Flores.

"I was in the war. Guess it was all that dust from the bombs Murrow has been talking about. Lot of Marines and Army got it in their lungs." I tapped ash onto the gravel. "Doc said a few months, but I think my time is running out quicker than that."

"Does Lynn know?"

"No." I looked at him seriously. "And you keep your damn mouth shut. Not even your wife can know."

"I got it." Flores twisted his lower lip between thumb and fingers. "That is the real business, ain't it? My daddy got it. Didn't know what to do with it back then, but there was one thing that helped. I don't tell people what to do, but you need to get straight with God. Yes, sir. Go to church. You can come with me this weekend. It will be like starting over again."

Flores could see I wasn't buying what he was selling, but something in that Catholic brain of his kept him going.

"It's a nice church. Mostly Irish, believe it or not. You ever even been to a Catholic church?"

I was married to Lynn in St. Philomena's, but it was not the church that sprung into my head when Flores asked.

"St. Ramon," I said.

"That in Hawthorne?"

"Kyushu."

That's all it took to send me back. All the way to the end of my time in the mountains.

■ ■ ■

Gardener forced the priest and the nuns to bury his men. It was a pitiful sight, watching those skinny nuns breaking their backs with the shovels. I think the yellow engineer was a Catholic, but he kept his mouth shut. When the bodies were in the ground, Gardener told them in Japanese to march back to Korano. That fat priest back-talked in that Dutch of his, and Gardener shot the ground by his feet. That sent him packing.

We watched them depart. A forlorn procession. They must have felt safe in that church, but it was Ishii, not us, who'd brought the war to their doorstep. He remained silent, watching, but called out to his sister at the last moment before she disappeared from view. I couldn't understand the Japanese. I wondered what I would say in that last moment. What do you shout out to someone you know you'll never live to see again?

When they'd gone, we began to climb. More than a thousand feet to the snow-capped summit of the nameless rock. Ishii said it was a holy mountain, but he wouldn't give us its name as he marched between Gardener and me. We followed a hiker's path for the first few hundred feet, but this dead-ended at an outcropping. Ishii insisted what we were after was at the very top.

"I can't go any farther," complained the engineer. "I'm afraid of heights."

It was a poor lie. He'd been with us through and over the mountains east of Sendai. We'd all grown used to narrow paths and perilous drops.

"Stay here," said Gardener.

The engineer did, watching us begin the more difficult climb up the nearly vertical rock face and into the morning's light. The mountain there was black beneath our hands, volcanic, like the sun-hot rocks of the Oscuras. From this height we could see for many miles, above the mossy tops of the surrounding mountains, into tiny villages waiting like grains to be plucked and harrowed by the advancing Americans. Their deeds were to the east of us. Smoke obscured the way to the sea, fires burning wherever our bombs fell, fires wherever our tanks and men arrived.

To the east it was deceptively peaceful. Villages disappeared into the dreamy mists, and the fog that swallowed the valleys made it seem as if the mountaintops emerged from snow. The world to the east was incomplete: golden where it peaked into morning's light and purple where it hid in the mountain shadows. At the borderland between light and dark there was a gray nothing, no visible details, but I could not tell if the world in these places was unfinished or already ending.

"It is beautiful," said Ishii, noticing my gaze. "I grew up in villages like those. Always misty in the morning, and the air . . . I have heard that men who spend their youth upon the shores of the ocean will live haunted by it their whole lives. My dreams are always of the mountains. No matter where my life takes me, I know my happiness is in these mountains."

I said nothing, but I must have betrayed my agreement with his sentiment.

"Do you dream of a place like this?" he asked.

"Not a place," I said. "Of a girl. Always her."

My foot slipped against loose stones. Ishii caught my arm and pulled me back against the cliff face. I stared down at the rocks plummeting away. They clattered from the mountain and disappeared into the mist.

"Do you have her?" asked Ishii, snapping me out of my vertigo. "Back in your home. In America."

"No," I said. "She is gone forever."

Ishii nodded. "I think these mountains will soon be gone. I was taught they were immortal, but I do not think so anymore. You have changed the world."

"Americans?"

"Yes." He hoisted himself up onto an outcropping of rock and helped me alongside him. "You have upset the order of things. Your atom bombs are many orders of magnitude more destructive than anything that has come before, and the project that created you is unthinkable. Producing men like automobiles to fight your wars. The Germans could not even begin to unravel the science behind it."

"You were there?"

"Yes," he said. "At Buhlendorf. Hoffman tried to unravel you there. And Mengele with his failed research on twins. Even Doctor Yakamura's fetal injections produced only short-lived freaks."

"I don't know what you're talking about," I said. "Whatever it is you think is going on here is wrong. I heard what you said in the church—"

"Hurry it up," Gardener, a confident mountaineer, called down to us from above. I offered Ishii a hand up. He looked at it for a moment before accepting.

"Thank you," he said. "Your face is the same, but you are not Gardener."

"There's no project," I said to Ishii. "You've got it all wrong. Somebody lied to you."

"Perhaps it is you who was lied to," said Ishii. "Why don't you ask Gardener about Operation Westward? Maybe he can tell you the truth."

An eerie cairn painted with Japanese characters marked the final approach to the mountain's peak. Gardener warned us that things would be treacherous for the last hundred feet. He climbed ahead, finding handholds in the bare rock and tying off ropes for Ishii and me to ascend behind him.

Halfway up I slipped. My fingers and one of my feet lost their grip in the same moment. I saved myself with a lucky kick of my boot and a turn of my hips that slammed me against the stone. Rocks clattered down around me as I scrambled for a new handhold.

I closed my eyes rather than look down. I imagined Lynn receiving a terse Army telegram stating that Casper Cord had fallen off a mountain. Would Gardener write that letter home, or would my death be added to the tally of some faraway battle?

"You all right?" Gardener called down.

"Yeah," I lied. "One minute."

I was turned sideways on the cliff and had to release one of my handholds and swing my body back into the groove Gardener was leading us up. My hand found new purchase, and I resumed the climb.

When we finally reached the summit, Ishii and I were exhausted, crawling up to the mountain's peak and onto the cold rocks, slithering the last few feet like salamanders. Our breath came out in steaming gusts.

Gardener stood over us. "Get on your feet. Both of you."

"Water," gasped Ishii.

Gardener unscrewed the top from his canteen and, staring down at Ishii, emptied its contents into his own mouth. He discarded the empty canteen and said, "No more stalling."

The view had a dizzying clarity, an expansiveness that shamed the mountains of New Mexico. The mountaineer's cabin was ahead, barely larger than an outhouse, with a shingled roof and walls made from wooden slats painted black. Its tin chimney was blackened with soot, and a camp lantern dangled from a hook beside the entrance. Japanese symbols were carved above the door and slopped with gold paint. We walked toward it with Ishii at gunpoint ahead of Gardener and me.

"Before you say anything," said Gardener conspiratorially, "be warned that Lt.

Col. Ishii is a silver-tongued devil. I know you were talking to him. He will confuse you and prey on your kindness."

"I've been around enough men stalling on their way to the hangman. I don't give a damn if you kill him. Ishii said something about Operation Westward. What is he talking about?"

"What did he say to you?" Gardener shook his head. "Damn it, Sergeant. Do I need to get out that green book again, show you all the miserable shit Ishii and his people were up to?"

"Don't mean we can't have miserable shit of our own," I said. "I know he's mixed up about what we are, but he knows something else. I can tell by the way you're spittin' mad that there's truth to it, so let's hear it. Aren't we supposed to be in this together?"

"Yeah, right," said Gardener. "Okay, Ishii wasn't lying about that. There is something called Operation Westward. The Air Force is running it out of White Sands."

"That's near the Pool," I said.

"Not my department."

"You know more than that." I prodded him with a finger.

"I know it's Shiftman's ball game. The Gideons are invested in it. The same crew that gave us the bomb. Some secret project that has something to do with rockets."

"Rockets? That doesn't make any sense at all."

"There are pilots they're training for Operation Westward. Warrens among them. Lots of the German eggheads we rounded up in Operation Paper Clip were sent to White Sands to work for the Air Force. Must be rockets. This is next-war business. Washington is looking ahead to the Soviets."

"Tell me the truth," I said. I stopped walking and jabbed my finger into Gardener's chest. He took a half step back.

"That is the truth," said Gardener, and he prodded my midsection with his pistol. "I'm OSS, not Air Force. I'm telling you everything I know about Westward. Don't you touch me again, or I swear I will—"

"It is just inside here," said Ishii. He was ahead of us, having reached the door to the mountaineer's cabin.

Gardener seemed to forget his quarrel with me and stomped past Ishii to the mountaineer's cabin. He took down the lantern hanging beside the door and lit it. Ishii and I followed him in. We stepped onto floors of frayed tatami and crowded around a table hardly big enough to play checkers on. There were no windows, only the light of the lantern that Gardener raised above his head. It swayed back and forth on its handle, creating movement in the shadows surrounding every object and on every face.

In the center of the table was the object Gardener had sought. He ran his fingers lightly over the lid before clutching it to his chest. Half-submerged in the swimming shadows conjured by the lantern, I saw that Gardener held a small tin box, green, painted with the image of a young girl and over her head *Vervains*.

Sirens blared, startling me out of the past. Three ambulances came speeding down the main access road to the front gate of Bishop's power plant.

"What the hell is that about?" asked Flores.

I didn't know, but I didn't like the look of it.

"I need to get inside." I dropped off the back of the squad car and turned to make a run for my Ford. Kapinski was in my way. He'd returned without my even noticing.

"Bad news," he said.

"Is she safe?"

"There's no girl in there," said Kapinski. "But there is a crime scene."

"I don't understand."

"Ethan Bishop is dead," said Kapinski. "Must have been a hell of a fight. Bullet holes everywhere. Him and seven other stiffs with their blood and guts all over the expensive furniture. At the moment, you're my only lead as to why the son of the richest man in California has been murdered."

The news was a rock in my guts. Kapinski wasn't taking any pleasure in my being wrong, which meant it really was as bad as he was saying up there. I only knew one man who could shoot his way through Ethan Bishop and his bodyguards and leave a homicide detective looking pale. One black hat and a giant, melt-faced freak beneath it.

"It wasn't me," I said.

"You'll have a chance to prove your innocence," said Kapinski, "but you brought us to a goddamn slaughterhouse. Flores, get him down to the station, put him in the stew. I'll have somebody drive his car to the impound."

Kapinski turned to walk away.

"Wait a second," I said.

"No." Kapinski leveled a finger at me. "No more games. You've dropped a mess into my lap that I've got to clean up. You used to be a cop, and I don't want to humiliate you, but if you leave me no choice, I'll get some of the boys to subdue you and put you in irons."

He waved to Flores and said, "Get him the hell out of here."

CHAPTER FOURTEEN

■ ■ ■

I've done things in life that made me feel lower than a worm. Killed people I shouldn't have, lied, cheated, even stolen. Nothing ever made me feel lower than what I did to Hector Flores that day.

We'd just left the Pit, headed for the station downtown. A long haul, longer because of the traffic. Plenty of time for me to get Flores into more trouble than he deserved.

He was headed west, about to turn the squad car onto the highway. I was in the back with my hands free as a courtesy. I put a cigarette between my lips and asked for a light. Flores used the electric lighter in the dash. I leaned forward to make it easy for him. As he brought the lighter up, I knocked it with my hand. It fell right into his lap.

"Christ!" He tried to grab the lighter off his lap. As he panicked and swerved, I leaned my arm past the bench seat and drew his gun from its holster. By the time he had the lighter and realized what was happening, I had his service revolver to the back of his head.

"Jesus, put it down," said Flores. "You don't mean that."

"Sorry," I said. "Ain't gonna happen. I'm too close to this now to let you lock me in stew overnight. I know where we go from here."

"You won't shoot me," he countered.

"Want to find out just how little you know me?" I lowered the pistol beneath the line of the seat but kept it aimed at him. "Now drive. Sunset Beach."

I gave him the freak's address. The bungalow where he'd kept Veronica captive. If he was the one who'd killed Ethan, then he'd have her there. If he wasn't, well, I was out of luck, and Flores could lock me up for threatening him. I'd even cop to it.

I'll never know how I missed the goddamn caravan we had on our tail. We pulled into the freak's neighborhood, right up to the bungalow, and they were on top of us. Flores hadn't even put the car into Park. A long black limousine pulled in behind the squad car, and two Mastiff cargo trucks trundled up to the front of the house.

"What the hell is this?" I said, but deep down I knew. I'd come to the right place and brought Harlan Bishop's men with me. The buzz cuts and dark suits came pouring out of the trucks with their shotguns and grease guns in hand. Elias stepped out of the limousine.

"Do not hurt the girl!" he shouted.

The buzz cuts surrounded the house like real cops, taking up positions around the property, kneeling or lying in the grass, steadying their weapons on the hoods of cars. Half of them went storming in the front and back doors. They shot the locks right off with their shotguns and piled into the perfect little California bungalow. Once they'd gone inside, the real shooting started. It flashed behind scarlet curtains and rattled out into the street.

Neighbors came into their yards, perhaps thinking it was a movie being filmed. They gawped and pointed. More gunfire chattered inside the house. Glass shattered out of the windows, and bullet holes punched through the door. A wounded man came reeling out the front, a gun limp in his hand, and he collapsed on the stoop. One of the buzz cuts waiting outside dragged him out of the way as the shooting continued.

Beneath the gunfire I could hear, but not discern clearly, the panicked shouting of the buzz cuts inside the building. Their terror must have been paralyzing when they realized they'd just leaped into a cage with a beast. A vicious one, right out of a storybook without a happy ending.

A man came crashing through the house's bay window, glass shattering all around him. His rag-doll body rolled in the grass and lay motionless. The curtains billowed through the window frames, and white smoke poured from inside the house. Gunfire continued to rattle from within.

"Got the girl!" came the call from the back of the house.

The men forming the perimeter began to withdraw to their vehicles. More men came around from the back, and I saw Veronica, held between two buzz cuts, her face sprinkled with blood. She was stricken by the violence. Screaming hysterically for the men to let her go.

Behind them, another man carried a body over his shoulder. It was wrapped up in a bloodstained sheet. A woman's red hair dangled from beneath the rolled cloth. They had Holly Webber's body as well.

I couldn't just sit there and watch them take Veronica. I threw open the door of Flores's car and started to get out. Elias was waiting for me with his own gun leveled.

"Stop right there, Mr. Cord," he said. "You've intervened enough in this matter."

"I won't let you take her," I said, bringing up Flores's gun.

"Ah, I'm afraid your options have been curtailed. You may lower your gun and do exactly as I say, or you may die. The choice is yours."

The moment I lowered my gun, Elias snatched it from my hand. He motioned over two buzz cuts struggling with the weight of the freak's limp body. Without his hat I could see that wispy hairs clung to his otherwise bald and heat-deformed head. One man had the feet and the other the shoulders. They dropped the freak unceremoniously into the street.

"He's still alive," said one of the buzz cuts. He lifted the freak's head up. "I don't know how. He's been shot fifteen times. Should we finish him off?"

"Leave him," said Elias, and then he indicated me. "And this one here as well."

"What about the cop?"

"Kill him."

Flores tried to drive away, but there was no chance. The rapid-fire pop of the grease guns echoed from the houses lining the street. The remaining onlookers screamed and ran inside, at last realizing they were not witnessing anything to be enjoyed. Windows shattered on the police custom. It swerved up onto the curb and struck a telephone pole, and the horn blew its singular ugly note. I ran to the car and saw Flores slumped against the wheel, clearly killed.

In my anger I turned to fight, but any hope of a suicidal confrontation with Bishop's men was gone. Their vehicles were already pulling away and taking Veronica and Holly Webber with them.

■ ■ ■

The police radio was buzzing with calls about the shoot-out in Sunset Beach. Two major crimes in one night had the LAPD out in force. Shoebox Fords with screaming sirens rumbled down every main artery. Foot cops watched intersections and mobbed the haunts of lowlifes with answers. There were checkpoints at the exits of the highways.

There had been a massacre at the Bishop power plant. A cop dead in Sunset Beach. The whole city was on edge, and all of the LAPD was looking for me.

I turned off the police radio and switched on the Cadillac's radio. The backlit dial glowed in the darkness of the car. NBC was playing "Archie." I turned through the dial until I found breaking news on KABC.

"We, ah, we wanted to correct a statement from earlier," said the newsman. "We are just getting word that the tragic shooting this afternoon at the San Pedro Power Station resulted in the death of millionaire industrialist Harlan Bishop and not, as originally reported, his son, Ethan Bishop. Los Angeles is in shock over this horrific rampage that claimed the lives of Harlan Bishop, police sergeant Hector Flores, and over fifteen others. I'm going to go to Tommy Hoolihan, KABC's man on the street, for his two cents. Tommy."

"Thank you, Chip," said Tommy Hoolihan. "My two cents is this: I guarantee you that when this whole story shakes out, we are going to find that it was either the Chicanos or the Negroes out of Power City who did it. Youth assassins are rampant and spreading as far as Sunset Beach? Tell me something I don't know. Bishop bottled up all those dangerous elements in—"

I switched the radio off. I'd parked the Cadillac beneath a half-built bridge, lights out, engine off. I was hiding out under part of the highway cloverleaf the crews had been working on for months. In among the tractors and trucks parked beside the road the Cadillac was just another work vehicle left to sit until construction resumed in the morning. Unless, of course, someone looked closely enough to realize it was a damn Cadillac.

The freak was sprawled in the backseat. I wasn't too sure why I'd brought him. Enemy of my enemy maybe. Hoping for some answers. While I was searching him for the keys to his big car, I'd realized he was alive. He was also a heavy son of a bitch and was bleeding all over the place.

As I was lifting him into the backseat, I'd figured out why he was still breathing. There was some sort of homemade metal vest stitched into his shirt. Half an inch of iron pounded into the shape of a man's chest. I'd seen the sort worn by bomber crews. The sort that didn't do a bit of good when a Jap was putting fist-sized shells through the side of your airplane. Worked out a little better for the freak. Looked like most of the bullets had torn holes in his coat and bounced or skipped along the body armor's curve and ended up in his legs and arms.

Still plenty of lead to kill a regular man. Even the big freak seemed on his way to bleeding out as he lay gasping and gurgling on the backseat of the Cadillac. He hadn't regained consciousness since I'd put him there, and I figured he would never wake up.

Without anyone to converse with, I'd spent the past hour going through my last pack of Bravos, nervously watching the lights of cars on the frontage road and trying to weave together the threads of Veronica Lambert, Harlan and Ethan Bishop, Holly Webber, and the big palooka drip-drying in the backseat. I thought I had it just about sorted. A theory that was working out.

"All right, listen to this," I said to the freak. "Tell me if I got anything wrong."

There was no answer from the peanut gallery. I continued.

"All along I was operating under the mistaken assumption that you were something new, some other sort of beast, on account of you being so huge," I said, "but you're not. You're a Warren, like me. Not only that, you're the Warren in the *Rex Rawhide* film with Isabella Webber. Her lover. Who else would be obsessively protecting her daughter's friend from Bishop?

"Isabella was with Bishop when she died. Maybe he stole her from you, maybe you split up, I don't know, but you acted to save her teenage daughter, didn't you?" I waited for an answer, but the freak only groaned incoherently. "Dirty work, creeping up to that poor family's house in Riverside. Did you kill them first or set the fire first and let them burn alive? That must have weighed on your conscience.

"Holly Webber was the last piece of Isabella left, so you got her out of Riverside and put her somewhere Bishop wouldn't find her. The whole time you were working for Bishop. Doing what? Work too dirty even for me? For Elias? When Holly was old enough, you paid for her to live in the city. Slipping envelopes full of cash under the office door of a sleazebag apartment manager in South LA. I can only imagine the sick peeping you did as she grew into a woman like her mother.

"Mind if I smoke another?" I pinched my last cigarette between my lips and looked back at the freak. His eyes were deliriously open, his lipless mouth parted, and bloody drool spilled down his chin.

"Thanks, bud," I said, and I continued with my theory.

"Your problem was that you didn't erase all of Holly's connections. You didn't take care of Veronica Lambert, Holly's best friend. So while Holly is living it up, bright young girl in the big city, all alone, she reaches back into her past for her good friend Veronica. Look-alike must have thrown you for a loop. Threw me for one too. But Veronica saw something, some artifact or picture Holly had, and she convinced Holly to blackmail Bishop.

"That's what happened out in Cranford." I cracked the window so the cool night air would suck some of the smoke out of the Cadillac. "Holly was blackmailing Bishop.

"She wrote him a letter, told him to drop the cash in the mailbox of an abandoned farm. They brought her the cash. Cash that flies like confetti out of her hands when she's run down. Blackmail money that ends up caught in the branches of the roadside scrub. Nobody was trying to kill her. You were trying to rescue her, weren't you? But you poor, big, scary beast. Look at yourself. You spooked her, and she ran for help. Ran for the road. Was it a random accident of some passing motorist, or was it Elias and his boys?"

"Them," the freak wheezed, nearly causing me to drop my cigarette. "It was them. Left the money in the mailbox. Came back to close the trap. Going . . . too fast. I should have . . . should have let Bishop . . ."

He paused, eyes glassy and damp with pain.

"Whiskey," he finally said.

There was a little Brown Barrel left in my flask. I handed it back to him, and he sat forward. Christ, the smell of the blood. It was as strong as anything since the trenches, since the massacre in that train back in Spark.

"Why protect Veronica?" I asked.

The freak slopped the whiskey into his lipless mouth. When he'd drained the flask, he answered.

"Holly loved her," he said. "More than friends . . . I . . ."

"She was a pervert?"

"No," he said. "A sister. Like a sister. As much as two people can feel for each other."

"Who are you to Bishop?" I asked. "I could never figure that out. I saw you leaving the power station in San Pedro. What do you do for him?"

"Judge," the freak wheezed.

"Buddy, I'm the damn Judge," I said.

"Frontier sheriff, Casper," said the freak, and he laughed. It was a bubbling, gurgling laugh that ended in a choking fit. The freak recovered and lifted his head. A translucent orange fluid was running out from a crack in the burn tissue on his head. "I am a policeman; you are a frontier sheriff. Last of the lone Judges. Bishop . . . saw our numbers . . . multiplying. Needed a force . . . to preserve the secret."

"An army?"

"Police," he reiterated. "He was right. I helped him . . . to keep the secret . . . to protect . . ."

He slumped back in the seat. I slapped him awake. His eyes came open again, reeling, pale marbles flicking back and forth in the livid raisin of his face.

"There are more like you?" I demanded.

He nodded, unable to talk. Bishop subverting the whole process of the Covenant was nothing new, but to learn he'd developed his own, separate enforcement arm was a shock to the system. I'd lived for over fifteen years figuring I was the only Judge, and here was a guy telling me we had a whole court system.

"One thing I can't figure," I said, "is why Holly Webber had my phone number. Did you do that?"

"Gave it to her . . . years . . . years ago."

"Why?" I demanded. "You told me to keep away."

"In case something happened . . . to me . . . I needed a man who would protect her." He looked away from me, out the window. "I knew . . . could trust you. Knew you . . . weren't . . . entirely Bishop's man. You were your own . . . your own . . ."

I was losing him.

"Snap out of it." I grabbed him and shook him. "You don't die yet, you son of a bitch. Wake up!"

His eyes rebounded from the gravity of unconsciousness. He peered right into mine and said, "Kyushu."

I let go of him.

"Gardener?"

"I . . . yes . . ." he said. "You left me . . . to die . . . but I lived. They put me back together."

"Ishii shot you," I said. "The cabin burned. . . ."

"Yes," said Gardener, and he leaned forward, his awful, melted face materializing from the darkness.

Atop the black rocks of the holy mountain. Gardener, holding that damn green box, Ishii stepping away. Gardener emptied the contents onto the table. I expected it to be filled with the letters Annie had exchanged with Gideon. I couldn't imagine anything else inside that box, but what was within made little sense to me.

"What is that?" I demanded, pointing to the papers and photographs stamped with GEHEIM that spilled out.

Gardener was ignoring me. He hung the lantern on a ceiling hook. He drew a flask from his pocket and began pouring strong alcohol onto the papers, overflowing the table and saturating the floor. I started toward him, my fists raised.

"Stay back," Gardener warned.

I smashed the flask from his hands. Gardener threw his Ronson onto the doused documents and photographs, and they burst into flames. Ishii seized his opportunity. He lunged at Gardener, throwing him against the wall of the cabin.

As they struggled, I tried to extinguish the fire. The flames were weak in the thin air, but Gardener had thoroughly doused the pages in the alcohol. Blue flames licked at my shoes. Cinders burst around my legs and ignited fire in the saturated tatami.

The fire was consuming typewritten pages in German bearing names like *Hoffman* and *Rascher*. There were photographs too, of Warrens, dead and naked on tables. Dead in a row in the uniforms of different services and even different nations. But there was something more.

"Kill him!" shouted Gardener as he wrestled with Ishii. "Kill him, damn you."

I ignored him, reaching into the spreading flames for the photographs. They were crumbling and burning, disintegrating before my eyes, but I glimpsed things that were impossible.

These were photographs of photographs, grainy and difficult enough to see if they were not also disintegrating in my hands. I glimpsed Warren Groves, his head in a pressure helmet. Another photograph was of a crane that held a golden sphere suspended in a familiar, rocky chamber. There was a photograph of a complex diagram, like two tornadoes meeting at the whirling tips. A crowded unit portrait of stoic men in Air Force dress uniforms, slightly different ages, slightly different haircuts, and the same serious face. My face.

The photographs had spilled from a single folder. As the fire consumed the last of the photographs, the folder's tab remained. Written in Japanese characters and then in English was the word *Westward*.

"Shoot him!" shouted Gardener.

He and Ishii were tangled on the floor in a fight to the death, surrounded by flames, nearly engulfed in them. Gardener was pinning Ishii down, but Ishii seized Gardener by the throat and began choking him. I found Gardener's pistol, and I aimed it at them, unsure which I wanted to shoot more.

The lantern, hanging up amid the creeping flames, exploded, showering the cabin in burning oil. I fired, unsure of which man I hit. I recoiled from the intense heat and ran outside. In moments the cabin was completely consumed, inside and out. I stood and watched it burn to a blackened pile of timbers. I was sure that both men were dead beneath the rubble.

"Westward," I said to Gardener, who lay dying in the backseat of the Cadillac. "What was it?"

"You want to . . . find out?" he asked. "Follow . . . Veronica. . . ."

"Where?" I said. "To Chatholm? Back to the power station?"

Gardener's smile was horrible.

"To New Mexico," he said. "To the Pool. He's going to make her . . . forever. And your . . . your answers are there."

CHAPTER FIFTEEN

■ ■ ■

There was an easy way back to New Mexico and a hard way back. The hard way was driving for a solid day, without rest, over mountains and into the desert, in a car being hunted by the police. The easy way was to put a gun into my mouth and blow my noodles out, erase all the scars, come back clean and new out of the Pool. I preferred that option.

Gardener, when he wasn't moaning deliriously, told me why that wasn't a bright idea. Bishop controlled the Pool and everything around it, he said. For those fifteen years I'd been doing his heavy work, Bishop and Shiftman and others had been turning Spark and the Pool into an industrial and military facility.

The war had granted them the special authority. Roosevelt had helped, and so had New Mexico's Governor DeWitt. It was all of it off the map, in a part of New Mexico officially known as White Sands Air and Missile Base. Lots of atomic-bomb checks paid for rail lines and paved roads in the middle of the desert, and Spark had become their secret place. The training ground of Westward.

"It's me," said Gardener. "I'm there. We're there . . . in Spark. The others . . . work for Bishop now."

Gardener's duplicates were covering things up and serving as Bishop's enforcers in Spark. They were the ones who had battered through the barricade to poor Beau Reynolds as we spoke on the telephone. I asked him what they might have done to Reynolds. How do you muzzle a man who can't be killed?

"Zeroed," said Gardener. "The Center." I asked him to explain what that meant, but he had lapsed into unconsciousness and could not be roused.

We were in the badlands of Arizona, sun boiling the desert, wind roaring through the open windows, when Gardener finally came awake again. He was nearly gone. His face was sunken and his lips cracked. The blood was dried all over him. I rolled the windows up so that I could hear what he was trying to say. I asked him about Operation Westward, but he wasn't answering.

"You have to kill her," he groaned. "If she . . . if she can't be saved. Kill her. Don't . . . let it happen to her . . . promise . . . promise me. . . ."

"I promise," I said. "I will kill her if I can't save her."

He was gone. Broadcasting to the Pool, to a newly made body, to become entrapped in Bishop's industrial complex. I stopped and buried the body in the desert. My lungs were aching, and the intense heat tired me after only a few minutes of digging, so he was buried in a shallow grave that would probably not keep out the scavengers. A single stone marked the location of the body. Already the wind was blowing dust across the trackless hardpan and covering the outline of the hole.

I bypassed Phoenix and Tucson. I drove through unmade lands where the sun did not shine, it scoured, a flamethrower intent on cleaning us out of the bunkers. In the dirty heights of the Santa Catalina Mountains I bought gasoline and something to drink. The boy running the gas pump complimented the road-worn Cadillac. He asked me if I needed a doctor.

"Shotgun," I said.

"Not here," said the attendant. "Try up in San Manuel."

No time. The longer I drove, the more the world receded. It passed along with rocks and leaning fence posts and disappeared into a single point in the Cadillac's rearview mirror. The horizon devoured the sordid, branching, endlessly recursive course of my 109 years. The wars and the betrayals and everything I'd lost, even my ancestral history spanning the darkness, over and over again, all stripped away by the desert heat.

I imagined there wasn't even a civilization to return to, only the cloud of dust behind the rattling Cadillac, swallowing up the road and erasing it like an Apache dragging a cottonwood bough behind his horse. The future was all that remained. As far as could be seen, that future was desert, baking and breaking clay beneath a pathless blue sky.

Here was New Mexico. The shape and colors of the mountains told me that much. My maps were obsolete and did not record the name of the road I was traveling. The useless black *X* I'd drawn in pen was no longer intersected by the vital world. There were always new maps. New ways to approach the mountains that never moved but could disappear if a highway turned in the wrong direction.

The dark shapes of distant mountains were born from nothing, hands lifting beneath a magician's cloth, heaving the bright desert into blue-black shadow shapes. The Red Lines and, more distant, the Oscuras. The music on the radio began to fade into static. After a few moments of crackling, a woman's voice resolved through the static reading a message. She spoke in a monotone.

"You are entering a United States Air Force restricted area. Turn back now."

The message repeated on an endless loop on every channel. I shut off the radio.

In the distance a condor took flight from the folded mountain rocks, soaring high above them, turning, defying the crush of the heat. Its huge wings were visible as a wheeling black line in the sky. It turned and flew directly toward me, toward my car, as if sallying forth to challenge me.

I reckoned it the biggest bird I'd ever seen. As big as that great golden eagle on Kyushu. It had a strange shape to its wings, as though it might be injured. I strained to see it more clearly, my vision going gray at the edges from the sickness. At that moment there was a loud explosion, and the car pulled violently into the oncoming lane. I resisted the urge to brake hard and smoothly guided the shuddering vehicle to the side of the road.

The cooking asphalt was soft beneath my shoes. The left rear tire was blown out, deflated tatters hanging from the rim, strips of whitewall drooping to the tarry black road. There was a trail of rubber scraps behind me. From the southeast, from the Tularosa Basin and Alamogordo and the White Sands Air Force base, came the steady drone of aircraft engines.

I stopped at the car's trunk, the spare tire leaned against my leg, the iron in my hand, and I observed in solemn awe as a pair of barrel-bodied fighter planes roared up from the basin. Some updated version of the familiar P-47 Thunderbolt. They passed overhead close enough for me to feel the beat of their props. They were in steep climbs, trying to gain altitude for some maneuver. I scanned the sky and realized they were rising toward the condor bird. They were turning, trying to get above it now.

The bird seemed to ignore them and swoop lower, still coming straight toward the road. Straight toward me. I realized this was unusual but could do nothing but watch, unable to move or look away as it grew larger and larger. The fighters passed it, and there was a black puff of smoke from each, and seconds later I heard the familiar chatter of .50-caliber guns. Black feathers or pieces fell from the bird, and it spiraled down toward the desert. The fighters began a wide circle to come around again.

The bird regained its senses only a few hundred feet above ground. It spread its wings and resumed its course, drifting lower and lower with each passing moment. The planes were coming around again, many miles behind it.

Almost too late, I realized it was coming for me again. I kicked the spare tire away and began running down the road. I could hear it. No engine, but a drumming, as if a deck of cards the size of a house was being shuffled. I glanced back, and my stomach lurched.

I recognized the cruciform shape of it, black on black, with flecks of glimmering red. It was the grasshopper idol come to life. I'd seen a glimpse of it while I was tied to a chair at Ian Bendwool's and had not even realized what it was. Now here it was in the light of horrible day, a massive insect, like a black locust with plump thorax and beating wings that glittered with iridescent red. Compound eyes bulged atop the armored shovel of its head, and arthropod mouth hinged open, drooling black as it came.

Was this creature from the Pool? Come from the other side as Beau Reynolds had said? Was this the beast, the demon insect, the keeper of that accursed place?

It seemed as though it might strike me down, or swoop and pick me up with the long hook-clawed legs dangling below it. It fell. It landed with great violence atop the roof of the Cadillac. It crushed the car's body and exploded the three remaining tires. Broken glass and shrapnel of auto body rained down on the roadway and raised puffs of dust in the surrounding desert. The car slewed sideways across both lanes. A hail of the glass beat against me and bounced from my shoulders and filled the indented crown and brim of my fedora.

The creature was still alive, trying to lift up, its legs flopping and spraying black liquid. It collapsed again atop the car with a screech of bending metal. I reached for my gun, but that was long gone. Somewhere underneath half a ton of Cadillac and however many tons of giant grasshopper.

I approached the stricken animal with great caution. This was a thing from my nightmare, alive and in the flesh for me to study. One more death was certainly worth the risk, but I'd rather not end up in the clutches of whatever new order reigned in the valley. The creature was still alive. I could hear the labored hissing of its lungs, spiracles venting, black blood spitting from its injured mouth.

The tessellated dome of one eye was punctured in two places by bullets, and more wounds stitched up its back. It lifted its head as I approached, languidly, like a sick horse. Articulated mandibles hung loosely. It was drooling such a quantity of the black liquid from its mouth that it overflowed the roof of the car and slopped and hissed down onto the pavement. There was no question it was looking at me.

The banded plumpness of its thorax arched up from the car, behind the armor of its folded wings. I stopped moving toward it. There was no stinger visible. Between the flexing segments were narrow bands of red and white. Long, stiff bristles covered its back. The wings were injured but began to thrum and beat against the bristles.

"Chiii chiiii chiiiii!" was the shrill sound of the vibrating bristles.

The creature cocked its head. I could hear the approaching buzz of the aircraft.

"Chiii chiiii chiiiii!"

"What in the hell," I said.

"W-warren," the creature's wings beat. "Warren. Warren Groves. Help. Help."

It began repeating this last, horrible, thrumming word again and again. Each time it finished the chirping syllable, it beat its broken legs against the car, as if for emphasis.

"Help? What can I do? What the hell are you?"

"Help!" it thrummed again and beat its broken legs against the car.

The sound of the aircraft engines pitched up and grew very loud. One of the planes was screaming down on me. I could see the winking lights of its guns firing. I had time to turn as the roadway exploded into flying stones and ricocheting bullets. I didn't look back. I ran as fast as I could across the road and leaped into the dust. I could hear the splintering, tearing meat sound and the steady hammer-rain against the car's body. I kept my face in the dirt until the shooting stopped and the planes roared by very low overhead.

Flames sprayed from the gas tank and spread quickly through the car's compressed interior. The locust creature atop the car was unmoving. Its body began to give off a greenish-black smoke that smelled like lobster innards. The juicier parts of its shell began to pop, chitin splitting along joints, flaking gray meat bursting from the split carapace. The black fluid on the roadway began to steam and sizzle.

I dusted myself off and set my hat onto my head. The foul smoke was growing thicker, the heat more intense, and I knew any effort to save the car would be wasted. More planes were roaring into the sky. Four fighters. Six. The shadow of a big four-engine bomber raced across the scene, momentarily darkening my upturned face.

A convoy of vehicles was emerging from a ramp up from the basin. There were black jeeps and olive-drab jeeps and big white trucks that I assumed were ambulances. They were coming on fast, but the convoy was still miles distant.

I was panicked by the sudden, lurching realignment of my foundational reality. Hard to make sense of what was happening around me. To reach the Pool I would have to evade the military—if that was what these people were—and cross the White Sands on foot. Spark was much nearer. I could see the buildings atop the looming slopes of Red Stem. The hills favored concealment in that direction.

I took one last look up at the planes weaving over the burning car, a last glance at the convoy approaching from the distance, and I ran.

■ ■ ■

Spark, the quaint town still lingering atop Red Stem when I'd passed through in '34, was gone. In its place were streets with sidewalks and row upon row of houses that reflected recent heights of suburban planning. All empty. The once-merry rows of houses and shops were sand-swept, a small park was desiccated, the playground equipment bleached almost white, the roads scoured of markings and cracked by the heat. No one had lived in this place, let alone maintained it, for months.

Somewhere, down a distant side street, a door banged open and closed at the whim of the wind. It was accompanied by the dissonant clinking of wind chimes. Advertisements for Lewis Licorice Sweets and Ogilvy Oil and other products under the Bishop umbrella suggested a company town, one that had never achieved its aim.

I followed the main street, keeping as much as possible to the shaded areas of the downtown. Tire tracks through the accumulated dust on this main road at least suggested recent activity. These tracks were numerous and large, indicating a mixture of vehicles but predominately trucks.

A huge structure stood where once Gideon Long's foundry had overlooked Spark. This was the terminus of the main street. It resembled an immense school or hospital. Perhaps a prison. I walked closer and saw it was surrounded by multiple layers of concertina wire sandwiching dead zones.

The gate to this structure was designed in a manner similar to Bishop's Chatholm estate. Woven vines of black iron spelled out simply CENTER. The gate was left open, and no one appeared to man the nearby tower constructed from wood. Nevertheless, I approached cautiously, expecting to be challenged by a guard. None appeared. There was only the wind howling over the unkempt grounds and the distant banging of that door. That emptiness unnerved me most of all.

As I made my way up the road to the concrete fortress, I recalled something Gardener said before he died. He said Beau Reynolds was "Zeroed," and he mentioned "The Center." Something about the way he'd said "Zeroed" gave me the heebie-jeebies. It was the way a normal person might spit out the word *"murdered."*

The Center stretched nearly to the edge of the mountain. Its institutional design of imposing concrete was embellished with black iron and recessed windows that seemed too narrow and high to be of any use. The main doors opened into a lobby stripped of its fixtures and its meaning. A floor map showing the locations within the building was covered in black paint.

I wandered the halls, searching the still and gloomy building for any signs of life. I passed warily between the squares of golden light cast through the windows. There were no electric lights turned on, although a glowing exit sign indicated there was still electricity. I came upon doors every few dozen feet, and some bore inscriptions that, presumably, had once described their purpose.

There was Trunk Theory, Trunk Plotting, Trunk Recovery, Autogenic Rehearsal, Implosion Depth Psychology, Aggressor Denial, Trans-Horizon Navigation, Electro Communication, Rhizopod Reproduction, Return String Determination, Non-Linear Circulation, Peristaltic Trunk Conduits, and my personal favorite, Universal Meat Origins.

Some of the words were familiar to me, but other than frequent use of the word *Trunk*, there wasn't much to help me discern an overall purpose, and the offices were empty. Some were carpeted and bore indentations where desks and large machines had once sat, but that was as close as I came to finding evidence of the contents.

I passed windows facing an exterior motor pool, and there were a few jeeps parked beneath corrugated shelters. I tried to place the view to the outside of the building so that I might return to that spot and, hopefully, get one of the jeeps started.

I came across a cafeteria stifling and heavy with the smell of old food. The eating area was very large, and all the chairs had been piled in a heap reaching up to the ceiling. The longest of the walls was decorated with a stylized mural of identical men standing in a line. Each had the same blond hair and strong jaw, and each was facing west, looking to a glowing horizon full of promise. The men were differentiated by the clothes they wore. One was a soldier, another a laborer, another a doctor, and the man in the foreground wore a padded white uniform and a stylized pilot's helmet over his head.

On the third floor I discovered a row of ten rooms, their doors close together, and each with PILOT stenciled on the door in gold lettering. Inside, the rooms were small and carpeted, and indentations in the carpeting suggested chairs and desks. Some walls bore the marks of framed photographs and holes from hanging nails, but the pictures were long gone. In the last room in the series I discovered a large wad of paper. I unraveled it and flattened it on the floor. *CONGRATULATIONS, TOM!* was spelled out in three-inch letters.

I was growing delirious from walking in the hot, unventilated building. I repeatedly passed several minutes shuffling from room to room without any idea of where I was going or what I was seeing. The stripped sameness of the halls and rooms was disorienting.

I came to heavy double doors of the sort used in hospitals to join wings or outbuildings. The doors were painted red, and there was a square of adhesive plastic, possibly a sign of some sort, that was defaced and illegible. There was no handle or bar to push open the doors, but I discovered a flat, metal button on the wall.

I pressed it. The doors swung open toward me, slowly and silently, sweeping all the way to the walls and revealing the large chamber beyond. It was much colder than the rest of the building, rising three stories and illuminated by light falling in dusty shafts through the yellow-tinted sunroof.

In the room's center, transfixed by the light so that its metal fixtures were golden, was an apparatus that was one part cockpit and one part cross-section of a bathysphere. Ten feet in diameter, its hull was covered with thick, golden paint, and the exposed interior revealed heavy reinforcing joints and lever-operated controls. The entire apparatus was suspended several feet above the floor by an industrial gantry. Stairs reached up to the cockpit to allow someone to climb inside.

The room was hollow, and my footsteps echoed as I approached the contraption. Up close the details of its construction became clear. Instruments including swivel-mounted "cameras" made from wood were controlled from the chair. Levers were labeled with words printed on pieces of tape. HATCH RELEASE, CAMERA I RELEASE, PILOT CAMERA RELEASE, TILT, ROLL, BRAKE. Scratched sockets in the wall of the spherical apparatus suggested gauges that had been pried out with a screwdriver.

I climbed the stairs and experienced a moment of leg-quivering vertigo at the realization that the apparatus was suspended above a deep shaft. I could see light reflecting from the surface of water far down the vertical shaft.

This was where the men were being trained for Operation Westward—there could be no doubt. Coupled with my experience at Bendwool's, I believed that Bishop and Shiftman were trying to travel through the Pool and out the other side, not by chance emergence, as my memory suggested, but by using some sort of capsule.

I'll confess, I've never liked science fiction pictures. Something about the rockets they fly in and the ridiculous ray guns doesn't suit me the way a good old war or detective picture will get my blood going. Even though I live an unusual life because of the Pool, I would have scoffed at something like this being possible. But with all that had happened over the past week, I could now believe just about anything.

I was examining a control pedestal with cranks and levers that seemed to control the flow of water into the shaft when I heard a bang. It was distant but followed by several more bangs. I leaped down the stairs and went limping out of the room with the training capsule. There it was again! Somewhere in the building something was making a lot of noise.

I searched out the source as the noise continued. Following my ears brought me to a ramp descending into the basement level of the building. It was dark, lit only by emergency bulbs casting a red glow reminiscent of the danger stations of a submarine. These were housed in steel cages. The walls in the basement were unpainted and unadorned, and the floors were bare cement. The hall sloped deeper and deeper, into a land of pipes and ductwork, beneath the building.

I reached a side passage and could see that it opened into a darkened room. Approaching carefully, I spotted a placard in the red glow of the emergency lamp. ZEROING.

A switch activated the room's overhead lights, and one by one long strips of fluorescents blinked to life. From floor to ceiling the room was covered in white tiles. There were drains set into the floor, and the surrounding tiles were stained brown. There was a single barber's chair and beside it a rolling instrument table bereft of any instruments. One wall was decorated with medical diagrams of the human skull and the human brain. Tall metal cabinets and drawers sat completely open and empty.

No, not entirely empty.

A second instrument table was topped by a cardboard hatbox. The top of the box was labeled with a neatly applied decal. In a calligraphic font it read, *HARROW MK. I.* Inside the box was a broken, handheld machine somewhere between an electric drill and the tool an optometrist uses to measure eyesight. The particular device did not work when I pulled its trigger control, but it was easy to imagine the device's u-shaped metal band held against a patient's forehead and a trigger pull activating the drill to enter his skull.

There was another bang. Very nearby now. It definitely sounded like a man pounding against something, possibly trapped.

I returned to the hall and sought the source of the noise. It came from beyond a door similar to the one leading to the training-capsule room. This time, the sign on the door had not been scratched off. It warned, *DO NOT OPEN WITHOUT ASSISTANCE.*

The loud thump shook the double door. What was I going to do? There was no assistance for me out there, so I opened it. It whirred and split and swung open toward me into the hall. I hoped to find Beau Reynolds.

I found a horror. I was immediately assailed by the overpowering stench of human filth and death. A man—a Warren—shuffled out of the darkness, his face gaunt, his nails bloodied. He moaned and came toward me, and I could see that his forehead bore the scabbed mark of the zeroing device called a Harrow. As my eyes adjusted to the deep blackness of the room, I realized it was vast and filled with shuffling men dressed in rags or nothing at all. Some were babbling, some beating their fists against walls, but many were drawn in my direction by the light.

"Beau Reynolds?" I shoved away the grotesque apparition of a man coming toward me. He fell to the floor and began writhing and moaning.

"Beau Reynolds?" My voice echoed in the depths of the blackness.

It was futile. The Harrow clearly reduced men to drooling idiots, and there would be no response to my shouts. All of them were Warrens, so there was no distinguishing them by appearance. Poor Reynolds was in there somewhere, or dead already, lost and locked away by whatever miserable authority ruled this place. Whoever it was, they had left no food or water for these men, and I could see that a number had perished already.

The sight of them coming toward me in a shambling wave was too much to stand. They were desperate and unable to communicate. Filthy hands grabbed at my clothes and pulled at my arms, and I retreated, afraid of being smothered by them or worse. They hooted unintelligibly as I fled, and I could hear them continuing to moan and scream long after I escaped from their sight.

CHAPTER SIXTEEN

■ ■ ■

Ahead of me, the dark Oscuras towered in all of their folded detail. Behind me, across the open desert, the military men were preoccupied with the barbecued grasshopper and the flattened Cadillac. The fire had so utterly consumed both that they probably figured I was dead inside the car. Only a single plane remained in the air, circling lazily overhead, but I had a feeling that as soon as those poor bastards from the Center came wandering out, the military would have their hands full rounding them up.

There was a road, four-laned, disappearing into the mountains. I approached across the desert, but there was no avoiding that road into the canyon. The entrance to the valley was dramatically widened. Some of this work was underway when I emerged in '34.

There was a gravel road and efforts to install some sort of building to house and deal with the immediately emerged. The flow of men coming out of the Pool seemed to be accelerating as more of us walked the earth. The method of drawing names from a hat had long since been replaced with a card-and-tabulator system similar to that of a factory. Draw a card and punch in to your new life.

Those changes did not prepare me for the extensive construction in the valley. The pueblos that had once lined the terraces were gone; the stairs were gone, all replaced with scaffolding and poured concrete. There were two paved ramps leading up to the cave entrance, which was itself widened even more. A second bore hole, far larger than the cave leading to the Pool, descended into the mountainside at ground level at a downward grade. This tunnel was accessed by a rail line that ran parallel to the highway-style road.

As had been the case for Bishop's version of Spark, this new construction was serviced by a number of shops advertising companies and products under the Bishop umbrella. The shops here appeared much more recently used but were nevertheless shuttered up. A number of derelict buses sat in a row alongside the road, and pallets of construction material were sheltered beneath heavy tarps. There was a huge flag-pole between the ramps; presumably once it had hoisted an American flag, but that was gone.

I parked the jeep near the flagpole and climbed the ramps on foot. A fly buzzed at my face, and I swatted it away. It buzzed back in at me, and I swatted it away again. I stopped in place. I turned, halfway up the ramp, and looked down at the shops and derelict vehicles. There were birds hopping to and fro in the dust, search-ing for bugs to eat. Flies were buzzing around the last bins of trash set out behind the shops. The wind shivered the tarps, and they rattled loudly as it gusted down into the valley.

The magic had been dispelled. The stillness that had once reigned was encroached upon by the natural world. I ascended the ramp as quickly as I could, wheezing and coughing, spitting sickness onto the ground. When I blinked, I witnessed echelons of false light glimmering in the vascular darkness. I fell to my knees at the summit of the ramp. The wind was whipping the dust into whirling ribbons and blowing grit into my eyes and nose and mouth.

I managed to get myself to my feet, swaying, staggering into the darkness of the cave. The sound of the wind grew louder here, scouring through the darkness like the hot air from a trumpeter. The wind was not just entering the cave but circulating. Ventilation shafts or possibly the additional excavation had clearly opened it up more to the elements.

The tunnel was now wide enough for a jeep, and I walked a thudding road formed from metal supports and wooden planking. The strings of miners' lights I recalled were replaced with the soft orange glow of sodium lamps buzzing every few feet. Signs warned me to watch my step or wear my hard hat or check the tempera-ture. The heat increased as I delved deeper into the mountain, but these were minor differences, not the searing furnace of before.

The cavern of the Pool was transformed. The mountain was excavated, the cham-ber dramatically enlarged to house an enormous gantry crane similar to but larger than the one used in the Center's training room. The Pool's surroundings were re-modeled to be more hospitable, with a garish WELCOME sign erected just behind sloping stairs descending out of view and into the Pool.

I walked to the edge, my footsteps echoing in the emptiness. I peered down, afraid, somehow knowing what I would see. Or wouldn't.

The Pool, the white cauldron of our unnatural birth, was gone. There was only a yawning blackness, a deep void that had once contained the liquid. I sat down on the lip of the stairs and dangled my legs over the void. I whistled, tunelessly at first but soon turning into an old French lullaby. Only knew the music, not the words.

I stopped my whistling and closed my eyes. There was only one way left. One path. I'd come all this way for nothing, but if the Pool still existed to endanger Veronica, then there was a way for me to get there. I reached for a last cigarette, but I had none. A last bite of Brown Barrel. My flask was empty.

"Good-bye, cruel world." I laughed, and I pitched myself forward into the pit.

Death was not so quick as I had imagined. I never guessed how deep the Pool was, but I learned at a terminal velocity, plummeting into the hollow darkness for many seconds, deeper and deeper, passing a light from the lower tunnel, deeper still, feeling the heat of the rock around me, all the way to the bottom. Accelerating into the rock that waited to cradle my flesh.

■ ■ ■

Bursting from the liquid, gasping, disoriented by the dreams I tunneled between and the cowl that surrounded my flesh. Hands lifted me from the cold ground, and I was carried to showers. Rough brushes and hot water scoured the membrane from my body. Men in white suits with hoses blasted away all of the filth of my creation.

Towels. Still hard to make sense of it. The light was so bright. I staggered along, allowing myself to be guided into a warm room with a padded bench. There were clothes here for me. They fit perfectly. How was that? Did they know I was coming? No, no, of course. All of us were the same size.

"Casper Cord," I said to one of the men helping me dress.

That was a name. A good name. My name before . . . My memories were returning. I shoved away the hands and tried to run for the door, but it was too late. More men entered the room. They were strong and forceful and held me upright. There was the sharp sting of an injection in my arm, and I began to slacken. My will to fight back dissolved into a gauzy pleasure, and I relaxed onto the padded bench.

Much later I was awakened. Ethan Bishop was there, dressed in a white tie and tuxedo. Or was it Harlan Bishop, assuming the role of his son at long last? There was no way to be certain. I was not sure it even mattered, the false son being as twisted as the father.

"So nice of you to announce yourself," said Bishop, leaning over me. "You'd forced us to quarantine every Warren emerging from the Pool to prevent you from running amok. Now that we have you, we can let those other poor fellows be on their way."

"Licorice?" Bishop offered me a wrapped candy. I took it from him automatically. "I think you and I should go for a walk."

Two Gideons dressed in white hospital coats lifted me to my feet, and both supported me and forced me forward as I walked alongside Bishop. We were in the gleaming halls of a newly built facility. It reminded me of the sort of place where an experimental aircraft would be built or some other precision machine, but it had the disinfected smell of a hospital.

"I wish you'd been here for the wedding," said Bishop. "Finally, the wedding

Annie deserved, not that pauper's church. Of course it was only a formality. She and I have had such a long and magnificent romance, it really was destiny, for her to emerge from nothing and for you, faithful Casper, to lead my bloodhounds right to her. But where were you off to? What took you so long?"

"Spark," I muttered.

"Of course!" Bishop snapped his fingers. "That would explain those poor, sick Warrens running wild in the desert. Troubled types, meant to be kept in the Center. General Shiftman was quite cross about that. A lot of explaining and covering up to do with his friends in the Air Force, but I consider what you gave me more than a fair trade."

"Where is she?" I demanded.

"Your friend was easier to spot than you," said Bishop as we stopped beside an observation window of the sort used in hospital nurseries. Inside was a Warren strapped to a bed. There was an IV running into his arm and a monitor with twitching armatures scribbling out his vital statistics. The Warren was youthful but had startling white hair.

"All of Milo Gardener's duplicates come out looking like that," said Bishop. "We're still trying to figure out why exactly. The others are so helpful, you know? Real go-getters committed to the cause. They serve in his honor. They call themselves the Gardeners. I like that, don't you? Weeding out the troublemakers. Tending the—"

"Let him go," I said.

"Eventually," said Bishop. "I have an offer for him. I think he may be convinced to cooperate when he realizes what a kindhearted man I am. How I can forgive past deeds and even give him a measure of what he desires most. He helped create the Gardeners, after all. I'd like to see him honored."

Bishop began to walk away. The two Gideon orderlies forced me to follow him.

We rode by elevator to a wood-paneled suite decorated with artifacts of the past. The ocean was visible from a picture window, a ship moving near the horizon, steam above its angled stacks.

"Where are we?"

"What?" asked Bishop. "Oh, you hadn't realized. Ha-ha, I'd thought you a detective. We're in San Pedro, of course. Power generation was always a cover for the construction."

"You moved it here? Why?"

"To possess it," said Bishop, and he seemed to grow annoyed. "This is what it wanted. To be near the sea. Could you not feel that yearning each time you emerged?"

"No," I said, in disbelief. "It doesn't talk to me."

"No, of course not," said Bishop. "You lack the connection we have with the Pool. You feel burdened by your existence, and we revel in it. Ah! Here we are."

We had reached a heavy door carved with delicate depictions of bathing women.

They were spirits of the water, nymphs and mermaids, frolicking in the surf and beneath the carved waves. Bishop opened the door with a key he took from his pocket.

The room was appointed in the height of cloying femininity. Flowers, real and decorative, covered every surface and wall. There was a luxurious four-poster bed within. Veronica seemed to float upon the ruffled bedclothes. She was resplendent in a white wedding gown. Her hair was teased into fat curls, and her breasts heaved within the corseted gown.

"She is my beautiful princess," said Bishop. "But I am no miser; I will share. There will soon be enough of her to go around."

Her eyes were open and staring up at the coffered ceiling and its brass fleur-de-lys.

"Could I talk to her?" I asked. "Alone?"

Bishop chuckled and said, "Of course."

He and his men left the room and shut the door behind them. I went to her on the bed, tentatively, afraid she might already be dead.

"Are you all right?" I asked.

"Casper?" Her head turned slowly. "You look so young. What happened?"

"It doesn't matter." I sat on the bed beside her and smoothed a lock of hair from her face.

"I'm married," she said, and she lifted her hand to show me an extravagant diamond ring with a gold serpentine band. "He took so many pictures. He said they were for the papers. There was a newsreel too." She reached and took my hand, her expression knitting into confusion. She squeezed my fingers. "I . . . I had a dream that I was swimming. There was water all around me, and I was falling deeper and deeper."

She described what could only be her descent into the Pool.

"It felt like the tide was pulling me apart until I was not in the water, I was of the water." She wet her lips. "It was beautiful. I could see everyone I remembered. My sister, Maxwell and Cecelia, my mother and father, Holly—they were all there with me, but my father told me to leave. I didn't want to, but I swam up out of the water. I leaped from the waves. I'm here now."

She looked at me earnestly. "Is that strange? Is that a bad dream?"

"No," I said. "It's a fine dream."

Her face abruptly contorted into an expression of panic.

"I can't leave here, can I? I can't!" She squeezed my hand so hard, it hurt. "They're with my sister. You have to go to them. You have to make sure they're safe."

"Who? Who is?"

"My children," she said. "Max and Cecelia. They're at my sister's house in Montebello. Will you take care of them? Promise me? Please! Promise me!"

I remembered. When I'd followed her after we first met. She went to the modest house in Montebello and was greeted by children. She lifted them into her arms and kissed their faces.

The door was opening behind me as I blurted out, "I promise."

"What's that?" asked Bishop. "Promises?"

He swooped in on her, and they kissed. The sight of it sent a shudder through me. His eyes cut to mine as he pressed his lips to Veronica's and slid his hand across her belly.

"Such a blushing bride!" he said, his lips marked red by her lipstick. "Well, my dear, I'm afraid you need your rest. Your friend must go now. Say good-bye."

"Good-bye," she said.

The Gideons in the white coats were already dragging me out of the bedroom apartment. Bishop was on my heels, closing and locking her into the room.

"Let me go." I fought against the orderlies.

"Of course." Bishop smiled. "Right this way."

The Gardeners were waiting on the other side of the door. There were three of them, dressed in dark suits, their faces mine but their hair the same stark white as the man I'd seen through the observation window. They easily overpowered me. Two of them held me pinned against the wall.

"I said twenty years," said Bishop. "But the Gardeners felt you needed the fullness of a life of peace and quiet."

There was a clicking of metal, and I realized one of the Gardeners was holding the device I'd found in the Center. He raised it toward my head, and I began to fight even harder, kicking and punching at the two men holding me against the wall.

"Now, now," said Bishop. "The Undercroft here is much nicer than the Center. You'll have plenty to do working down there. Lots of jobs to keep you busy. You'll be a productive member of society again."

The metal cradle was cold against my forehead. Calipers closed against my temples, further immobilizing me in the device. The Gardener operating the Harrow pulled the trigger, and the machine's drilling mechanism began to whir loudly.

"I will see you in fifty years or so, Mr. Cord," said Bishop. "Enjoy your rest."

The bite of the drill into my flesh was a minor pain, followed immediately by the searing heat of the Harrow against my skull. I squirmed, still fighting it, but no matter how much my body moved, my head remained immobilized within the device. The heat on my skull was excruciating. I screamed, and there was a pop and . . .

1973

■ ■ ■

The Sister

TRANSCRIPT OF A RECORDING OF A MEETING BETWEEN THE PRESIDENT AND ADVISORS IN THE OVAL OFFICE ON MARCH 20, 1973

Participants: PRESIDENT (POTUS Ronald Whiteacre), **HEIDEMAN** (White House Chief of Staff Bert Heideman), **KISSINGER** (National Security Advisor Henry Kissinger), **BISHOP** (Civilian Economic Advisor Ethan Bishop)

PRESIDENT: Well, I'm trying to figure out with Bishop what the strategy should be on this, uh, Westward (*unintelligible*) the real problem here.

HEIDEMAN: You know my position on that, Mr. President. I'll, uh, be happy to repeat it in front of him: cut him loose.

BISHOP: Thanks.

PRESIDENT: I've been a friend of his family for twenty-five years. I can't do it.

HEIDEMAN: Then you'll face a bloodbath in the midterms over this freak show. You'll give O'Neill the votes he needs to start articles of impeachment.

BISHOP: The President said he can't do it, Bert.

PRESIDENT: I stand by that. I'd like to be paid back with some goddamn honesty. Uh, the . . . give me my glasses . . . The, uh, *Post* from this morning, front page, has pictures. You and a retired general named Shiftman, you and Greenwald, you and some engineer working in Alabama. There's even a picture of your father as a young man. All of them identical.

KISSINGER: There are also the military men, the Lieutenant Gardener, and the, uh, fighter pilot from the cinema.

HEIDEMAN: And the women.

KISSINGER: There is also the matter of the photographs the Israelis passed to CIA. From the Jewish slave doctor working at Buhlendorf. Very incriminating if those leak.

PRESIDENT: What about that, Ethan? How much of this is true, and, uh, how much is bullshit?

BISHOP: I'm afraid they're on to something, Mr. President. Those leaked files are real. Some of the details are wrong, some of the pages missing, but real. Operation Westward was more than rocket tests in the desert.

PRESIDENT: So I had guessed. So, what was it?

BISHOP: My father began the project under a different name, without the military's help, during the Great War. He was experimenting with medical rejuvenations for injured veterans. Ways to regrow limbs and heal lungs burned by gas. It worked, after a fashion, but the treatment had some unintended side effects, including, I am sorry to say, the political consequences for you, Mr. President.

KISSINGER: The situation is graver than you know. Your therapeutic explanation will not pacify the Soviets. Brezhnev has deployed tanks to the border in East Germany. The Fulda Gap is threatened because they believe the President has violated the laws of decent science to forge an army.

HEIDEMAN: We need to go a step beyond cutting Bishop loose. We need to arrest him and his cronies, seize his assets (*cross talk*)

BISHOP: Not nationalizing my goddamn (*cross talk*)

HEIDEMAN: (*cross talk*) show of authority is the only way we (*cross talk*)

KISSINGER: Mr. Bishop has too many assets to seize.

PRESIDENT: So what do we tell them? The, uh, press corps are like piranhas every day in the goddamn briefing room. There's blood in the water, and they're not going to stop biting until their bellies are full of meat.

BISHOP: If Montague can't handle the heat, then you go out there.

PRESIDENT: And say what? What do I tell them?

BISHOP: The truth.

HEIDEMAN: Christ, no.

PRESIDENT: These duplicates, uh, how many of you are out there? And the others?

HEIDEMAN: Last night CBS was talking dozens.

BISHOP: Our conservative estimate is around two thousand.

PRESIDENT: (*unintelligible*)

HEIDEMAN: You son of a bitch (*unintelligible*) and let the So-viets drop an H-bomb on White Sands.

BISHOP: The Oscura facility is abandoned. Woodward dredged that much up following the money.

KISSINGER: Mr. Bishop, you say your conservative estimate is two thousand. What is your liberal estimate?

BISHOP: Over eighty thousand.

HEIDEMAN: You want us to tell them that? Tell the press and the Russians you've grown a division?

BISHOP: No, I want the President of the United States of America to go out there tomorrow and tell them the truth.

KISSINGER: So you said, but what truth is it you want the President to tell?

BISHOP: I'll stand beside the President while he tells the American people that immortality belongs to the United States. Tell them that at San Pedro my scientists and the US Government have perfected a treatment that can make a man live for-ever. We can cure any disease, stave off the ravages of time, and restore every friend, or enemy, of the United States to youth and health. We can make Brezhnev twenty again if he asks nicely.

HEIDEMAN: Madness. I'll not be a part of this.

BISHOP: We can do more than build an army. We can preserve the world's firsthand knowledge indefinitely. It sells itself. The Founding Fathers, Edison—they all could have been saved. It is the power to control the course of human history. And they have to come to us.

KISSINGER: These are strange times. If this is correct, we would wield tremendous influence here and abroad by offering the treatment or withholding it.

HEIDEMAN: Mr. President, please, you're not seriously considering this, are you?

PRESIDENT: Eloise. My sister. Have you met her?

BISHOP: Yes, just once, at the picnic before *The Cremation of Care*. She is a beautiful young woman.

PRESIDENT: That was a long time ago. She's forty, and she's dying of bone cancer. Horrible (*unintelligible*) the, uh, process of that, her face . . . I don't recognize her when I go to see her. I don't want her to die. Do you understand me?

BISHOP: Absolutely. I can fly her to San Pedro, and she will be on her feet in a day. And you'll announce it to the world?

PRESIDENT: If you can save her, I'll sell your damn treatment to the world.

BISHOP: I always knew my father was right to pick you. It's a deal, sir.

PRESIDENT: I don't want her to end up like you. No more new lines of these duplicates.

BISHOP: Don't worry about that. It's all taken care of, Mr. President. Everything will be fine.

2006

■ ■ ■

The Mother

CHAPTER ONE

■ ■ ■

Polly gave the order with a single tone over the radio. They moved in on the apartment from both ends of the hall and wrapped up the lookouts before the surprised type twos could alert their gang. Breaching was easy. Bad Tower was full of cheap doors, kicked in a dozen times, patched up, never replaced. The team's battering ram slammed into the locked door of unit 2814 and compressed a semicircle into the wood. The second blow broke loose the dead bolt, sent splinters and strips of wood cladding flying into the apartment, and smashed the door wide open.

"Pit Security! Hands up!" Polly's cop-voice was honed by a half dozen years of no-knocks raids.

The beams of their flashlights stabbed through a haze of wood particles and illuminated the confused angles of the apartment interior. Fetch was first. His jaw was set, his gun up. He went through and didn't ask again to see the hands. Nobody was grabbing air, so he opened up with the matte-black carbine against his shoulder. The rapid-fire boom of the gun was painful in close quarters. A shaggy-haired type two stood dumbfounded in the face of the onslaught. Shots chewed foam from the arm of the decaying sofa beside him. He stared at the flashing gun and died.

The dead man's friend, another type two, cast aside a plate of microwave slop and fled into the kitchen, spilling through trash and empty bottles. Men and women screamed in the deeper darkness of the apartment. Polly knew the sound. Junkies always made that same animal wail of fear as they were torn out of their highs by danger.

Polly advanced past Fetch, her vision tinted by the amber curve of her shooting glasses, a trickle of scarlet hair spilling from beneath her helmet and over her forehead. She stalked into the kitchen. Her boots crunched in the trash. The dupe fumbled in a drawer for something. She put two rounds into the small of his back and threw him away from the cabinets. Dead batteries, packets of soy sauce, and a Stillman holdout in the drawer.

He was still breathing, neck bent awkwardly against the lower cabinet as he writhed in open-mouthed pain. His skin was pale and glistening with sweat. She put a thumb to his cheek and sagged open his lower eyelid. Shivering pupil. It was the fever of the bliss. The first scrawls of blood vessels were visible beneath his waxy flesh. He was a fresh addict. Maybe three or four days.

"This is big," said Fetch over his radio. "Get over here, Foster."

She cuffed the dying junkie and left him in the trash on the kitchen floor. They would clade-type the bodies later for retrieval at the Pit.

Fetch, Canton, and Nineteen were against the wall near the entrance to the hallway. The stench of squalor was billowing out of the darkness, bringing with it the strong musk of the distillers. Every window was blotted out by electrician's tape. Canton aimed his flashlight down the hall, passing it over a trunk of cables snaking into the darkness. They were hacked into Bad Tower's grid, a sure sign there was a major distiller in use. Open doors yawned on both sides of the hall.

"Looks like your informant was right," said Fetch. "Goes on forever like that."

"They've cut into the surrounding units."

"It's a nest," said Canton. "We need everybody in here."

Polly clapped him on his shoulder. "Fine, get them up here, but we're going in now. Before these maggots burn the caps."

She went first. Two of them came at her, one from each door, tube-fresh type-two maggots, heads still shaved from processing. One of them was still wearing the jailbreak-green of his Los Angeles Rejuvenation Center coverall. They were armed with wrenches and knives. She put a shot into each, center mass, left them flopping and gasping on the floor. She swung the gun around and into the room on the right.

The overhead bulb was a useless, jagged eggshell. The beam of her gun light played across overturned nursery furniture, a moldy doll, sagging carpet, and a pool of brown water. Crayon scribbles decorated the peeling wallpaper. The dusty smell of the spore was in the air. She checked the detector clipped to her belt. Still green.

"Left is clear," said Canton.

Polly picked up the doll and shook off some of the filth. One cantilevered eye blinked as she turned its head.

"Right is clear," she said, and she dropped the doll back into the water.

Two more rooms. Someone had been using dozens of broken-down cardboard boxes as a bed. Cases of a chemical fertilizer called Magic Grow. Maybe something to cut the drugs with. The other room was a flop. Single-sized mattresses and filthy sheets. Needles, ashtrays, food wrappers, and empty bottles of Brown Barrel—the usual accumulation of junkie garbage.

The rest of the maggots hiding in the apartment had fled behind a door. She could hear them shouting and banging on the other side.

"Give it up," Polly shouted. The voices on the other side went silent. "Nobody else needs to get hurt. It's only five years in the cannery for distilling. Come out with your hands up, and we'll get this over with."

There was no answer. Polly motioned for Canton, and he hammered the door again and again with his ram. The door broke completely from its hinges after only a few blows, but it was held in place and upright by an unseen weight. The junkies must have wedged something big and heavy against it. She motioned for Canton to stop. He leaned the ram against the wall and hunched over, panting from exertion.

"Jensen will be up in five," said Fetch. "We can have him blow it."

Five plus another minute or two to get charges set, reckoned Polly. Plenty of time to burn the caps, break down the distillers, and dump all the bliss down the drain. Weeks spent running this place down, and they'd be no closer to the supplier and his grow op. The Bishops were breathing fire about bliss. They wanted to clamp it down before word got out to metro that dupes were brewing something new and nasty.

"We can't wait. If they destroy all the evidence, we lose our leverage. We need to make them give up the grower."

"We can't get through this." Nineteen traced her gloved fingers down the door frame.

"Right," said Polly, and she rapped her knuckles against the wall beside the door. "We'll go through here."

The drywall was deformed from water damage and decades of mold. Once Canton put a hole into it, they got their hands in and pulled crumbling chunks of drywall out. The frame inside broke apart. The wood was nearly black and soft with rot. They cleared a space big enough for a single person to enter.

Polly scored the back of the drywall with her knife and motioned for Canton's ram again. She raised her gun, and so did Fetch and Nineteen. The drywall exploded in a single hit, showering the surprised junkies with dust and bits of rotten wood. One of them had a big old gun that fired with a painfully loud thunder that set everyone's ears ringing. Canton staggered back, grabbing at the gory path of the bullet in his jaw, flaps of skin wobbling between his fingers and blood gushing down the front of his uniform.

Through the drywall dust and smoke Polly spotted the fat-ass type one with the iron. She smiled. Didn't see the type ones in Bad Tower too often. She thumbed to three-round and squeezed off six shots into his center mass. He shook and spun away, flopping boneless on the floor, the gun flying from his hand. She went in through the ragged hole in the wall, popping bursts into two more dupes trying to flee with plastic jugs filled with brown liquid.

A type three with wide eyes and hair matted into dreadlocks came at Polly from behind the refrigerator they were using as a barricade. She had the sharp-edged face of a cheap cut job and a kitchen knife in her hand.

"Worm has got us, bitch," the junkie girl screamed. "It's gnawing at our guts, and you can't see it. You think this matters? You dumb. You fucking dumb."

Polly batted the silver blade away and threw the woman to the ground. Bliss did funny things to the way the junkies perceived time. She'd heard it all before in bliss detox, waiting for the junkies to clean up and answer her questions. These moments, reality, didn't matter much to them. Just some television joke, blink of an eye, compared to the time-distorted, epochal high of the bliss.

"Offa me!" The woman kicked and scratched and scampered back to her feet. She howled and came at them again like a feral animal.

Always that little bit harder to pull the trigger on one of your own, but Nineteen did it for Polly when the knife flashed again in the junkie's hand.

There were no more targets. One of the dropped jugs was open and sloshing its contents onto the floor. There was no mistaking the smell of gasoline.

"They were gonna torch it," said Nineteen.

"Canton?" asked Polly.

"Hurts! Can't fucking talk right." His consonants weren't connecting through the wounded meat of his jaw.

"Quit talking," said Polly. "Nineteen, get him downstairs."

Nineteen was a type three. She was young, plus three or four, slender in all the places Polly had managed to thicken out with muscle and fat in her plus eight. Number names were always lucky, so Polly liked to have her around. Nineteen helped Canton to his feet, and they disappeared back up the hallway.

Fetch was a type two. Young face, just plus one, but an old cop. He still had some of that past-life arrogance. He came swaggering through the hole and stood beside Polly, strapped down with all his cop gear, radio on his hip squawking away. He checked his spore detector like a cowboy eyeing the watch clipped to his vest. Polly could smell it too. Strong enough to catch a whiff through the gun smoke and spilled fuel.

The apartment they entered was a reversed mirror of the one they'd breached coming in. They were near the kitchen, sink full of the sort of cheap pots, pans, and copper tubes used in small-time cook houses. Straight ahead was the door out. To the left was the living room full of more flops. There were too many mattresses to belong to just the people they'd already encountered.

"What's with all the dolls?" asked Fetch.

Polly slid the shooting glasses from her eyes and dropped them across the curve of her helmet on their elastic band. She approached the pile of toys. They were ugly and cheap, American made from Undercroft plastic and dressed in mismatched outfits. The tangle of limbs unnerved her.

It was unusual finding anything for kids. Maybe in the shanties, maybe up in Carson or Torrance, where the ever-creeping fingers of Bishopville mingled with the old suburban housing of the snowflakes, but the worker blocks were the heart. No kids. Nothing but dupes.

Kids being here meant unspoken rules were breaking down.

"Check your fire," said Polly. "The last thing we need is a flake getting her skull ventilated."

It mattered when the flakes died. Snowflakes had families and people who cared. The Gardeners didn't haul off the leftovers. Their little snowflake bodies didn't come gurgling back out of a tube in the Pit. Polly didn't like to think about it. Didn't like to think about the families.

"Over there." Polly directed Fetch to the gaping hole broken into the next-door unit.

They stepped over the bodies and approached the dank entrance to the neighboring apartment. The detectors began to glow yellow, orange, and then a flashing red. They chimed warning tones that grew louder and more urgent with each step they took toward the wound broken through the wall. Polly tasted the chalk of the spores in her mouth. She tried not to breathe it in too deeply. If she were a flake, she knew, she'd already be dead.

Unseen lights glowed faintly blue in the neighboring unit. Polly ducked her head beneath the jagged edges of broken wood and nearly fell straight into the hole through the floor. The entire floor was warped by moisture, descending from all sides into a conical depression where the carpeting and floorboards had given way and collapsed into the level below. The light was coming from down there. She shuffled as close as she dared to the sloping edge and leaned down over the softly glowing pit.

"What is it?" Fetch was hanging back from the edge. "They got the distiller down there?"

They did have a distiller down there. A monster cobbled together from an industrial pressure washer and steel flasks. She hardly noticed. She wasn't sure how to explain what she was seeing to Fetch. "It's bad. It's the caps. All . . . all of them. Alive. These are the growers. It's a grow operation."

Fetch said something else, but she couldn't answer or even really hear him. It was as if she looked upon the surface of another world. Soil was piled in a mound, and fungus grew in pale stalks that branched out near their tops and ended in the fat, luminous fruit of the caps. She had never seen them alive, only cut and dehydrated in the bins distillers kept. The round fruits glowed blue and pulsed, light to dark, in gentle, eerie patterns of synchronization.

She stared at the pulsing light for seconds before she realized the stalks were growing out of the mossy white bodies of children. Men and women too, but Polly saw the children clearest. They lay half-buried in piles of fertilizer, their limbs sticking out, patches of visible skin pale and gaunt, their eyes milky, and their open mouths furry with the spore grass.

A little girl, her head half-submerged in the loamy black soil, still clutched a Betty Brighteyes doll to a gingham dress with her tiny hands. The threads of the fungus pierced her flesh and sprouted from her shoulder and neck. Her head was tilted forward, chin against her chest, and her skull opened as if the caps had burst from within her brain. The girl's face was lit by the sweeping pulse of the fruiting caps. The segmented white body of a millipede slowly traversed her cheek.

"What is it?" Fetch asked again.

She ignored him and struggled to operate her radio.

"Twelve . . . ah, twelve-ten, this is seven-ninety. I'm going to need the meat wagon." Her throat was painfully dry. "I need . . . there are a lot of bodies in here."

"Say again, seven-ninety," Jensen's voice crackled back over the radio. "Casualties, you say? We got Canton coming down. He'll be all right."

"Are you okay, Foster?" asked Fetch.

"Snowflakes." She tried to count them. "There's, ah, fifteen." She shuffled closer to the precipice to count them more accurately. "Sixteen. Maybe more. I can—"

The warped floorboards creaked and shifted. Polly cried out in panic as her boots lost traction. Fetch reached for her, but he was too far away. She plunged face-first into the luminous fungal carpet. The soft, degraded bodies of the children cushioned her fall. The stalks broke, and the caps split open and smeared her with oils of phosphorescent sapphire.

It was raw bliss, unrefined and undiluted. Her skin went cool. She shuddered out of sync with time as the ecstatic milk of the fungus began to melt through her flesh.

Polly screamed. She knew in some dim recess of her overwhelmed brain that she was overdosing. The pleasure burned through her and coruscated against her skin. She tore at her collar. She arched her back and kicked her legs. Her sense of connection with the flow of time was unraveling.

Her body tensed and released, and she reached a plateau, attained and inescapable, pulsing and radiating in time with the luminous blue fruit. It was pounding in repeat. Echoing. The strobe-lit faces of the dead children. Fetch, blue-faced, peering down and shouting something too slowly to be understood. The hiss of spores bursting into the air. The beat of an invisible heart, again and again for one hundred years.

She kept screaming long after Jensen's men loaded her into the ambulance.

■　■　■

Wesley Bishop's hands were shaking. Sweat beaded his forehead, and an hour of frustrated tugging had deconstructed his hairstyle into a mad scientist's crown. Difficulties? Yes, of course. Bad news? He handled it. The haranguing was what made it all so intolerable.

He slammed open the door and exited into the parking concourse. It was jammed with limousines and dark sedans. Chauffeurs raised their heads like dogs at the sound of a whistle. Bethany followed Bishop from the air-conditioned monolith of the Nations Unies and into the sticky Copenhagen summer. She was composed and fashionable, blond hair in a clockwork French twist, expression unmoved by the drama.

Schumacher, the diminutive man from the State Department, was chasing after Bethany's clicking heels. He was doughy, pale, pushing glasses up his nose, slicked-back hair curling instantly in the humidity—the North American jelly-backed bureaucrat emerging from its aboriginal forest.

"Get my fucking car," said Bishop.

Bethany was already dialing her pocket telephone. She held the device to her ear and searched the long-bodied Citroens and Daimlers for an American-made vehicle.

"It could be worse," said Schumacher. "The French might have refused to use their veto in the Security Council and forced us to stand alone."

Bishop chose not to look at Schumacher. He snapped open his cigarette case and pinched a gold-banded Bravo between his lips. A deep inhalation did some to steady his nerves. His shoulders relaxed, he leaned against the granite façade of the UN building and exhaled a stream of smoke. It lingered, limpid in the heat. He put on his sunglasses before finally turning to Schumacher. The wonk from State was fiddling with a piece of chewing gum.

"You didn't warn me Berezin himself was going to be there. You let them ambush me in there. Half the fucking world just watched the Chairman of the Supreme Soviet call me the devil." Bishop took another drag from his cigarette and flicked it away into the concourse. "Literally. He called me the devil."

"Loose translation," said Schumacher. He winced at the sound of his own voice.

"I'm a proxy for all the duplicates, a straw man, and they're trying to use us as a pretext to invade the United States. Why are you so calm about it? If you don't work for me, and you don't, then you at least work for your country. Show some backbone."

Schumacher folded the piece of gum into his porcine mouth and tossed aside the foil wrapper. "You need to take the deal. Let their inspectors—"

"Private business is not subject to UN law. I didn't sign their treaties."

"We've been over this, Mr. Bishop. I spoke at length with you and your lawyers. They're demanding inspections. We can block this nonsense with the peacekeepers— that's just posturing—but you have to relent. Cooperate with them. It will be a small team, UN, not Russian or Chinese. Show them what you need them to see, and let them write up their reports. Those things always fall into an area too gray to be acted on."

Bishop said nothing else. The car was rounding the concourse to pick them up, and his mind was already moving on to the evening's distractions.

"The needs of the American people and the needs of your company are not exactly concordant. You have to give a little in a situation like this," said Schumacher.

Bishop communicated his disagreement by slamming the limousine door in Schumacher's face.

Later, deep in the interminable night, ensconced behind walls of Nyhavn hotel glass, Bishop sprawled on the bed with a prostitute named Miael, his cheek resting on the dark, flat drum of her belly. The midnight harbor congealed beneath the mast lights of antique ships. Aromatic hints of the slow sea—salt, old fish, ropes wetted and dried a thousand times—mingled with the exotic spices of Miael's skin, the chrome finish of the furniture, leather of the chairs, and oiled timbers of the ceiling.

He stared at that ceiling with one eye, unwilling to lift his cheek or turn his body. In the darkness between recessed lights he sensed the presence of the apex. There was the moment of greatest achievement, a black snake of shadow, only revealing itself incrementally, finally, as he plummeted away from it.

There were declines before, troughs to every wave, but he could sense the difference. Final acts were beginning. Waves of pestilence. Forces aligning against him, transnational and growing in power, rising to the drumbeat of a new sort of war. *Peacekeeping,* they called it in the UN, but he knew what war looked like. Even if Berezin's vitriol was posturing, the world was ready to sink its hungry jaws into the United States and tear out the beating heart of Bishop Unlimited.

And on top of it all, the drugs were wearing off.

"I am falling," he said, feeling it literally, vertiginous sensations of his crumbling high, incandescent, breaking apart into the night like a meteor in the sky. Flashing in his vision, erasing the serpentine shadow. He needed more, something stronger, something that wouldn't give up on him midstream. When he needed it most. "Any bliss?"

Miael didn't know what he was talking about. She shook her head and smiled, then ran her long fingers over his forehead and into his salt-and-pepper hair. Bliss. He'd seen pictures of it. Tantalizingly different. Poisonous to the flakes. Precious. Glowing. Pictures of what it did to people, to dupes, killed them in a way so ugly that it only increased his desire to sample the drug.

No bliss. Not for him. He opened the leather satchel Patrice, his bodyguard, had left him for the night. Bethany knew about the bag and forbid him certain indulgences. No more opiates. No more speed; it made him do stupid things on the telephone. Patrice knew better.

He settled for tranquilizers designed for animals. He broke them up and snorted them from a one-of-a-kind table made from a twist of yellow glass. When he felt them begin to deaden his limbs, he forced himself up and staggered out onto the tiles of the suite's promenade. Music and car horns mingled with the soft, lethargic murmur of the harbor. Miael tried once to pull him away from the balcony, but he leaned over it, laughing down at the cars and pedestrians a dozen stories below.

He clambered up onto the railing and swung over to the other side. His toes caught the edge of the balcony, and his hands were clinging to the polished stone railing.

"If I let go," said Bishop, "it won't matter."

Miael pleaded in French for him to come back onto the balcony. He teased her by jerking his arms and pretending to lose his grip. She screamed, lunging uncertainly forward and back, finally collapsing in the doorway, sobbing in the gossamer of the billowing curtain.

"Let someone else have it," said Bishop, dangling by one hand. He'd taken someone else's place. He'd dissolved the shareholders' board. He'd made himself, once more, the sole proprietor of the world's largest corporation. He swung by a single handhold, hair blowing over his face, his smile showing white in the darkness. "I'll go see the bottom. Let some other maggot put his hand on the tiller. Any one of us could preside. Any one of us."

He shouted again and again down at the cars. At the lights of ships. Some of the pedestrians were pointing up at the lunatic hanging from his balcony. He decided it was time to let go, and so he did, expecting to meet the pavement below and begin it all over again.

Patrice caught Bishop by his wrists and heaved him over the balcony railing. Bishop's naked back scraped painfully on the stone. The big Acadian dropped him on the tiles, barked an order in French for Miael to leave, and summarily ended the night's festivities. When the girl was gone, Patrice stood over Bishop and smiled, not unkindly, the specifics of his expression camouflaged by the tiger pattern of a Creeptown face tattoo.

His long, tanned arms were corded with muscle and embellished with more tattoos and scars. He was leather, denim, and snakeskin forming a man. A flake. The gutter-bred antipode of the security professionals imported to rarefied Copenhagen by the diplomatic corps.

"Ya, you got bit by dat babette, podnah. Make Miss Bethany turn red, she know I gave you dem pills." Patrice carried him to the suite's oversize bed. "Gwon getcher head down on de pillow an forget about dis place. We home to Los Angeles in de tomorrow."

"Don't ever . . ." Bishop swallowed back the growing lump in his throat. "Don't ever let me come to Copenhagen again . . . or I'll . . . have you . . . killed. . . ."

"I give dem Gardeners knots in dey belly if a try an' chew on my bones." Patrice folded his arms over his chest. He watched Bishop's head weaving drunkenly.

"Maybe . . . you're right. . . ."

Bishop emptied the contents of his stomach across the bedspread and rolled onto the floor. He began snoring almost immediately.

Later, rinsed and dressed, somewhat less ill, Bishop found that the foggy gray of morning suited the humorless architecture of the Lufthavn. He waited in private runway enclosure D smoking cigarettes, buttoned too tightly into a designer raincoat and sweating. Still early, still not quite boiling, but it was going to be another hot and humid day. Patrice was asleep on his feet. Bethany was talking on her pocket telephone. The jet—his jet—was approaching slowly through the misting rain, toward the boarding stairs, the reflected taxi lights trembling in the puddles on the runway.

"Something is happening in San Pedro," said Bethany. "A Rapid Response action is ongoing at Tower Thirteen. Milo says they have found a grow operation for bliss."

"Isn't that what they were looking for?" Bishop didn't care about the source of bliss, he just cared about tasting it, but Milo's recent obsession was discovering how it was produced.

"Things have gone wrong, and a number of snowflakes are dead on the scene. The Gardeners are already there. Milo says there's a problem. You should talk to him."

"Tell him to clean it up," said Bishop. "We can talk about it when I get back."

Her conversation with Milo was consumed by the whine of the approaching jet engines. The plane rolled to a stop, and ground crew began to position the boarding stairs by hand. Patrice pushed the luggage cart toward the aircraft. Though eager to be on his plane and away, Bishop waited, unwilling to brave the blowing rain until the last moment.

"He's insisting I ask you again," said Bethany, leaning so close to Bishop that he could taste the bitter flower of her perfume. "He says that a cleanup will be very ugly."

"Milo Gardener"—Bishop started out into the rain, holding his hat on his head against the jet wash—"is already extremely ugly."

"Sir?"

"Tell him to do whatever it takes," said Bishop. "I don't care if he has to wade through an ocean of shit. And get Schumacher on the telephone. I accept his deal. The UN can send their people to California, and we will be very accommodating."

Bethany's response was lost to the noise of the plane. He was very much looking forward to a handful of sleeping pills and dreams of blue phantasms. Visions of a milky white Pool lit by bliss. Maybe he would finally learn firsthand the lure of its pleasures.

COMINTERCEPT – SOVNET - ELECTRONIC TEXT - NOENCRYPT - BLACK LABEL

FROM: Dr. Guillermo Delgado@UN Disaster Assessment and Coordination (UNDAC)
TO: Dr. Robin Burns@UNDAC
SUBJECT: Something Big

Robin,

I hope you had a chance to look through the 2004–2005 CDC field study. Their evidence was always obfuscated by the political situation in the United States, but their raw data cannot lie. As you suspected, Los Angeles was ground zero for the past three major epidemics, including hemorrhagic staph. The only conclusion possible is that these diseases are carried and spread by the exponential growth in North America's poorly-understood duplicate population.

Myself, Dr. Robichaud, and Secretary-General Lee have been lobbying hard for access to the San Pedro site to investigate these outbreaks. The last reports from our UN field offices in the area prior to our precautionary evacuation suggest wide-scale contamination of the ecosystem by unidentified, invasive microorganisms.

Robin, we have the access we've been wanting for five years. The governor, the President, even the head of the corporation that owns the LARC, Wesley Bishop, have all relented. I need you now. I know the personal cost and the danger I am asking you to accept. I can think of no better person to make the trip to Los Angeles. You can have whoever you want for your team—you have the full support of UNDAC—but I desperately need you to lead this from the ground.

We all know how critical the situation has become in North America. Harvest what specimens you can, native and invasive, catalogue *in situ* behavior, and assess the threat posed globally. Information is our only weapon in developing an action plan for Continental Europe and Asia.

Despair may be reigning in the General Assembly, unrest marching in the streets, but we do not have such luxury. Spore counts are low but rising in Beijing and Berlin and Moscow. Militaries are straining at the leashes held by civilian governments. Paris is still beautiful for now. Let's keep it that way.

We will relocate your children to the emergency evacuation point in Seattle to the government bunker in Vladivostok. They will be safe. The Soviets will cover all expenses, and the only concession they have asked is to include a team member from their biological vault in Ostrov Gallya.

I do not have a second choice for this job.

Best,
Dr. Guillermo Delgado
Managing Director
UNDAC

COMINTERCEPT – SOVNET - ELECTRONIC TEXT - NOENCRYPT - BLACK LABEL

FROM: Dr. Robin Burns@UNDAC
TO: Dr. Guillermo Delgado@UNDAC
SUBJECT: RE: Something Big

Guillermo,

Absolutely not. I'm never going back to that hellhole.

Thanks,

Dr. Robin Burns
Field Operations Supervisor
UNDAC

CHAPTER TWO

■ ■ ■

Polly Foster remained catatonic for days, lost in the phosphene world of blue fungus. Her nightmares twisted the heaps of dead strangers into her children, long-ago Max and Cecelia, abandoned with her sister, lost to the crush of time and multiplication, never to be touched again. She first perceived reality again from outside her body, a blue-tinged world of nurses coming and going, the Pit Security representative, a lawyer from Bishop Unlimited.

She emerged slowly, dazed, greeted with legal documents that she signed against the objections of her doctor. Nausea and headaches lingered, the medication they gave her for detox made her itch, but she was otherwise physically fine.

A very nice type three with a smart suit and her hair up in a little bun informed Polly she was reassigned. Something had happened; no one clearly explained it, not the type three, not the HR representative on the telephone, not the lawyers. She heard pieces of the story. There was a fire in the unit in Bad Tower. The grow op was destroyed—something about spilled gasoline and an unsecured weapon.

"They're gone," said the lawyer. "Your team is gone. Jensen's men too."

It didn't make sense. How could they disappear in a fire? Wouldn't they just come back? There were no answers to the metaphysical questions, but the flakes on the TV news blamed her. She was "the focus of a continuing investigation into what went wrong at Tower Thirteen."

Someone in the company had leaked the information to the press that she was in charge of the operation, the sole survivor, an incompetent named Pollen Foster. It was her unsecured weapon. Her decision not to take care of the gasoline spill. They even had her photograph from crash training. Her frozen smile seemed mocking in the harsh light of tragedy.

She was released from the hospital. Home felt rearranged, as if the floor plan had been reversed, as if she'd burst through a back wall and entered her apartment all wrong. She met Mrs. Valdez in the hall the next morning. The old woman smiled and said something nice. A fat tabby cat arched its back and rubbed against the woman's stocky leg. Polly couldn't stand to hear the kindness. Didn't want to talk to a flake.

■   ■   ■

Rapid Response had no use for her. They flushed her down to Corrections Emergence. It was a place where careers went to die. Misfits shepherding zeroed dupes back into an unfamiliar world, coaching them through the gap caused by their sentence, and turning them back into productive members of society.

She despised the corrections job and clashed with her coworkers and supervisors. They were defeated by their low-impact world. She was a bird caged with rats. They shifted her to dealing with the long-term corrections cases. Ten years, twenty years, and more. Idiots zeroed in the '70s who had never seen a pocket phone or one of the Chinese computers businessmen carried. Revolutionaries and Communists from the '60s, emerging young and bleary-eyed, not understanding their war was long-lost.

Every day, every case, Polly wanted out. She was willing to walk Creeptown busting pickpockets and hookers, handle riot control, work the walls. The dispassion with which each boss rejected her requests only inspired more contentious letters and phone calls. She returned to an apartment she could no longer afford, outside the cordon in a flake neighborhood; she hurried past Mrs. Valdez waiting in the hall, and she dreamed each night of the blue flames surrounding her, the dead bodies of children breaking open in her hands, crumbling into the dust of the spores.

■   ■   ■

The exterior elevator ascended the Bishop Unlimited spire's slope through a wall of lingering pollution. Gray ceiling became gray floor, muffling the sound of the world below so that all Wesley Bishop heard was the cool hiss of the elevator air conditioning. He was alone in the car, agitated by another restless night. He wore a robe of white silk, lambskin zori, sunglasses, and the stink of chlorine in his hair. He wanted nothing more than to escape to the serenity of the rookery.

There would be no respite. Bethany was waiting at the summit of the spire, watching him approach through the windows. He imagined her chastening words. He waved, but she did not return the gesture.

She was a striking woman, possessing a long, narrow nose and a wide mouth with razor lips that matched her elongated figure. Her strangeness suited her couture, Bathymere heels clicking on the Grecian tiles, rippling as she moved beside him in her black Ooseaco business chic with its Fibonacci swirl of white and gold embroidery curling from the sheaf neckline down to the hem of her asymmetrical skirt.

"What is it?" he asked.

She said nothing. By his sidelong glance he observed the subtle tightening of her lips, the curl of her brow, and he knew she was especially cross. They climbed the stairs to the garden, rising into the blue-green shafts of sunlight. Beneath the acres of tinted glass, a narrow littoral of pinewood decking faced an immaculate sea of white sand. Tenders dressed in traditional black samugi rose from benches and assembled along the perimeter of the garden. They bowed to Wesley in unison, rakes at shoulders.

Wesley kicked aside his sandals and shed his robe onto the boardwalk. Nude, he crossed the deck and descended the few steps into the garden, pausing as he always did to wriggle his toes in the cool white sands before marching through the manicured desert. Bethany followed him, carrying her heels pinched in one hand, her other occupied with a bound ledger.

Each step they took sowed disharmony in the garden and disturbed the concentric ripples radiating out from the Oscura rock sculptures. The largest of these sculptures, a rough obelisk carved from volcanic rock, was built with material exposed to the earliest atomic tests. It produced measurable radiation. Wesley had no doubt his droll predecessors had waved Geiger counters over it to amuse guests.

They reached the dais at the garden's focal point, and Wesley settled into the plush caterpillar of a massage chair. He was as unashamed of his nudity as Bethany was unimpressed. She stood over him, blocking his light long enough to be a nuisance.

"And here you are, literally darkening my day," he said. "What is it you want?"

She folded her legs and sat, but did not rest, in the chair beside him.

"You have been avoiding Milo." She opened the ledger. "He's made nine calls and visited twice."

"Perhaps a letter next time?"

"The United Nations team you agreed to entertain will arrive in six days. To my knowledge you have made no arrangements for them. Milo is quite upset that you have not given him instructions."

"I hoped he would figure it out himself." Wesley availed himself of the nearby bar. He scooped a handful of ice cubes into a rectangular glass and doused them in Pernod. He sipped through a straw and caught sight of Bethany's disapproving glare. "It's after ten."

"Patrice told me you were frolicking in the Pool until three in the morning," she said. "We've had this talk before. Your self-destructive behavior is your business. I only care that you are doing your duty as the head of this company. If you're avoiding Milo, you're not doing your job."

Wesley pointedly drained the glass before replying.

"Fine." He tossed the glass over the railing of the dais. The tenders scurried to pick up the glass and each individual ice cube and comb away the marks left in the sand. He waited for them to retreat back to the deck. "Let's start with these phone calls I've been receiving from half the middle-managers in the Pit. There was something on my desk, something about a type three from one of the Rapid Response teams Milo decided to liquidate. Foster, I think it was. She wants a transfer from—where was it?"

"Corrections Emergence."

"Yes, that. Transfer her to the Gardeners' authority. I want her to be our liaison to the United Nations team. Tell Milo to give her whatever she needs—cars or whatever—and prepare her a believable itinerary."

"That does not sound wise," said Bethany. "I hesitate to speak for Milo, but this woman knows about how the fungus cannibalizes normal humans and is ingested as a drug by the duplicates."

"So do you," said Wesley, "and you're not even a duplicate."

"My point is that she has damning information. Why place her in the midst of international inspectors?"

"Because I want Milo to kill them all," he said, and he stretched back into the massage chair. "This will be so much more convenient if they are in the same place at the same time. I don't care where or how he does it, so long as it is believably accidental and absolutely inescapable. I can't fathom why he left her alive at all."

"If you kill the UN team, there will be a cloud of suspicion. The Russians and the Chinese won't stand for it, and your domestic enemies will be empowered."

Wesley shrugged.

"They will send another team," said Bethany.

"And perhaps the second time Berezin will think better than to bully me."

■ ■ ■

Polly stood beneath the buzzing fluorescents of Mr. Kim's Quick Grocery, searching for something to fill her pantry. The basket over her arm, like the shelves, was nearly empty. She found a few expired boxes of pasta and canned corn, tamarind candies, Mexican sodas, and a bottle of ketchup. Mr. Kim's son watched her shopping from behind his counter. The candy and cigarette displays were empty; the rack for the easily-pocketed flasks of booze was barren.

It was nearly curfew, and Mr. Kim's son wanted Polly to leave. He wanted her to leave always. He hated dupes. She didn't know why, but most flakes had good reasons. Personal reasons.

Salted beef strips. A Korean pickled meat. A bag of rice that was ridiculously overpriced.

"That it?" he asked, staring as she slid the basket across the counter.

It wasn't. She bought cat food. All they had. Paid in cash and didn't complain when Mr. Kim's son shorted her two dollars.

She left the shop and began the walk home. At a busy intersection she caught a glimpse of her reflection in a car window and realized she was grinning like an idiot. One of the Gardeners wanted to meet with her about her transfer requests. One more day of Corrections Emergence and she would be returned to duty of some kind—she was sure of it. Her life would be back on the path she had planned.

She veered away from the busy street, avoiding the congestion of a police action that was blocking traffic. LAPD cruisers and black SWAT trucks surrounded a flophouse. Whoever was inside was lucky it was the police instead of the National Guard.

Polly's neighborhood was old: white fences matched the drooping white leaves of the dying palm trees. The bungalow apartments were emptying out as the fear of the spores drove out tenants. More broken windows and gang tags, fewer lights in the darkness.

Mrs. Valdez was still there and awake. Her TV spilled flickering blue through the curtains of the second-floor window. Polly passed through the gate and ascended the stairs, carpet baked with the smell of cigarettes, past her own apartment, to the door of her one and only friendly neighbor. She knocked lightly, then heard the heavyset Mrs. Valdez rise from her recliner and tread over to the door.

The door opened without hesitation, and Mrs. Valdez greeted Polly in her housecoat and fluffy white slippers. She was stout and ill-formed, with too much hair on her face and too many moles and little bits of skin, a hunched posture, thick legs, and a smell that hovered between shampoo and cat urine. A gold crucifix dangled above the dark valley of her cleavage. Mrs. Valdez matched her unloveliness with a particularly potent blend of friendliness and generosity.

"Polly," said Mrs. Valdez, "it is so good to see you. But late. You should be in bed. Did you eat? You need to eat. I made some broth. I could thaw a chicken."

"I brought you some groceries." Polly hefted the paper bag toward Mrs. Valdez.

"Oh, come in." Mrs. Valdez shuffled aside and held open the door. "You're so nice to me."

Polly tended to avoid the stout old woman. The occasional smile or hello in the hallway of the apartment, coming or going quickly, was apparently enough to make an impression on Mrs. Valdez. Polly was a "nice girl."

Polly entered the knitted preciousness of Mrs. Valdez's cramped apartment, redolent with cat smells, past meals, and the faint flower of an overwhelmed airfreshener. The warm yellow of antique lamplight was sucked into the gloomy sponge of mementos. Every wall was a shrine to her family; bright photographs of grandnieces and nephews, handsome men in military uniforms, women in wedding gowns, an older photograph posed in an orange grove, extending all the way back through Mrs. Valdez's lifetime to a gauzy picture of a man and a woman, expressions flat, their features painted with false color. Her parents.

No such clear lineage existed for Polly. No ever-growing list of family members. At least not ones she chose to recognize.

As she stepped inside, it was as clear as ever to her that Mrs. Valdez did not leave her apartment. Complex systems, of movement and storage, had accumulated around her daily rhythms. She raised a thick leg over a stack of old magazines that nearly tripped Polly up, leaned sideways to shut off the television, and swiveled her hip at just the right moment to avoid a tea table piled with brightly-colored plastic toys.

"Do you want some coffee? I make you some coffee." Mrs. Valdez brought her into the kitchen. The walls were decorated with images of saints, the Holy Mother, and Presidente Salazar, the last president before Mexico's partition. The old woman found a clean kettle and cleared space on the stove to begin boiling water. She spooned instant coffee into teacups.

Polly unloaded the paper bag of groceries into a cupboard.

"You can put the cat food here," Mrs. Valdez said, pointing to the table. "Señor Romeo get out, but he be back. I leave the window open for him."

"Your cat is gone?" Polly stacked the cat food into towers of tins.

"Yes." Mrs. Valdez nodded gravely. "He go away sometime when the siren made the sound and scared him. He does not like loud noises. I hate sirens too."

"They keep you safe." Polly finished emptying the bag and folded it up. "Do you know what to do when you hear them?"

"Have to stay inside."

"That's right. And close your window. There are dangerous things in the air when the sirens make that sound."

"On the radio the man said that you put poison in the air to kill people. He said that the Army needs to come and shoot you. I don't know. You're a good girl, Polly. You didn't do the poison, right?"

The kettle began to boil, and Mrs. Valdez waddled back to the stove. Polly knew the sort of man on the radio that Mrs. Valdez was talking about: one of those political talkers who spewed nothing but invective. Some, like Gordon Savage, were openly advocating a military action, demanding blood vengeance against the duplicates. Their counterparts on television, slightly muted in tone, had a similar effect.

"No," said Polly. "I didn't put the poison into the air."

But Polly knew something that would drive the talkers to new heights of anger. She knew where the dupes in places like Bad Tower were getting the raw ingredients for their drugs.

"That is what I say to my son." Mrs. Valdez slid a coffee in front of Polly and shoveled in a healthy spoonful of sugar. "He is with the Army up north. On the big cannons in the Hollywood hill. He says like the man on the radio, but I tell him he listen too much to the radio. And the news."

"You heard about me?" Polly sipped the coffee.

"No." Mrs. Valdez clapped her hands together. "I heard man on news say your name, something about a fire, and I say no. I turn him off. They lie all the time."

"It's okay," said Polly.

"No, they lie and make up stories. I will not watch him anymore. Put on channel three instead."

Mrs. Valdez took a long sip of coffee and then asked, "I watch baseball. Do you like baseball? I don't remember. My nephew plays baseball."

Polly knew about Chico Castro. It was a long story she'd heard before, about how he was called up to play for the LA Bombers and ruined his career riding in a car with a hard-drinking friend. The one-car accident had left Chico unable to play. Polly didn't mind hearing it again. She smiled at all the right spots and shook her head sympathetically when Mrs. Valdez grew emotional. The story ended, as Polly knew, with a miraculous tale of a lottery ticket bought with Chico's last dollar.

"It was only the smaller prize," Mrs. Valdez finished, "and he took it back to Algadones. Now he has a wife, six kids, and he has four bathrooms in his house. And a boat. I will go ride on it someday."

Polly returned to her apartment and crawled into bed, her stomach full of bad coffee and thawed chicken poached in broth. She felt plugged back in. Someone had taken the time to connect her back to the world and convince her, in a small way, that not every story had an unhappy ending.

She closed her eyes and began to imagine Chico Castro and his boat. Her fantasy swam into a dream reality. The deck was sun-warmed beneath her bare feet. Placid waters unfurled in every direction. Chico waved from behind the pilot's wheel. He was smiling, bronze-skinned, and muscular, incredibly handsome. He called out, but his voice did not make any sound. He frowned.

She was very aware of the sound of her breathing and the noise of the ocean. The soft lapping of waves against the side of Chico's boat became as hollow as the slosh of water in a bathtub. A single ominous note began to howl in the distance. The bright day began to darken. The noise drowned out every sound, growing louder and louder, until it was a familiar whine.

Polly opened her eyes, her body seized by waking tachycardia, and the spore sirens howled to life across the city of Los Angeles.

COMINTERCEPT - TELEPHONE - NOENCRYPT - GREEN LABEL

06/19/06 - 14:48:07 PST - Partial Machine Transcription

Subjects: Dr. Robin Burns **<Robin>** (SSO subject, Copenhagen, Denmark), Nathanael Burns **<Nate>** (spouse, Chengdu, China)

<Robin> I thought you liked the white one with the corset.

<Nate> I like them all, but the blue one is the most fun to take off you. Bend you over the couch in the den and use my teeth to pull that thong out of—

<Robin> Stop! Nathan, my God. Not now.

\<Nate\> Or do you like it better when I—

\<Robin\> Nathan, stop it. I mean it.

\<Nate\> I miss you.

\<Robin\> Don't say it like that. Not today. I have something serious I need to talk about.

\<Nate\> I don't like the sound of that.

\<Robin\> I'm . . . Guillermo is sending me into the field.

\<Nate\> Oh, Christ. Here we go.

\<Robin\> I need you on my side.

\<Nate\> Did you volunteer? You're always so eager to hop on a plane.

\<Robin\> That's not fair.

\<Nate\> What about the kids?

\<Robin\> That's . . . they're being transferred to the safe zone in Seattle.

\<Nate\> From Montreal? No. Absolutely not. Seattle is practically ground zero.

\<Robin\> If there were any other—

\<Nate\> When they say "safe zone," they mean "right next to the fucking unsafe zone." No. The kids can come stay with me.

\<Robin\> Can they?

\<Nate\> (inaudible)

\<Robin\> What about your mother?

\<Nate\> She's gone.

\<Robin\> Where? If she went to the summer house in Nice, we can send them there. The South of France has barely been touched.

\<Nate\> She's dead.

\<Robin\> Oh, honey, I'm so sorry. What . . . when did it happen?

\<Nate\> They notified me yesterday. There was an outbreak of hemorrhagic staph in Bismarck. She caught it at the grocery store, blood contact, not even the airborne kind. I don't know how it happened, but she was dead so fast, there was no chance. I can't get through to the Patels or Ms. Walczak. Anyone in her building. The police aren't helpful.

\<Robin\> The funeral?

\<Nate\> They burned all the bodies.

\<Robin\> What can I do?

\<Nate\> When do you leave?

\<Robin\> Tomorrow.

\<Nate\> Everyone is so far apart now. Promise me you won't go away. I can't lose any more people over the telephone. Not you.

\<Robin\> You won't. I promise.

\<Nate\> Where are they sending you?

\<Robin\> Los Angeles.

CHAPTER THREE

■ ■ ■

He ascended from a deep darkness. First willful flexing of muscles. The first thought of *Here I Am*. A breathless mouthful of sour mud. Lightless, airless, compressed. Squirming bodies. Sucked into a conduit feet-first, tender flesh beaten against unforgiving tubes. Something heavy and soft wrapped up in his arms. Mud becomes water. Scream rendered as choked gurgle. The head-sickness of realization. *This is. How long . . .*

Others all around. Reaching, screaming, tangling together. Threaded grass of hair, long hair, swims across face. Grasping at arms and hands and feet and breast. Vomited into the rusty trough of a sedimentation tank. He held an animal—a dog, fur clotted with filth as he cradled it in his arms. Groaning. Suffocated bodies beneath. Still struggling to make sense of sensation. Vomiting white onto a pile of living flesh. The dog breathing against his cheek. A soft cry within its chest.

Bright lights overhead, moving overhead. A man above with ghost-white hair points to a man with ghost-white hair below. The man below is extracted by crane hooks, limp, rising slowly above them, dangling like the engine of a car. The amplified squawk of a voice giving instructions. Oh, God, the hoses. Pressurized to strip skin. Blasting away the white remnants of cowls. Toppling men and women from the pile. Rubber boots and rubber aprons. Men standing on the faces of others. Rubber hands grasping and pulling him out. The dog was still in his arms.

"This one came out with a fucking pet."

One of the men in rubber boots stepped on backs and faces, climbing out of the tank, and came over and tore the dog from his arms. When he resisted, purely out of instinct, the man beat him with a cudgel and shoved him to the floor.

The man carried the dog through a door. Klaxons sounded. He peered back into the rusted hull of the sedimentation tank. A hatch was opening. They were crying for help. The youthful, terrified faces of men and women he did not recognize. Who were they? The sluice gates opened, and the remnant mass was herded away by the flow of water. Washed down into the depths. The doors closed on the tank.

How long . . .

He marched in a daze through old hallways, once clean and hospital white. Year upon year, decade upon decade of dripping feet on tiles. Ever greater quantities of flesh through the birth canals. Epochs of invisible filth materializing in gray grids and scuffed trails. The file was joined by others from other tanks and became a shambling mass prodded by rubber-suited wardens, their identities concealed by gray respirator masks.

He could see his face repeating. A few of the girl. Many of the Bishops. They trudged drunkenly, without protest, without concern for modesty, passing beneath grates of misting water that cleared the last of the debris clinging to their bodies. They sat slack in the chairs of a hundred barbers as their hair was removed with buzzing clippers. He gazed at the sullen face of the Bishop across from him as peels of hair dropped to his chest. *"On your feet."* Rising as one. Shuffling out, shoulders itchy with shorn hair, beneath another screen of water to wash it away.

Shoving hands pushed him through a doorway. He was isolated in a room. Small and imperfectly lit by failing fluorescents. Cold and naked still. A single spot of blood on his temple. He sat in the small, uncomfortable chair. He tried to remember, but there was a great black void in his memories. He perceived the past as if it were at the end of a long tunnel, distant images and memories echoing and distorted by the tunnel's length. He had been here before. Looking for her. Looking for . . .

Her.

The door opened, and there she was, still beautiful, but her features harder and receding beneath years and fat. He remembered that face but not her name. Her generous proportions bustled beneath a dark military uniform. She wore a pistol and a cudgel on her hip. He did not recognize the military patch on her arm. FOSTER was printed across her left breast on a name strip.

She said nothing and set about fitting a machine cuff around his forearm. He could not speak. She closed a collar around his throat that cinched his air and forced him to breathe shallowly. He tried to speak, but she ignored him as she lowered a crown upon his head.

The cuff at throat and arm pinched him, and he could feel needles entering his flesh, a small measure of his blood siphoned through curling hoses. After a moment there was a hiss of pressure, and three televisions blinked. Glowing green letters scrolled over darkness. The crown was heavy upon his head and connected by trunks of electrical cables to the televisions.

CLADE 11784-3C flashed in green text upon the first television. MONOPHYLETIC PROTEIN SECRETING B-TYPE. 101 OF 101 ANTIBODY MARKERS.

"Your blood looks good," Veronica said. "Brain waves are off, slow to recover."

The second television displayed a name.

CORD, CASPER.

The third television displayed yet more information in quivering green letters.

INFORMATION VIOLATION, SEDITION, CORRECTIONS, UNDERCROFT, LIFE SEN-
TENCE. NO EARLY RELEASE.

"Do you remember this name?" the woman asked, tapping her finger on the center television without actually looking at the screen.

Yes. It was his name. The third screen was his sentence, pronounced by Ethan Bishop, and she . . . she was . . .

"Veronica," he said, numb-mouthed, pleadingly, a thin stream of drool falling from his lips.

"No," she said, and she adjusted an alligator clip on the crown that held his head. "That name doesn't belong to anyone anymore. I want you to tell me your name."

"Ver . . . Veronica?" He tried to lift a hand to her face but found it held down to the chair by a fabric strap around his wrist. When he managed more than a single word, his voice was bleeding and dragged behind a truck. "Veronica. Veronica . . . what happened to you?"

She sighed as if his question was exasperating. "Are we really going to play this game"—she paused to read the name off the television—"Casper Cord?"

She faced the television and stood with her back to him for a long while. An odd typewriter made of beige plastic lay on a shelf beneath each television. Her fingers clicked at the keys.

"It really is you. I've never seen one this old. Maybe you do think I'm Veronica." When she stepped away from the television, it displayed the date and time of his last memory. 4:08 AM, June 29, 1951. "Whoever you are, I need you to repeat the name. We have to follow the script."

He felt mentally and physically exhausted from trying to communicate with her. His shoulders flexed, the result of shrugging with his arms strapped in place. "Casper Cord."

"Casper Cord, you have paid your debt to society. Pit Security Department of Corrections Emergence hereby releases you from the Undercroft, returns you from zeroing with all mental faculties and agency restored, and hereby permits you to resume emergence. Do you accept that you are a free man? Please say yes to receive your complimentary clothing and emergence stipend."

"Yes," Casper said, and he hung his head.

Veronica placed a small cardboard box on his knees. She removed the crown from his head, unstrapped his wrists, and freed him from the cuff and collar. Blood welled from the needle pricks left on his forearm.

"A unique identifying phrase will be issued for you momentarily. Please look into the camera and wait for the flash to receive your new Master ID."

She pointed to a camera recessed in the wall behind a pane of thick glass. He stared at his distorted reflection in its lens, head shaved, face young, and the camera flashed. As he blinked out the after-image, he saw the television screen that displayed his name blanked. A moment later the words NINETY-NINETY appeared in place of his name.

"Double-number name. You are very lucky." Machinery clattered unseen within the wall for several seconds. It ceased, and a small plastic card snapped out of a gap beneath the camera. Veronica passed it to him, and he took it, feeling the warmth of the plastic, smelling the newness of it. His photograph seemed made from a mosaic of tiny squares. An odd, shimmering strip above his name, Ninety-Ninety, was filled with repetitions of the word and the digit 2.

"Get dressed. I will be back in a few minutes to escort you out."

Within the cardboard box was a green coverall stenciled with LARC across its shoulders, a pair of rubber sandals, and a red card similar to his ID card but with a stylized version of the Bishop company logo. *Welcome Back!* printed in italics above a serial number in raised lettering. It was a "debit card," which meant nothing to him. Beneath this was a small booklet, stapled at the spine, entitled, "Long-Term Emergent's Startup Guide to the World, 2006 Edition." The cover was a confusing photographic collage depicting unfamiliar people, events, and inventions.

Fifty-five years.

He dressed, wondering at how he could remember nothing. The coverall fit perfectly. He stuffed the booklet and the strange cards into its pockets. The rubber sandals weren't rubber at all. There was a rippled texture within, and the material felt tacky against his skin. He sat back down in the chair and waited.

Veronica's kids—what were their names? He could not remember their names. She'd made him promise. Matthew? Malcolm? Would they still be alive?

"All set?" Veronica—the one with FOSTER on her name strip—was standing in the doorway, arms folded across her chest.

No. Something else was missing. When he emerged from the pit, he had something with him, but he'd lost it in the confusion. It snapped back into his addled brain. He had many questions, so he chose which one to ask carefully.

"Where is my dog?"

"Huh?"

"I had a dog with me when I emerged. They took it from me."

She didn't seem to believe him, but he pressed the issue. She relented. "All right, let's go look for your dog."

She told him to stop calling her Veronica, to call her Foster. When he started to ask her about the kids, she rounded on him and drew out the cudgel. She pushed the end of it into his sternum and walked him back against a wall.

"Their names pass your lips, and we're done looking for the stupid dog. Then, just for doing me the favor of dredging up some bad memories, I'm going to give you knots to take with you to Creeptown."

She didn't seem to be bluffing, so he went quiet and followed her through the corridors searching for the dog. She moved differently than Veronica, less sex appeal but more swagger. She was confident, joking with some, stern and commanding with others, never the sort to stare at her feet. Occasionally she snapped to attention and saluted someone else wearing a black uniform like hers.

"Where are we?" he finally asked, confused by all the turns they'd made down corridors narrow and wide, empty and packed with shaved-headed emergents.

"We just left Outflow Processing, corrections wing. The bad boys and girls end up there. Like you, mister fifty years. There's a concourse up ahead that will take us to OA, Outflow Anomalies. I'm guessing your dog got caged up and stuck in with the really weird stuff that comes out. "

Casper stumbled trying to walk and crane his neck at a file of men and women ascending a staircase into a gallery that opened high above. An elevator whisked past horizontally several floors up, adding to his bewilderment.

"There's so many of us," he said.

"Too many. You'll find that out soon enough. Once I'm done with you here, you get dropped in Creeptown. I'd advise you to keep going, north or east, and don't look back until you can't see Los Angeles anymore."

"That bad?"

She hooked her fingers through the handle of a door made from green glass, turning back as she opened it and favoring him with a noncommittal raise of her eyebrows and a pinch-lipped smile.

They arrived, after an interminable walk, at a double security door sharing halves of the stenciled word ANOMALIES. Foster swept her plastic ID card through a slot beside the door. There was a magnetic disengagement of locks, and both doors swung open into the hall with a pneumatic hiss. The room beyond, vast and low-ceilinged like an endless basement, was a cacophony for every sense.

The fluorescents cast their clinical whiteness through air thick with pulverized dust. Jackhammers were pounding away behind rows of industrial shelves, sparks spattering through the ventilated shelving and dancing across the chalky floor. The shelves were stocked with items like the evidence room at the police station, cardboard boxes with paper tags, just the paper tags for things too big to fit in cardboard boxes.

He followed Foster into the shelving, taking in passing details like a cardboard box labeled HUMAN TEETH (LOT) and a moth the size of his hand pinned to a dusty card reading BIG MOTH. There was a pickled mouse in a jar of green fluid, the card noting FOUND IN CAVITY. A cardboard file box overflowed with corroded wires twisted and knotted into meaningless symbols.

An entire shelving unit was gutted to make room for a twelve-foot glass-sided tank filled with murky liquid. Casper paused at the tank, searching for a card that might identify its contents. There was a strong chemical odor surrounding it. He gave the tank a gentle push, and the liquid within sloshed. There was a momentary slap of yellowed flesh against the side of the glass.

"Leave it alone," said Foster.

The tank was covered with an iron lid too heavy to lift. There was a small sliding panel in the top like a speakeasy's slot. It was rusted into place, but a swift strike from the heel of his hand dislodged the corrosion and popped the little door open. The sloshing liquid was as dark as pitch. He leaned down.

"Get the hell away from that," said Foster, clamping a firm hand on his shoulder. Before she could yank him away, the fleshy body in the tank rolled—in which direction, he was not sure —and as a fin revolved out of the water, he was confronted with a pickled cluster of rheumy eyes—two large, sixteen small. He recoiled in revulsion as much as from the yank Foster gave him.

"What the hell was that?"

"Stuff floats out of the Pool sometimes," she said. "Maintenance brings it here. Usually it's fucked-up maggots, inside out, no eyes, that sort of thing."

She guided him back onto the path through the aisles of storage shelves. The sound of a nearby saw made him strain to hear her voice.

"Sometimes it's not people." She hooked her thumb at the tank. "Something like that comes out, maybe in parts, maybe just one part, mutation or something, I guess, not my department. Flops around on the maintenance deck for a few minutes and usually dies. If it doesn't, somebody makes sure it dies. They bring it here, chop it up if they have to, and process it for storage. It's considered a prime job for Maintenance."

They passed beneath a yellowed fish's jawbone hanging from stanchions lost behind the forest of lighting strips. Whatever the jaw was from was easily big enough to swallow a man. He craned his neck in a vain search for a paper label.

"When did this business start?" he asked.

"They've been doing it as long as I can remember," she said, holding open a gate into a secure area of the storage. "It's been happening more lately, I guess just because more of us come through every day bringing weird junk with us."

"Us," he said quietly. "How many of us have come through?"

She answered, but the zip of a saw stole the sound of her words. He was pretty sure she said three hundred thousand, which made him a little queasy. They passed workbenches where men and women were preparing anomalies for the shelves, preserving them in strong-smelling fluids, fabricating cages, mounting in display boxes, screwing bones into placards, stuffing the loose hides of animals, and attempting to arrange meaning from the broken pieces of pottery and unidentified machine parts.

The worn nature of the anomalies reminded Casper of the sort of thing anyone could find washed up on a beach, but alien, as if the deepest sea had churned and released ancient shipwrecks, drowned sailors, crashed airplanes, and a haul of sea creatures that lived as strangers to the light of day but were discovered clattering in the surf.

"There's the man," said Polly. She was walking with purpose toward a big man dressed in blue coveralls beneath a forge apron, gray beard hiding his throat, filthy welding goggles over his eyes. He wore a dusty bandana over the Medusa's nest of his dreadlocked hair. Foster waved to him, and he looked up, the glowing joint of metal reflected in the lenses of his goggles.

The big man snuffed the torch with a puff of gas and hung it from its cradle. He propped the goggles up on his head, revealing the pale circles in the grime on his face. His eyes nestled deep amid wrinkles.

"Polly!" He greeted Foster with a big hug. Their arms intertwined. They spoke too quietly for Casper to hear over the sound of the machines, but after a few seconds she turned and brought the man over to Casper.

"This is Grinch," she said. "Used to be PitSec. Not bad. Lousy shot, but he could talk a confession out of a spore siren. Grinch, this is Ninety-Ninety. Fresh-brewed."

"I see," said Grinch. He pinched the carbonized finger of his work glove in his teeth and shucked the glove off to offer Casper his hand.

Casper was shaking the man's callused hand when he realized that Grinch was a Gideon. Old and worn in strange places, a much harder sort of man than he ever imagined Gideon being, but he was for sure of the same blood. Casper's handshake went limp, and he found it impossible to return the old man's friendliness.

"Ninety-Ninety has been in the cannery for a long, long time," said Polly. "Longest I've seen."

"When?" asked Grinch.

"Fifty-one," she said. The year was clearly fraught with some meaning the man immediately understood.

"Sorry about that, bud." He clapped a hand on Casper's shoulder.

"I had a dog with me," said Casper. "They took it."

"All right, for you and Polly, I'll check." Grinch shed his remaining glove and took Polly and Casper over to the lone clear space on a workbench otherwise crowded to overflowing with various screws, tools, and spiral machining scraps. There was another beige typewriter keyboard attached to a television, and Grinch began to clatter away as easily as any pool secretary Casper had seen, pausing only to turn his head and light a cigarette. Something called a Bravo Licorice Mild.

"Yeah, dog is in live holding, brought in about ninety minutes ago. We get dogs more often than you'd think." Grinch turned and blew out a stream of smoke and looked meaningfully at Casper. "White ones keep bobbing to the surface or getting sucked into the outflow tank."

"The Indian dog?" asked Casper.

Grinch tapped a finger against the side of his cauliflower nose. "We get so many, we dump them right back in. Don't worry, yours isn't one of those. Says white and black. It's on tier two by the birds. I put in a hold, but I'd hustle my ass over there in case some maggot forgets to check the computer and decides to dump it back into the soup."

"You're gold," said Polly. She gave Grinch a kiss on his grimy cheek.

"What are you doing in Corrections anyway?" Grinch asked as she pulled away. "This about that thing on the news?"

"Yeah. It's a long story."

"Well, I don't watch the news. Too depressing. You tell me the story sometime over drinks."

"I'll be back on the street soon. I bitched to the right people and landed an audience with one of the white-hairs."

"Now, there are some monsters I wish we'd never created." Grinch looked at Casper. "But you'd know better than me."

"It's good, They wouldn't call me in if they weren't planning to do something about my complaints."

"Careful," said Grinch. "The nail that sticks up gets the hammer."

Tier two was more of the same, with a focus on live animals—at least in theory—in cages. There were terrariums full of cave crickets and millipedes, cages thick with bats, birds, rabbits, even the occasional dog and cat. The animals were somnolent; few lifted their heads as Polly and Casper moved among them; few ate or made any noise at all. Some seemed dead, and the smell of excrement and decay was repellent.

Polly didn't seem to know the men and women working in this area. She bounced from one to the next, asking for help, Casper shuffling behind her as if he'd just been in a car accident. She eventually stopped a harried-looking duplicate of herself. The woman's face was younger and leaner than Polly's, her hair pulled tightly back except for one curling lock that kept falling into the woman's mouth. Her arms were shrouded in elbow-length rubber, and her chin dipped beneath the filter mask she wore around her throat. When Polly flagged her down, she was pushing a bin cart heaped with the dead bodies of hundreds of pigeons.

"If it came through in the last six hours, it'll be in Processing," said the woman. "After that it'll either be in the stacks for the Gardeners or in the queue for Euth."

"Processing" suggested the industrial nature, but not the brutality, of what was occurring. Panicked animals in cage-topped bin carts were pushed in through a strip door and wheeled into a parking area to await handling by crews from Anomalies.

"Cozy place Bishop has built." Casper ran his hand over the prickly crown of his head. "I really need a cigarette. You got one?"

"No," she said. "Let's just find your dog. I've wasted enough time with this today."

A gangly Warren—Polly referred to him as a "type two"—with a bandage across half his face finally helped them with more than just a pointed finger. TWENTY was stitched across the breast of his coveralls. He looked like he'd taken a blow to the head;

it was misshapen, as if part of his skull had been removed. He typed at the keyboard attached to a television, demonstrating none of Grinch's speed or skill. At last he hammered out the right keys, and the television flickered and displayed an alphanumeric code. It was gibberish to Casper but clearly meant something to Twenty.

He motioned for them to wait by his sorting station and disappeared into the stacks of recently processed animals. He returned a few minutes later with a dog on a leash. It was a medium-sized breed, white with black spots, one covering its left ear. It was a friendly-looking dog with big, expressive brown eyes. It heeled and sat beside Twenty as he passed the leash over to Polly.

Casper knelt and scratched at the dog's head affectionately, but this prompted no reaction. It had cleaned the cowl from its body, so he cleared a few leathery strips remaining atop its head. It stared at him, unblinking, and he felt a growing unease. The dog's eyes were not brown, as he'd first thought; they were a shade of red, and, more disconcerting still, he recognized the black and white pattern in its fur.

It was Ringo.

FLAGGED - ALERT - FLAGGED - ALERT - FLAGGED - ALERT - FLAGGED - ALERT

REDACTION NOTICE 6/10/06 4:09 PM
Pit Maintenance Incident 7889-40

An obstruction formed at the inflow aperture of emergence channel D5. A maintenance team routed to clear the obstruction reported a single mass of hard material. D5's inflow aperture depth of 950+ necessitated the deployment of a side-scan buoy in plated pressure sheath. Images produced indicated, as before, a homogenous mass, exactly 10 feet in diameter, sealed, with slight indentations in the surface. Recovery armature deployed, but the flow pressure holding the object to the aperture exceeded fail load. An engineering team consulted, and two armatures were deployed, clearing the obstruction. D5's gate was closed, and positive buoyancy lifted the sphere to the surface of the maintenance lid quickly.

Obstruction was spherical, AU-clad, evidence of minor damage, but hull and seals intact. Buoyancy suggests a large hollow cavity within. Serial number 707-1950 and WESTWARD stamped in cladding. Sent to engineering.

ENGINEERING ADDENDUM

Object s/n 707-1950 WESTWARD recovered at depth 952 feet. Protocol followed, no attempt made to open the object, Gardeners contacted and retrieved object.

GARDENER ADDENDUM

Fifth object in two weeks. Serial number matched Operation Westward archives. Launched June 1, 1950, Oscuras.

Object opened. Control surfaces undamaged and appear almost new.

As before, audio and film archives blank, pilot's logbook contained single log entry written in English on first logbook page, intended for date of launch. Ink matches pilot's mission pen. Message as follows:

Deep water rises.
Abandon your spire.
It is coming.

CHAPTER FOUR

■ ■ ■

The Pool boiled with hunger. Beneath a wellhead of intake pipes and high-pressure skimmers, the surface spanned three hundred feet and descended in a conical shaft penetrating into the mantle rock. It was capped by a domed lid of jointed concrete supported by steel rib-beams. The side of this lid that faced the Pool was lined with a microlayer of insolvent gold known as shield paint. The coating was used on any object intended to come into contact with the Pool's highly corrosive fluid.

The obverse side of the lid formed the white-painted floor of the maintenance vault. It was a vast, curiously low-ceilinged chamber filled with sodium-lit gantries and high-pressure pipes. It smelled of marrow and echoed with the ceaseless churn of the Pool beneath the lid.

Wesley Bishop sat in the uncomfortable backseat of a maintenance car, wishing he had died in his sleep. His office desk was piled with charts and reports describing an unraveling scenario he desperately wanted to escape. The last diversion he would have chosen would be a trip to the maintenance vault, and yet Milo, chief of the Gardeners, thought to drag Bishop from between the tangled legs of his bedtime friends and force him into the heat and ugliness of that exact place.

Though Bishop's thoughts often wandered toward suicide, he never wanted to go near the Pool. He hated even being reminded it existed. Being this close to it, hearing it speak from beneath the floor in gurgles and sloshes, was intolerable.

The only place worse was the Fane. He'd made the mistake of visiting the Fane out of curiosity only once. You could look through several feet of gold-treated glass and see the thing at the bottom of the Pool. Oh, yes, he'd had more than his share of nightmares about that little trip. The memories were a gift to all his misbegotten duplicates.

The maintenance car thudded over a rail track as it traversed the acreage of access hatches and parked inspection teams, bound for the bulging hillock at the lid's center.

"Sorry about the rough ride," said the type two driving the car. "They've been laying cables and tracks all week to move stuff around."

The summit was ringed by maintenance cars and lit by a semicircle of bright halogen lamps. Between the parked vehicles and generators he glimpsed shimmering gold and the white hair of the Gardeners. There were armed PitSec men and women and a gaggle of engineers in bright coveralls poking at items spread out upon a tarp.

Milo was waiting to greet him, his expression as grave as ever, his heavy brow knit with worry. He was stooped, shrunken with age, but still tall, his white hair pulled back from his face and held with a silver band. He favored a black cassock coat and wore a badge of office around his neck on a leather cord. The stag's-skull badge was popular among the Gardeners, and in Bishop's experience the entire freak-order of white-haired Gardeners fancied themselves more hunters than weed-pickers.

Bishop did not share his predecessor's reverence for the Gardeners. He viewed them—and Milo especially—as melodramatic buffoons. Relics of a superstitious age. He entertained their eccentricities as long as they were useful. They were utterly ruthless and sworn to loyalty to the corporation, and he used them for the dirtiest of work, so long as they conducted their perverse ceremonies out of sight.

"Mr. Bishop," said Milo, and he offered Bishop a hand out of the maintenance car. Bishop refused it.

"Why are you haunting the maintenance vault?" Bishop straightened up and wiped machine grime from the seat of his pants. "No, a better question: why have you dragged me out of bed to join you in this miserable place?"

Milo began walking with him toward a central perimeter of privacy screens.

"I hope you read my communication yesterday."

"Admiral Haley and his carrier group parked off the coast? We built that carrier at the Brunel Yard in San Diego. That fat Unionist bastard is making noise to set himself up for his future political career."

"I informed you of CSG-9's blockade position three days ago."

Something else. Something about maintenance reports. Spark? Was that involved? He had been sleepwalking with opiates when the document appeared on his desk.

"I didn't read it, then," said Bishop. "I have a lot on my mind. A lot of important documents. Bring me up to speed."

An armed sentry stepped aside, and Milo parted the privacy screen for Bishop. They ducked into the ring of lights. The gold sphere was larger than he remembered. It was dented and scraped, but its protective cladding had survived whatever journey it had undertaken through the caustic liquid of the Pool. The cockpit of the Operation Westward craft was opened and surrounded by engineers in white coveralls poking and prodding at its interior. Bishop stopped just inside the perimeter, struck by the golden brilliance of the machine reflecting the halogen lamps.

Milo waved with a hand at a tarp spread upon the floor. There was the body of a type two, stretched out, still zipped into his flight suit, the rubber cup of his oxygen mask hanging beneath his chin.

"One came back?"

"The Westward craft have nearly all returned, all at once, regardless of their launch date," said Milo. "He is the first pilot we've found."

Bishop overcame his shock and joined Milo beside the dead pilot.

"He looks well-preserved." Bishop moved the mask partly covering the pilot's mouth. His lips were blue, his flesh ashen, but he did not look a day older than the man who had departed in 1950. "The others were empty?"

"Yes, but there was a message in each vessel's logbook. 'Deep water rises. Abandon your spire. It is coming.' The message in this vessel's logbook was slightly different."

Milo handed the logbook over. The pages were clean and white; the message Milo described was neatly printed but awkward, the letters misshapen and connected in odd places. Beneath this message was another one, larger, scrawled haphazardly but in the same style.

" 'Sorry, Warren Groves. Here was not meant for your flesh.' " Bishop read it aloud. "What does that mean?"

"My men will autopsy the body," said Milo. "His personal camera was in his pocket. Perhaps there is more evidence there. The message seems to imply his destination point was inhospitable. A toxic environment."

"A planet?"

"That is a reasonable assumption. Trunk theory does not speculate about the destination point at the other end of the peristaltic conduit. It was always possible these pilots might not arrive at all or might arrive and die quickly."

"Let's talk to the dead pilot. Where is he now?"

"Presumably," said Milo, "he regenerated upon death from the nearest Pool."

Bishop gazed down at the ashen face of the pilot and imagined the man's air dwindling, his mask filling with aching exhalations. Dying in agony alone in the tiny capsule.

He actually felt a little sorry for the stupid type twos who volunteered for Operation Westward, traveled through the trunk at impossible odds, saw some incredible planet, and ended up in a loop of asphyxiation deaths. Regular men were considered heroes for dying once for their country; this poor idiot was out there somewhere, still dying.

"We'll build him a statue or something. Put it out front of that rocket museum in New Mexico."

"Very well," said Milo. "What do you intend to do in regards to the warning?"

"I intend to do nothing." Bishop shoved the pilot's logbook back into Milo's hands and started to walk away. Milo fell in behind him. "We do not know who sent the message, we do not know their motive, and we do not know what they're warning us to do. Unless you know something I don't."

Milo gripped Bishop by the shoulder and turned him around with ease.

"Do you not feel it?" asked Milo. He cocked his head, a smile slowly splitting his lips. "She is restless now, more than ever before."

"Increase the water flow," said Bishop.

"The Pool's turbulence and these warnings are part of a pattern," said Milo. "Even if you have not read my reports, you know this to be true. They are linked to the increase in anomalous matter emerging from the Pool, the pandemics of hemostaph and PPD, the spores, and the mycoforms. Junk and living things are being pushed out of the Pool like debris thrust through the water by the bow wave of a ship. A very large ship."

"We have ships of our own," said Bishop. "I am very tired of people trying to intimidate me. I won't be frightened of some specter passing us notes in bottles."

"A change is coming." Milo leaned in, almost eye to eye, demanding Wesley's full attention. "And I do not believe we can stop it."

■ ■ ■

The PitSec cruiser creaked on its heavy shocks, its interior swimming with the familiar smells of a police vehicle: seat leather, gun oil, the hot plastic of the radio, air freshener canceling the lingering whiff of the last lowlifes to fill the back. Casper's view of Polly from the backseat was partially obstructed by a mesh divider. The uncanny dog was beside him, still and silent.

They ascended from the Pit by way of the motor pool's corkscrew ramp and emerged into daylight in the shadow of one of the familiar cooling towers. Casper blinked away the gray light and took in the immense structure, its paneling outlined by weathering, rust stains where the tips of rebar showed through the eroded concrete. It was ugly but somehow reassuring. Good to be out of the Pit, in the open air, in the shadow of a landmark he at least recognized.

They weren't actually in the shadow of the tower at all, he realized, but beneath some much larger building, elevated like the barrel of a cannon firing at short range. Vast, dwarfing the four cooling towers, seemingly constructed from spurs of steel and acres of green glass. The scale of it reminded him of the spires on the other side, the same yawning openings along its flanks, paddle-shaped balconies spilling into the open air. The sun caught in the green glass and dazzled his eyes. He averted his gaze, blinking away the afterimage of the monolith haunting his vision.

The buildings of the San Pedro Atomic Power Station, much more numerous than he recalled, had taken on a hardened, bunker quality. The facility was surrounded by a fifteen-foot perimeter wall backed by walkways and gun platforms and unwelcoming guard towers. As the cruiser emerged through the main gate, a time-consuming process in itself, a quintet of helicopters whooped overhead, hammering the sky as they disappeared north, heading toward a Los Angeles he doubted he would recognize.

The arterial road was thronged with men and women, mostly duplicates, on foot and gathering in shacks made from corrugated metal, sections of brick, aluminum siding, and wooden slats. Here and there old signage constituted walls or doorways and reflected the fading remnants of advertisements for products familiar to Casper. Among the many duplicates there was a profusion of facial tattoos, piercings, and ugly surgical modifications. Two women offering their bare breasts up to the passing traffic seemed to have simply cut their faces with knives to leave interesting scars.

"Creeptown"—Polly raised her voice over the din of honking horns and shouting pedestrians—"starts right outside the gates and runs all the way to Carson City. That's about where the Army cordon is."

"For what?"

"Spores," she said, and she pointed out a side window at a bullhorn siren attached to a defeated-looking lamppost. "Have the whole city on edge. Deadly stuff for the flakes. You'll see them in the air if it's bad enough. Look like particles in pond water. You don't have to worry about them. They don't make us sick."

A black armored vehicle rumbled past, its slope-nosed chassis creaking on eight fat rubber tires. A man wearing mirrored sunglasses and a uniform similar to Polly's, with the addition of an armored vest, stood in the top hatch of the vehicle, scanning the crowd from behind a pintle-mounted machine gun.

"This is bad," Casper said. The more his face repeated in the crowd on either side of the car, the more isolated he felt. "How the hell did it end up like this?"

"Simple." Polly hit the light strip and blasted the horn to clear more of the pedestrians from the road. "We just kept coming, and we didn't stop."

The metal cage enclosing the cruiser's side windows stippled Casper's view of the shanties. The slum of Creeptown had devoured every familiar street and landmark Casper recalled, encrusting the city in a visually inscrutable mass of rusty sheds, billowing tarps, cat-whisker antennas, junked cars, garbage, and people. So many goddamn people.

Polly navigated the cruiser through the crush of the slum toward evenly spaced apartment towers starkly invading the sky. The rust-brown shanties remained, following the roadways and side streets, the grimy foot traffic becoming less respectful of the cruiser. Dense, multitiered aggregations of shanties gathered at the base of each tower the cruiser passed. The color and the profusion of the slum, contrasted with the singular immensity of each tower, reminded Casper of piles of fall leaves spreading beneath trees.

"I'm supposed to let you out here," said Polly. "Truthfully, you'll never make it out alive. You've been in the cannery too long."

There was a small pond of brown water, foamed and reforming from the passage of a truck, a heap of trash, sifted for anything useful, rotten pieces of food and paper wrappers pressed into the mud, fat bundles of electric cables under tension descending from the tower like guy wires and exploding at ground level into a root system of black veins, caught in a cluster of sloped sheds, roofs of corrugated tin, walls of plywood and translucent plastic sheeting offering a cataract view inside of the shapes of men and women, blinking lights from a television, steam gusting from a cook pot and discoloring the edge of a plastic wall. Nothing marked this little spot as any different from the others.

Casper realized Polly was watching him. She did not smile, but there was faint bemusement to her expression.

"I'll take you somewhere safer," she said, and she put the car into motion again.

"What did they do to me?"

"Read the manual. Shoulda been in the box I gave you. Still have it?"

Casper checked his pocket and brought out the stapled chapbook. He waved it by the divider so she could see it.

"Good," she said. "It's mostly full of shit, propaganda about the company and America, but it tells you the basics. You used to be a detective, right? Use those skills to figure out what's a snow job and what's straight."

Casper flipped the booklet open to a random page. It displayed a simplistic black-and-white cartoon of the American flag. A soldier, a boy, and a dog were standing in a row and saluting the flag. Something was off about it. Six rows of stars, nine stars in each row. Ten stars in the sixth row. He closed the book.

"There's a soup kitchen, St. Philomena's, on the other side of the cordon." Polly turned the cruiser down a side street to maneuver around a stalled truck. "You can get a meal and a bed there. It's one of the few places that will take in dupes. Just don't expect the flakes to like having you around as company."

"I've heard of St. Philomena's before," said Casper. He married Lynn there. A flash of happy memories was swallowed by the thought that she was surely dead fifty-five years later.

Casper stuffed the booklet back into his pocket. He looked over at the dog. It was staring right at him. It reached a paw out and placed it on his leg just above the knee. Something about the way it blinked and lifted the paw and set it down again was deeply unsettling.

"What do I do?" he said, not wanting to stare at the dog anymore.

"That's up to you, Ninety." Polly was watching in the rearview. "Like I told you before, if it were me, I would get as far away from LA as fast as possible. You're gonna learn that the flakes don't like you, especially outside the cities, so stick to the main highways and head east. Maybe head for Las Vegas or Dallas—lots of dupes there—or somewhere in the Midwest maybe. Chicago got it real bad with a strain of hemostaph last summer. Housing is probably dirt cheap if you can find work."

"Do you have a . . . is there a number where I could call you? I haven't seen too many friendly faces, and—"

"No," she said, pronouncing the finality. "I'm not an emergence counselor. I'm not your parole officer. If things play out the way I intend, I'm not even gonna be in this job in a couple of days. From the moment you leave this car, you make your own way in the world."

North of the towers and the shacks, tent shelters and improvised hovels continued for several miles before gradually diminishing, first into empty lots and abandoned properties waiting to be overtaken, and then disappearing entirely into a bulldozed strip of jumbled concrete, masonry, and metal.

Military trucks formed the outer perimeter of the cordon, blocking all lanes of traffic, parked across the road to force those approaching the checkpoint barricade to weave slowly back and forth around the trucks. The barricade was constructed from infill barriers heaped with broken concrete. A heavy-gauge gate on rolling wheels spanned one lane of traffic. There was a rectangular guardhouse building, prefabricated, larger than seemed necessary, set flush against the barriers, its plastic siding partly hidden behind a warning sign displaying checkpoint rules and a map of the cordon. A long antenna emerged from the guardhouse, curved by the limp weight of a Confederate battle flag.

The cruiser's arrival interrupted conversations among the soldiers manning the checkpoint. All of the men wore gas masks, but tension visibly poured into their posture, and they set rifles against the barricades. Casper reckoned facing a squad or more of riflemen behind cover was never a pleasant experience. As if to add to that thought, one soldier swiveled the long barrel of a machine gun toward the PitSec car, his upper body protected by the folded shovel of the gun's shield.

"Park the car in the red zone, and turn off the ignition." The message was boosted almost to feedback by the low fidelity of the loudspeaker, but Polly understood. She slowed the cruiser, easing into the rectangle painted on the roadway in front of the gate. She shut off the engine.

"Remain in your vehicle, and do not make any sudden movements."

Casper studied the cordon sign. *You may be required to provide a blood sample* was printed alongside a simple picture of a syringe and a red drop of blood. In bold lettering was the warning: OFFICIAL TRAVEL ONLY.

Beneath these warnings was a map of the military cordon zone. From this checkpoint, marked with a red star, the line ran west to the Pacific and east, inland to Long Beach, south from there to the ocean again, neatly isolating the San Pedro Atomic Power Station, the housing towers, and the rusty accretions of Creeptown. A far-reaching curfew sealed the cordon completely during overnight hours.

A soldier emerged from the guardhouse, and the gate was opened enough for him to pass through. His appearance did little to ease the tension.

He wore desert camouflage trousers bloused into boots, his forest-pattern BDU jacket completely unbuttoned and inside out. The jacket was open; his dog tags hung against a white undershirt. He was not wearing the gas hood like the other soldiers, which caused the straps of his gas mask to bunch up his hair and force down the top of his left ear. His combat webbing was unbuckled and sagging under the weight of spare rifle magazines, a compact radio, the case for his gas equipment, and a pistol in a shoulder holster.

The soldier lifted a palm-sized device hanging from his belt, and a light on it flashed green-yellow. He let it drop on its lanyard and crossed the last few feet to the driver-side door of the cruiser.

"These guys are 114th Infantry, upstate, National Guard," Polly whispered urgently. "They aren't regular Army. Keep your mouth shut."

The soldier's feet scraped grit on the pavement as he drew up beside the cruiser's window.

"Turn back your vehicle, ma'am," he said, his voice muffled and shaped by the cup of the gas mask. "Official business only. You know the evac rules."

Polly held up a badge or card of some sort. She pressed it to the glass.

"I can't see that through this basket." The soldier rapped his knuckles on the bottle-break cage. "Step out of the vehicle. Just you. Leave any weapons inside the vehicle."

He took a step away from the car door. Casper could not see his face from the backseat, just his torso. The soldiers behind the barricade were not moving their heads or talking. It seemed unusual discipline for something as routine as a vehicle arriving at the gate. A radio crackled inside the guard post; it went unanswered, maybe just crosstalk on the channel.

The dog growled softly.

"Keep it quiet," said Polly, laying her pistol and baton on the front seat. "Just stay calm. Nothing is going to happen."

She clambered out of the cruiser. She was talking to the soldier, but Casper could not hear what was being said. She passed the ID card to the soldier. He looked at it, flipped it over, handed it back. They continued talking. Casper leaned forward, straining to hear what they were saying. There was a sudden flurry of movement. Polly was wheeled around and slammed facedown on the hood of the car. Casper tried to open the door, but it was locked.

The soldier was right behind her, pressing in, kicking apart her feet. Casper couldn't see her upper body behind the protection plate over the windshield, but now he could hear what she was saying when he leaned forward up against the partition.

"You do not want to do this," she said, her anger contained.

"Shut up, bitch," the soldier said. "Piece of type three meat dangling in our faces, huh? I fucked one of you in South Texas, you know that? Did you feel it? She called herself Persimmon, and she was a cheating whore. You know her?"

"No," said Polly.

"She wasn't any good." The soldier ran a hand down over Polly's backside. "We'll let you through, sure. Sure. Once we're done with you."

She grunted as if she'd been hit. The dog whined on the seat beside Casper.

"Carefully consider the actions you are about to take." Polly spoke with police authority, loud and crisp. "I am with PitSec. Whatever you have planned, it's not too late to stop it."

"You think anybody is gonna miss a couple dupes?"

"It doesn't—"

He slammed his fist against the hood with a loud bang. She replied with hostile precision.

"This is Post number fifty-six. It is printed on the sign. You are a lieutenant with the one-hundred-and-fourteenth California Army National Guard, Eightieth Infantry Brigade Combat Team, First Battalion of the One-hundred-eightieth Infantry Regiment. You operate out of Fort Orland. How many nights have you spent in those gray longhouse barracks with the shingled walls? Do they still have that shitty shopping mall in Orland?"

"Shut up," he said, and he drove a knee into the back of her thigh.

"This will not go well for you. I want to be very clear on that. If you kill us, we will be back. I will remember every detail, every scrap, the temperature, the exact time, the Brown Barrel on your breath, the gold wedding band on your finger. I will come for you, Lieutenant, along with all my buddies in Rapid Response. It won't be hard to find you. We will come driving up here, or to Orland, in the dead of night. The door will explode without warning. Your kids will be screaming, your wife will be facedown on your kitchen floor, and we will drag you out into the night, and that will be the last they see of you, but it will not end there. You will wish it did, but it will not. We will drag you and your little posse down into the Pit. I know you have heard the stories about what happens there."

"Shut the fuck up." The soldier hit her again. "You fucking freaks. Shut up."

"It's worse than that." Casper could hear the pain in her voice, contained by her willpower but unavoidable. "Worse than . . . anything you can imagine. I am a killer, Lieutenant, and I won't give up on you if you go through with this."

"This is our side now, bitch. You don't go through anymore. You don't . . . we will fuck you up. You don't go through to our side. We're taking it back, and you don't go through."

"Can and I will," she said. "Draw the blood, do the test like you're supposed to, and we'll forget this ever happened. We'll be on our way. Chain of command doesn't have to know. Your wife doesn't have to see—"

He hit her again, hard enough to startle Casper. The dog barked.

"Don't talk about my fucking wife." The soldier stepped back. He hesitated.

"I'll forget all about it," Polly repeated.

The soldier abruptly pivoted away and staggered back through the gate and into the guardhouse. Polly stood up cautiously, still covered by the guns of the other soldiers. She rubbed her ribs.

Two more men came out from behind the barricades, jogging with rifles slung and red hard-shell cases in their hands. Polly opened the back door of the cruiser. Casper blinked up at the light, at her, at the tension crimped into her features. He reached a hand out to touch her. She pulled away.

The guardsmen popped open their boxes full of individually wrapped needles and test kits. They took off their masks—one, to Casper's surprise, was a Warren— and they performed quick blood draws on Casper and Polly. As his blood was filling a tube, he tried to catch her eye again, but she wouldn't look at him.

"I'm sorry," said the soldier drawing Polly's blood. He was a lanky Warren, gas mask pushed up on his face, heavy black prescription glasses on an elastic band around his head. He seemed too old to be a National Guardsman. "This isn't how we operate. He's . . . a lot of them have lost family."

Their blood samples swirled in the test vials. They turned cloudy pink.

"No spore," said the Warren. "They're clean."

Polly said nothing until they were back in the car and driving through the gate.

"Fucking flakes deserve this," she muttered. Casper remained quiet.

It was a different world beyond the cordon. There were patches of churned dirt that suggested that buildings and asphalt had been removed to make way for the perimeter. Boxy, prefabricated mobile homes were assembled in parks, housing for the soldiers now manning the checkpoints. Trucks filled with regular Army troops rumbled past, their gas masks newer, cleaner, and their guns like a void against the stark white of their arctic camouflage smocks.

Civilian vehicles moved on the streets. Unique, normal humans walked the sidewalks along with duplicates. A few businesses remained open, markets and watering holes, entrepreneurs toughing it out despite military warnings barking out of the sirens attached to the light pole on every corner.

"What happened to you?" asked Casper.

"Nothing," she said. The police radio burbled with reports of a crime in progress.

"You're not who I remember," said Casper.

The cruiser pulled up at a stop light, and she turned her head, her profile limned by the sun visible through the window strip.

"You're damn right I'm not. Don't try to cast me as her. Forget about Veronica Lambert. She's dead."

The light clicked to green, and traffic began to move again. Polly returned her attention to the road, and the cruiser rumbled on.

CHAPTER FIVE

■ ■ ■

Milo Gardener met her in a plain hotel conference room in downtown Los Angeles. Every Gardener she ever met in the line of duty was strange, with Pool-born white hair and unusual mannerisms, but Milo Gardener was downright unnerving. Words emerged from his time-flaccid lips as if spoken by a faraway child. Though hunched, he was imposing and not enfeebled by his advanced age.

"I have requested you," said Milo, "for a special task. We are in need of a shepherd to tend to a flock of visitors from the United Nations. Despite your recent difficulties, I believe you are well equipped to see to the security of these guests and to ensure they see what we want them to see."

Milo embellished the importance of the job to her without seeming condescending, yet she was left with the distinct impression that he wanted her as a tour guide. Still, it was an improvement over spending her days seeing addle-brained type twos out of the cannery. She agreed to take the job.

"You now work for me." Milo stood. "I expect superlative performance from all of my employees, but I do not doubt your ability to meet my expectations. I will be contacting you with an itinerary. The UN-chartered flight will arrive tomorrow night. In the meantime, begin preparing a security detail that can travel lightly, inconspicuously, and quickly."

She shook his hand, surprised at his weak grip and delicate fingers.

"I will be thorough and professional," she promised.

His hand lingered on hers, his leather-clad fingers cold against her palm, but he said nothing else. She was transfixed by his blue eyes and wondered how much of a man like Casper Cord was within a strange creature like Milo Gardener. He pulled away abruptly and departed.

She returned to her neighborhood beneath a gloaming gray sky, columns of smoke rising within the cordon and farther east, where the Army supposedly operated a field crematorium for victims of spore outbreaks. Sirens howled distantly.

Curfew was coming, and there were few cars on the streets. A retriever dog with a collar appeared from a side street and ran north along the curb. It trailed a frayed leash behind it, and its eyes were wide and showed white. It jerked and dropped low to the ground as a heavy-lifting helicopter passed overhead. Its eyes and ears followed the thudding Doppler of the rotors.

The light was on upstairs in Mrs. Valdez's apartment, and Polly discerned from the moving shadows that her elderly neighbor was up and about. After her last visit and the subsequent nightmare it had inspired, she felt increasingly concerned about the old woman. They were not far from the cordon, and the entire area was under threat of a spore storm. Almost everyone but dupes was gone or in the process of leaving, but poor, hapless Mrs. Valdez was caught up in the inertia of her life and was not going to evacuate.

Polly climbed the stairs and discovered the door to Mrs. Valdez's apartment slightly ajar. In the dim light she made out a black smear on the door frame beside the knob. She leaned in and realized it was blood, congealed but not yet dried.

"Mrs. Valdez?" she said, and she opened the door with the toe of her boot. "Mrs. Valdez, are you all right?"

The apartment was as she remembered, too cramped and disorganized to spot anything out of place. She took a step inside, nearly tripping over a stack of magazines. There was a strange odor in the air, earthy, sour in her sinuses, like the marrow stench of the Pool edged with decay. Fat black flies buzzed against the windows and overhead lamp.

"Mrs. Valdez?" Polly stepped over a sliding stack of photo albums. The top one flopped open to pictures of a funeral of an elderly man. The images were bleached with age. She picked the album up and closed it. When she returned it to the stack, she saw that where it had fallen was a blood smear on the carpet and the rough outline of a shoe.

She searched for something, some sort of weapon, in case there was an armed intruder. She hefted a jar filled with pennies from a shelf. It weighed enough to do some injury. She kept quiet and stepped more carefully. All of the lamps in the apartment seemed to be on, although the piles of mementos and bags filled with ornaments obscured the direct light.

There was more blood, smeared by fingers on the edge of a door frame. Bloody paper towels and enough blood to pool on the linoleum of the kitchen. There was an empty tube of antibiotic ointment and first-aid tape on the kitchen counter beside the sink. A narrow hallway delved from the kitchen into the darkness. Rooms opened on either side, and there was a third door at the far end of the hall. There were bloody footprints everywhere on the hall carpeting. They beat a foul path from one door to the other and back to the door at the far end of the hall.

Polly took a halting step onto the carpet, forced to stand in the blood. She froze. There was a repetitive clicking sound, almost like a ratcheting, followed by a soft thump. It came from the room on the right. Her heart slipped in her chest. She raised the jar of pennies and advanced, moonlight showing the way around a dresser and into a small bedroom dominated by a queen-sized, four-poster bed of solid wood. The lamp was overturned in her path. Her feet crunched in broken glass.

A strip of light was visible at the bottom of the adjoining door. Shadows paced back and forth. A bathroom, probably, and behind it, softly, the ratcheting sound again, this time ending in a slow scrape against the door. The noise repeated several times and began to seem less mechanical and more like the chattering call of an insect or amphibian. Her stomach tightened, and Polly tasted acid in the back of her throat.

She approached the door and listened. Something was definitely breathing on the other side. It thumped loudly and shook the door. Polly reached a hand out to the knob. It was sticky with blood. She lifted the jar of pennies up high and steeled herself for what she might find.

"Miss Polly?"

Polly nearly dropped the jar of pennies at the sound of Mrs. Valdez's voice. She caught the jar with both hands and turned to find Mrs. Valdez slumping in the doorway of the bedroom.

"Mrs. Valdez, what happened?" Polly went to her and helped her stand.

The old woman was out of breath, her hair matted with sweat and her eyes heavy-lidded with exhaustion. Her dressing gown was disheveled and bloodstained, and the entire length of her left arm was wrapped up in paper towels.

"Mr. Romeo come home," said Mrs. Valdez. "He hurt really bad but he okay now. I give him a bath. He is sleeping in the bathroom to get well."

Polly brought Mrs. Valdez into the kitchen and sat her down at the table. In the full light she did not seem so badly injured.

"He did this to you?"

"He so scared. He scratch me when I carry him. He did not mean it."

"I need to see what he did," said Polly. Mrs. Valdez shook her head petulantly. "If you don't show me, we have to call an ambulance, and they won't be gentle. I will be gentle."

She was almost as afraid to see what was under the bandages as Mrs. Valdez was afraid to show her. People infected with the spores were known to conceal the spreading white growth until it was too late to remove the infection or amputate the limb and save their lives.

"Okay," said Mrs. Valdez.

She pinched her lips and closed her eyes. Polly knelt beside her, slowly unwinding the paper towels covering her arm. The first layers unfurled easily. Blood began to show through in spots. The towels were darker and darker and sticking to the injuries. Polly peeled them back gingerly. Mrs. Valdez winced as the final layers were removed.

There was no telltale white of spore growth. There were dozens of deep scratches and gouges as well as unusual bite marks—paired holes that seemed too closely grouped—that were swollen and oozing clear liquid. Polly soaked a towel with purified water from a bottle. The swelling and redness became more apparent when the blood was wiped away.

"This already looks seriously infected," said Polly. "We need to take you to a hospital before you become sick."

"No!" Mrs. Valdez pulled her arm away and stood up from the chair. "On the radio they say the hospital you go into, you catch the sickness, and the Army takes you to burn you. I not going in there. No. You can't make me."

"You could die."

"If I die, I go here in my house with my family." Mrs. Valdez said. "I love Mr. Romeo. I stay with him."

There was no hope of moving the stout old woman against her will. Polly doubted an ambulance would even show up this close to the cordon. Maybe the Army or the police, not that she would resort to involving them.

"Okay," said Polly. "I have a first-aid kit in my apartment. Let me go get it for you, and I will do what I can for your arm."

Mrs. Valdez nodded. Polly hurried out of the apartment and up the stairs. She had a hard-shell emergency medical kit she'd swiped from Rapid Response years ago. It included some powerful antibiotics that should stave off the infection. When she returned to Mrs. Valdez's apartment, she found the door shut and locked. She pounded on the door and called out to Mrs. Valdez, but there was no answer.

"I know you can hear me, Mrs. Valdez," said Polly. "Don't be afraid. I am leaving my first-aid kit outside your door, and I am putting a note with instructions on what to use to make sure that arm doesn't get badly infected. Do exactly what these instructions say, and you should be okay."

Polly did as she said and slid the kit against the door.

"Please use it," she said as she leaned her head against the door. "It might save your life."

She retreated and waited at the top of the stairs for some time, the corner of the kit visible. After many minutes the door opened, and the kit disappeared into Mrs. Valdez's apartment. It was a small victory, but one that might save her elderly neighbor's life.

Polly struggled to sleep. She was distracted by thoughts of the United Nations visit and the odd responsibility being given to her by Milo Gardener. The assignment did not make sense. Why shuffle her off to the woebegotten depths of Corrections Emergence and, in the span of a couple of weeks, turn around and give her such a critical assignment? The possible reasons troubled her.

When she managed to suppress such concerns, her mind drifted back to the vision of Mrs. Valdez and her arm. She pictured the strange bite marks—two holes only separated by an eighth of an inch—and the puffy flesh surrounding each wound. The image in her memory was accompanied by the soft ratcheting sound she had heard from the bathroom, rising and falling, punctuated by a thump that shook the bathroom door in its frame.

■　■　■

Splayed out upon the table, the type three called Violet Vex slowly became the meal. This was her purpose, she insisted, and therefore it was her desire. Her assistant had administered a spinal anesthetic so that she might remain conscious until the moment of death, watching her guests with blue eyes outlined in black, encouraging them to take a second helping of her thigh or the meat of her arm.

Several of the guests departed before she was even served. It was, after all, an intolerable sight for a normal human, who perceived only the gory human frailty, not the beauty of her sacrifice and the serenity to be found in the living mutilation of a human body. The enjoyment of consuming another human's flesh, no matter how willingly offered, was even further beyond their comprehension.

When those with weak stomachs had departed—mostly type twos and the handful of normal humans invited to attend—the remaining dinner guests mocked their exit. They saluted one another as courageous and selected cuts of hamstring and gluteals, pectoral and trapezius, with even greater relish.

Wesley Bishop sat at the head of the table, beside the head of Violet Vex. She watched her vivisection in a mirror suspended above her to advise the servers in their knife work. She talked with Bishop frequently and insisted he be served the choicest cuts.

"Dig deep," she instructed the type two carving her chest. "The lean muscle is best."

While this Grand Guignol was under way, a video was projected on the long wall of the rookery's main dining room. Footage played of Violet Vex wearing a jogging suit and running along sunlit mountain roads, crossing streams, walking through idyllic pastures, and lying nude upon a beach. These scenes were punctuated by montages of her eating, stuffing herself full of rich foods to provide just the right "marbling of my succulent flesh," as she narrated.

The butchers began to part bone and strip away planks of quivering musculature to reveal the organ meats. Violet, features pale and sunken, voice barely more than a whisper, finally spoke her last.

"I must depart," she said, her body shaking from the sawing of the knives. "I wish I could remain to enjoy the main course. I am . . . slipping away and hope for . . . a pleasant meal . . . may I sustain you . . . as . . . friendship sustains . . . us all."

She breathed her last. Her cheek gently dropped against the table. One of her assistants changed over the video to a lingering wide shot of her literally walking into the sunset with *Thank you* written over the image in golden script. The guests clapped as her mutilated carcass was draped in a lavender sheet and the cuts of meat, piled high upon platters, were stacked onto carts and wheeled off to the kitchen to be cooked.

"Without a doubt, your most extravagant party yet," said Idol Constantine, the famous type one movie star. "A toast to our gracious host."

Idol raised his glass, but Wesley Bishop stood, raising his own in a toast.

"To Violet Vex," Bishop saluted with his glass, "for providing us with such a welcome distraction from our troubles."

The toast was enthusiastic. The guests, luminaries of the world, heads of subsidiaries, duplicates from the upper echelons of American society, were epicureans seeking ever more extreme indulgences. Tonight's meal of performance artist Violet Vex would go down in legend.

When the trays heaped with sizzling meats arrived from the kitchen, there was another round of applause. The room filled with the aroma of cooked meat. Tureens of blood gravy were joined by plates heaped with asparagus, potatoes, and other vegetables. Violet Vex's chief assistant promised, "Everything on your plate was nurtured personally by Miss Vex."

Bishop sawed off a steaming morsel from her pectoral steak and savored the nuance of her flavors. Her meat reminded him of suckling pig. The guests cleared their plates. There was a commitment to gorging, a desire by each diner to pay a debt incurred by Violet Vex's sacrifice.

No amount of acting or self-assurance could overcome the instinctive human revulsion to cannibalism. Even starving men gagged on the flesh and blood of men. Not so for his guests. The time given to them by the Pool had removed such human inhibitions as surely as did the war rituals of benighted tribes of man-eaters. Fat tongues patrolled greasy lips; teeth tore into thigh and limb and crispy skin. Browned muscles parted to knives. Preparations of organ meats quivered on rising forks.

When the meal was finished, servers arrived and cleared the table once more. Bishop and his guests retired to the lounge for a *digestif* and found Violet Vex waiting for them. Her type's red hair was hastily dyed a glossy black, cropped mannishly, and parted at the side to match her previous style. Her blue eyes were darkened with teardrop outlines of mesdemet. Her body, restored to softness, was tightly swaddled in a garment of red-tinted plastic wrap that mashed her inherited contours out of shape.

The guests saluted her and congratulated her on her vision. They drank Arak from antique Syrian vessels belonging to the collection of a museum that no longer existed. They surrounded Violet Vex and ingratiated themselves.

Bishop felt the axis of the evening tilting toward his entertainment. He self-medicated from tablets he probably was not supposed to be mixing with the sharp, licorice-flavored alcohol. He drank too much, said things he should not, put his hands places they did not belong, and ended the party slumped on a couch, watching the last guests trickle out for the long walk to the elevators.

Violet Vex remained. She was hardly drunk at all as she unwrapped herself and came over to him on the couch.

"You promised to respect my artistic vision," she said, and she deposited her shapely bottom in his lap. "Your man, Patrice, would not allow my dessert course."

"Not my fault," said Bishop. He knocked over empty cups in search of one with something to drink.

"The custards were laced with cyanide." Violet wound her fingers into Bishop's hair. "I was going to make every guest a participant in the performance. Instead, what do I have?"

He took a drink. She yanked his head back, the Arak spilling out of the corners of his mouth. Her eyes glittered in the low lighting.

"A limp-dicked drunk, my supposed patron." She kissed him. The shape of her lips was well-known to him but their movement unfamiliar and new; she excited him despite the haze of pills and booze. When she had her fill of his kiss, she sat back on his knees and tousled his hair as if he were a child.

"You really should have let me kill them."

"You have two million dollars," he said.

"Now, why did you say that?" She got up from his lap. "Now I can't fuck you. It would be too transactional."

He pushed himself up from the couch and took her hand. "Tomorrow I will get them all back in this very room, and you can kill them however you'd like."

"You're so romantic," she said.

The rookery was a catacomb of personal apartments and private lounges. He and Violet Vex found one, black lacquered walls and recessed furniture, and became entangled in the billion-thread-count sheets, working up a sweat, moaning though neither one was having any fun. The perfunctory sex ended with anticlimactic separation, and they lay alone beside each other, filling the small bedroom with the smoke of exotic cigarettes and the soft murmur of their breath.

"I want my own clade," she said. "We deserve it. The Vexes. Artists. We can start a commune or something. I'll move to Napa."

"I don't involve myself in that sort of decision." He sat up, showing her the tanned flesh and freckles of his back. The liquor was being replaced by a headache. He craved pills or some sort of distraction better than Violet Vex could offer him.

"But you could involve yourself." She sat up behind him and insinuated her arms around his chest. She hooked her chin in the crook of his shoulder. "There's a whole scene of duplicate artists out in Napa. Canyon makes wine, Elation runs a raw-food restaurant, and all the breeds of creatives gravitate to them. A very funny bunch. Very self-satirizing. And mostly my duplicates."

He did not reply. She ran her hand down to the useless muddle of his lap and gave him a gentle squeeze. She inclined her head so that she was looking into one eye.

"Do you know BronQ?"

"No," he said, and hr flicked ash into the chrome cup of the ashtray.

"He's amazing. Type twos are very rarely so talented. He does nothing but abstract portraits of Annie Groves, over and over again. He does these triptychs of her transforming into—"

"I want to show you something," said Bishop.

He harbored no particular fondness for Violet Vex. She was one of many satellites orbiting him, usually distant, occasionally drawn in by the gravity of circumstance, but she was there. In that moment he wanted to show someone.

"Of course," she said. "What is it?"

They dressed in silk kimonos torn from hermetically sealed bags and exited the apartment. Patrice trailed behind them in the halls but did not follow them into the darkened dome of the observatory. The antique telescope—dreadfully boring in Bishop's mind—was gone, removed to make room for his latest object of interest.

The golden Operation Westward vessel rested atop the observatory platform. With a flick of a switch it was illuminated by powerful lamps, the light reflecting warmly from its restored surface. The hatch was opened and facing the door.

"It's a treasure," said Violet. She was drawn into the room by the vessel's glow. She ran her fingertips along curved seams and leaned her head and shoulders into the cockpit. "It's beautiful. Is this a space capsule?"

"Close enough," said Bishop.

"How does it work?" she asked. She was already climbing into it, sitting in the cushioned seat, strapping the harness over her shoulders, and fiddling with the capsule's control surfaces. Bishop helped her secure the five-point harness. Her kimono caused some difficulty. She solved it with her lack of modesty. "It's like the Venera ships the traitors used."

She was referring to the reviled clade of type twos who defected to the Soviets in the 1970s and became cosmonauts. They all perished, boiled alive, participating in deadly Venus landings in the 1980s. By then the Gardeners were good at catching deviants when they emerged from the Pool. The reborn cosmonauts were captured and interrogated. The Soviets never received their promised debriefings from the defectors. Venera was considered a failure for the Soviets, and Bishop's predecessors ensured that the traitors remained zeroed in the cannery.

Violet shifted in the seat with a creak of leather and let her fingers roam the mechanical controls.

"There are no computers," she said.

"It's much simpler than a rocket." Bishop leaned into the capsule. "And it is old."

Bishop demonstrated for her the Euler control stick that operated the rudder and recessed dive planes. There was a switch to activate the electric motor, a lever to release diving weights, hatch releases, a roll-top cargo bin, and controls for internal and external recording equipment. Everything still functioned. The blank film and audio tape recovered from the capsule were still being analyzed by the Gardeners. The canisters hung open; the reel heads and other internal mechanisms lay exposed.

Violet wrinkled her nose. "It has an odd scent. What is that? Scorched wires?" Bishop ignored her question.

"I traveled to the Fane once," said Bishop. "Have you heard of it?"

"A room at the bottom of the Pool. Outside the Pool."

"It is the room that cradles the Pool's nadir," he said. "It is so hot and so deep, you must wear an insulated cooling suit like an astronaut. When you leave the laboratory, you follow a curving tunnel chiseled through the bedrock. There are beautiful formations of crystal as big as a house. They swim in the heat. Every step is tiring. The air hisses constantly into your helmet, cold enough that it hurts your face, but if your skin touches the glass of the helmet, you will be burned.

"There's something else, more oppressive than the temperature. You can feel it, through the rock: first a pressure behind your eyes, the magnetic pull of the iron, then as you near the Fane, it becomes invisible hands squeezing your brain."

"It?" Violet fidgeted with the control stick.

"The Mother," said Bishop. "She's there at the bottom of the Pool, much denser than the surrounding fluid. The scientists call her the Threshold Mass. The Gardeners have built a macabre chapel devoted to her in the Fane. They conduct ceremonies in there, human sacrifices of a sort, to appease the Mother."

Violet studied him as if trying to judge if he was joking.

"The baked skull of a stag is mounted to the wall." He diagramed with his hands. "It hangs above two hatches. The upper hatch is painted red and only a few inches across. It opens easily. The lower hatch is much larger, big enough for a man to crawl through on hands and knees. For as long as I have been CEO, the larger hatch has never been opened. I will not allow it. I have nightmares of the consequences of opening it. The smaller hatch covers a portal, a view of the Mother herself. Gold-tinted lights penetrate the churning column of fluid.

"She is vast. Smooth and pale, like the belly of some great beast. I watched the bodies rise from her as gossamer, thin as hairs, weaving and bending into the figures of men. There were so many emerging that she quivered. As these wire men ascended, they gathered bone and flesh until they were you and me and all of the rest of us, disappearing from view as they rose to the surface. The whole while that I watched, I could feel her weight pressing at the edges of my mind.

"The scientists long held that there was more to her, that something was being missed. The idea was that the Mother was just a small part of some larger entity, a great unseen Thing that extended beyond our capacity to detect. The scientists in New Mexico dreamed up all sorts of theories and ways to test them.

"This capsule"—he patted his hand against the frame—"was one of ninety built during the 1940s to test their favorite theory. Trunk Theory. The capsules, the training, the experiments all fell under the rubric of Operation Westward. My forebears proceeded with the secret assistance of the US Government, which had, by then, been infiltrated and influenced by our kind."

"They talk about these things on the discussion nodes," said Violet.

"I'm sure you're right. Most of the theories leaked to the public not long after President Whiteacre exposed our kind. Those theories were methodically discredited as conspiracy fantasies. The Soviets believe them, which only further discredits them in the eyes of all free people.

"The capsules like this that launched in the late 1940s to test the theory entered the Mother and disappeared. They passed through the Threshold Mass, seeming to confirm Trunk Theory. And then . . . nothing. No communications were received. No pilots returned from the Pool, and no capsules bobbed to the surface. Weeks became months became years, and there was no sign of the capsules. The project was abandoned."

"So why did you keep this one?"

"I didn't," said Bishop. "It returned to us. They all did, quite recently."

"Where was it?"

"That was *my* question," he said. He crossed to the light switch and shut off the powerful lamps surrounding the capsule. The fading heat of the filaments survived for a few seconds before darkness engulfed the room. The stars became gradually visible through the panes of the observatory dome. The brightest appeared first. More stars became visible incrementally until the whole cloth of the sky was dusted with countless flecks of radiance.

"All of the Westward capsules returned to us empty, except this one. The pilot was inside and dead. He'd never left the capsule. He died wearing his oxygen mask, sucking his last breaths from the capsule's dwindling supply. After he succumbed, the capsule was opened, and someone used his camera to capture a series of photographs of the sky. They returned the camera to his pocket and returned the capsule to the Pool."

Bishop studied the night above them. Violet unbuckled her straps and crossed the room to join him.

"Right there," he said quietly. "It's small. Just below the bright white one. Its name is a string of numbers. Based on the position of constellations in the sky of the photographs, that is where this vessel was."

Violet took a little assistance to find the star in the sky. She saw it, or pretended to, and asked, "How far is it?"

"Impossibly far," he said. "It would require countless centuries for the Soviet's fastest rocket to reach that star. I was told it took only seconds to cross the trunk to the destination."

"So the Pool is a way to travel between places," she said. "Send another capsule."

"There is no way to control the destination. The capsules can only follow the coincidental flows. That they were apparently scattered to different locations means there are multiple destinations, tributaries maybe. The Pool is part of a network of unseen rivers crossing the stars."

"Why did none of the other capsules produce pictures?" she asked.

"Maybe there is no reason," said Bishop. "Or maybe this one was the only one to reach a destination, out of all ninety, close enough to see the same stars as us."

■ ■ ■

Casper Cord stirred beneath the plywood. He crawled on hands and knees into the dirt, amid the debris of a demolished building. His body ached. The dismal air was heavy in his lungs. It was still night, but the lot was bathed in the eerie orange of the sodium street lamps.

The dog was awake and staring at him, unmoved from where he had left it.

"Good morning," Casper said.

He pissed in a gutter and scratched the stubble growing on his face. He wanted to crawl back under the plywood and stay there. Maybe he would eventually scatter into the trash strewn around the abandoned lot.

An Army truck rumbled past, slowing down and playing its searchlight over the rubble of the building. He knew enough to keep his head down. After a few moments the diesel engine shuddered, and the truck moved on.

He drank from a pail of hydrant water and washed his face in what was left. The dog followed him, never making a sound or pleading. When he turned around, the dog was always there.

"Goddamn it, why are you following me?" he demanded of the dog. It cocked its head as if it understood the question. It almost seemed that it might answer him. Instead it lay down and rested its chin on its front paws. Casper shook his head. Animals were supposed to have more sense than to climb aboard a sinking boat.

At first light he wrapped himself in the cheap blanket they'd given him at St. Philomena and made his way back to the gray Gothic church. Families of flakes as well as a group of type twos and threes formed a line that reached around the block. They kept apart from one another, and Casper kept apart from them, as he had his first night. He refused to stand alongside the other duplicates. He resented what they had done to Los Angeles while he was away. The flakes would not have him. They turned away and stepped back as if he might spread a disease to them.

"I do smell pretty ripe," he said to the dog. He patted its head.

Not everyone in the line had the look of a refugee. There were a few men and women queued up behind him who seemed out of place. The men were hard types, bald heads showing fresh-shaved skin, prison tattoos on their arms and necks. They were laughing and drinking from jugs of homemade wine and had not noticed him yet. He figured it was only a matter of time.

The doors opened right at five, and the line moved quickly and then stopped. The skinheads tossed their bottles of wine into the street. The line moved. Casper shuffled forward. One of the girls said something about the dog, but Casper couldn't hear what. He kept his eyes on the heels of the man ahead of him. A surprisingly cold wind penetrated the blanket draped over his shoulders. The line moved. Casper shuffled forward.

"How much for the dog?" asked one of the men behind Casper.

He kept his head down. The line moved. He shuffled forward. The skinhead repeated the question. A heavy hand fell onto Casper's shoulder, S-I-E-G tattooed across the knuckles. The line moved. Casper shuffled forward, pulling away from the hand. He was close to the door. He could hear the clang of silverware and the murmur of voices rumbling inside St. Philomena's cafeteria.

Not close enough.

"Motherfucker." The skinhead grabbed Casper and turned him around.

He was an ugly one. An asymmetrical head, a chin that was an inch too long, a mouth full of teeth placed in haphazard, jagged rows. Three teardrop tattoos by his left eye, red suspenders worn over a white T-shirt, surprisingly clean, tucked into black denim. Bulging, muscular arms sheathed in a graveyard of sinister white-power tattoos.

The dog snarled and bared the cage of its teeth at the skinhead.

"Fucking green meat." The smile made the man uglier. "I can tell by your haircut. How'd you get a pet so fast, green meat? What you doing here?"

"Just trying to have a meal," said Casper.

"What, you mean one of our meals? Cuz you're going in ahead of us, that means you're taking one of our meals. Right?" The ugly one's friends agreed with him. "That's okay, though. We're civilized and respectable, ain't that right, Van?"

"Yeah, you're right." Van had a shaved head and a pasty moon face monstrous with acne.

Casper was stalling, sizing up the skinheads. There were six of them, four men, two women. They all looked dangerous in their own way. He figured he could take the big one asking about the dog, and probably the next one, Van, wearing a leather jacket too small for his husky body. After that the odds weren't good. If they had knives, the odds were terrible.

"So we make a deal, green meat. A dog for a meal. Looks like a good dog." The ugly one reached a hand down, and the dog snapped at him, prompting laughter from his companions. "Might have to kick some manners into his stupid ass."

No point stalling any longer.

"Just get on with it, you rats." Casper brought up his fists. "I've tangled with worse."

"That's enough of that." The voice was loud, but when Casper turned, he saw it belonged to a man scarcely five feet tall. He wore the coat and collar of a Catholic priest, ruddy faced, eyes large and bright blue behind a thick pair of gold-rimmed spectacles. "Freddie, you want to eat, you leave this one alone. There's enough for all of you."

The priest guided Casper away from the skinheads and into the church. The soup kitchen was plain, full of crowded folding tables and the savory smells of stew, baked rolls, potatoes, and vegetables. Families and groups of young people were already tucking in to cafeteria trays heaped with generous portions. The line was moving efficiently past the kitchen, where men and women in aprons ladled up each component of the meal.

"I saw you in here last night," said the priest. "I'm not very good at telling you from the others, but I remembered the dog. What's your name?"

"Casper."

"And the dog?"

Casper had to consider the question. "He's not Ringo."

The priest chuckled and said, "No? How about Lennon?"

"The Communist?"

"That's the one," said the priest.

Casper shrugged. "Sure, Lenin it is."

"I'm Father Woodhew. Just Father to most. I apologize for those boys out front. They're always coming here looking for a fight. " The priest took a small cookie out of his pocket. He bent low and held it cupped in his hand. The dog snuffled it out of his palm and accepted a pat on the head as it crunched away. "If he messes in here, you'll need to clean it up in a hurry. That's just the thing could start a donnybrook. I say, for now you find a seat with some of your kind. Most folk won't like you too much, and it can be hard to make friends."

The priest deposited Casper in the back of the line feeding past the kitchen.

"I need to welcome everyone," said Father Woodhew.

"Do you have a cemetery here?" asked Casper. "For people who go to this church, I mean."

"There is a small cemetery behind the church, but we haven't buried anyone there in a long while. Not since the seventies at least. Do you have a relative interred there?"

"I don't know."

"I'll get the record," said Father Woodhew. "You wait in line."

The priest threaded his way through the cafeteria. Casper looked around at the line. The couple ahead of him, heads and shoulders draped in wool blankets, looked back, saw he was a duplicate, and pulled their children in tightly against their legs.

The line stopped and started and advanced slowly. With each shuffling step the savory aroma of the buffet grew more overwhelming. The dog whined and licked its chops.

"It does smell good," said Casper.

Father Woodhew returned with a folio bound in time-worn leather.

"This one goes all the way back to the forties. If you need something older I'm afraid I can't help you tonight. If you come back tomorrow—"

"This is what I needed," said Casper.

He knew what he would find before he found it. No Lynn Cord, because she had resumed using her maiden name. She was Lynn Short. Born 1911, Died 1962. A beloved sister and aunt.

When he exhaled it felt like more than just air leaving his lungs. Casper closed the book and passed it back to Father Woodhew. The priest squeezed Casper's hand.

"If they are buried there then they are with God now."

He received his tray of food and searched the tables for an open seat that wasn't adjacent to someone staring at him with hatred. A slim, light-skinned black man with a spotty face and uneven, dreadlocked hair looked up at Casper and quickly looked away. There was an open seat next to the man, beside a very heavy white girl who was wrapped up in conversation with the people she was sitting with.

Casper took the opening, weeding his way through the crowded row between the tables and dropping heavily into the chair beside the black man. All around chairs squealed against the floor as men and women abandoned the table and moved away from Casper. Some of them shoved him in the back as they pushed past carrying their half-eaten trays of food.

Only the black man remained, shoveling food into his mouth. He was wearing a puffy winter coat, ripped across the shoulder, and he smelled like cigarettes and sweated booze. A plastic grocery bag stuffed with clothing was tied around his forearm by a heavy piece of white rope.

"Casper." He didn't bother to offer the man his hand.

"Don't think you can talk to me," said the black man. "Everybody in here wants to kill you. Even the dupes you was supposed to sit with."

Casper began to eat. The food was institutional grade, which suited him just fine. He was ravenous. He stared at the tray, but he could feel the eyes on him all around the room. The weight of the dog rested on his feet.

"Man, I swear you got a death wish, coming here," said the black man. "Don't try to Rosa Parks with me. Nobody makes the rules. You sit with your kind, we sit with ours."

He stood but did not immediately depart.

"You can have my biscuit," said Casper. "You don't even have to stay. Just tell me your name."

The man with the dreadlocks hesitated. He eyed the crusty biscuit and licked his lips. His skinny fingers swept over Casper's tray. The biscuit was gone, disappearing into the bag tied around the man's wrist.

"They call me Bottles," he said. "And don't try to sit near me never again."

COMINTERCEPT – CIVILIAN/MILITARY UHF/VHF – IN THE OPEN - RED LABEL

7/02/06 - 9:01:39 PST - Partial Machine Transcription

Subjects: AF 996 (Aeroflot International Flight 996), **WALLACE** (USS *George Wallace* CATTC), **BREWER 14**(USMC MH-54, Transport), **HAVOC 53**(F-18J, Escort)

Aeroflot International Flight 996 is a chartered civilian aircraft departing Vladivostok and over the Pacific bound for LAX. UMSC MH-54 transport helicopter BREWER and F-18J multirole fighter HAVOC are launched from the aircraft carrier USS *George Wallace.*

WALLACE: Civilian aircraft Aeroflot 9-9-6, this is the USS *George Wallace* tower. You are entering our CAP space. Maintain heading and altitude.

AF 996: Ah, repeat, USS *Wallace*?

WALLACE: Aeroflot 9-9-6 en route to LAX, maintain heading and altitude. This is the United States Navy.

AF 996: I copy that, US Navy.

AF 996: (*cockpit crosstalk*)

WALLACE: AF 9-9-6, maintain heading, descend to three thousand feet.

AF 996: Descending to three thousand.

AF 996: Uh, US Navy, this is 9-9-6. There are fighter plane aircraft visible off port wing.

HAVOC 53: Aeroflot, good morning. Me and HAVOC 5-4 are going to see you in safely.

AF 996: Okay, we do not want the trouble, US Navy.

WALLACE: AF 9-9-6, drop speed to two hundred knots.

AF 996: Okay. Slowing to two hundred knots, US Navy.

BREWER 14: Aeroflot 9-9-6, this is BREWER 1-4 coming in low and slow on your seven.

AF 996: Copy, BREWER 1-4. We do not see you on radar.

BREWER 14: AF 9-9-6, that's just fine and dandy. We'll be there.

AF 996: Very well.

BREWER 14: AF 9-9-6, *Wallace* CATTC is going to hand off to the civilian controller. Follow their vector in, but I want you to halt on your landing runway and remain in place. Do not taxi. Do you understand?

AF 996: BREWER 1-4, we are not supposed to do this.

BREWER 14: Just tell me you understand, AF 9-9-6.

AF 996: We copy you, BREWER 1-4. Land and do not taxi. Is there any other instruction?

BREWER 14: We'll see you on the ground, Aeroflot.

CHAPTER SIX

■ ■ ■

Los Angeles International Airport was empty. Its runways and tarmacs were a concrete desert. Minutes could pass in its bright caverns during which not a single passenger walked the concourse. The ghost life of its facilities continued. Escalators climbed and fell, shops remained open, security stood ready, and janitors and ticket- counter employees continued at their jobs.

Outside its terminals, beyond the silent food court and shopping plaza, there was a security perimeter maintained by the Army. A handful of business flyers, private jets, and cargo aircraft were still operating. All other civilian air traffic was routed well north and south. Protestors camped in the parking lots and occasionally attempted a run on the front gates. They were inevitably forced back by the security— mostly duplicates—supplemented by a detachment of military police.

A convoy of matte-black armored carriers arrived in the passenger drop-off area with a blast of horns and the lurching gurgle of idling diesel engines. The Rapid Response teams loaded inside the vehicles were under orders to create a spectacle. Hatches banged open, sergeants barked commands to dismount, and squads of security troopers charged out and deployed in full tactical gear. They faced a jeering crowd of onlookers. The confused airport security watched and, unsure of how to react, decided to do nothing.

Simultaneously, a quartet of unmarked vans arrived at a chain-link side gate manned by a pair of uniformed guards. Identities were verified, and the gate rolled open. The vehicles slipped inside without anyone noticing. Polly Foster was in the lead vehicle.

The vans fanned out and halted on the tarmac at Terminal Three. Polly stepped out into the still morning. The quiet and the retracted Jetways lent the terminal a forlorn atmosphere, like the docks of a drained lake.

A pair of fast, low-flying military jets shook the sky as they passed overhead. Polly was searching for them when she spotted the wide-bodied Antonov on approach. It wallowed in the air, sliding side to side above the shimmering river of the landing strip.

It was a beast. It dipped lower, and its four jet turbines whined. Smoke gusted from its rows of tires as it touched down, finishing a long deceleration and halting on the nearby runway. It was only as its powerful engines cycled down that Polly heard the thudding of the helicopter following it in.

She recognized the Poseidon, the naval version of a military Griffon helicopter. It was flat gray and bore no markings. It circled above the stopped Antonov once before descending to the runway. The moment the helicopter's wheels touched concrete, a bristling contingent of Marines in city-pattern fatigues spilled out of its doors.

This was not how things had been arranged. There was no provision for a deal with the military. Polly thumbed her radio.

"Head for the Antonov. We'll meet them on the runway. Keep your safeties on."

She expected to meet the UN team leader, Dr. Robin Burns. What she was greeted by instead was a polite but insistent United States Marine Corps sergeant. He was an imposing and extremely fit African American with FUNKWEED stitched on the breast placard of his city-pattern vest cover.

"Let us through," said Polly.

"I'm sorry," said Funkweed, "Captain Dryson will have to talk to you first."

He kept his tone respectful and his carbine pointed at the ground, but he was physically blocking her from approaching the Antonov. The helicopter lifted off, leaving behind a full squad of Marines—Force Recon, by the looks of their gear and patches—to secure the ponderous Soviet transport aircraft.

"This was all arranged with the Army," said Polly. "They're in control of this facility. Colonel Ford? Do I need to get him down here?"

"This is a Marine Corps operation," said Funkweed. "I'll salute an Army man if you'd like to haul him down here, but I take my orders from the captain, and he said nobody gets on that plane."

Polly studied the squad of Marines. They were unusually fit and disciplined, even for Marines. Each man was not only in peak physical condition but almost the same height and build. None of them were duplicates.

They took up positions around the aircraft, not threatening but making it apparent that if she or anyone else tried to interfere, there was going to be an intense disagreement. She ordered her escort teams of two men per vehicle to remain in the vans.

Only Sergeant Funkweed was relaxed. He folded a stick of chewing gum into his mouth and leaned his wrists over the back of his slung weapon.

"All the palm trees are dead." Funkweed gestured to a row of denuded trunks planted along the fence a few hundred yards across the tarmac.

"All the trees within a hundred miles are dead," said Polly. "The leaves turned white and dropped off weeks ago. That's the sort of thing the UN team might be interested in."

"You think?" He grinned and snapped his chewing gum.

"Yeah, I think."

"You should tell them," he said, "when Captain Dryson is done with 'em."

Buzzers sounded from within the belly of the Antonov, and, with a sustained whine of hydraulics, the aircraft's blue nose began to rotate up and over the cockpit, gradually exposing a cargo hold filled with equipment and boxy European land rovers. The trucks were painted white and stenciled with the UN lettering in black.

A lanky Marine officer and several civilians stood at the top of the Antonov's ramp. The Marine descended the ramp with the nose cone still rotating into the open position. Polly and Funkweed approached him.

"You must be the detachment from Bishop Unlimited," said the Marine officer. "The name is Captain Everett Dryson."

"Polly Foster. I'm from Rapid Response, not Bishop. It's an autonomous subsidiary."

"Still a subsidiary." Dryson exchanged a grin with Funkweed.

He shook Polly's hand assertively. He was tanned and self-assured. He wore a pistol in a shoulder holster. His long, plain face was unapologetic, his eyes unwavering beneath dark brows. His confidence, meant to calm, only rankled Polly further. Act like the boss, and people will treat you like the boss. She was familiar with the trick.

"You and your men need to leave," she said. "This was arranged through Colonel Ford's office and in cooperation with Third California Mountain. I am the security liaison for the UN inspectors. That was the deal."

"Deals like that are above my pay grade, Miss Foster. Even above Colonel Ford's."

"Admiral Haley?"

"Maybe even above him. This inspection deal wasn't with the company or the Army; it was with the United States government. Somebody way above me was worried that, respectfully, some folks here might not put the security of these interlopers at the top of the agenda."

So this was an ambush and an insult on top of that.

"It's understandable," he continued. "I'm sure everyone in Los Angeles has a lot on their minds. They don't need a babysitting job added to that. We'll take it from here."

The civilians were wandering out of the Antonov's belly and onto the runway. There were a lot of them, dressed in jackets and photographers' vests, bleary-eyed in the bright sunlight. Polly recognized a handful of them from the briefing documents Milo had given her.

"I am responsible for the safety of these people, and I don't want this to turn into a fight, Captain. Tell your men to stand down and back away from the aircraft. You can call in your helicopter and leave peacefully."

Polly made no move for her sidearm, but the threat was understood by Dryson and Funkweed. Their smiles disappeared. Their posture shifted. They were taking her seriously.

"I would seriously advise against trying to force the matter," said Dryson. "This aircraft is under my protection, and you need to step away."

"You don't have any dupes on your crew," said Polly. "No type twos?"

"No," said Dryson.

"That's too bad." Polly reached slowly and deliberately for the radio on her belt. "We come in pretty handy when the odds are hopeless."

Dryson smiled again, and the expression was pinch-lipped and humorless. He unfastened the strap securing his pistol in its holster. Sergeant Funkweed was now holding his carbine as if he intended to use it. Despite the threats, Polly raised the radio to her face and keyed the channel.

"I've asked the drivers to unload the vehicles." The words were hard-edged and came from a diminutive woman pushing her way past Funkweed. "I need you people to move. You're blocking the way."

Polly recognized her as the inspection team's leader, Dr. Robin Burns.

The details from the briefing files rattled through Polly's head. Burns was a Harvard-educated blood specialist, worked with Mayo and then assisted on pandemic studies for the CDC. A brush with death saw her enlisting her skills with the United Nations. Mid-forties, married, husband an avowed Communist working for the Chinese, two children living somewhere in the French Canadian enclave.

The formidable CV was matched to a woman not a crumb over five feet. Robin Burns was slim, naturally pretty in a delicate manner that seemed better suited for a life of leisure. She was obviously doing everything possible to ignore her own good looks. Her graying blond hair was swept back and tied. Instead of makeup she wore a pack strapped to her shoulders that bulged with equipment, and she wore sensors and sample equipment on her belt. Fists on hips, she swept her harsh glare over Polly, Captain Dryson, and Sergeant Funkweed.

"Settle it," said Dr. Burns. "I want to do the best possible job in the least amount of time, and I don't need your cock-waving getting in my way."

"Ma'am." Captain Dryson saluted her respectfully.

"Don't salute me, you fascist." She gestured to a caramel-skinned giant of a man wearing a blue uniform picking his way through the aircraft's formidable luggage. "Get your Marines, and help Rukundo and the others load up the trucks."

Dryson complied enthusiastically, marshaling his men and joining the UN scientists in packing up the white land rovers. That left Polly staring down Dr. Burns.

"You're from the company." Dr. Burns spoke with an indistinct, Midwestern American accent. "Foster, was it? I was told that to get access to your facilities, we need to cooperate—catch more flies with honey, that sort of thing. I'm not much of a honey sort of gal. I apologize in advance for my brusqueness, and I hope you understand, for this job to be finished, I need full access."

"I will do my best," said Polly.

"And I hope that's good enough. If it isn't, I might have to rely on these jarheads. Captain Dryson expressed his eagerness to make sure we get everything we need."

Dryson and his Marines assisted Rukundo and the crew of the Antonov in loading up the land rovers. Polly allowed the equipment to be carried in the UN vehicles and insisted the scientists ride in her security vans. Dr. Burns overcame her resistance to the idea in a show of magnanimity.

Polly attempted to familiarize herself with the UN team as quickly as possible. There was Dr. Burns, serving as the team leader, an Indian pathologist named Dr. Nandy, and a friendly, almost flirtatious, botanist named Dr. Madeleine Roux. Polly had little luck remembering the names of the others even though she'd read them from the briefing documents.

There were more than twenty scientists in all and half again as many technicians, drivers, and Rukundo, their internal security expert. He looked to be in his early thirties. Perhaps because of his great stature and calm demeanor the scientists and even Dr. Burns deferred to him. His placid demeanor amid the nagging scientists reminded Polly of a tree being fought over by squirrels.

When the lengthy introductions had been finished, one man remained unidentified. He was skulking in the background, near the land rovers, fiddling with long cases of yellow plastic.

"Who is that?" asked Polly.

"That is Mr. Sokov."

Konstantin Sokov was a last-minute addition to the debriefing list. A "biological archivist," Mr. Sokov was also a Soviet. Milo had not even included a photograph.

In the flesh, Sokov was perfectly Russian. He possessed a heavy brow and a high forehead exaggerated by his receding, oiled hairline. It was difficult to determine his age. Polly thought anywhere from thirty to fifty. He wore eyeglasses in heavy black frames. The prescription made his blue eyes enormous.

"Good to meet you, Polly Foster." He spoke with a thick accent. "It is very beautiful to be here today. I look forward to good expedition."

"Have you been to America before?" asked Polly.

Konstantin's answer was an uneasy laugh and a shake of his head. He retreated to the aircraft to oversee the loading of his sample cases. The land rovers, five in all, emerged from the Antonov's belly weighed down with equipment and personal baggage. The uniformed drivers were under Rukundo's supervision. He marshaled the UN vehicles into an idling row, each land rover stuffed to the windows with duffels and equipment cases.

"Good?" he asked Polly.

"That will work fine." She motioned for her vans to join the formation.

Rukundo insisted on riding in the security van with Dr. Burns. Polly wanted Konstantin Sokov in her van as well, and he ducked his head and clambered dutifully into the backseat. Captain Dryson offered her no choice and rode beside her, a carbine resting between his boots in the vehicle's foot well. The other scientists were distributed, along with an uncomfortable mixture of Marines, among the remaining security vans.

The convoy of vans and UN vehicles departed LAX without further incident. Milo's office had prepared a specific itinerary for the arrival, and the first stop was a check-in at the desolate UN offices in Redondo Beach. They were close enough to the cordon to hear the Army trucks and close enough to the edges of Creeptown to smell the refuse.

The haunted remainder of the local UN staff was in a rush to leave, saying their hellos and good-byes in the same sentence and fleeing in an assortment of overloaded vehicles. The borderline panic clearly unnerved the visiting UN scientists. Dr. Burns was given keys to the offices, only to discover that everything, even the fixtures, had been stripped out and looted by the fleeing staff.

"We can provide you with office space on-site," said Polly.

Her reassurance did little to ease the growing tension among the scientists. There were mutterings of abandonment by the UN. Second thoughts were given voice. One man swept a spore detector of unfamiliar design around the office. The device trilled and flashed red, and he cried out in alarm, "Contamination! Twenty-five P-P-M!"

The scientists inside the office building spilled out into the parking lot and began throwing open the doors of their vehicles. In a panic, they opened emergency cases, spilling medical equipment into the parking lot as they grabbed for gas masks and hoods. Polly checked the small fob detector clipped to her belt. It wasn't even showing yellow.

"Your equipment is too sensitive," said Polly.

"All right, calm down." Dr. Burns raised her voice to be heard over the commotion. "Everybody! We all knew some level of exposure was a guarantee. Unless some of you have traumatic, gaping injuries, you are well below the danger threshold of three hundred. Be smart, and you should be safe."

"*Should* be? You *should* have distributed masks at the airport." The UN scientist who'd complained was a stout, pale man, and he spoke with an Irish brogue. His broad face and curly mop of hair disappeared beneath the black rubber of a hooded mask. He said something else, but it was too muffled by the canister filter to be heard.

A few of the others followed his example. The remainder, still holding masks and hoods, in the process of opening cases, looked to Dr. Burns indecisively. Dryson, Funkweed, and the other Marines watched the drama unfold and did not react. Their gas equipment remained stowed in the packs around their waists.

Dr. Burns took the detector from the man who originally discovered the contamination and waved it in the air like a dowsing wand. She followed the invisible trail of spores to a greasy smear on the walkway in front of the office building. The detector was trilling sharply.

"It reads over one hundred P-P-M here," she said, and she leaned her face down near the smear. "It's nothing. Some dropped food or a dead animal. I'm breathing it in, and nothing adverse is happening to me. We're in no danger from these readings."

Her demonstration seemed to calm the scientists. Even the Irishman grudgingly shucked off the gas hood. He started to return it to the case, but Dr. Burns stopped him.

"No, you were right, Liam. We should distribute the gas equipment to everyone now so that if we have a real emergency, we will be prepared." She saluted the scientist. The foam-packed, commercial gas equipment was quickly distributed to the scientists and their drivers. Rukundo reminded those who needed help how to put on the gas mask and tighten its straps. Polly joined Dr. Burns near the greasy smear with the high readings.

"You handled that well. We can get them loaded, and I'll show you to your hotel."

"No, I want to get started now," said Dr. Burns.

"Fine," said Polly. "I will distribute copies of the itinerary prepared for this afternoon, and we can start on it now."

Dr. Burns walked with Polly over to one of the open land rovers and popped open the lid of a medical kit. It was packed with sample tubes, gauze, forceps, sterilizing foams, and chlorine spray known to neutralize the spores if applied directly. Dr. Burns plucked a syringe from the shaped tray of the medical container.

"I researched you when I heard you were going to be our liaison. Most of you duplicates are slippery, hard to single out one from the other unless you want it that way, but you were recently involved in a spore-related incident."

The frost of anxiety crept up Polly's back and raised gooseflesh on her arms. Her heart thudded wildly. How could this woman know about what had happened in Bad Tower? Not even the news media had managed to uncover those events, and Milo had given her strict instructions—menacingly strict—to keep quiet about the events of that day.

"I'm, uh, not sure what you mean," said Polly.

"Your medical records were submitted to the United Nations at my request. You were recently treated for spore contamination. I realize the spore is not lethal to your kind, that you produce antibodies we can hopefully isolate to develop a treatment, so you must have been exposed to massive amounts if you required hospitalization."

"Yes," said Polly. "I was caught in a spore storm. The streets went white."

"Yes, I've seen footage of spore storm events. My hope is that since you survived such a massive dose, your body might be producing very high levels of the antibody. I would actually like to begin our inspection with you, Miss Foster. A full medical exam would be nice once we are situated, but for now, a blood sample would be very helpful."

Polly hesitated. Dr. Burns fixed her with an unwavering stare. Aware that the exchange was being watched by Captain Dryson, Polly rolled up her sleeve and offered her arm to Dr. Burns.

■ ■ ■

About a third of a hamburger. Nine French fries. A napkin smeared with congealed ketchup. And, what was that, a cockroach? No, a piece of fried crust from an unidentified pastry. Casper laid the garbage picnic out on the table of a cardboard box. Lenin, formerly Ringo, watched the ritual with apparent interest, cocking his shaggy head with each rearrangement of Swiftee Burger refuse.

"The only way I'm going to be able to choke this down," said Casper, "is if you stop staring at me."

He threw a French fry past Lenin's head to distract the dog. Lenin whipped his muzzle to the side and caught the thrown nugget in his jaws, swallowing it without chewing.

"Not bad. Try this one."

Casper threw the fry much higher and with greater force. The shape of the potato was ill-suited to a breaking fastball, so he put a lot of muscle into the throw to overcome the aerodynamics. It was gone before he even knew which way it was going. Lenin dropped to the dusty ground and licked his chops.

"You should go out for the Yankees, kid."

Mentioning a baseball team was an unpleasant reminder of all the years he'd spent living as a brain-scrambled stiff down in the bowels of the Pit. Did the Yankees still play ball? Who won the World Series in '51? Hell, who won it in '91?

He threw Lenin a last fry and shoveled the remainder into his own mouth. They were cold and greasy. He swallowed them in one unpleasant gulp and hoped to keep them down. The dog was a natural catcher; maybe he could start a sideshow act at a circus, if those still existed. He stuffed the burger down his gullet—even worse than the fries—and wiped somebody's old dish towel across his lips.

Casper was aimless. He'd spent time in his past lives as a drifter, hopping trains and looking for work in faraway towns. That was different. There was nowhere to go in this world. His purpose, felt so keenly up until the gaping hole in his memory, was gone. He sprawled listlessly on cardboard in the empty lot, down behind the barbed-wire brambles of a few dead bushes, and he listened to the city beginning to move around him.

There was still traffic and commerce, even though it felt like the whole place was about to be bombed. The distant warble of a siren now and then added to that atmosphere. The Army trucks and the occasional tank made him think the bombing might have already begun.

Casper tried to reconnect. He sought out his old house in Hawthorne but the neighborhood was replaced with garish retail outlets long since taken over by the military to use as staging areas. The LAPD headquarters he used to work in was unrecognizably modernized and fortified. He tried to find out more of what became of Lynn, but the newspapers and county archives were no longer operating. Just as well. He feared the details might drive him to further despair.

Even Ciro's was gone, replaced with a plaza and a statue of men standing atop a tank commemorating THE BATTLE OF THE RÍO TLALNEPANTLA. FEBRUARY 19, 1978. He read the inscription. *The 9th US Armored Division and 4th California Volunteer Infantry Division battled pro-communist forces for control of the bridges over the Rio Tlalnepantla. Six hundred and fourteen brave Americans gave their lives that day to protect Democracy and crush the last strongholds of the illegitimate Mexican dictator Valentín Campa Salazar and his revolutionary movement.*

The more he learned about this world, the less he liked it. Each day he ended up right back where he started: alone, homeless, sprawled on a piece of cardboard, waiting to draw flies.

The sky, colorless and bright, was a blank sheet in the typewriter for him to bang out his last note to the world. Suicide being a futile pursuit, he discussed it openly and often with his canine companion.

"Maybe I ought to jump in front of a bus," he said to Lenin, who remained sitting by his side. "They're bigger now. Did you see those things? Bet those big wheels would turn me into paste."

He wanted a drink. A real belt in the guts. Something better than the dregs of beers he found in the same Dumpster as the hamburger.

"Nah, if they swerve, maybe they'd just hit my legs, crush 'em up. Don't think I could stand that. I'll just go up to one of those Army pukes who put hands on the policewoman. Tell him he shits sideways, and see if he'll plug me full of holes."

Casper scratched the dog's head and looked into its red eyes flecked with black.

"No, you're right. I'm not the sort of guy who offs himself. Not unless it'll save him a plane ticket." He felt around in his pockets for the chapbook that was in the emergency kit Polly Foster had given him. It was creased in the middle from the way he'd been bending it the night before while trying to use a discarded tire as a toilet.

" 'Chapter three.' " He read aloud, picking up where he'd left off. " 'Social Changes.' I hope this one is better than the map chapter. Whatever happened to 'walk softly and carry a big stick,' right? Now we just club everyone over the head with it."

Lenin curled up and tucked his muzzle against his tail. His position allowed him to continue to stare at Casper.

" 'The United States of America has undergone many changes since your incarceration began, fundamental alterations to the fabric of our society. All races, without exception, are viewed as equal and permitted to intermarry with whites.' Well that's different, right?"

Casper cleared his throat.

" 'Segregated facilities have been abolished since the Social Justice Act of 1981. Duplicates have enjoyed the right to publically marry with non-duplicates since the

Affirmation of Rights Act of 1985. As of 1997, clade typing—delineations of duplicates based on behavioral and other factors—is featured on the drivers' licenses of
fifty-three of the states and the Oaxaca and Yucatan Territories.'"

He lowered the book from his face, intending to say something to Lenin. Instead,
he spotted a very attractive type three walking on the nearby sidewalk. She was
physically different from Veronica or from the cop woman, Polly Foster. She had
more bounce to her step, lighter hair, ridiculously big breasts, and a face reshaped by
surgery or some other means, yet she was still the same woman. The same legs, he
realized. She reminded him of a cartoon version of Annie.

Casper whistled appreciatively. The woman, seeing him as a leering derelict lying
on cardboard, cinched her purse a little tighter under her arm and hurried away.
Casper sighed and let the book fall into his lap.

"Looks like I've lost my charm," Casper said melodramatically. "Nothing to do
now but curl up and die. Maybe I could find some rat poison to chew on."

He drew the blanket from St. Philomena's over his head in hopeless jest. The
sounds of the city grew very quiet. More quiet than they should have.

"Casper Cord."

The voice was distant, its intonation flat. It was the hiss of wind-stirred leaves
echoing in a dead canyon.

"Casper Cord." Louder, the shape of the words assumed an improbable complexity. A multitude of tiny brushes painting the words upon a canvas. "Casper Cord.
Prepare yourself. It is almost upon you."

Casper tore the blanket from his face. He intended to confront the ominous
speaker but was not sure what he would find waiting for him.

Horns on the nearby streets as traffic continued to move. A car weighed down
with luggage and too many passengers motored past the lot, its engine chugging
under protest and its undercarriage scraping the street. A helicopter sounded in the
sky. There were no pedestrians. No one within earshot.

No one there at all.

Except the dog.

■   ■   ■

The Pool had given birth to a giant. It lay facedown with its long arms at its sides,
still draped in the clotted membrane of its birth envelope. It was something like a
man but three times as large, flesh soft and purpling as if in an advanced state of
decay, shoulders, back, and limbs bulging with muscles.

The length of its arms and the proportions of its body reminded Wesley Bishop
of a gorilla, but its bald head was comparatively tiny. It was as small as a normal
man's head, a pallid egg of flesh traced with livid capillaries that showed through the
remains of its birth cowl.

"Have you ever pulled up a freak as big as this?" asked Bishop.

The man he asked was an unusual type one with graying hair and an unkempt beard that fitted his greasy workman's coverall. The name GRINCH was embroidered over his breast.

"Not alive. It took two of the cranes to haul it up," said the bearded man. "It was still thrashing around a little bit. Trying to breathe. Lucky it wasn't more alive, I guess. Looks like it could have done some damage."

"Why did they bring you in?"

"They wanted somebody from Anomalies to take a look and tell them what to do. I was going to contact the Gardeners—"

"No. You did the right thing calling me first." Bishop covered his nose and mouth with the perfumed handkerchief to keep out the stench of the decaying giant. "So what do we do?"

The type one in the coveralls shrugged his bony shoulders.

"Very helpful," said Bishop. "Have them turn it over. I want to see its face."

Grinch called up to the crane operators to rotate the giant onto its back. Men from the maintenance crew took hold of the dangling hook blocks and dragged the lines over to the prostrate giant. They secured lifting slings around and beneath the tree-trunk width of one of the giant's arms and one of its legs.

At a signal from the floor the winching commenced, and motors in the cranes began to whine. The giant's arm rose awkwardly backward, and the giant began to turn. Its other arm slid beneath the massive torso. The movement stopped, and the crane winches grew louder as they fought to overcome the resistance. It seemed the cranes were outmatched until a muffled boom of dislocating bone echoed through the vault, and the arm slid beneath the turning corpse.

The giant's body crossed over the fulcrum of the crane, and gravity carried it the rest of the way onto its back. The corpse flopped over with a jarring impact that shook the vault. The cranes gently slackened the cables holding its arm and leg upright until they settled onto the floor as well.

Bishop, Grinch, and a few of the bolder men and women from the maintenance crew approached the giant's head. It had only surfaced from the Pool in recent hours, and yet the smell of decay was overpowering. The barrel of its chest was banded with muscles, but the skin was falling away, slipping off the muscle and bone like wet cloth, peeling to the floor in glistening strips. There was a soft hiss audible as they approached. Faint tendrils of vapor rose from its flesh as if it were cooking.

"It is disintegrating," said Bishop. "The air in the vault is reacting with its flesh."

"That smoke could be poisonous," said Grinch.

Bishop continued closer to the giant, his footsteps splashing through the pool of viscous fluid surrounding the creature. The others followed a few wary steps behind him. The smell permeated the cloth Bishop held over nose and mouth and set his eyes to watering. It was the miasma of ocean rot, of strange, deep things on stranger shores.

The maintenance crew was very quiet as Bishop crossed the last few paces to the giant's head. Even the Pool, so tumultuous of late, was calm beneath their feet.

The giant's shoulders and back were so massive and its head so small that the back of its head, though dangling, did not touch the floor of the vault. The immense beast's physiology was less similar to a man's than it at first seemed. The arms were jointed only once at the elbow, with no wrists and very crude hands. The sloughing flesh revealed slabs of withering muscles far more numerous than a man's body might possess. The legs were powerful to be sure but were dwarfed by the arms. The creature possessed no visible genitalia between those legs. The face was dark, its features concealed by the membrane of the cowl.

Bishop crouched beside the hillock of its shoulder, intent on removing the cowl covering its head.

"Don't touch it," said Grinch.

"Quiet." Bishop flexed his hand and reached for the cowl. He pinched the yielding husk between thumb and index finger and lifted it slowly from the beast's face. The suction released, and the creature's visage was unveiled.

Bishop's stomach lurched at the sight. A gasp rose from the maintenance crew, and a few of their number backed away.

The flesh of the giant's face was gray-black and covered in stiff bristles. Two bulbous black eyes dominated the upper half of its face. Several smaller eyes were located on either side of its head and in a row of four beneath the large, domed main eyes. A pair of segmented chelicerae, like those of a venomous spider, dangled from the lower half of the giant's face. Black fangs, big as knives, tipped each grotesque limb and curved inward to rest against the creature's disintegrating chest.

Bishop furrowed his brow and studied the horrible face. Revolting though it was, he did recognize something of it. There was a long-ago dream, forgotten until this moment, of creatures like this, stitched and restitched, howling as they charged across a twilit battlefield zippered with trenches, slagged emplacements, and shell-pocked bunkers.

He imagined this muscular giant among them, moving at great speed, bellowing from its arachnid mouth as it charged and leaped over earthworks, taking hold of beams of tilted steel and brachiating through the tangled frame of a ruined fortification. He was caught in the midst of a savage battle between these creatures.

Mortars thundered through the air and shook the earth. He heard the pop and whoosh of poison canisters, smelled the acrid purple gas that crept across the trenches. The fighting giants became ghosts moving silently through the clouds of poison. He felt the sudden oven heat of invisible rays sweeping through the air, passing overhead, and incinerating whatever they touched.

A giant loomed above him, straddling the trench where he emerged from a chugging culvert of white liquid. It peered down at him curiously, its eyes polished marbles of black, its huge chest heaving beneath a uniform of bloodied rags. It reached down into the muck for him, its hand large enough to enclose his chest.

In a rush of smoke, vaporizing sinews, and popping, cooked bones it was split in half by a heat ray, its entrails spilling out, its sectioned body flopping into the trench all around him. The giant yet lived. A smoldering mound of flesh dragged itself toward him with one arm. It screamed at him, its face split open and drooling green-black fluids. Bishop screamed in answer and could not draw breath. He looked away, looked away and cradled the bottom of the trench. He suffocated in the stifling air, his skin smoldering and effervescing like that of the dead giant.

"Do you recognize this thing?" asked Grinch.

The question dragged him back to the vault, to the rot-softened face of this dead thing. No. He could not be sure. Increasingly he believed that these moments, creeping back into his memory, were real events occurring on the other side of distant Pools, distant and fading death dreams across the trunk space, indistinguishable from lies conjured by his desires. Or maybe they were nothing. Maybe just his fear creating a fiction of this monstrosity and his knowledge of the Westward capsules.

He discarded the fleshy membrane of the cowl and turned to confront the type one from Anomalies.

"It's just another one of your freaks," said Bishop. "Maybe a bit bigger than usual. Haul it—"

Grinch shouted a wordless warning. Bishop half turned in time to see the decaying paw of the giant reaching for him. It caught him around his chest and squeezed hard enough that he felt his ribs compress. He was dimly aware of flying. There was a hard landing. Hard enough to hurt, not hard enough to do any lasting damage.

The giant howled and was up and moving around the vault. Men and women screamed, first in terror and then in agony. There was a sound like tearing cloth that Bishop later discovered was the shredding coveralls of workmen as they were pulled apart by the giant. One of the cranes was felled with a resounding crash.

When Milo and his Gardeners finally arrived, they found the giant once again, and finally, deceased. Having rampaged through the maintenance vault, it had spent its final moments beating uselessly on a hatch separating the vault from a surface access tunnel. Grinch and a few workmen survived, and Bishop, somehow un-harmed, was found buried in a heap of entrails. Gardeners helped him up from the grisly debris.

"Am I alive?" asked Bishop, wiping gore from his face.

"You are, sir," said one of Milo's white-haired clade brothers. "Shall I get you a doctor?"

Bishop was already walking away, slopping loops of someone's intestines from his shoulders. His hair was stuck flat with blood. He stopped and looked at his shaking hands.

"Patrice," he said to no one in particular. "I need pills."

■ ■ ■

Polly took them where she was supposed to take them. She drove them downtown and paraded them through the Enhanced Care facility managed and operated by Bishop's pharmaceutical subsidiaries. They sat through brain-numbing videos describing the facility and then witnessed, firsthand, the advanced procedures being used to save victims of the spores.

The UN team asked questions of their appointed tour guide, Dr. Chandrasekar, a portly Indian physician in a white coat. He wore thick glasses, and his face was defined by angular lips and pronounced jowls that belied his youth.

"Where do you get these patients?" asked Dr. Roux.

"What are the survival rates for your treatments?" asked a dark-skinned African UN doctor.

"May we view the remains of the deceased?" asked the pathologist, Dr. Nandy.

Dr. Chandrasekar answered the questions deftly. When he could provide a positive answer that reflected well on Bishop, he brought attention to it. When a line of inquiry threatened to expose an unpleasant truth, or one of the scientists demanded more evidence than he was providing, Dr. Chandrasekar relied on his clearly honed public-relations skills to deflect their questions and distract them with additional information. The UN team was provided with storage boxes filled with medical records, test results, and descriptions of the success or failure of various treatments.

"It will take year to read this," said Konstantin Sokov. "Eh . . . maybe ten year."

Dr. Burns watched from the back of the tour group, glowering at Polly when their eyes met, clearly dissatisfied with the stage-managed introduction. Near the end of the tour Dr. Burns took Polly by the elbow and escorted her into the women's restroom. Once inside, she wheeled on Polly, jabbing her fingertip into Polly's sternum.

"This production does not satisfy the agreement," said Dr. Burns.

"I heard some very effective treatments described," said Polly. "You met the little girl who was cured by—"

"I met one little girl out of how many?" Dr. Burns folded her arms across her chest. "Just giving me a clear and current infection rate would be more helpful than the past two hours."

"I am taking you places that I was told would be helpful."

"Told by whom?" Dr. Burns did not wait for Polly to answer. "This is a field study, Miss Foster. An inspection cannot be led around by its nose, and our results will not be crafted by such obvious public- relations efforts."

Polly sighed and said, "What do you want from me?"

"A chance to get at the truth," said Dr. Burns.

Their next stop was even less satisfactory.

Reclaimed park, read the item on Polly's itinerary. The park was located three blocks off the walled ramparts of the I-10, on La Cienega in Culver City. The vans and UN vehicles parked in a line along a street shaded by living trees. The park comprised a few acres of healthy vegetation including grass, lush trees, and planters full to bursting with vivid flowers.

"Just three weeks ago this park was the site of several casualties and a serious spore storm," said Polly as she walked the UN team into the bucolic park. "There are photographs in your packet of the storm. As you can see, the park was saved from destruction and serves the community once more."

"Where is community?" asked Konstantin Sokov.

Polly was stymied. It was a fair question. The park was empty, and the surrounding businesses, although nice, were open and vacant or, more often, were shuttered. The situation deteriorated quickly. One scientist realized the green grass was freshly sodded. Dr. Nandy pointed out that the trees were larger in the original photograph.

Liam, the paranoid man from before, discovered the most damning evidence. Black scoring was apparent in the cracks between the paving stones of the park's walking path. Whoever had power-washed the stones had not completely scrubbed the proof that fire had been used to clean out the park.

"And we're supposed to be impressed by Bishop's scorched-earth policy?" asked Liam.

Dryson and his Marines had remained respectfully separate from the scientists, observing their actions and watching for danger. Dryson clearly enjoyed watching Polly struggle.

Annoyed by the itinerary's failed attempts to mislead, Polly corralled the scientists back into the vans and started the convoy moving again.

Their hotel was downtown, atop Bunker Hill in the former Palisades Hotel building. When the pandemics made convention-going in Los Angeles unfeasible, Bishop bought the luxury hotel and had it renovated to his own tastes. The twenty-story tower was refurbished in austere, dark, ultra-modernism, with recessed lighting, echoing spaces, and brutalist fixtures visible through its façade of smoked glass.

The staff was mostly duplicates with an apparent dress code of pale skin and severe hair styles. The concierge, a young type one with an arrow of hair atop his shaved head, sported an intricate facial tattoo depicting stylized winds. The rooms were on the second floor, facing north toward the dreary military emplacements in the Hollywood Hills. They were well-appointed in the European fashion.

Hotel porters and the drivers began unloading and hauling luggage and personal equipment from the trucks and into the hotel. The scientists became preoccupied with directing their own belongings to the correct room. The hallway was packed with people moving in different directions. Frayed nerves and a long flight soon gave way to shouting.

Dryson and his Marines, intending to camp in the lobby, nevertheless entered and searched each of the rooms. Polly watched them work, curious as to their intention. Were they expecting a firefight?

"Miss Foster." It was Dr. Roux. "I need to speak to you."

The doctor approached her through the twisting flow of porters and scientists. The busy confines of the hall forced her close to Polly. The Frenchwoman seemed too young to be a doctor. She was beautiful, her curly auburn hair glamorous, her utilitarian clothing worn in a complimentary fashion. Her smile was untouched by the grind of the day.

"Uh." Dr. Roux's closeness and gaze made Polly uncomfortable. "Yes, of course, we can go down to the lobby."

"Just there." Dr. Roux gestured to the door of one of the rooms. "We can speak privately in there."

Dr. Roux's fingers brushed against the back of Polly's hand. She followed Dr. Roux but remained wary of the woman's intent. She was stopped in the doorway of the hotel room by someone calling out to her.

"Hey! Miss Foster!" It was Liam. "What the hell are you on about? We need to have it out. You're wasting our time."

"We wanted to talk." Dr. Burns appeared from the flow of porters. "In here is fine."

She chased Polly into the room and seemed surprised to discover Dr. Roux there as well.

"Madeleine." Dr. Burns addressed Dr. Roux. "I need to have a few words with Miss Foster. If you could, take Dr. Cochrane down to the lobby and see if you can get everyone situated with meals. I'm sure they would appreciate that."

Dr. Roux creased her lips to hold back any objection. She nodded curtly and departed with her arm hooked to the reluctant Dr. Liam Cochrane's elbow. Dr. Burns shut and locked the door behind them.

"I approached this from the wrong direction with you," said Dr. Burns. "You're trying to do your job and protect your employer—I understand that. It's what anyone would do in your position. I'm not one of the conspiracy theorists who believe duplicates are part of some hive mind. I've worked and been friends with several over the course of my career. There are duplicates working with the United Nations."

"We get around," said Polly.

"Yes, that's rather the point, isn't it? As you have multiplied and distributed yourselves globally, you have brought with you waves of pandemics to which you are immune but native populations are not. This latest, these spores and their accompanying . . . habitat? Ecosystem? This is more troubling. And that is why we are here."

"I understand that," said Polly.

"I hope so. We are here to save lives, perhaps millions of them. We are not here to embarrass Mr. Bishop or any of his subsidiary entities."

"I said I get it." Polly was growing tired of the lectures. "And I said I would do what I can to help. Anything within my power."

"Get me inside." Dr. Burns spoke quietly.

"We have lab facilities in the Pit. I will take you there tomorrow."

"No." Dr. Burns waved her hand to dismiss the offer. "We need to see how your process works. I have read that you are generated from a liquid medium and—"

"That is off-limits even to me."

The Gardeners tightly controlled access to the Pool itself. Even the maintenance teams were forbidden from getting any closer to the surface than the maintenance vault above the Pool.

"If we could take samples of the medium, it might unlock every one of these mysterious diseases. Ten minutes. You do not even need to allow all of us inside, just myself and Dr. Nandy."

"No." Polly started toward the door. Dr. Burns grabbed her wrist and turned her back.

"Get us to the Fane."

The use of the word shocked Polly. The Fane was a rumor even among the duplicates, presumed to exist but never seen. She had never imagined she would hear it mentioned by a flake.

"That . . . what you're talking about is not real." Polly's laughter concealed her unease. "I can't take you somewhere that doesn't exist."

She opened the door and set foot into the din of the bustling hall, nearly bumping into Captain Dryson in the process. The taciturn Marine was joined by Sergeant Funkweed. Dryson was holding a small cardboard box against his chest. It rattled when he shook it and held it out to Polly. It was mostly empty, but the bottom was a tangle of wires and transistors.

"In the telephone receivers, in lamps, stitched into pillows," said Dryson. "I think we found them all. I'm sorry you won't be able to snoop on these people's personal communications any longer."

COMINTERCEPT – TELEPHONE - NOENCRYPT - GREEN LABEL

06/30/06 - 06:46:22 PST - Complete Machine Transcription

Subjects: Dr. Robin Burns <Robin> (SSO subject, LARC, USA), Clayton Burns <Clay> (son, Seattle, WA), Evelyn Burns <Eve> (daughter, Seattle, WA)

<Eve> Hi! Mommy, we had eggs.

<Robin> The real kind?

<Eve> From a chicken. They have all sorts of animals here, and Mr. Treacher lets us pet them.

<Robin> Is Mr. Treacher nice?

<Eve> He's all right. He sorta smells like Daddy's shoes. He said we can do a play this weekend.

<Robin> Are there other kids?

\<Eve\> There are a bunch. And they all speak English! One girl named Dorothy has all of the Little Critters including the gold and silver.

\<Robin\> What's that?

\<Eve\> Little Critters. Santa gave me the zoo set for Christmas.

\<Robin\> Oh, yes, with the tiger and the monkeys.

\<Eve\> That's right, and those are all back home, but I brought Horus the Hippo and Boris the Bear. Aaaand . . . I forgot what I was going to say . . . because of the helicopter.

\<Robin\> That's okay, sweetie.

\<Eve\> There is a bubble on the roof, and I can see a helicopter landing, and it has two spinny things. It's really, really neat, and I want you to see it.

\<Robin\> I will soon. I have to finish my work here, and then I can come get you, and we can go home.

\<Eve\> Clay wants to talk to you.

\<Robin\> Okay, bye-bye, Evie. I love you.

\<Eve\> Love you too!

\<Clay\> Hey.

\<Robin\> Hey yourself. How are you doing?

\<Clay\> You mean how am I doing being dragged away from my friends in the middle of the summer and stuck at a petting zoo full of six-year-olds? I'm doing great.

\<Robin\> I'm glad to hear you haven't changed your attitude.

\<Clay\> When we get home, can I get a metro bike? Franky and Jean have one.

\<Robin\> A motorbike? We'll talk about it when I come get you.

\<Clay\> The news is pretty messed up.

\<Robin\> What's going on is serious.

\<Clay\> Are they aliens?

\<Robin\> They're alien species, not space aliens. It's just a phrase. No spaceship.

\<Clay\> One of the ladies who works here was crying this morning.

\<Robin\> It'll be all right. I promise.

\<Clay\> [inaudible]

\<Robin\> You're going to upset your sister. I need you to be an adult right now.

\<Clay\> I . . . okay, Mom.

\<Robin\> I need to go now, honey.

\<Clay\> Can I call you tonight?

\<Robin\> I will call you when I can.

\<Clay\> I love you, Mom.

\<Robin\> I love you [unintelligible]

CHAPTER SEVEN

■ ■ ■

Polly was drawn from the deck of Chico's boat, moored in the crystalline blue waters off the Playa Los Algadones, by the whine of the sirens. Coming awake in her gray apartment, she realized the sound was not the distant muezzin call of nightmares. These sirens were close, though the howl was oddly muffled.

She clambered barefoot from bed. Umbral light filtered through the curtains, and wind rattled the windowpanes facing the street. She staggered to the largest picture window and drew back the diaphanous curtains.

Her window was dark with the mass of the spore grass sprouting from its surface. A network of vermicular roots crisscrossed the glass up the sides of the window frame and burrowed into the mortar between bricks. These roots supported dense thickets of white leaflike plants. In the gaps between tufts of spore grass the street was visible as a desolate snow globe.

Dead trees, cars, streets, buildings, and even telephone wires and chain-link fences were coated in the white growth. It was a living, gently moving carpet, growing over every surface. A neglected mailbox crumpled suddenly beneath its weight. She watched as the grass crept slowly up the sides of the building across the street, covered a street lamp, as roots spilled out and squirmed up to the cornices above her window. Spores circulated in the air, swirling and rising and falling like snow. The siren howled on, defiant, slowly disappearing into a beard of spore grass dangling from the electric transformer.

The spore grass was not the only thing growing. In shaded corners and from beneath garbage heaped in an abandoned lot, slender white stalks sprouted above the spore grass, at the tip of each swaying frond a dark bud no larger than a pea, soon to blossom and grow into luminous blue fruit. She tamped down the fearful memories that came rushing up.

Polly retreated from the window. She remembered Mrs. Valdez, alone in her apartment, sleeping with the window open. The imagined plight of Polly's neighbor gave her a proactive way to focus her thoughts.

"Mrs. Valdez!" She bounded down the stairs to the elderly woman's apartment. "Mrs. Valdez! You need to come out."

The door was locked. She beat the heels of her hands against the door and screamed for the old woman until her throat hurt. There was no answer. If only she had the ram Fetch had used to break open that door in Bad Tower. She used her shoulder instead, running it into the door again and again. It hurt, but at last the upper hinge broke loose, and she was able to kick out the lower hinge. The door fell into the apartment with a crash of breaking glass.

"Are you okay Mrs. Valdez? It's Polly! It's—"

The window was open in the cluttered main room of the apartment. Spore grass was growing over tables and chairs, across the carpeting, over light fixtures, up and over the many precious photographs of Mrs. Valdez and her family and to the ceiling. White stalks tipped with buds grew from a bowl of candy as if placed there in decoration. The sweet, fleshy scent of the spores was overpowering. Polly covered her face with her nightshirt to keep from gagging.

The spore grass blurred the divisions between rooms, consuming the natural lines of the apartment in its homogenous mass. It struggled to grow more than a foot onto the floor of the kitchen, but thick tufts sprouted from open cabinets, filled the sink, and covered the ceiling with tiny leaves. The hallway leading to the bedrooms was dark. It was damp and plaint beneath Polly's feet.

"Mrs. Valdez?"

The door to the bedroom was ajar. A TV was playing a cartoon, casting shifting blue light over the unmade bed and unkempt floor. The spore grass was growing intermittently. It encircled the television, reaching down to border the screen and dripping from the dials. The bedspread was dark with blood. The spore grass was growing visibly across it, unfurling pale threads and creeping up them like frost, reinforcing the treads with more, creating a solid mesh of underlying roots for the dense fungus that would soon follow.

There was a sound from the bathroom. A sound like shifting, wet fabric followed by a thunk. The door was closed, the crack at its base clogged with more of the growth.

"Mrs. Valdez, are you in there?"

A weak voice answered her.

"I can't hear you, Mrs. Valdez. You need to come out of there. We need to get you somewhere safe."

Polly's shoulder was hurting after breaking through the front door. She did not know if she had it in her to smash through another door. If it came down to it, though, she would find out rather than leave her neighbor to die in the bathroom.

"Please, open the door."

"Go away," the voice faintly gurgled. "Go away, Miss Polly."

"If you're infected with the spores, it's okay; they can remove them." She thought back to the little girl cured at Bishop's Potemkin hospital. "There are treatments that work. Please open the door."

Liquid sloshed, and a groan echoed through the bathroom. Wet cloth slapped against the tiles. She imagined Mrs. Valdez heaving herself, fully clothed, from the bathtub. Instead of the sound of the turning doorknob, there followed a loud, organic ratcheting sound and a pained cry.

"No, no, please, Jesus," said Mrs. Valdez, her voice wet with fluid. "*Dios me libre*."

There was no further answer, so Polly began to kick the foot of the door. It was not so sturdy as the front door, and the lock tore out of the plywood frame. The door only opened inward a few inches before colliding with something soft. It was dark and smelled of candle smoke and human filth. The light of the cartoon on the television spilled into the bathroom, living in the mirror and revealing the long-expired prayer candles covering the countertop.

"Stay back," said Mrs. Valdez, heaving herself into the darkness of the bathtub.

Polly switched on the overhead light, and it spilled through the stained drum of the fixture as murky red. The tiles of the bathroom were smeared with blood, the toilet heaped with red-black filth and draped with torn clothing.

Mrs. Valdez was an unrecognizable horror inhabiting the bathtub. She was bloated to three times her stout frame, her body split open as if burst from inside, naked flesh rancid with blood and sores and livid stretch marks. Her inner meat— clotted yellow fat and scabrous muscle and even organs—lay exposed beneath the useless flaps of her skin. She wallowed in a tub of excrement and blood, her eyes black with renal failure, her lips pulled back from gory teeth.

"He did not mean it," she said.

Mrs. Valdez's plump tabby cat lay with her in the tub, bits of fur still clinging to the loathsome, fleshy body beneath. It was attached to her breast and flayed abdomen by numerous hooked barbs that covered its bloated, limbless, caterpillar-like body. Its head was an eyeless black button equipped with a pair of flexible tubes through which it sucked fluid from Mrs. Valdez's dying body.

Polly vomited into the sink. Her sickness drenched writhing animals. The sink was a cradle for miniatures of the creature in the bathtub, squirming creatures with short, fat little legs and bodies covered in barbs. Some rolled on the floor and wriggled in the bathtub, crawling up the ruins of Mrs. Valdez's legs.

"Go away," moaned Mrs. Valdez. "Go away. I love him. He doesn't mean it. Go away!"

The largest of the creatures suckling from Mrs. Valdez retracted its feeding appendages from her flesh and lifted its smooth head to face Polly. It began to rhythmically flex its body and emit a ratcheting sound that filled her with dread. She fell back, closed the bathroom door, and stumbled out of the apartment, vomiting again across the white fur of the spore grass. It had nearly entombed everything in Mrs. Valdez's apartment.

■   ■   ■

"Some things rear up and hiss at ya," Patrice had once explained about bayou wild-life. "Quiet is when you got to be afraid. If a critter mean business, he gwon juss bite."

Patrice stood beside the door with his shoulders leaned against the wall. He was chewing a hangnail. It was a laconic posture that Wesley Bishop reckoned made Patrice the latter sort of bayou animal.

Wesley sat in the room once used for meetings of the now-defunct shareholders. High in the spire, the room's wraparound floor-to-ceiling windows afforded a breath-taking view of the port and coast all the way to Long Beach. Not on that morning. The city sprawling below was lost in the gray haze, like poured smoke, and only a black crescent of the Pacific showed through the vapor.

The oversized table, meant to seat twenty, hosted only three. Bishop sat at the head, Bethany at his side, and at the far end of the table, Milo Gardener sat with his back to Patrice.

"Have you ever been up here?" asked Bishop.

Milo folded his gloved hands on the table.

"Your predecessor did not feel the shareholders needed to know about my activities for the corporation."

"I agree," said Bishop. "I have even more contempt for them, which is why they are no longer here. But I suppose you're wondering why you are. How rare is it that I call upon you and not the other way around?"

"It is infrequent."

"Yes." Bishop snapped his fingers. "You're usually very self-sufficient. I suspect that if I dropped dead and another of my clade climbed from the swamp to take my place, you would hardly notice."

Milo said nothing.

"I was awakened from a very happy dream by a telephone call from Admiral Haley." Bishop leaned back in the chair and propped his Illio Maglia wingtips on the table. He picked a piece of lint from his suit. "Do you know what he had to say?"

Milo did not react to the question.

"He gave me forty-eight hours to allow someone named Captain Dryson and the UN inspectors, whom I was assured would be dealt with, into the depths of this facility. Into"—Bishop bared his teeth as he overenunciated—"the Fane."

One of Milo's white eyebrows flicked involuntarily.

"I didn't know what to tell him. He was very belligerent, and he has that little flotilla parked out there in the Pacific. Very threatening. I said I would think about it, because I was mad. I do not react well to ultimatums like that."

"I am at your service, Mr. Bishop." Milo bowed his head obsequiously. "What would you like me to do?"

"Pack *The Republic* up with explosives and drive it into Haley's aircraft carrier," said Bishop.

Milo nodded and began to stand up.

"Seriously?" Bishop looked to Bethany for support. "This guy was going to drive my boat into an aircraft carrier. Are you a moron?"

"It was your command," said Milo.

Bishop struggled to remember his center and not throw something at the old man across the table from him.

"Sit down." Bishop waited for the old wraith to settle back into his chair. "I was practically smashed into jelly in the maintenance vault yesterday by a freak, and I am not going to be bullied by some flake with fancy epaulettes today. He has given us a deadline. Forty-eight hours to bare our darkest secrets.

"Here is what I want you to do: fucking kill them. Dryson and the UN team. Zero that bitch from Corrections Emergence. No more waiting for the right moment or making it look like an accident. I want you to put these people in a room and fill them with holes until their fucking hearts stop pumping blood. Is that clear enough? Do you get what I want you to do?"

Milo nodded. At a gesture from Bishop, he flowed out through the door. Patrice followed him into the hall. There was something else Bishop wanted from Milo. Something he did not want Bethany to know about.

Something had to be done to help him relax.

■ ■ ■

Polly discarded Milo's itinerary. Studio City? Lunch at a three-star restaurant in Santa Monica? That sort of distraction became sickening in light of what had happened to Mrs. Valdez.

She rallied Captain Dryson and the UN inspectors, and the convoy rolled out, headed south for the cordon. She did not explain where they were going or what they would see. She could feel Captain Dryson studying her from the passenger seat and did not care. She was resolute. Silent. Her expression carved in cold stone.

"Miss Polly."

The manner of address caused her to slam on the van's brakes. It was Rukundo in the backseat, blue beret in his hand, his long arm draped over the back of the seat and his body leaned toward her. He peered at her from beneath a brow stitched with concern.

"What?" she asked.

"Please, you seem very angry. You do not tell us where we are going."

"To the Pit," she said.

The van fell back into silence, and she continued driving. It was what they had demanded, at least the best she could do, but they now realized what they were getting. The streets were emptied of all people. The neighborhoods closest to the cordon showed signs of fires; entire blocks were gutted, and the streets were discolored by vivid stains from the toxic chemicals used to kill the spores.

They reached the military cordon, and a young National Guardsman, barely more than a child, stepped up to the window. He demanded their business. Satisfied with their answers and credentials, he read a script from a white card that warned, "Exiting the cordon may not be possible. If you test positive for spore contamination or attempt to bypass the cordon, you will be dealt with by military authority as established by Presidential Order. Do you have any questions?"

"Yes," said Konstantin Sokov, leaning past Dr. Burns to be heard by the soldier. "Could I please use your gun to shoot myself at this time?"

No one laughed at the joke, least of all the boyish guardsman. Polly rolled up the window and continued on into the dead zone and beyond, through the squalid expanse of Creeptown. The streets, suddenly boiling with life, smells, and sounds, bewildered the UN team. Duplicates threw stones and trash at the vehicles as they wound their way through the confusing network of side streets.

Captain Dryson communicated on his radio to the other vans for his men to stay alert. He lifted his weapon from the foot well and scanned the shanties and walkways for danger. Konstantin Sokov appeared sickened, Dr. Burns observed more clinically. Only Rukundo did not appear upset.

"I know this place," said Rukundo. "It is like Biryogo of Kigali but more. It is market and living place where the unwanted go. Those with not much."

"A ghetto," said Dr. Burns.

They passed beneath the ominous tower blocks with their base towns and elaborate murals. Face gangers appeared to challenge the convoy. They displayed their tattoos and showed menacing gang signs. Some held guns but were smart enough to keep them pointed at the sky. Polly did not doubt that Dryson and his Marines would flood the base towns with automatic gunfire if the convoy came under actual attack.

"They have places like this in Soviet Union." Konstantin was oblivious to the danger. He pressed his cheek against the window to peer up at the buildings towering all around them. "They plan the city with many apartment from the start. Without so much . . . ah . . . what is word for things around these building?"

"Garbage," said Polly.

Just beyond the tower blocks the detectors in the vans began to sound a spore warning. The scientists and Marines hurried to don their gas equipment.

"Should you stop?" asked Konstantin.

"Spores move," said Polly. "We need to move too."

The detectors flashed yellow and then red. The convoy passed through a stretch of rusted shacks and stacked shipping containers. White spore grass was climbing the corners of the structures, devouring wood and rubber features of the improvised architecture more quickly than the bottle-glass windowpanes or corrugated metal. It was not nearly as bad a storm as the one that had engulfed Polly's street, but she could see the spore dust drifting in the air; aggregations like snowflakes burst apart on the van's windshield.

"Look there," said Konstantin. He pointed at two men, shirtless and laboring to cover a rain cistern with a tarp. Their identical physiques suggested a pair of type twos. They stopped in their task, eyes covered by goggles, noses and mouths hidden beneath flapping scarves, and they watched the convoy drive past. One of them men waved at the passing vehicles.

The UN scientists knew of the hyperbolic towers and the immense, angled cantilever of the Bishop Unlimited building looming over San Pedro. They had seen such places in videos and photographs; meager preparation for what they beheld. These were man-made Grand Canyons, awe-inspiring when their scale was revealed in person. Birds wheeled beneath the spire's overhanging rookery. Sunlight broke diagonally through the upper layers of the glass and cast an acre of pale rectangles of green light over the chapped hull of the nearest cooling tower.

The offices prepared for the United Nations team were located in an unused hospital outbuilding. The facilities were dated and barren, with hardly more furniture than the stripped UN offices in Redondo. There was a mortuary, a few hospital rooms, and desks outfitted with obsolete electrical computers.

"This will suffice," said Dr. Burns. If she was upset, she did not betray it. "Dr. Nandy, if you can set up in the mortuary, I believe Dr. Cochrane has already collected some animal samples."

"Let me know when you are finished," said Polly. Dr. Burns waved her hand, already distracted by another question about where to bring in a pair of heavy centrifuges.

Polly stood aside while the scientists began hauling in their equipment. The Marines and her drivers assisted. She planned more for the excursion but wanted to give the UN team a chance to acclimate and prepare so they could get the most out of a journey into the Pit itself. All the way up to the Pool, if she could get them that close. It would take her most authoritative voice and more than a little subterfuge, it would probably cost her this new job, but the maintenance vault was her ultimate destination.

The Fane, however, remained out of the question.

■ ■ ■

Casper Cord wiped himself with napkins purloined from an abandoned Swiftee Burger and folded the "welcome back" chapbook under his arm. He was sick almost constantly and worried about catching something that might last from the garbage he'd been eating. Some of the stuff—brightly colored fried corn and candy that tasted like medicine—he figured might have made him sick fresh out of the package. His old guts weren't used to any of this. Not that the rest of him was a better fit.

He stuffed Bishop's book of depressing lies into the pocket of a beaten-up, paint-spattered old duster coat. The good thing about being a filthy, half-crazy derelict was that most people looked away. Not many people to do that, but he hated it when they stared at him. He could see their pity.

He remembered, seemingly a couple of weeks ago, using the john in Ciro's, tipping the Negro attendant for a spray of cologne and a fresh Bravo. Now he was shitting in a ditch and digging through trash for plastic lighters so he could suck the last nicotine from a collection of cigarette butts. He flopped down on his cardboard. It was still early morning, still cool, and he wanted to go back to sleep. Lenin was awake and staring at him again.

"Say something for yourself," said Casper. "Do something useful instead of sitting there giving me the creeps day and night. Don't I feed you?"

Lenin licked his chops and looked expectant. Casper tossed him one of the last morsels in the bag of scavenged food. The dog caught it easily and swallowed it without chewing.

He was sick of the dog. He wasn't sure if he was going crazy or if it was something the dog was doing, but half the time when he covered himself to catch some sleep, he heard a voice. Real creepy, soft, not even like a person talking, like an animal or a tree or something making a person's words.

"You've got no idea what I've been through." Casper stirred his finger in a tin can full of cold coffee. "I found the woman I loved killed. Fell in love with her twin. Told she was dead all over again. I've seen a giant bug—"

The dog barked.

"That's right, you stupid mutt, a giant bug, and I had my goddamn brain drilled out. Been stuffed down in a hole with nothing to think about for fifty years while the world moved on without me. Now here I am, a bag of bones somebody dug up when they were building a house. It's not that I feel sorry for myself . . . "

The dog was still staring intensely at him.

"Well, all right, so I do feel sorry for myself. What else is there to do? You tell me that. What about you? What's your story?"

The dog did not answer. Its merry stupidity infuriated him. He tossed pebbles at its face.

"Talk, goddamnit!" He threw a bigger chunk of concrete, and the dog, ears pinned back, yowled and leaped out of the way. "Please. Please talk to me. Say it to my face. Say whatever it is about what's coming to my face so I can know I'm not losing my goddamn mind."

"You're losing your goddamn mind."

Casper knocked over his coffee in his rush to get up from the cardboard. An interloper had crept onto the abandoned lot he had claimed as his own turf and walked to within a few feet of his campsite. It was the rangy mulatto with dreadlock hair.

"Bottles," said Casper.

"Yeah, you remember that, so I guess you ain't all crazy," said Bottles. He was grimy but lacked a full layer of filth compared to what Casper had already accumulated. He covered the last few feet to where Casper's cardboard was laid out on the ground. There was a half-buried pot filled with ashes. Casper had built a fire in it to make coffee the night before. Bottles kicked it once and harrumphed at the lack of fresh smoke.

"What do you want?" asked Casper.

"My man, you don't have to be all hostile like that." Bottles sat down on the milk crate and warmed his hands in his breath. "It's a social visit. You're the new face in the neighborhood. Well, the new person belonging to that same old face. Truth is, I never seen a dupe so low. Not one that made it out of Creeptown."

"Don't need your pity."

Casper picked up his tin can of coffee and salvaged the dregs of his twice-brewed grounds. He bent over the dead fire and stoked it, trying to bring back the flames. It was no use, and there was no more paper around to start the fire going. Bottles eyed the stain spread down the shoulder and back of Casper's threadbare duster.

"Ain't pity," said Bottles. "More like a zoo or something. Goddang, is that throw-up all over that coat, man?"

"Not mine."

Casper felt the weight of the chapbook in his pocket, and he drew it out. It was cheaply printed on crude stock. Just the sort of thing that would burn nicely. He tore out the half he had already read and fed it into the fire bowl. A flick of the lighter, and the pages were burning. Casper squinted at Bottles, the fire warming one side of his face. He shook the fire-blackened tin can full of grounds at him.

"Want a cup of coffee?"

■ ■ ■

The facilities being occupied by the UN team adjoined a simple canteen. It was sparsely equipped, stowed like a closed restaurant, the cabinets and countertops garish blue and yellow and red. It was a relic of another era covered in a patina of dust. Polly switched on the lights and flipped a chair down from one of the tabletops.

She sat down, sick in the pit of her stomach. Since the spore storm that morning she had experienced a sense of detachment from reality. Her mind had collided with the impossible, and it was as sudden and profound as the aftermath of a severe car crash.

She reminded herself of the facts by sliding her fingers into the pocket of her uniform trousers. It was still there, soft, yielding to her touch, slightly warmer through the plastic than the fabric surrounding it. Could it still be alive? Surely it had suffocated in the bag. Or did it not breathe at all? She gave it a squeeze, and it squirmed slightly in her grasp.

"Miss Polly. Good to see you." Rukundo entered the canteen and approached the table Polly was sharing with three stacked chairs. "May I sit with you?"

"Of course," she said, quickly withdrawing her hand from her pocket.

Rukundo took down the chairs and arranged them around the table. He found a kettle in the cabinet and put water on the stove. Another cabinet contained an assortment of LARC mugs featuring logos and slogans—THE WAY THINGS USED TO BE—dating back to the late 1970s. Rukundo selected one of these from the cabinet. He took a leather pouch from a pocket of his shirt and opened it on the counter. He transferred pinches of dried leaves from the pouch to the coffee cup.

"Black tea from home. I am very particular about it."

Rukundo was very handsome. He was thin of body and face, big eyes the color of honey, an elegant manner, and a softness to his voice that was slightly feminine and beguiling. The uniform he wore, dark slacks and a pressed white safari shirt with a blue beret, suggested military, but Polly was unfamiliar with the insignia. He joined her at the table.

"Are you in the military?"

"I am part of the African Coalition Peacekeepers." He spoke with an exotic French accent. "I was allowed into the special security unit."

"You mentioned Kagali in the van. Is that Kenya?"

"Rwanda." He looked away when he said it.

"Where do you come from? A city?"

"No. It was very small. There was a man in my village who was very old. Older even than your Mr. Bishop. All of us wondered how he grew to be so old, so I went to his house and knocked on the door. He said to me 'Rukundo, come into the house.' He had so many wrinkles that you could not even see his eyes. And I asked him, 'What is your secret to being so old?'"

"The old man said, 'One, I drink only black tea from leaves grown in the highlands,' and he gave me some tea. 'Two, I eat only almonds with their skin boiled off,' and he gave me a bag of boiled almonds to take with me. 'Three is most important,' said the old man. 'I never argue with anyone.' And I was cross and said to him, 'That is it? This can't be. There must be some other secret to your great age. Some magic or prayer.'

" 'Yes,' said the old man, 'you are right.' "

Rukundo stared at her, very serious, and then burst into loud, hitching laughter. Polly began to laugh as well, finally separating the joke from the tone with which Rukundo told it.

"Something funny?" asked Dr. Burns.

She entered just as the kettle began to boil. Rukundo ducked his head as if caught doing something mischievous, and he hurried to deal with the whistling kettle.

"Nothing at all, miss," said Rukundo.

"Miss Foster," said Dr. Burns. "You wanted me to get you when we were finished."

"Yes," said Polly. "Before I take you into the Pit, I need to speak to Dr. Nandy. I want to show her something."

Dr. Burns brought Polly to the newly operational mortuary. Dr. Cochrane and Dr. Nandy were sorting through a pair of coolers filled with bagged, dead animals apparently infected with spores. Polly touched the thing squirming in her pocket.

"What is it?" asked Dr. Nandy.

"I don't know," said Polly.

She placed the sealed bag from her pocket onto the nearest mortuary table. The creature, the size of her fist, pale and plump, wriggled like a grocery-store pork chop in a bag wet with blood. Its proboscides curled against its body, and the coarse bristles covering its segments tented the bag.

"Where did you find this?" asked Dr. Nandy, leaning over the bag and holding her spectacles to her face.

"In my apartment building," said Polly. "It ate my neighbor."

COMINTERCEPT – SOVNET - ELECTRONIC TEXT - NOENCRYPT - BLACK LABEL

FROM: Konstantin Sokov@UN Disaster Assessment and Coordination (UNDAC)
TO: Ianka Sokov
SUBJECT: my trip

My beloved Ianka,

I hope you are in Vladivostok and that your family has arrived safely. I am sorry I could not be more truthful earlier about where I was traveling. The situation in California is very complicated, but I have collected many clean samples already. Before I am done, I will fill the vault beneath the black rock of Cape Tegethoff with the essence of this country. I do not know if science can ever remake it, but I know it is worth preserving.

We were brought to the place called the Pit, and I was given an office. I am not wanted. There was a great excitement over a specimen, and I was not included.

I remained in my office and realized I could see the ocean. Beyond the brutal architecture of the fortress walls there is an area, still restricted by fences, that contains a long stretch of coast. After a bit of sneaking I escaped outside, beneath an open sky, out from the shadow of the towers, and was at last standing upon the shores of the Pacific Ocean.

These were not the sunny beaches of California girls in their bikinis. No surfers or swimmers. I was near the busy industrial harbor of San Pedro with its steady flow of cargo ships and refugee boats. The thought of so many vessels coming and going in the midst of disease quarantine filled me with pessimism.

All along the water the beach grass was brown and dead. The branches of salt trees and shrubs were heavy with sprouting fungus, leaves and trunks stained white with disease. The strandline was fouled with bull kelp and other seaweed, discolored and turning to mush, ignored by the hundreds of gulls overhead. Dead birds and fish rolled in the surf.

I brought in my pockets a few capsules to collect specimens, and I filled these with bits of healthier kelp and native amphipods burrowing in the sand. The sand fleas beat their backs against the curve of the plastic capsule. There were a few glistening jellies, and I discovered one small enough to fit into a capsule. I doubt any of these samples will prove to be free of contamination.

I came to a finger jetty of haphazard concrete slabs, and I climbed upon the awkward jumble of blocks to have a better view of the ocean. The tiny inlets formed by the overlapping stone blocks were filled with the decaying remains of tidal animals. The hollowed shells of crabs floated upon the surface, sucked in and out by the waves, and beneath were the bloated cucumbers and starfish, whitened and downy with coats of disease.

Not everything was perishing. A bloom of scarlet phytoplankton was visible a hundred or so meters from shore. As the waves rolled through this mat, they became vividly red and yellow and came crashing to the beaches to deposit some of the plankton. Fish leaped in a frenzy to devour the plankton, their excitement drawing the gulls in the gray sky.

A ship moved swiftly through the growth, its prow like a knife through the red meat of the plankton bloom. The ship's superstructure was an angled slab, and its billowing stacks were recessed almost completely into its hull. This was a military vessel. There were no apparent weapons, but above the superstructure sprouted the whiskers of a dozen antennae and the spinning dish of a radar system.

The vessel's name was painted above the scarlet bow wake of churned plankton. *The Republic*. It scattered the gulls, cut across the ocean, apparently impervious to what was happening around it, and I became very melancholy. It was a war machine of iron to combat an army of ghosts. I fear the Americans misunderstand the terms of the engagement.

CHAPTER EIGHT

■ ■ ■

It was just as well that the specimen Polly brought occupied the UN inspectors long into the evening. While they discussed the results of various tests in hushed tones, she pored over a detailed map of the spire to determine their best approach for the maintenance vault. When time came at around 8:00 PM, she assembled the UN scientists and marines at the main door of the outbuilding like children waiting to go to recess.

Polly had told the menagerie of UN scientists to travel lightly. They did not listen. They lined up to depart with backs bent beneath packs and carrying heavy cases filled with their scientific instruments. Even the Marines were bogged down in their gear.

She went down the line, lecturing each person individually and demanding they trim down what they intended to bring. When she finished each lecture, she handed the recipient bright yellow boots and gloves and a bright orange coverall. The boots and gloves were oversized rubber; the coverall was cheap, artificial, and smelled of long-term storage.

"Love, no offense"—Dr. Cochrane shook out the coverall and held it up to his stout frame—"but looking like a Christmas orange is a shite disguise."

A few of the doctors murmured their agreement.

"You cannot be disguised," said Polly. "You will be entering a closed facility with a closed population of duplicates. Better to not hide at all, pretend to belong by standing out. Stay calm, stay quiet; if we are stopped and you are asked any questions, you will defer to me. If we are taken into custody by Pit Security, you will comply. Do not try to run or fight."

She looked pointedly at Captain Dryson and added, "No weapons of any kind."

"You heard her," said Captain Dryson. He began taking carbines from his men. "Hand them over. No pistols, no grenades. Don't hold out on me."

"You sure this is a good idea, sir?" asked one of the Marines.

"Button it up, Romero," said Funkweed. "Captain Dryson gave you an order."

Dr. Burns, far more agreeable since Polly had handed over the specimen, added her own weight to Polly's instructions. There were no further questions. The scientists brought minimal equipment, the Marines none at all save for a single deployable hard case filled with radio equipment.

They crossed the freight artery, stopping the traffic of the reclamation vans, the flat-faced waste-disposal trucks, and the deliveries of perishables for the extensive housing located underground. The six-lane road branched into a dozen ramps that descended into the loading bay. There was an entrance at ground level and a translucent security kiosk occupied by a single uniformed guard. Polly did not wait to be stopped; she approached and showed her credentials to the scruffy type one in his Plexiglas cube. He buzzed the magnetic locks on the door, and Polly ushered the scientists and Marines into the loading area.

They traversed the cavernous bay by walkways layered between the overhead ventilation fans and the slow river of trucks idling beneath their feet. Trucks stopped in loading areas to be serviced by container cranes and forklifts. Three lanes of trucks continued on and disappeared into branching tunnels lit in wheeling flashes of headlights and taillights.

High above this shuddering ballet, the smell of diesel fumes was intense. The fans, large as trucks themselves, drowned out all other sound when they activated. The suction they created stole Polly's breath and pulled at her clothing as she directed her companions beneath each spinning blade.

The so-called Undercroft was a honeycomb of administrative offices and processing areas for emerging duplicates. Polly did not dare try to pass through these, as they were densely populated and, in the case of the processing, considered sensitive. The central trunk of elevators was similarly a danger spot. She opted instead for a path through a heating tunnel crowded with ductwork. They encountered only the occasional, slightly bewildered type two or three. No one challenged them.

They emerged from the tunnel onto a grated platform high above the floor of the ventilation hub. The hub was a hot, dry chamber filled with the roar of pump turbines drawing geological heat up from the deepest tunnels. Even walking out of the heat tunnel and seeing the machinery of the pump turbines perilously far below was dizzying.

"We go down." Polly pointed to the visible railing of stairs. It was flimsy and never intended for through-traffic.

"I hope it's down at a non-terminal pace," said Dr. Cochrane.

The metal frame stairs were bolted to a concrete structural pylon, and each step from each member of the team made the zigzag stairs bounce like a spring. The Marines dealt with the precarious conditions, but several of the scientists panicked.

"No," pleaded Konstantin Sokov. "I am afraid of heights. I cannot. I will faint. Leave me."

Dr. Burns tried to cajole him to the staircase, but he clung to the entrance of the heat tunnel like a child afraid of Santa Claus. Polly knew there was no going back for Sokov. Not by himself. He either had to be forced to go down the stairs, or they would all need to turn back.

"It's all of us or none of us," said Polly.

It was Funkweed who broke him loose. He wrapped him up in his burly arms and, pushing off from the wall with a combat boot, he pulled poor Sokov out onto the quaking platform. Their momentum nearly took them over the railing. Funkweed dropped Sokov onto his feet at the head of the stairs.

"March your ass down those stairs," said Funkweed in his best drill sergeant voice. "You baby. You think I ain't scared? I don't even like climbing a ladder. You think I like this? Grow up, Ivan. We have to do it, including you."

That seemed to break Sokov out of his despair. He stood up ramrod straight. His mechanical response to Funkweed's shouting suggested a military past.

"Yes," said Sokov, and he began to march down the stairs. Funkweed followed closely behind, but no further prodding was needed.

The air at the chamber's floor level was desert hot and punctuated by bursts of even greater heat as workers opened hatches on the pumping machinery, exposing the baking temperatures being siphoned from the depths. The men were clad in dun-colored coveralls and wore hard hats and protective gloves. Their uniforms were dark with sweat and grime. They toiled as machines, paying no mind to the interlopers.

"We've been at it for over an hour. We need to rest." Dr. Burns mopped sweat from her face with a kerchief. The scientists leaned on one another or sat upon the dusty floor.

"We go on," said Polly.

It was another hour, trudging through more heating tunnel and on into a forgotten warren of storage offices for low-level administrative clerks. The rooms and corridors were appointed in the fashion of an office of the 1950s, with narrow halls, decorative incandescent light fixtures, and wooden-framed doors of frosted glass stenciled with job titles like JUNIOR BURSAR and SENIOR DISTRIBUTION MANAGER. The only piece missing from the mosaic were the windows and slatted blinds facing downtown Los Angeles, New York, or Chicago of half a century ago.

The office was populated by a colony of type ones in cheap business attire and a handful of type threes acting as secretaries. They were clearly put out by a large group of snowflakes in sweaty work clothes traipsing through their domain. Polly's map took them through halls cluttered with boxes and interrupted conversations among identical men in identical shirtsleeves and identical ties. As they rounded a corner, following a sign directing them to the stairs, a type three dropped a romance novel onto her desk and disappeared behind a door stenciled with the name BOB DENIM and the title INTERMEDIATE OFFICE SUPERVISOR.

"You." Denim, a burly type one, stepped out of his office shouting. "Type three.

What are you doing with these people in my office? You can't be in here. They can't be in here. Get out of here."

Polly signaled for the procession to halt behind her. Secretaries put down their distractions, and doors opened all along the hall as type ones poked their heads out to see why the boss was yelling.

"We are on official business," said Polly. She lifted her clearance badge in its laminated holder. Bob Denim squinted at the card and shook his head. He picked up the telephone receiver from his secretary's desk and began to dial.

"I need to call Mr. Hopper," he said. "He'll straighten you out. You really can't be in here with those people."

Polly flattened her finger in the telephone's cradle.

"The Gardeners sent me," said Polly. This produced an immediate reaction from Bob Denim. His anger disappeared, and he straightened up.

"These people are being taken to processing," said Polly. "Deep processing. The kind nobody comes back from."

"My supervisor still needs to talk with you."

"Who should be told about this? Your supervisor or my supervisor?" She stepped back from him. "Go ahead and make that call if you need to."

His thought process was pantomimed on his face and in his body language. He looked at the phone, scowled, looked at Polly, and, bereft, appeared about to whine. Instead, he hung up the phone.

"Well, okay, then." He raised his voice. "This checks out. Official business. Carry on."

Shamed by his confusion, Mr. Denim retreated into his office. Polly and her charges proceeded to the stairs and descended, at last, to one of the approaches to the maintenance vault. The footpath was only wide enough for two to walk abreast and, though built from concrete slabs, seemed poorly put together. The slabs were uneven, and long cracks split the walls and curved up into the ceiling. Occasional dusty showers of concrete flakes clattered down onto their heads and shoulders.

It was not the approach used to move large material in and out of the maintenance vault, nor was it the jeep track used by the maintenance crews, although this could not be avoided entirely.

The narrow footpath crossed the jeep track—two lanes of hardtop in a curving tunnel—and it was so quiet, she heard the distant gurgle of the Pool and the buzz of the lighting twenty feet over their heads. It took more than a minute to usher the scientists across the track. There should have been at least one vehicle coming or going in that time.

"There should be traffic," said Polly.

The scientists were too footsore and overwhelmed to care, but Dryson took an interest.

"What do you mean?"

"They run smaller anomalies out through the jeep track. They should be driving them out in boxes and returning almost constantly."

"What do you mean by this 'anomalies'?" asked Sokov. His brow was furrowed, and he was polishing sweat from his glasses. His eyes seemed tiny and dark without the benefit of the lenses.

"I mean junk, debris; weird things."

"Like the parasite you brought for Mrs. Nandy?"

"No." She hesitated. "I mean, freak things, sometimes, but messed up dogs, cats, rabbits. Rats. Giant fish or something."

"A giant fish?" Sokov returned his glasses to his face.

"It's all junk. Mistakes. I haven't seen anything like that parasite." She was annoyed by Sokov's questions and the way his watery eyes seemed to be pleading. "We need to keep moving."

"So why aren't they driving them in and out like you said?" asked Dryson, following her as she pushed her way to the head of the column again. "What reason could they have for stopping?"

She did not know the answer to that. The thought that anything could halt the steady traffic in and out of one of the most vital parts of the Pit was a cause for grave concern.

"I don't have an answer for you," she said.

Near the vault entrance the footpath widened into a chamber, low-ceilinged, no more than twenty feet wide, but long enough to accommodate all of the scientists. There were chairs, low tables, ashtrays, and even vending machines stocked with candies and sodas. After crossing through the oppressive depths of the Undercroft, the scientists, though relieved to be able to sit for a moment, were nevertheless put off by the amenities, as if they were a trick.

Polly checked the small version of the guide map she had brought along. A line drawn in grease pencil marked their course to this point. The entrance to the maintenance vault was down two levels and through heavy security doors. There was no more bypassing of security points possible. The UN team would have to clear a security checkpoint. She rehearsed a more detailed version of the story she had given to Bob Denim. As long as a Gardener was not manning the checkpoint, she was confident she could bully her way through.

Dryson sidled up, peering over her shoulder at the map.

"Not much farther," she said.

"Good," he said. "They're past the point of complaining, but they've just about had it."

"Let them rest for a bit. I need to scout ahead." She thought about leaving Dryson in charge—he obviously expected to be left in charge—but she called out to Rukundo instead. He came loping over to where she was standing. "I need you to take care of everyone. Let them have a drink and rest their feet. You are in charge."

"Me, Miss Polly?"

"I trust you."

Dryson rolled his eyes and rejoined his men. Polly set off down the stairwell, her feet echoing in the lonely concrete enclosure. There was an odd smell in the air, almost as if something had burned. The stairwell opened into a plaza that reminded her of a parking garage. A security wall separated the stairwell and a pair of large elevators from the doors leading into the maintenance vault. There was only one way in or out, and it was through the metal detectors of the checkpoint, similar in design to the translucent box at the loading bay.

The kiosk was empty. She approached cautiously, ducking beneath the back-and-forth ropes of the queue. The metal detectors chimed and flashed red as she passed through them. Papers were scattered out of the open door of the checkpoint. The smell of smoke was even stronger here. Polly slipped quietly to the nearest pair of doors opening into the maintenance vault. She tested the handle. Unlocked. She could hear the Pool churning through the door, feel it beneath her feet.

She opened the door.

The huge vault was quiet but for the rumble of the Pool. The vault's domed floor rose to a hill in the center and partially obstructed her view of the opposite side of the chamber. Jeeps were parked haphazardly. Cranes were deployed as if work had stopped suddenly. A tangle of metal that appeared to be another crane had been pushed aside by a tracked earthmover, its metal shovel still buried in the junked crane.

White halogen lights were directed at an open maintenance panel a dozen feet across. A crane was positioned above the open panel. An immaculate, golden sphere belted with weights dangled beneath the crane as if it were about to be lowered into the Pool. It swayed gently from side to side.

There was no one in the vault.

Polly approached the open panel. The tempestuous noise of the Pool grew louder with each step. She splashed through spilled motor oil, careful not to lose her footing, until she was standing at the mouth, loud as a waterfall, looking down into the poorly illuminated Pool. Dimly, she perceived its muddy surface, twisting and reforming, reeking of old bones and earthy, inner flesh. It was warm and sickening.

She turned to walk away, stopped, realized the slick she had taken to be spilled oil was a long trail of blood. It collected at the open panel and dripped into the roiling liquid.

She took out her pistol from its holster and ran back to the stairwell, searching as she went for any signs of danger. Her breath was ragged as she took the stairs two at a time and banged through the door and into the holding area where she had left the UN inspectors and Dryson's men.

Too late.

"Drop your pistol." The order came from a white-haired type two with a face crisscrossed by scars. He was aiming a folding machine pistol at the head of Dr. Burns.

Polly hesitated. The UN team and Dryson's men were on their knees, hands folded behind their heads. Sergeant Funkweed was laid out on his back, lip and nose bloodied, with a Gardener kneeling against his chest and holding the barrel of a pistol to his forehead. There were too many Gardeners to count.

"Now." The Gardener menacing Dr. Burns shook his gun insistently. Dr. Burns stared at Polly, betraying no reaction to the threat. Slowly, submissively, Polly lowered her gun to the floor.

The Gardeners were freakishly white-haired, clad in riding boots and cloaks of unusual design, silver stag's-head badges worn around their necks or pinned to their collars. Some bore brutal scars or strange tattoos. They all carried weapons.

"Pollen Foster." Another Gardener approached her from the side. He was wizened and moved slowly, did not carry a weapon, but she felt afraid of the power he represented. He was Milo.

She scrambled for an excuse.

"I was ordered by Mr. Bishop to—"

"Do not waste our time with your fable. I know exactly why you are here, Miss Foster. Better than you, I'm afraid. As for Mr. Bishop, he has given us explicit orders to murder everyone in this room."

■ ■ ■

"In about five minutes," said Bottles, "they're gonna open up the cots. There's a big rush, everybody wants a bed, but there ain't enough. The trick is, what I do is, you go back to the kitchen right then, and they give you a bag of food. I know this other place, man, it ain't far. It's a lot better than a cot. It's got electricity and a toilet and everything."

Casper liked the idea of using an actual toilet and maybe cleaning up. It was an appealing offer, but he did not trust Bottles, not yet. The man was after something.

"And you're going to take me there and jump me for that debit card," said Casper, wiping his face with a napkin. "Try to steal my dog. Is that it?"

"Naw, not at all. You got it wrong. You're oversuspicious of people who are extending a hand of friendship."

Casper held on to his suspicion. Bottles yammered on, talking about Pittsburgh and somebody named Carlos, asking questions, trying to feel out what Casper might have worth trading or selling. He offered Casper a pair of tennis shoes for his rubber sandals. They smelled as if they were taken from a dead man. He tried to trade Casper a liter bottle of water for the debit card, pointing out how the container was still sealed and describing the filtration process used to ensure it was spore free.

"I guess that don't matter to you." Bottles put the water back into his bag.

The tables began to empty, people carrying their trays back into the kitchen and depositing them in a steady clatter of plastic and clink of silverware into wash bins. When each person dumped his tray, he moved, with family and friends, to double doors opposite the entrance. The doors were closed and apparently locked.

"Waiting for the cots," said Bottles. "Finish your turkey, man, or give it to me. We'll go get seconds, and I'll show you a much better place to hang out."

Casper spooned the gravy off the turkey and passed the piece beneath the table. He felt the lash of Lenin's tongue as the dog delicately pulled the hunk of meat from his fingers. Once the dog had finished the piece, Casper followed Bottles back to the kitchen. Across the room, the double doors swung open, and the people crowding them pressed into the adjoining room. Father Woodhew could be heard shouting for cooperation, a stone in the flow of a mighty river of desperate families hoping to find a bed for the night.

"Here we go," said Bottles. He put on a big smile and, true to his word, sweet-talked the tired kitchen staff into ladling plenty more food into a couple of foam clamshell containers. "Oh, you tell that Denise if she is here tomorrow, I might ask her to marry me if she makes another sweet-potato pie. God bless you all. God bless you."

"That sweet-potato pie is nasty as a dead cat," said Bottles, once they were out of earshot. "Now you come on, we'll go out the side way."

They passed through a metal side door into a narrow alley between the courtyard wall and the rearmost buttress of the church. The sky was a deep blue, sunset blue, seeming darker because of a harsh light above the church door. That door thudded closed behind them, its lock clicking with finality.

"You found yourself another pet." It was the big, ugly skinhead who had accosted him during an earlier visit to the church. He and his gang were blocking off the alley. All of them, even the girls, were brandishing weapons; chains, knives, and the leader, the ugly son of a bitch, wielded the curved black blade of a machete. "I'm gonna cut your head off, dupe. I'll just take a couple fingers from the nigger."

Casper brought up his fists, but his estimates from days before were all wrong. The fight was over quickly. Casper was caught wrong-footed, his swing skipping off the side of the machete, deflecting the skinhead's weapon but failing to disarm the man. The fat skinhead called Van slammed Casper sideways, elbows in his kidneys, against the bricks, driving him to his knees.

Bottles retreated against the door, turning his back and sheltering his face from the laughing girls and their knives. Casper registered kicks, steel-toed, bruising his legs, arms, and sides. The machete would come soon. He knew what it was going to feel like from a brief visit to the Philippines that had ended poorly.

Casper was facedown on the pavement, the world trickling, bouncing in and out of darkness with each distant blow against his ribs or back. The girls were laughing still, slashing at Bottles with their knives, peeling ribbons and tufts of padding from his coat, sprawling him on the ground atop his smashed boxes of food. Everything went dark, but Casper was still aware. He could dimly feel them still beating him and hear their voices.

And he heard them when the screaming began.

FLESH soft and weak, lacking chitin or tarsus or limbs enough for the violence of my kind, but, oh, the jaws. They are small and leveraged to rend muscle and sinew, long bone wound with cords, inheritor of power. The liquor of my veins is potent, propelled on shuddering meat, enriched by countless glands, and distilled by reflexive terror. I suck their smell in through my snout, and I know every contour of them, every movement by the vortices in colorless, perfumed smoke.

In the white stone antechamber of the boreal spire of the Sub-Regnant Queen the 702nd, the Cardinal Betrayer, Usurper and Defiler of the ways of true hatching, I faced ninety-nine warriors of her brood. They were strong, honed in the old violence and the old ways, shells scarred from battle, drunk on their queen's richest honey.

Through beam and chisel and, by second moon's height, through mandible, I extracted the pulp of each warrior. I cored their husks and burned their nerve cords into jelly. I was VIOLENCE. I was a champion of my kind, like Warren Groves, but of the hard shell and inner flesh.

The soft meat of humans does not stoke fear in my mind. Their way is slow and anchored to the soil. There are no venoms or beams, only crude metal tools. I welcome battle. Praise her name, my Regnant Queen, long gone into water. Praise her and answer this TREASON with VIOLENCE.

I discover great speed in this flesh. I leap and seize with rows of curving fangs. Their throats and groins and bellies are soft. Their limbs snap apart into morsels. I strum their tendons with my jaws.

Stricken faces, pale, wide-eyed, screaming. I KILL WELL. Humans are gurgling, thrashing for the meat I have taken from them. Their fluid is warm on my face and on these quills that do not speak. One human female runs. She sees me for what I am. She is too slow, too soft.

Her death scream inhabits the night. Impossibly loud to my senses. The hot gush of arteries, molten on my snout, on my tongue. Her fluid scent is nuanced, layered as my own would be if this flesh was opened up. DRINK. DEVOUR. It is the will of the flesh, bestial, but I accede, beyond resisting the impulse, filling my belly with a stew of meat and venous brine.

I AM FOREVER AND WILL BE a champion. Victorious once more. Head dampened with the liquid of my enemies. Snout dripping with their gore. I remain restless with lingering urges for violence. Casper Cord lives. The other human, who does not attack, is watching. He has escaped death and yet learns of other things to fear. I clean my mouth with the dexterous muscle of my tongue and stare into

his tiny, glistening eyes. The meaning of my flesh to him is transformed by
impossible acts. He gazes upon me and trembles.

"This?" Wesley Bishop took the tin box from Patrice. It was heavy. Glass clinked
and rasped within. "He gave you this?"

"Gwon get a look inside," said Patrice. "I check it out. Dass de right one."

"This is her box."

Bishop sat down upon the bed and traced his fingers over the faded paint. The
pretty portrait had nearly gone, but the word was still legible. *Vervains.* He could not
remember the specific sound of her voice, but he could recall that moment, hands
touching across the metal lid, sliding it open to show him how she kept his letters.

"Tings got ya wrong, podnah?" asked Patrice.

"No," said Bishop. "Go on. Speak with Bethany. I think there remain preparations before our departure."

"Don't overimbibe on dem. Ya gotta keep ya head on ya shouldas."

"Only one," said Bishop.

Patrice left and knew not to disturb Bishop further unless there was an emergency.

Bishop sat in the quiet darkness. He tried to picture Annie caressed by the sun,
tried to conjure her as completely as possible without contaminating her features
with the many images of Veronica Lambert that occupied the nearer terrain of his
memory. Annie slipped away, and he pictured Violet Vex, waggish, pale, hair black
as ink, and Pollen Foster, more like Annie, just as unlucky, but hard at the edges.

His inability to summon Annie caused pain that he wanted numbed with pills
or drink. Instead, he opened the lid of the tin box and took out one of the faintly
luminous vials of bliss. Each vial held only a few drops, swirling within the glass like
a mixture of glowing pigments and oil. The vials smelled sweet and foreign, the
delicacies of a faraway land with a trace of the chalky spore odor. He unscrewed a
vial and lifted it to his mouth. He took a deep breath, the glass poised against his
lower lip, an antique clock softly ticking on a nearby shelf. There was no turning back.

He tipped the vial, and the cold liquid spilled across his tongue. There was a
sharply bitter taste that lingered only a moment. The fluid was gone. He reclined
upon the bed and felt nothing. There was only the sound of his breathing and the
tick of the clock. Both sounds became concordant, slowing, gaining in texture and
meaning, until he perceived geography derived from the steadily stretching moments, an expanse invisible during the normal passage of time.

When he lifted his head from the pillow, he was not at all surprised to find the
walls and furniture replaced with darkness populated by blue traceries, shifting,
meaningful, but describing no manmade features. He laughed. Burning, smoking
shapes effervesced at his feet. He enjoyed the display, wondering at the ultimate,
incandescent form they might take.

The fire shapes burst in a wave of heat and further whooshing smoke and revealed themselves as Harlan Long astride the gray horse Apollyon. Both were alive, though they possessed the sunken features and livid markings upon the flesh of the dead. Their eyes burned with azure light.

"My son." Apollyon spoke with his father's voice. "I am come to see you off."

"No!" Bishop moaned and slid away across the bed.

"This lie you have built is at its end. It is finished." Apollyon stepped its forelegs onto the bed and stood above him, triumphant, and roared, "Usurper!"

Bishop recoiled. He tried to escape from the horse, for he knew it spoke truth. The drug found time where none existed, expanding the hallucination into the frozen places it eked out between clicks of the antique clock. The effects of the bliss lasted less than an hour. Wesley Bishop perceived months tormented and mocked by his father, fleeing them through phosphorescent streets of blue light, pursued by laughter and the stone horse Apollyon.

■　■　■

Milo Gardener did not kill them on the spot. His men ordered the scientists and Marines to their feet and began marching them down the stairs and to the elevators. Captain Dryson and a few of the other Marines had received minor injuries and were handled with greater care than the scientists. Only Sergeant Funkweed, mouth badly bloodied, nose clearly broken, had sustained any lasting injury.

"I am sorry," said Rukundo. "I could not stop them."

A Gardener shoved him past Polly and down the stairs.

"You as well," said Milo, and a pair of Gardeners with folding machine guns flanked her.

They followed the bedraggled column into the elevator. It was a deep-diving freight elevator, just barely large enough to accommodate them all. Its control panel was equipped with a red box marked with the silver stag's head symbol of the Gardeners. Milo inserted a key and opened the box.

"Where are you taking us?" asked Dr. Burns.

"Where you wanted to go." Milo operated the controls inside the box and closed the panel. When he stood to face Polly, he was smiling. "I am taking you to the Fane."

The elevator shuddered into motion. Some of the UN scientists cried out softly as the car began its long descent into the deepest of the Undercroft.

"Why?" asked Polly.

The elder Gardener signaled to one of his men, who provided him with a small flask. He took a sip from it and wiped the water from his lips. He crossed to where two men held Sergeant Funkweed upright. He was still breathing, but his chin rested against his chest, and blood occasionally dripped from his face. Polly realized he was missing teeth.

"I am afraid you have been doubly misled, Miss Foster. This man is not who he claims to be, nor are his companions. They are a unit of Admiral Haley's special-operations force. They are Navy commandos, not Marines, and the man who called himself Sergeant Funkweed"—Milo lifted Funkweed's slack face with two gloved fingers—"works for one of those droll Washington agencies with an invisible budget."

"He's lying," said Dryson.

Milo ignored the comment.

"They communicate using a very pernicious cipher. My men have only cracked a handful of their transmissions. These transmissions are, curiously, always one-sided. They report"—Milo pushed the deployable radio case the Marines had brought with the toe of his boot—"but no one replies. Their goal all along was to get to the Fane. To destroy it, I presume."

"I don't know what you're talking about," said Dryson. "We are here to protect these people."

"If that was your only task, then you have failed," said Milo. "But I believe you mean what you say. Only your friend, the erstwhile Sergeant Funkweed, knows exactly what was intended, but I think we have him figured out now."

"You never answered me," said Polly. "Why take us down to the Fane just to kill us?"

Her question wrenched sobs from the most terrified of the UN contingent. Milo blinked as if surprised that she had not already reached the conclusion he intended.

"I intend to help Sergeant Funkweed accomplish his mission, of course." Milo clapped a gloved hand onto Funkweed's shoulder, and the beaten man lifted his head, one eye pasted shut with blood. "I will help him destroy this place."

■ ■ ■

"Don't look at it," said Casper, helping Bottles to his feet. They pushed through the carnage that filled the alley. They endured the inside-out stench of dead animals, their feet slipping in loops of viscera dragged across the asphalt, splashing in blood pooling in every fissure, gallons upon gallons of it, decorating ten feet up the walls of the church in abstract sprays of crimson.

Casper stooped to pick up the skinhead's machete from the mess. It fit his hand, the wrapped horn of the handle still warm. He shook meat from the blade.

Bottles was catatonic, a smashed foam tray tilted, forgotten, in one hand, sloshing gravy out its buckled sides as Casper pulled him out of the alley. The gore even sickened Casper, who thought himself inured to extravagant violence by decades of war. No, it wasn't the violence. The sick tightness in his gut was the fucking dog. Its tail wagging, its blood-soaked mouth hung open wide, tongue flexed and throbbing, panting and looking at Casper expectantly as though the mangled bodies were sticks it had fetched for him.

He was afraid to even acknowledge the dog. As they fled the church and disappeared into the night, down streets scabbed with refuse, human and otherwise, Casper knew it was right behind them. He could hear its nails clicking on the sidewalk.

They hurried aimlessly, past abandoned businesses, through ethnic neighborhoods clinging to life, through sudden campgrounds spilling from parks and ruined buildings. They weaved through crowds, demonstrations, chanting, mob anger, lines of police deflecting stones with metal shields, streets without electricity lit by burning cars.

They climbed a quicksand ramp of trash over a concrete barrier to cross a highway Casper did not remember. The traffic did not stop for them. Cars and trucks roared past, wind sucking at their clothes, horns blasting, men and women screaming insults out the windows. All traveling in one direction: away from the cordon.

Casper was exhausted from dragging Bottles. When they reached the other side of the highway, he collapsed against the stoop of a building missing its second and third floor. A furniture store maybe—there was a weather-beaten couch surrounded by the wooden wall frames hung with scraps. The stoop was substantial and dark and out of the way. It was a chance for Casper to catch his breath.

There were sirens in the distance, police, ambulance, and, farther away, the ominous, droning wail of the alert sirens. What did that mean, he wondered. Garbled warnings, inscrutable and foreign, echoed over the city night. Helicopters tore at the sky, pale blue beams lancing down into the neighborhoods below. One passed nearby, and Casper felt the whoop of the rotor in his chest, a thudding arrhythmia shaking his injured ribs.

"Where are we?" asked Bottles, rubbing his eyes. He squinted up as the helicopter's searchlight swept over them without lingering.

"I have no idea. Toward the ocean maybe. Are you all right?"

Bottles hesitated, answering the question for himself before replying with a nod. He seemed absurdly normal to Casper, as if his brain had completed its own cordoning procedure of recent memories and effectively shut those areas off.

"Come on, man," said Bottles. "I know a place. Don't want to be out after dark in this part of town."

"Which part of town?"

Bottles studied the neighborhood. There were a few apartments, boarded shops, a Korean restaurant gutted by fire, the nearby buildings smeared with the black grease of its immolation, and a row of cars that looked as though they had been crushed beneath a tank tread. Someone was shooting a gun, rapid fire, not too far away. The helicopter that had passed them over was thudding back in their direction. The bright headlights of Army trucks appeared from an intersection. Harsh light washed over the crushed cars and stretched hard-edged shadows down the street.

"I guess it don't really matter," said Bottles.

They continued into the depths of night, the dog at their heels.

CHAPTER NINE

■ ■ ■

The Threshold Mass Lab was located more than six thousand feet underground. It was composed of a series of refrigerated chambers, experimental laboratories, pressure locks, and monitoring stations gleaming white with chrome fixtures and the most advanced computer equipment Polly had ever seen. And it was in a shambles.

The Gardeners marched the UN inspectors and the Marines through the corridors. Signs of fighting were everywhere. Walls were splashed with blood, and the acrid smell of gun smoke lingered wherever they turned. This was a coup, she realized. The Gardeners had murdered the scientists and heavy security guarding the Fane. Whatever Milo's intentions, he was no longer obedient to the corporation and the line of Bishops serving as CEO.

"Why are you doing this?" she asked.

"Bishop created the Gardeners and bought my loyalty all those years ago with a tangible promise." He did not stop walking or look at her. "He gave me the body of Holly Webber, blood of mine and Annie Groves, and promised me I could restore her to life. By my own hand I have carved her up and fed her to the Pool. I have seen her return hundreds of times an empty shell. No matter what effort, no matter our devotion to the Mother, she will not come back to me."

"So this is revenge?"

Bishop stopped and motioned for the other Gardeners.

"Separate the killers," he said, directing his men to two conference-sized rooms filled with computer equipment. Bullet and blast damage scarred the walls and furniture. Some of the electronic screens were holed and dark. "We will bring them out one at a time to prepare them so they might all bear witness."

He laid his hand, almost kindly, on Polly's shoulder.

"You were her friend, Veronica," he said. "You remember her alive. I envy you that. When I touch her . . . each piece of her, each toe and finger, each lock of hair, each pickled morsel fills me with longing darkened with sorrow. You must understand this in some small way. You lost Max and Cecelia."

It was the burden borne by all of her flesh. She felt the heat of the last memory of her children at her sister's house, in the yard. They were playing, the sound of their laughter like swings swaying on the power of kicked legs. The fleeting fire of sunset turned them to burnished statues. And then cold, blue waves of time and strange circumstance closed over her recollections.

"I see it," said Milo. "In your eyes. You are as beautiful as her, Veronica, but you are not her. You can never replace her in my heart."

Others came and took her gently away from him, leading her into the room filled with the UN scientists. Each of them was dealing with the situation differently. Some cried; some hung their heads in acquiescence or leveled empty stares at screens overflowing with computer information. Konstantin Sokov sat alone, staring at a photograph of his wife. Dr. Cochrane and Dr. Nandy embraced as old friends and spoke in private conversation.

"Miss Polly," said Rukundo.

She joined him, Dr. Burns, stoic as ever, and Dr. Roux behind a long conference table littered with papers, concrete dust, and shrapnel twists of plastic and metal. The carpet beneath the table was saturated with blood.

Dr. Roux threw her arms around Polly without warning and buried her face in Polly's bosom. Tears dampened the pretty French doctor's face. She cried and hugged Polly tightly. Though surprised, Polly returned the gesture as best she knew.

"It will be okay, Dr. Roux," she said.

Dr. Burns and Rukundo looked away as if the sight of Polly and Dr. Roux embracing made them uncomfortable. Polly soothed Dr. Roux with a hand on the back of her head.

"*Mère!*" Dr. Roux's cry was muffled in Polly's chest. "*Mère! Vous me manquez enormement!*"

Polly was still cradling Dr. Roux to her chest, trying to calm her, when a pair of Gardeners returned to the room. They singled out Dr. Nandy and Dr. Roux, as well as two other scientists Polly did not know well, and pulled them from the room. Polly objected, but they ignored her. Dr. Roux screamed and reached out for Polly as she was dragged from the room.

When her cries had receded and fallen silent, the scientists looked to Polly expectantly. Some faces were hostile, others supportive. She had no consolation to offer them. The Gardeners returned soon after, and four more, including Rukundo, were marched out of the conference room.

Weary, emotionally drained, Polly sat down beside Dr. Robin Burns and at last noticed that the woman shared her exhaustion. Her skin was pale, her features drawn tight with stress.

"Are you afraid?" asked Dr. Burns.

"If they kill me," said Polly, "I'll come back. I am afraid for the future. For the city. I grew up here."

"I know," said Robin.

"Yeah, I guess they teach about us in the schoolbooks."

"They do, but I'm a little old for that. I read up on the three of you before we came. I wasn't sure how closely we would be working with you. I'm glad it was you. Instead of a Warren or a Gideon."

"I never knew the old names until later. After I'd . . ."

"After they forced you into the Pool?"

"It wasn't like that." Polly allowed her anger to show, but it wasn't at Robin. Not really. It was anger at the confusing way her many lives had unfolded.

"I'm sorry," said Robin.

"It was . . . do you have children?"

"I have two children, a son and a daughter. Evie and Clay. She's still my little girl, and he's starting to think he's a man."

"I didn't know."

Robin's smile was forced. "It's always hard to be away from them. I've been assured they are in a safe place. Seattle."

"The farther from here, the better," said Polly.

She realized belatedly that she was pushing Robin in an uncomfortable direction. She cursed herself. She should have known better than to talk about danger to her children. She changed the subject.

"What about you? Are you scared?" asked Polly. "For yourself, I mean."

Robin leaned her head back against the wall and sighed.

"About . . . fifteen years ago . . . wow, fifteen already? Let's say when I was young and beautiful, I was assigned to do some research in Alaska. Nothing like this, not even epidemiology. I was a junior scientist, and it was work with the natives on wildlife census information and populations. A lot of extinctions back then. Arctic wolves, certain types of seals, whales, and we were afraid polar bears were gone too. Habitat loss and pollution.

"As soon as they told me I was going, I went to the used bookstore near my house and bought a big, thick travel guide to the Alaskan wilderness. It was an old brown hardback with yellowed pages and cracks in the spine as if someone had really tucked into it. Printed in 1965. There was a lot of good information in there, but the chapter that will always stand out to me is this chapter near the end called 'Avoiding Bear Attacks' about avoiding and surviving polar bear attacks. Lots of practical advice, list of things to have with you, like a pistol to frighten the bear, common-sense advice like 'always pay attention to your surroundings' and 'never turn your back on a bear.'

"At the very end of the chapter there were a few paragraphs telling you what to do if the attack couldn't be avoided. How to survive it. The author said, and I'm paraphrasing from years ago, 'The first thing you think when you are attacked by a bear is that this cannot be happening. You must stay calm and realize that it is happening. You are being killed by an animal force that cannot be reasoned with. It's much stronger than you. The only way to overcome death is to convince the bear that you are dead. You must go limp and pretend to die in its jaws, and no matter how great the fear or pain, you must be perfectly quiet.'"

"I don't think that would work too well in this situation," said Polly.

"Maybe not." Robin's gaze was far away. "I'm sorry, I got a bit lost remembering that trip."

"Did you find what you were looking for?"

"It was inconclusive. We found markings that might have belonged to an adult polar bear. We never saw a fresh trail or a live bear. As far as we know, they have been wiped out by human habitation, extinct outside of zoos."

"At least those are still around," said Polly.

The door opened, and several Gardeners piled in, separating the remaining scientists into manageable groups and escorting them, by twos and threes, out of the conference room. Polly was afraid, despite her previous arguments. Robin Burns must have shared the sentiment, for as they were escorted through the corridor, she took hold of Polly's hand and squeezed.

■   ■   ■

Downtown Los Angeles glowed. Traffic moved in orderly grids. Military trucks did not patrol between the immense office towers. It was almost like the city was still alive.

Bottles brought Casper to the southernmost edge of downtown. It was a dark worksite, surrounded by chain-link and plywood. A sign depicted a mainsail of blue glass and banded silver. The Azure Tower, coming 2001.

The building was unfinished, construction halted, according to Bottles, "When the economy got fucked up." The exterior of the lower floors was finished with polished metal and Gothic flourishes, too big to be easily looted, that reminded Casper of a larger-scale version of St. Philomena's. The building ascended several floors, mostly intact, before receding into girders strung with billowing tarps, half walls and safety cages, and finally ending entirely in a jagged, steel jigsaw. An unfulfilled promise to the city skies.

Two massive cranes stood idle nearby, skeletal sentinels defending the gates of the incomplete tower. As they passed beneath them, Casper picked out details of broken struts and disconnected hydraulics that suggested the cranes were waiting to be scrapped, not waiting to resume work.

Bottles sought and found a sun-bleached rectangle of plywood, nailed into a window frame, apparently unmarked. He worked the toe of his shoe beneath it and pried it out at the bottom. It was nailed in the other three corners, but he was able to open it wide enough for Casper to duck inside. Bottles followed him into the darkness, glass crunching underfoot, closing the plywood behind them, but not before the dog scurried in as well.

"Don't talk to nobody," Bottles warned.

The sprawling ground floor of the building was occupied by dozens, maybe hundreds, of squatters. There were families of normal humans mixed in with a lot of dupes. They crowded into unfinished rooms, lay in sleeping bags in the dry fountain of the lobby, and talked quietly around fires burning in the empty sockets of never-potted plants. A woman—a Veronica, Casper realized—wrapped in a blanket, wearing a stocking cap and layers of filth, upended a bucket full of shit down the empty shaft of an elevator.

The secret place Bottles had described at St. Philomena's was revealed at the bottom of three staircases, in the stinking bowels of the building, behind a riveted access panel cleverly made to pivot.

"Ain't showed nobody this for a while. Come on, you gotta crawl."

They descended through a tunnel, at times so cramped not even the dog could stand, and they were forced to go on their bellies. The stifling heat of it at first reminded Casper of the cave in New Mexico, but the deeper they went, the cooler and fresher the air became, until Casper could hear rushing water and the dirty smell of city rain.

"Watch your step," said Bottles. "We're getting to the ladder."

The shaft ended abruptly, the space yawning open into a dark space echoing with the sound of rushing water. There was faint yellow light glowing from fixtures bolted into the stone walls, and Casper was able to see a ladder set beneath the access shaft descending to a ledge. The cavernous space was some sort of massive, high-tech storm sewer. A central channel was flooded with rushing water, but it was clearly designed to accommodate a much larger capacity.

"It goes all the way to the ocean," said Bottles, an expression of pride on his face as he helped Casper down off the ladder. "I walked it when I first found this place."

The dog leaped down from the shaft, into the rushing water. Casper thought for a moment it would be swept away—he wished it would be—but it pulled itself out, shaking off the moisture before rejoining them.

"This a storm sewer?" asked Casper.

"I figured, but like none I seen before," said Bottles, leading Casper deeper into the tunnel. "You could drive a truck through here. Two maybe. It ain't finished out east— stops in this big pit that seems like they're not working on it anymore. Lets you off right downtown. But, man, you go the other way, you can go all the way to Sugarside and sit there and watch the sun go down over the boats. I do it sometimes. Did it yesterday. Most of the boats are gone now, just a real big one, like a Navy ship, and some stragglers."

There was a maintenance door, heavy but unlocked, that opened into a power and flow-control shed. It wasn't a big space, ten feet by seven or eight, hemmed in by pipes but partitioned into more than one room by hanging sheets and builders' plastic. It smelled of perfume poorly masking sweat and urine, and beneath that a complexity of warm metal pipes, machine grease, corrosion, mold, and long-ago meals soaked into the porous concrete.

Soft music played behind a curtain printed with cartoon ducks. Old music, crackling with AM distortion, old enough that Casper felt he should know it, but he didn't. The walls were built up with shelves made from plywood and bent wire, each supporting a bewildering assortment of junk.

"A lot of it comes floating down from above." Bottles picked up a tin can filled with toothbrushes, pens, pencils, and combs. He showed it to Casper, put it back, and picked up a toy made from articulated, brightly colored plastic. "A lot of it I got to go get myself."

"David?" a soft voice called out, barely louder than the sound of the rushing water and the gentle music playing from the radio.

"Toilet is in there." Bottles pointed to a door frame hung with plastic sheeting. "I got to see Carlos."

He immediately passed through the hanging sheet covered with ducks. Casper inspected his cramped surroundings again. The dog was lying in the open doorway, at least somewhat rinsed of blood by the flow of water. There was a milk crate topped with a beaded cover, a table made from layers of cardboard, and the hot plate with a surprisingly clean but well-seasoned soup pot on the burner.

Casper sat down on the milk crate and took out the chapbook of propaganda Polly had given him. He became almost immediately distracted, straining to listen to the conversation Bottles was having. He pushed aside the sheet just far enough to get a finger in and peer through to the other side.

Carlos was propped up with pillows beneath him and heavy blankets over his body. He was dark-haired and heavy browed, slight, young seeming, handsome under better circumstances. His face was pale, his eyes sunken and dark, and his flesh waxy. He was gaunt; the smell of piss was emanating from him, and something else, medicinal but not quite covering a rancid odor like rotten meat. Casper had witnessed cancer do that to people he loved. It would have done it to him if he hadn't ended it first.

Bottles shifted empty plastic containers and old magazines aside and crouched next to Carlos, talking so quietly that Casper could only hear every few words. Bottles stroked Carlos's head tenderly, feeling his cheeks with the backs of his fingers, talking in an affectionate tone that nevertheless betrayed his concern. He offered the smashed clamshell of food, but Carlos shook his head. Bottles emptied the contents of the bag and tried to cheer Carlos with the various things he had collected.

"Who is that with you?" asked Carlos, his voice fragile.

"He is a friend. I met him at the church. He's an okay guy. Good guy."

"Just a friend?" There was jealousy, teasing but evident.

"He is a good man, only a friend. Don't worry your head." Bottles reached for the bottom of the blanket covering Carlos, but Carlos seized his hand.

"Not now, please," he said. "It was better this morning."

"That's because I scraped it. You got to let me check. I can put some more medicine on them."

Carlos let go of his hand. Bottles lifted the sheet, and as he did, the rancid-meat smell intensified, and Casper caught sight of red, suppurating wounds covering Carlos's feet up to his shins. Tufts of white threads sprouted from the wounds, anchored in the gory ruins of his limbs. Some of these vermicular thatches were large enough to grow broader near the tips of each thread, forming translucent diamond shards, like leaves of frosted glass. Bottles was as transfixed as Casper by the horrific sight.

"He's watching," said Carlos, his feverish eyes on Casper.

Casper dropped the sheet back into place.

They continued their conversation in hushed quiet. Casper could only follow the general ebb and flow, the increase in pitch or the occasional word. When Bottles finally emerged from the sheet, his eyes were puffy and red, and he was still wiping away tears with his fingertips.

"I got to go," he said. "You get some sleep. Lock the door. When I get back, I'll knock five times. You got to let me in."

"You're trusting me?"

"No choice." Bottles unscrewed the lid from a water bottle and took out a small wad of cash. The money was different colors, red and orange bills, a large green one. Casper recognized Benjamin Franklin on a hundred-dollar bill but could not place the other portraits. Bottles stuffed the money into his pocket.

"Where are you going?"

"Man"—Bottles turned, his brow cinched tightly, his lips curled in a snarl—"you mind your fucking business, and quit with the questions. I got to get medicine, okay? And you are not invited. You are not . . ."

Bottles sighed. Casper took out his debit card and pressed it into Bottles's hand.

"Take it," he said, and Bottles did take it, wiping his tears again, feet shuffling into the tunnel. The door clanged shut, and the room became very quiet. Casper was alone with the sounds of the dying man.

■ ■ ■

The refrigerated prep area was all white tile and chrome panels and heavy glass doors. Rukundo, Dr. Roux, Captain Dryson, and all the others who had disappeared were there and dressed in puffy white insulated suits. Except they were similar to the padded suits warn by cosmonauts, with hardened helmets and glass face-plates. Large backpacks and thickened joints restricted movement so that they even had the ponderous, bounding gait of a cosmonaut on the moon.

The Gardeners dressed Polly and Robin quickly, handling them almost like small children as they directed their arms into sleeves and closed pressure clamps without regard to complaints.

"Where is Sergeant Funkweed?" asked Polly, realizing he was the only man missing.

"He possessed some information we required," said Milo. "He gave us what we wanted, but he is no longer in a condition to participate."

The Marines bristled at this comment. It sickened Polly as well. Despite their initial differences, she rather liked Sergeant Funkweed. The thought of him being tortured in strange ways by the Gardeners did not renew her own hopes for a happy, or at least survivable, ending.

A young Gardener, maybe only days out of the Pool, lowered a domed helmet over Polly's head and engaged the seals. The outside world was abruptly muted, and the loudest sound was her breathing and the click of an air circulator. Each suit was connected to three hoses feeding in cold air from a backpack unit, coolant liquid to pouches in the lining of the suit, and evacuating heated air.

"The temperature beyond the door has increased recently as high as 350 degrees. It is currently 268 degrees." The Gardener spoke into a headset that relayed his voice into their helmets. "The suit is self-sealing, but if you tear it open, there is a good chance you will die. Be mindful as you walk, and do not make sudden movements."

They were joined by similarly-equipped groups of Gardeners. The Gardeners brought with them a long, insulated case resting atop a wheeled cart. It was the size of a coffin. The Gardeners distributed themselves among the UN inspectors as the entire group began a deliberate shuffle toward the airlock.

Movement in the suits was plodding and uncomfortable. Despite the painfully cold feel of the coolant pockets and the cold air, Polly found herself sweating in the helmet. These awful contraptions were like a faded childhood memory of wearing a snow suit. This suit, with its rigid joint protection, was even worse. Bending at the elbows and knees took concerted effort.

The heavy airlock door cycled slowly closed. There was a hiss of equalizing pressure as the outer door opened. It only took a moment for the heat to hit her. Their suits crackled and clicked as the polymers expanded. The rocky corridor was revealed by the rotating door, lit yellow by lights recessed in mineral-tinted domes.

The underground world was alive with the heat. Steam lifted from rocks; drooling strands of plastic hung from the ceiling where the temperature spike must have liquefied the fixtures. The air shimmered, and the rocks seemed soft at their edges. Polly could feel it now. Fingers of heat reached between the packs of liquid coolant in her suit like swords finding weaknesses in a suit of plate armor.

The voice of a Gardener crackled over the helmet radio. "Get moving."

She trudged slowly, minding her step. The corridor curved gently around the lowest point of the Pool. There were handholds built into the rock walls, and the floor was textured to reduce the chance of someone slipping. They passed beneath a toothy forest of pale stalactites.

"I wish I'd thought to bring my camera." Dr. Cochrane's voice sounded weak and nasal over the radio.

"Your camera would have been ruined already," said a nearby Gardener. "Don't worry. There are cameras watching your every step."

They trudged on, following the curving corridor. Huge quartz crystals jutted from the red rocks of the wall. The pink formations of rock reminded Polly of the color of strawberry milkshakes from Swiftee Burger. The thought of a cold sip from one seemed only to make the heat reach deeper through her suit.

Moving was a great labor, and the exertion showed in the way each person's arms now hung limp and heavy at their sides. The walls of the corridor ahead were covered in sheets and scraps of paper. The group divided to follow the walls on either side, looking at the papers. Some papers were new and white, the writing clear; others were colored by the mineral gases or marred by heat damage to the inks used in writing. Many of the sheets were decorated with elaborate illustrations of nature scenes and animals, of esoteric symbols. Polly stopped at one, a drawing of a Veronica, amateurish but very detailed.

"They're tombstones," said Polly. "These are the people who have died and been returned to the Pool."

"Why? You just come back," said Dr. Cochrane.

"Please, Liam," scolded Robin.

"Keep moving," said one of the Gardeners flatly.

CHAPTER TEN

■ ■ ■

Casper read the propaganda chapbook for a while, about the wars in Vietnam and Mexico, Central America, the Philippines, and the Middle East. The fight against the Communists and the Muhammadins. There seemed to be endless wars with political and humanitarian motivations poorly concealing the true fight: a global war for the domination of resources.

He turned off the lights, all except for an electric lantern kept beside Carlos, glowing brightly enough to give color to the cartoon ducks. There was just enough space for Casper to lie with his feet on either side of the toilet and his head beside the metal maintenance door.

He rested but did not sleep. He listened for the sound of Carlos breathing. There were long pauses between each rattling intake of air, a high-pitched squeak at the edge of each exhalation. The cadence was frequently disrupted by rattling coughs.

The man surprised Casper by recovering from a particularly brutal fit and then asking, "Hey. Are you still there?"

"Yeah," said Casper.

"My name is Carlos. I'm," he trailed as if considering what to say next. "I'm with David."

"The name is Casper Cord."

"It's weird sending him off for medicine," said Carlos. "Used to have all I needed. You know, I was an EMT. They called in every ambulance when it hit. It was one of the first, maybe the first real big one. There were already crews there when we showed up. It was an elementary school in East LA. We had masks and gloves in case it was hemostaph, but it—"

Carlos's cough burst through his words, a fluid lung spasm that continued for several seconds. Once he regained his composure, he took deep breaths before continuing. "It wasn't hemostaph. The kids were all on the ground, right there on the playground, three classes of them, and these teachers freaking out. The other kids were watching through the windows of the school, their faces in a row along the windows of the classrooms, watching us try to save their friends. I wish the teachers would have kept them away, but they were . . . they were all outside with us."

Carlos went silent. Casper listened to him struggling to fight back a cough. Carlos steadied himself, took a few more deep breaths, and continued.

"I thought it was pollen, you know, when it caught a beam of sunlight. Like the air was all chalky. There was more and more of it every minute we were there, and these kids, man, they were fucked up. Seizing, eyes rolled back in their heads, tearing at their skin. There was no time to stop and assess. Then it started growing on them. Wherever they scratched themselves open, so fast it was like their bodies were full of the bristles, man, the white weed."

"The blood," said Casper. "I remember."

"Yeah. It likes open wounds a lot, open mouth or eyes, mucous membranes— that's how it got all those teachers. We kept telling them to get back, but they wouldn't stay away. I just brushed my pant leg against a little girl, flat-lined, working the bag on her. Partner doing compressions. He got it all over his hands and arms. By the time we had that girl and two others loaded in our unit, it was starting. I . . . I don't know . . . they corralled us, the military, tried to cut it off of us, which works for a while, but the others kept dying, so I got away. Holding me was pointless any-way—it was in the air—but I sometimes wonder if I might have been better off. Maybe I—"

More coughing. Prolonged this time.

"If I'd stayed, maybe one of their doctors might have found something. I've lasted longer than most. Got some . . . got a partial immunity maybe. Maybe at least going through this would have meant something to someone."

Casper turned onto his side and slid the curtain open a little. Carlos's eyes rolled slowly to regard him. There was foam at the corners of his mouth. His nose was bleeding.

"You didn't send Bottles to get you medicine, did you?"

"I did," said Carlos, "but it's an antibiotic in high demand. He'll never find it."

"You might be surprised; he seems pretty resourceful."

Carlos chuckled, which caused a silent hitching in his chest as he stifled more choking.

"I didn't want him to watch this happen. I can feel it, growing all the way up my thighs, onto my stomach. It's only an hour or two now. Maybe even less. You can . . . it moves, it grows so fast, you can feel it moving on your body, then it gets cold. Burning cold.

"You did this to me, you know." Carlos smiled. "Not you, I mean. Your kind. I've read the CDC reports at the hospital; all of these invasive diseases have infection patterns radiating out from that fucking rejuvenation center. The spore came from there. That place you all are hatched from. It's . . ."

Carlos's head lolled to the side, and drool spilled from his lips. He began a rhythmic motion of arms and legs, violent at times, that dashed the radio to pieces and startled Lenin from his sleep. He stopped, finally, but continued to make a terrible gurgling sound as he struggled to breathe. It was several minutes before he came fully awake, disoriented and frightened, staring up at Casper, who had tried to position him to breathe better.

"I saw this disease before," said Casper. "Far away from here in a strange place."

Casper confessed the whole thing to Carlos, relating every detail, first of the other side, and more broadly, of his experiences, even the truth about the strange training apparatus, the Harrow, and the trepanned prisoners in the Center. He rambled, stretching back further, to the Pool, to its discovery, to Spark, and to Annie. He looked down every so often to be sure Carlos was still alive. As he finished the tale, he saw the white creeping up Carlos's neck, growing onto his jawline and over the cartilaginous portions of one ear.

"I heard it," said Carlos. "It makes it better in a way . . . I . . . please . . . take me to . . . take me to where the tunnel ends. I want to see the outside."

It was pointless to argue a deathbed request with the man, so Casper carried him, the dog following along by his side. Carlos was like a skeletal bird, hollow and fragile, his arms dangling uselessly, his limbs sheathed in the bristling pelt of the spore grass, his eyes rolling as he passed in and out of consciousness. The white material appeared soft but was brittle and burned wherever it touched Casper's body. It did not take root in his flesh.

He traced the path from the maintenance room west until he could hear the surf rolling in, louder than the rush of the drain water.

"I can hear the ocean," Carlos said with a dreamy smile. They reached the end of the tunnel, and the view of the night sky, spangled with countless stars, and the marina, dark, full of ships bobbing gently in the tide, was moving to both men.

There was an outflow ramp, which would have made possible the descent from the tunnel mouth down to the rocky shore below, but Casper dared not attempt carrying Carlos down the slippery concrete. Casper braced him against the tunnel's central pillar, the cool night air ruffling his hair. Casper watched the time-lapse unfurling of white threads up Carlos's chin, around his mouth, wriggling into his scalp, his nostrils, but his dark eyes remained untouched.

"My mother . . ." Carlos said something in Spanish before continuing in English. "My mother, she was very religious, always believed she would die when the world was ending. I thought it was silly. She died from a bad heart years ago. But I understand it now. I understand why she wanted that."

"Why is that?"

"To follow the tide out to sea," he said. "To be carried away with everyone and not be alone. To not die alone."

Casper was not sure when Carlos passed from merely being quiet to being dead. Casper gently stretched his body out on the concrete, but he did not want to leave this view of the ocean. Carlos was right about that. The Pacific was speaking, reminding him of the immense power the world still contained. He leaned the side of his head against the wall of the tunnel, mesmerized by the reflections in the water and the cool air.

"He chooses death." The voice was soft, flat, and unaffected by the stone walls of the tunnel, but completely clear to Casper. "He is correct. Heat builds, the depths stir and churn, and the deep waters will devour land and sea. Fluid and flesh, the ichors of every living thing, consumed. The outcome of its arrival is inevitable. Your spires will break, the earth will heave and crack open, it will consume the marrow of this place, and unique humans, rich with purpose and meaning, are its greatest craving."

Casper was afraid. Without looking, he knew the voice belonged to the dog, and he knew it was revealing its true self to him, that the thing within the flesh of his old dog was exposed, glowing coals in an open furnace, casting rippling aurora light along the moisture-darkened tunnel. If he turned and looked upon its face, he might go mad.

"What are you?" Casper asked quietly, trying to still his fear.

"I am friend, Casper Cord, who is Warren Groves, who is the champion of this place, trapped in deep waters with me. I am long-ago thing of faraway place, another kind, protector of a dead queen, guardian of a forever thrall of the waters. I am reificant. Intent trapped in deep water, I wear the flesh of your dead animal. A corpse-thing shunned by the water. We have met before. I have tried to be the voice of warning."

"The grasshopper," said Casper.

"I am from the other place. You have been there. You have witnessed as I have witnessed the great ruin of my kind. You walked on two slow legs through the city by the sea. It was once greatest of our cities, our capital. The spires of this place were largest, the scholars the most learned, the warriors, the mightiest and most fearless. It took six hundred days to incorporate us, to adhere us to the gestalt, ravenous, extending infinitely, unseen but yawning. A well of deep water."

"The Pool," Casper said, his words eaten by the crashing surf against the rocks. Foaming water climbed the drainage ramp. His head was beginning to ache. "It's doing something, spreading these diseases like Carlos said."

"Diseases first," said the grasshopper. "Sessile things follow to make the air ripe. Already coming. Danger blooms. Slavering jaws collected from countless places. Wise things, full of meaning, cruel and savage, stalking your fallen spires. Their hunger is its hunger."

"Why?"

"The water flows and fills the cracks, to beckon, to dissolve and incorporate. It is the bodies within that give this water purpose, and it is this purpose the water seeks. Life, Casper Cord, like yours and mine. Sentient life is the most precious resource."

"Why?" said Casper.

"A stone cannot be heroic. A chasm of ice deep enough to swallow this place cannot stir the spirit of the sky. Only intelligence imbues meaning. The water bends and flows and fills the cracks between, crosses void, offers eternity as its honeyed trap. Your kind has sworn this pact."

"How can . . ." Casper's head ached fearsomely. "Tell me . . . how can we stop it?"

"Through the eyes of strange flesh I have witnessed things impossible in the context of my kind. I have lived as other flesh. Other places I have been, the water has been before. This place is the first I happened upon quickly, before the fall, the next sentient to be tempted to the water's edge. The long-ago people of the desert met me first, and I learned their words and sang them with quills. Warning, Casper Cord, was heeded, and these brave humans chose death over eternity. They chose extinction over servitude. You, the others, have not chosen the same. The tipping point has been reached, and you must prepare."

"To fight?" Casper leaned his head into his hands.

There came a clicking sound, almost scornful. When the grasshopper spoke again, its voice was very close behind Casper.

"You are champion of your kind. A human. It is a body without flesh, it is mindless and infinite, it cannot be overcome with violence. It is too late for sacrifice, but you must prepare."

"For what?" Casper tore at his hair.

"A champion must deny meaning to the water. This place is lost. Your kind is lost." A dry husk rasped against stone. "You must prepare to flow with the water to the next place, to warn the next kind, to deny meaning to the water. You must take on new flesh."

"How?"

There came no answer. Casper asked it again, and still it did not answer. The scudding sound of rubber on concrete echoed up the tunnel. A voice called from far away.

"Carlos!"

The dog was sitting on its haunches, staring at Casper with red eyes flecked with black. It did not look away as Bottles approached from behind.

"Casper, what . . . what happened?"

"I'm sorry."

Casper stepped up to him and tried to hold him back, but it was a futile, weak-limbed gesture. Bottles tore through his grasp and ran to the edge of the tunnel. Carlos was by then completely engulfed in the white of the spore grass. It spilled from his body and planted itself along the floor around him. Bottles stopped short, realizing that to touch his dead lover meant death. He fell upon his knees and hung his head and did not rise again for a very long time.

Casper and the dog could only watch.

■ ■ ■

The corridor opened into a stone chamber, painted red and filled with rows of rock benches. The rock walls were adorned in carved figures and patterns. As they stepped into this chamber, Polly became unsteady on her feet. A tightening sensation enclosed her skull, but from inside her helmet, as if something was squeezing the soft fruit of her brain. Someone was whispering to her, a chorus of soft susurrations.

"Do you hear that?" she asked. No one admitted to hearing it.

The Fane was small. Three wide steps up to an indentation in the rock wall. There was a black hatch low to the floor clamped shut by several heavy locks. There appeared no way to open this hatch. Above that, at roughly face height, a smaller red hatch with a hand-grip to lever it open. An elaborate symbol was carved into the stone above the red hatch. It was the skull and branching antlers of the stag.

"This is not what I expected," said Dr. Roux.

"It is a chapel," said Konstantin.

"You worship this thing?" asked Captain Dryson.

"We venerate her and commune with her," said Milo. "Do you not feel the Mother, pressing into your skull like fingers in soft clay?"

The snowflakes did not feel it. Polly did not admit to feeling it, though she still heard the soft whisper of unintelligible voices.

"The effect becomes more pronounced when you open the viewing aperture," said Milo. He ascended the rough stairs and operated the smaller hatch's locking mechanisms. Unearthly, moving light appeared behind the glass. Even through the gilded portal she felt it. Polly laughed and felt a rush of hormonal pleasure. The scientists and soldiers yelped with dismay.

"Ow, fucking hell!" complained Dr. Cochrane. Others sagged against the walls or one another. The ragged breathing and the hastened click of their respirators sounded over the radios. It took several seconds for the group to level out.

"What is happening?" demanded Robin.

The Gardeners ignored her question. They began a methodical process of unfolding a red velvet cloth and spreading it upon the rocky floor beneath the larger hatch. They lifted the insulated coffin from its cart, and four men carried it to the red cloth. The Gardeners assumed a formation, standing like soldiers in parade rows between the cloth and the scientists. Milo was visible above them, standing atop the stairs.

"You may begin," he said.

"Yes, brother," replied the Gardeners surrounding the coffin.

Rukundo moved close to Polly and took hold of her sleeve, tugging it gently. He gestured back down the tunnel. Escape was his intent. She gestured to the cameras in protective bubbles. Rukundo tugged more insistently, not daring to speak over the open radio channel. The Gardeners were involved in some bizarre ceremonial opening of their insulated coffin. She wondered if someone intended to climb inside it.

Milo began to speak loudly, his tone and posture that of a seasoned preacher.

"Without form or limits," began Milo, "we revere your waters, which pass through stone and cross all gulfs. We are the instructions of men, derived from your flesh and your blood. We are your water. We are eyes to see and hands to touch for you on this earth. We are your mouths to speak on this earth."

"Mother, be praised!" answered the chorus of Gardeners.

Polly watched in disbelief as Milo reached up to the clasps on his helmet and unsealed the cuff with a hiss of releasing pressure. He tossed aside the helmet. His face was immediately red and shimmering in the heat.

"Come forward, brothers," he said, and the front ranks of the assembled Gardeners joined Milo at the head of the stairs. They carried hammers and chisels and immediately set about pounding the chisels into the gaps on the larger of the two hatches.

"Mother, we free you. We release you from your cage and crack the shell that holds you. We present a great sacrifice and beseech you, call forth the spirit of Holly Webber from her surviving flesh."

The four Gardeners standing at attention beside the insulated coffin opened the lid. Steam rushed out in a gasp and evaporated almost instantly, exposing a naked and badly mutilated body. It was gray with decomposition, its features softened as though it had been brined. Polly's stomach lurched as she realized the lipless face was Holly Webber. This was her original corpse.

"I"—Milo swayed unsteadily—"I give myself to you. I give my brothers to you. I give this place to you, so that you may become unlimited. So that your waters . . . your waters will overtake the sea."

He descended the stairs and laid a hand upon the grotesque carcass of Holly Webber. He lifted that quivering hand and let it fall. The men behind him beat their hammers against the chisels in unison. A crack, loud as a cannon shot, sounded through the Fane.

Polly began to back away, fearful that the hatch might release a torrent of fluid into the chamber. She collided with Rukundo and realized the others were already backing away as well. The two halves of the hatch opened outward on flaking hinges, slowly, heavily and with a resounding wail of fatigued metal. Their inner doors were smooth gold. The inner ring of the hatch was similarly clad in gold. The opening hatch revealed a luminous pearl of white fluid as large as a weather balloon.

"My God!" cried one of the scientists.

The vise of pressure on Polly's brain suddenly burst within her skull, and Polly experienced ecstasy like nothing before in her life. She dropped to her knees, looking at the face of it, beautiful, bulging slowly out of the lower hatch, extending in a fluid column, its form stretching past the Gardeners and moving toward Milo. Everything it touched—papers, the discarded helmet, the velvet cloth—boiled away like steam.

The scientists, even the Marines, were screaming, scrambling away in a confusion heightened by the disorienting effects of the Mother's presence.

Milo, his face beginning to blister, barely able to stand, nevertheless reached out a hand as if to touch the approaching mass. The fingers of his suit burst, and the flexible material curled up his dissolving arm. His limb became smoke, and the Mother, pouring into the room, seemed to inhale it. He fell back, leaning heavily against the table. It gathered its mass, squirming out into the room and creating two floes that began to encircle the coffin and Milo.

Some of the Gardeners stepped back to avoid the Mother. Others fell to their knees and allowed her to overtake them or stepped into her milky surface and hissed as their entire bodies dissolved into smoke. Polly, transfixed by the sight, quaking with tremors of pleasure, was dimly aware of arms taking hold of her and pulling her away from the viscous mass still pouring out into the Fane.

The hatch—open doors and the protective ring—boiled away, gold peeling and falling to the floor. Chalky dust steamed from the widening hole. Alarms sounded at the sudden concentrations of spores. The fog became so thick, the Gardeners began to disappear. The grass sprouted over the walls and erupted millions of wriggling tendrils over the heated rock.

The last thing Polly saw as Rukundo dragged her away from the Fane and around the curvature of the tunnel was the encircling Mother collapsing in on Milo and the remains of Holly Webber. A moment later the world began to shake.

■　■　■

They buried Carlos beside the ocean, just out of reach of the waves breaking on the stony shore. The sun was rising behind them, and the sky and ocean were of the same color, divided by a curling meridian of white foam. When it was done, they went to the edge of the water, and, though the stones were sharp and the flooded tide pools unpleasant with life, Bottles took off his shoes and threadbare socks and walked out into the surf. After a time Casper shed his sandals and joined him, the ragged edge of coral against his toes, the jelly of some tidal creature beneath his heel.

Bottles was staring at nothing, at the elapsing night, at the new day unveiled in a gradient, the gentle lifting of the house lights following the performance. Casper's gaze was drawn to the marina at Sugarside, a quarter mile distant, the many bobbing lights he had believed were the masts of ships by darkness revealed as buoys and mooring posts. Only a few vessels remained, but behind them, beyond the ship canal, almost out to the farthest breakwater, was the shape of a warship.

It was long and low to the water, painted a stark white and liveried with blue. It flew an American flag but no naval standard. Casper studied it for some time. There appeared to be people in blue uniforms moving on the decks, but none of them stayed outside very long.

"*The Republic*." Casper read the ship's name aloud.

"It's been there for a few days," said Bottles. "A week maybe."

"What is it doing?"

Bottles shook his head and began to walk back to shore, stepping gingerly over something that pricked his toe.

"Showed up one morning right as the spores were getting real bad. Sometimes it leaves and patrols around. I used to catch it coming back in toward the marina. They can park it up close at the end of the main pier, but they mostly just sit out there."

They splashed out of the water. Bottles took a seat on a stump of chipped concrete and began rubbing the grit from his feet before putting his socks back on.

"I got him that medicine." Bottles stopped trying to fit his second sock over his toes. "I had to sell all my liquor and your card, man, but I got it for him. I knew he was tricking me, getting me out of here so he could die like a fucking dog, man. Die alone."

"I was with him."

"That almost makes it worse. He didn't have much use for your kind. Thought you caused all this disease and stuff."

"He went peacefully," said Casper.

"Naw, that's not true. He fought it the whole time. Days would go by with nothing, and then the next day he'd wake up, legs all covered in it, screaming about dreams he was having." Bottles beat two fingers against his temple. "It got into his head. Like it was growing in there too, giving him fevers so he saw things. Thought I was the devil one time . . . and . . . ha-ha . . ."

Bottles was done talking. He wiped at his eyes, and they finished putting on their shoes in silence. As they were finishing, the rocks around them seemed to dip, like a trampoline depressing beneath their feet and then snapping back up with a release of tension. Rocks clattered down around them; car alarms began honking in the distance. It came again, shaking now, and Casper knew it was an earthquake, not as strong as the initial shock but oscillating rapidly.

Heavy stones rolled down and crashed among the rocks of the artificial headlands. Buoys bobbed violently up and down in the marina. Casper heard glass breaking and the clatter of masonry collapsing, followed by the sharp bang of something falling from a considerable height.

"Goddamn," said Bottles, steadying himself on a stone post. "I been through harder shakes than this, but the fucking thing just keeps going."

It felt like a minor earthquake, but it had already gone on for a minute and was still shaking, quivering up into the bones unpleasantly, scattering loose rocks down from the cliffs. *The Republic* seemed unmoved by the temblor, but many uniformed men were out on the deck, pointing inland.

Casper's view of whatever it was they were pointing at was obstructed by the ramp leading up to the drainage tunnel and, behind that, the embankment of piled stone too steep to easily climb. He was staring up, straining to see something, when the smoke appeared, moving swiftly on the wind, a shuddering caterpillar of black smoke crawling its shadow across the shore. He inhaled the tang of burning diesel, the smell of foundry and deep earth, hot stone, grit in mouth, and the smell of marrow.

The seared stench of human marrow wafting out to sea.

■ ■ ■

"Are you aware of the 2004–2005 Pandemic Study conducted by the CDC?"

Misha Rosen's question jarred Bishop out of the gathering stupor. How could she have that study? He had gone to staggering lengths, done very difficult things, to ensure that study disappeared from the face of the earth. Misha continued before he could respond.

"Allow me to quote you something from it. 'Type-D Pandemic Pneumocystis and Hemorrhagic Staphylococcus follow almost identical outbreak patterns, with first cases reported in the area of San Pedro and South Los Angeles, radiating out geographically, following normal travel patterns.' It goes on, Mr. Bishop, to state that the only logical conclusion, and I will quote again, 'is the emergence of immune disease-bearing duplicates from within the Los Angeles Rejuvenation Center.' "

"That document is a fake, most likely circulated by groups with a bigoted, anti-duplicate agenda."

"Experts have authenticated it," said Misha, but Bishop was bullying ahead and speaking over her.

"For you to parrot the rhetoric of hate-mongers, for you to serve as a propaganda mouthpiece for anti-American bigots like Berezin and the Chinese, against a fellow American, well, this is appalling. It's disgusting." Bishop reached to tear off the microphone on his lapel, thought better of it, and surged to his feet. "I'm not going to sit here, allow you to come into my place of business, and commit this . . . this blood libel against my people. Do you have any idea how much we have done for the United States?"

He shook his finger at Misha, his gaze flicking from her smug face to the glass Cyclops of the camera.

"Harlan Bishop built this country into the world's only superpower. Look around you. At your camera. At your TV set. Our designs. Our factories. Our jobs we give to you. Our enterprise has transformed an isolationist yokel into the king that straddles the continents. We have fought in wars, fought and died for this country, in great gory heaps, and I will not let you scapegoat my brothers and sisters for every ill in this world."

"Not every ill, just the diseases and the spores," said Misha firmly.

"There are treatments, cures," said Bishop. "PPD and hemostaph are no longer death sentences."

"These treatments were developed by your company," said Misha, "with improbable speed."

"All of our resources were focused on dealing with the crisis."

"Two years after the PPD outbreak in 2000 and six months after the outbreak in 2003 you went to market with treatments. You released the vaccines as if you were sitting on thousands of gallons of the antibodies."

"We saved millions of lives."

"You made hundreds of billions of dollars. Your company profited on diseases you introduced, unintentionally or otherwise, and your fortunes grew amid global pandemic, recession, and chaos. Should we expect Bishop Unlimited to come to market with a cure for the spore sicknesses?"

His fury was spent. He slumped back into his chair.

"Get out. Take your Communist sympathies and your damn cameras, and get out. I won't hear another word of your racist slander."

"One more question," said Misha. "Are you prepared to respond to Admiral Haley's forty-eight-hour—"

The room began to violently shake, and Misha's words were forgotten midsentence. The first shockwave was powerful enough to knock artifacts from shelves and stagger some of the TV crew. The cameraman became ensnared in the cable snakes trailing from his equipment and tipped over backward. Light stands fell and dragged down the blackout curtains. Daylight streamed in, stabbing into the stricken faces of the crew.

The mousy sound woman from the World Insight crew yelped and leaped toward the desk, narrowly avoiding being crushed by a falling barrister case weighed down with books. It boomed to the floor, loud as a cannon shot. Patrice hurried into the room and pulled Bishop away from the window.

"It's all right," said Bishop, shaking off his bodyguard's hands. "It's just a minor tremor. This is California. We're used to this sort of thing, right? Let's just all stand clear of furniture or fixtures. It will pass quickly."

It did not.

CHAPTER ELEVEN

■ ■ ■

Businesses and apartments emptied into the streets, and Casper, Bottles, and the dog walked among the teeming masses. There were injuries, scrapes and bruises mostly, bleary-eyed hordes coated in brick dust and cradling wounded limbs. The earthquake had shaken loose every emotion. Men and women laughed, cried, called out in panic to one another, searching for lost comrades, lost children, among the confusion of bodies. It was bewildering, a scene of too many personal dramas to process.

Car alarms were still honking rhythmically. The sirens of emergency vehicles moved on unseen streets. Bottles peeled away from Casper and found two men he recognized standing together. One was a handsome, light-skinned black man with a neatly-trimmed goatee and dark glasses. The other was a summit of a man as dark as molasses, bald, shirtless, broad-shouldered and rippling with muscles, his expression unchanging, his biceps decorated with the illegible blots of prison tattoos.

"Let him go," said the dog. Casper could feel it revealing itself again, crawling against his neck, the shifting colors of it playing up and down his arms. He stood still in the middle of the crowded street, the dog at his heels, and its unearthly presence went unnoticed. The frantic conversations surrounding him receded to a murmur.

"What do you want?" asked Casper.

"I know your thoughts. I have steeped in them for longer than you know. You crave violence. This is your nature. Your purpose, like mine. You desire to rend human flesh."

"Bishop," said Casper.

"Who is Gideon Long, who has succumbed to the deep waters like so many of your kind. It is too late for this notion of revenge. All that remains is the deep water. It is here now."

A Warren brushed past, and Casper saw the concern in his eyes, the worry as the man's gaze flicked to the dog. He clearly sensed more than the others, his gaze lingering on the dog, his mouth working as if he wanted to say something, but he stumbled on past, looking back as he was sucked away into the crowd.

"The white dog." Casper recalled the dog in the desert of New Mexico, its eyes startlingly blue. "Was that you? Why would you lure us to the Pool?"

"It was not me," said the dog. "The waters have consumed many kinds from many places. Some are like Gideon Long and take pleasure in the power it gives them. They repay it with their ravenous desire to witness and consume. You have known the ones that wore the flesh of the white dog. You knew them in the fallen shells of the spires of my kind. They pursued you to the shores of the Surata. You know this because I saved you from them."

Casper remembered. Scrambling, bleeding, through the echoing boulevard of the dead city. Pursued by a clattering horde of white-skinned creatures with bulbous blue eyes and inverted limbs. Above them, descending from the pyroclastic skies, the cruciform shape of the grasshopper, knocking them away, freeing him to leap into the churning white ocean. The cruciform shape, repeating again and again on the ceiling of the cave, on the ceiling of a white-painted room, the grasshopper idol crumbling in his hands, not clay at all, but the long-ago shell of something that had once lived.

"How do I stop them?" asked Casper.

"Stop who?" Bottles asked, returning to his side,

"Someone I've known for way too long," said Casper.

A black bird streaked above the rooftops, disappeared, flapped back into view, racing parallel to the street and drawing cries of alarm from the crowd below. A second bird joined it, the two animals pirouetting together, seemingly fighting over a morsel.

They weren't birds at all, Casper realized. Their bodies were black, featherless; their wings were membranes taut over a visible framework of bones. The dark flesh of each wing receded to a line of gray, the trailing edge becoming a waggling comb of luminous blue flesh. Their heads were fused to their bodies, tapered and triangular, powerful, snapping jaws oversized and awkward, like those of deep-sea anglers.

With a last clatter of jaws competing for a ribbon of meat, the pair of flying creatures spiraled out of sight. A fluttering, pink curl of fabric drifted down, and Casper realized it was the torn remains of a coat sized for a child's body. He gripped the wrapped handle of the machete he had taken from the skinhead. It made him feel more secure to hold it, more secure still to draw it from his waistband as though he might hack a path through the crowd.

Children began to wail, and adults verged on panic. The smoke was again blowing overhead, stiflingly heavy with diesel. Some people were filtering back into buildings despite the fear of another earthquake.

The distant whining of the spore sirens began, rising in volume and intensity to a howl. The oppressive noise spread from one corner to the next, the wail becoming louder and louder with each new siren, until the very nearest siren began to cycle.

As the ugly tone blanketed the street, the men and women crowded there began to cry out in fear, yanking children by their hands, grabbing for belongings and stampeding in a dozen directions at once. It was an aimless, mob convulsion. All around Casper and Bottles people were trying to escape the warning din. There was no escape; the dirge played from sirens on every corner throughout the city.

"We got to get out of here!" shouted Bottles. He swung his head, eyes wide and white, searching for an escape, shoving and cursing against the tide of bodies. "Come on, man. Come on!"

The dog was unconcerned by the men and women running past on both sides, unworried by the droning sirens and the strange birds. It sat on its haunches, its mouth open in a coincidental smile, pink tongue lolling, watching Casper with the rusty marbles of its eyes. The dog, the grasshopper, wanted him to return to the Pool. Abandon the only man who was anything like a friend to him.

"It is a body without flesh," the grasshopper had told him of the Pool. "It is mindless and infinite. It cannot be overcome with violence."

If the world was truly lost to the creatures of the Pool and there was no escape to be found, then it was Casper's duty to follow the dog's advice and return to the waters. To leave this place for the next. He'd spent his lifetime walking away from responsibility whenever he couldn't solve a problem with fists. It's what the dog wanted him to do now. Abandon his race, his world, and find his way to another to confront the Pool there.

Casper surveyed the panic-stricken crowd. Bottles tugged at his sleeve and urged him to run. The dog waited, seeming to know he would choose to abandon the city and return to the Pool. No. Not again. Not this time.

"Philomena's," said Casper, grabbing Bottles by the shredded arm of his coat.

"No, man, that's too far!" Bottles resisted and tore free of Casper. "Seven, eight blocks. Almost straight toward the cordon. That's where all this shit is coming from, right?"

"There are families and kids at the church. I have to save everyone I can. We'll get them down to Sugarside and commandeer a boat."

"There ain't no boats left down there except that big one."

"Then that's the one we'll take."

Bottles stopped struggling. Sustained gunfire rattled in the distance. Something exploded, and a fresh column of smoke burst above the buildings. Dozens of the black creatures swooped overhead.

"Yeah," said Bottles. "Yeah, that's right. Like an ark, man. Like Noah in the flood. We can save some fucking people from this shit."

■ ■ ■

They did not escape the Fane unscathed. Marines and scientists died beneath falling rocks, trapped, unable to be rescued as Polly and Dr. Burns and the others ran headlong from the overflowing Mother. Spore grass spread like white fire, racing along walls and floor. The earth heaved, tunnels twisted, and fissures split the bedrock, crushing men and women beneath enormous chunks of stone.

The rolling cog of the airlock was broken loose, and they charged inside, scrambling over shards of rock, deafened by the percussion of huge boulders raining all around them. The inner airlock would not fully open. Rukundo and Captain Dryson and Polly pulled with all of their strength. Dr. Cochrane added his weight, and the airlock turned, opening just wide enough for a man in a bulky cooling suit to pass.

The young Gardener appeared at the door, machine pistol in hand. The sound of the gun firing was lost in the roar of the earthquake. Tufts of padding and coolant fluid sprayed from Dr. Cochrane's body as he reeled and collapsed back into the airlock. Blood sloshed into the glass dome of his helmet. He arched his back, fingers twisting into claws, legs kicking out straight, and then he lay still.

Polly smashed the gun aside before the Gardener could fire again and pushed him into the lab. A spreading spider's web of cracks decorated the shuddering concrete walls. Partitions disintegrated in falls of shattering glass. The floor heaved and rolled, and the white tiles broke loose like the scales of a fish. Electronic monitors were falling from their moorings. Smoke poured from burning equipment.

The lights, already reduced to emergency lighting, fell completely dark. The only remaining illumination was the spotlights built into the coolant suits.

The Gardener lost his grip on the machine pistol, and it went skittering away on the floor. Polly fought him hand to hand. She was well-trained but slow and inept in the suit. He utilized sweeping, flowing, martial-arts movements but was unable to land a blow with sufficient force to hurt her. Captain Dryson settled the matter by dashing open the man's skull with the corner of a television monitor.

They found Sergeant Funkweed dead in a bathroom, arms bound behind his back. The Marine's radio was beside him, fully deployed, its antenna routed through the main antenna running all the way to the rookery.

Dryson tried to tell her something, but there was no communicating amid the noise. He began to recover the radio equipment. It would take him several minutes. She pulled him away and toward the elevators.

It was impossible to account for who was missing or dead in the chaos, but a stream of scientists and Marines emerged from the collapsing tunnel system and followed Polly and Dryson back to the elevator shafts. It was the only way back to the surface. The elevators were not functioning. Though they were physically intact, it seemed the force of the quake had triggered a stoppage to prevent cars breaking loose in motion.

They huddled in the elevator room. Dust and smoke filled the corridors, making it impossible to see or communicate at all. She felt rooms collapsing as huge chunks of concrete tore loose and flattened the contents of the laboratory. Brakes screamed above them in one of the elevator shafts. Smoke puffed from the doors. Despite the safety stoppage, a car was falling from high above. A moment later one of the three elevators exploded out from its doors in a gory tangle of steel and human remains.

Polly expected the Mother to flow into the elevator chamber behind them, washing through the rubble and turning everything it touched into smoke. The quaking stopped. In the dreadful silence that followed, their respirators clicked over radios. The moving spotlights of their cooling suits created a high-relief collage of the ruin enclosing them.

"Everyone stay calm and stay put," said Polly.

She took an account of the survivors. Dryson, Dr. Burns, Rukundo, and more than a dozen scientists and Marines had survived. Dr. Cochrane was dead. Polly presumed all those missing were dead.

"Help us," crackled over the radio. "Help us, please. I am here with Mr. Sokov. We are trapped."

"It is Dr. Roux," said Dr. Burns.

"Leg is hurt," moaned Sokov. "Fucking rocks have fallen . . . ah . . . on my leg."

"Do you know where you are?" asked Polly.

Dr. Roux described their location. She could not place it. The Marines seemed to possess incredible situational awareness and immediately knew the room she was describing.

"I can get them," said Captain Dryson. "It's near where they stowed their weapons when they changed into these suits. Those might help as well."

Mistrustful that he would be concerned with arming himself in this situation, Polly insisted on accompanying them. Two of the Marines remained behind to help Rukundo and the scientists get the elevator working again.

They backtracked over tumbled slabs of concrete. They passed from the jumbled angles of collapsed corridors into a tunnel of pale fronds and a carpeting of soft, fleshy spore grass beneath their boots. Ahead, the darkness was lit blue by bliss fruit gently swaying on long stalks.

"There's something moving," warned one of the Marines.

Humpbacked crustaceans scurried through the fungal undergrowth. They were the size of puppies, carapaces white with segmented shells displaying blue details at the hinges. Gently moving antennae beat the fronds ahead of them, and their eyes were iridescent yellow and white. They possessed short tails like an armadillo's.

"They look like rats crossed with crabs," said another Marine.

Their starting-and-stopping movement was reminiscent of rat behavior. When they seemed to detect the Marines, they scurried away in different directions, disappearing into impassable corridors and beneath furniture.

"Be careful," said Dryson. "We don't know if those things bite."

"Does what bite?" asked Sokov over the radio. "What is out there?"

Rather than describe the animals over the radio, Polly attempted to comfort Sokov. They were getting close, and she told him that. The wariness of the Marines showed in their body language as they continued past some of the hiding places of the so-called crab rats.

"Ahead on the right is where they stashed their weapons," said Dryson. The door he indicated appeared passable. "Give me two minutes, and we'll salvage what we can."

"Quick as possible," said Polly. "If it's blocked in there, you call it off."

Dryson handed her the machine pistol taken from the Gardener. He clapped her shoulder and then led his men through the door, shoving aside wood already beginning to smolder in the heat. Every surface was smothered by spore grass, and the floor, thick with it, was increasingly treacherous. Her cooling suit's shoulder-mounted spotlights only penetrated a few meters into the smoke and foglike spore clouds. Dryson and his Marines grunted with effort as they moved debris.

"I can see their guns. There's another blockage inside. I think we can move it to get to them, but it's going to take another minute."

"Forget it," said Polly. "We need to get Sokov and Dr. Roux."

"Yes, get Sokov. Please!" It was Sokov.

"We don't know what's down here with us." Dryson's voice was strained with effort. "And we don't know . . . ah . . . know what's . . . nmph . . . what's on the surface."

"Something out here," said Polly.

A shape coalesced out of the fog ahead. A human figure, moving awkwardly, not clad in one of the insulating suits. Polly snapped the machine pistol's stock into place and raised the weapon to her shoulder. She realized she could not fit her gloved finger through the trigger guard, and she fumbled to tear off the insulating garment.

"What is it?" asked Sokov.

The figure loomed out of the smoke. There was a pop of equalizing pressure as Polly found the release on the glove. She shucked it off and discarded it into the swaying spore grass at her feet. The heat was terrible, like holding her hand inside an oven. She pushed the thought aside and fitted her finger through the hot metal of the trigger guard.

She raised the weapon to her shoulder just as the figure came into view. Redskinned, blistered, it was a nude woman. Polly thought for a moment it might be Holly Webber, restored to life by the Gardeners' ceremony.

"Help me," moaned the woman, and she collapsed into Polly's arms. Polly lowered the unconscious woman to the floor.

More figures were emerging from the smoke. Shambling, burned raw, a steady stream of duplicates was approaching.

"What is happening to me?" cried a type two as he sank to his knees in the spore grass.

"Help me, God!"

Another scalded type three slumped against the wall, her skin peeling back and sticking to the hot stone. They were moaning and shuffling toward her.

"Get out here, now!" said Polly. "Some of the duplicates are emerging here. We need to move."

"Jesus, your hand," said Dryson, appearing in the doorway. Polly's hand was red, as if she had held it under a scalding hot tap. He was even more horrified to find the duplicates approaching like the sorry procession of victims of an atomic attack.

"We can't help them," he said.

"You don't have any fucking idea," she snapped at him. "We need to get to Sokov and Dr. Roux before the whole place is overrun by these people. They will just keep coming and coming by the thousands."

"We've almost got the elevator working," said Dr. Burns. "There was an override and—"

"Just get it going, and don't tell us about it," said Dryson.

They rounded a corner, shoving aside the pitiful duplicates, and reached the door behind which Dr. Roux and Sokov were trapped. A single, flat slab of concrete had fallen from above and speared deep into the flooring. Dr. Roux reached her arm out of the door.

"In here," she said. "I see you."

"Get them out," said Polly. "I'll cover you."

Blisters were already forming on the backs of her fingers and hand. The metal of the gun was so hot, it seemed even worse than the baking air. More of the duplicates followed her light, faces and horrifying bodies emerging from the fog, pleading as she shoved them aside. There was something else. It was smaller than a man, moving cautiously among the staggering duplicates.

"Hurry it up," she urged.

There was more than one of these hunched creatures coming toward her. Their long strides and strange silhouettes filled her with fear. She took aim as best she could through the helmet.

"We've got it!" shouted Dryson. "On your feet, Sokov! Come on."

It was too late.

The first of the creatures emerged from the spore fog. Her first impression was of a skeletal man with chalky white flesh. But it was smaller than a man and walked hunched low. It was propelled by over-articulated legs with reverse knees and long shins that flexed behind its body. Its forelegs were clawed and equipped with a bony protrusion behind the hand that resembled a knife's blade. Its elongated oval face turned toward her. Its huge eyes, separated by a bulging snout, were blue but reflected yellow in the light.

"Shit," she said, and she began firing.

The creature's head snapped back, and its brains painted the wall. Pink folds and blood slithered in strands from its shattered skull and dripped into the spore grass as it fell. The others bounded toward her like insects, faces splitting open to reveal bony plates that clicked and chattered in their lipless mouths. She fired again and again, actually stepping toward them, punching bloody holes in their bodies. They toppled and skidded across the floor. Some flailed in the grass, their blood spurting out and darkening the vegetation.

Screaming. The panicked screaming of Dr. Roux. Polly had no time to look back. She fired the last of her bullets into one of the creatures, and it dropped at her feet. She grabbed the hot barrel in her gloved hand and swung the machine pistol like an axe, shattering the skull of the next creature to step into range. Behind her, a Marine shrieked in pain.

There was another approach to the room, and the creatures were swarming in from that direction. Dryson and his men desperately struggled to tear off their gloves and brandish the machine pistols they had recovered. As she watched, one Marine fell beneath one of the creatures as it punctured his suit with its bladed forelegs and opened his belly up in a gush of coolant fluid, blood, and entrails. Red spurted from his mouth and filled his helmet. The creature began devouring the man alive.

Polly had no time to help Dryson or his men. She smashed aside another of the creatures. It thrashed in the ever-thickening grass. She stomped her boot down and crushed its head beneath her heel. Another creature pushed her aside, running for the Marines. Dryson turned just in time to see it and blast it with his gun. Another creature stalked past Polly, paying her no heed in the same manner that they moved past the scalded duplicates moaning in the corridors.

"Get them out of here," she cried. "They won't stop coming. You have to retreat."

Dryson and his men were already moving, leaving behind two of their own amid the mounting carnage. Polly got to her feet and clubbed another of the creatures as it bounded past. It screamed with surprise at her attack. She smashed its jaws and face until the horrible clatter of its jaws ceased.

Polly fell in with the Marines just as one of the creatures leaped over a dying comrade and threw itself into their midst. Its bladed forelimbs sliced open Dryson's throat, missing his neck but opening his suit up. Blue coolant fluid arced under pressure like a severed carotid, and Dryson choked into the microphone and lost his footing.

A Marine shot the creature, but not before it droves it bony blades into Dr. Roux, spearing her in her midsection and pulling down as it withdrew the protrusions. Polly caught the young woman as she fell. Her body was limp.

"*Maman*," gasped Dr. Roux. "*Désolé. Maman.*"

Polly took hold of her reaching hand. Dr. Roux's glove was sticky. She was missing fingers.

"*Maman*," Dr. Roux whispered, and she turned her awkward helmet to look at Polly. Her smile was dreamy. She died.

"Let her go," said Dryson. He held his damaged throat with one gloved hand and fired his machine pistol on full auto. The muzzle flash was blinding in the narrow corridor. His men, only two now, both injured, were firing alongside him. "Take Sokov, and get out of here. Get the elevator going."

She did not linger. She scooped up a dead Marine's weapon in her badly-burned hand. There was no time to argue against Dryson's bravado. He knew the sacrifice he was making. She lifted Sokov beneath his arm and helped him limp back to the elevator. It was not long before screams and static burst into the radio. The guns fell silent.

Dr. Burns and the others were already loaded inside the elevator. Polly heard them coming after her and piled into the elevator so hard, she knocked over poor Dr. Nandy. Rukundo, operating the controls, knew to close the doors. The scientists quailed at the fleeting glimpse of the creatures swarming into the corridor and running at the elevator. And then they began to ascend.

Out of one hell and into another.

■ ■ ■

The offices were in turmoil in the aftermath of the earthquake. The elevators refused to descend to ground level, and the stairwell was full of panicked workers, stampeding over one another. Patrice escorted Bishop, Bethany, Misha Rosen, and the crew from World Insight through the chaos.

Employees pleaded for help. When they got in the way, Patrice shoved them aside or hit them with slaps and told them, "Get!"

Bishop knew it was all caught on tape by Misha's cameraman. He operated under the belief that nothing Patrice could do to his cowardly office staff could be more harmful to his company's reputation than the interview.

The floor security officers in their PitSec uniforms were milling uselessly around the security station. Patrice bristled. Bishop bullied his way into the security station alongside Patrice to get a better feel of the situation. Officers working the camera monitors were speechless with shock at the scenes unfolding across their screens.

Two of the hyperbolic towers were partially sunken into the earth, and steam emerged from fissures in the surrounding structures. The cameras did not cover the Undercroft, but the monitors displayed confusing scenes of strangeness and violence throughout the lower levels of the building. Spore grass was covering most surfaces in the lobby. Duplicates wandered in a daze. Flake employees lay convulsing on the floor. The main cafeteria was filled with obscuring smoke. Inhumanly large figures moved through the billowing gray. The PitSec motor pool was partially collapsed, and gunshots could be heard over the ambient microphones.

"The loading docks are clear," said Bishop, but as he tapped a finger on the monitor, a black mass surged up from the tunnels. He thought it to be liquid until it rushed past the camera and he saw it was thousands, perhaps millions, of individual birdlike creatures, half as large as a man, swarming out and into the open air.

"The roof," said Bishop. "We evacuate by helicopter. It is our only possible option." Patrice agreed.

"Get Milo on the telephone," Bishop instructed Bethany. "I want to know how he allowed this to happen and what he intends to do to make it better."

Milo never answered. The phalanx of PitSec men beat a path through the office and to the spinal elevator. Bishop had an override to the safety lockout, and, despite aftershocks, he was able to disengage the lockout and get the elevator started to the rooftop helipads.

"My God." She pressed against the glass wall of the elevator. "Look at that. Harvey, get a shot of it. Do we still have the live feed to New York? Are you getting this, New York?"

Bishop and the cameraman both leaned against the glass to see what she was referring to. One of the partially collapsed cooling towers was breaking apart, shedding avalanches of concrete onto the crowds of people escaping from the building. Something was arising from the dust surrounding the fallen structure. It slithered up from beneath the building as a bolus of immense, headless snakes.

As they watched, it lifted out of the dust, the snakes revealing themselves as a beard of tendrils attached to the elephantine body of a creature rising on a pair of stiltlike legs. It was a dozen stories tall, its head studded with black eyes that rotated and blinked like those of a chameleon. The tendrils slithered and played across the flank of the nearest standing tower. Brickwork crumpled, and loose blocks shivered down the slopes and exploded among the fleeing pedestrians.

A stream of translucent bells, almost like bubbles, issued from the fissure created by the elephant creature as it strode away. This gossamer swarm twisted and spiraled into the air in an unbroken chain.

"This can't be happening," said Bethany. "This is not really happening. What is this, Wesley? What the fuck is this?"

He had no answer for her.

They arrived at the rooftop helipads and divided into two groups to be conveyed out of danger by the waiting helicopters. These short-range aircraft would deliver them to *The Republic*, waiting at Sugarside, which would allow Bishop to escape farther from the calamity. The pilots conducted preflight checks and began to spin up the rotors on the helicopters.

Heavy fighting was breaking out in the city. Gunfire chattered, and heavier artillery boomed from the cordon line. Whatever these creatures were, they had already encountered the United States military.

"Let's go, boss man," said Patrice. He lifted Bishop into the helicopter and handed him a pair of noise-canceling headphones for the aircraft intercom. Misha Rosen and her crew piled into the helicopter with him. The PitSec team climbed into the second helicopter. He would have preferred a detachment of Milo's selfless warrior cultists, but the fools weren't answering his calls.

Patrice reached a hand down to help Bethany into the helicopter. She waved him away. Her pinned hair was unraveled by the downwash from the helicopter.

"I can't go," she shouted into the roaring turbines. "My sisters are in the city."

"We can make arrangements for them. I will send men to pick them up." Bishop found himself more afraid of living without Bethany than facing the nightmare in the city below. "We can get them to safety."

"No," she said, clutching his day planner to her chest. "I'll see you off, but Patrice has to take care of your ass from here."

"Please, be sensible," he said. Patrice held him back from climbing out of the helicopter to bring her aboard.

"Right now, I want to be with my family, not an idiot child like you."

Bethany handed him his day planner at the last moment before the helicopter lifted off from the pad. She watched them depart, lonesome on the windswept roof of the spire. As the helicopter turned away, gaining altitude, Bishop realized that creatures were scaling the outer surface of the tower. They were duplicates of the creature that had attacked him in the maintenance vault. Some bashed in windows and leaped into the offices; others were climbing with ease, ascending all the way to the summit of the building.

"We have to go back," said Bishop. "Land the helicopter."

Patrice twisted in his seat to face Bishop and the crew from World Insight. He lifted his headset.

"Dyin what ya want? Dat it? Nuh-uh. Ain't turnin dis round."

"I command it," said Bishop.

"She done made her nest," said Patrice, settling the headset back onto his head. "Ain't do nobody no good get da whole of us et by dem tings."

They lifted clear of the Pit compound as anarchy spread beyond its walls. The pair of helicopters wheeled north, gaining altitude to avoid a twisting black cloud of flying creatures. Artillery batteries flashed from their positions in Hollywood. Streams of multiple-launch rockets arced through the air, bright missiles curving from launchers and into the Pit, to burst among the carnage already under way.

The helicopter banked, and Bishop witnessed the fighting below them. All along the cordon the military was engaged with monstrosities. Tracers spilled into the air, and rockets exploded among apartments and throughout the rusty brambles of Creeptown. Convoys of troops moved to stem the tide of breakouts, and tanks shuddered along the elevated highways, panning their turrets from side to side and firing at targets of opportunity.

He was so intent on watching the action beneath the helicopter that he almost missed the diaphanous spheres drifting up into the air all around them. Each glistening sack of air contained a dark green nucleus, no larger than a tennis ball, suspended in its midst. One of the sacks drifted close by the window, and Bishop saw that the nucleus was a collection of closely-packed organelles fringed with wriggling cilia. It drifted up, toward another, and as they came closer, they each accelerated as if attracted by magnetism.

More spheres lifted from rooftops, gleaming in the sunlight, clotting together into a whirling, lifting balloon shape. This quickly adhered to another aggregation and grew in length. It began squirming through the air in a motion that suggested purpose and reminded him of the rise and fall of a Chinese dragon.

Without warning it twisted its colonial length and spiraled in their direction. It moved with breathtaking speed and fell upon the lead helicopter. The rotor blade dashed many of the sacks to pieces. Hundreds and thousands more poured through the windows and door, and every person in the helicopter was carried away. They did not fall; they dissolved inside the mass. Clothing and flesh and bone disappeared in seconds and colored the serpentine colony translucent pink. Bits of metal and plastic dropped from within the creature. The serpent broke suddenly apart. The spheres drifted away from one another and settled toward the ground.

Without its pilots, their companion helicopter banked hard right, directly into the path of Bishop's helicopter. Patrice shouted a warning, and the pilot pulled hard on the stick. The engine whined in protest as they gained altitude. The helicopter disappeared below Bishop's view.

The landing strut clipped the rotor of the pilotless aircraft. High-velocity shards burst through the helicopter's floor, shredding the pilot into gory ribbons and perforating the ceiling. Smoke billowed out of the engine and was sucked into the cabin. The aircraft plunged. Lights went red all across the control panel. The automated voice of an altitude alert began chiming, "PULL UP! PULL UP!"

Patrice, coated in the pilot's blood, possibly injured, attempted to gain control of the helicopter. The engines had lost all power. Misha Rosen and her crew were screaming. Bishop's sigh of resignation was lost to the howling airframe as the helicopter plummeted to the street below.

Patrice fought the stick to the bitter end, but it was to no avail. The helicopter smashed into the street, what was left of the fixed landing struts buckled, the canopy exploded, and the metal frame of the helicopter deformed around Bishop. The forward cabin crumpled, instantly killing Patrice. Misha Rosen was impaled on a dislocated crossbar of the helicopter. The cameraman and producer were flung beneath the wreck. The helicopter shrieked and skidded along the ground for most of a block, smearing their bodies to jelly.

When it had finally come to rest, Bishop realized its new geometry trapped him on the ground. Misha Rosen was alive but unable to speak. Eyes wide and disbelieving, she gripped the bar impaling her chest. Her face twisted in anguish. She tried to speak and never did.

Bishop's back was an agony of fragments. It was broken, and he knew it. One wrong move, and shattered vertebrae might pinch his spinal cord and paralyze him. His body from his armpits up was still in the helicopter, caged by the wreckage, but his legs and bare stomach were outside the helicopter on the street. The hot metal of the helicopter clicked as it cooled around him. He slipped easily into unconsciousness and hoped he would never wake up again.

CHAPTER TWELVE

■ ■ ■

They rode the elevator up from the depths. The scientists clung to one another and moaned with fear at each new shock felt through the dangling cable. Polly Foster shed her insulating suit. The elevator was swampy with residual heat and thick with the cloying, marrow smell of the Pool. She was hardly able to flex the fingers of her right hand because of the second-degree burns.

Dr. Robin Burns crouched beside Polly and began tearing strips from the lining of her coolant suit to wrap Polly's hand.

"I'm sorry," said Polly. "Dr. Roux was . . ."

"She shouldn't have been here," said Robin. "I didn't find out until we were already in the air."

"Find out what?"

"Does this hurt?" asked Robin as she began wrapping Polly's burned hand.

"No." At least the pain had stopped. All of her nerve endings were cooked. "What did you find out about Dr. Roux?"

"Dr. Delgado's office was supposed to vet every candidate I suggested." Robin continued wrapping Polly's hand, her motions made awkward by the thick gloves of the coolant suit. "I suppose they did not pry into personal lives. I knew Madeleine from a field study we did in Greece. I thought I knew her."

Robin tied the bandage off on Polly's wrist. She stood, and Polly saw the stress etching her features. Sweat or tears dampened her cheeks.

"Dr. Madeleine Roux was an orphan. Her parents were killed in an air accident almost thirty years ago. She was adopted and became very attached to her new mother and was distraught when she, too, died only last year. That mother was you, Polly. One of your duplicates."

The overwrought embraces and meaningful gazes now made sense. Polly experienced an unexpected wave of loss.

"I suspect she came to try find her actual mother. You were the next best thing."

"She never would have found her," Polly said bitterly. "When we die, we forego our past identities."

"I would imagine that is not entirely impossible," said Robin.

Polly tried to imagine doing it, and she had to agree with Robin. She still dreamed of her children all these years and identities later.

The elevator opened onto the central elevator plaza. The lights were extinguished, and the immense chamber was consumed in spore grass and softly glowing bliss fruit. Mycelial fans, bright like coral, swayed in the currents of moist, cool air. Columnar macro-fungus ascended above them, anchored on roots as big as human limbs, creaking as they grew, opening a canopy of fleshy, gilled umbrellas over their heads.

Crab rats scurried through the undergrowth. Strange vegetation pulsed in the dark and created hypnotic patterns of varicolored light. Here and there mounds of fallen debris, overgrown with vegetation, created hills and valleys soft with the quivering fronds of spore grass. Confused, naked duplicates wandered in the alien garden.

"Stay close together," said Polly. "Keep the duplicates away from us."

As they ascended toward the surface, they encountered venting gas polyps, the sticky tongues of carnivorous flora, fronds that seemed to whisper with human voices and grotesque scenes of death and destruction. Polly kept the team moving through it all.

Screams echoed in the distant halls, and the aftershocks, though much weaker, continued to shift the floor beneath their feet. Such rumbling was compounded by a steady drum of surface shocks. Polly believed they were explosions from bombs or artillery. The two surviving marines, Hudson and Romero, agreed with her assertion.

All approaches to the lobby entrances were cut off by fallen debris or impassably overgrown with alien vegetation. Polly took them out the way they had come in, climbing the muffled barrel of a truck tunnel to the loading bay. The sounds of the outside world filtered down the tunnel: the crash of explosions, distant chatter of machine guns and automatic cannons, and the crowing of thousands of birds.

The source of this crowing became clear as they escaped from the tunnel and into the loading bay. The walkways high above them, which they had crossed hours before, had become the roost for thousands of enormous black bird creatures. Scores of the bat-winged animals rose from their perches high above and swooped down to pick at dead bodies strewn among the grassy trucks. They were as big as any raptor but grotesquely alien in their details.

"Move slowly and don't be afraid of them," said Polly, hoping her advice was sound.

"We should take a truck," said the Marine called Devereux.

"Yeah, man," agreed Hudson. "I can rig it up, and we can ride right out of here."

Polly vetoed the idea. Even the least contaminated of the trucks was buried under spore grass. To drive it, they would have to scrape off the windows or drive blind. They stayed close to the trucks and advanced into the loading bay. The grass-entombed vehicles supported a menagerie of tiny insects and jelly-bodied creatures as prey for the crab rats. There were also slow-moving black animals, the size of two spread hands, that seemed made out of bent wires. These collapsed in upon hapless jellies that crawled beneath their limbs.

"Remarkable," said Dr. Nandy. "It is a complete ecosystem, deployed ready-made."

"It is wonderland of nightmare," said Sokov, limping along near the back of the group.

"Quiet," said Polly.

They passed seizes of the alien birds squawking and waving their wings at one another. The birds stood on the backs and bellies of the dead scattered across the roadway, peeling pink ribbons of meat from the corpses and fighting over organs. A few seemed to notice Polly, but they did nothing more than watch her from multiple pairs of eyes as their wide, flexible jaws snapped up strands of human meat.

They reached the last of the trucks remaining before the ramps ascended out into the open air, and Polly called for a halt. From her vantage she could only see the sky, stormy with smoke and sallow glimpses of daylight. The sounds of battle had receded to the distance. The ramp out of the loading bay was broad but congested with hundreds of the crowing birds. The loading crews must have attempted to flee and perished there in great numbers. The only way out was through the mass of birds.

"We go single file," said Polly. "Very slow. Very careful. No sudden moves. Follow me."

She walked deliberately, mindful of her footing on the debris. The first of the birds saw them and lifted into the air. They squawked their contempt and returned to their roost up near the ventilation fans. Polly proceeded in among the feasting birds. Some watched or flapped their leathery wings with irritation. Robin was immediately behind her, the line extending single-file down the ramp, winding between the groups of birds as they neared the surface. In one spot the line was forced to climb over the bodies. The fresh meat displaced awkwardly beneath their boots. The tension was sickening. It manifested in the hitching breaths the scientists took, audible over the suit radios.

They were almost there. Polly was able to see the damaged heap of the nearest cooling tower and the fires raging through an outbuilding that had once served as a barracks for workers. Polly stopped and turned to say something to Robin, following on her heels.

"Ah!" The cry came softly over the radio. Polly could do nothing but watch as one of the scientists crossing over the bodies lost his footing and fell directly into a mass of feasting birds. The scientist's flailing limbs collided with the birds and spooked them into the air. The surrounding birds were not so easily frightened. Several took an airborne hop, landing atop the fallen scientist.

"No! No! God!" the man screamed.

Polly did not even remember his name, but she recognized his voice as one of a small contingent of Dutch computer-modeling specialists. His fearful pleading became hysterical, agonized screams as the bird creatures began testing him with snapping jaws. Up above, the birds roosting had taken notice, and by ones and twos they were beginning to descend toward the fallen scientist.

"We have to do something," pleaded Dr. Nandy.

"Shoot those motherfuckers!" said Hudson.

She raised the machine pistol and aimed at the mass of birds. The scientist's flailing, bloodied limbs were visible among them. There were far too many of the creatures, and they were gathering in ever greater numbers. He was doomed. She lowered the weapon.

"Run," said Polly, deciding as she spoke the word aloud. "Run, goddamnit! They'll kill us all!"

They ran, escaping the frenzied beasts into the tumult on the surface. They could not outrun the screams of the poor scientist. He continued gurgling over the microphone until a last, long, hitching breath. Static faded in and out at the limit of the radio's range, intermingling with a repetitive click of the scientist's helmet being moved as the birds feasted on his body.

Fires raged out of control. Alien vegetation crept over the ruins of buildings, softening their edges, transforming the canyons formed by the roads into abyssal trenches teeming with lurid, strange life. Something enormous was rampaging just beyond the wall, partially visible through thick smoke. The scientists gawped in disbelief at the panoramic scene of alien destruction.

One of the creatures that had attacked them in the Fane came bounding over a mossy car, its jaws chattering. Polly fired a burst from the machine pistol and knocked it into the grass. The gunfire roused the scientists from their stupor. She wanted to head straight out of the Pit along the main access road. Sokov and Robin urged them to cross among the overgrown vehicles and ruined buildings and return to the outbuilding where their equipment was stored. Polly demurred, but Sokov was adamant.

"All archive samples in building. If I do not recover, then what is point?"

She gave in to them. The outbuilding was damaged by an artillery shell but largely intact. Abandoned cars and trucks filled the street. A trio of PitSec armored carriers were halted in front of the building, hatches thrown open as the crews had bailed out. One was gutted by fire, but the remaining two seemed intact.

"B-T-R," said Sokov. "I drive in army."

The safety they might afford was too tempting to pass up.

"We'll take them," said Polly, "and escape north. Get your samples, Sokov. They'd better be worth it."

■ ■ ■

The sunken highway called the 10 ran inland from Sugarside, but Casper warned Bottles away, fearing the concentration of refugees trying, too late, to flee Los Angeles. Desperation was dangerous. Instead, they navigated side streets in their course toward St. Philomena's. Lenin followed obediently at their heels. Casper was aware that with each passing moment more violence was erupting throughout the city. Distant gunfire grew closer. The whistle-crack of artillery passing overhead was unmistakable.

"That's them big guns," said Bottles. "It's on now. Oh, hell, is it on."

Attack aircraft soon followed. Casper did not recognize them, but he knew of their function. Stub-winged carrier jets first, screaming in low and firing missiles and bombs in the area of San Pedro. Attack helicopters and heavy bombers arrived minutes later, carpeting strips of Creeptown as far north as Carson with incendiary bombs. Something was fighting back. Before long helicopters and jets began crashing into the city.

Bottles pointed skyward as a bomber, big as a jetliner, engines burning and trailing black smoke, came rumbling down for a hopeless emergency landing on the 405, completely packed with refugees. Casper imagined the horror of families trapped in cars and vans as the enormous jet smashed into them. The jet dipped below the line of the surrounding buildings. He felt the impact, and a moment later an immense fireball curled into the sky.

There was nothing they could do. They continued on through absurdly desolate streets echoing with the dirge of the spore sirens.

"I don't like walking out with them sirens going," said Bottles. He tied a patterned handkerchief over his nose and mouth. "You might have got your shots, but I can still catch it. This do-rag ain't gonna save me if shit gets bad. Let's go inside like everybody else and wait for them to shut off."

"There's no time for that," said Casper. "If we go to ground here, you're a dead man."

Casper's argument was won as a mass of screeching black bird creatures appeared above their heads like bats issuing from the mouth of a cave. They ducked beneath the eaves of a long-shuttered dentist's office and waited for the birds to pass by overhead. Gunfire erupted from nearby streets. The sound of breaking glass and screaming accompanied the passing birds.

When the birds had moved on, Bottles and Casper continued. They soon came upon the body of a jet pilot hanging from a city lamp by his parachute. The birds, or some other animal, had shredded his legs and stomach to strips of cloth and meat with white bones showing through. He still clutched a pistol in his hand. There were shell casings on the street beneath his dripping carcass.

Bottles realized that Casper was going toward the dead body and objected. "Don't touch that shit, man. Let's go."

"He has a spore mask," said Casper. "And a gun."

He pried the gun loose from the pilot's hand. It was a small automatic, but the magazine was empty, and Casper could not find spares in any of the pilot's remaining pockets. To get to the mask he had to climb the pole and hang on to the pilot's parachute webbing with one hand. It was a grotesque act that squeezed out blood and produced posthumous sighs from the corpse.

"Hurry up, man. Somebody is coming. A truck or something."

The dog barked in agreement.

Casper opened the clasps for the mask and shucked the rubberized hood up and over the pilot's head. The hose was connected to a chemical rebreather strapped around the pilot's chest. Something rumbled just around the corner.

Bottles was right; a truck was coming, and it would not be wise to be caught looting a downed pilot if it was the military. He let the mask dangle and fumbled for the strap securing the rebreather around the dead man's chest.

"Now or never," said Bottles, practically dancing with nerves.

Casper almost had it. He glanced up at the pilot's face, ghastly pale, lips and nose reddened by fresh blood. Eyes open, glassy, but staring at Casper. The pilot's lips moved. He blinked. Casper lost his balance and fell, tearing loose the rebreather as he dropped on his back into a pool of the pilot's blood.

The trucks, two of them, rounded the corner fast enough that their wheels screeched. The lead vehicle swept its headlights through the smoke haze and over the scene in the street. Bottles and the dog were nowhere to be seen. Casper had no time. He went limp and hoped that amid all the blood he would look like another dead body.

The trucks slowed as they passed the lamp post, their wheels only inches from Casper's sprawling arm. The trucks were full of National Guard. They were breaking and fleeing. Deserting. They did not appear to even have fought. Their gas hoods were package fresh, and their equipment was not dirty. They must have heard a nightmare unfolding over the radio and decided to pack it in.

In his experience, cowards were the most dangerous. They resented being caught.

One of the soldiers leaned over the railing of the open-topped truck. He passed so close by that Casper could see his eyes through the tinted lenses of the man's mask. He leaned his rifle over the side of the truck and aimed the barrel at Casper. He fired once. The bullet struck the road and buried itself in the soft asphalt. A shrapnel of pebbles buffeted Casper's face.

"What are you doing?" shouted someone in the truck. "Get back in the truck and stop fucking around, Hammond."

The vehicles rumbled past, their taillights reflected in the quivering metal back of a stop sign. When he was certain they were gone, Casper sat up. Bottles and Lenin rejoined him in the street.

"You all right?" asked Bottles.

"Yeah." Casper tossed the heavy rebreather to him. "Put that on."

Casper wiped away the blood beading on his cheek. When he looked up at the lamp, he found the pilot was dead but still staring right at him.

By the time they arrived in sight of St. Philomena's Gothic steeple, the world was enfolded in black smoke. Sheets of flame tore at the southern skies. The aircraft had been destroyed or chased away, and the sounds of front line fighting were drawing ever closer. Artillery continued to shudder overhead, but in sporadic salvos rather than its previous, steady barrage. The sirens continued their dirge for the city of Los Angeles.

The doors of the church were shut and barred. Only after pounding for more than a minute did a peephole slot open up. Eyes appeared and surveyed Casper, Bottles, and the dog. The peephole slammed shut without comment, but Casper and Bottles beat their hands against the door until it opened.

They were not greeted by Father Woodhew at all, but rather a mob of angry men and women brandishing household implements as weapons. The dog growled. The crowd surged out of the church's open doors, ignoring Bottles to lay their hands upon Casper and drag him roughly into the building. Father Woodhew appeared behind the angry mob, begging for them to stop, but it was no use. Their angry cries to "kill the dupe" and "string him up" echoed in the lofty chapel. They beat and kicked Casper until he fell to his knees amid the pews.

"Stop it!" shouted Bottles. "We came to help you! Stop it! You're gonna kill him!"

"That's the idea. Just be glad you're not next." The heavyset man who growled the response swung a rake handle and beat Casper over his back as he tried to stand.

A noose was slipped around Casper's neck, and he was dragged to one of the crossbeams. The rope was thrown over the timber, the slack pulled taut so that he was lifted to his feet. He grabbed at the noose, fighting to get his fingers beneath it.

"I will kill them." The voice belonged to the dog. "It is not a certain thing. They are many."

"No," said Casper.

"Yes, you dupe motherfucker!" shouted the man with the rake handle.

"Then surrender to them your flesh," said the dog. "It has no more value. It is a passing thing belonging to all intent that shares the water. All that matters is the state of your discrete electricity. It will become fire and fill new flesh. I will show you the ways of the reificant."

Casper forced his fingers beneath the strangulating noose. He was rewarded with a blow to the stomach with the end of a table leg that nearly made him pass out.

"Hang him high!" shouted a man.

"They did this to us!" shouted another.

"Let God have him!" shouted an old woman.

"Save them," Casper gasped. "Got to . . . save them."

"You'd better pray to your devil god," said the heavyset man. "Cause you're the one needs to be saved."

Casper's feet lifted up off the floor. The rope cut into his fingers and neck in equal measure, and he lost his breath. All of it began to darken and grow quiet. Bottles and Father Woodhew were still pleading for the crowd to stop. Men, women, and children were still screaming for his blood. It all receded into quiet shadows.

"They are doomed." The voice was still with him. "You cannot save them. This place is lost to the waters. Come with me now, and we will save the next people to walk the next place."

"Please." Casper found his voice no longer hoarse or constricted. "They're my kind. Don't you need me to cooperate?"

"I cannot force you," said the dog.

"Then I will cooperate. I will go with you. If you help me save them."

The world was almost dark. The only remaining light was the soft incandescent glow of the dog below his feet.

"You will travel through the water to the next place?" asked the dog. "You will become reificant, to take on new flesh, even if it cannot be your own?"

Casper was not sure of the exact meaning of the dog's words, but he saw no alternative. He would go with it wherever it needed him.

"I give you my word."

Unearthly light unfolded around Casper. He fell from the rope and to his knees upon the floor. Manifesting in the midst of the angry mob, standing above Casper, the dog became the reificant within its flesh, revealing in burning, radiographic detail the widespread wings and upright shape of a twelve-foot-tall insect. Exoskeleton and organs and looping entrails phosphoresced in black and brilliant purple, electric red, and burning gold.

The hemolymphatic throb of each organ was visible through the others. It was alive in exquisite, overlay detail. It was, at once, beautiful and terrible to look upon. The mob was transfixed by its terrible beauty.

Father Woodhew fell to his knees and cried, "Praise Almighty God! Behold His messenger!"

Casper sucked air into his aching lungs and tore the rope from around his neck. He rose from his knees and stood before the burning tracery of the grasshopper. It seemed to envelope him like a cage, and he realized that the dog had moved to stand beside his leg. He scratched its head as one by one the men and women in the mob fell to their knees. Even Bottles prostrated himself.

"Our salvation is at hand!" cried the fat man who had beat Casper with the rake.

"I'll try," said Casper, his voice hoarse.

He would lead them to the waters at Sugarside and save as many as he could.

■ ■ ■

Wesley Bishop awoke slowly, wondering at first why he was asleep in a junk heap and then recalling his predicament. His upper body and head were pinned inside the wreckage of the crashed helicopter, his suit and shirt bunched up in his armpits, while his bare stomach and his legs and feet extended into the street on which they had crashed. His back was broken, and even the slightest movement was agonizing.

His right arm was completely trapped beneath the deformed rear of the cabin, but he was able to free his left arm enough to touch his face. His fingers came away coated in blood, but it was not his. The helicopter had rolled onto its side as it came to rest. Misha Rosen, dead and impaled by a piece of the helicopter structure, was now hanging above him. She was cooperating with gravity to empty all of her fluids onto his head and shoulders.

Bishop cried out for help. He listened for an answer, but there was only the steady whine of the sirens and the confusing din of gunfire and explosions, seemingly all around him. A vehicle drove past. He heard it slow and called out to it for help. His only answer was a long blurt of gunfire very nearby, followed immediately by the squeal of tires.

Bishop shouted himself hoarse, and no one came to save him. He began visually searching the helicopter's interior for any means to either free himself or kill himself, though he did not favor the thought of reemerging in the midst of this calamity. There was a flare gun intended to signal *The Republic* to come to shore. The wrecked helicopter stank of hydraulics and fuel, and he might be able to set it ablaze and kill himself that way. He reached for it, but no matter how he shifted his body, he could not reach it. His gaze fell upon something closer and much more reassuring: Patrice's snake-leather bag of pharmaceutical goodies.

He extended his arm all the way out to his fingers across the fuel-dampened wreck of the cabin. The tips of his fingers brushed the snakeskin bag. He stretched, pain exploding in his fractured spine, but only managed to push it a bit farther away. He pushed up on the helicopter's body, minutely shifting the multi-ton frame and allowing him a scant centimeter to slide his body. He reached again for the bag, but this time, as he extended his arm, Misha Rosen moved above him.

He cried out in surprise. Her arm was swaying very slightly as it dangled, limp, from her shoulder. *No*, he told himself, *she is dead, and you are imagining things.* He looked back at the bag, tantalizingly close, and gave her one last glimpse.

A pale length of arm darted into the helicopter, clawed fingers reaching above his head and tearing into Misha Rosen's slack face. The hand withdrew with a quivering hunk of meat. A moment later Bishop caught sight of a naked man, legs all wrong, bounding past the deformed bubble of the helicopter's cockpit. Another appeared, lingering this time, peering in to reveal a face that was not human at all but a hairless, leporine face with bulbous blue eyes and jaws filled with bared plates of translucent bone.

They appeared in great number, crawling all at once into the helicopter's wreckage. They insinuated themselves through narrow openings, reaching out and tearing hunks from the dead reporter and the mangled corpses in the front of the cockpit. One came very near to Bishop. It sniffed at him, flaring nostrils slits and touching his face with its cold hand, but it withdrew, seemingly uninterested in him. They snapped at one another over choice bits and began tearing out Misha Rosen's entrails in a frenzy. The helicopter filled with the bestial sounds of gorging and the carcass smell of organs.

Bishop wished they would kill him. Wished they would sink their strange teeth into his throat and tear it out. He was not afraid of pain or death and did not want to watch such savagery any longer. At the limit of his sanity, a gunshot mercifully rang out and struck one of the creatures. He became aware that rumbling vehicles were nearby, and the helicopter was suddenly shaking with the impact of dozens of bullets. The creatures screamed and began to flee. Some died in the process of escaping and lay thrashing beside the helicopter.

The shooting stopped, but the vehicles did not immediately move on. Boots crunched through debris. Men were talking, voices muffled by respirator masks.

"This is one of Bishop's private helicopters," said a woman, her voice clear.

"Yes," cried Bishop. "Yes! I am here!"

A head covered in a spore hood leaned in above him, near Misha Rosen's mutilated carcass. It ducked back out, and after a few moments they had cleared the crumpled door above him. He was still trapped, but they at least had a view into the helicopter. A familiar woman's face appeared in the door. She was wearing a Rapid Response uniform, and her face was serious and marked with abrasions.

"Thank Christ," Bishop sighed. "Please, get me out of here. I have a ship waiting in Sugarside. It will take us to safety."

The woman smiled. She did not move to free him.

"What a lucky find," said the woman. "I'm Pollen Foster. You sentenced me and about thirty innocent people to death."

Foster? Yes, he remembered her. The woman from Bad Tower. Milo's loose end.

"No," said Bishop. He panicked and stammered for a response. "No, I was against that. I told Milo that it was a foolish idea. That you would, ah, that they would just send more UN inspectors. That it would be messy. It would be too messy to kill your team in Bad Tower too. I tried to veto him, but he is a monster. He is—"

She aimed a machine pistol in at his face.

"There's more of them coming," said one of the men wearing spore masks.

Her smile darkened, and she withdrew the gun. Her face disappeared.

"Wait," he said. "Don't leave me here with those things."

She was walking away with the men.

"Please!" he screamed. "Please! I'll tell you how to signal my ship!"

She reappeared in the door. "Speak quickly."

"There's a flare pistol, just there." He gestured weakly with his free hand. "Fire it twice. Two green flares, and they will come to the docks. Free me, and I'll—"

"We'd have to cut you out of this. We don't have time."

Bishop licked his dry lips. She pushed away from the door frame, intent on leaving.

"Please, have mercy," He gestured to the snakeskin bag. "Just leave me that. It has my medicine."

"You don't deserve it," she said. She nevertheless reached into the helicopter and handed him the bag. He clutched it to his chest with one hand and thanked her again and again. He continued to thank her even after he heard the doors slamming on the vehicles and the engines revving and rumbling away.

The pale creatures crept back to the helicopter. They crowded around it in even greater numbers than before. Jaws snapping and hissing, they leaped atop the wreck and pried open the metal. The helicopter shifted painfully against his chest. Alien faces appeared at every possible entry point. Hands reached in and tore wet strips from Misha Rosen. Bishop fumbled the bag open. He stared at the watery blue eyes swept by nictitating membranes.

Something about these creatures was familiar. Like wolves. Like that fucking dog that started all this. He could see it in their watery fish eyes. That same thinking. Watching from the rippled spine of a gypsum dune. Watching him fall and suffer.

"Get away from me," Bishop moaned.

They did not ignore him this time. Strange hands tore at his clothes, hitching his trousers painfully and tearing them open. He gasped as jaws closed on his muscular stomach and his thigh. They bit off his toes like ripe fruit. Their jaws clicked and clattered and sawed into his tender flesh. The pain was excruciating.

He reached into the snakeskin and felt the hard, cool shape of vials. No pills. No powders. Only the oily blue of the bliss filled the hand that he brought out of the bag and to his face. He screamed, delirious with pain, for it seemed to go on and on, and he seemed no closer to death. Their hands were inside his body, pulling out pieces, consuming him slowly. The only escape from the agony was what he held in his hand.

Quivering fingers unsealed the vial, and he brought it to his lips. The bliss poured into his mouth and was absorbed through his tongue. He felt the snuffling breath on his thigh, on his shriveled cock. No, he pleaded. Die before it happens. No. I cannot endure that. Alien jaws snapped shut. Pain exploded in his groin; hot, liquid, stretching and tearing away the flesh. He was submerged in the agony of castration, fading into the blue landscape of the bliss, and still he did not die.

Death would take many days, pursued through traced geographies of pain by his father and the laughing horse Apollyon.

■ ■ ■

Polly opened the hatch and thrust her head and shoulders out of the PitSec armored vehicle. She could almost hear the ocean, they were so close, but the city had become unrecognizable. Damage from the earthquake and military action was impossible to differentiate. Rubble was consumed by the explosion of life.

The convoy had passed from a graveyard of destroyed military vehicles and into a luminous realm of mycoflora, the sky blotted out by the gilled caps pulsing with circulating liquids. The buildings lining the street were difficult to distinguish beneath a fleshy carpet of adhesive basidiospores.

The drone of the sirens was muffled. The alarm of a car bleated from within a hedge of pale mycelial threads. The vermicular roots squirmed across the roadway, and, as she watched, their gathering weight smashed through hidden windows.

The variety and scale of flora was oppressive. Sweet smells of the fruiting bodies drifted through the air on the currents created by respiring fungus. Crustaceans scuttled out of the roadway and gathered beneath delicate, veined fans. Maggot things like those that killed Mrs. Valdez worried at the carcass of a dog. Larger things slithered, half-seen in the loathsome crowd of surrounding fungus. She sensed these creatures observing her, their menace palpable, but they did not act. Perhaps they were afraid of armored vehicles. Perhaps they had already eaten.

They proceeded, following the map she still carried, but soon she was forced to halt because of an obstruction. The ruptured curl of an immense fungal cup drooped across one lane. The roadway and surviving buildings were stained by a wash of carmine liquid from the cup's interior. Black flecks and scraps clung to the curb and gathered in a leafy clot against the storm drain.

"What do we do?" asked Sokov, calling from the hatch of the vehicle he was driving.

Hundreds of bones enrobed in scarlet flesh scattered the road. There were limbs still partially connected by sinews, skulls, wet and glistening, and lurid mushroom stalks already sprouting between the meaty spokes of a ribcage. The quantity of bones spilled out of this velvety cup was sufficient to make a dozen or more complete skeletons. Bits of metal—keys, belts, coins—were strewn about and shined to glittering silver by the enzymes that digested the unfortunate men and women.

She felt sick. Were they dead already? Did they perish in the earthquake, or did they succumb to contagion? The thought of even one man alive and trapped within the fungal cup as the enzyme began to work was too much for her to consider long.

"We drive on," she finally answered.

There was no choice but to drive through. The pale, questing fingers of mycotic fronds were torn away. The solid rubber tires of the armored vehicles slipped with filth. She could hear the human bones crackling beneath them.

After a moment, Robin joined her in the cockpit. The gas suit she wore was pulled back from her face.

"You shouldn't take that off," said Polly. She tapped the yellow warning light blinking on the spore detector. "Every time I open the hatch, I let some of it in."

"It's too late for that," said Robin. "I'm afraid when we were underground I somehow ruptured my suit. I've been hoping . . . I'm already infected."

"We can cut it off," said Polly.

"It's long past the point of amputation." Robin lifted her arm. She had surreptitiously bandaged it in Dr. Nandy's mortuary. She showed the wrappings to Polly, and the spore growth was showing through the gauze. "I can feel it in my lungs, which means it's in my blood."

"The treatment," said Polly. "We can turn around and take you to the hospital that Bishop was operating."

She knew as soon as she spoke the possibility aloud that it was ridiculous. Dr. Chandrasekar's treatment was a farce. If it ever worked at all, it was only because of immediate surgery. Polly had never seen anyone recover from spores in the blood.

"No," said Robin. "I will die. I can't bring this infection with me onto that ship. I should not even be in this vehicle with everyone else."

Polly began to argue again, offering other farfetched possibilities, but Robin stopped her and said, "Let me tell you again about my son and daughter."

She took a wallet out from her pocket and opened the snap. She produced a photograph of a young boy in knee-high socks and a soccer uniform kneeling beside a ball on a grassy field. He was handsome and had hair as sandy blond as his mother's.

"That's Clayton, from a few years ago," said Robin. "He's older now. His birthday is the nineteenth of June."

She slid the photograph out of the wallet and passed it to Polly.

"I can't take this."

"You have to take it." Robin slid out another picture, this one of an ecstatic little girl on the back of a Shetland pony. She handed it to Polly. "It's from Evelyn's birthday last year. I call her Evie. We were in . . . never mind, it's not important. Her birthday is the tenth of February."

Robin leaned her head against the carrier's hull. The infection was spreading so quickly across her arm that Polly could see the tiny fronds of the sting grass unfurling like little worms and widening into minuscule feathers of white."He likes heavy-metal music and motorbikes and Chinese food. She likes horses and collecting toys and . . . there's a song I used to sing with her . . . I can't remember it now. The one time it matters."

"I know songs," said Polly. "Don't worry. It's okay."

"That's it. 'Don't Worry, Be Happy.' She likes that song. And macaroni and cheese."

"Every kid loves that," said Polly.

"They are in the UN safe zone in Seattle. You have to reach them. They may be evacuated to Vancouver or to the Soviet military bunkers in Vladivostock. If not there, then to Ostrov Gallya, beneath Cape Tegethoff. It is where the UN has built the biological vault. Konstantin knows the way."

"I will find them."

"Promise me."

Polly looked her in the eye and said, "I swear I will find Clay and Evie, and I will get them out of this."

Robin took other photographs out of the wallet, including a family picture and a photo of herself and her husband, a gray-haired man in a tweed suit. She took off her wedding ring and a necklace and passed them all to Polly. She put them into her pocket and hugged Robin with the arm she was not using to drive the armored vehicle.

When Robin separated from the hug, she lowered the mask back over her face to conceal her emotion.

When they reached Sugarside, Polly guided the armored vehicle down a switch-back earthen ramp to the parking area, which ran along the marina and dockside shops and restaurants. The area was teeming with people. Men, women, and children. They were waving and signaling to a long, low vessel that lay at anchor out in the waters. Those at the rear of the crowd turned their attention on the PitSec armored vehicles. She expected the crowd to assail the vehicles with stones, but they waved in a friendly manner.

Polly opened the hatch and was met with welcoming cries.

"What is going on here?" she asked the nearest people.

"We followed an angel," said a young, dreamy-eyed woman. "He came to save us."

She pointed up the dock to a tall man with a shaved head and a grimy, paint-stained coat. His back was turned to her. He was waving a bedsheet wrapped around the handle of a rake back and forth to get the attention of the vessel anchored out near the breakwater.

"Get everyone out." Polly spoke to Sokov over the radio. "Stay together. I'm not quite sure what's going on here, but we're out of gas, and it's our best bet."

The people gathered along the docks were supernaturally calm. Only a few were equipped with any sort of spore masks. They extended handshakes and hugs to the scientists as Polly guided them through the crowd, toward the man waving the makeshift flag. There was a dog and a skinny man with dreadlocks standing along-side him. He turned as she reached the marina's docks.

"Ninety-ninety," said Polly.

"Call me Casper." He shook her hand, was unsatisfied with that, and decided to hug her.

She was dumbfounded, but the dog was the same, and the man, other than a few ugly scabs on his face and a growth of stubble, was the man she had dropped off at St. Philomena's. As if to confirm this, Father Woodhew approached out of the crowd.

"Polly Foster? Is that who you are?"

"Yes, Father." She embraced him. "These people need to cover up. The spore storms will be spreading here soon."

"There's a ship at anchor out there," said Casper. "I've been trying to signal it for the last ten minutes, but they just watch us through binoculars and do nothing."

The Republic was waiting for Bishop. She was three hundred and fifty feet in length and had the look of a military vessel. She was liveried in bright white, and her single middle stack was blue capped by red. A red, white, and blue yacht ensign was flying from her masthead. Small radar turned above the pilot house, and figures could be seen moving within the illuminated interior. Men were gathered on the deck in dark uniforms, some with weapons and some with ropes to pull the ship in closer to the dock.

Polly did not hesitate. She took the flare pistol out from her pocket and fired two green flares to signal their arrival. The crowd in the lot cheered as if watching fireworks. White smoke began to emerge from the funnel of *The Republic,* and she shortly approached the main pier. The men on the deck of the ship immediately set to work mooring her against the dock.

"Who goes there?" One of the crewmen shouted a challenge from the deck as Casper and Polly marched out along the dock at the head of a column of scientists, Marines, and families. Everyone on the crew was a duplicate.

"We're coming aboard," said Polly. "Mr. Bishop has told us to take his place on this ship."

The crew shouted up along a human chain, calling for the captain, and soon a dashing type one in a blue pea coat emerged from the pilot house. He walked to the gunwale and leaned upon it with his elbows. He surveyed the menagerie gathered on the dock. He seemed to remember his station, and he took a rumpled white hat from his pocket and settled it upon his head.

"I suppose we should lower the gangplank," he declared. "Come on aboard with you. I'm Captain Fellows."

Smiles broke out on the weary faces as they filed out across the gangplank. Robin said her good-byes to her fellow scientists, though no amount could ever satisfy the gravity of her situation. Polly had to force herself to release the woman from her arms. When she'd gone over to the gangplank to board, she found Casper and his dog bidding farewell to the dreadlocked man they called Bottles.

"I'll save you a seat at the table," said Bottles. He paused as he crossed the gangplank and waved a final farewell.

Polly indicated Robin, sitting alone on the pier. "She is staying. She has the spore disease."

"I'm staying as well," said Casper.

"What? I don't know these people. I have to take this ship to Seattle."

"Take it to Seattle," said Casper. "I had to get them to the ship, and now I have another obligation. I will stay with your friend until it is time for her to go."

Polly cast a lingering look at Robin, chin up, gazing out across the waves lapping at the dock's stone pilings. The sun would be setting soon. Polly crossed over the gangplank and onto the immaculate deck of *The Republic*. The dashing Captain Fellows was waiting to greet her. He shook her hand vigorously.

"Good to have you aboard," he said. "You will be treated like Mr. Bishop himself. My vessel is at your disposal."

The weight of sadness tugged at Polly's limbs as she stood on the afterdeck and watched the dying city of Los Angeles recede beyond the horizon. All around her were smiles and joyous embraces. For those escaping certain doom, these were the happiest moments of their lives.

■ ■ ■

Later, as the sun fell against the crashing sea, Casper Cord held Robin Burns in his arms.

"I want to see the sunset," she said, and then she fell into a prolonged spasm of choking coughs. When she recovered, she smiled weakly and added, "It had better hurry."

The white of the spore grass had crept across her limbs and body and up her neck. It cradled her chin and sent roots questing above her jawline. Though the sun had nearly slipped below the horizon, he doubted the scientist would see her wish granted.

Behind his shoulder stormy clouds of smoke hung over the city. The atmosphere reminded him of the volcanic ruins of the grasshopper's world. The parking lot was overgrown with white, and the stalks of blue fruits quivered in the lee of the armored carriers.

A faint yellow glow appeared in the highest clouds above the city. Its light flickered within the clouds as it passed through them toward the veiled ruins of Los Angeles.

"What is that?" asked Robin as the rumble of engines became audible.

The glow passed out of the ceiling of clouds and revealed itself as the line of a missile, descending at great velocity for San Pedro. Several more glowing missiles speared through the smoke all across the area, plunging at equal speeds, like the fragments of a falling star. The dog wagged its tail.

"It's the sunset," said Casper.

The stars flashed and light built upon light. Casper, Robin, and the dog were transformed into smoke. The Pool, vast and deep, was freed from its manmade imprisonment by the fire. Its water flowed out and began to overtake the sea.

■ ■ ■

The sky above the horizon was lit with lingering flashes and those aboard *The Republic* heard a rumble of distant thunder. Some suspected that this was the end of Los Angeles, but none spoke of it. Through the night they heard jets and saw strange lights in the sky. Just after midnight a terrible screaming began to issue from an unknown source in the darkness. The children were taken below decks. The crew played searchlights across the ocean and the sky looking for the source. It was never found and most agreed that was just as well.

The following morning Captain Fellows notified Polly, Rukundo and the others that the ship's radar had detected large surface returns. Admiral Haley's fleet was only a few miles west. None of the vessels were answering the radio.

"Should I avoid the area?" asked Captain Fellows.

"We'll take a closer look," said Polly. "Very carefully."

By mid-morning they spotted the first of the picket ships. A destroyer called *Porter*. The sea was hidden beneath a dense, white fog. The gray vessel was listing slightly and did not respond to visual signals. They passed it by at a distance of a few hundred yards. Nothing moved and the ship was dark. Soon they spotted other vessels in similarly ominous states. One ship, a supply vessel, was burning out of control. An explosion sent flaming debris arcing into the ocean. There was no sign of lifeboats or any survivors in the water.

"We should go away," said Rukundo. "This place is not safe."

Polly agreed. The surviving Marines insisted they continue. They had friends aboard Haley's flagship, the immense aircraft carrier *George Wallace*, and that vessel had just appeared on the horizon, apparently undamaged. The ship was big as any building Polly could recall. It, like the others, did not respond to any signal. The Marines and a few armed crewmen from *The Republic* lowered a motor launch into the fog and boarded. After more than three hours they returned.

The boat was raised from the surface. The stricken expressions of the returning men as they came aboard was enough to silence questions. It was just as well, none of the men would speak of what they saw. Captain Fellows conducted a rigorous, private debriefing of his crewmen and decided to keep the details to himself.

"On to Seattle," said Captain Fellows. "Pray to God we get there before what wiped out Haley's fleet."

The journey took three days. During that time the many refugees from St. Philomena's crowded around civilian band radios, listening to stations along the California and Oregon seaboard as they reported on the spreading disaster. Panic was leading to misinformation.

The harried radio announcers reported every scrap of information, even if it contradicted others. The military was falling back east, leaving the civilians in California to either follow them or perish. Tanks were mounting offensives from Nevada. The President was dead. The President was safe on Air Force One. Some units were mutinying. The military was massacring duplicates in Nebraska. A plane took pictures of San Diego and it appeared as if a thousand years have passed and a strange jungle has grown up in place of the city. Earthquakes wracked the Midwest. The Chinese were in Florida. The Soviets were in Alaska. The acting President requested their military advisors.

Konstantin Sokov was permitted to use the long range radio to communicate with Vladivostok. The connection was intermittent and vulnerable to the increasing atmospheric interference. For a day a military officer named Gergiev beckoned him to come to the bunkers and promised to reunite him with wife. On the second day, after hours of blackout caused by a roiling storm, Sokov received a terse message advising him to head to the biological vault beneath Cape Tegethoff.

"Ostrov Gallya is last hope," Sokov later explained at an early-morning conference. "It was built to survive world war. Nuclear missiles. If they tell me to go there it has already become very bad in Vladivostok. Maybe everywhere."

"Then we find who we can in Seattle," said Polly. "Robin's children are my priority, but we pick up any survivors we can, along with provisions, and sail for Ostrov Gallya. How many can they accomodate?"

"All." Sokov was holding his thick glasses and massaging the bridge of his nose between thumb and fingers. "Was built for thousands."

They reached Seattle that afternoon. Captain Fellows navigated *The Republic* through a refugee fleet of fishing trawlers, cargo ships and pleasure craft fleeing for the false safety of the ocean. The port was packed with those who could not find a ship. There were so many that Captain Fellows anchored *The Republic* a half mile from the Port of Seattle. Polly, Rukundo and a detachment of armed crewmen were ferried to shore by launches. The boats would return to pick them up when Polly fired a signal flare.

Order was crumbling in the city limits. There were few signs of the spores or any of the alien life—some black birds and the deflated bells of aero plankton—but entire blocks were consumed in flames and the downtown appeared to be a war zone. Crazed looting was going on. Polly and Rukundo moved among the chaos unnoticed. The military units meant to hold the city were joining the looters or already fleeing along with most of the civilians, their tanks lashed with furniture, televisions and cases of booze.

They witnessed vile crimes of opportunity. Murders, executions, beatings, mob justice and attacks on women. Some of this violence was too much to bear. They came upon the steps of a public library where a group of policemen, both black and white, seemed to be preparing to execute a number of young black men. Polly motioned for the others to stop and began to formulate a plan of attack.

"We cannot help them," said Rukundo. "This place is in darkness. Now men turn to beasts and there is no place for the righteous. We must go."

Rukundo seemed to speak from firsthand knowledge. Polly obeyed the calm peacekeeper and they followed him down an alley and away from the miserable scene. Shots echoed from the library plaza behind them.

It wasn't much longer before they found the UN safe zone. Polly felt sick. The gate and guard posts were demolished. The geodesic dome of the central building was hardly more than a metal frame. Smoke poured from the upper floors of the brick outbuilding and a long, glass-fronted welcome center was being picked over by looters. Glass crunched underfoot. Polly fired her weapon and scattered all but the most determined looters.

"What do we do now?" asked one of the type twos from *The Republic*.

"Their names are Clay and Evie," she said. "They're the reason we're here. Search in pairs."

The dead and dying were everywhere, victims of the sudden brutality consuming the city. Horrors lurked behind almost every door of the compound. The worst were the children. When Polly came upon some of the men responsible Rukundo could not restrain her. She gunned them down where they lay and left their bodies sprawled in empty bottles of booze.Night was falling. The fires in the outbuildings were worsening and the automated spore sirens were beginning to wail an uneasy dirge to the south. Polly was become more frantic with each passing minute.

"You will go back to *The Republic* now," said Rukundo. "I will remain and will find them and bring them to you."

She appreciated Rukundo's courage. She showed him the pictures once more to remind him of their faces.

"I will not go back without them," she said.

Five minutes later Rukundo found them, along with fifteen other terrified children, herded into a maintenance space beneath the floor. One of the UN guards had hidden them there before fleeing. The children were dehydrated and scared beyond tears, but once they realized Polly and Rukundo were not like the looters their tiny hands reached out for comfort.

Clay was the oldest boy among the children and probably the worst off, because he understood more of what was happening. He didn't speak, but Evie, her eyes bright, took hold of Polly's hand and asked, "Can we go away from here?"

"Far away," said Polly. "Somewhere safe."

COMINTERCEPT – MILITARY UHF/VHF –
IN THE OPEN – BLACK LABEL

08/01/06 - 07:01:39 PST - Machine Transcription
Subjects: ??? (Unidentified subjects)

Signal received in the open. Standby recording engaged.

???: Hello? Is anybody there? Hello? Please help us. My daughter is sick. I don't know if—hello? Is anyone there on this frequency? We found this radio in an Army truck. There are four of us alive. The shelter in Springfield is not safe. Do not go to Springfield. Please, if you hear this, please come rescue us. There's a big hill here. We're gonna climb it. We're going to high ground. We're going to . . .

???: (unintelligible)

???: I love you, Mom. I love you. I know you can't . . . I hope you're okay. I love you.

???: So long, everybody.

EPILOGUE

■ ■ ■

Her promise to Robin Burns was fulfilled. Evelyn and Clay Burns were safely ensconced in the immense biological vault beneath the black horn of Cape Tegeth-off. They were joined by the other children from the UN safe zone and the survivors of St. Philomena's. They would share the vault with the archivists and villagers from the nearby work camp. The isolated arctic geography and winter glaciers might keep the vault safe from the alien species. It was a sealed system, producing its own food and purifying its own water. It derived its power from geothermal turbines.

No duplicates were allowed inside. *The Republic* had set sail toward Alaska, following the Aleutians to the mainland in search of other survivors. Captain Fellows had not been optimistic. Even the NOAA weather beacons were quiet.

Polly Foster slept soundly beneath the trackless, dim blue sky of Ostrov Gallya. Her teeth chattered, and her face, exposed to the elements, was stiff with the cold. It was almost midnight. The frigid rock beneath her had worked its way through the insulation of her sleeping bag.

She clambered to her feet and groaned at her soreness. The sound of her own voice startled her. She tried to stoke the embers of her last fire back to life. No luck. She would have to gather more wood and start a new fire.

Her pre-pack food was gone. Her water was nearly gone. She searched her bag and found a sugarless sweetener packet. She savored the powder as it dissolved in her mouth. Sitting on the mossy earth beside the pack, she watched the puffins circling over the eastern cliffs.

Her vigil outside the vault was nearing its end. If she remained sitting, watching the birds, she would freeze to death in hours. She could feel the insidious cold beginning to numb her entire body. Soon she would feel warm. Happy. She could die that way.

No.

She got to her feet again and gathered up her belongings. The emergency sleeping bag, the flare pistol, the radio, the plastic sheeting dripping with condensation, and the extra clothes she'd brought over from the ship. The machine pistol was heavier than she recalled. She thought about shooting one of the puffins and starting a fire to roast the bird. She thought about pounding on the heavy door of the biological vault and begging for Konstantin or Rukundo to let her inside. Rukundo might do it if she begged enough.

That line of thinking was dangerous. She had to go before she succumbed to desperation. She shouldered her bag and her gun and set off in the direction of the Tegethoff settlement. Spore grass was taking over the rocky slope down to the sea. The needles of the pines were white, the trees dead or dying, festooned with the gossamer strands of alien vines. Here and there the crab rats scurried underfoot, turning over saltlick quartz and scraping off the colonies of bacteria beneath.

The fecund mycotic jungles would swallow the island soon enough. There were pale stalks rising among the trees, glowing caps, curling fronds and fleshy cycads that dripped with poisonous sap. The cold was no match for the febrile pulse of alien vegetation.

No sign of the pale men. Somehow, she knew, they would find their way to the island. To every corner of every map.

The settlement of Tegethoff, originally built to contain the biological vault, had changed dramatically in the few days she'd spent camped outside the vault. White encrusted buildings up to the second floor. The outlines of the streets were disappearing beneath the blanket of spore grass, pale red fungal fruits, stalks and glow plums, and the pods of the floaters, waiting to launch their dust into the air and give birth to the gas bag colonies.

The movement of a door caught her eye. It was only the wind, but she approached anyway. She found a tiny library, walls taped with drawings from children, varicolored carpet partly overgrown with mycelium. Papers gathered in drifts. The shelves were stuffed mostly with books for children. Letters cut out from construction paper and taped to the wall spelled out WELCOME in English and Russian. Canadians and Soviets had once worked together in this settlement.

A sheet of paper crumpled under her boot. She picked it up, then brushed off the spore dust. It was a schedule of library events. Yesterday Mary Tologanak had demonstrated kakivak fishing spears for the children. In two weeks Fedor Chernienko, the author of *Skies of the Mother's North*, would be conducting a reading from his book on amateur astronomy. There it was, printed on that discarded paper: the last bit of future waiting to play through the reels.

Polly searched the librarian's desk—paper clips, rubber stamps, ink pads, pens, pencils—it was full of little human things that would never be made again. She found a Goodnut bar in the drawer. It was frozen hard, so she put it down the pocket of her inner layer of trousers. She gathered some books she thought she might like to read and stuffed them into her pack. She considered taking some of the political books for kindling but could not bring herself to burn any book.

She went out into the street and watched the sun that never left come up over the eastern coast. The cold wind off the ocean blew her hair behind her head in copper limbs that burned with the sunlight. Gold spilled over the shore and the powdered carcasses of dead whales and sea lions. They seethed with the scavenging crab rats. Gulls circled above, crying with hunger but afraid to land on the shore. The tide was thick and writhing with the entrails of alien eels. Spore grass was everywhere, breaking through windows, growing up rain spouts and onto the roofs of the houses. A spore fog hid the horizon, and above it stretched a vast cloud of translucent aeroplankton moving with the air currents.

There was a sense of passing. It was the loss of man's dominion but also of all the beauty that had once inhabited the world. She was a stranger to this place. The gulls and puffins were as doomed as the whales and sea lions and the trees. It was only a matter of time.

Polly wandered the streets, calling out to the translucent creatures passing high overhead and beckoning to the pale men that never came. A noise brought her to a house clinging to one of Tegethoff's rocky slopes. Here the cape was so steep that the foundation was built on timber pilings like the pier at Sugarside. She climbed the staircase to the door. It was torn from its hinges. Gone. The frame of the door hung broken, and pieces of aluminum siding were scattered amid the white grass. From within she heard a loud clicking followed by a clatter of dishes and pans.

She entered with caution, the machine pistol at her shoulder, unsure if she sought death or sought to inflict violence on some alien creature. She stepped as lightly as she could, thankful of the heavy carpeting. She was careful to navigate around an overturned end table and the fragments of a broken flower vase. More debris. A Soviet-style television and photographs of a Slavic family. Unopened letters with Cyrillic writing and a child's raincoat. More clattering from the kitchen on the far side of the house. The thudding, careless movement of something large. Her heart strained in her chest.

She rounded the corner down a hall and nearly fired her gun at a skittering family of crab rats. They scampered across the carpet and disappeared into a floor vent. The ceiling light fixture was broken and strewn across the hall. Despite her best efforts, glass crunched beneath her boots. Something wooden snapped in the kitchen. The house groaned under the weight of whatever was in there.

She reached the end of the hall, pivoted, and flattened her back against the kitchen cabinets. It was only a few feet away now. She used her teeth to pull off the glove covering her shooting hand. The creature emitted an earthy odor. She could hear the thrum and hiss of its breathing. It was rooting through the food, looking for something to eat. She searched for its reflection in some object so she could see what it was and where it was in the kitchen.

The dirty chrome of a toaster reflected just enough that she could see the dark bulk of it, beside the table, standing amid the upright skeleton of a wooden chair as though it had tried to stand on it. It was so large and black, for a moment she thought it might be a bear of some sort. No. The legs: long and too many joints. Something familiar about it. She flicked the safety of the machine pistol, took a deep breath, and stepped out to face the creature.

A short, startled intake of breath. It froze, a chewed corner of moldy bread caught in its mandibles. The deflated sack of bread was held pinched by segmented tarsus. Black pupils moved within the rusty red hemispheres of its eyes. Its head cocked to one side, and it regarded Polly.

She projected human emotions onto its reaction. Surprise, for certain, but there was something else. It lowered the bag of bread to a table strewn with domestic debris. It took two heavy steps to turn to face her. The chewed corner of bread still dangled from its mouth. It looked embarrassed.

Polly couldn't help herself. She lowered the barrel of the gun, and she laughed. She laughed so goddamn hard, she had to lean against the kitchen counter for support. It was the most ridiculous thing she had ever seen. A twelve-foot, gray-black grasshopper, fat body and awkward limbs completely filling this wrecked kitchen. Caught eating bread. As ashamed as a little kid caught with his hand in a cookie jar.

It watched her work through the paroxysms of her emotion. She hunched over, wiping tears from her eyes. She gasped for breath through the last convulsions of her desperate laughter. She let the folding machine pistol hang from its strap, and she reached into the waist of her pants. She brought out the body-warmed Goodnut bar.

"I've never seen one of you before," said Polly. "Is this what we do now? Raid someone else's pantry?"

She pulled off her other glove and unwrapped the candy bar. The chocolate was soft and parted easily as she divided it with her fingers. The alien watched intently.

"Will I be rooting around some poor little space man's kitchen?" She avoided more laughter. When she blinked, tears were still falling from her eyelashes. "Here, have some."

She held out half of the Goodnut bar. She could feel the snuffling of air through rigid holes on its face. The chewed bread fell from its mouth, and it cautiously leaned its head down toward her, the projected shapes of its pupils never looking away from her face. Its mandibles delicately grasped the candy bar. It lifted its head and raised a limb to its face to support the melting morsel.

Polly found an overturned chair amid the smashed cereal boxes and tins on the floor, and she set it upright. She sat down, facing the insect. It was holding the Goodnut bar as if uncertain it was edible. She made a show of unwrapping her half, holding it up to her face, and sticking it into her mouth. Almost, but not quite—too much to be chewed at once.

The warm candy was the sweetest thing she had ever tasted. It was the past in every speck, and she appreciated it in its fullness. She was aware of the generational efforts conspiring in its production, the strata of techno-ingenuity to breed and plant and gather and shell and boil and salt and sweeten and blend and robe in milky chocolate and wrap in glistening, impermeable, brightly-printed polymers. One-time thing. Now unwrapped, discarded, floating away on the wind, dissolving in her stomach and becoming a part of her.

She chewed with her mouth open, showing the alien thick steam gusting up from her gullet with each breath. She swallowed the tacky lump and gestured for the alien to do the same. The candy disappeared into its mouth as though hoisted up by ropes. There was no chewing or outward sign of pleasure. Could it know the taste?

"It's good," she said.

After a moment the alien raised a forelimb and reached out a three-tipped claw to her. It wavered in the air a few inches from her knee. The alien moved its fatter, hindmost legs in a strumming motion across setae on its back. The vibrating bristles produced a sound between the shrill chirping of a cricket and a dissonant human voice.

"*Tk clk crrrk crrk,*" it said.

"I don't understand you," she said.

"*Tk clk crrrk crrk,*" it repeated. "*Trr ssrrk llk.*"

The massive insect seemed intent on making her understand. She shook her head, still not grasping its meaning.

"*Tk clk crrrk crrk.*" It reached up its other forelimb to a pattern of iridescent chitin between its eyes and traced the shape with its claw. For the first time she noticed the pair of small, round eyes set between the larger facetted domes. "*Tk clk crrrk crrk. Tk clk crrrk crrk.*"

She slid the machine pistol off her shoulder and laid it on the nearby counter. She stood and took the creature's extended claw in her cold-pinched hand. The claw was hard, but not as hard as she expected. The many segmented plates allowed it to flex and flatten. She smiled up at the broad wedge of the creature's face and shook the claw up and down. Whether or not it understood the gesture did not matter.

"Polly," she said. "Polly. My name is Polly."

"Ppppp-ooooolly." Her name sounded bizarre being formed by the quivering bristles on the alien's back.

"It's good to meet you," she said.

And it was.

■ ■ ■

Wesley Bishop was alive and reconstituted for the hundredth time that day. He climbed over the squirming flesh of naked bodies. Familiar faces beneath his hands, crying for help, begging for death. They baked in the radiation emanating from the heat-fused ruins of San Pedro.

He tore the cowl from his eyes and stared up from the gutted pit of the central pylon. The Pool was open to the sky. Shrieking swarms of black birds flapped out from the liquid, tearing at their own cowls, twisting by the hundreds up into the yellow-black daylight. Massive things were stirring within the liquid depths. They rose on shaky limbs and shook off the gelatin membranes of their birth.

All the types were being born from the Pool in an endless tide. There were men and women from the Undercroft. Forever young starlets and scientists once kept locked in the cannery with all the criminals. They were released into a world they did not comprehend. They pulled themselves over one another, clawing up hills of the living and the dead, working their newly-made bodies up the fractured innards of the birthing pipes, and scaling the rubble into the nightmare that was once the LARC.

Bishop clawed hardest of all. He was always good at finding his way to the top. By any and all means, by gouge and claw and step and kick, he made his way to the top. He stood naked in rubble, howling winds rippling his hair. The newly made duplicates buffeted him as they streamed past. Other creatures were scaling the sundered honeycomb of the Pit, joining their human brothers in the landscape the Mother had created for them.

Looking out across the hills of ruin, Wesley Bishop spied a heap of slag that so resembled a horse, he decided, at last, he did not care for this place anymore. He craved something else. He craved more than ruins. He wanted beautiful skies and narrow, cobbled streets. He yearned for sumptuous dinners and warm nights with pretty girls. He required new lands to lay claim to.

Bishop returned to the Pool's shores and waded into the hungry liquid. It hissed on contact with his flesh. He began to dissolve and, as he did, imbued the serpent with his desire to escape where Apollyon could not follow.

I inhabit the spaces between, flowing with deep water to all its shores. I rise on human bones and flesh beneath skies consumed in the storms of nebulae. When I am choked by poison or seared by distant suns or freeze atop the airless mountain, I remake myself as new things.

I am the flesh of woven bone. My sky has torn loose, and the earth heaves with liquid fire. I am one of few, sentinel upon the surface, protector of the softer things beneath the crust. I rise and warn of the coming of the deep water. My words are not understood, and I am cast into the fire.

I am the machine-being, one of the engines that endured the long-ago destruction of my creators. I am a component in the millennium work of transforming all a planet's resources to navigate the stars. Deep mines have found the water. My arrival offends the pulsing crystal stacks of logic cores. I am made to answer for my existence. I do not speak this language, and I am disassembled.

I am warm and still. I process the soil and enrich it with my excretions. I cling to roots of the primeval forest, completing a century's climb to the surface where I will become a hard-shelled thing and live only for one day. It is my only chance to speak to the trees and warn that their roots will soon touch dangerous waters. I sing with a voice deep within my body, and I do not know if the forest understands my words. The hard-shelled things are simple, and the trees are faceless and silent like all trees. I crumble; my husk will nourish the forest, and I will not know for another century if they have heeded my warning.

I am Casper Cord. A champion of a dead race. Warrior of a lost country. I am reificant. I travel the waters that flow between and emerge in ten thousand distant places with my story fixed inside new flesh. My memories, my prejudices and wars, my cities, my music, jokes, my people and places, my injustice and hunger for more. All my memories remain vivid in the deep water.

When I set foot upon a faraway stone or crawl on segmented belly through the tunnels of a strange ship, I will always love Annie Groves in all the names she took and regret the terrible deeds I have done. I will always have fought in wars and betrayed friends and burned whole cities with bombs. I will transport it all with me when I emerge. I will bring my country wherever I venture.

I will bring the message to all flesh that finds the water.

BEWARE.

ACKNOWLEDGMENTS

∎ ∎ ∎

This book would not have been possible without the support of my wife, Michelle, and that of my entire family, who put up with me turning into a horrible shit for quite a lot of time. In addition to being a novel, *Liminal States* was a multimedia collaboration. Friend and longtime collaborator Josh Hass inspired and motivated me with his artwork related to this project. His perspective on the characters influenced my concept of them almost as much as my own ideas. Dan Sollis was ingenious and completely generous with his time and formidable filmmaking talents. His influence on the project manifested in every stage and facet. Robin Stoate's music (as Conelrad) played constantly during the writing of this novel, and I hope to work with him again. As always, I must thank Rich Kyanka, who gave me my first big break as a writer and continues to support my freedom to write bizarre things for SomethingAwful.com. There is no other Web site quite like it.

And thanks to you, for reading this book all the way to my acknowledgments. Who actually even does that? It's you, my friend. You. God bless you.